THE SHAAR PRESS

THE JUDAICA IMPRINT
FOR THOUGHTFUL PEOPLE

THE FORTUNE

A SHAAR PRESS PUBLICATION

SEEKERS

A NOVEL BY LIBBY LAZEWNIK

Published by **SHAAR PRESS**
Distributed by MESORAH PUBLICATIONS, LTD.
4401 Second Avenue / Brooklyn, N.Y 11232 / (718) 921-9000

Distributed in Israel by SIFRIATI / A. GITLER
6 Hayarkon Street / Bnei Brak 51127

Distributed in Europe by LEHMANNS
Unit E, Viking Business Park, Rolling Mill Road / Jarrow, Tyne and Wear, NE32 3DP/ England

Distributed in Australia and New Zealand by GOLDS WORLD OF JUDAICA
3-13 William Street / Balaclava, Melbourne 3183 / Victoria Australia

Distributed in South Africa by KOLLEL BOOKSHOP
Ivy Common / 105 William Road / Norwood 2192, Johannesburg, South Africa

ISBN 10: 1-4226-0646-5 / ISBN 13: 978-1-4226-0646-9 Hard Cover
ISBN 10: 1-4226-0647-3 / ISBN 13: 978-1-4226-0647-6 Paperback

Printed in the United States of America by Noble Book Press
Custom bound by Sefercraft, Inc. / 4401 Second Avenue / Brooklyn N.Y. 11232

For Menachem, with love

Through thick and thin,
In the dark places and the light,
Partners always.

Acknowledgments

In the life of every novel, elements are introduced of which the author has no personal knowledge. I am indebted to Dr. Erik Roskes, a forensic psychiatrist practicing in Maryland, for sharing his expertise with me and for affording me a glimpse into that fascinating place where the criminal justice system meets up with the science of mental health. Thank you!

I am grateful to the dedicated people at Shaar Press — most notably Shmuel Blitz — for pointing an unerring finger at the story's weak spots and standing firmly behind me throughout the long process of bringing the novel to fruition. Michelle Katz, I appreciate your light but professional hand in editing the manuscript, as well as your enthusiasm as a reader. Judi Dick, as always, you have your "finger on the pulse". Your input has been invaluable. Eli Kroen, the cover is a work of art. Thanks for your flexibility!

My heartfelt thanks to my family for bearing with me through the ups and downs of creating a work of this size and, most of all, to the One Who provided me with the ideas, creativity and stamina to see it through to completion.

Libby Lazewnik

March 2008

"Better for me
is the Torah of Your mouth
than thousands in gold and silver"

(Psalms 119:72)

Westward, Ho!

(Rallying cry of the American pioneers)

Prologue

New Mexico, 1849

A single, straggling cactus plant was growing right up against the saloon wall. Esther Mindel could see it clearly from the other side of the dusty street, where she and her companions were huddled in the meager shelter of the hotel porch. The cactus looked oddly out of place against the saloon's weathered wood — defiantly so, as if to say, *I've been uprooted from my natural habitat — from my true home, the desert beyond the outskirts of this little town. But I will survive anyway! I will survive …*

Esther Mindel wondered if the same could be said of herself and her companions.

They, too, had been uprooted from their homes. They had crossed a turbulent sea in search of refuge and a better life in America. What cruel twist of fate had taken their innocent bid for safety and prosperity, and turned it into a nightmare?

The most that could be said of the impending disaster was that it would not be the kind of end that any of them had envisioned.

Back in the *shtetl*, beyond the natural menaces of illness and starvation it had been a drunken Christian peasantry that constituted their gravest threat. Here, thousands of miles away in an arid, alien landscape, a very different enemy threatened. But death attended this encounter just the same. Esther Mindel could smell it coming.

"Get back!" someone whispered fiercely. She started. Unwittingly, she had drifted off the wooden porch — for a better view of the cactus, perhaps, or in an unconscious desire to meet her fate halfway. Wordlessly she retreated deeper into the shadows, closer to her people, where the pungent stench of their fear mingled with her own.

The hotel was a no-nonsense affair. There was little in its appearance to tempt the holiday-seeker. It was designed to offer a bed and two solid meals a day to hardy pioneers en route to parts west and whatever destiny might await them there.

The group to which Esther Mindel and her husband belonged, though following the Western trail like so many before them, could hardly be called "hardy." They were bearded men and kerchiefed women, not long out of Eastern Europe and piteously vulnerable in this harsh, open country. Each of them had the same worried eyes that scanned the horizon without surcease, and ears that strained to catch the dread thunder of approaching hooves.

They had come to escape the pogroms and the poverty of their native land, intending to settle down to a quiet, anonymous peace among their brethren on America's eastern shore. The timing of their arrival had changed all that. It was 1849 — and gold had been discovered in Sutter's Mill, California.

Everywhere, dreamers were abandoning the east coast for the far west. This band of newcomers, dazed by the rapid-fire changes in their lives, allowed the dream to scoop them up as well. They had traveled across the sea in pursuit of simple security; having arrived, they found they wanted more. The glitter of that far-off gold beckoned to them as it had to so many others. An unlikely group of "Forty-Niners," they paused to catch their breaths for only a few short weeks before once again hoisting their bundles and trekking west.

One of those bundles consisted of a small Torah scroll; most precious possession of Hershel Baumgarten. Hershel was considered by his fellow emigres to be something of a scholar because he knew how to read a page of Gemara a little more adeptly than the others. He had carried the scroll in his arms all the way from Eastern Europe, and all through the dreary, uncomfortable months on the trail. But his arms were empty now, on this last stand of the last leg of their disease-ridden, disaster-prone journey. He had recently been ill and had barely recovered as yet; weakness coursed through him in waves as he waited hopelessly with Esther Mindel, his wife, for what was to come.

The Indians were on the warpath.

Esther Mindel felt a stirring behind her. Half-hidden by her skirts were two small figures with two very frightened faces: a small boy of 6 and his sister, a year younger. The children clutched at their mother as though she might stave off the danger that with each heartbeat was drawing closer. Even as the exhausted group held its collective breath and prayed for a last-minute miracle, it became all too obvious that none was coming. Not their deliverance, but their doom, was galloping their way.

They were too tired to run any longer, too debilitated by illness. Already their numbers had been horrifically thinned during the demanding months on the road. There had been some talk of escape, but it was halfhearted talk, empty air without substance. This was the only town for miles around. Stretching ahead and behind them was the forbidding, desertlike landscape, with its towering red cliffs and plunging canyons called *arroyos*. The Jewish travelers were too weak to continue grappling with such a hostile territory. Even the hot Southwestern sun, so much more relentless than the sun they had known back in Poland, seemed to have become their enemy. It suffocated them, and sapped their will.

Esther Mindel stared at the cactus against the saloon wall and thought, *We've come too far. We've stepped over the edge of our world. We don't belong here …*

But greed — or its gentler face, the longing for the security that prosperity offers — had propelled them westward in pursuit of gold. It had brought them here, to this little town near the shores of a small, sparkling lake and the rushing waters of the Pecos River, to fight, or die fighting, with their backs against an alien wall.

The town, it was said, had been bypassed once before and spared an expected attack. The same thing might happen again now, despite the appalling tales that had reached the townspeople's ears from the few survivors of the current rampage who had found their way here. Those townspeople were holed up in their homes now, for whatever protection their four walls and their shotguns might offer. But Hershel, Esther Mindel and their companions had no place to hide, and they would no longer run. When action moves beyond the realm of practical possibility, it becomes easier simply to wait, and to hope.

And so, with resignation, they huddled on the graying, weather-beaten hotel porch, tending the tiny flame of hope ... and waiting.

They were not kept in suspense for much longer. Before many minutes had passed, the dreaded sound came at last: the galloping of many, many hooves. The force of that collective horsepower caused the ground beneath the Jews' feet to tremble, as though some determined housewife had decided to shake out the great mattress of the earth and be rid of them all.

After that tense prelude of offstage sound, the curtain rose at last on the final act of the tragedy. Over the crest of the hill, framed by a piercingly blue sky, came wave after wave of screaming Apaches. A line of horsemen filled the horizon from end to end, blotting out the sun.

Esther Mindel gasped, her eyes rolling upward in the beginnings of a swoon. Then, at the urgent touch of her children's hands, fresh resolve seemed to pour into her — a miracle in itself. She breathed deeply and remained steady on her feet. With a fleeting glance at her white-faced husband, Esther Mindel set in motion the desperate plan they had devised for just this moment, when all hope was lost.

She crouched quickly and whispered, in Yiddish, "Run away to the cave, my dears. You know the one I mean, right? Where we were yesterday. Run as fast as you can — and don't stop for a minute!"

"But — but ... you and Papa —" the boy stammered, while his little sister stared with great, grave eyes that were already filled with the premonition of catastrophe.

"RUN!"

There was something in the mother's voice that precluded argument. Anyway, there was no time. Father and mother gave the children a swift, hard hug and a little shove to send them speeding on their way. With a last, frightened look over their shoulders, the boy and girl ran through the hotel's rough foyer and scrambled onto the sill of a small, rear window. There they swayed for a perilous moment before jumping safely to the ground. They started up to the path that wound its way into the cliffs.

Across the sunbaked earth they ran, two small creatures racing ahead of their own shrinking shadows, taking what meager concealment the scrub oaks offered and climbing until their legs ached. Behind them lay the town, where terrified screams mingled with bloodcurdling Apache shrieks. But the children did not stop running to wonder whose screams were echoing in their ears. By this time, nothing could have stopped their legs from pumping in an almost mechanical fury. They had gone beyond fear, beyond grief, to a place where nothing existed but motion and speed.

The cave loomed just ahead.

A great, twisted cactus partially blocked the entrance, providing excellent camouflage. But the little boy remembered the way. He had been here, with his father and a few of the other men, just yesterday, when word had come that the Indians were on the warpath. All had been quiet overnight, and in their innocence the party had descended into the town in search of food. Too late, they had realized their mistake. Their last mistake in a long, dismal line of mistakes.

The boy grabbed his sister's hand to pull her into the mouth of the cave, though she hung back, loath to leave the bright day for the darkness inside. He picked his way carefully over half-seen boulders until he was sure that they were not visible from the entrance. The children crouched in the darkness, listening to the gradual slowing of their heartbeats. They were safe here. The only way anyone could find them would be by walking right inside.

Unfortunately, some three hours later, that was exactly what happened.

A pair of Mescalero Apaches (These two did not belong to the Jicarilla tribe that had attacked the town. Those warriors had already galloped on to fresher fields, once their bloody work was completed.) were passing bareback on small-boned ponies when they noticed the marks the children's feet had made as they had clambered up the trail. Curious, the older of the two motioned for the other to dismount. They tethered their ponies and followed the signs to the mouth of a cave, its entrance half-hidden by a huge, straggling cactus bush. Pushing this aside, they went in.

With wonder they beheld a boy and a girl, both very pale in the gloom, with thick brown hair and eyes of an unusual, hazel color. The children, surprised in their sleep and dazed with drowsiness and despair, made no attempt to hide. The older of the two Indians glanced over at his grown son beside him, then back at the children. Though their faces seemed to the children to have been carved from granite, some information was apparently exchanged in that glance. The older one crouched down beside the fugitives and held out his hand.

Neither the boy nor the girl took it. But both stood up at the Indian's beckoning, reassured perhaps by a steadiness in his eye, or else simply resigned to their fate.

Slowly, stiff from their long wait in the dark, they followed the Indians out into the rose-colored light of the sinking sun.

Part One:
Blazing Trails

Chapter 1

I.

We can't go on like this, Tova Bernstein thought, as the siren wailed its ghastly, all-too-familiar lullaby. *Something has got to change.*

She held Gila's hand tightly as the ambulance drove up their street and finally screeched to a stop outside their red-brick Brooklyn home. Her husband, Nachman, was gripping the child's other hand just as hard. In the center, trying to breathe, stood Gila. At 8½ years of age, this would be her eighth trip to the hospital by ambulance. And that was not counting the times without number her parents had taken her to the emergency room under their own steam.

As the paramedics leaped out with their stretcher and equipment, Nachman leaned closer and quipped softly, for Gila's benefit, "Your chariot has arrived, madam." Gallantly, Gila tried to smile. It broke her mother's heart to see the way she struggled for a moment to respond, before the greater struggle — to get air into her starved lungs — made any other effort superfluous.

Within seconds, Gila was lifted into the ambulance. To the EMT's query, Tova said tiredly: "Asthma." Even before they started moving, a shot of epinephrine was administered. The parents were relieved to see Gila's breathing ease slightly by the time they reached the hospital doors, as the fast-acting hormone relaxed the child's muscles and opened constricted airways.

The emergency-room routine was a familiar one, but the anxiety was always fresh: cold, piercing, a knife in a mother's heart. Tova ran through the familiar drill with the physician on duty. Epinephrine usually did the trick when Gila suffered one of her attacks; that is, it helped clear her lungs and let her breathe again. But it wasn't solving the problem.

"Stress often brings on an attack in asthma sufferers," the efficient, young doctor told them, just as if they hadn't heard this a thousand times before. Didn't they already try to reduce the level of stress in their home to the barest minimum? It was no use; you can't control all things, all the time. It might be an incident at school that triggered an attack. Sometimes it was simply Gila's own nature, so placid on the surface, so deeply feeling on the inside. Who could tell what would strike her sensitive heart the wrong way, starting a chain reaction that stole the very breath from her small lungs?

They discussed changing the dosage of albuterol that she took daily through a spray-dispensing nebulizer. The ER physician concurred with Gila's own pediatrician that a higher dose posed too great a risk of undesirable side effects.

"Another thing you might consider," the doctor said, "is a change of scenery. A warmer, drier climate has been known to work wonders for asthma victims."

Nachman nodded. "We've heard that," he said in his pleasant way. "It's not easy, you understand, to uproot a whole family. We'd hoped that, as she grew older, Gila would ..."

"Start getting better on her own?" the doctor finished for him. He shook his head. "At most, she'll learn to control the attacks better. With conscious stress-reduction, the acute asthma episodes will hopefully abate. But make no mistake: The attacks will continue."

Tova pondered these words as they rode home afterward in a taxi. Night had fallen while they had been inside the hospital, absorbed into its timeless, well-lit medical universe. "The attacks will continue." It was a decree that doomed them to sharing their home with an ever-present enemy — an insidious and persistent enemy that had targeted their precious middle child. Tova rested her head against the window, but the cool touch of the glass did not refresh her. Reality pressed in, relentless. *We can't go on like this,* she thought again, despairingly. But what recourse did they have?

Neither Gila's three older siblings nor her three younger ones showed any sign, thank heaven, of the illness that had troubled her since babyhood. Much to Gila's frustration — she intensely disliked being in the limelight — her condition caused the entire family to revolve around her with alarming frequency. Each new attack turned her into the epicenter of a fierce, domestic earthquake. Together they would ride the wave of fear and worry, and together slide toward the dizzying relief of recovery, to emerge afterward shaken and weak. It was an unpalatable state of affairs — if not an unbearable one. Where was the solution?

Tova glanced over Gila's head at her husband. The very sight of Nachman, with his curly brown beard, solid shoulders and eyes so wise and warm behind their gold-rimmed glasses, always had a reassuring effect on her. It reassured her now. And yet, she knew that Nachman was as helpless as she was in the face of the asthma.

She waited until they had pulled up in front of their house, paid the driver and escorted Gila inside. She waited until their other children's greetings had been offered and their questions answered and their fears allayed. She waited until each and every one of them was finally tucked into bed and even Shana's ubiquitous reading light turned off. It was only much later, when all was quiet and she and her husband were seated on adjoining couches in their comfortable, blue-and-beige living room, that she turned to him and said, "Nachman, we can't go on like this. You know that, too, don't you?"

Slowly, he nodded.

The nod frightened Tova. It was as if, in her secret heart, she had been hoping that he would show her a way out of this impasse; that with a wave of his magic wand he would make everything right. The slow, ponderous nod was a confirmation of her own, deepest fears.

"I know," he said. "Something's got to change. The question is: What?"

"Let's sleep on it," she said. It was wishful thinking: Though the hands of the clock stood at 11:30, she felt wired and wakeful. Insomnia would be her companion tonight.

"I'll do better than that," Nachman said with sudden resolve. "I'm going to talk to the Rosh Yeshivah."

Tova made an impatient gesture. "What do you expect him to suggest — that we pick up and move to Arizona or somewhere? He won't want to lose you, Nachman. You're the best *maggid-shiur* he has."

"What will he suggest?" Nachman echoed with a smile. "If I knew that, I wouldn't have to ask him — and he wouldn't be the Rosh Yeshivah."

They said their good-nights and pretended to go to sleep. Tova counted 20 breaths before she heard Nachman sit up and say casually, "Guess I'll go learn for a few minutes."

"I can't sleep, either," Tova sighed. She watched her husband head downstairs to his tiny study, where in the presence of his beloved holy volumes, he would find solace and distraction from his anxiety. She herself was at a loss for a similar distraction.

She tried reading, knowing in advance that it would be no use. After looking at the same paragraph for the sixth time without processing a word, she checked her bedside clock. Just after midnight. The dead of night, when all the world lay wrapped in slumber — or ought to be. Tomorrow she would pay a steep price for her overalertness now. It would be a day of heavy eyes and snapping nerves, a day of surviving rather than moving forward.

But tomorrow would have to take care of itself. Tova had her hands full dealing with the present. She got out of bed, paced restlessly across the room and ended up at the window. How to pass the mind-numbing minutes or hours until sweet sleep finally came to claim her?

As she stared gloomily into the unresponsive night, inspiration struck. Why hadn't she thought of it before? There was one person who would certainly be awake at this hour. For her friend Heidi, in her Manhattan high-rise, midnight was — to use her own favorite expression — the shank of the evening. Back in high school, Heidi had always been good for a late-night call. The years had not broken that pattern.

Without a second's hesitation, Tova reached for the phone.

II.

Heidi Neufeld lifted her head from her work and stretched her arms toward the ceiling. She felt the slight cramp in her neck ease and a pleasant sense of relaxation take its place. In the window opposite her desk she saw her own reflection, dark eyes staring back at her with an almost baleful intensity. She switched off her desk lamp — and, immediately, the reflection was replaced by the island of Manhattan, spread beneath her in all its glory.

The city was spangled with yellow lights that twinkled like earthbound stars: stars that never winked out, though the sky turned from charcoal to black and back to charcoal again. Only in the fading, pre-dawn gray would those lights be dimmed, but by then Heidi would be fast asleep. Or so she hoped.

Heidi did not enjoy sleeping. Every minute that was not purposeful, energetic and goal-oriented was, for her, a waste of that most precious commodity: time. According to her mother, she had been that way since birth. "Heidi? She's always been such an active child. Nonstop motion, morning to night — and often way past that, too."

According to her father, with whom she'd been very close until his death two years earlier, the problem was that Heidi was reluctant to face herself in the dark. The way he put it was, "You're afraid to think."

"But I do think! I think morning, noon and night. My *job* is to think!"

He had merely offered his calm, serious gaze and, smiling, shaken his head.

Her job was to think. She was paid an inordinate amount of money per hour to think up tax loopholes for a glittering roster of corporate clients. And, in her own opinion as well as that of the partners in the law firm where she worked, she earned every penny that she billed. So what if lying alone in the dark for more than a few minutes made her break out in a cold sweat? She preferred working till she was too exhausted to … well, to think.

She had reached this uncomfortable point in her reflections and was about to attack the files in her briefcase with renewed vigor, when the phone rang. She glanced at the clock: 10 past midnight. Who could be calling at this late hour? Picking up, she offered a tentative, "Hello?"

"Hey, Heidi."

"Tova! So late? Not that I'm not thrilled to hear from you, of course."

"Of course you are. Knowing that you'd be up to your elbows in tax law, I decided to relieve you of your agony for a few minutes." Tova's laughter sounded frayed.

Heidi caught the strained note in her old friend's voice, the voice of someone working hard to fend off encroaching despair. Frowning, she switched the light back on. "What's going on, Tova?"

A sigh. "It's Gila."

"Again?" The force of her dismay lifted Heidi to her feet and propelled her across the room. Beyond the circle of light cast by the desk lamp, the study — officially designated as the apartment's "second bedroom," but rarely used as such — was at once plush and functional. The carpet was thick, the furniture modernistic and functional. The color scheme, olive and black, was almost masculine, alleviated only by the occasional gold accent. At the window was a thin-slatted horizontal blind that Heidi hardly ever closed. With the lamp shining again, her reflection in the window had sprung back to life: a night creature on the prowl. Receiver clamped firmly against one ear, she listened to Tova with her characteristic focus. Though the hour was so advanced, she was still fully dressed — except for her shoes, which she always kicked off the moment she walked through her door.

"Yes. Again. The attacks seem to be coming more frequently these days." Tova did not trouble to hide her pain. "Maybe it's school. She's in the third grade now. I guess the stresses just mount as you get older …"

"You *guess*?"

This won a reluctant chuckle. Heidi smiled briefly into the phone, then asked, "What does the doctor say?"

Another sigh. "The usual. The epinephrine's causing a rapid heartbeat — or, as Gila puts it, 'My heart is running a race.' Anyway, it's not a solution, only a Band-Aid … though thank heaven for that!" She paused. "Nachman says he's going to talk to the Rosh Yeshivah. I suppose it's something to do."

"Maybe more than that." Surprisingly, in someone so wedded to a highly secularized lifestyle, Heidi's faith was rock solid. Though Tova was married to a rebbi in yeshivah — a *maggid-shiur*, no less — it was often Heidi who bolstered her belief in their Creator's ongoing benevolence. And that, Tova realized wryly now, was probably the real reason she had picked up the phone to dial this number tonight.

"Let's change the subject," she suggested. "I need a distraction. So, what's new in *your* life, Heidi?"

"Since last week, you mean?" They had enjoyed a good, long chat then, over Tova's sinkful of dinner dishes and Heidi's work-laden desk. "Nothing new. I went out with a brain surgeon the other night."

"Oh?" Tova's interest quickened. "How'd it go?"

"Let's just say that he sounded a lot more interesting on paper than he turned out to be in person. The guy has neurons on the brain!"

Heidi's laughter sounded carefree. Tova did not share her friend's apparent lightheartedness on the subject of marriage. She worried incessantly over Heidi's continued single state. At 35, the sands were fast slipping through the hourglass. Didn't Heidi care?

Old friends though they were, Tova never knew — and, if Heidi had anything to do with it, she would never know — the effort it took to create that carefree impression. Heidi had spent long years cultivating that particular, nonchalant laugh. Even now, even with Tova, who could generally read her like a book, it worked.

Tova made a token attempt to steer her friend straight. "Really, Heidi. I don't know what on earth you find to laugh about. I wish you would take this seriously! Don't you *want* to get married? And what about children?"

"Of course I want to get married. I've just been too busy to get around to it so far, that's all. And you know how much I love kids."

"Too busy!" Tova snorted. "Busy wasting your time, that's what!"

"Now you sound like my mother."

Tova was contrite. "I'm sorry. I didn't mean to lecture you. And I don't mean to imply that your life, or your work, is a waste of time. I'm just worried about you, Heidi. I don't want to see you alone anymore."

I'm worried about me, too, Heidi thought but didn't say. *And I don't want to see me alone anymore, either ...*

As for the accusation that she had been wasting the substance of her life, with a profound inner shudder she pushed that away as just too painful to examine.

Aloud, she said, "Since we're quoting my mom, I'll just end with her usual: 'Hashem will help.'"

"Amen," Tova said fervently.

But not as fervently as high-powered attorney Heidi Neufeld echoed the word a moment later, having hung up the phone and regained her solitude.

After that momentary lapse into weakness, she threw herself back into her paperwork with a ferocity unparalleled even for her. There were still hours to go before night gave way to the pastel pink of a new dawn. She planned to work through most, if not all, of them.

Across the Brooklyn Bridge, deep in the wilds of Flatbush, Tova resigned herself to the silence and her own, comfortless thoughts. But the conversation with Heidi had accomplished one thing. As she lay unsleeping, listening to the relentless march of her ticking bedside clock — she had the old-fashioned, wind-up kind, with a jangle to wake the dead — she had her worry over Heidi to dilute her worry over Gila.

Somewhere between 2 and 3 a.m., worn out with anxiety, she dropped into oblivion like a stone into a deep, deep lake.

Nachman Bernstein, her husband, was made of sterner stuff. Never one to need much sleep, tonight he found himself moving past even his own limits. He pored over his Gemara, ostensibly refining tomorrow's *shiur* but actually doing what Tova had been aiming for in her call to her friend: looking to strengthen his faith even as he courted distraction.

It was approximately 4 a.m. when he realized he was not going to sleep at all that night.

Along with that realization came another one. Somewhere in the interval between sitting down at his desk and the present moment, the nature of his activity had subtly changed. He was no longer just learning, or even just distracting himself from his anxiety over his little girl. Something else was going on. Intrigued, he paused to analyze this.

Then he saw: He was engaged in preparation. He was getting ready; for his talk with the Rosh Yeshivah, perhaps — a man he revered. But it was more than that. With her words that evening, Tova had planted a seed. "Something has got to change."

That was it: He was waiting for change, preparing for it. Like a soldier digging his trench, he was tensed for the whistle of the first, oncoming shell. He didn't know how it would arrive or from where, or whether it presaged good or ill — but change was coming. And Nachman, amid a steady stream of learning followed by fervent early-morning prayer, was gearing up to meet it.

III.

I t was a tired but clear-eyed Nachman Bernstein who knocked on the Rosh Yeshivah's door later that morning.

To walk into that familiar room was, in itself, to shed a burden. It was a feeling similar to tucking one's hand trustingly into that of a wise adult. There was no need to speak; merely being in that room, near that great man, was a sweet, flowing wine that went straight to the head. It went to Nachman's head, at any rate. He felt an inner settling, as if some uneasy sediment was beginning to find its place.

Rabbi Greenfeld, the Rosh Yeshivah, looked up at him and smiled. "*Shalom aleichem*, Nachman. Sit down, sit down."

Nachman pulled up a chair and faced the Rosh Yeshivah across the cluttered desk. Physically, the two men were not dissimilar: Both had midlength beards, Nachman's a vibrant brown and the Rosh Yeshivah's streaked with silver. Both were strongly built and radiated a presence that transformed them into natural leaders. What made Rabbi Greenfield a Rosh Yeshivah and Nachman Bernstein a *maggid-shiur* was an indefinable depth in the former's personality: a spiritual profundity that contrasted with Nachman's more matter-of-fact approach to life. Nachman deeply respected the man under whom he had studied since his teens, and with whom he had worked to build this small but flourishing yeshivah in Brooklyn.

"You're troubled," the Rosh Yeshivah said with his characteristic discernment. "Tell me the problem."

"It's my daughter, Gila. You know, she suffers from asthma? It seems to be getting worse rather than better as the years go by. My wife and I are beside ourselves, rebbi. We need to do something, to make some sort of change. But what?"

Rabbi Greenfeld nodded somberly. "What do the doctors suggest?"

"The usual. Less stress. A drier climate. But how can I prevent any stress from entering my child's life? Life *is* stress!" It was not often that Nachman was betrayed out of his usual equanimity. That he was speaking in this vein today told the Rosh Yeshivah just how worried he was.

"I see. And — the second option? A drier climate?"

Nachman shook his head in frustration. "How can we move, rebbi? This yeshivah is my life. My kids don't know anything but New York. They have their schools here, and their friends. Besides, where would we go? How would we live?"

"The Torah is your life," the Rosh Yeshivah corrected gently. "And children adapt easily to new places. They make new friends." He paused. "How does your wife feel about it?"

"Tova? About … moving?" Nachman didn't understand exactly how the talk had veered onto this track. "We — we haven't really discussed it. It didn't seem like a feasible option."

Rabbi Greenfeld sat back in his armchair, gently fingering his silvery beard. From beyond the office walls came the reassuring clamor of young men learning Torah in the adjoining *Bais midrash*. The sound, for Nachman, had always been the essence of joy. Though he felt far from joyous at the moment, the sound offered its own brand of comfort, and he permitted himself to take it.

"It's my turn now, Nachman," the Rosh Yeshivah said. "I've got a problem, too."

"R-rebbi — has a problem?" Nachman was startled.

"Yes. Listen to the story. Some time ago — a few weeks, no more — a man came to see me. A very, wealthy man. A man approaching the end of his life, who wishes to create some lasting monument to that life before he leaves this world. Something meaningful; something that will endure. And what is more meaningful, or more enduring, than the study of Torah?"

As this was clearly a rhetorical question, Nachman maintained a respectful — though intensely curious — silence.

"He came to me to discuss an idea he had. He thought of founding a *kollel* in a place where there was no *kollel* before. To plant a seed of Torah in a neglected field, so to speak. This man will undertake to fund the *kollel* and to support the families who agree to be a part of it." Rabbi Greenfeld eyed Nachman keenly, challenging him to take up the sword.

"A — neglected field?" Nachman repeated slowly.

"Can you think of a place less imbued with Torah than … New Mexico?"

"New Mexico …?"

"It's next door to Arizona. Dry and warm during the summer, dry and cool in winter. People with conditions like your Gila's move there every day." Rabbi Greenfeld waited.

"I — I don't know what to say." Nachman looked, and felt, thunderstruck.

The Rosh Yeshivah leaned forward. "Say you'll be the *Rosh Kollel*, Nachman. Say you'll take your family, and several other families, out to New Mexico. Actually, I was exaggerating when I called it a neglected field. There's already a Jewish day school out there, and even a tiny new Bais Yaakov-style high school for girls. The plan is for the *kollel* to form the kernel of a future *mesivta* for boys — slated to open, possibly, as early as next year."

Nachman shook his head, dazed. Out of the thousand-and-one questions whirling through his brain, he managed to ask one. "Can you tell me about this place in New Mexico?"

"It's a fairly large town on McMillan Lake, near the Pecos River in the southeastern part of the state. The climate is perfectly suited to people with respiratory problems. Pinchas Harris is the rabbi of the only shul in town. His wife serves as principal of the girls' high school I mentioned. I think you'll find them congenial people to work with, Nachman."

Numbly, Nachman nodded. "It sounds … interesting."

"Marvin Fleischmann — that's our benefactor — wants us to move on this as quickly as possible. He'd like to put money down on the building site as early as this summer. In the meantime, while construction takes place, the *kollel* would share facilities with the shul."

"I — I'll have to talk this over with my wife."

"Of course. But if you do decide to take on the job, we will want to work quickly, to get the *kollel* up and running as soon as possible. *Rosh Chodesh Elul* is the target date."

Nachman roused himself. "'Quickly' is the operative word for Gila, too." The numbness was wearing off, and a tentative excitement rushed in to replace it. Nachman flashed a boyish smile. "You know, rebbi, this could be a real possibility!"

"I believe it is. And, if you decide to accept, I have some suggestions for other *kollel* candidates. Starting with Efraim Mandel."

Involuntarily, Nachman frowned. Under Rabbi Greenberg's steady gaze, his face gradually cleared. "Efraim Mandel," he repeated, his tone carefully neutral.

"Exactly. They're expecting a new baby, and their financial situation is becoming desperate. This is strictly in confidence, of course."

"Of course."

"I think the new *kollel* will be just the ticket for him." Rabbi Greenberg leaned forward, catching Nachman's reluctant eye. "Efraim Mandel is the sort of man who thrives most when he's needed. Here, he's a small screw in a big machine … Out there, he would be important. Needed. Respected. I think it will bring out the best in him. The community will benefit from his talents, Nachman. You'll see."

"If the Rosh Yeshivah says so." Nachman was unconvinced. But all of this was too premature; he hadn't even consulted Tova yet. The Rosh Yeshivah seemed to read his mind, for he leaned back in his chair in a way that spelled "end of discussion."

"By the way," he said, with a smile rarely seen but unusually endearing, "you didn't ask me the name of the town."

"Oh, that's right," Nachman said, sitting up straighter. "Well, what's it called?"

"You're not going to believe this. It's Lakewood." The Rosh Yeshivah's smile grew broader. "Lakewood, New Mexico."

IV.

Money, money, money. It was always about money. Everything in the Mandel household — the testiness, the quarrels that erupted over nothing, Efraim's compulsive snacking, Etty's compulsive house-cleaning — revolved around that single, tension-making reality. Money — or rather, the lack of it.

Sometimes Etty thought that even their Shimi's learning disabilities were money related. At any rate, it would take a good chunk of it to hire professional tutors who might make a difference. Tzirel, 9, was a placid, average achiever who spent a good deal of her time plugged into her Game Boy or some other electronic game. Chanala, in the first grade, seemed to be a blessedly normal student, and Ora was of course too young even for nursery school. As for Meir, their *bechor* — here Etty's face relaxed its rigid lines in a moment of sweet *nachas* — no one could complain about *his* school record! Just bar mitzvah, he was at the top of his class. His rebbi's praises at their last parent-teacher conference could not have been more effusive.

And then there was Number Six (as Etty privately thought of her un-born child). There lay the real problem: the proverbial straw that might very well shatter the camel's back. This baby was wanted and it would surely be loved, but there was no denying that it posed a problem. There wasn't enough money in the Mandel household to stretch seven ways; make that eight, and that camel's spine would be just about ready to crack open in three different places.

She gazed with dissatisfaction around the kitchen. She had just fin-ished scrubbing it squeaky clean, though to the uninitiated it would have appeared squeaky clean even before she had begun. Seeing that there was nothing left to be done here — unless she decided to empty out the refrigerator, but it was a little late for that tonight — she moved into the front hall. Her eagle eye made out a certain dinginess in the floor tiles there. Out came the mop and the Pine-Sol. She had work to do.

The apartment was unimaginatively decorated, with a decor that her friend Tova Bernstein had once laughingly dubbed "contemporary *chinuch*." Bland, overused couches, a faintly, scarred coffee table and a threadbare rug were the high points of the living room; the dining room consisted of a long folding table topped with a discreetly covered slab of wood and flanked by 10, comfortable folding chairs. The curtains, once bouncing and pretty, had faded in keeping with the rest of the decor. Overall, the effect was homey, snug, inexpensive — and *clean.*

Etty plied her mop with a vengeance, taking her frustrations out on the hapless hall floor. The mop glided silently over the tiles. Stroke, stroke, stroke, went the sopping strings, in time to her own inner threnody: *Money, money, money* …

It wasn't as if Efraim was on a ladder to more earning power. No, he was staying right where he was, giving his modest *shiur* and being grateful for his monthly paycheck. She couldn't understand why he wasn't more popular with the *bachurim*. Nothing like that Nachman Bernstein, for instance, who could rarely be seen without a train of hangers-on asking him questions, basking in his smile, or content just to hover near. What did Nachman Bernstein have that her Efraim didn't have?

The answer — though Etty was loath to supply it even to herself — could have been summed up in a single, Hebrew word: "*chein*" … That elusive quality that is part charm, part grace, and wholly a gift from heaven. The sort of supreme likability that Nachman Bernstein had in buckets, and in which Efraim Mandel — and his wife, Etty, too, for that matter — were dismally deficient.

Surprisingly, for such an uncharming couple, they had very well-liked children. Shimi, despite his lackluster academic record, was king of his class with his easy ways and gap-toothed grin. Tzirel had a devoted best friend to provide company whenever she wanted it. Chanala enjoyed a lively social life with her fellow first graders, and even little Ora, at 3, was the hub of her playgroup. Only Meir, the eldest, had a bit of his parents' too-serious air and their insensibility to social nuance. Being at the top of his class went a long way, however, to compensate for the fact that, at 13, he had few close friends.

The floor was nearly done when Efraim's key jangled in the lock. Without being told, he wiped his shoes on the outside mat and then, for good measure, removed them. Like the rest of the family, he had been well trained. Etty glanced up from her mop to murmur, "Hi."

Efraim's greeting was similarly understated. It had been a long time since he'd been able to muster up much excitement over anything; least of all, coming home at night.

If asked, he'd have been hard put to explain just why this was so. The house was always tidy and clean when he walked in the front door, and the younger children were tucked into bed. He enjoyed his learning sessions with his oldest son and derived considerable satisfaction from Meir's progress. There was nothing displeasing in his wife's conversation, either. If really pressed to put his finger on the reason he found his home so disheartening, he would have had to admit that the place served as a constant reminder of his own failure.

A man of average talents, he had gone about as far as he could go in this yeshivah and he had no real hopes of interesting anyone else in hiring him in a more prestigious capacity. At a dead end: that's where he was. Was it any wonder that his heart sank as he walked through his front door, and that he could find little to smile about even when no actual crisis was in the making? Gray is a dull color for a life.

And so, while Etty strained her wiry arms to push the mop just a little harder — using small, vicious strokes that spelled a death knell to the tiniest speck of dirt — Efraim carefully bypassed the wet patches in the hall and wandered into the kitchen to fix himself a consoling snack. He had been in need of a great deal of consolation in recent years, as his waistline testified. His almost nonexistent waistline, by this time … The two of them, Efraim and Etty, looked like a caricature — a modern-day Jack Spratt and his wife, in reverse. Efraim was shaped more like a balloon than anything else, while his wife, even when expecting, resembled a tall, angular pin, primed to send the air whooshing right out of that balloon …

Not that Etty ever consciously attempted to deflate her husband. She was openly supportive and worked hard not to criticize. It was her air of defeat that did him in. It was her unspoken words that sent him scurrying into the kitchen night after night, in search of a comfort that was really no comfort at all.

Into this scene of quiet desperation, the phone rang.

Etty called softly from her corner, "It's all wet here. Can you get it?"

"No problem," Efraim called back. He put down the hunk of choco-late cake he had just sawed off and went to the phone.

"Hello?"

"Hello, Efraim? It's Nachman. Nachman Bernstein."

Neither Efraim nor Etty knew it, but their most heartfelt prayers were about to be answered.

V.

"**M**azel tov! Mazel tov!"

The four middle-aged people seated around the restaurant table lifted brimming glasses of wine to the smiling, younger couple at their center. Asher Gann, the male half of the young couple, asked with academic interest, "Do you still say 'Mazel tov' after six years of mar-riage?"

"Of course you do!" his mother declared. She took a sip of wine and set her glass down. "This is your anniversary, isn't it? What else should we say but 'Mazel tov'?"

Asher could think of lots of things. "Tough luck" would have been one of them. "There's still hope" would have been another. Glancing at his wife, Rivi — without whom he seriously wondered if he would be capable of drawing breath — he saw at once that she was thinking along the same lines. But of course she was. That was what made the two of them so special.

Each knew exactly how hard it was for the other to celebrate yet an-other anniversary without the prospect of a baby in sight.

The ambience in the restaurant was discreetly luxurious. The light-ing was dim, the tinkle of cutlery muted, the waiters silent as ghosts and helpful as genies. Tears glistened like tiny diamonds in Rivi's eyes as she gazed at her parents, her in-laws, and finally, her husband. "It *is* a 'mazel tov,'" she said. "A 'good fortune.' We're so lucky to be here, all together and in good health. We have everything going for us." She spoke defiantly, as though challenging anyone to argue with her. At the same time, there was a wistful note that only Asher caught. He watched her being brave and hopeful, as she always was, even when he himself was falling apart inside. A couple of diamonds gathered at the corners of his own eyes.

"That was a good meal," his father, businessman Benny Gann, announced, leaning back in his seat. "This place is a real find. I'm going to start bringing my clients here."

"You do that," his wife said comfortably. The pearls in her ears and around her throat were testimony to her husband's success in his field and his generosity on the home front. Rivi, across the table, wore a more modest, but no less genuine pearl necklace, her *chasan's* wedding gift to her six years earlier. Asher had wanted to buy her other pieces of jewelry since then, but she'd always protested that, as a yeshivah couple, it was an extravagance they could ill afford. Both of them preferred to ignore the fact that their parents would have loved to shower them with luxuries, had they only been willing to ask.

"You can buy me something when we have our first baby," she told him once, back when they had been married only a year and hope was still a bright, glowing thing not yet tarnished near-black. But fashion trends in jewelry had come and gone since then, and she was still wearing the same, pearl wedding-necklace for special occasions ...

Rivi's mother was a pleasant woman who shared her daughter's fair coloring, but not much else. Temperamentally, they had little in common. The mother was matter of fact, where the daughter was idealistic, and she lacked that instinct for the lovely and exotic that made Rivi such a fine artist. However, being a mother, she immediately picked up on the despondent undercurrent beneath the couple's cheerful air. Hurriedly, she said, "Dessert, anyone?"

Asher wanted dessert. Rivi didn't. She never wanted dessert, which was why she looked nearly ethereal. The quality derived from more than merely her size, however. Her large, gray eyes seemed to see things that other people didn't. Asher had learned that they saw beauty where it was not obvious, and grace where it was all but obscured. This beauty and grace emerged in her paintings, which adorned the walls of their little home. At the persistent prompting of family and friends, Rivi was beginning to seriously consider having a modest public showing of her work. "Maybe I can sell some of these pictures," she had told Asher the previous night, "though it would break my heart to part with a single one of them."

"Your parents would buy the whole collection, if you'd let them — all, that is, except the ones *my* folks would insist on buying. Then you could see the pictures whenever you wanted, in their homes."

"Not much satisfaction in that," Rivi said, with a smile.

The creative satisfaction in her life came from her painting, and Asher was more grateful for that than he could express in words. While other young wives of their acquaintances pushed strollers and exchanged child-rearing tips, Rivi stood in their sun-washed, second bedroom — her "studio" — creating art. It had begun as something to fill the empty hours; a way to make use of her empty hands in her empty house. By this time, it had become much, much more.

But it broke his heart. All the passion and the creative spirit she lavished on her painting was misdirected, waiting in vain for its proper outlet. Rivi was a natural mother who, bewilderingly, found herself without any children to mother. Asher remembered one night, a year ago, waking up in the darkness to see Rivi sitting straight up in bed, blinking in confusion.

"Where are they?" she had cried softly. "Where did they go?"

"Sssh. It was only a dream." Asher had had to bite his tongue from adding, "They didn't go anywhere, Rivi. They just haven't come yet ..."

Slowly, as the meal wound to a close, he felt a hard seed of anger begin to form inside. It was an anger aimed at nothing, because there was no enemy, but it was anger nevertheless. It grew more pronounced as his father and his father-in-law argued, predictably, over who would pick up the tab, and swelled to ominous proportions as they each donned their coats and stepped out into the frigid, January night. The wind, gaspingly cold, rushed up to him and slapped his cheeks, but did not succeed in cooling his rage. The stars — ice chips floating in a smooth, dark drink — did not shine half as brightly as his fury.

He was angry at the status quo. Angry at doing nothing — as though, somewhere along the line, he had meekly accepted "nothing" as the sum total of his fate. As soon as they were in their own car, away from any ears that might overhear, he turned to Rivi with a determined gleam rarely glimpsed on his easygoing face.

"Rivi, what you said in there about 'mazel' made me start thinking. Maybe it's time for us to make a change. You know what they say: *'Meshaneh makom, meshaneh mazal.'*"

Rivi was startled. "You mean — leave the yeshivah?"

"Maybe."

"But what good would that do? You'd be miserable. Nothing would really change."

He shook his head almost violently. The usually humorous blue eyes flashed with a fire that had been building slowly for six years.

"We can't go on like this, Rivi, don't you see that? Going on year after year, waiting and crying inside and pretending that everything's fine … The doctors haven't been able to help. So far, *davening* hasn't helped, either. Maybe we need a change." The words sounded lame even in his own ears. Still, the flame refused to die. It smoldered on, searing him on the inside, demanding action.

Rivi watched him, wondering. She could not recall the last time Asher had spoken so passionately about something. He seemed charged tonight, as though an inner switch had been turned on that was out of his control now, and it was all he could do not to race away on its current.

Was she being too passive, too accepting of her lot? As a child, she had loved reading books about pioneer families heading west to forge a new life on the endless prairie. It had been the descriptions of the journey by covered wagon that had intrigued her most. The rhythms of that long journey — patient, steady, determined in the face of whatever waited round the next bend — had seemed to suit an inner vision of her own. It was a vision of courage and stoicism, combined with a heady, human mixture. She had always viewed sheer endurance as a shining virtue. Was she wrong? Was she missing the point somehow? Was it time to stop enduring and begin acting?

Should she and Asher take their world and turn it upside down: upend the furniture, scatter the pillow feathers, do a thorough spring-cleaning of their life to see what it looked like afterward?

"It's something to think about," she said finally. Asher saw by the look on his wife's face that he had upset some delicate equilibrium in her. She needed time to assimilate the question he'd raised, to grope her way around it to a conclusion she could share.

That was all right. He could wait. As he started the car, he reflected that about the only thing he had learned to do these past six years was to wait.

If the Mandels lacked that elusive quality called *"chein,"* Nachman Bernstein thought as he picked up the phone to dial, Asher and Rivi Gann had been blessed with it in abundance. The Ganns' number rang four, five, six times. He was about to hang up, when the receiver was snatched off the hook and a breathless voice said, "Yes? I mean, hello?"

"Asher? Is that you?"

"Yes, it's me. Who ...?" The voice was familiar, but Asher couldn't quite place it.

"This is Nachman Bernstein."

Asher's face lit up. He saw Rivi, cheeks pink with the cold they had just left outside, hang her coat in the front closet and then signal for him to hand her his own. Shrugging out of his overcoat, he said into the phone, "Oh, hello, Reb Nachman. Sorry for the way I answered now — we just walked in. We were out celebrating our anniversary."

"Oh, really? Mazel tov! What number is this?"

"Six."

The number hung heavy as a dead weight between them.

Without the least sign of embarrassment, and every sign of quiet empathy, Nachman said, "You know, Asher, I have a thought for you to mull over. *'Meshaneh makom, meshaneh mazal ...'*"

Asher nearly dropped the phone.

"What is it? What's the matter?"

"Nothing. It's just that ... I was just saying that same thing to my wife."

Nachman chuckled. "Then maybe you'll be receptive to the proposal I'm about to make you. I hope you will be."

"Proposal? This sounds interesting."

"I hope it will be. I need you, Asher. In New Mexico."

For a moment, Asher wasn't sure he'd heard correctly. "Did you say — New Mexico?"

"That's exactly what I said. Can I come over to fill in the details?"

Dazed, Asher nodded into the phone. Quickly, feeling foolish, he said aloud, "Of course! Any time."

"Good. I'll be right over." Nachman paused. Then, with a mixture of jocularity and seriousness, he added, "This could be just the thing for you, Asher. You know what they say: 'Go West, young man!'"

The words seemed to echo in the New York living room long after Asher had hung up the phone and gone to find his wife, to tell her that they were expecting a special visitor with an extraordinary proposal.

VI.

Many hundreds of miles to the southwest, Bobby Smith stepped out of the adobe apartment building in which he lived. *If you could call it living,* he thought sourly, picturing the room he'd occupied since his return from Albuquerque. Rickety old bed, tired dresser, stained sink with matching stains on the floor underneath. Not exactly what he'd dreamed of when he left the reservation and set out to conquer the world.

He had gone to the big city to seek his fortune, and had returned home empty-handed. He attributed his failure to bad luck, which had seemed to dog his footsteps both in the job market and at the casino table. Bobby was a gambler; at least he was when he had the funds with which to gamble. But reality, as they say, is a harsh taskmaster, and reality's chalkboard held a stark formula: No job, no paycheck; no paycheck, no casino. Good jobs, the kind that Bobby considered worthy of his considerable, though as-yet-unplumbed talents, were not easy to come by. No one in Albuquerque, at any rate, had offered him one.

He needed cash, lots of it, and then he could make the big time at last. The trouble was, he needed to eat, too. Which was what had brought him back, in the end, to the reservation where he had grown up. Back to this miserable reservation with its smell of stagnation. Both his parents were dead; his closest remaining relative a disinterested aunt subsisting, like far too many other Native Americans on the reservation, on her welfare check. Bobby was on his own, empty in the pocket, and right back where he'd started from.

It was enough to sour anyone.

In this edgy, dangerous frame of mind, he stalked toward the nearest bar for a drink or two, and maybe a game of pool. He would give it another day or two — a week at most — and then start making plans again. Bobby Smith was great at plan-making. It was the carry-through that all too often tripped him up.

Except for the streetlights, the reservation was plunged in darkness. Electronic music blared from this window or that as Bobby passed, then faded way behind him. The occasional raised voice sounded indistinct to his ears. Though he couldn't see it, he could sense the desert stretching beyond the settlement's perimeter: ancient, serene, untouchable. The cliffs and *arroyos* and scrub oak were as familiar to him as his own face, as natural to him as breathing. He had tried to turn his back on them. He'd run away to the big city (as folks in these parts referred to Albuquerque) in an effort to recreate himself. In the end, though, the ancient homeland had called him back. It had snapped its fingers, and here he was.

His obsidian eyes narrowed. *Not for long*, he promised himself. He would escape this dead-end prison yet. He would find a way to make a bundle of quick cash and then off he would go, to where the lights glittered and the cars were fast.

Out of the shadows between two buildings stepped a hulking figure. "Big Jim" Littletree came up alongside, suiting his step to Bobby's. Bobby grunted a hello. Big Jim beamed. "Hi, Bobby. Where're you going?"

"The Black Feather."

"I'll join you."

Bobby neither encouraged nor discouraged him. The two had known each other ever since they were boys, when Big Jim — known only as Jimmy then — had punched out a kid who had dared to bully skinny little Bobby Smith. Bobby had grown considerably since then, but Jim still seemed to regard him as his special charge. Though Bobby didn't need the protection anymore, he didn't mind the company. The fact was, Jim admired him. He thought Bobby was smart as a tack and was willing to follow his lead anywhere. Given his reception by the rest of the world lately, Bobby couldn't help but enjoy that.

A dirty, neon sign heralded their destination. Bobby pulled open the door to the slap of smoky air flavored with alcohol. With Big Jim right behind him, he went inside.

Four drinks and two pool games later, he was ready to go.

He had bet on one of the games, and won — both the game and $50. Maybe his luck was beginning to turn at last. Feeling several notches taller than when he walked in, Bobby led the way outside. The night had turned colder, the air crisp and very dry. Above their heads, every star glittered like a tiny piece of chipped glass. *Anyone break a window up there lately?* he thought, and chortled at his own humor.

"What's the joke?" Big Jim asked, ambling along beside him like an amiable giant. Jim's hair needed a wash and his belly hung over his belt like a half-depleted sack, but his smile was friendly and he radiated goodwill.

Bobby was about to return a curt, "Nothin'," when the screech of brakes and a muffled thud made him look sharply around. Beside him, Jim gasped.

Bobby hesitated. Then, with an impatient shrug, he moved forward, making his way toward the huddled figure lying at the curb.

That decision was about to change his life forever.

Chapter 2

I.

Seated at the head of his dining-room table, Nachman Bernstein looked around at the others. The families that planned on being part of the new *kollel* were meeting to discuss the move. Tova sat at his right, with Etty Mandel and Rivi next to her. On the other side of the table sat Efraim Mandel, looking nervous, and Asher Gann, looking ebullient. Three men, three wives. *A small kernel*, he thought. Then again, didn't mighty oaks from tiny acorns grow?

Covertly, he studied their faces. Despite his nervousness, Efraim Mandel was clearly glad to be there. In the day or so since Nachman had broached the idea of the New Mexico *kollel* to him, Efraim appeared to have become charged with new life. He seemed more alive in the *Bais midrash*; he smiled more often and appeared uplifted. This was reassuring to Nachman, who had his secret reservations about taking this man as his partner in such an intensive new enterprise. The Rosh Yeshivah had made it clear that he wanted Efraim Mandel in. Fervently, Nachman hoped that Rabbi Greenfeld saw something in the man that he himself did not.

Etty Mandel, Efraim's wife, wore a fixed, polite half-smile. Nachman didn't know her very well. She and Tova, he knew, were on terms of casual friendship. An energetic woman, a real helpmate to her husband. With a mental shrug, he passed on to the Ganns.

Here he was met with bright eyes and eager smiles. If Rivi's were a trifle more subdued than her husband's, it was a small enough difference as to make no difference. Asher was like a charger on a leash, straining to be let loose. Here was one fellow he was glad to have at his side as he set off to face the unknown.

A last look at his wife. Tova met his glance and nodded: Let's start already! He grinned and cleared his throat.

"Ladies and gentlemen," he intoned solemnly, "I'd like to take this opportunity to welcome you all to our humble home — and to the first meeting of the 'Lakewood *kollel*,' Southwest. Though, of course, that won't be its official name. We don't want to step on any toes."

"Names don't matter for now," Asher Gann said eagerly. "So tell us more, Nachman. How soon do we go?"

"What are the living conditions like?" Etty Mandel spoke up.

"And the stipend? What's the stipend?" This from Efraim, speaking rather more loudly than was necessary.

Asher threw him a laughing glance. "Oh, leave all that for later, Efraim. This is so exciting! Let's talk about the kind of community outreach we'll be doing."

"That's easy for you to say," Efraim huffed, cheeks reddening. "I can't afford to leave 'all that' for later. I happen to have a family to support."

Now it was Asher's turn to flush. "Sorry," he said shortly. A light seemed to have gone out of his eyes.

Nachman gazed at his two potential colleagues in dismay. Not five minutes into their first meeting, and already Efraim had ruined things! Making that comment about having a family to support, when he knew that Asher had been waiting six interminable years to start a family of his own! There were some people, he reflected, who served — and not always consciously — as a species of human poison ivy. He caught Tova's eye. She reached for the coffeepot and lifted it in a maneuver clearly intended to defuse and distract. "Coffee, anyone? Or I can make some tea ..."

Rivi jumped up to pass the cake, while Etty sat with the same stiff, little smile, torn between outrage at her husband's behavior and an overwhelming sympathy for his position. Efraim *did* have five children to support with a sixth on the way, while the Ganns did not yet have a single one. Then again, he might have phrased things more diplomatically. Watching him, she saw Efraim struggle with that same realization.

"I'm sorry, too," he told Asher, not without some difficulty. "I didn't mean to offend anyone. It's just that — well, money *is* an issue for my family, especially right now ..."

"Of course!" Rivi Gann said softly, a plate of cookies clutched in a hand that she was keeping steady by sheer force of will. "Etty, would you like one of these? My contribution to this meeting. They're home made — and very good, if I do say so myself."

"I'm sure they are," Efraim answered in his wife's place. He reached over to the cookies and snagged a couple. "I see you've taken advantage of your free time to become a superb baker." He recited the blessing and took an appreciative bite.

Tova could hardly bear to look at Rivi's face. In a very cheerful voice, she said, "Why don't we let Nachman present things in his own way? I'm sure he'll cover everything that any of us may be interested in hearing. Won't you, Nachman?"

Her husband nodded. It took half-a-dozen swallows of coffee before he could trust himself to speak.

"Now," he said, taking the reins back into his own, capable hands, "let's get down to business. Housing, stipends, schooling, shopping, community outreach. Everything and anything you might want to know before making up your minds to hop on board."

Nachman and Tova saw the last of their guests out in a spirit of almost palpable relief. Though Asher Gann had made a determined effort to behave naturally during the remainder of the meeting, it was clear to everyone that he could barely bring himself to meet Efraim's eye. As for Rivi, she had remained her gentle, friendly, slightly ethereal self, whatever feelings she may have harbored clamped firmly out of sight.

"Honestly!" Tova exclaimed the instant the door closed. "*How* is this going to work? Did you hear what Efraim Mandel said to Rivi? 'Free time' ... I tell you, my heart just went out to her."

"That," Nachman said heavily, "was Efraim being tactful." He went over to an armchair and sank into it.

Tova took the couch. "Nachman? Tell me honestly: Is this going to work?"

"It has to work, Tova. It's the only option that makes sense for us. I just wish the Rosh Yeshivah hadn't been so insistent on including Efraim. There's trouble brewing there, I can feel it."

Tova nodded sympathetically. "But you're a good leader. You'll find a way to make the team work smoothly." The words emerged more as a question than a statement.

"I hope so." He was uncharacteristically somber. "With Hashem's help, I sure hope so ..."

On the upstairs landing, unseen, their two daughters crouched at the bannister, listening. Their father had told them about the *kollel*, of course. The boys had been excited. "We're going out West to seek our fortune," Ta had said, and that had been enough to ignite a fire under them.

Shana and Gila, on the other hand, were far more ambivalent.

Shana didn't want to go. More than anything in the world, she didn't want to go. She was at the near edge of adolescence, just tasting the terrors and pleasures of establishing herself in the growing-up world of her peers. While she was not especially enamored of Brooklyn, it was home. Life was feeling strange enough, these days, without the added strangeness of a new home and the discomfort of having to make new friends. The prospect of trading comfortable, old Flatbush for Lakewood, New Mexico was no less horrifying a prospect than settling on Mars.

Judging by her parents' expressions, she saw that they were having their problems with the whole idea, too. She turned to her sister, Gila, the cause of all this unpleasantness. *Look!* she wanted to say, blinking back tears of frustration and rage. *Look what you've done to all of us. This is all your fault!*

Then she saw Gila's face, and knew that she didn't have to say a thing. Words were unnecessary, because Gila was already staggering under the same crushing burden of guilt that Shana had been so ready to dump squarely on her young shoulders. The "fortune" they were setting out to seek was Gila's restored health, and the family's peace of mind. So what, really, was there for her to feel guilty about?

It was the asthma that was the true criminal here, not Gila. Not sad, guilt-ridden Gila, involuntary uprooter of families and unwitting dealer of misery to older sisters. It was not really Gila whom she blamed for this disaster. Not the little sister she loved with such a fierce protectiveness, and who suffered so much at the hands of an illness that threatened repeatedly to steal the very breath from her body.

So Shana pressed her lips tightly together to keep the words inside, and closed her eyes just as tightly to hold back her incipient tears.

The idea that had so cruelly shaken up her world had been broached only a day ago, but already Shana was learning to let her love precede her pain.

II.

He saw a huddled figure at the curb, and the taillights of a heavy vehicle careening away out of sight. *One drunk on the ground, knocked there by another drunk at the wheel,* Bobby Smith thought grimly as he went to bend over the shapeless form in the gutter.

Grunting with the effort, he turned the figure over so that he could see its face. He recognized the hollow, gray-stubbled cheeks and the shoulder-length gray hair with its streaks of white, though the rheumy, dark eyes were closed. It was Old Henry Jones — he preferred to be called by his Indian name, but, for the life of him, Bobby couldn't recall what it was. Henry was a fixture in the Mescalero reservation — especially in his own special corner of the Black Feather bar and pool hall. Bobby had seen him there tonight, alone as usual though not averse to a bit of company, nursing his drink with the skill of long practice to make it last.

"It's Henry," Big Jim breathed at Bobby's shoulder.

"Yes. The old fool stepped into the street without looking. I'm surprised this didn't happen years ago."

A small knot of people were beginning to gather at the scene. Someone pointed at a thin trickle of blood, black in the light of the street lamp. A puddle of spilled oil near the huddled body glowed with rainbow phosphorescence.

"Somebody call an ambulance!" Bobby shouted irritably at the gawkers. A man in a business suit whipped out a cell phone and self-consciously began dialing.

While they waited for help to arrive, a cold rain began to fall. Like magic, the crowd dispersed. Bobby remained, as well as Jim. Bobby was held in place not by compassion but by sheer necessity: As the icy drizzle had begun to revive the injured man, his black eyes had opened and one bony claw clamped onto Bobby's hand with surprising force. Henry hung on tight as, with sheepish looks and muttered good wishes, the last of the spectators drifted hurriedly away to find shelter.

"Gee, it's cold out here," Big Jim said.

"Oh, is it?" Bobby snapped. "I hadn't noticed."

His sarcasm was wasted on Jim. Shivering, the big man merely hunched his shoulders and bowed his head, prepared to stoically wait out the weather.

Bobby himself was not nearly as patient. *I'll give that ambulance another minute*, he thought, *and then I'm out of here.* No old drunk was going to hold him hostage until he turned into a block of ice.

The siren's welcome wail seemed to electrify Old Henry. His eyes, which had been fluttering shut, flew open again. As the siren grew louder, his grip on Bobby's hand tightened cruelly. "Don't leave me," he whimpered. "Don't let them take me away all by myself."

"You're not a baby," Bobby snapped. "What do you need me for?"

"He's scared, Bobby," Jim whispered.

"Thanks for the information." Bobby was getting angrier by the minute. Couldn't a guy even walk down the street without getting mixed up in some dumb fool's business?

Apparently not. The two EMTs, wearing rain gear as they hopped out of the ambulance with a stretcher and oxygen apparatus, seemed to take it for granted that Bobby would accompany their patient back to the hospital. Under the pressure of this expectation, Bobby, with ill grace, gave in.

"Is there room for me, too?" Jim asked.

The stockier of the two paramedics shook his head. "Sorry. You can meet your friends over at Memorial later, if you like."

"He" — Bobby jerked his head at Old Henry, now lying supine on the stretcher — "is no friend of mine."

Nobody was listening. The stretcher was lifted into the waiting ambulance. Reluctantly, Bobby entered after it. Jim gazed forlornly after them, massive shoulders hunched in sodden misery.

"See you later, Bobby," he called, waving a beefy hand.

Bobby replied with a dour nod. The ambulance doors swung shut. As the vehicle began moving down the slippery street, he felt the claw-like grip on his own hand again. Sighing, he turned to face the old man.

Henry's eyes were wide open. "Am I gonna make it?" he rasped.

Bobby wasn't sure if the old man even knew who he was, or if he was no more than a vaguely familiar face, an available hand to clutch in a crisis.

"I don't know," he said brutally. "Maybe. Let go of my hand, man. You're hurting me."

The pressure eased fractionally. "You're my friend," the old Indian mumbled. "You came with me. You'll take care of me."

Bobby shrugged.

"I'm gonna tell you a secret … what's your name again?"

"Bobby," Bobby said shortly.

"I'm gonna … tell you a secret … Bobby." The injured man paused, wheezing heavily. His breath was coming faster now, as though impelled by some inner agitation. The paramedic on the stretcher's other side leaned closer. "Take it easy, fella. Don't get yourself all excited now. You've been in an accident."

Old Henry turned his head so that he was facing away from the EMT and looking directly at Bobby. "Tell you later," he mouthed.

"Sure," Bobby said, surreptitiously checking his watch. "Whatever you say, old man."

The siren shrilled on as they sped through the rain.

III.

Heidi checked her makeup one last time in the small mirror she kept in her top desk drawer, stood up and walked across her office to the door. Her heels clicked across the polished floor, then padded silently over the exquisitely beautiful Persian rug. It was time for the weekly conference at the law firm, and it would not do to be late.

Normally, these meetings energized her. During the short walk to the conference room at the end of the corridor, her mind would be at its peak, sorting, selecting and cobbling together facts regarding the briefs with which she was presently involved — facts that she would present in a concisely efficient manner at the meeting. This morning, however, the smoothly functioning piece of machinery that was her brain seemed lost in an odd torpor. The usual bounce in her walk was conspicuous by its absence. She had been battling a headache since waking that morning.

Actually, the headache had made its appearance the night before, when her oldest and best friend, Tova Bernstein, had called with the stunning news that she and the family were relocating to New Mexico to start a *kollel* there. "For Gila's health, you understand. We were running out of options."

For Gila's health. Heidi did understand. But the news had thrown her into an unaccustomed turmoil. It had reminded her, forcibly, that *she* was running out of options, too. What was she going to do without Tova, her oldest and best friend: her lifeline?

Stop it. Shaking her head in an effort to banish both the headache and her unwanted thoughts, she strode into the corridor and toward the conference room.

"New Mexico. That's a long way off," she had said on the phone last night, straining for lightness when her heart felt as though it had turned to solid concrete.

"Don't worry. Just get yourself engaged, and I'll be back in a flash to dance at your wedding!" The offer was laden with all the things Tova wasn't saying. Heidi had ignored them, asking the expected questions, moving the focus adroitly away from herself. This was something she was very skilled at doing.

She had always prided herself on her strength. No matter what was happening — or not happening — in her personal life, the facade of the perfect lawyer must never be tarnished. Heidi entered the conference room just behind two silver-haired partners chatting in undertones — both of them dressed in expensive three-piece suits, discreet ties and matching airs of self-importance — and just ahead of another junior partner like herself. The junior partner looked young and eager, sharp nose pointed straight ahead like a bloodhound on the scent — of … what? Heidi wondered suddenly. What *is* he after? What are we all after?

Like a swarm of gnats, the strange and unbidden questions swarmed around her and refused to desist. Heidi was grateful when portly Earl Flaxen, the firm's senior partner and son of its founder, cleared his throat and opened the proceedings.

Instantly, she was caught up in a swirl of legal jargon: tax coups, court maneuvers, gains and losses and more gains. When it was Heidi's turn to speak, she was able to render a modest account of a recent triumph that had saved an important client a great deal of money and consequently made him very happy. This made Earl Flaxen happy, too. He and his silver-haired cohorts beamed. Someone called out, "Good girl, Heidi." The other junior partners looked chagrined: Heidi's triumph dimmed a bit of their own luster. "It's a dog-eat-dog world out there," she remembered a law-school professor telling her class one day. "Just be careful who you take a bite out of. He may come back and chew you to pieces one day …"

Somehow, her victory did not make her feel as triumphant as she would have expected.

It's the headache, she thought, to explain the odd malaise that had gripped her all morning. That, and … the prospect of saying good-bye to Tova. As she winced at the thought, her neighbor — Kimberly Stone, an associate with frosted hair, extremely high heels and even loftier ambitions — leaned over and in a solicitous whisper asked if she needed a Tums.

"I'm fine." Heidi forced a smile. She had a sudden vision of Kimberly as a sleek, golden snake, coiled to spring. Her eyes moved along the table. Earl Flaxen, at its head, resembled a sleepy lion, deceptively relaxed but possessed of an enormous, latent power that rendered him immensely dangerous. John Spinner, the senior partner at his right, wore gold-rimmed bifocals shading the eyes of a hungry tiger. Evelyn Habelard, on Flaxen's left, frequently bared her white teeth in a smile that was equally predatory. Heidi shivered. How had she stumbled into this jungle? And how did one hack one's way out?

Since when had she ever wanted to?

The headache intensified.

As yet another associate tendered his report, her thoughts drifted back to Tova. She would miss her friend, no doubt about that, but Tova's news had touched a chord that went much deeper than that. This major change in her friend's life underlined the unchanging nature of her own. Tova and Nachman's decision was forcing Heidi to take a good look at the choices she herself had made. The puzzle pieces that she'd long ago forced into what she had believed to be the correct picture seemed not to fit anymore, and she wasn't sure why. It was as though an unseen hand had stamped a thick, red, "*Wrong!*" across the test paper of her life.

As though by some mysterious compulsion, she found herself reviewing those choices now.

Here in the chrome-and-glass headquarters of Flaxen, Domb and Tremaine, she was a rising star. Like the office itself, she was all glitter and efficiency. A bright and well-oiled legal machine, that was Heidi Neufeld. Within the context of this encapsulated world she looked right, she behaved right, and — most of the time — she felt right.

In her rare moments of relaxation, she was also a devoted Auntie Heidi to the children of her sister and two brothers, all of whom lived in the Greater New York area and all of whom, though younger than she, had married years before. Playing that role for her nieces and nephews, bearing gifts, smiles, and lending an attentive ear to their childish stories and complaints, all of that felt right, too.

The trouble was, neither role satisfied her. Neither was enough. And even both together still fell short …

"That's it for now," Earl Flaxen boomed from his place at the head of the long table. "Get those billing hours up, ladies and gentlemen!" He ended every meeting with this injunction. "That's all till next Tuesday." Rising painfully to his feet — Flaxen suffered from arthritis, high blood pressure, clogged arteries and a host of other by-products of a too-indulgent lifestyle — he lumbered to the door, the usual three or four partners trotting in his wake like satellites of a silvery sun.

Heidi took her time following. She seemed to be moving through a different medium today, as though she had been transplanted to an alien world and was having difficulty adjusting to its atmosphere. But it was the same world she had inhabited for the past 11 years, since her induction fresh from law school. Heidi Neufeld, third in her class at Columbia Law, smart and ambitious and hard driving. What a catch!

She had allowed herself to be caught. And now she was a little fish, swimming around and around a pond that regarded itself as vast and terribly important, but was really (she thought sacrilegiously) in the overall scheme of things, quite small. Insignificant, even. A pond that left her well fed but strangely malnourished, as though some vital nutrients had been leached from its waters.

The intermittent headache settled into a dull, relentless throb. She felt suffocated, on the verge of drowning. How long had it been since she had broken through the pond's glassy surface and looked — really looked — around her? How long since she'd squinted in the light of a sun-drenched morning or felt the caress of a carefree wind?

But fish don't do those things. They dare not lift their heads from the waters of the home pond. To do so is dangerous. It could even be fatal.

Contrary to her usual practice — a sandwich and Diet Coke at her desk — she took an extra-long lunch hour, lingering over lasagna and cappuccino and then taking a circuitous walk back to the office through a small but pleasant neighborhood park — a tiny, green handkerchief tucked into a pocket amid the skyscrapers. The fresh air did little to lift her spirits; she seemed to carry a bubble of sluggishness around with her everywhere she went.

Why? When had the practice of law — and the life of Heidi Neufeld — changed from a thing of joy and pleasure to an insufferable burden? It had happened so gradually, it seemed, that the transformation was upon her before she was aware that anything was happening. She was a successful, upwardly mobile attorney with very bright prospects. Certainly she was making more money than any of her high-school classmates. She had used her brains, her stamina and her considerable personality to follow her dream.

Well, I'm living the dream, she thought, as a startling sob rose out of nowhere and made a passer-by raise curious eyebrows. *Now what?*

No one had ever told her that the question even existed. That there was life on the other side of the rainbow. That the pot of gold she'd found there, as promised, would not be enough.

Not enough. That seemed to be the theme of her day.

The day plodded on to its conclusion. Usually among the last to leave, she abandoned her office at just 6:30. She rode the subway to her luxurious apartment on the Upper West Side, hanging on grimly to the commuter strap and trying not to scream out loud as a very heavy gentlemen in gray pinstripes stepped on her toe. The short ride left Heidi feeling as drained as if she had run an all-day marathon. She stepped out of the station into a chilly evening. Clouds chased one another across a pewter sky in a game of wind-tag, until it was time to turn into her own building and let the cold, marble interior and artificial light blot out the sky.

She rode the elevator to her floor, dragged herself through her front door, kicked off her shoes and sank gratefully into an easy chair. A lamp was perched at just the right angle behind her left shoulder, and the book she was in the middle of reading lay waiting at her elbow. She ignored them both.

When the phone rang and the caller ID told her that it was her mother, she ignored that, too. She didn't want to speak to anyone until she managed to throw off this inexplicable mood and began to feel more human again — least of all her well-meaning mother, antennae ever tuned to her oldest daughter's frequency. Heidi was not ready to broadcast her feelings yet, even to those nearest and dearest to her. How could she, when she hadn't the slightest clue what they were? She was receiving a signal from the distant lighthouse of her own heart, but she had forgotten the code.

I won't work tonight, she thought with a flash of rebellion, glancing venomously at the crammed leather briefcase she'd brought home with her. *I'll read a book and go to bed early.*

That was her resolve when the night was still young. Hours later, when the stillness had intensified and the unwelcome thoughts continued to rush at her despite her most urgent attempts to push them aside, she found herself reaching for the briefcase with a greedy, almost desperate haste.

She gazed out at the glitter of Manhattan, then switched on her desk lamp and faced her own reflection. Both, at the moment, filled her with equal revulsion.

Turning away from the window, Heidi poured herself a cup of coffee, then sat down and attacked the first legal brief like the old friend, or enemy, that it was.

IV.

Rabbi Greenfeld was looking pleased.

"I'm delighted," he told Nachman Bernstein frankly. "Just delighted. This *kollel* is going to be a beacon of light in the Jewish Southwest."

Doubtfully, Nachman asked, "*Is* there such a thing?"

The Rosh Yeshivah laughed. "There is — and there will, with Hashem's help, continue to be. You and your group will be among those who make certain of that. Now tell me." He leaned forward, suddenly sober. "How's it going?"

Nachman began to outline the steps that he had taken so far. He described his meetings with the prospective *kollel* members. Though he left out Efraim Mandel's remarks to the Ganns at the general meeting and did his best to delete any other reference, however oblique, to his most prominent headache in setting up what he was beginning to think of as "the team," Rabbi Greenfeld's next words made him realize that he was either less adept at concealment than he had hoped, or — more likely — that his Rosh Yeshivah was an exceptionally astute man.

"And Efraim Mandel? How have he and his wife taken to the idea?"

"Oh, they're thrilled. They were apparently ripe for a change. The Ganns, too — for different reasons." He and the Rosh Yeshivah exchanged a knowing look. Asher and Rivi's childlessness was a source of pain to everyone who knew the couple.

"We still have an opening for a fourth member," Rabbi Greenfeld reminded him now. "I take it Leib Shneiderman didn't work out?" "No. His wife is very attached to her family and is dead-set against moving away. I didn't get the impression that Leib himself was all that eager, either."

"Moish Hausman?"

"No good. His elderly father just suffered a stroke. He's got to stay."

"Yes, I know. Well, keep your eyes open, Nachman. We'll start with three couples if necessary, but a fourth would make the workload easier all around."

Nachman nodded.

"And now," the Rosh Yeshivah smiled, reaching for the phone. "I think introductions are in order. Ready for your first conversation with Pinchas Harris? As rabbi of Lakewood, New Mexico's only Orthodox shul, he's been the backbone of much that has been accomplished in the community so far. The two of you will be working closely together."

"I'm as ready as I'll ever be."

Nachman watched as Rabbi Greenfeld located the listing in his old-fashioned Rolodex and punched in the number.

After six or seven rings, the Rosh Yeshivah left a message on Rabbi Harris's cell phone. "I'll try his house, too, though neither he nor his wife is likely to be home at this time of day. She's principal of the girls' high school out there, you know."

"Amazing that such a small community can support a Bais Yaakov high school. Even a very small one."

"'Tiny' is the word. And it *is* amazing — and awe-inspiring. There's nothing that can't be accomplished if you want it enough and *daven* hard enough. Remember that when you're out there, Nachman."

Nachman nodded. He tried to picture the tiny Bais Yaakov in the tiny town, perched on a lake between a desert and a river, but found himself entertaining instead a mental image of his daughter's tall, brick school building in the urban wilds of Flatbush. The contrast, and his imagination's inability to encompass it, made him smile. Never mind; soon enough, all these people and places would come alive for him. Right now they were still only names and addresses on a Rolodex (though shortly to become entries in his own Palm Pilot).

The Rosh Yeshivah recorded a second message, then disconnected. "I left him both your numbers, as you heard, Nachman. I had hoped to make the introductions personally, but I'm sure you'll do fine on your own." Behind the wire-rim glasses, his eyes twinkled.

"I'll do my best, rebbi," Nachman promised.

"You always do, Nachman. You always do."

As he let the door of the sheriff's office swing shut behind him, Rabbi Pinchas Harris pulled out his cell phone and checked his messages. While he'd been meeting with Sheriff Ramsay, Rabbi Greenfeld had called from New York. About the new *kollel*, no doubt. Listening to the message, Pinchas heard the name Nachman Bernstein, along with some phone numbers. He recognized the name as that of the new *Rosh Kollel*.

I'll call back tonight, he thought. *Given the time difference, I'll probably catch him at supper.* A good time to get hold of a busy man, as he knew from experience. Sometimes, the only time ...

He was drained and frustrated from his recent encounter with the Lakewood, New Mexico police force. Not that he blamed Ramsay. The sheriff had proved much more sympathetic to the shul's problem than Pinchas Harris had expected. Still, when all was said and done, Jack Ramsay hadn't offered much more than sympathy. And it was clear to the rabbi that more than that was needed. Much more.

Compulsively, he drove past the shul on his way home, though he could have made the trip more quickly by another route. He slowed down in front of the single-story, brick structure with its distinctive winged roof, so graceful and inviting only yesterday — and today so hideously disfigured by the ugly, red scrawl in foot-high letters: JEWS GO HOME.

Sheriff Ramsay had said that he had his eye on some local Native Americans with a gang history. Both of them knew that no arrests would be made. Graffiti did not qualify as a major felony, and given the size of Lakewood's minuscule police force, it would be filed away as a "pending" case until a more serious offence occurred to revive it.

A hate crime, that's what it is, Pinchas Harris thought angrily. He pressed down on the gas pedal as though he wished it were the perpetrator's face. Someone always hates the Jews. One would have thought that here, way out in the wilds of the American Southwest, their little community might have escaped all that. But he should know better. There was no escape — either from the curse of being a Jew, or the blessing. They would be hated until the redemption, when the whole picture would change and light would pour down where darkness now reigned. Comforted by the thought, he drove away slowly, leaving the hate-scrawl behind him. He would have Dr. Ben, the local Jewish pediatrician and a *gabbai* of the shul, hire someone to scrub that wall right away. By the time the morning *minyan* straggled in, it would be a blank slate once again.

He grimaced; not exactly the most apt metaphor. The last thing he wanted was for his shul to serve as a blank slate for any passing scrawler with hate in his heart.

The Harris's house, like most of the others in town, was a single-story, stucco structure, cream colored with deep maroon shutters at the windows. Twin pots of vivid red geraniums greeted him as he headed up the front path. He forced himself to stop just before he reached the door, to breathe deeply and banish his gloom. No sense in bringing the taint of that ugly scrawl into his precious home.

He wore a determined smile as he walked in. His wife saw through it at once.

"What's the matter?" she asked sharply. "What happened?"

As a couple, there was an uncanny resemblance between them. People sometimes mistook them for brother and sister. Pinchas and Penina Harris were nearly the same height, both of sturdy build with reddish hair and light complexions prone to sunburn. Both had pale, gray eyes, though only Penina sprouted a field of freckles across her nose in summer. She was the more practical of the two; Pinchas was the visionary, the idealist in search of new pastures to plant with spirit and meaning. He had found such a pasture here and had cultivated it almost single-handedly, in fact. Both he and his wife took great pride in their modest but steadily growing shul. It pained Rabbi Harris to share his painful news with his wife.

Grimly, he told her about the graffiti.

"Did you go to the police?" Penina asked at once.

He nodded. "Sheriff Ramsay was helpful — and unhelpful."

"Meaning what, exactly?"

"Meaning that he completely understands my distress, shares my outrage, and so on and so forth. But what can he do to catch the perpetrators, or to prevent it from happening again?" He spread his hands in uncharacteristic bitterness. "Zilch. That's what."

Penina was silent. She felt as if a fissure had opened beneath her feet. Something that had seemed rock solid and dependable had suddenly developed an ominous crack. Their tiny, precious community was threatened.

Pinchas had his shul, but she had her high school to worry about as well. Apart from some vague rumblings of anti-Semitism in the community when they had arrived — rumblings faint enough to be safely ignored — they had never had any outright trouble before. Was this a one-time occurrence, or did it predict the end of an era?

In some trepidation she faced her husband, to ask him what he thought. But Pinchas had turned away; he was at the fridge now pouring himself a cold drink from a plastic pitcher.

"Ramsay did say he'd pass the word on to a Native American lawyer who may be able to help. Steve Birch is the name. A Mescalero. He comes from the reservation, though he lives here in Lakewood most of the time. Apparently, Birch has acted before as a sort of liaison to the 'white' communities in the area. He may know who the perpetrators are, or at least be able to warn us of any more unrest."

"So the Sheriff thinks it was the Mescaleros who did this?"

Pinchas Harris shrugged. "Maybe — and maybe not. There are Indian gangs and non-Indian gangs around. Toss a coin ..."

A hissing sound from the stove had Penina scuttling in that direction with a gasp. With a quick twist of the burner knob her pot of soup, on the verge of boiling over, subsided.

"Got a call from Rabbi Greenfeld today," Pinchas remarked, clearly glad to leave the other subject alone. "He wants me to make myself acquainted with Nachman Bernstein — the new *Rosh Kollel*."

Penina sank into a chair with a tired bark of laughter. "Some welcome he's going to have. Better get someone to wash off that graffiti ..."

"I'm planning to. Right now, in fact. And then I'll call Rabbi Bernstein."

"Are you going to tell him about the hate message?"

Pinchas hesitated, then shook his head. "What's the point? This was the first incident of its kind. I hope it'll also be the last. Sheriff Ramsay is hopeful, too."

What Penina Harris thought of such hopes did not need to be said aloud. Her expression said it for her.

But her husband wasn't looking. He was focused on his cell phone, dialing his *gabbai's* number. Soon the hateful words would be washed away, and along with them — he fervently hoped — the need to remember that the whole thing had ever happened at all.

V.

Steve Birch looked thoughtful as he hung up the phone. He took a turn around his postage-stamp living room, contemplating the conversation he'd just had with Sheriff Ramsay. With the reservation less than 30 miles from town, this was not the first time the Mescalero had been implicated in a Lakewood crime. This was the first hate crime, though. A departure from the usual line of petty theft, shoplifting and joyriding. It was a departure he did not like.

JEWS GO HOME. The words conjured up an image of bearded rabbis in long, black coats, alongside a contrasting one of a turbaned scholar in a striped Egyptian robe. He had once come across such a picture of the venerable scholar Maimonides, and in the absence of any real working knowledge of Jews, had adopted that image as a rather illogical stereotype.

He had met Jews since then, of course. There was a whole community of them in Lakewood now; a small community, but one that seemed to have settled in comfortably. He saw them at the supermarket, and occasionally exchanged polite nods with them at the gas pump. These Jews were neither turbaned, nor for the most part, bearded. Except for the yarmulkes on their heads, he might have taken them for almost anyone else. The women, of course, were a different matter: The mere fact that they wore unrevealing dresses even in summer lent them an exotic air. Beyond this, he knew virtually nothing of the Jewish people.

JEWS GO HOME. Why would anyone — Native American or otherwise — want the Jews to leave Lakewood and go "home," wherever that might be? Who had scrawled that hate message? Some storekeeper who felt threatened by impending Jewish competition? Or, as the sheriff believed, local youngsters infected by a hitherto inactive strain of Southwestern anti-Semitism?

Steve frowned. If it *had* been youngsters, and if those youngsters belonged to his reservation, he wanted to know about it.

He strode into his diminutive kitchen and poured himself a single glass of dry, red wine, his nightly ration. It was a rule of his never to drink more than one glass when he was alone. Look at what had happened to his stepfather. Old Henry had once been a reasonably stable member of society. Now he was — to put it baldly but with a sad adherence to the facts — a drunk.

He took the wine back to the living room with him. Decorated in taupe tones, the room was a muted echo of the landscape outdoors. Steve Birch pulled open the sliding glass door and stepped out onto his narrow balcony. He owned this little place on the reservation as well as a larger apartment in Lakewood. This balcony faced the reservation's eastern rim, with the foothills of the Sacramento Mountains a brooding presence at his back. Before him lay a vast, flat darkness that somehow breathed with a life of its own. The smell of the desert filled his nostrils and a desert wind ruffled his hair. That hair might be Indian-black, but the eyes were different: a medium greenish-brown, with a darker, brown ring around the perimeter. His skin, too, held a pallor unusual in a Native American. "Paleface," the other kids used to taunt him when they were kids. Sometimes, Steve believed, he had more than just a pale face. He had a pale soul.

From the start, he had been different.

For one thing, he was a reader. While the other kids on the reservation dreamed about making it big — about piles of money, or acts of daring based subconsciously on the old Indian legends they treated with such disdain — Steve was curled up with his books, becoming acquainted with a much wider world than the one allotted them by the U.S. government on this desolate New Mexican tract.

His father had died when Steve was just a boy, and it hadn't been very long before his mother, strange, dreamy-eyed Alice Birch, had remarried. The marriage had seemed to young Steve not so much an active choice as an acquiescence — a disinclination, or inability, to argue her way out of Henry Jones' repeated proposals. Henry hadn't been bad, as stepfathers go, but Steve had rejected him as a role model. His true model was an amalgam of all the literary heroes he had come to revere in the course of his reading: strong but wise, brave and steadfast, always kind and never, ever irresponsible.

He had won a scholarship to the university, and made that a springboard for law school. The United States government had been more than happy to sponsor the studies of an ambitious Native American. He had graduated fifth in his class. Job offers poured in, but a sense of loyalty to his downtrodden people had brought him back to the reservation, where he ran a far-from-thriving law practice that catered mostly to his fellow Native Americans, with a smattering of "outside" clients who had heard of his reputation and sought his expertise.

Gradually, he had begun to serve as a sort of missing link between the redskin community and the paleface one. It was an unofficial role, but one he relished. Fostering peace between differing peoples seemed to him a worthwhile goal. That was something else that had always set Steve apart from his playmates: his penchant for lofty goals. Henry, his stepdad, had laughed at this tendency and wondered from where it came. Alice, his mother, had merely smiled at him with her sad, dream-filled eyes and said nothing.

Alice was gone now, and Henry was drinking his life away in the reservation barrooms. Steve was still unmarried, living alone. He could have enjoyed a higher and much more pleasant standard of living off the reservation, or even away from modest Lakewood; stubbornly, he refused to leave. The big city might offer more diversion, but here, he felt, was where he could do some good. He had few regrets and a great many hopes.

In the most secret places of his mind, Steve Birch harbored a private, almost mystical sense of things still to come. It was like a voice whispering in his ear, telling him that his life was still in the process of unfolding. What lay at the heart of the mystery he could not guess. Like an origami creation, he would not know what waited in store until the last fold was in place and the creation finally spread open for his pleasure and wonder.

Whatever it was, he knew in a deep and very certain way that it was going to be more beautiful than anything he had ever encountered before in his life.

Setting down his empty wineglass, he went to the phone to make a few calls. He had several contacts who might know something about the message scrawled in blood red on the synagogue wall. If so, he would soon be paying a couple of calls to some of the pueblos in the neighborhood.

VI.

Steve Birch stood in the dingy hallway, facing an equally dingy door. He checked the name on the faded sign against the slip of paper in his hand, then knocked.

There was a pause while indeterminate voices sounded from within. When the door was finally opened, he was welcomed by a toothless grandmother who offered a gaping smile to attest to her harmlessness. Long, white hair straggled on either side of her wrinkled, walnut face. She made a good front, Steve thought with appreciation. But he was far more interested in those inside.

"Is this the home of Al Barker?" he asked politely.

"Al's my grandson." From the dim recesses behind her wafted the aroma of slightly scorched cornbread. "What you want him for?"

She might as well have asked, "What's he done now?" Steve read in her tone an apprehension rooted in long, painful experience, with truant officers, irate neighbors, the police. Gently, he said, "I just want to talk to him. Is he in?"

Grudgingly — the toothless smile was nowhere in sight now — the grandmother stepped aside to let him in. There was no need to introduce himself. Everyone on the reservation knew Steve Birch ... and some had good reason to avoid him.

Young Al Barker was apparently intent on avoiding him right now. There was a scuffle at the rear of the meager apartment, as though someone was trying to hide. Had the apartment not been situated on the fourth floor, Steve would not have been surprised to hear the scrape of a window opening, and then the thud of sneakers as they landed below and raced away into the night.

"Come on out, Al," he called pleasantly. "I just want to talk."

Sixty seconds later, a sullen shuffle of those same sneakers heralded Al's entrance onto the scene. He was about 19, tall, thin and greasy haired. One ear sported an earring and one forearm boasted an indecipherable, aquamarine tattoo. He scowled at Steve and said nothing in greeting.

Steve was content to provide the opening remarks. "Sit down, Al. Let's have a chat."

Al remained where he was, slouched against the wall in his overlong T-shirt and faded jeans. A highly charged wariness came off him in waves: the aura of a hunted animal, poised for flight.

"All right, stand if you want. Mind if I sit?" Without waiting for an answer, Steve selected the least rickety looking of the chairs and sat down. "I hear you've become quite the artist, Al."

A guarded curiosity entered the teenager's eyes, but he didn't speak.

"Someone's been decorating the walls of the synagogue over in Lakewood. I hear it has your signature on it."

Al narrowed his eyes and still said nothing.

"You and your buddy … Joe Fenway, isn't it?"

Still no answer. Steve dropped the pleasant demeanor. He leaned forward and fixed the greasy-haired delinquent with a steely eye. "We've all looked the other way when you've gotten into scrapes till now, Al. They've been relatively minor scrapes. You've got a difficult family situation, not much money, and — well, boys will be boys. But this is serious. Hate crimes are real trouble. Trouble, as in prison time. Get me?"

Al looked away.

"We've got enough on our plates without sending hate messages to other people," Steve said, still leaning forward but less menacing now, and more persuasive. "Those Jews have a right to worship, just as you have a right to do the things you like to do … as long as they don't hurt anyone."

"I din' hurt no one." Al offered his first contribution to the conversation, if it could be called that.

"Yes, you did. You've hurt an entire community, you and your buddy Joe. *If* what I heard is true. Was it you, Al? Did you paint those words on the synagogue wall?"

"So what if I did?" Al shot back. "Din' hurt no one."

Steve sighed. He knew all about the emptiness that was Al's life, and the lives of his friends. With no real future on the reservation and scant hope of ever making good in the big world outside, they often turned to alcohol, drugs, petty crime — anything to lend a touch of color to their drab lives and to foster the illusion that they mattered. Even hate, he figured sadly, could lend that illusion.

He stood up. "I got a call from Sheriff Ramsay over in Lakewood. He's upset over what happened, real upset. I wouldn't want him to come out here to the reservation, looking for someone to let all that upset out on. Would you?"

Al, having apparently talked himself out, went back to saying nothing.

"Al." Something in Steve's voice made the teenager lift his eyes, which had been for the most part riveted to the grimy floor. Holding them with his own, Steve said with quiet emphasis, *"I don't want this kind of thing happening again.* For your sake. Understand?"

Slowly, with obvious reluctance tinged with a grudging but equally genuine respect, Al nodded.

"Good. Nice seeing you, Al." Steve went to the door and, with a pleasant nod for the grandmother peering out at him with frightened eyes, saw himself out.

Chapter 3

I.

"The only thing I don't like about this move," Asher confided to his wife as they sat at their kitchen table making lists, "is leaving Avi behind."

"I know," Rivi said, biting her lip. Her tender heart never failed to break when she thought of her husband's closest friend, Avi Feder. Avi's wife, Yocheved, was very, very ill. The doctors held out slender hope for her, especially now that she had slipped into a coma. It was unbearable, seeing the once vibrant, young woman failing a little more every day. And even more unbearable, if that were possible, was watching Avi struggle for so long to cope with the unimaginable reality that was collapsing in on him like a tower of bricks.

"Our parents, too, of course," Asher added, though with less regret than Rivi would have shown had she been the one to express the sentiment. Asher had been chafing to get away on his own for a long time now. Longer than he was aware, perhaps. For him, this opportunity in New Mexico was a clarion call to leap into the saddle and gallop off to conquer new worlds. Leaving one's parents behind was regrettable, but only to be expected. It was the way of the world. He would miss them, of course, but the imperative to move on was irresistible. He glanced sideways at Rivi, hoping she felt the same way.

She didn't. She wouldn't tell him so, however. *Her* imperative was to support her husband's dream, provide a secure backdrop, help him to be productive and happy. She would miss her mother and father terribly, her in-laws only slightly less. "Hopefully, they'll come out often to visit," she murmured. "And send for us to come see them, too."

"Sure," Asher said easily. "Now, back to this list. Do you really think we should sell the couch and the dining-room set and buy new stuff out there?"

"Absolutely. Why *schlepp* along more than we have to?"

He laughed. "You always were a minimalist, Rivi." He slanted a sly look across the table. "So, what if I were to suggest that we leave behind your easel and painting supplies?"

The look of horror on her face made him laugh even harder. It took her a moment to realize that he was teasing.

"Perish the thought!" she exclaimed, with an answering twinkle. "I'd never survive New Mexico without them. Besides, I want to paint out there. I hear the scenery's breathtaking."

"Well, we'll find out soon enough." They were to take a short pilot trip to their new home the following week — the first couple in the newly forming *kollel* to do so. Nachman Bernstein and Efraim Mandel's teaching responsibilities at the yeshivah precluded either of them from making the trip at this time. "You'll have to report back to us," Efraim had said unhappily. "Etty's going to want to hear every detail."

"You bet I will," Asher had replied, with a forced heartiness; he hadn't forgotten Efraim's hurtful remark at their meeting the previous week.

It was winter in New York: an unending chill that dug deep into bones and froze fingers when they touched unheated steering wheels in the morning. What was the winter like out there? Cool, someone had told him, but never very cold. Clean air — great for young Gila's asthma, and not a bad bonus for the rest of them. Asher felt his spirits rocket to new levels. It was going to be torture, counting off the months till summer. And if he knew his parents and Rivi's, they were going to beg that the couple postpone the move till summer's end instead of letting them fly off at its start, as he longed to do.

"Let's make the most of our time here," Rivi said softly, as though reading his thoughts. "I hate when a decision has been made to leave somewhere or end something, and the present becomes — nothing. Like a troublesome fly you just want to swat away."

"Okay," Asher grinned. "We'll make the most of our time here, by planning our move to New Mexico!"

Reluctantly, Rivi shared his laughter. As she leaned back in her chair, she caught sight of the kitchen clock. Nearly 8 p.m. Her head jerked up, staring at the time in horror. She leaped to her feet and began whipping around the kitchen like a mad woman. Rip off that apron, turn off that burner, find that handbag ... "Oh, no! Visiting hours are almost over at the hospital. I'd planned to run over and sit with Yocheved for a while. I told Avi I would ..." She ran to the front closet for her coat.

She was halfway out the door when the phone rang. Some instinct made her pause despite her hurry. She watched Asher amble over to the phone and lift the receiver.

"Hello? ... Oh, hi, Avi. What's —"

Asher's face changed color. It turned first white, and then a sickly green. At the door Rivi leaned against the wall, her breath coming in quick, painful gasps. She wanted to clap her hands over her ears, so as not to hear the words she knew, without knowing how she knew, would emerge from her husband's lips next.

They came. Rivi's hands hung limply at her sides, and not over her ears, so she heard them with a sickening drop of the heart: the kind of drop that comes with the knowledge that something has shattered irrevocably.

"*Baruch Dayan emes*," Asher whispered.

The funeral was held on a sunny, windless morning. It was a day that sang of life and the joy of living. A day to make you squint and shade your eyes against an impossibly blue sky. A day when death seemed no more real than a dream, something to be tucked away in the shadows because it had no place in this bright, beautiful world. Every cotton-puff cloud, every blade of grass, conspired to make this ceremony a travesty.

In an attempt to hold back the tears, Rivi clenched her fists until they hurt. The effort was futile; the salty drops flowed unchecked. Where was Yocheved today? She should be standing here beside them, relishing each long, cool breath. Not in a wooden box, being lowered respectfully, and with such tender care, into the earth's waiting arms.

Asher, standing beside the bereaved widower, was stunned by the enormity of his grief. He had known Avi Feder since they were boys. They had collected marbles together, and climbed trees, scraped their knees and endured identical scoldings for tearing their pants. They had done their homework together and forgotten to do it together; they had shared their *shidduch* ups and downs and danced jubilantly at each other's weddings.

Now the twin trail had ended. Avi Feder, aged 28, was a widower. A vital phase of his life had slipped away, never to be recaptured. Asher stole a glance at his friend. Avi looked 10 pounds lighter than Asher's mental image of him, and so pale that the single, blue vein throbbing on one temple stood out in harsh contrast. A stab of guilt twisted in Asher's heart. How could he leave Avi at a time like this? Six short months from now, could he simply pack his bags and fly off to New Mexico, leaving his bereaved friend to cope alone with the cold, new world into which he'd been so tragically catapulted?

He shook his head. He wouldn't think about that until he had to. There was plenty that he could do for Avi right here and now. Plenty of comfort and sympathy to offer, though he realized — because he knew Avi so well — that it would be a long time before any form of consolation would find its mark. He and Rivi accompanied Avi, Avi's parents and poor Yocheved's parents back to the apartment, where the mourners were fed the traditional hard-boiled eggs. Only family members and very close friends stayed till the end of the day. It never occurred to Asher to be anywhere else.

Their flight to New Mexico was scheduled for the middle of the *shivah* week; Asher canceled it. Every morning he was present as part of the *minyan*; at his lunch break he was sitting beside Avi again. Supper was eaten with Avi, and Maariv was *davened* at the *shivah* house, followed by the rest of the evening spent at his friend's side. Avi rewarded his devotion with looks of sorrowful gratitude and the occasional wan smile.

Asher knew that the full impact of his loss hadn't even begun to hit the bereaved man yet. Avi looked dazed — like a prizefighter, reeling from a blow, who believes he can still get up and fight again.

It would take some time before he realized that this particular fight was over.

II.

Avi Feder walked into his house and closed the door softly behind him. It was the first time in nearly two weeks that he had the house to himself. The week of mourning had ended several days before, and he had just returned from taking his parents and in-laws to the airport. In stepping over the threshold, he was symbolically taking possession of his home again — and his life. Though, to be honest, he wasn't sure he wanted either.

The house rang with emptiness. The bitter bile of grief rose to his throat as he contemplated life without Yocheved.

Mingled with the grief was fear. He would have died rather than admit it to even his closest friend, but Avi was terrified of facing life alone. In marrying, he had cut the bonds of dependence that had bound him to his mother and father. In their place, his wife had become his security. Yocheved had been his shield against loneliness, his partner in joy and adversity. As a brand-new widower, he felt as insecure as a child again, but without a child's ability to run into his parents' arms for safety. He was a man fully grown and knew he must stand on his own two feet, wobbly as they felt just now. He must face the world with spurious courage, hoping that no one would ever guess at the little-boy panic that welled up in him at the mere prospect of going it alone.

He sank into a deep armchair, letting self-pity engulf him and rob him of the brief spurt of energy that had carried him out to the airport and back. Alone now, there was no need to pretend. Abandoning the armchair, he went to the couch and lay down, head on one arm and feet on the other. Sleep would be nice.

But the blackness that descended on him had nothing to do with sleep.

It was a long blackness. It lasted for weeks, and he struggled through it alone, hardly noticing Asher and Rivi's solicitous calls, their visits and invitations. All these were irrelevant, because other people were irrelevant just now. All that mattered, all that existed, was his pain.

It was a giant pain, a skyscraper of a pain that filled his horizon and blotted out any other view. Avi made no attempt to see around it. With his characteristic doggedness — a trait that was first cousin to courage, though he would have been the last person to call it that — he trudged stoically into the very heart of his anguish, avoiding nothing, ducking none of the blows, but taking them full on the chin.

The weeks took their toll. Always slender, he became gaunt. The circles under his eyes, born during the long vigil at his wife's bedside, seemed to become permanent. He forgot to knot his tie and neglected to tie his shoelaces. Sometimes, he nearly forgot to breathe. Wherever his Yocheved was, he had one foot in that place as well.

It was Asher who finally dragged him back. Asher, with his bluff, direct manner, offering his friendship because he could offer nothing else. Asher seemed to be there at odd moments, when Avi least expected him. He would wake from a sleep that was no sleep, held fast in the grip of his nightmares, to find Asher beside him with an invitation to supper. More to allay his friend's concern than anything else, he forced himself to take part in the conversations that Asher insisted they have. Asher seemed not to mind, or notice, that they were one-sided conversations. Asher talked, and Avi listened … or pretended to.

Asher talked mostly about New Mexico, and the new *kollel* being planned there. At one point, Avi dimly registered a break in the continuity of Asher's presence: The Ganns had flown out to Lakewood to investigate, firsthand, their soon-to-be new home. When they returned, Avi heard about a lake and a river, about sunbaked canyons and desert cactus, about a shul and a day school and a sweet, little community perched near the southwestern rim of the United States.

A strange place, it seemed to the bemused widower. A place that was outside the world he knew. Toiling through the dense fog of his own private limbo, he welcomed anything that was separate and apart from the world where he had experienced such a grievous loss. He began to listen more attentively.

One day, just a little over two months after the funeral, Avi found himself thinking about Lakewood, New Mexico in a different way. Instead of seeming like part of a vague story he had once heard, the place began to take on an immediacy, an almost physical presence. He could practically smell the arid tang of the desert, sniff the pungency of sage and mesquite, hear the soul-chilling howl of the coyote. Was it a howl of pain or of loneliness? Whichever it was, Avi sensed an echo in his own heart. He thought for a long time. Then he went to the phone.

"Asher?" he asked, when his friend's voice sounded on the line. "About the *kollel*?"

"My *kollel*? In New Mexico?"

"That's the one."

"Well, what about it?"

Avi drew a deep breath, and stepped gingerly back into the land of the living. "Count me in."

III.

The preparations started slowly, then grew gradually more frenetic as each household got ready for the move in its own way.

Tova Bernstein's mode of preparation was to do a little packing and a great deal of powwowing. She held a slew of family conferences, formal and informal, planned and spontaneous, at any hour of the day or night. It was not uncommon to find Tova perched on the top stair leading down from the second-floor landing, engaged in earnest conversation with Shana or Chaim or Gila. The kitchen table became the focal point of marathon group discussions. In these sessions she opened the floor to her children's questions and concerns, and did her utmost to answer and allay them. A fleeting glimpse of a downturned mouth, the merest whisper of a sigh, was enough to engage the mother in an earnest heart-to-heart talk with whichever child seemed less than completely happy with the impending change.

It was Shana who minded the most.

"It's a difficult age," Nachman reassured his wife, when she confided her ongoing frustration in helping her daughter cope. They were sitting at the kitchen table, sharing a quiet cup of tea after an especially hectic day in which they'd hardly managed to exchange more than a few hurried words. "She's bound and determined to believe that her life has been ruined. There's nothing to do except let her see that it hasn't been." He paused. "But it's going to take time."

Tova nodded unhappily. Time moved in a different way for her and Nachman than it did for their 14-year-old. For Shana, the prospect of even a day — no, make that an hour! — away from her friends was agonizing. Expect her to smile at a move that would tear her away from them, more or less permanently? Tova was far too realistic for that.

"Will there be other girls for her to be friends with out there?" she asked anxiously, and not for the first time.

"Ought to be. There's a small — a very small — Bais Yaakov-style high school, just right for Shana to start in the fall." Nachman had told her this before, but he knew she needed to hear it again. Asher Gann and Avi Feder, between them, had agreed to homeschool the older Bernstein boys and Shimi Mandel next year. The year after that, if all went well, the new *kollel*-sponsored *mesivta* high school would open its doors — just in time for their Chaim to be part of the first ninth-grade class.

Tova was still consumed with her anxieties over Shana. "What if the school's not up to par? What if she doesn't fit in? What —?"

Nachman held up a hand. "No 'what ifs.' We'll deal with each hurdle as it comes. If we find that something doesn't work, we'll look for a way to fix it. There are out-of-town high schools for girls with dormitories, you know …"

Tova straightened with a jerk. "Send Shana away from home? Never!"

Wisely, he kept silent. "Never," he knew, is a relative word. You take what life hands you and do whatever may be necessary in response. Just as they were doing now, with this gigantic move in response to Gila's condition.

Tova knew this just as well as he did. Which was why he kept silent. No need to rub his wife's face in the loamy grime of reality. Life would handle that job just fine, all on its own.

Etty Mandel's approach was far less verbal and far more tactical. With her relief at this golden opportunity to fuel her, she attacked the house in military fashion, determined to make this the most efficient and cost-effective move in recorded history. And she intended to have the whole thing completed well before her encroaching due-date made her cumbersome and slow.

Every closet was turned out, every drawer upended, every article of clothing and kitchen utensil rigorously inspected. Those that passed muster made their way into one of a row of carefully labeled cartons lined up like suspects against the living-room wall. Prudently, Efraim and the children kept out of her way. Months before the move was due to take place, Etty had just about sorted her home to death. The enemy was well on its way to a state of utter subjugation.

Every now and then, when the house was empty, Etty would pause in the midst of her work and stand quite still, feeling waves of happiness flow over her. She wished she could scoop her youngest up in her arms and hold her pressed to her heart, whispering into the sparse, fragrant hair, "Thank you, thank you, thank you ..." Her family would have been hard pressed to recognize the no-nonsense wife and mother in Etty's suddenly softened eyes and radiant smile. These alarming symptoms had always disappeared by the time the others got home, replaced by Etty's usual businesslike, almost stern, demeanor.

Of Tova Bernstein-style talks there were none. The Mandels weren't that kind of family. What discussions they had revolved around practical matters. If Shimi was upset at leaving his native city, his school and all his playmates, or if Tzirel was heartbroken at leaving behind her devoted best friend, no one knew about it. Their mother didn't ask, and they didn't volunteer the information. They had long ago learned to keep such things to themselves.

And when Shimi began to repeatedly act up in class, to the point where he was sent home with a letter of reprimand for his parents to sign, no one asked him why. Instead, he was grounded for a week in punishment, though after only five days, Etty, out of her mind with the effort of keeping her restless son entertained indoors, surrendered and reduced his sentence to time served.

The Ganns' trip out west was a success. Asher and Rivi returned home with glowing reports about the town that was soon to be their new home. At another hastily cobbled-together meeting, this time in the Ganns' living room, they shared their impressions.

"The scenery is breathtaking," Rivi said over coffee and homemade Danishes. "The sky's incredibly blue, with canyons that plunge so deeply, that sometimes you can hardly see the bottom, while the cliffs soar right up into the sky. And then there's the flat plain along the Pecos River, with a mesa popping up out of the blue every so often. That's a hill with very steep sides but a flat top. The view must be amazing from up there … There's a kind of freshness to the air — a desert-y feel, but not oppressive because it's dry. I saw a flock of geese, and a really interesting group of birds that someone told me are called sandhill cranes. Apparently, they migrate to New Mexico for the winter —"

"That's all very nice," Etty Mandel broke in. "But we're not geese, and we're not going to live in a canyon. What's the housing situation like?"

"Terrific," Asher told her, determined to be polite. "We looked at several very comfortable homes within walking distance of the shul. Affordable, too — nothing like the prices we have to contend with around here. Rabbi Harris and his wife were more than helpful, taking us around and show-ing us the ropes." He went on to describe the day school, the girls' high school and — again, at Etty Mandel's request — the shopping.

As the *Rosh Kollel* designate, Nachman thanked the Ganns for their pilot trip and for this informative meeting. He went on to discuss vari-ous details of the learning programs he hoped to implement with them in the Lakewood, New Mexico community. The air was thick with flying comments and opinions. Only Avi Feder was silent, a ghost among these vital people.

The others were forward looking, ready to blaze a new trail for *Yiddishkeit*. He, newly bereaved, was simply looking for a way out of the maze of pain in which he was wandering. Even now, he sometimes woke in the morning to an instant of peace, a fraction of time in which his loss was not uppermost in his mind. When memory returned to shatter the peace, there was always the tiniest sense of surprise. His wife had been ill for a long time before the end, but death has a way of striking with a sudden arm, to sweep even the most prepared off their feet.

Nachman registered the silence, and turned to him with a smile. "I'm sure I've said this before, Avi, but welcome aboard."

"Thanks," Avi said with a smile. His decision to join the *kollel* had astonished even himself. He hoped it was a good one. They said the New Mexican air was healing. Maybe, with Hashem's help, he would someday join Gila Bernstein on the recovery list.

It seemed a long shot, but Avi Feder knew that he had nothing to lose.

IV.

"Chaim, get the door, will you?" Tova called from the kitchen. It was her late-Friday-afternoon voice, the words striving for a semblance of measured control but betraying themselves by the rising note — a kind of frantic squeak — at the very end.

Chaim went to the front door and opened it for Aunt Heidi. Of course, she wasn't really his aunt, but what else do you call such an old friend of your mother's, someone who's been around ever since you can remember, and by all accounts, even before that? Though Aunt Heidi was like no aunt he'd ever seen. Even on a casual visit she was always high powered, as though she were leading a business conference instead of dropping in on old friends. If he hadn't known her forever, she would definitely have made him nervous.

Heidi Neufeld smiled at her honorary nephew and held out a bottle in a sparkly bag. "Put this in the fridge," she ordered without ceremony, a smile tossed over her shoulder to turn the command into a request. As always, Heidi exuded an air of brisk authority. She might be wearing a simple skirt and blouse in place of her usual tailored business suit, but it made no difference: Aunt Heidi was a lawyer, through and through.

Heidi followed Chaim into the kitchen, where she helped him locate (not without difficulty) an empty spot for the wine in the groaning refrigerator. Then she hugged Tova. "What can I do to help?" she asked, rolling up her sleeves. "Just throw me an apron, Chaim, would you?"

Chaim, who was beginning to feel like an unpaid paralegal, tossed her the requested item and beat a hasty retreat from the kitchen.

"Oh, it's so good to see you, Heidi," Tova said, as her pot of soup began to bubble over and the fragrance of overdone kugel wafted from the oven. "Not that I have time to see you right now," she added hastily, grabbing a pot holder and advancing on the stove.

"We'll talk later," Heidi agreed. She turned on the water in the sink and started on the huge mound of dirty pots and utensils waiting there. Tova was definitely not the clean-as-you-go type of homemaker.

With her friend's help, Tova managed to have the food cooked and warming peacefully on the *blech* with a full 15 minutes to spare before candlelighting. "Bless you, Heidi," she sighed, dropping into a chair. "I'll run up and shower in a minute, but first — oh, my aching feet!"

"You should talk," Heidi groaned. "Have you ever seen what I have to wear to work? High heels, each and every day. Some of them higher than others, but all of them sheer torture."

"Why do you do it, then?" Shana asked curiously, having wandered into the kitchen in search of her mother.

Heidi shrugged. "Gotta climb the ladder, sweetie."

"What's that supposed to mean?"

"It means that Aunt Heidi is ambitious to succeed at her job," Tova explained. "And she knows the magic formula: Dress for success!" Thoughtfully she surveyed her daughter, who was wearing a fairly new knit outfit that the two of them had bought in a painstaking bout of shopping, and murmured, "Then again, don't we all do the same thing?"

"*I* don't!" Shana said, tossing her still-damp hair.

"Don't you? Don't you care what your friends think of clothes? To be considered well dressed is a kind of success for you girls, too."

Seeing Shana's flush, Heidi said hastily, "Okay, let's not get personal here. The real reason I wear high heels, Shana, is because I like the way they look. But, boy, do I pay the price! Nothing that a good, long soak won't cure, though."

She grinned at the girl, who somewhat grudgingly grinned back. Shana remembered why she'd come into the kitchen in the first place. "Ma, where do you keep the safety pins?"

Tova told her, and Shana exited to finish dressing. Tova struggled to her feet and started upstairs, while Heidi went into the guest bedroom, nearly as familiar to her as her own Manhattan high-rise, to prepare for a night and a day of perfect contentment.

Shabbos was wonderful, as it always was when she spent it at the Bernsteins. She could be another Heidi here, away from the pressures of work and image-making. Even the time she spent at home with her parents was not stress-free in quite this way — not as long as she clung to her single status. She understood her family's desperate desire to see her happily married, but knowing it and liking it were two very different things.

At the Bernsteins, she could, literally and figuratively, kick off her shoes and relax. She adored the kids, she respected Nachman, and she simply and devotedly loved Tova. From their very first meeting, as teenagers, the two had clicked. There was something about Tova — an openness, and a matter-of-fact acceptance of who her friends were — that was, for Heidi, a life-giving elixir.

They talked in snatches throughout Shabbos: one long conversation that began Friday night when the men were in shul, carried on over coffee Shabbos morning, and continued in snatches before and after their Shabbos naps. At the *Seudah Shelishis*, which Nachman and the boys had at shul, Tova and Heidi raised their voices in the kind of harmony they had relished back in high school.

"The two of you still sound great," Shana remarked as she doled another dab of potato salad onto her plate. It was on the tip of her mother's tongue to point out that serving oneself a great many tiny portions does not fool the body into thinking you're eating any less; prudently, she refrained. In any case, Shana was not overweight; she only thought she was. This was one battle Tova declined to join.

It was a regretful Heidi who said good-bye that night. Standing by the open front door, with her expensive leather overnight-bag at her feet, she hugged Tova again. "I still can't believe you're moving all the way to New Mexico!" The move, and new *kollel*, had of course been the main topic of conversation all Shabbos. She wailed the words humorously, but there was tragedy in her eyes. "When do you leave, exactly?"

"The week of *Rosh Chodesh Av*. Exactly five months from now." For the first time, Heidi noticed the clown on the door, the traditional harbinger of *Adar* at the Bernsteins. *Rosh Chodesh*, she remembered, was tomorrow.

"Too soon," she complained. "And way too far."

Tova made a face. "I agree with you there. I don't want you so far away, Heidi. What will I do without my favorite Shabbos guest?"

"I'll fly out."

"Often, right?"

"But of course. I'll be a frequent flyer to end all frequent flyers."

The two women smiled at each other. A night wind came to ruffle Heidi's thick, brown hair. Impatiently she brushed it back from her forehead. "Wait here." She picked up her bag, and was gone.

She was back a minute later, minus the bag and struggling to hump something else up the stairs. "I left this in my trunk over Shabbos," she puffed. "I saw it on sale and decided it would make a perfect housewarming gift for your New Mexico place."

Tova gazed down at her friend's offering. "This" was a brightly striped patio umbrella, ideal for shading tender skin from the harsh, Southwestern sun. "Heidi!" she laughed in astonishment. "Where in the world did you find this in the middle of the winter?"

"The best time to shop for summer," the lawyer said. "Got it at a tremendous discount. This is top-quality merchandise, you know."

"I don't doubt it. Thank you, Heidi. We'll think of you every time we sit under it." Tova made a mental note to buy a patio table first thing, to prop up this umbrella.

"You do that. Though I call first dibs on it when I come visit."

"It's a deal."

Heidi sketched a smiling salute and started for her car. Tova remained where she was, framed in the doorway until her friend was out of sight.

The memory of that Shabbos lingered as Heidi strode into the office Monday morning. As usual, she made directly for the coffee machine. There she met her colleague, Kimberly Stone of the frosted hair and heels even higher than Heidi's. Kimberly didn't look good this morning. In fact, at second glance, Heidi saw that she was just one short step away from haggard.

"Out partying all weekend?" Heidi asked as she poured her coffee.

"Are you kidding? I was busy juggling two kids, four briefs, and at least three social obligations I had absolutely no desire to meet," Kimberly told her, munching moodily on a donut. "Some party."

"Well, at least you can look on the office as a vacation."

"Some vacation. With this constant pressure to bill more and more hours." Kimberly looked up suddenly, as though seeing the other woman for the first time. "You know, I envy you, Heidi. No husband, no kids, no family responsibilities. You can rack up those hours to your heart's content — and still have time and energy left over for fun and games." She sighed. "Lucky you."

Heidi pictured the Bernstein Shabbos table, with Nachman at the head playing benevolent despot when the kids got out of hand, Tova scurrying around trying to serve the meal before the little ones became too drowsy to eat, and the kids being kids, talking and fighting and telling silly jokes and singing too loudly and usually off-key. Then she thought of her home office, and the desk where a pile of legal briefs waited patiently for her, night after night, like the most loyal of friends.

"Lucky?" she echoed hollowly. "You think so?"

"I *know* so," Kimberly declared. "Take today, for instance. I had to take Cyndi to day care with a nose that was running like a faucet, and my Eddie's playing a soccer match that I'll have to miss."

"Why?"

"Why? You know the answer to that as well as I do. Can't fall behind. What would Mr. Flaxen say? Gotta rack up those billable hours, girl!"

She stuffed the last of her donut into her mouth, mumbled a mournful farewell and vanished in the direction of her own office.

The area around the coffee machine was momentarily deserted. Heidi sipped her coffee, thinking over what her colleague had just said. Up until a very short time ago, she'd have agreed with it. "Lucky" was just the way she would have described herself. She had it all: upwardly mobile career, a fantastic income, a wardrobe women gnashed their teeth over and as much of a social life as she wanted.

She thought suddenly of Shana, and a question occurred to her: If Shana had been *her* daughter, would she have chosen herself as the girl's role model?

Abruptly, she put down her mug and started rapidly for her desk. She didn't want to think about the answer.

V.

The whirlwind of the emergency room had given way to late-night quietness on the ward. Old Henry was lying in a high white bed, tubes and wires snaking out of his arms, nose and chest. His skin was a ghastly color and his eyes — when he troubled to open them — were a sickly yellow and bloodshot at the same time. *Not a very savory sight*, the nurse thought as she checked his vital signs. She glanced at the younger man, sprawled in a chair at the patient's side, asleep with his mouth turned down, as though discontented even in his dreams.

Bobby Smith stirred at the nurse's approach. She smiled professionally. "I gave him something to ease the pain. He'll sleep easier now."

"Guess I'll be going, then." He began to drag himself up from the chair in which, unwittingly, he'd fallen into a doze a few minutes before. Old Henry, he had been told by an earnest young doctor, had sustained internal injuries and must be kept in the hospital for further tests. That was fine with Bobby. He cursed his luck for involving him in this business in the first place. The sooner he got out of here, the better.

With another professional smile, the nurse left the room. Bobby was about to do the same, when a bony hand shot out and clamped onto his wrist with a viselike grip. Despite appearances, Old Henry was not yet asleep, and his hold was surprisingly strong. He had something to say.

"Listen, young fella ... Bobby?" he said urgently. "Listen to me ..."

Bobby made a futile effort to shake the hand off. "Why don't you go back to sleep? You can talk tomorrow."

"No ... now. Don't know ... how long I got ..."

"You're gonna be fine," Bobby said impatiently, resisting the impulse to wrench his wrist free. "Go to sleep, old man. We'll talk in the morning." *Right*, he thought scornfully. As if he'd willingly walk into this place again anytime soon ...

"No. *Now*." The old man's voice was thready but surprisingly insistent. "It's about ... somethin' good. About ... treasure."

This got Bobby's attention. Slowly he sank back into his chair, which he pulled closer to the bed. "What treasure you talking about, Henry?"

"Family treasure ... Wife's family, that is." Henry's eyes were wide open now, and fixed on Bobby's with a strange intensity.

"Your wife's family has a treasure?"

"Listen," Henry said again. He paused as a paroxysm of coughing took hold. Presently, wheezing, he tried again. "Old story ... Wife got it from ... her mama ... who got it from hers ... and so on ... back a long way."

"What story?"

"Treasure ... in the cave ..."

"What cave? *What cave?*"

"Treasure in the family ... Alice's family. She was s'posed to tell *her* daughter ... only she never had none. Only the boy."

Bobby leaned forward, lips compressed in excitement. What did he care about Alice or her daughters? "Tell me where the treasure is, you old fool!" he snapped.

Henry didn't seem to mind the epithet. It seemed doubtful that he even heard it. He was intent on pursuing some train of his own.

"Alice's boy ... Steve. Nice little kid ... but always preachin' at me these days. Tellin' me I drink too much. He's right ... But who wants t' be preached at ... all the time?"

It was with difficulty that Bobby restrained himself. He breathed hard through his nose, trying to hold onto his patience. "Where — is — the — treasure?" he hissed.

"That's why I'm tellin' *you* ... 'stead of Steve."

"Steve Birch? Is that who you're talking about?" Bobby knew that Old Henry and the lawyer were related somehow.

Henry nodded jerkily. "Alice's boy ... my stepson. He was s'posed to be ... a daughter, y'know ..."

What was that supposed to mean? The old man was wandering in his head. Bobby had no time for this. He brought his face to within inches of the old man's, intent on moving the talk back on track. *Treasure ...*

"*Where?*" he asked.

The look that Old Henry flicked at him was surprisingly alert. "In the caves. You go have a look ... Bobby. Find that treasure. You been good ... to an old man ... I been all alone in the world ... since Alice went. No one cares 'bout ... ol' Henry anymore." A tear trickled down one weathered cheek and landed on the pillow by Henry's head. He seemed danger-ously close to descending into a pool of whining self-pity.

"Henry, tell me which caves. There are caves everywhere!"

Another coughing spasm racked the old man's chest. His face turned even grayer, and for one brief moment, he seemed incapable of catching his breath. Bobby waited with rising impatience. He wondered if there was anything to the story. He remembered Henry's wife. Alice had been — different. The same way Steve Birch, her son, was different. Nothing you could put your finger on, but in some elusive way removed from the other Mescalero Apaches. If anyone might have a family secret hidden in the mysterious mists of time, it was not hard to believe that ethereal, dreamy-eyed Alice would be the one.

The spasm passed. Old Henry lay with a heaving chest for several agonizing seconds, exhausted by the mere act of drawing breath. Bobby was about to ask again, when the old man opened his eyes, fixed them on his own, and said distinctly, "Find it, Bobby. I want … you to have it. You're … my friend …"

"But where do I find it?" Bobby's voice had a frantic edge to it as he leaned over the patient's face. "Describe the place to me, Henry."

But Old Henry was past describing anything. His eyes closed with finality now, and presently the room was filled with his wheezing snores.

Bobby left. He found Big Jim waiting for him down in the lobby. He brushed aside Jim's questions. "Leave me be. I'm thinking."

Big Jim had the greatest respect for Bobby's thinking. He fell into a reverent silence, suiting his step to Smith's as they walked out of the hospital into the cool, arid night.

Jim had brought his car. It was an old jalopy, its seats held together with chicken wire and a horn that didn't work, but it would take Bobby where he wanted to go. Which, at the moment, was as far away from this place as possible. Hospitals gave him the willies.

Jim had put seven miles on the odometer when Bobby finally spoke. "Jim, you 'n me are about to strike it rich!"

"Really? How so, Bobby?"

"There's a great big treasure waiting for us, over in the caves near Lakewood. We're gonna find us that treasure — and live like kings!" He had already decided that Big Jim's strong arms and unquestioning devotion would be useful to him in the search.

It never occurred to Big Jim to question Bobby's prophecies. However, he was curious to learn their source. "Old Henry tell you about it just now?" he guessed shrewdly.

"Yes. He wants me to be the one to find it. Guess he loves me like a son ... just 'cause I went along to the hospital with him in that ambulance." Bobby gave a shout of laughter. "Cheapest road to treasure *I* ever heard of!" He felt elated, away from that sour-smelling sickroom at last and on his way to a future lined in gold.

Big Jim had thought of something. "What about Steve Birch? Old Henry's his stepdad, isn't he?"

"What about him? Steve's out of the picture. Old Henry told me so, see? So you just keep your big mouth shut, you hear?"

"Sure — sure, Bobby. I won't say a word."

"Not to Steve, or to anyone."

"You can count on me, Bobby."

He was exultant. The black ribbon of road seemed to be rushing him headlong to meet his great good fortune. He pictured gold — or diamonds, maybe — tucked away in a hiding place in those ancient caves for generations ... waiting just for him. A sense of destiny joined with his greed; the combination filled him with a heady elixir of excitement. Talk about a short cut to success! He could forget petty jobs, irritable bosses and nonexistent bonuses. He was about to strike it rich. And no one, he told himself smugly as he leaned back in his seat and watched the parade of rosy visions march across his mind's eye, deserved it more.

He fell asleep planning a visit to the hospital again next day, to see if he could dig up any further details about the treasure and its location. He intended to pump Old Henry dry.

But morning brought the news that Henry was not talking. Sometime in the night he had slipped into a coma. The doctors weren't saying much, but given Old Henry's age and general state of deterioration, the prognosis was not good.

Bobby cursed his bad luck. No point making the trip to the hospital now. He would be better off spending the day looking for some kind of work. He barely had two cents to rub together.

Besides, he told himself as he got ready to face a morning that had promised to be a first step toward a golden tomorrow but was now just the start of an ordinary day, Old Henry had probably been hallucinating or something. Delusional, that was the word, after the knock on the head and all. Not that the old man was very coherent even at the best of times. Combine an empty bottle with a knock-down accident, and it wasn't likely that Henry had been talking any kind of sense at all.

It was probably all a pack of moonshine, Bobby thought, jamming his nearly empty wallet into his pocket and starting out the door. *Nothing but wishful thinking. Just an old man's pipe dream.*

Probably.

Chapter 4

I.

All the planning, the meetings, the packing and the leave-taking were finally behind them. They had arrived.

It was August, and New York's dripping humidity had been magically replaced by a totally different, arid heat. The flight, the twilight drive through an exotic landscape to their new town, the hasty supper and the exhausted falling into bed — all these were behind them now, a blurred dream. These past few days, the children, like Tova herself, seemed to be living in a state of suspended animation; one in which the old reality was still very much with them and the new one had not yet quite taken hold. Their presence here felt more like a temporary visit — "My Summer Vacation in the Southwest" — than actual real life. Perhaps that was the reason for the children's unusually subdued behavior since the move. They weren't talking much, and more important for their mother, they weren't fighting much, either. Even Shana was doing her sulking in silence.

Unpacking was an ongoing process, purposeful but leisurely. If it took them a week, or even two, to put things in order, so what? The kids had no school and the bulk of the parents' communal responsibilities had not yet begun. There was a great deal of shopping to do, as well — odd bits of furniture to fill in the gaps in their new and larger home, towels and dishcloths to replace the worn-out ones left behind in the East ... and a white, plastic patio table and chairs for the backyard. The moment this was delivered, Tova asked Nachman to plant Heidi's big umbrella right in the center. As the pole dropped neatly into its designated hole, Tova felt a sense of comfort — almost as though her friend were standing beside her instead of going about her lawyerly affairs a couple of thousand miles to the east.

She would wake up at odd moments of the night and wonder where she was. Her children, apparently, were suffering from the same sense of disorientation. "I keep forgetting we moved," little Yudi complained one morning. "I keep waking up and wanting to know where my old room is!"

Tova recalled this with a smile as she put her shopping list in her pocketbook. It was Thursday, time to stock up the pantry. Whatever may happen in life — whatever crazy twists of fate may overtake a family or a country or the globe — stomachs must be filled. It was the one bright spot of sanity in what, at moments, felt to Tova like an almost surreal situation.

"Gila!" she called at the door. "Hurry up, sweetie. Let's check out the supermarket." She paused. "Unless you've changed your mind and want to stay home with Shana and Chaim?" Gila had never been big on walking, and walking was just what her mother was planning to do now. Nachman had taken the car that morning. Tova might consider herself on vacation, but her husband was already busy with *kollel* matters — foremost of which was finding a suitable property on which they might build. Marvin Fleischmann, their benefactor, was insistent on this point.

"I don't know how many more years I have left on this earth," he reminded Nachman in a phone call, sealing their pact. "I want to see both the *kollel* and the boys' yeshivah in action, in their own building, before my time comes." And Nachman had given him his word that, if his own efforts had anything to do with it, Fleischmann would.

"Coming, Ma," Gila called back from upstairs. "Just a second."

"Fine. I'll wait outside."

Stepping out of the whitewashed, stucco house that had become "home," Tova Bernstein stood blinking in the blinding sun, struck by the strangeness of it all.

This place was — alien. There was no other word for it. There was no whiff, no reminder, of what "home" used to mean. No redbrick Brooklyn buildings, no sensibly numbered streets or rows of familiar shops selling items useful to an observant family. The air seemed to shimmer whitely around her on the sun-baked street. Everywhere she looked were dust and rock and plants whose names she didn't know. The very sky looked different, as if it belonged to some other race of creatures. *At how many different skies had the Jewish people gazed up over the millennia*, Tova wondered, in a philosophic vein unusual for her.

The air smelled different, too: drier, tinged with faint, foreign scents. Desert scents. Their home was near the edge of town; just past the shoulders of the houses across the street was a vastness that made Tova's heart twist. Never before had she felt her own — and the Jewish people's — exile as keenly as she did here, on her own, still-unfamiliar doorstep in Lakewood, New Mexico.

What am I doing here? she thought. In all the months leading up to the move, it had been she who had dealt with everyone's questions and insecurities. But what about her? What about the friends that *she'd* left behind, and the pleasant home, well worn by memories, that she'd been forced to abandon? Who was going to make sense of it for her?

Behind her, the door opened again. Gila stepped out into the sun, blinking just the way her mother had done a moment earlier. The girl breathed deeply of the dry air, as though she knew how beneficial every atom was to her delicate lungs. In actuality, however, Tova doubted if her 9-year-old really understood much of that. All Gila knew was that her family had moved to New Mexico to cut down on all those distressful visits to the emergency room. Here, her parents had promised, she would be well. They had cut ties pleasant and even precious to them — all because of her. The young girl had carried that knowledge out here with her, a twin burden of relief and guilt.

She smiled up at her mother now. "It's nice here."

Suddenly, the queer, oppressed feeling — the sense of alienation — fell away. The strangeness was still there, but not the desolation or the need for comfort. This place *was* the comfort. Tova looked at her daughter, blond hair gleaming in the sun and round face so innocently happy, and a surge of an echoing emotion filled her own heart. Watching Gila, her mother knew the joy of new beginnings. The joy of hope ...

So what if everything she saw was foreign to her? She was not alone. Sharing the strangeness was her husband, Nachman — the rock that anchored them all — and her darling children. Most important of all, Gila would be healthy here. She would, literally, breathe easier in this place. That made everything worth the cost.

And then there was their mission: reaching out to lost Jewish souls, building something enduring in this isolated corner of the American continent. There was so much to be done, and such fun to be had in doing it! People to meet, functions to plan, classes to give, things to see. It was with a smile on her face that she said, "Let's go, Gila. We've got things to do!"

They started down the street toward the supermarket, some three blocks away.

Tova didn't mind the fact that Nachman had taken the car today. She welcomed the opportunity to walk. Before too long, she was determined to get to know every inch of Lakewood. If this was going to be "home," she was going to make sure she *felt* at home!

One block into their trek, the cell phone in her purse rang. Tova was tempted to ignore it. She wanted to relish this first outing on foot, and her daughter's silent but friendly company. Another ring. With a sigh, she pulled the phone out of her bag and flipped it open, stilling the monotonous melody with a brisk, "Hello?"

"Tova? It's Heidi."

"Heidi! How're you doing? I miss you!"

"I miss you too." Heidi sounded odd — as if she were half-asleep, though it was midmorning back in New York. "Can't really talk now. I just wanted to hear your voice ..."

"Heidi, are you all right?"

"I'm fine. Just fine. Life's just hunky-dory, isn't it?"

"Heidi —"

"I really do have to run, Tova. Just wanted to let you know I'm thinking about you. The place sounds terrific. Stay in touch with more details, O.K.?"

"Sure, Heidi. But —"

"Bye ..." The connection was lost.

Tova frowned at the phone, which glinted back at her in the fierce summer sun. What was *that* about? Heidi should be in the thick of her workday right now, over her head in files and torts or whatever it was she surrounded herself with at the office — and loving every minute of it. Somehow, Tova had the impression that her friend was not in the office at all. Half-asleep, she'd sounded ... in the middle of the morning ...

The phone rang again. With an effort Tova pushed the mounting worry from her mind as she automatically scanned the phone's caller-ID screen. It read: "Harris."

"Hello?"

"Mrs. Bernstein? This is Penina Harris?" The voice ended on an upward note, a question mark. *Do you know me?*

Tova smiled into the phone. "Hello, Mrs. Harris. The rabbi's wife, right?"

"Right. My husband met you all at the airport the other day, but I haven't had a chance to see you yet. That's why I'm calling."

"Well, how nice!"

"Is this a bad time?"

"I'm just on my way to the market. On foot, I may add. It's the only way to get acquainted with a new place, I always think."

A chuckle. "I agree. Though walking takes time, and that's one thing that always seems to be in such short supply these days ..."

"I know what you mean. Nowadays, using your feet is something you do for 'exercise' — not to get anywhere. Right now, though, I'm enjoying every minute of it." She smiled down at Gila, who gave a little skip and smiled back.

Penina Harris cleared her throat. "Tova, chatting on the phone is fun, but maybe we can do this more conveniently — and certainly more pleasantly — in person. I'd like to invite you and your family to join us for Shabbos lunch?" Again the interrogatory note.

"Of course!" Tova smiled into the phone. "We'd love to come. I'm hardly done with the unpacking, so cooking for Shabbos is not going to be that easy ..."

"Don't bother. Didn't my husband tell you? We have a committee for that sort of thing. Someone will be bringing around your Friday-night *seudah*."

"Really? How nice!" Tova's heart warmed at the thought. "Now I really feel welcome."

"You should be. We've been waiting for you people very eagerly, you know. The *kollel's* generating lots of excitement around here — not to mention the new *mesivta* high school that's in the works ..."

They chatted a few minutes longer, until the supermarket's doors loomed just ahead of Tova. Regretfully, she said, "I guess I'd better concentrate on the shopping now. Oh! I forgot to ask which *hechshers* you use out here."

"My goodness." Penina Harris sounded irritated. It took a moment for Tova to realize that the irritation was directed inward, back at Mrs. Harris herself. "I really should have spoken to you before this — helped you find your way around," she apologized. "It's just that ... well, as principal of the girls' high school, I sometimes find myself almost too busy to think. I've been really snowed under this week — going from one crisis to the next, it seems. How we're going to open up for business in just a few weeks is beyond me ..."

"I understand," Tova said quickly. "Please don't give it a thought. If you could just fill me in right now, I'll get through the shopping with no problem at all."

Penina filled her in. Tova memorized the information, then hung up with an exchange of friendly farewells. Belatedly, she remembered Gila, plodding so patiently along beside her all this time. Snapping the phone shut, she buried it in the depths of her pocketbook.

She smiled down at Gila. "All right, sweetie?"

Gila beamed back. "Fine, Ma!"

Taking her daughter's hand and swinging it as she went, Tova Bernstein marched into the supermarket to purchase the commodities that lie at the physical heart of any home: food.

II.

"**N**ice house," Chaim Bernstein commented as, ever the trailblazer, he led the family up the path to the Harris's front door.

"It's bigger than ours," his brother Donny noted without rancor.

Gila said softly, "But ours is a prettier color."

Tova waited for Shana to say something, but her oldest daughter kept her lips mutinously shut. Though dressed in her Shabbos best, Shana looked definitely unfestive. The clues were in the way she carried herself these days: head low, shoulders hunched protectively, smile nonexistent. Tova sighed and tried to catch her husband's eye. But Nachman had just swooped down to catch one of their 2-year-old twins as the child darted, laughing, right into the street. Luckily, on this sleepy Saturday morning there was no traffic in sight. Both Moshe and Boruch — better known as Mo and Bo — had been blessed with a welldeveloped sense of adventure that called for constant vigilance. With Bo held in one firm grip and Mo in the other, Nachman Bernstein overtook his older sons in a few swift strides and stepped up to the door.

This was opened almost immediately by Rabbi Harris himself. Beyond him, they had a glimpse of a smiling, aproned Penina Harris. There were no children in sight.

"Empty nest," Penina confided in the kitchen a moment later. Her eyes held a gleam both humorous and resigned. "We have three kids. Both boys are away at camp, and it's back to yeshivah after that. Debby, our oldest, is married and living in Denver." She spread her hands, one of which was clutching a pair of salad tongs. "It's just the two of us now. Hope your kids won't be bored."

Tova said that her kids were never bored. A crescendo of laughter from the living room reached their ears, as though in confirmation.

Rabbi Harris was in his best entertainer's mode when the women entered to put the finishing touches on the dining-room table. His funny anecdotes were being very well received by the Bernstein children — and not only the children, Tova noticed. Nachman was grinning broadly as well.

Penina Harris was a competent, if uninspired, cook. The Bernstein boys were grateful for the plain, hearty fare — chopped liver that looked and tasted like chopped liver, and not some mysterious melange of vegetables chopped, sauteed, and mixed out of all recognition; a "normal" salad — that is, one featuring things they could identify and call by name — and innumerable bottles of their favorite soft drink to quench their thirst. Gila, too, ate happily enough, maintaining her usual contented silence.

If Shana picked at her food and said only as much as was absolutely necessary for courtesy's sake, Tova could only hope that, in the ruckus that her other children were making, their hosts didn't notice.

"So, you're here at last!" Pinchas Harris said, rubbing his hands together with a huge smile. "You must have a million questions, Rabbi Bernstein —"

"Please. It's Nachman."

"Nachman, then. What would you like to know about our little town?"

Nachman and Tova exchanged a look. "Everything!" they said together.

Pinchas chuckled. As his wife busied herself in the kitchen again — she absolutely forbade Tova to join her this time — he launched into a vivid description of some of the highlights of their tiny community.

"My wife, you've met. She's principal of our little Bais Yaakov. We're very proud of it — and of her, of course. Who would ever have expected a high school like this out here in the middle of nowhere? But Penina had the vision to see it. We had a handful of girls in the community, all within a year or two in age and all in desperate need of a good, religious high school."

"Were these newly observant families?" Nachman asked with interest.

"Well, by and large. Except for a few *frum* families that somehow stumbled upon us for one reason or another, the rest of the Jews in town were — and many still are — uneducated in Judaism. Unreached … but by no means unreachable."

"And you've tried to reach them."

"Well, we try. There's been an amazing response. A Jew, in his soul, wants to be a Jew! Membership in our shul started out as a trickle. Now — eight years later — we've got 100 families on the list, and we're still growing." Rabbi Harris paused. "Of course, only about 40 of those families are actually mitzvah observant. But they've all got a strong Orthodox affiliation, and that's important."

"Beautiful," Nachman murmured appreciatively.

"We think so ... Well, we've also got our day school — six years old now, and growing by leaps and bounds, *Baruch Hashem*. Run by a brilliant but unassuming woman named Simi Wurtzler. Married to Yehoshua Wurtzler, our resident computer pro. Works as a consultant around these parts ... You'll find a lot of overlap on the shul's and day school's Board of Directors. There's Nate Goodman: fine young man, very interesting character, an attorney by profession, plays the piano like a dream and lives just a couple of blocks from your place. Ben Sadowsky's a pediatrician; he practices out of Memorial ... The two of them are my *gabbaim* at the shul. I couldn't ask for better!

"Sammy Cohen is an industrialist, gives incredible amounts to *tzeddakah*, practically supports this whole house of cards all by himself ... And then there is Abe Rein. *Doctor* Rein, I should say. He earned his Ph.D. at Columbia." Pinchas paused for effect. "Abe's a forensic psychiatrist."

"A — what?" Tova asked.

"Forensic psychiatrist." Rabbi Harris was clearly enjoying the moment, as proud as if he'd invented both the profession and its local, observant practitioner. "That basically means a person who studies the criminal mind. Abe's an expert, works with our county penal system. He has some interesting stories to tell."

"I'm sure he does," Nachman said. "I'm looking forward to meeting all of them." He leaned forward, thanked Penina Harris for the bowl of *cholent* she'd just passed him, and said, "How are the relations between Jews and non-Jews in the town?"

It was nothing — the merest fraction in time. But that fraction, as Tova and Nachman agreed when comparing notes later, was charged with an electric current powerful enough to light a bulb. Penina Harris seemed to stiffen slightly. Her husband carefully did not meet her eye. He turned to Nachman, addressing his question.

"Oh, it's basically fine," Pinchas Harris said expansively. "Just fine. Of course, there have been minor incidents. Neighbors of the shul complaining about the lack of parking on the block during *minyanim*, or a

Simchas Torah celebration a little too loud for their taste — that sort of thing. Sheriff Ramsay, our local lawman, is sympathetic to our needs. But complaints like these have prompted us to urge that the new *mesivta*-slash-*kollel* be located just outside town, rather than in its center. No need to get the locals' backs up."

"Luckily," his wife said, relaxing slightly, "Rabbi Greenfeld has found a sponsor."

"Yes," Nachman smiled. "He has. And that sponsor has given me the green light to go ahead and find the most suitable site, and get the ball rolling on construction. We're all anxious to see this thing up and running as quickly as possible."

"If anyone can do it," Pinchas Harris said sincerely, "I'm sure you can."

Himself a visionary, a fervent idealist, he deferred with a sincere admiration that bordered almost on awe, to the kind of resolute and practical strength that Nachman Bernstein seemed to typify. This was the very best kind of marriage of the spiritual and the worldly: a man with one eye on heaven and the other on the road to be traveled. A doer.

Recalling his own silence on the subject of the hateful graffiti on the shul wall, he felt a pang. But all that had happened six months ago. The trashing of Goldman's Grocery a couple of months back, and Harry Rosenberg's smashed car window just last week, *might* have been the work of ordinary teenaged hoodlums, and not a Jew-centered message at all — even though something looking suspiciously like a swastika had been smeared in paint on the windshield ...

No use frightening these good people, he told himself, uncomfortably aware of his wife's scrutiny as he went on speaking. Penina was all for "putting our cards on the table," as she expressed it. But Pinchas disagreed. Talking about things, bringing them out into the open, only lent them weight. It made them come alive, somehow. And the last thing he wanted in his lovely Lakewood was the specter of anti-Semitism springing out of the shadows. Acknowledged. Alive.

So he continued doing what he had been doing for the past half year. He put it out of his mind and said nothing.

III.

"What a nice couple," Tova said as they slowly walked home later. Shana and Gila each had a twin by the hand — Mo and Bo were adamant in their rejection of the double stroller, which turned every family walk into an exercise in patience — while Chaim and Donny were telling young Yudi a story that was making his round blue eyes even rounder.

"Very nice," Nachman agreed. There was a tiny frown between his eyes.

"What's the matter?" Tova asked.

He hesitated. "I just had the feeling that Pinchas Harris was hiding something."

"I know. I felt it, too."

"It might be nothing ... probably is. Still ..."

"If it was nothing," Tova completed the thought, "why hide it?"

Nachman nodded, clearly unhappy. "Well, I guess whatever it is will come out sooner or later. Things usually do."

"That's all?" Tova demanded. "'Things usually do'? Where's the burning curiosity? Don't you even *want* to know what's going on?"

"Of course," he smiled. "However, at the moment, I don't know. And I'm not about to press Pinchas Harris about it. So ..."

He didn't finish his sentence, and he didn't have to. Tova knew him too well to try and change his mind. Yudi skipped back to share the tall tale his big brothers had just fed him, and the parents' attention was firmly engaged for the rest of the way home.

The moment she finished cleaning up after Shabbos and herding her little ones to bed, Tova went to the phone. She had been turning over in her mind Heidi's strange call on Thursday, and itching to call her ever since.

Heidi's home number rang and rang. *Maybe she's out on a date*, Tova thought hopefully. New York was in a different time zone, two hours behind New Mexico. Had she called too early? With mounting impatience she gave herself another half-hour, then tried again. Still no answer. She decided to try Heidi's cell phone. Just to make sure her friend was "all right," she thought vaguely, leaving the parameters of her unease undefined even to herself.

This, too, rang on unanswered. Strange, she reflected. Heidi usually kept her cell phone with her at all times. In fact, she liked to paraphrase the poem about the child and his shadow, saying, "*I have a little cell phone that goes in and out with me/And what can be the use of it is more than I can see* ..." Except that Heidi did find her cell phone useful. It was her aide, her secretary, and sometimes even (Tova privately thought) her companion.

She left a message on both phones. Then, after a brief hesitation, she looked up Heidi's parents' home number and dialed that.

"Mrs. Neufeld? This is Tova Bernstein speaking. How are you?"

"Oh — Tova!" Was she imagining it, or was that relief she heard in her friend's mother's voice? Mrs. Neufeld, who had long ago mastered the art of small talk, had no patience for it tonight. With uncharacteristic directness, she asked, "Were you looking for Heidi?"

"As a matter of fact, I am. I've tried both her phones —"

"Don't bother. She's not answering."

"What?"

Mrs. Neufeld drew a long, quivering breath, then let it out in an audible sigh. "Heidi's on vacation, Tova. A spur-of-the-moment thing. She suddenly seemed to get — I don't know — fed up? She had so much vacation time coming to her, piled up over the past three years at *least*. So ... she took it."

"Where'd she go?" Tova didn't know if she should be happy that her hardworking friend had finally decided to take some time off, or anxious over the suddenness of it all. This was not like Heidi. She was the archetypical planner, the tourist who never budged from home without a meticulously typed itinerary and everything booked in advance.

"That's just it — we don't know. She wouldn't tell us. She said she needed some time alone ... and that she'd be in touch." Mrs. Neufeld sounded on the verge of tears. "Only, she hasn't."

Tova's heart leaped up in alarm. "Not at all?"

"Just a brief call on the first day, to tell us she was going ... wherever it is she's gone."

Tova's heart gradually ceased its mad jig. This didn't sound quite as terrifying. Heidi just wanted some privacy. Nothing so terrible about that.

Still, if she were strictly honest with herself, she'd have to admit that she shared Mrs. Neufeld's concern. It didn't sound terrible — but it wasn't exactly reassuring, either. What was Heidi up to? Recalling the way her friend's voice had sounded on Thursday, anxiety welled up again.

"When did you say she left, Mrs. Neufeld?"

"I didn't say. It was Thursday. She apparently woke up that morning and decided she needed a vacation. Just like that."

Just like that. To Tova, it sounded ominous. She longed to speak to Heidi in person — and she had a strong feeling that Heidi felt the same way. Why else had she called?

On the other hand, once she'd called, why hadn't Heidi said anything about what was on her mind? What had she been thinking about?

"Mrs. Neufeld," Tova said earnestly, "if Heidi does call again, would you please tell her I phoned? Tell her to call me, please. Any time of the day or night. I — I really need to speak to her."

"I'll tell her," Heidi's mother said heavily. "*If* she calls."

The "if" dangled between them like a flag at half-mast, and seemed to linger in Tova's consciousness long after she'd hung up the phone.

It was much later that night, as Tova was enjoying a last cup of decaf before heading for bed, when she heard the noise.

It was a loud noise, halfway between a thud and a crash, and it came from outside, just beneath her window. The backyard.

"Nachman," she whispered, poking her head in the dining room, where her husband sat with an open Gemara in front of him. "I heard a sound outside. As though something crashed in our backyard."

His brows lifted. "Are you talking UFO's, Tova?"

"Of course not. But I did hear something. Come on, let's check it out. I'm scared to go alone."

He stood up and followed her to the back door. A security light, pale and diffuse against the deep black of the Southwest night, cast its dim illumination over the patio. By that light, the Bernsteins saw what had caused the noise that had so startled Tova.

The large, heavy umbrella — Heidi's gift to them — lay sprawled on its side on the plastic patio table.

How it had come to fall was a mystery. There was no breath of wind to topple it, no rowdy children around to give it an accidental shove.

"Must have been loose," Nachman shrugged.

Tova stared at the overturned umbrella with a secret, almost superstitious, dismay. Heidi's umbrella, once so proud and erect, head toward the sky, had inexplicably toppled. The sight seemed like a confirmation of Tova's most pressing fears. When, oh when, would Heidi call her back?

IV.

The following week, the Mandels arrived in town.

They came in a blaze of triumph — and apprehension. Efraim Mandel, for all his gratitude for the opportunity that had come his way, was nervous as he had not been in years. For a man not noted for his flexibility, adjusting to a new role in a new and very different place constituted a monumental challenge.

Etty, his wife, was hardly less nervous. She felt as if she were about to walk into a party where she knew none of the other guests, was ignorant of the party games and was dressed all wrong for the occasion. In her usual response to a challenge, she rose to fantastic new heights of organization, marshaling her husband and children and their belongings out of New York and into tiny Lakewood, New Mexico with all the dispatch of a general mustering his troops or, it sometimes seemed to her, a frustrated shepherd herding a flock of recalcitrant sheep. And she did it while nurturing a newborn infant, born to the delighted family just three weeks earlier.

Layala was the newest princess, reigning in serene aplomb amidst a blaze of adoration. Dark haired like Efraim, but with Etty's gray eyes, she was acclaimed a beauty from her first day on earth, and jealously protected even by 3-year-old Ora, newly catapulted into big-sisterhood by the newcomer's arrival.

There had been some talk on Efraim's part of their moving earlier in the summer, to allow Etty to settle them into their new home before giving birth. Etty had been adamantly opposed. "I'm not good for anything in my ninth month," she declared. "After the baby's born, I usually bounce right back onto my feet. Give me a couple of weeks, and I'll be rarin' to go."

With some reservations, Efraim had agreed. He usually agreed to her plans where they concerned the home front; practicality was her strong point, not his. He was secretly relieved at her take-charge attitude, which allowed him to adopt a more passive role in the move — a role that he wore like a comfortable old suit. It freed him up to use his energy for his own, private worrying.

It also allowed him to become his children's confidant. They whispered their fears to him in a way that they were wary of doing with their mother. It was Efraim who learned the real reason behind Shimi's bad behavior these last few weeks.

"It's my bar mitzvah," Shimi told him, as together they packed *sefarim* by Etty's strict guidelines. "Who's going to be there now? I won't know anyone in town."

"You'll make friends," Efraim said, reaching up with an effort for a *sefer* on the highest shelf of the old bookcase. It was harder than it should have been for a man his age. He glanced ruefully down at his girth. *I should start a diet*, he thought, as he'd done so many times over the years. *Exercise, too ...* Then he promptly pushed both well-worn thoughts aside and focused on his son.

"I'm getting homeschooled this year, right?" Shimi went on. "That means that, except for Chaim and Donny Bernstein, no classmates. My bar mitzvah's at the end of January, Ta. That'll give me — what? Four-and-a-half months to make enough friends to make my bar mitzvah look like anything. It'll be embarrassing!"

Efraim, as a father, was not always attuned to his children's moods or emotional needs. On the other hand, insecurity was something he could understand.

"Shimi," he said with an impressive gravity, "trust me. You're the kind of kid that makes friends anywhere. People *like* you. Mark my words: By the end of January you'll have a bar mitzvah that'll be the talk of the town."

For the first time since he'd heard of their impending move, Shimi's eyes began to sparkle with hope. "You think so, Ta?"

"I know so!" With a shrug, Efraim added, "You'll make more friends in that time than I will, that's for sure …"

A peer might have offered a disclaimer — a comforting response to Efraim's self-assessment. But Shimi was only 12, and blind to a father's vulnerability. Grinning from ear to ear, he said, "You know something? I bet you're right! I guess I will make some friends by then. Anyway, I've got the Bernstein kids. They'll be there."

"Of course they will." Efraim began pulling down books again, each move straining his bulk and deepening the sheen of dampness on his face. "Of course you'll have friends. You'll have a great bar mitzvah, Shimi. Mark my words."

Etty, noticing her son's cheerful demeanor at dinner that night, calmly appropriated the credit. "Nothing like a little work to make a child forget his silly moods," she told her husband later.

Efraim just smiled.

They stepped exhausted from the plane, surrounded by a sea of bags and boxes. Three-week-old Layala hadn't stopped crying the whole way — or at least, that was the way it had felt to her distraught family, and to most of the other passengers as well. Etty and Efraim had taken turns holding her, patting her, changing her diaper and feeding her. This last action proved their undoing: The moment the feeding was over, the baby had vomited violently. Fortunately, this took place in the tiny airplane rest-room, so the damage was contained. Etty handed the baby to Efraim while she efficiently cleaned up the mess (smiling an embarrassed apology to the various women who entered the restroom only to stop short, appalled, at the sight of the mess). Layala's tears, however, continued unabated.

"Maybe she's coming down with something," Etty said worriedly, as they waited for an unoccupied porter to help them with their luggage. "I'd better find out about a good pediatrician, first thing."

By the time they reached their new house on Freemont Avenue, it was late afternoon and Layala seemed to have settled down. Exhausted by her own exertions, she was asleep on her father's shoulder as the family walked into the rambling, white-stucco structure for the first time.

"Wow!" Shimi said. "This place is neat! Look at that curvy staircase!" He started up the stairs, yelling, "I get to pick my bedroom first!"

His older brother, Meir, was after him in a flash, with Tzirel and Chana Perel on his heels. There was the sound of raised voices from above, though whether the clamor was one of excitement or dissension, the parents could not yet tell.

Etty sat down on the steps. Though she had "bounced back" from the birth just as she had expected to, the gargantuan task of making this move had sapped her energy in a way she didn't like. Also, she couldn't ignore the fact that this was not a first child but a sixth; she was getting older. Like a physical burden, she felt the weight of the long months of preparation that had led up to this moment. Wearily she steeled herself for the ordeal of unpacking and setting up that still lay ahead.

The moving truck had already been here (with Tova Bernstein on hand to let them in) and there were furniture and boxes everywhere — in all the wrong places, of course. Efraim, taking pity on her, said, "Relax a few minutes, Etty. The boxes won't run away."

She was actually tempted. It was the thought of how much more tired she was going to feel later that made her straighten her shoulders and say with a sigh, "No, if it has to be done, it may as well be done now." She took the baby from her husband, laid her tenderly in her stroller to continue her sorely needed nap, and turned to survey the mess. Then she cupped her hands to her mouth and called, "Kids! Downstairs — now! We've got a lot of work to do!"

She had hardly begun issuing jobs when there was a stir at the front door, which was standing wide open to the street. Moving shadows mingled with the brilliant sunshine that poured through the door. Etty, work clothes dusty and kerchief askew, stared in dismay.

The entire Bernstein family had come over to welcome them to Lakewood.

V.

Etty's first reaction was to step outside and slam the door shut behind her. How could she let anyone see the house looking this way? She never invited visitors into her home unless it had been cleaned to within an inch of its life. As she spent a great deal of her time cleaning — even her windows were washed biweekly — welcoming guests was not usually a problem. But today, of all days! How could she play hostess with cranky children, nothing in the house to eat and a disaster area of packing crates at her back?

She hung back, at a loss, as Efraim stepped up to greet the newcomers on behalf of them both.

"Nachman! How nice to see you, all of you." Efraim smiled and spread his hands. "Well, we're here."

"*Shalom aleichem*, Efraim! And all the Mandels!" Nachman Bernstein boomed. He had a habit, when uncomfortable, of becoming rather hearty.

To Etty, Tova added, "We're delighted to see you all. So how was the flight?"

"Um, it was fine." Etty hesitated, then blurted, "Please excuse the mess. What you must be thinking …?" She flushed.

"What I'm thinking," Tova said comfortably, "is how nice it is to see you! As for the mess, what else do you expect on moving day: neatness and order? Not even you can work that kind of miracle, Etty!"

As always, Tova's casual warmth had the effect of melting Etty's reserve. Smiling at last, she stepped back to allow the newcomers into her domain. In her mind, a formula clicked into place: A house was not a home until you got out your scrubbing brush and scoured every inch of it. Ergo, this place was not yet her home, and nothing to be ashamed of. Relaxing further, Etty asked Tova about her own family's trip the previous week. She proudly showed off the baby, and both women exclaimed over how much she'd grown.

Shana undertook to stay behind and watch the twins, politely — if with a trace of the sullenness that had become habitual with her these days — declining Efraim's invitation to join the grand tour he was forming. Bashful Gila elected to stick close to her older sister. With his own two sons trailing behind, Efraim launched a tour of the house for the benefit of Nachman and his boys. "I'm hardly qualified to show you around yet, though," he said. "I barely know the place myself yet."

In short order, the boys detached themselves from the men and settled, shouting and laughing, on the swing set outdoors. Tova had brought over dinner for the Mandels, and had stocked the fridge with all the necessities to carry them over the next few days. Etty was grateful but stiff: She hated being beholden to anyone. Gradually, however, under the influence of Tova's flow of bright prattle, some of the stiffness eased.

The two women were a study in contrasts: Etty, tall and gaunt, had aquiline features set in perpetually wary lines, as though she suspected some wild thing of lurking just around the corner, ready to undermine her carefully orchestrated life if she wasn't quick enough. Tova was shorter and more petite, with a quick laugh and astonishingly swift mood changes, reminiscent of clouds drifting over and then away from the sun. Because Tova's warmth and openness did not represent a threat to Etty, she was the only woman among Etty's yeshivah acquaintances with whom she enjoyed any semblance of friendship.

For Tova, Etty represented an enigma, and her own polar opposite. As to their being "friends," let it suffice to say that Tova's definition of friendship began where Etty's left off.

After a while, the men joined them in the kitchen. The four adults sat around the table, eating Danishes, drinking coffee out of the thermos Tova had brought, and swapping news. The talk soon turned, naturally, to the new *kollel* and the planned *mesivta*.

"Marvin Fleischmann — he's the man sponsoring this whole undertaking, you know — wants to get the ball rolling on the high school as soon as possible," Nachman said, taking a steaming sip from a disposable hot cup. "The *kollel* can use the shul in the meantime, but the *mesivta* will need more spacious quarters."

"For which he's willing to shell out a small fortune," Efraim said, in open wonder at the power of a well-filled pocketbook.

"He's near the end of his life," Nachman explained. "Money means little to him at this point — and time, everything." He paused to enjoy a bite of Danish. "I've already been out with some realtors, looking at likely properties just outside of town."

Whatever he had expected in reaction to this casual remark, it was certainly not the dead silence that descended on the Mandel couple. He and Tova exchanged a look, surprised and anxious.

"You couldn't wait for Efraim to get here?" Etty asked finally. Her face was white and set.

"What?"

"Oh, never mind." Etty put down her mug and made a gesture of dismissal. "It doesn't matter. We'll get by. We'll do whatever we have to do."

"Etty, what are you talking about?" Tova pressed, leaning forward and trying to read the other woman's expression.

Etty hesitated, as though debating the wisdom of saying anything further. Finally, fatigue — coupled with genuine outrage — brought down her guard. "Well, it seems to me that Efraim might have been invited along. He *is* the senior member of this *kollel*, after all."

"Etty," her husband said sharply. "Nachman's the *Rosh Kollel*, remember?"

"But you're older. You've been at the yeshivah longer." There was a flicker of genuine pain behind the sternness in her eyes. She had endured years of seeing her husband bypassed at the yeshivah in favor of younger, more charismatic men. Was the same fate going to dog him even out here? It suddenly seemed too much to bear. The adventure — the triumph — of this move lost a bit of its luster. Something in Etty Mandel sagged in a kind of despair.

Tova said quickly, "This was just a preliminary viewing, you know. No decision has been made yet. Of *course* Efraim will be invited along on future outings. You, too, if you're interested."

"That's right. You just weren't here yet," Nachman put in helplessly. "And Fleischmann was putting pressure on us to get the ball rolling ..."

It was clear to them both, however, that their words were not sufficiently palliative for Etty's pain. Nachman glanced at Efraim, who shook his head ruefully and then looked away, as though to indicate that he did not disagree completely with what his wife had said.

There was a moment's tense silence. Visions of discord and resentment reared their ugly heads in all four minds. Then, with truly impressive courage, Etty cleared her throat and mustered a smile.

"Oh, well, I'm sorry. I didn't mean to throw a wet blanket over this celebration. Everything's fine. Everything's great! We're here, and we're going to make this *kollel* the best thing that's ever happened to Lakewood, New Mexico." She glanced pleadingly at her husband, then around at the others. "Right?"

Stumbling over themselves in their haste to agree, the Bernsteins assured her that she was absolutely correct. Efraim swallowed a huge chunk of Danish and asked, "Have you met any of the community members yet, Nachman?" The men began to discuss prospective classes and learning groups. Tova and Etty, relieved to have hurdled a difficult moment, launched with rather forced animation into a discussion of such practical amenities such as shopping and pediatricians.

The adult Bernsteins took their leave soon after. Nachman and Tova agreed to let their two older sons stay behind to enjoy the Mandel boys' company for a while, and to lend Mrs. Mandel a hand where needed.

It was with mixed emotions that Etty saw them off. She felt proud of the way she had carried off the scene earlier, although she had been the one who'd created it in the first place. An old chewed-up bitterness churned inside her, along with a determination to somehow spit it out at last. She wanted this new phase in her family's life to be wonderful. She just wasn't sure how to make it so.

With a sigh, she decided to leave the boys where they were for the moment; she lacked the energy to induce them to work just yet. She and Efraim would start the job of unpacking on their own, shouldering the burden the way they always had: with a great deal between them left unspoken, but side by side. Together.

Chapter 5

I.

Her cell phone was ringing again.

Automatically, Heidi lifted her head and checked the readout. It was Tova. Surprise, surprise ...

Tova had been ringing her on the average of once every couple of hours for the past three days. (Heidi's mother had given up after Day 1.) Each time, Heidi looked at the name on the readout — and let her voice mail pick up. She listened to the increasingly urgent messages her old friend left for her, but she didn't call back. Picking up the phone and dialing Tova's number seemed beyond her strength, a herculean task too daunting to contemplate. Tova would require explanations and reassurances, both of which were in short supply for Heidi at the moment.

She let her head drop back onto the motel-room pillow, her eyes traveling to the window. The curtains were nearly, but not quite, drawn. It was high noon, and the sun was shining in a bright and cheerful sky. Heidi regarded both sun and sky with neither approval nor disapproval, only with an immense detachment, as though observing the scene from some point in outer space.

This same detachment had driven beside her all the way from New York, and had taken up residence in this motel room with her: uninvited, but not unwelcome.

She smiled, vaguely surprised at herself even now. She hadn't planned on taking a vacation. Heidi Neufeld didn't take vacations. She never stole a single, precious moment away from her vital life's work of preparing meaty legal briefs and billing fat-cat corporate clients for all they were worth. She was part of the law-office furniture, among the first to arrive in the mornings and often the last to leave. That was why she'd been so astonished when, upon waking last Thursday morning, she had realized that she did not intend to go into the office at all.

In a dreamy way, she had pondered the possibility of calling in sick. Then, with a shake of her sleep-tousled head, she decided that no, that wouldn't do. She was not going to be sick today. She was going on vacation.

She packed a few things in a bag and made, what was necessarily, a difficult call to the office. That is, it would have been difficult, had she been the Heidi who cared about such things. As it was, she hardly remembered what she told them, except that she wasn't coming in for a while. An indefinite while. She was taking a vacation.

Once, years ago — it felt as though it belonged to a different lifetime — she had eschewed time off. Fresh out of law school, newly hired by the law firm of her dreams, she had walked into her office on her first day on the job as though it were a Garden of Eden and the world could offer no greater delight. She had chained herself to her desk, a willing prisoner. While her friends had, one by one, married and become (in her view from the heights) more or less domestic slaves, she had sweated away in her own, airy skyscraper of a dungeon and believed that she couldn't be more free.

No, she hadn't taken many vacations in her years with Flaxen, Domb and Tremaine. Apart from Shabbos and the Jewish holidays, she'd been the most dedicated slave the firm owned. Well, she was taking one now. A real, honest-to-goodness vacation — a spur-of-the-moment vacation, which ought to be the best kind. Let someone else bill her clients for a while. Let someone else sit at her desk and admire her view, assuming they had a free second to spare for admiring views. Let someone else mark their initials on her file folders. Heidi Neufeld was unavailable.

She looked around at her apartment with a stranger's eyes. Had she really lived here all these years? A few minutes spent tossing a few items into an overnight bag, and she was ready to walk out the door. Why hadn't she realized before that life could be this simple?

She stepped out and headed for the elevator, giving herself a mental pat on the back for remembering to lock the front door behind her as she went. A few minutes later, she was seated behind the wheel of her car. On her way.

Just where she was going, she hadn't a clue. Busy avenues and noisy traffic snarls turned eventually into a bridge winging its way out of Manhattan Island. Very soon, pretty, tree-lined roads took over. Roads to lead her ... where?

Gradually, two words formed in her mind: the Poconos.

She was going to the Poconos.

It was a place she had never been to before, though the name had always triggered her curiosity, along with an undefined longing for the sort of relaxation she had never offered herself. The Catskills she knew well enough, having spent most of her childhood summers there along with the rest of Jewish Brooklyn. She had enjoyed those summers, thought she'd never returned there as an adult. But it was not the Catskill Mountains that called to her now. It was that other range, with the name that breathed of mystery and escape. The Poconos.

She made two calls from her cell phone while still navigating New York. It was as though she knew that, having left the city behind her, she would find it increasingly difficult — if not impossible — to maintain the old, familiar connections. One call was to her mother, who was bound to worry when Heidi became unreachable; the other went to a number with a 505 area code: Tova Bernstein, in far-off New Mexico. She did not say much to either of them, but the two, brief conversations seemed to liberate her.

She gave herself another mental pat for remembering to call them. Then she put the phone away and did not think of it again.

There were other delays, hardly noted before they were gone. Traffic backups at roadwork sites, a stop for a soft drink and a restroom, and another in early afternoon to break her fast. Hours later, her car pulled up in front of a motel. Behind the nondescript block of rooms — each one with its door painted a different, faded pastel hue — soared green-clad mountains, the western sun already settling on their shoulders. Night was closing in and she was hundreds of miles from the place she called "home." It suddenly seemed very important that she be safely behind one of those pastel doors before the sun sank finally into darkness ... The first cycle of darkness to greet her new, unrecognizable self.

Her credit card was produced, her name signed in the register, and her bag slung over her shoulder as she followed the matronly proprietress down the outdoor lane in the deepening twilight. "This is it," the woman said, handing her the key to Number 28. Heidi took it with a sense of almost mystical significance. She hardly listened as her companion proceeded to outline various attractions available for tourists in the area. She was not a tourist — though what, exactly, she *was*, she didn't know. Thanking the woman, who was inclined to be chatty, Heidi stepped into the room and closed the door firmly behind her.

Her new "home" was a squarish, neatish, plainish room, with an adjoining bathroom and a closet equipped with nonremovable hangers and extra blankets. The suit Heidi was wearing had probably cost about as much as all the furniture in the room combined, but that did not detract an iota from her satisfaction with everything she saw. Except for some chips and a chocolate bar early that afternoon, she hadn't eaten all day, but she was not the least bit hungry. Tired, that's what she was. It had been a long drive. A long, long day ...

Watershed. The word came unbidden. Today had been a watershed in her life. Something had changed for her today. Something big. Significant. What lay on the other side of the big change was still wreathed in fog. A distant thrill of fear coursed through her, something to observe rather than to suffer. Throwing her pocketbook down among a packet of brochures on a bland, round table, she flung herself onto the bed for a nap.

She had been lying here, more or less continuously, ever since.

There were brief forays for food — tuna, mostly, with the odd tomato or cucumber, some fruit, and once, a package of frozen bagels which she air-defrosted and then devoured in quick succession until they were gone. She drank water out of the tooth glass she found in the bathroom, waved the chambermaid away in the mornings, stared through the window, and slept. She slept a great deal.

In a vague way, she thought that she must have suffered something — some sort of emotional malfunction. A "nervous breakdown," to use familiar terminology. Though she didn't feel nervous at all! She didn't feel anything. That was the best part of this vacation. She didn't feel. Nor did she think. Daddy had always said she'd do anything to avoided thinking. Well, here Heidi didn't have to avoid it: There was simply nothing to think about. She was merely existing. She was floating, like an astronaut in space, or a specimen in a bottle. Floating, one did not have to think at all.

The phone rang every few hours, reminding her with a dull pinprick of pain that a world still existed outside this room; that there were people who cared about her and expected her to care about herself. She ignored its summons. This was no time to be asking her to address things. She was on vacation!

She turned over with a yawn, noting as she did that her food supply (stored on the plain, round table among the disregarded brochures) had dwindled to a single can of tuna and one very soft plum. She would have to go shopping tomorrow, to stock up. The prospect, this tiny plan, gave her a pleasant sense of comfort. She was taking care of things. She was taking care of herself. She might be a bit drowsy these days, a little fuzzy around the edges — but basically, she was fine. Just fine.

When the phone rang yet again, she was tempted to pick it up just to let Tova know how fine she was. In the end, though, it was too much trouble to answer. So she just let it ring, while her eyes fluttered closed until she was asleep.

Eventually, the phone's battery wound down. She did not bother to recharge it.

II.

"I do not want to be a third wheel," Avi Feder told the Ganns firmly, as they stood contemplating their new home on a sun-drenched street in Lakewood, New Mexico. The taxi from the airport had just let them off here. Avi had intended to continue right on to his own rental apartment some blocks away. He hadn't counted on Asher's intransigence.

"What in the world are you babbling about?" Asher Gann asked. "Come on, man — in you go! We want your opinion about this place. We bought it in about five minutes, back on our pilot trip last winter."

"I'm almost scared to see it again," Rivi admitted. "What if we've made an awful mistake?" It was a small house — a "cottage," she called it in her mind — set back from the street behind an unusual garden, all pebbles and tiny bonsai trees in decorative planters. It had been the garden, and the fairytale-like snugness of the place, that had won Rivi's heart. With her heart in her mouth, she stared at it now. Was it right?

She closed her eyes for a moment and when she opened them, it was her own, sweet cottage again, just the way she had remembered it through all these long months of planning. A smile crept across her face and she gave a tiny nod, as though greeting a friend.

Asher was unlocking the front door with an air of proud, self-conscious ownership. Behind him, Avi still hung back. Asher rounded on him. "Would you *please* stop being an idiot and come inside, Avi? Afterward, we'll go over to your place and help you get set up."

"I can set up myself, thanks," Avi said stiffly.

"Of course you can." Rivi smiled. "We'd just love to help, that's all. I hope you'll let us. There's nothing more fun than setting up a new home, don't you think?"

Avi didn't have to answer, because the other two had already swept him eagerly inside. Despite his own, bleak mood (his bleak state of mind would be more like it; he owned only one kind of mood since Yocheved had died), he could not help smiling at the Ganns' delight. Soon, he found himself sharing it. The house was small but compact, with a pleasant flow of rooms and a good exposure to the sun that rendered the space light and airy. Rivi wandered from one room to the next in ecstasy, planning the decor and the arrangement of their furniture in the same way that she visualized a painting on a still-blank canvas.

The house had three bedrooms, one of them clearly the "master" one. "The computer can go here," Asher planned cheerfully, sticking his head into one of the smaller bedrooms. "There's enough space for a high-riser, too. This'll be a fine combination study/guest room."

Rivi nodded, only half-attending. Her eyes had strayed to the other bedroom, directly across the hall. Without volition her mind began filling it with furniture: a crib, a changing table, a pretty white dresser with gold knobs. The walls became palely tinted — the actual color was flexible in her mind — with a matching pattern marching along the border where wall met ceiling. Pastel curtains fluttered at the window, where a breeze was making the mobile above the crib revolve lazily in place ...

"Rivi? Hello? ... Earth to Rivi! Where have you been?"

She started at her husband's voice. The room into which she was staring was empty. Not a stick of furniture or a single homey knickknack relieved its barrenness. There were no curtains at the window ruffling in the breeze. There was no breeze. Only this hot stillness, suddenly suffocating ...

She turned away. "Sorry about that. Just daydreaming, I guess ... I'll go check out the kitchen." If her voice was pitched a little higher than normal, neither of the men noticed. While she examined her kitchen, they went out to inspect the garage. If Rivi spilled a few tears as she communed with stove and refrigerator, there was nobody there to see her do it.

At the end of 10 minutes they were back together again, all three expressing their general approval with the house.

"And now," Asher announced, "we're off to Avi's place. I'll bet Rivi has some good tips on how to make the place look like home in no time." He stooped to swing his friend's traveling bag over his shoulder. Avi nodded, drawn and sad despite his best intentions. Seeing it, Rivi felt a pang. How dare she shed a single tear over what she didn't have, when she had so much already! She had Asher, and he had her ... while poor Avi was alone. She threw a doubtful glance at his face, set in its white lines of misery. Would he have been better off staying back East, near his family? But he'd been determined to come. He had seemed eager to escape the scene of his former happiness — and his bereavement.

She heaved a tiny sigh. No one can plumb the depths of another's heart, to know which words hurt and which may offer comfort. The most you can hope for, after years of marriage to one person, is to become familiar with certain signposts, clues to that hidden map ... But poor Avi had no one to read his signs now. No one to try to traverse his inner map or join him in trudging its private roads. That, Rivi realized with a shudder of compassion, was the true definition of "alone."

Turning with a bright smile, she said, "And afterward, you'll come back here for a potluck supper, right?" They had brought along food supplies to last until she acclimated herself.

"We'll see," Avi said evasively.

But, as things turned out, none of them had supper in the Ganns' new house.

Scarcely had they set foot in Avi's modest one-bedroom apartment, which featured a postage-stamp-sized porch off the bedroom and a ship's-galley kitchen, when a peal at the door scared them all out of a year's growth. Rushing to open it, Avi was confronted by a horde of laughing, talking faces. Familiar faces, most of them. It was the Bernsteins and the Mandels, come to say "Welcome home."

"We must've just missed you guys coming out of your place," Nachman Bernstein told the Ganns with his warm, infectious laugh. He looked around at the minuscule living/dining room. "Well, we might have had a little more elbowroom back there — but we're all friends, right? None of us minds a little crowding over supper!"

Tova and Etty went into a happy huddle with Rivi, Tova talking a blue streak and Etty throwing in a word of clarification or correction as needed. Rivi listened, nodding and smiling. Soon the women spread a tablecloth over the dining-room table (the apartment had been rented furnished) and began setting out the food they'd brought. Coolers were emptied, paper plates, cups and plastic cutlery distributed and soup poured out of large thermoses. A heavenly aroma of mushrooms and spices rose in the air, as though consecrating the place with the seal of friendship and good food.

Sniffing appreciatively, and looking around at the friendly circle of faces — the adults eagerly discussing plans for the new *kollel*, the children alternately joking, bickering and falling on the food as though they hadn't eaten in a year — Avi felt a hard knot inside him begin to soften. This was a good thing he had done. A new beginning, a fine mission, and good people with whom to carry it through. He listened to the babble of voices rising to fill the empty rooms and, with a pang of dread, thought of the silence that would take the place of this warmth and camaraderie later tonight. Firmly, he shook his head. He wouldn't think about that now.

"Pass the crackers, please?" he called down the table. Someone obliged. He set to, letting the good taste of soup and crackers make up the whole of his reality — at least for the moment.

Excitement was at a fever pitch among the pioneer *kollel* families. Nachman fairly crackled with energy and ideas. He had outlined a schedule of *shiurim* for the four of them to deliver to the local, Jewish homeowners. He'd planned the schedule in conjunction with the Rosh Yeshivah and, long-distance, with Rabbi Harris, keeping each of the *kollel* members' strengths in mind.

Charismatic Asher Gann would tackle the youngest group: older teens (if any could be induced to come), singles and young marrieds. Avi Feder, who was developing decided expertise in the area of *halachah*, would offer courses in practical Jewish law to both men and women in the community. Efraim Mandel would teach the more established householders, people who came not in search of spiritual or philosophical adventure as much as a genuine and inner-directed desire to learn. As for Nachman himself, he would deliver a general talk every Thursday night, as well as conduct classes in Gemara and Jewish thought to those who had made it past beginners' level.

Rivi was drafted to design an eye-catching flyer describing the offered schedule of classes. The flyer would be sent out to every name on the shul's mailing list. She planned to do this right away, before the new school year began in a couple of weeks. She was also going to do some part-time teaching in the day school this year. Simi Wurtzler had called her while they were still in New York, explaining that the school had not yet been able to afford an art teacher. "But now that you're coming — sort of a built-in art *maven* — I'm going to make sure the Board budgets for one," the principal had promised.

She had made good on that promise. Rivi faced the prospect of teaching her self-taught craft with a mixture of joy and trepidation.

Tova mentioned that she was toying with the idea of looking for part-time work herself. "Mo and Bo are still a handful," she said. "I hate to inflict them on some unsuspecting babysitter. On the other hand, they are old enough to be away from home for a few hours each day. Wherever they go, they'll always have each other."

"What kind of a job are you looking for?" Rivi asked.

Tova shrugged. "Make that future tense, please. I haven't even thought that far ahead yet. My first priority is getting the house in shape and everybody settled in. Then comes the start of the school year, and then the *Yamim Tovim*. I won't even dream of undertaking anything else until all that is behind me."

Etty Mandel hit the only sour note of the evening, and she did it in the privacy of the diminutive kitchen, with only Rivi to hear.

"Whew! I'm tired," Etty remarked as she rinsed empty pans and serving utensils in the sink with her typical efficiency. Beside her, Rivi dried. The children had the foresight to bring along a couple of board games and were happily engaged with them in the living room while their parents chatted. Tova, with a sleepy twin on either knee, had excused herself from kitchen duty.

"Tired? I'm sure I don't know why," Rivi said lightly. "You've only moved cross-country. A snap!"

"There's still so much to do." Etty handed Rivi another dripping utensil, unresponsive to the younger woman's gentle teasing. "I tried to be ruthless when we were packing up, throwing away as much as I could. But there's still so much *stuff*!"

"I know what you mean. I'm not looking forward to unpacking. Asher tries to be helpful, but he has no idea where things go, bless him. If I let him at the boxes, I'm liable to find my Teflon pots in the breakfront."

"I don't know what you're complaining about," Etty said dismissively, hands moving like lightning through the streaming water. She seemed impatient of Rivi's complaints, oblivious to the fact that Rivi had only voiced them in a comradely spirit, as a sharing of Etty's burden. "There's just the two of you — two adults. No one to get underfoot or undo what you've just spent hours doing. No baby to start crying and vomiting just when you think you've got her settled for the night."

A second later, she seemed to hear what she had just said. A slow flush crawled up her cheeks, staining them a dull, unbecoming crimson. Her hands kept working mechanically, reaching, rinsing and passing things to Rivi without meeting her eyes.

The silence stretched. At last, when she couldn't bear it any longer, Etty peeked sideways at Rivi and burst out, "Oh, I'm sorry! I didn't mean —"

"It's all right." Calmly, Rivi continued her rhythmic wiping with no sign of discomfiture. Etty glanced at her again, wondering what she was thinking.

What Rivi was thinking was, *Poor Etty.*

Poor Etty, with so much bitterness inside. Such a deep pool of resentment, lapping at times as high as her chin — while, below, tangled strings of seaweed-envy wrapped around her legs, sucking her down, down ... When what she needed most of all was to let herself rise bobbing to the surface, past the gloom and up into the light of day where it's so easy to see that none of it need ever have mattered at all ...

The two women finished their washing-up in silence. All too soon, various mothers and fathers began the job of collecting their protesting offspring. It was time for the men and boys to head to shul for Minchah and Ma'ariv. The others — mothers, girls and small children — dispersed to their new homes; in Rivi's case, so new that it wasn't until Tova had pulled up in front of her house that she realized she was there.

III.

It was mid-August: time of the doldrums, of constant tyrannical heat, and a dryness that seemed to make your insides stick together. Bobby Smith slouched angrily down the street, jangling the few coins in his pocket and wishing there were more. More coins, more green bills, more to look forward to than another dismal stint in Holson's Hardware, stacking goods on already overcrowded shelves.

It was only a temporary job, of course. Bobby Smith was destined for much greater things. But a guy had to eat, and Holson was paying him enough to keep body and soul together while the wheels of his mind spun in fruitless circles, seeking a way out. A way out of the reservation, out of his limited future. He stumped home in an ugly frame of mind. Bobby Smith was fed up.

The fridge was nearly empty, because he'd used the better part of his last paycheck on pool and whiskey instead of food. Now his stomach growled. Bobby slammed a fist into the blank, white door. Why couldn't anything ever work out for him? *Where was the way out?*

As if by magic, he was shown the way at that moment. The phone rang.

He almost didn't answer. There was no one he wanted to talk to right now, with his empty stomach screaming in protest and his nerves as raw as an uncooked potato. Potatoes … cornbread … Sharply, he jerked his head back as though to banish all thought of the food he didn't have. The call, whoever it was from, would at least be a distraction. Two steps brought him over to the phone.

"Yeah?"

The voice at the other end was polite, professional. "Is this Mr. Robert Smith?"

"Bobby Smith, that's me. No one calls me Robert."

"I'm sorry, sir. Mr. Smith, I'm calling from Memorial Hospital. We have a patient here, a Mr. Henry Jones. He's been asking for you."

"What do you mean, asking for me? The old man's been practically in a coma for months!"

"Well, he's wide awake now." A certain asperity had crept into the nurse's voice. "And he's been asking for you. He seems quite anxious to see you, to the point where the doctors felt he ought to be humored for the sake of his health. He mustn't become agitated, you know. His heart is still very tricky at this stage …"

Bobby was not interested in Old Henry's heart. His first impulse was to shrug off the request. Why drag himself all the way down to the hospital, just to see an old man he hardly knew? But something stopped him from brushing off the nurse and her call. The memory of a single, shining word. *Treasure* …

"All right, I'll come down and see him. When's a good time?"

"Our visiting hours this evening are between 7 and 9 o'clock. Or you can come tomorrow morning, from —"

"I'll be there tonight." Might as well get it over with. And who knew? Maybe Henry would have something to tell him that would help him sleep better tonight, without the help of his usual two or three whiskeys. He hung up, mulling over the prospect. It was probably all hogwash — an empty dream generated by an aging, liquor-addled mind.

Then again, maybe not ...

Forget the empty fridge. He would run to the decrepit, little grocery down the block and ask Mrs. Thomas to extend him a bit more credit until payday. He would fix himself a sandwich, then make his way over to Southwest Memorial Hospital. Old Henry had woken up from his long sleep, and one of his first concerns, if the nurse was to be believed, had been to ask to see *him*. Old Henry had something to communicate to Bobby Smith, and Bobby Smith was growing more and more curious to find out what it was.

The elevator door slid back to reveal a bland hospital wall with one of its ever-present directories, white on black. Bobby remembered where Old Henry's room was. He made his way there now at a rapid clip.

He found the door he wanted and strode right in — only to check himself.

Old Henry already had a visitor.

Steve Birch, in an uncomfortable-looking orange plastic chair, turned his head at Bobby's entrance. The peculiar, brown-rimmed hazel eyes widened a little as he saw the newcomer, but his greeting was polite. "Good evening ... Bobby Smith, isn't it?"

"Yes, it is. Uh, I'm here to see Old Henry. He 'specially asked to see me."

"Oh?" An eyebrow lifted in surprise. "Any particular reason?"

Belligerently, Bobby snapped, "Does there have to be a reason for visiting a sick old man?" He would bluster his way through this, waiting for that palefaced Indian, Birch the lawyer, to go away and leave him alone with Henry. He'd nearly forgotten that Birch was related to Henry.

"Hey, Henry. How you feeling?" Bobby asked, leaning over the patient.

The old man looked awful. He was as pale as Bobby had ever seen him, with about a hundred new lines etched onto his already well-creased skin. Tubes snaked out in every direction, including one from Henry's nose. But the black eyes above all the tubes were gazing directly at him, and there was a tired smile of welcome in them.

"This is — my friend — Bobby," Henry said, in a pathetic parody of a hostly introduction. "Bobby — this here's — my stepson ... Steve."

"We know each other already, Henry," Bobby said impatiently. Hadn't the old man heard them talking to each other just now? He began to entertain serious misgivings about this whole visit. Old Henry was obviously not all there. The past few months in a semicomatose state must have robbed a few marbles from an already depleted supply. Trying not to betray his mounting disgust, Bobby said, "Glad you're awake, Henry. How soon till they let you out of here?"

"My stepfather is still a very sick man, Bobby," Steve said quietly. "His heart is dicey and his kidneys are failing."

"What about his mind? They check to see if he's still thinking straight?"

Steve shrugged. "He's sound enough — for a man whose brain has been pickled in alcohol for more years than you've been on this earth."

"Has he been telling you ... about anything special?"

"Special? What do you mean?"

Bobby backed away from the risky topic. The urge to probe the extent of Steve's knowledge about a possible, hidden treasure had been too strong to resist; now he had better put it away before the lawyer got suspicious.

"Oh, nothing." Bobby's eyes strayed back to Henry's face. "Guess I'll go find me a chair and visit a bit."

Steve took the hint. Standing, he buttoned his jacket and leaned over the old man in the bed. "Sleep well, Henry. I'll be back to see you tomorrow. Same time, same place ..." He smiled, inviting his stepfather to share the joke. But Henry just stared back stonily, unresponsive.

Bobby had paused to witness the interchange. "What's with him?" he asked curiously. "Is he mad at you or something?"

Steve shrugged. "He's mad at anyone who tries to tell him that he's got to change his ways if he wants to go on living. Starting with his 12-drinks-a-day habit."

"Maybe he doesn't want to live," Bobby suggested, only half in jest.

"Maybe not," Steve said, not in jest at all.

With a murmured good-night, Steve Birch left the room.

Bobby straddled the chair the other man had just abandoned. Meeting Henry's eyes, he found them fixed on his own with an intensity all the more pronounced because his eyes were so deeply sunk in the hollows, above the prominent Indian cheekbones.

"Come ... closer," the old man wheezed.

Bobby inched his chair right up to the edge of the high hospital bed.

"Remember ... what I told you ... day I came in here?"

"I'm amazed that *you* remember." Bobby was itching to get to the point, but he knew there was no use hurrying Old Henry.

"The treasure ..."

Bobby leaned so close that he could feel the old man's breath on his face. "What about the treasure, Henry?"

"In the cave ..."

"Yeah, you told me that part. But which cave? Where? How do I find it?" He held his breath. The last time he'd asked this question, Old Henry had lapsed into unconsciousness. He'd been only halfway in the world of the living in the months since. This was Bobby's first chance to get the information he was after.

Henry's eyes were riveted on his. "Lakewood," he whispered.

"Lakewood? You mean, down by Pecos River?"

The old man shook his head. "No ... other side. Up ... in the bluffs ..."

Bobby was not very familiar with the terrain around Lakewood, a small, pretty town perched on the shores of Lake McMillan. But that was something that could be very quickly rectified.

"Tell me more, Henry. Describe the place to me, exactly. There must be lots of caves over there."

"Big cave ..." Henry shook his head. His breathing grew more labored and his chest heaved. "You find it ... not Steve. Nice boy ... once. Now ... just preaches at me. Don't do this ... don't do that. No more drinking ... What kind of ... loving stepson ... is that?"

Bobby did not want to discuss Steve Birch. "The cave, Henry," he said urgently. "Describe the cave."

Useless. Old Henry's mind had wandered into a different groove and there it was stuck, like an old-fashioned phonograph playing the proverbial broken record.

"Thinks he knows ... better 'n me ... Never would listen to what ... I tried to teach him. Thinks he's so smart ... All them fancy schools ... degrees ..."

"Henry! Get with it, man! The treasure!"

"Don't know exactly ... what the treasure is ... but it's beautiful. Alice said so ... Been in her family ... generations ..."

"And it's in the cave?" Bobby prompted.

"The cave." Suddenly, Henry's expression altered. It became focused, alert. "You find that cave, Bobby. Find the treasure. I want you to have it. Steve ... he don't deserve it."

"I'll find it," Bobby said between his teeth, "if you'll just tell me more!"

"I'm sorry," said a crisp, feminine voice at his back. "Visiting hours are over. I'm afraid you'll have to leave, sir."

It was all Bobby could do not to lash out at that professional face with its pasted-on smile. "I'm not finished here yet. Gimme another minute or two." He turned back to Henry.

"I'm *sorry*, sir. You'll have to leave *now*."

Bobby ignored her and leaned over Henry again. But, as though in collusion with the clock that had decreed visiting hours at an end, the old man's eyes had closed.

"What're you sleeping for, old man?" Bobby snapped. "Didn't you get enough sleep these past two months?"

There was disapproval added to the firmness in the nurse's voice as she reiterated, "You'll have to leave now, sir. The patient needs his rest."

Grudgingly, Bobby scraped back the flimsy chair and rose to his feet. "I'll be back tomorrow," he said. It sounded more like a threat than a promise.

"You do that!" the nurse said brightly, obviously relieved to see the last of him tonight.

But the next day found Bobby's plans changed. He woke up elated, his mind filled with glittering visions of treasure. He could almost feel the rasp of gold against his fingers, and the tickle of gems against his palms. That treasure was as good as his already. Tonight, he would get the rest of the information out of Henry, and then he'd be on his way ...

On impulse, Bobby decided to skip work and celebrate instead. How could he be expected to concentrate on inventorying stock, with his life poised to make a 180-degree turn, right into the future he had always dreamed of?

Instead of spending the day at Holson's Hardware, he spent it in the pool hall, winning a few dollars and downing a series of strong drinks in rousing good humor. The upshot of all of this was that, instead of driving out to Memorial Hospital that evening, he lay sprawled in his bed, sleeping off the effects of his little party. Old Henry waited in vain for his newfound friend to return that night.

It wasn't until the next morning, with his head shrieking in agony from the world's worst hangover, that Bobby Smith's phone rang — nearly finishing off his head in the process — with news from the hospital. News that told him, sadly and irretrievably, that he had celebrated too soon.

Steve Birch looked for Old Henry's great buddy at the funeral, but Bobby never showed.

IV.

He was having the dream again.

Steve Birch was asleep in his Lakewood apartment, on a quiet side road not far from Main Street. This was where he stayed whenever the reservation began to feel stifling. He never questioned his need to escape the reservation which was, after all, his natural home. Following an instinct too compelling to resist, he had simply gone out one day and purchased this modest, second home.

It was a pleasant place, simply but tastefully furnished in the desert hues he favored, and it suited him to the core. After a no-frills meal of spaghetti and salad, he had gone to bed peacefully enough that night, and had been enjoying a much-needed rest, when the familiar images began to intrude, ripping his peace to shreds with their own peculiarly potent power.

It was not the first time he had dreamed something of this sort. The first time, the dream had come after an unsatisfying day spent on the Mescalero Reservation, where Steve had been a spectator to the tribe's annual July 4th ceremonial.

There was a quality to the dreams that set them apart from the usual garbled nighttime visions. They possessed an unusual clarity, and a coherence that made them like the telling of a tale. It was as if Steve were seated in a darkened theater watching a play acted out for his benefit, or listening to a story read aloud for his ears alone. Both times he awoke with an unshakable conviction that what he had seen had actually taken place. His mind had not been constructing a casual fantasy, but viewing an actual scene that had its roots in reality.

He had watched the Apache dancers on the reservation that Independence Day. Usually at these ceremonies Steve was, if not a passionate observer, at least a noncommittal one. Indian lore substituted in his life for faith, organized or otherwise. Though he had long ago relegated the lore to the realm of fairy tales, it continued to draw him, however feebly, with the sense of history it offered. Anything was preferable to feeling utterly anchorless in a vast impersonal world.

So he had attended the ceremonial that summer, the way he did every year — only this time, there was nothing noncommittal in his reaction. As he watched the dancers' painted faces, and their feet stamping their age-old rhythms against the backdrop of garish tapestries, for the first time he felt a powerful antipathy — a rising nausea that first startled and then threatened to overwhelm him. The revulsion was directed not so much at the Indian dancers as at the fact that *he* was there, watching them. He felt out of place … dislocated … lost.

Before he had a chance to analyze the unexpected hostility, it vanished — and was replaced by crushing grief. He was beset by a piercing sense of having lost something of inestimable worth, a gem of priceless value. And the saddest part was that he didn't even know what it was.

These emotions rose and fell with the speed of a one-two punch, and when they'd passed, Steve felt as bruised as a felled boxer in the ring. He had risen shakily, ignoring the glares of other spectators who resented his departure in the middle of the show, and made his way back to his apartment — in Lakewood, not on the reservation. Too tired to think, he'd flung himself on his bed and fallen instantly into a deep sleep. And while he slept, he dreamed …

He dreamed of two children, walking hand in hand into an Indian camp. They had the tentative manner of reluctant outsiders. It was an old-fashioned camp, with tepees in place of the reservation's adobe buildings, and the Indians gathered around were dressed in the clothes of a century and a half earlier. The boy seemed slightly older than the girl; the hand that was not clutching hers was curled into a fist of helpless defiance. Gently, fearfully, he led his sister (for that, the dreaming Steve knew with certainty, was who she was) into the center of a circle of curious eyes. Just behind them stood the two Indian braves who had brought them there.

The older man spoke to his fellow tribesmen in fluent Apache. Steve, the slumbering observer, understood every word. The Indian explained that he had found the two young ones in a cave, abandoned and alone. The tribe knew of the massacre that their brother Apaches had perpetrated that day. They knew, too, that these children did not belong to the town that had been attacked. Their clothing was foreign; their look was foreign. And those of the Mescaleros who spoke a few words of English soon discovered that these children knew even less of the American tongue than they did. Upon being questioned, the children returned a rapid-fire rush of words that none of the others could comprehend.

A woman past her first youth pushed forward. The dream-Steve, observing from the edges of the crowd, somehow knew that she was a recent widow, her husband having succumbed to a rattlesnake bite while walking alone in the desert. A man of eccentric habits, he had eschewed company on these solitary rambles — and here was his reward.

But the wife was no less eccentric, it seemed, than her husband had been. Pushing forward to stand before the tribal chieftain, she began to address him in an urgent undertone. Steve could hear every word. She was asking for the children.

"My man is departed. I am left husbandless and childless. Please give me these young ones, to raise as I would have raised my own."

"And if you were to marry a second time?" the chief asked quietly, the black eyes narrowed in sympathy and reflection.

The Indian woman stood a little straighter. "Any man who wants me will have to take my children as well." Already, they were "my children" …

And so they became. Steve saw the chief give his consent, then watched the woman lead the two small figures into her tepee. And that, for several weeks, was the last he saw of them. His nights had been untroubled by any sequel to that disturbing dream …

Until now.

In the same Lakewood apartment, asleep in the same bed, Steve dreamed his second dream. It possessed the same startling clarity as the first one, and the same vivid sense of reality.

The Indian boy looked about 13, though sometimes it seemed to Steve that he might be a year or two younger. In the dream he followed the boy about his day, watching from a distance as the young brave trained in archery and knife-throwing, rode bareback with his friends, wolfed down the cereal that the women had pounded and cooked over a smoking mesquite fire, then flung himself down on the ground for a brief nap before starting all over again. Steve never got close enough to look the boy directly in the face. From the rear, or at a distance, he looked like any other young Apache — slightly less sturdy than the rest perhaps, but not markedly so. If his hair was dark brown instead of Indian-black, the difference was hardly noticeable.

Sometimes the girl came into the picture, too. She hovered at the edges of the dream, seeming to communicate with her brother with passing glances only. Mostly she stayed with the women, pounding maize into cornmeal, stringing ornate bead necklaces, sewing moccasins and tanning hides and drawing water. There was little chatter with the other Indian girls, Steve noted. This one kept to herself a great deal. There was a frail, wistful air about her that set her apart.

Excitement charged the camp. With the first tang of autumn on the wind, the braves were preparing for the big yearly hunt. This time — for the first time — the 13-year-old was to be allowed to come along. Following behind in the ghostlike way that dreamers have, Steve sensed the boy's suppressed emotion: a wild exhilaration, tinged with fear. He watched the boy hone his arrows to a fine point and polish his knife until it shone.

When dawn broke, gray and dreary, the boy was among the first to rise. He stood aside from the others for a few minutes, mumbling to himself

what looked like a brief prayer. Then, thrusting his knife into its sheath
with an adult gesture that sat comically and a touch pathetically on his
far-from-grown-up shoulders, he strode over to where the men and a few
other lucky youths were devouring their breakfasts. Mesquite smoke rose
acridly on the chill air. Nearby the horses munched their corn, sleek and
groomed, nostrils flaring as though they could already smell the buffalo
they'd be pursuing this day.

The boy sat down with his bowl, but he did not eat right away. While
Steve, invisible, crept up beside him, the boy lifted his eyes to find his
sister. As though at a silent signal, she looked up, too, and gazed across at
him from her place with the women. For the first time, Steve got a good
look at their eyes.

Both pairs of eyes, brother's and sister's, were deep set, and filled with
a nameless sorrow that tore at his heart. But this emotion — so carefully
clamped down all the rest of the time, and glimpsed only in this unguard-
ed moment at danger's edge — was not the thing that shocked Steve most
of all. What shook him to the core was the color of their eyes.

They were not black as obsidian, as good Indian eyes should be. Instead,
they were that mixture of brown and green known as hazel, with a darker-
brown ring around the perimeter. Unusual eyes.

They were also exactly like Steve's own.

He woke with a shudder.

His pajamas and sheets were soaked with sweat. For a few dazed moments he lay chilled to the bone, reliving the dream, wondering at it,
fearing it. Then, almost savagely, he got up, ripped off the sheets and
remade the bed with fresh ones.

It was 5:30, at least an hour before his alarm clock was due to wake him,
but he knew that, for now, sleep was a thing of the past. A quick shower
was what he needed, to wash away the bitter taste of the dream … though
he knew from long experience that it would take more than water, however hot, to do that. He had been having this dream, at intervals ranging
from a couple of weeks to a couple of years, since childhood. Curiously, the
frequency of the dream had stepped up since the day, some eight months
before, when Sheriff Ramsay had called on him in the matter of the anti-
Semitic hate message found scrawled on the synagogue wall.

Who was the boy? And what role did the sister play in all of this? He would have thought, after all the times they'd met in his nocturnal wanderings, that he would know more about them than he did. But all he knew was what he saw, which was disturbing enough. Who these people were, and what might be their connection to him, remained a mystery as elusive as the world of dreams itself.

With resolution, he put the night behind him. He was due in court today; an 18-year-old youth from the reservation had been apprehended with an illegal substance in his possession. There were mitigating circumstances that Steve intended to bring to the attention of the court; still, he doubted if he would be able to talk his way out of a conviction this time. The most he could hope for was a bit of understanding when it came to sentencing.

Two cups of coffee later, he was out the door. Though he tried to ignore it, the scent of burning mesquite stayed with him all the way to the courthouse.

V.

"**H**ey! I saw that!"

"Whaddaya mean? What'd I do?"

"You know very well what you did!" The voices were rising to a fever pitch. Shana and Donny were fighting again.

Tova's hands froze in the act of folding a shirt. Fleetingly, she remembered their first few days in Lakewood, when the newness of everything had dulled the edge of her children's normal behavior patterns. They had generally been cooperative then. Hardly a quarrel had broken out, let alone a full-scale fight.

But that had been then. Right now, gazing at the waiting mound of clean laundry on the bed in front of her, the mother considered her options.

She could stalk into the living room, scene of the battle, and ask for explanations. She could arbitrate, adjudicate and, it was to be hoped, finally orchestrate a little peace and quiet.

Or she could stick her head under her pillow and pretend that she hadn't heard ....

"You are *too*!" Shana's voice rose shrilly. "You're out, and you know it! You're such a cheater!"

"*I'm* a cheater? What about the time you moved two of my checkers when I wasn't looking?"

"That was a joke, O.K.? It also happened about two years ago!"

"I have a good memory," Donny said stiffly. "Anyway, that's no excuse."

"Well, for your information, what you did just now is *nothing* like that. It's just — plain — cheating. And I don't play with cheaters!"

"So who asked you to play? You're the one who butted in when Chaim and me were starting a game ..."With a sigh, Tova put down the shirt and went out of the room. This was cutting a little too close to the bone. Donny, bless him, was about to hit a nerve that was very raw with Shana just now. He was on the brink of reminding her that she was the new girl in town and had not yet met anyone her own age with whom to hang around, which was why she was reduced to playing with her younger brother in the first place. Back in Brooklyn, Chaim and Donny had rarely even seen Shana on a Sunday afternoon and, if they did, she was only half-glimpsed, camouflaged amid an animated group of friends.

School's starting soon, Tova reminded herself as she approached the living room, where the quarreling voices had reached a new crescendo. She'll be with other girls then. She'll make friends.

If we can all survive that long ...

She paused at the entrance to the living room, entranced all over again by the decor. No decorating expert herself, she had not set her hopes very high in this move. She would transfer their ordinary furniture from New York to New Mexico, and that would be that.

Then Rivi Gann had stepped in.

It had been at one of their meetings, back in Brooklyn. In the lull before everyone arrived and settled down around the table, Tova had shown Rivi pictures of the house they had purchased in Lakewood. It had been Nachman who chose it, with the help of the Harrises and a real estate *maven* in the community by the name of Phyllis Pergoda. Rivi had been enchanted by the layout of the rooms.

"See how much light comes in through these big windows! And the flow of the rooms makes for such an airy feel, even more spacious than it really is. With the right colors on the walls and floors, the effect will be just stunning." Rivi handed the photos back with a smile.

Tova handed them right back. "Talk," she commanded. "I have absolutely no sense of these things. What kind of wallpaper and rugs should I order? And how do I arrange the furniture for the best effect? Help, Rivi!"

Rivi was delighted to help. On her and Asher's flying visit to New Mexico, she went so far as to visit various purveyors of wall and floor coverings and a furniture establishment or two.

"I've even found the perfect light fixtures for your main rooms," she told Tova on her return. With deft hands, she sketched her vision of Tova's new home. It was hard to say who was more ecstatic with the results, Tova herself, or her unofficial interior designer. Rather awkwardly, she offered to pay Rivi for her expertise, but Rivi waved the offer away with the closest thing to anger that Tova had ever seen her display.

Now, standing at the entrance to the living room that was Rivi's handiwork, Tova marveled anew at the gracefulness of the lines — the "flow" that Rivi had talked about — the beiges complemented by delicate pastels in the cushions that accented the darker, hardier solids of sofa and easy chairs. The whole effect was one of peace and harmony. An effect which was, at the moment, being grievously ruined by her offspring.

"For your information, mister know-it-all —" Shana shrieked at her brother as Tova walked in. Donny was sitting back on his heels, glaring at his sister across a disheveled checkerboard, a heated retort ready to spring to his lips.

"For everybody's information," Tova announced, forcing herself to keep her voice level and calm, "this game room is hereby closed for the duration."

"The duration of what?" Donny asked, diverted.

"The duration of this quarrel, for one thing. If necessary, the duration of your childhoods ... I will not have this silly bickering going on in my home. If the two of you can't play a game without fighting, then don't play at all."

"That's fine with me," Shana said, standing up and brushing off her skirt as if to rid herself of the germs of her brother's presence. "Who needs to play with little kids, anyway?"

Tova prayed that Donny wouldn't reply, "*You* do, obviously." To head him off, she said hastily, "Donny, why don't you ride your bike a while?"

"It needs air."

"Well, use the pump. Maybe Chaim'll want to go biking with you."

The idea appealed to her active son. The only reason he'd confined himself indoors today was because Chaim was busy with a model airplane set and had not been available to join him. In light of his encounter with Shana just now, he was clearly of the opinion that even solitude was preferable. He scampered off to find his bicycle pump and his big brother, in that order. Maybe Chaim was done with his model and would join him outdoors.

When Donny had disappeared, Tova turned to Shana. There was a dangerous look in her daughter's eye, one that elicited pity but dared you to express so much as a syllable of it. A tricky age, 14 — compounded by an equally tricky situation. Tova drew a deep breath.

"Sweetie, I was thinking of heading out to the mall. Maybe we could find something nice for Yom Tov. We planned to go shopping in New York, remember? With everything as hectic as it was, that didn't work out."

"So what else is new?" Shana grumbled.

"A good attitude would be nice." Privately, Tova added, *Not to mention a good friend ...*

She didn't have to say it out loud. The misery in Shana's face reflected everything her mother was thinking. Shana wouldn't admit her pain. She wanted to be the good girl everyone expected her to be. Instead, her unhappiness trickled out in a million tiny ways every day: in renewed nail-biting, a habit she had broken two years before; in monosyllabic answers to any question of a remotely personal nature; in picking pointless quarrels with her siblings. Optimistically, Tova had decided to offer the shopping trip as a kind of universal pick-me-up. It's hard not to smile when you have a new dress to wear.

That rule might hold true for most girls; Shana, for her part, was wondering why in the world she should bother dressing up, when there was no one in this whole hot, sleepy town to notice — let alone care — what she wore.

She looked up to find her mother's eyes fixed expectantly on her. After a brief hesitation, Shana shrugged and said, "Okay. I'll go." *As though,* Tova thought wryly, *she was bestowing a favor ...*

The phone rang while Tova was waiting downstairs for Shana to get ready. It was Nachman.

"What's the matter?" her husband asked at once, attuned to her mood even across the telephone wires.

Tova glanced over her shoulder at the stairs, feeling absurdly like a conspirator in her own home. "It's Shana," she near-whispered. "Miserable, miserable Shana ..."

She could almost hear her husband's mind click into focus to consider the ongoing problem of their oldest child's discontent. They had both talked themselves dry on the subject. They'd tried to cheer Shana up, to encourage her, to hold out hopes for a bright future even here, so far away from where she wanted to be. But words, however numerous and eloquent, had done no good at all. Miserable, miserable Shana ...

When Nachman spoke again, there was a note in his voice that told Tova he had made up his mind about something. "Listen, Tova. It's no good trying to sugar-coat the situation. Fact: Shana doesn't want to be here. Unfortunately, there's a second fact that she has to take into account: the fact that she *is* here. And reality always wins."

"Sometimes after a long and bloody battle," Tova sighed.

"What we have to do," Nachman plowed on, ignoring his wife's pessimistic lapse, "is engage her interest. New Mexico is her reality, at least for now. Let's help her realize that, and stop fighting it."

Tova asked the relevant question: "How?"

Nachman's smile came through over the line. "I have an idea. I'll be home in a few hours. Then we'll see ..."

"We're going to the mall to look for something for Shana to wear on Yom Tov. A spur-of-the-moment decision, in the course of trying to avert World War III between her and Donny. She's in no great mood, though. Wish me luck ..."

A light footfall behind her made her turn swiftly, intensely glad that she had kept her voice down. Shana stood there, hair brushed, neatly dressed, and with absolutely no animated spark in her eyes. She might have been on her way to the dentist's instead of going shopping for a holiday wardrobe. Tova forced herself to smile brightly at her daughter as, in her ear, her husband's voice in the phone murmured, "Good luck, Tova. See you later."

"Thanks. Bye." She hung up, widening her smile into a caricature of gaiety. "Ready, Shana?"

Unenthusiastically, Shana nodded. As she fetched the twins and let the other children know they were going, Tova prayed that Nachman's idea — whatever it was — would bear fruit. Otherwise, no matter what the weather outside, it was going to be a long, hard winter at the Bernsteins' place.

"Shana, I'd like you to meet Mrs. Helen Sadowsky. Mrs. Sadowsky, this is my daughter, Shana."

Shana mumbled something in reply, still caught in a net of surprised bewilderment over this strange visit. Only minutes after her homecoming from the mall with her mother — both of them laden with packages that had had the effect of slightly and temporarily brightening her spirits — her father had walked in and announced that there was someone he wanted Shana to meet. Tova shot him a startled glance, a question in her eyes. Smiling, Nachman said only, "I'll tell you all about it later. I'm anxious to get the ball rolling on this."

What "this" was, and just who she was going to meet, remained a mystery to Shana as she and her father drove through town to a rambling house at the outskirts. Beyond this street lay Lake McMillan, surrounded by the usual arid landscape dotted with mesquite and scrub oak. The low-lying growth looked like scribbles on a large flat page. In the background was the highway's muffled roar. The house to which her father led her featured a formidable-looking cactus garden that somebody was obviously tending with love. Some of the cacti plants were in flower, red or yellow or bright purple blooms peeking incongruously out of the thorny surface. The house itself had a slightly shabby but self-respecting air, like a scrupulously groomed horse put out to pasture. Shana allowed herself to be led, her curiosity piqued.

The door was opened by a middle-aged woman in wire-rim glasses, with dimpled cheeks and a friendly smile. She was wiping her hands on the front of a voluminous apron when they came in, and holding aloft like a welcome banner a long wooden spoon which she'd forgotten to put aside when the doorbell rang. Shana soon saw that the rest of the place was as homey and unintimidating as its mistress. A hasty glimpse around the living room showed her sagging, comfortable armchairs and low tables piled high with books and magazines. The whole room was like a vast cushion: a place to sink into and put your feet up, where there was always something interesting to read at your elbow and a good smell wafting in from the kitchen while you were reading it. Despite herself, Shana's heart warmed to the room: and also (she peeked shyly upward) to the woman of the house.

"Mrs. Sadowsky is the wife of Dr. Ben Sadowsky, the pediatrician we'll be using," Nachman told her. "But she also plays a very important role in her own right. Mrs. Sadowsky is the town's head librarian."

"There's only one public library in town," Mrs. Sadowsky laughed, "and I happen to be the senior employee there. You make it sound much more glamorous than it actually is."

"Head librarian," Nachman Bernstein repeated firmly. "I thought, Shana, that it might be interesting for the two of you to meet. Mrs. Sadowsky is also — in an unofficial capacity — the town historian. She knows everything there is to know about Lakewood and the surrounding area. And the two of you have something in common, something that you both love: books."

"That's right. I'd be thrilled to have you come over now and then, especially before you get into the swing of things at school," Mrs. Sadowsky said comfortably. "My husband's a doctor, you know, and between his private practice and his hospital rounds, I'm alone a good deal of the time. We could meet either here or at the library. You can even lend a hand at the library, if you want. We're always a little understaffed."

Nachman held his breath without seeming to, as he waited for his daughter's reaction.

To his astonishment — though he carefully kept this from showing in his face — Shana didn't hesitate.

"Thanks," she said, smiling shyly at the librarian. "I'd love to." Her gaze wandered again into the inviting living room, with its heaps of books and sink-into-'em armchairs. "Can we start now?"

Three minutes later, having promised to pick Shana up whenever she was ready, Nachman Bernstein was on his way home to tell his wife about the start of a miracle (or so he devoutly hoped) in the making.

VI.

That week, the last before *Rosh Chodesh Elul* and the *kollel's* opening, was a busy and productive one. In many ways, it was a happy one as well. This was a getting-acquainted time, a cautious inching toward familiarity with their new town and their own role in it.

Nachman Bernstein put the finishing touches on the schedule of classes that the *kollel* would be offering the Jewish public, and held earnest meetings with each of his fellow *kollel* members to see that they got off to a good start. Tova busied herself with their new house and getting her children ready for school. Shana would be attending the fledgling Bais Yaakov, while Gila and Yudi were enrolled in the day school's fourth grade and kindergarten, respectively. Chaim and Donny — along with Shimi Mandel — were to be homeschooled at the *kollel* by Asher Gann and Avi Feder.

The week had its points of drama. During one lively game of hide-and-seek, Yudi and Bo went missing for all of 30 minutes, only to be found, after a frantic search, in a dark corner by the furnace room, happily munching graham crackers from a box they'd found on a basement shelf. Gila, though apprehensive about starting the fourth grade in a new school, did not have a single asthma attack. And Shana eagerly continued her visits to Helen Sadowsky, her first friend in Lakewood.

"This is an interesting part of the country," the librarian told her that first night, when they were both snugly ensconced in two of the huge armchairs in the Sadowsky living room. They held matching mugs of hot cocoa. A plate of cookies sat ignored on the coffee table, almost lost among the books and magazines scattered there. "New Mexico was a latecomer to the United States: She's the 47th state to join the union. But she's got a long, long history before that. Did you know that Santa Fe — that's a city up in the northern part of the state — is the oldest seat of government in the United States? The Spaniards who ruled this part of the country built their Palace of Governors there in the 16th century. And *El Camino Real*, the 'Royal Highway' running from Sante Fe all the way down to Mexico City, was the very first road built by the Europeans in what would one day become the United States. It was first used in 1581! Imagine."

Shana tried. Her imagination boggled at the antiquity of it all. What had people worn in those days? Did they drive carriages or ride horses? She pictured haughty Spaniards with pointed black beards trotting down the Royal Highway on beautiful dark horses of noble breeding.

Mrs. Sadowsky went on, "Do you know that New Mexico is where the first atom bomb was built and exploded? In fact, nuclear power — for use in space rockets, electricity and our country's defense — is one of the country's major industries. Los Alamos, not far from here, is a big laboratory where government scientists work on military and non-military uses for nuclear power. A good deal of research is done up in Albuquerque, too."

Shana nodded politely. She hesitated, then asked the question that was uppermost in her mind. "There are a lot of Indians around here, aren't there?"

Helen Sadowsky leaned forward, eyes sparkling. "It's interesting that you should ask that. Indians have always played an important part in the history of the American Southwest. After all, they lived here long before white settlers came and forced their way in. But here's an intriguing point — and rather a sad one, I've always thought. The Indians had no concept of land ownership. They thought of themselves as caretakers of the land, no more than that. When the white settlers came and offered to buy the land from them, what the white men thought of as a 'sale' was, in the Indian mind, merely permission to use the land for a while. Like good children, they believed in sharing. That might explain why the exploitation was so easy to perpetrate. The Indians just didn't have a clue."

"You sound sorry for them."

"In a way, I am. Too many of them live on welfare today, and are plagued by all sorts of societal problems." The librarian paused. "Though they did manage to wreak plenty of havoc in their time. Especially the Apaches. Did you know that there's a big Apache reservation not far from here? It belongs to the Mescalero tribe. Actually, it's the only reservation in this corner of the state. The others are far to the north and west."

Shana nodded. "My father says the reservation's about 30 miles away. But we've seen some Indians right here in town."

"There aren't many employment opportunities for today's Native Americans on the reservation," Mrs. Sadowsky told her. "Many of them have 'gone urban,' moving to Albuquerque or other big cities in search of jobs. Some have even found their way to little Lakewood ..."

"Tell me more about the Apaches," Shana urged. Her initial bashfulness had entirely melted away in this perfect room, in the company of this woman, who was turning out to be not only a warm hostess but also a fountain of fascinating information.

"The Apaches were fierce fighters," Helen Sadowsky said slowly. "Initially, they were primarily hunters and food gatherers. They hunted game: deer, antelope, rabbits. They picked cactus fruit, piñon nuts, edible roots. They had no permanent homes, preferring to travel in small bands, searching for food. Mostly, they lived in brush shelters and tepees."

"I've seen pictures of those," Shana volunteered.

"Who hasn't? But not all Indians lived that way. Others lived in caves in the cliffs. Cliff dwellers, they were called. You can still see some very ancient cave homes up near Sante Fe."

"So the Apaches weren't fighters?"

"Not at first. After a while, though, they began to raid their Navaho neighbors for food and other goods. The Navaho were more settled, more prosperous."

"Didn't the Apaches fight the white men, too?"

"Yes. They fought the Spaniards, and later on the other white settlers who had come to take over their territory. In the latter part of the 19th century, an Apache warrior by the name of Geronimo led attacks on settlers and soldiers in Mexico and the Southwestern United States. Ever heard of him?"

"Sure!" Some months ago, on learning of their family's impending move to this part of the country, her brother Donny had adopted that name along with a new identity as an old-time Indian chief. The game — which included a great deal of "weapon" brandishing and earsplitting war whoops — had flourished until their father had declared Geronimo banished, for the sake of peace and their eardrums ...

"When things became too hot between the white men and the Indians, the government rounded them up and moved them all onto the San Carlos Reservation in Arizona. The Apaches earned a reputation as savage fighters. Geronimo escaped the reservation and fought United States troops for a while, before returning to the reservation. Then, in 1882, he and other Apache warriors fled to the Sierra Madre, in Mexico. They set up hidden camps and used them as a base for bloody raids on both sides of the United States-Mexican border. Finally, our Army got the better of them, and in 1883 Geronimo and his men surrendered." She paused. "Geronimo was the name the Spaniards gave him, by the way. It was not his Indian name."

"What was his Indian name?"

"Goyale. It means, 'the smart one.'"

However smart he may have been, Geronimo did not succeed in liberating his tribe to live as they once had, free and untrammeled by any foreign government. Shana couldn't decide if she felt sorry for the Apaches or appalled by them. Both, really. She could understand their outrage at having their land taken away, but who could condone all those terrible massacres?

She picked up her mug of cocoa, which had grown cooler by now, and peeked at the librarian over the rim. "You know so much about everything."

Helen Sadowsky smiled. "I'm interested in everything." She leaned forward. "But what especially interests me are clues to a possible Jewish presence in these parts, as far back as a century or two ago."

"Was there any?" Shana's eyes grew wide.

"Hard to say. Most Jewish immigrants to this country stuck to the urban belts, where they could worship together and earn some sort of a living. There were not too many Jewish farmers, and certainly not very many Jewish pioneers. But there may have been some."

"I'd love to hear about them," Shana exclaimed. In some, small corner of her mind, she listened to herself with a measure of astonishment.

When was the last time she had expressed this much enthusiasm for anything?

Before her parents had told her they were moving her out to New Mexico. That much was certain.

Then it was time to go home. Her father came to fetch her in the car. Shana did not volunteer much during the drive back, but her air of contentment was a relief to both her parents. She fell asleep thinking about Indians and tepees, and woke to the sound of hammering. Her brothers were using the last of the golden summer days to put the finishing touches on a treehouse they were building in the forked limbs of the big old cottonwood in their backyard.

The Mandel boys were helping. Even Meir Mandel descended from the heights of aged superiority to offer advice. What use the treehouse would be to any of them once the school year began, Shana didn't know. But they were having fun, which was more than she could say for herself at the moment. It was too soon to visit Mrs. Sadowsky again today, and school didn't start till next Tuesday.

For the first time, Shana thought about the first day of school with a smidgen of anticipation. The long lethargy had begun to lift, and the cloud of fury was dissipating, too. Holding onto anger is an exhausting activity, and Shana had a feeling she was going to need all her energy in the weeks to come. Maybe school wouldn't be so bad. A small school might even be kind of nice. She would wait and see …

Nachman and Tova were cautiously elated at the change. Though Shana was still far from content with the drastic changes in her life, they believed that progress of sorts had been made. Some two weeks after moving here, the girl had finally consented to dip her big toe into the waters of Lakewood, New Mexico.

It was a start.

Part Two: Smoldering Threat

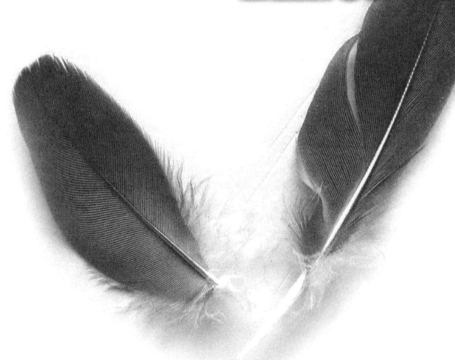

Chapter 6

I.

On the Bernsteins' second Shabbos in Lakewood — the first for the other *kollel* families — the shul threw a gala lunch in the newcomers' honor.

The meal represented a concerted, community-wide effort. Committees of Sisterhood women and girls had lovingly prepared the food, set the tables and fashioned the flower-shaped place cards that poked their heads up beside each plate. Before the meal began, Nachman Bernstein and his colleagues were introduced to various members of the Lakewood community: "our pillars," Rabbi Harris called them.

There was Dr. Ben Sadowsky, a pediatrician and founding member of the shul board. A quiet man with a genial demeanor, "Dr. Ben," as he was fondly called, shook Nachman's hand warmly and welcomed him to the community. "I get them when they're young," he quipped, referring to his little patients. "Afterward, they're all yours."

Nate Goodman was next: a tall, dark attorney with intense eyes, a shock of curly black hair beneath his kippah and an unexpectedly disarming smile. "Just what we need around here — some fresh blood," he said, the eyes boring into Nachman's as though taking his measure.

"Seems to me you've already got some high-caliber *old* blood," Nachman remarked, with a smiling glance at Rabbi Harris, beside him.

Rabbi Harris held up his hands in laughing protest. "Believe me, I was the first one to jump at the idea of a *mesivta* and *kollel*. A one-man show is not at all what I'm after. As far as I'm concerned, fresh blood — and the more of it, the better — is just the ticket!"

Next, the rabbi introduced him to Sammy Cohen, a prosperous industrialist who had the distinction of being the only *Kohen* in town. "That makes me a mighty popular man around Yom Tov," he told Nachman, giving him a hearty handshake and gripping his arm at the same time. Cohen was on the short side, sturdily built, slightly balding, businesslike and friendly in equal measure. Nachman murmured, "I'll bet that's true the rest of the year as well!" before Rabbi Harris swept him on to the next board member. "Another doctor, but not a medical one this time," he explained. "Abe — Dr. Abe Rein — is a forensic psychiatrist."

Nachman peered curiously at the professorial figure before him as they shook hands. Dr. Rein had a smooth cap of hair, graying at the edges, and he wore bifocals through which a pair of remarkably steady eyes looked out at the world. "Does that mean what I think it does?"

"That's right," Dr. Rein nodded, his smile cool and courteous. "I spend my time talking to criminals to see what makes them tick."

Nachman shuddered. "Better you than me ..."

"He's got some fascinating stories," Pinchas Harris said. "You should get together sometime, just to hear them."

"When my wife feels ready for Shabbos guests," Nachman promised, and had the pleasure of seeing the psychiatrist's smile deepen, "I'll take you up on that."

Last of all, just before it was time to sit down to the *seudah*, was their day-school principal, Mrs. Simi Wurtzler. Tova Bernstein had already made her acquaintance, and was glad to introduce her husband.

"We'll all be working for the *klal* together," Nachman said pleasantly. With her eager manner and air of indefatigable energy, it was easy to see how Mrs. Wurtzler had risen to her present position. "May it be a long and fruitful relationship."

"*Amen!*" Simi Wurtzler cried. "Tova, this is great! I'm going to do my best to cultivate the boys in my school for the *mesivta* — and the *mesivta* can groom them for the *beis midrash* and *kollel*. We'll become a full-service town ..." She shivered in a kind of dreamy ecstasy. "Who would've believed it, just a few years back?"

Whatever remark either Tova or Nachman might have made in response was obviated by the need to find their seats. The meal commenced in the shul's spacious social hall, amid a babble of talk punctuated by the clink of silverware and the clattering feet of small children too restless to spend the communal Shabbos *seudah* doing anything as mundane as eating. Tentatively, old-timers made overtures to the newcomers. Before long, various personal conversations had been struck, and the first notes in a symphony of future friendships could be heard quivering faintly in the air.

Most notable — to Nachman, at least — was the instant rapport that seemed to spring up between Avi Feder and attorney-*gabbai* Goodman. The two unattached men took adjoining seats at the table and kept up a more-or-less continual dialogue throughout the meal. Nate was an accomplished pianist, Nachman remembered, and Avi had recently taken up the violin. Nachman caught his wife's eye and knew that she had also noticed. A gladness crept into his heart: Avi, still groping for stability in his bereavement, needed the warmth of friendship to fill the void in his life.

Rabbi Harris made a short welcoming speech between the *cholent* and the dessert, then cleared his throat and glanced down to where an elderly man was sitting on his right. Nachman Bernstein was seated on the man's other side.

"And now, I'd like to introduce a special guest; a man who has flown in from New York especially to be here with us this Shabbos. The man behind the *kollel* and the planned yeshivah high school for boys; the man who had the vision to see potential in our own little town, and the get-up-and-go to start turning that potential into a reality. Ladies and gentleman ... Marvin Fleischmann!"

The elderly man rose slowly to his feet. He was tall, and gaunt almost to the point of emaciation, but the eyes beneath the silvery cap of hair were bright and alert. When he smiled, which he did now, the beaked nose and severe lines of his face were softened.

"Thank you, Rabbi Harris," he began in a gravelly voice. "It's a pleasure to be here …"

He gave a terse talk, lasting no more than four or five minutes, in which he outlined his plans for transforming the spiritual landscape of tiny Lakewood. He spoke of a plot of land just outside the town limits, of a modest beginning and eventual expansion. Around the room, faces were riveted in rapt attention. It was like watching a mythical fairy godfather descend, magic wand poised for action …

"As for the actual substance of what the *kollel* will be offering your community," he ended briskly, "I'll step aside to let the expert speak." He waved a hand at the man seated to his right. "I give you Rabbi Nachman Bernstein, your new *Rosh Kollel!* Reb Nachman, please." With a brief incline of the head to acknowledge the burst of enthusiastic applause that rent the air like a thunderclap, he stepped aside with a gracious half-smile to make way for the younger man.

Nachman Bernstein stood up and took Fleischmann's place, gripping the old man's hand warmly en route. Watching him, Tova felt her heart burst with pride. Such a genuinely modest man, her husband, but in his capable, unassuming way so ready to use whatever talents and abilities Hashem had granted him for the sake of his people! Impulsively she turned to see her daughter's face and caught Shana gazing at her father with just the same look as she knew she herself was wearing. As though she sensed her mother's observation, Shana turned her head. Their eyes met and held. There was an instant's clarity, a shared understanding of how they felt about the man at the podium, and how it bound them to him and to each other. Tova's heart swelled: This was the first real moment of connection she remembered having with Shana since … since she and Nachman had announced the move to Lakewood. Silently sending her thanks heavenward, she turned her attention back to her husband.

"Please believe me when I say that it is my great and sincere pleasure to be here with you today," the new *Rosh Kollel* began. "I don't think I need to tell you how very different Lakewood, New Mexico is from my native Brooklyn, New York. Our little *kollel* has its roots in a place that is overflowing with Torah, *Baruch Hashem*. We are glad to bring the flowering of those roots here to you, because you've asked for it. Because you've prepared the soil for it to flourish. Because Torah is something that you thirst for and want to learn more about." He paused, both with emotion and with the timing of a natural speaker. "I know that I speak for my colleagues when I say that it is my privilege to be here. And my honor." He waited politely for the wave of applause to crest and subside. Grinning, he added, "But the teaching goes both ways. Every teacher learns from his students. I've already had my first lesson." Into the curious silence, he deadpanned, "I've learned how to make my first Spanish omelet!"

Laughter, more applause, and then Nachman launched into the meat of his talk: a brief but pithy lesson gleaned from the weekly Torah portion, followed by a somewhat lengthier introduction of his fellow *kollel* members and the various classes they would be offering the Lakewood community. By the time he resumed his seat, the shul members felt as though they had known him forever. Once again Tova felt the smile creeping straight up from her heart and into her eyes. This one, she shared with Nachman.

And then, almost before they could turn around, Shabbos was behind them and the earnest work of the week lay ahead. On Monday, *Rosh Chodesh Elul*, the *zeman* would begin; community classes were scheduled to start the following night. But first, on Sunday, a very exciting field trip was planned.

"Marvin Fleischmann has invited the entire *kollel* — wives and children included — to join him and the realtors tomorrow for a final tour of the prospective site. If he's satisfied, he'll give the okay to start planning and construction." Nachman's eyes sparkled. "We're going places, folks!"

That night, he phoned Efraim and Etty Mandel to extend his personal invitation for them to join the outing. Efraim was hesitant.

"I don't know if we'll be able to make it, Nachman. It's Meir's last day home before he goes to yeshivah. The next day, we take him to the airport and put Meir on the plane to yeshivah in L.A. The *zeman* starts the day after that."

"Can't you make it for even a little while?"

"I'll talk to Etty. She'll be going crazy packing Meir's things, preparing a fancy farewell dinner — busy, busy, busy. I don't know if she'll want to drop everything to go on a picnic. But I'll ask."

Nachman did know what Efraim meant. Etty Mandel had a way of infusing even the most innocuous situation with some of her own edgy tension. On the eve of seeing her eldest son off to yeshivah for the first time, she would be like an unlit powder keg.

"Well, see what you can do, Efraim. We'd love to have you there. In fact, Marvin Fleischmann might take it amiss if you don't at least show your faces. Solidarity and all that."

"I'll use that argument to try and convince my wife." Efraim sounded dubious.

"Where will Meir be flying from?"

"Albuquerque. That's a full 160 miles from here. It'll be an all-day round trip."

"Well, we'll miss him for sure. Please tell him that I wish him *hatzlachah* in his learning. Are you planning to bring him back for Succos?"

"Unfortunately, no. We can't afford the airfare again so close to the beginning of the *zeman* ... He'll be staying with my wife's sister in L.A. He has cousins his age there."

"I'm sure he'll enjoy it, though he'll miss you all, of course."

"Yes ... Well, I'll keep you posted about tomorrow. If I don't make it, please be sure and tell me all about it afterward, O.K.?"

"I certainly intend to do that, Reb Efraim," Nachman promised.

Hanging up a moment later, Nachman let his mind dwell on the next day's pivotal meeting. Though it would take place outdoors, complete with picnic fixings and cameras, the final decision on the site of the new *mesivta* and *kollel* building would be made then. Nachman would use the day as an opportunity to solidify his relationship with Marvin Fleischmann, without whom none of this would be possible. He found the old man crusty but approachable; there was already a burgeoning sense of mutual respect between them.

After tomorrow, Nachman hoped that Fleischmann would fly away with a positive feeling about the brand-new *kollel*, a feeling that would be reflected in a steady flow of support in the future.

II.

Southwestern New Mexico enjoys little rain even in the winter; in the summer, dry skies are almost a given. Tova and Rivi could pack their picnic baskets with light hearts. Avi Feder, who'd insisted on being in charge of dessert, had raided Lakewood's supermarkets for kosher cookies of every description. "One day, I'll bake the cookies myself," he had pledged on the phone as they laid their plans for the next day. "It's on my list."

Avi had a long list of things he intended to do "one day," to make his unwanted independence more bearable. A widower for nearly nine months now, he was finally ready to acknowledge his new reality. Ready to accept that this — for the moment, at least — was all there was.

Since baking his favorite chocolate-chip cookies was still beyond his capabilities, Avi turned instead to his newest hobby: the violin.

Just why he'd chosen this most difficult instrument to comfort him in his loneliness, he found it hard to say. Perhaps the haunting quality of the violin's voice spoke to something lost and wandering inside his own psyche. Whatever the reason, when after four or five months of bereavement the fog began slowly to lift and he found himself once again capable of taking an interest in anything, he decided to take up an instrument. After learning all day long, he did not want to spend his quiet evenings with the printed pages of a book or newspaper, however relaxing. Chatting on the phone had its limitations as well, especially since his closest friends were people caught up in the joys and vicissitudes of family life.

He turned instead to music.

At first, he was a passive listener, letting the notes he loved wash over him in a healing balm. After a while, though, he found himself itching to play a more active role. He would become a student of music. He would take up the violin!

Now, some three months later in his tiny, new apartment in Lakewood, he picked up his case with tender, careful fingers, undid the clasps and gazed upon the instrument.

The violin gleamed in its case like a jewel on black velvet, reflecting the care he gave it. Carefully he reached in to pick it up; slowly he brought it to his chin tucking it in place as he reached for the bow.

The phone rang.

He paused, nerves jangling. For a fleeting instant he contemplated the beauty of a universe without telephones. Then, reflecting that it was probably his mother calling, wondering why he hadn't been in touch on this *Motza'ei Shabbos*, he hastened to answer.

"Hi, Ma."

She returned his greeting unsurprised: Caller ID had become old hat even to her, a woman who generally resisted the encroachment of modern technology on her life. "Avi. How are you, *sheifeleh*?"

He winced at the endearment. Didn't she realize that he was no longer 5 years old?

Apparently not. "*Sheifeleh*, I have wonderful news. Mrs. Erlanger has given me a name for you."

"I already have a name, Ma."

"Very funny. Listen to me, this is important. She gave me the name of a wonderful girl, for a *shidduch*." She did not give him an opportunity to offer the usual protests. "It's time, Avi. It's been nearly nine months. If a baby can be born in that time, can't you be ready to start dating again? You need a wife. It's not good to be alone, *sheifeleh*."

He sighed. She meant well, he knew. But could he give birth to a new heart in nine months? A heart that would not cringe at the thought of letting a stranger in … A heart so shattered and scarred that it sometimes felt like a mound of glass fragments and not a beating, feeling thing at all.

Out of nowhere came a memory. An ordinary Friday night, two years or so ago, with the table already cleared — a quick job when there were just the two of them dining — and the food put away. They had moved into the living room, he and Yocheved, with reading material and tall, cold drinks of iced tea. Neither of them spoke much. The silence was restful. But all along, Avi was aware that he was not alone, that his wife was in the room with him, turning a page, chuckling a little at something she read, occasionally looking up to share a passage with him. An ordinary Friday night, when he'd felt a sudden, poignant piercing in the region of his heart. He remembered thinking: This is home. This is my family. This is happiness.

He had thought the happiness would last forever ...

His mother's voice broke through, as though from a great distance. "Avi? Answer me, *sheifie*. Say yes. Or at least let me tell you about her."

He felt as reluctant as ever to hear her out, but suddenly it seemed easier not to fight. His mother, as well as other well-meaning acquaintances, had for months now been exerting a nearly unrelenting pressure on him to put himself back into circulation. He could almost hear the choir of breaths that would catch in excitement when various matchmakers were informed that he'd agreed to step back into the ring.

The loneliness was debilitating. If only to banish that, he *was* ready to date, though not with any real hope of anything more. Given his still-limping emotional state, the gesture, he believed, would lead exactly nowhere. But that wasn't his fault, was it?

They said their good-byes. Mrs. Feder was eager to start the round of phone calls that would jump-start her bereaved son's life. Avi left all the details to his mother. He had no demands or preferences, because he had no hopes. In the little apartment in Lakewood, New Mexico, the first tentative notes from his violin floated out into the silent air.

One note went sour. Carefully, he played it again, correctly this time. He would need to find a music teacher here, but he was in no rush. He had no ambition to become a virtuoso. Plenty of enjoyment was to be had from merely playing the few simple songs he had mastered while still in New York. Maybe, when he'd honed his skill a bit, he could play duets with Nate Goodman, the lawyer/*gabbai* he'd met at lunch today. With relish he played his songs over and over, each note offering its modest packet of pleasure to the ear.

Unfortunately, his next-door neighbor did not share Avi's tastes. Before a quarter of an hour had passed, old Mrs. Richie was tapping irritably on the wall connecting their two apartments. Her message was crystal clear: "I'm trying to go to sleep. Quiet!"

He glanced at his watch. Nine forty-five. Some people had early bedtimes. With a sigh, he stopped playing and tucked his violin back into its own bed.

The walls of his apartment stared back at him, sightless and indifferent. He really should buy a few prints to dress up the place. Somehow, he had not yet mustered the energy or the interest. Decorating had always been Yocheved's domain ... Deliberately moving his thoughts away from that painful, tender spot, he paced the house restlessly. The evening pressed in on him.

He toyed briefly with the idea of giving Nate Goodman a call — the fellow intrigued him, and his conversation had been intelligent and stimulating — but he was reluctant to intrude on Nate's evening when they were still hardly more than new acquaintances. He was so bored that he even considered dropping in at the Ganns unannounced. As always, an innate pride held him back. It was this stiff-necked pride that prevented him from, as he termed it, making a nuisance of himself. Asher and Rivi might very well have plans of their own tonight. Although, on second thought, it was more probable that Rivi was busy in the kitchen, preparing a feast for tomorrow's picnic.

At the thought, his spirits rose. He was looking forward to tomorrow, and that was no small thing. For a long time after his Yocheved had gone, he had looked forward to nothing at all.

The day was a complete success. Marvin Fleischmann, attended by his secretary and a phalanx of eager realtors, stood in the blinding light of the New Mexico sun and pointed, emperorlike, at his future domain.

"This is where we'll build," he told Nachman and the others, with a broad gesture that encompassed a snug tract of land lying in the shelter of the cliffs. The tract was open to the east, where Lakewood lay about a mile away, and Lake McMillan, and then the Pecos River, winding its slow way down to the Gulf. To the northwest were the sheltering cliffs— purple, gold and crimson — that ran in a line roughly parallel to the town. To the south lay open desert.

Fleishmann entered into rapid-fire discussion with the realtors, ordering the requisite land survey, discussing the need for construction crews and capable foremen. "I'm leaving this in the hands of the realtors," Fleischmann told Nachman. "They'll provide ongoing supervision of the construction and refer any questions to you. I don't want to make you take valuable time away from the *kollel* in order to visit the site on a regular basis — spot checks should be fine. I'm going to institute a system of checks and balances to make sure the job gets done in a responsible fashion."

Listening to the wealthy entrepreneur, Nachman had no doubt in the world that the job would get done just as Fleischmann wanted.

After that came the fun part of the outing. As Fleischmann and his people departed to the realtors' office to hammer out details before his private jet bore him back East, out came the balls, frisbees and picnic baskets. In the shade of the same cliffs that would shelter the new yeshivah building from the west wind, the women spread their blankets and set out the food. Even the children were tempted by the array, which included fresh sandwiches and fruit, tasty leftover Shabbos fare, and Avi's cookies.

At last, satiated, the men sat talking desultorily in one lazy group and the women in another. The little Bernstein twins were uncharacteristically quiet for the moment, busy with some imaginary game of their own. Yudi Bernstein clamored for a family frisbee match, which Chaim Bernstein organized: brothers against sisters. He wished that Meir and Shimi had shown up, but their family had yet to put in an appearance at the picnic. Shana complained that two against three wasn't fair, to which Donny countered that Yudi, being only 5 and incapable of catching a frisbee to save his life, didn't count. The match was on!

When even the sight of flying frisbees palled, Chaim asked his father if he and the others could go exploring. "Just up that path there." He pointed at the nearest cliff, pockmarked by caves. "We'll be in sight most of the time, and within shouting distance." He knew his parents' rules all too well.

Nachman gave his permission.

He watched with a hand shading his eyes as his two older sons and two daughters began toiling up the trail. *My intrepid explorers,* he thought fondly. With a pang, he realized that the summer and its gift of lavish family time was over. Tomorrow the *zeman* began, and the daunting job of creating a new institution in a new place. He would hardly have time to so much as look at his children for a while … Seeing Gila glance back over her shoulder, he smiled and waved up at her. Gila's placid face broke into the unique smile that she saved for her family, the one that showed a large chunk of her heart along with the two rows of pearly teeth. Then she turned back, trotting to keep up with the others.

Chaim, as always, led the way. They were pretending to be pioneer woodsmen, though anything less resembling woods in this spot would have been difficult to find. Shana, friendlier than she'd been in days, threw in a suggestion now and then, but she was content for the most part to let her brothers do the talking. She was enjoying the walk, the unfamiliar sights and smells and the parched air that felt like the inside of a clothes dryer. Not a sound reached them from the group below. There was no one in the world but themselves, bravely exploring new territory. With a start, Shana realized that right now, at this moment, though so terribly far away from her friends and everything she had once known and held dear, she was not actively unhappy.

The rattle of a dislodged pebble was their first hint that they were not alone. In the sunbaked stillness, the sound was as loud as a gunshot.

III.

Chaim looked around, suddenly a little nervous. His younger brother, Donny, and his older sister, Shana, were half a step behind him, with 9-year-old Gila struggling along in their wake like an afterthought which, he had to admit, she often was.

But the sound had come from a different direction: to the left and a little above the trail where Chaim was leading the way. Pausing, he squinted up at the insistent blue of the sky, slashed through with spires of reddish rock. A dry, hot breeze fanned his face as he stood very still, listening intently. In the blazing sunlight, his shadow lay sharp and black on the path. Fronds of desert foliage waved like fingers from crevices in the stones. Scrub oak and stunted mesquite trees dotted the harshly beautiful landscape. Here, where the trail curved leftward, Chaim and his companions were temporarily hidden from their parents' view. He waited, straining to catch the sound again.

"Who's there?" he shouted at last, not really expecting an answer. Just behind him, Donny started to say something and then abruptly fell silent. Shana gasped in sudden panic. Another shadow had just stretched across their path, longer than Chaim's and looking, if possible, even blacker. All three children leapt back as if stung.

The man who stood in the path was not dressed in deerskin and feathers, but Donny and Chaim and Shana knew just from the shape of the man's jaw and the color of his hair that here, indubitably, was an authentic Native American. He was sturdily built, wearing jeans and a white T-shirt, and with coarse black hair that nearly touched his powerful shoulders. Dark, impenetrable eyes looked right at the children and seemed not to like what they saw.

A second man popped out to join the first. This one was Indian, too. He was nearly a head taller than the first, and far heavier: just plain fat, to put it baldly. The buttons of his plaid shirt had to work hard to meet in the middle. His hair was shorter than his companion's, and his eyes rounder, with a good-natured and slightly stupid look.

"Who are you?" Chaim demanded, blustering because he was afraid of betraying just how terrified he was. At 12, he was the oldest Bernstein boy (though not the oldest child in the family; Shana, two years older, had that distinction). He was the brave one: the trailblazer. Thrusting his hands into his pockets to hide their shaking, he met the long-haired Indian's eyes squarely and tried not to blink.

"We belong here," the man said slowly. His eyes seemed to be carved from stone, and they never left Chaim's. "We're from the Apache Mescalero reservation." He waved an arm westward. "But you — you're intruders. Go back where you came from!"

This was too much for Shana. Indignantly, she said over Chaim's shoulder, "What do you mean, intruders? We live here, right down there, in Lakewood! That's a whole lot closer than your reservation." After her talk with Mrs. Sadowsky, her father had helped her locate the Apache reservation on a local map. It was nestled in the foothills of the Sacramento Mountains, more than 30 miles away.

This little speech seemed to sap the last of her courage. She stepped back, and Donny moved up to stand like a human shield in front of her. He continued to stare at the strangers, struck momentarily dumb.

"That so, little lady?" the man sneered. And his companion, with a rumble of laughter that started deep in his drooping belly, echoed, "That so?"

"Yes." Chaim spoke calmly, with just the slightest hint of a waver in his voice. "And besides, our father's school is buying property right at the foot of these cliffs. So we do have a right to be here."

Something flickered in the black eyes. The first Indian hesitated, then seemed to make a conscious decision to retreat from his hostile stance. Flashing a smile that was very white and suddenly charming, he asked in a tone deliberately neutral, "So, just what might you kids be doing here this afternoon?"

Donny finally found his tongue.

He remembered what his father had told them, six long months previously in New York, when they had been contemplating this move. Somehow, it all seemed to be tied up with this hot, hot sun and these strange, deep canyons — *arroyos*, Ta had said they were called — and the soaring red cliffs, and these two black-haired strangers whose faces fit all the pictures of the Wild West that he had ever seen.

"We're seeking our fortune," he told them.

"Really?" the fat Indian exclaimed. "So are we!"

His companion elbowed him sharply, making him grunt in pain. With a smile that even Gila — toiling up and around the curve into sighting distance now — could tell was patently false, the first Indian said, "Well, never mind. You kids enjoy yourselves. We'll be going."

And, just like that, they were gone.

"Wow!" Donny breathed, eyes shining. "I always heard that Indians can move like the wind, but I never thought I'd see it for myself!"

Chaim was troubled. "I don't like the look of those two."

"Me neither," declared Shana. "Come on, let's go back."

"But we haven't finished exploring!" Donny protested.

"We can always come back another time," Shana said. "We live here now, remember?"

Reluctantly, the 11-year-old turned and followed his older siblings back down the trail. Gila walked beside him, blond haired and round faced and quiet. She was curious about the encounter she'd just glimpsed, but it was not her way to ask questions. Most things she learned by staying quiet as a mouse, and listening.

Nachman and Tova, apparently, had had their fill of sitting idly over the remains of their picnic. Or perhaps it was the twins, growing restless, that galvanized them into action. Some 50 yards below them on the trail were the children's mother and father and the three little ones. The group was moving slowly up in their direction, with Mo and Bo on kiddie-leashes to prevent them from hurtling themselves off the cliff tops, something they were absolutely capable of doing.

As the children hurried down the trail, the enchantment of sun and sky and the towering cliffs began to work their spell. Even before they reached the rest of their family, their apprehensions had nearly dissipated. Donny spotted a speckled rock that he was almost sure was uranium, and ran ahead to ask his father what he thought. Rabbi Bernstein stroked his beard and said that uranium was indeed one of New Mexico's natural resources, but he wasn't quite certain if this rock qualified. When Shana did begin to tell her mother all about the Indians, her manner was far less urgent than it would have been five minutes before.

"I don't like you kids talking to strangers," Tova said worriedly.

"You and Tatty were just a few steps behind us," Chaim said. "And besides, we didn't really get a choice in the matter. They just sort of ... appeared ... right in our path!"

"Just like real Indians," Donny said ecstatically.

"Silly! They *were* real Indians," Shana told him.

"Well, make sure you stay away from strangers in the future," their father said firmly. "Indians or not."

Mo chose that moment to run circles around his twin, entwining him in coils of plastic leash and making everyone laugh. Danger seemed a million miles away.

Up among the caves that dotted the cliffs, the two Indians watched them. The plumper one was still rubbing his side where his friend had poked him.

"I don't like this," Bobby Smith said.

"Big Jim" Littletree looked at him. "They're just kids, Bobby. They won't bother us."

"It's not the kids I'm worried about. It's their parents — and the others. Where one family moves in, others will follow. You heard what the kid said, didn't you? There's a school looking to buy this property. A Jewish school, by the likes of them."

"How do you know they're Jews?" The very word was exotic to Jim, who had never seen one before. He hadn't even been certain that such things existed these days.

"I met some of them up in the city. They move in packs, those Jews. And they're looking to buy in this area. That means they'll want to build the place up. That's not good."

"No," Jim agreed. "No good at all." He paused. "Why not?"

"Because we need a clear field to do our searching, that's why not! Do you want a bunch of people around when we find the treasure? Wanting to share it with us, maybe? Or worse?"

Big Jim frowned. "So what do we do, Bobby?"

Bobby's eyes were not surly now. They were just very black and intensely thoughtful. A fly bobbled past, brushing his cheek. Bobby swatted it away with a powerful sweep of the arm. "I don't know yet," he said slowly. "But we're sure going to have to do something."

"Something about that family?"

"Them — and the other Jews."

Jim said, searching for a ray of hope, "We don't know for sure that there'll be others."

"Oh, they'll be coming. Where there's one, there'll be more. Till now, there's only been a trickle of them. One synagogue, a school, a kosher section in the supermarket. But these guys are new. They're looking for property out here." For the first time, Bobby turned to look his companion straight in the eye. "We've got to make sure that doesn't happen, Jim. Get my drift?"

Big Jim nodded.

Though the Bernsteins were a long way off by this time, some trick of the wind carried a brief bubble of high-pitched laughter up to where the two men sat. Jim glanced quickly at his friend. The fly zoomed back, and this time Bobby swatted it viciously, as if he wished it were the voice he'd just heard.

"We've got to get rid of them," he said.

Jim thought about this. "So we can seek our own fortune, hey?"

"Yeah. So we can seek our fortune." Bobby looked around at the surrounding cliffs, all of them riddled with caves, and all of the caves filled with the possibility of the treasure. He had a clue — one little clue, but it was enough. Some deep, inner voice told him he was getting closer.

To facilitate their search, Bobby and Jim had leased a cheap room in Lakewood. It was ill lit and shabbily furnished, with suspicious scrabbling sounds behind the thin plaster walls that no amount of mousetraps seemed to be able to eliminate. Bobby hardly noticed. This was only a way station, a brief (he hoped) stopping place on the way to the land of his dreams.

By night, he and Jim drank to their future success. By day, equipped with flashlights, ropes and pickaxes, they tackled the southernmost caves in the cliffs west of Lakewood, intending to move in a steady line to the north until they hit upon the treasure. It was hard work, and tedious. Jim was not exactly a sparkling companion, which made the work all the more dull for Bobby. He was almost tempted to send Jim away and root about on his own — almost. But he needed the big man's muscle, it was as simple as that. To get it, he had been forced to promise Jim half the booty.

When the time came, he would figure out a way to keep the bulk of the treasure in his own pocket. That, he reasoned, was only fair. Old Henry had confided the secret to him alone. It was his.

By midsummer, Bobby was beginning to feel intensely frustrated. They had searched caves large and small for a couple of weeks now, and found no sign of gold or any other precious commodity. Still, he was determined to continue. Old Henry had been so certain, so convincing with his gasping, wheezing story of treasure waiting in the dark for patient decades. Bobby would not give up. The search would go on.

Jim, the eternal follower, was resigned to doing whatever Bobby did.

On this blazingly hot day in late August, they had just reached a promising-looking bank of caves set high in the bluffs overlooking Lakewood. They'd been on the point of resuming their search when the children had appeared out of nowhere; "to seek their fortune," the kid had said. His sister spoke of their father who, she said, was looking to buy some property in these parts.

The news came as a blow to Bobby. Buying property meant developing tracts of land, which meant bulldozers and surveyors and building crews. Secrecy would be impossible. Why couldn't those Jews buy property on the other side of town? Why couldn't they be like everyone else and head for the pretty lakeshore? He gritted his teeth and silently cursed the bad luck that had crossed their paths.

After his initial dismay, Bobby's resolve stiffened. He was not about to let all this work, and the chance of a lifetime, slip through his fingers because of a bunch of Jews looking for a promising bit of real estate.

"We've got to get rid of them," he repeated. The thin lips, no stranger to cruelty, curled down with steely resolve. These cliffs belonged to him. These caves — and especially the one cave waiting to give up its secret — were his. He'd almost come to believe that the treasure was his birthright, planted there from the beginning of time to make up for all the ill luck that had dogged his steps since he first set foot on the stage of the world. The treasure would make up for everything.

His eyes were fixed on the caves they had not yet searched. He could almost taste the gold he hoped to find in one of them. Of course, it might not be gold. *It might be jewels, though gold was more likely*, he thought. *Spanish gold, maybe, from centuries past.* All he had was the one word, a veiled but alluring promise: *Treasure*. It was sparkling just around some corner, waiting for him.

"No one's going to take that away from us," Bobby said with soft menace.

Far below, the trail looped around the skirt of a cliff and the Bernstein family popped back into view. Like ants they looked from up here: tiny, colorful ants winding unevenly in a row. Bobby's eyes narrowed to slits. With deadly emphasis, he repeated, *"No one."*

IV.

The Mandels appeared just as the others were packing up to go. Efraim was disappointed to learn that Marvin Fleischmann had already left the site. With an uneasy glance at his wife, he murmured, "I thought he'd still be here."

"What a pointless trip," she sniffed. "I had to leave everything on the stove to run out here and Fleischmann's not even around any more!"

"Why we couldn't just have enjoyed the picnic and had less of a fancy dinner, I don't know," Efraim said with a trace of petulance. "Meir would have enjoyed this just as much."

"So that's the thanks I get for slaving for my family!" Etty looked and sounded outraged, edgy and worn out.

"Sorry," Efraim muttered. "I just would have liked to be here, that's all." He would have liked to shake their benefactor's hand, and to let Marvin Fleischmann see that he, Efraim Mandel, was an integral part of this mission. Instead, he had been conspicuous only by his absence. The fates seemed always to conspire to shove Efraim into the background.

Hastily, Nachman stepped into the breach. "Anyway, we're glad to see you now. Look around, both of you. What do you think of the view? This is where we're going to build. Fleischmann confirmed the choice this afternoon."

Etty made a determined effort to relax, to be a good trooper. Looking around her, she saw the cliffs, the desert vista and the sky, now tinged with pink at the edges, hovering over all like a vast, protective blanket. "It *is* pretty," she admitted. "But different. All that cactus ..."

"The inside of the building's going to look a little different, too," Nachman said with relish. "Fleischmann's hired an architect who's planning to design a place that will flow with the setting, so to speak. No brick high-rise here. Fleischmann was insistent about that."

"Well, I'm sure it'll be very nice, whatever it is." Already, Etty's thoughts had moved on. She glanced at her sons, chatting with Chaim and Donny Bernstein, and double-checked on her girls. The baby was asleep in the stroller beside her. "Efraim, if nothing's happening here, I think we'd better head home."

Shimi, when informed that the brief outing he'd been promised had just become even briefer, registered a protest. Etty was adamant. Coming up against the wall of his mother's implacable will, he tried switching gears. "Can't Chaim and Donny come over for a little while, then? To — to say good-bye to Meir?"

Etty considered. "All right. Just till dinner's ready. Remember, it's Meir's good-bye dinner."

A small cloud settled in Shimi's eyes: as if he could forget! For weeks now, it had been "Meir" this, and "Meir" that. Though how was that any different, really, from the way things had always been in their house? Meir was the golden boy, the top of his class, the child who could do no wrong. His older brother's very existence threw Shimi's less obvious abilities into even deeper shade.

But Shimi had long since learned to live with this particular ball and chain. A moment later, the cloud was gone and he was racing back to the Bernstein boys to extend his invitation.

Rivi Gann, meanwhile, had unpacked some of the leftover picnic cake. She offered it to the Mandels.

"None for me," Efraim said. Motivated by the move, he'd been slowly, though steadily, shedding excess pounds for weeks. Happiness over the impending change had done him all the good in the world. Etty beamed proudly as he refused what would once have proved an irresistible lure.

"Or me," she told Rivi. In a lowered voice, she added reproachfully, "Put it away. Don't tempt him!"

Flushing, Rivi obeyed. Etty looked around for her children. "Well, it's been nice …"

"One second," Nachman broke in heartily. "Before you go — a toast! A toast to our new *kollel* and our new building!" He picked up a bottle of Coke and began pouring lavish cupfuls from the pile of cups Tova had provided. Reluctantly, Etty accepted a cup. Efraim was more eager. Avi Feder, Asher and Rivi Gann and all the various children were soon holding brimming cups of their own.

"*L'chaim!*" Nachman boomed, holding his cup high in a salute to the unfamiliar terrain that they were about to make their own. "To the *kollel!*"

"To the *mesivta!*" his son, Chaim, shouted.

"To friendship, and hard work, and high hopes!" Asher Gann cried in a sudden burst of poetry. Of them all, he was possibly the most excited over their joint venture.

"To a fresh start," Avi Feder said quietly.

Efraim Mandel, aware of his wife's eyes on him, strained in vain for something witty or meaningful to add. Finally, he burst out, "To us!"

To his surprise, this seemed to go down beautifully with the others. With smiles and nods, they drained their cups of soda. Tova felt her heart twist in a queer exaltation. The others, judging by their expressions, seemed to feel it, too: a swift, charged uplift that took them right out of themselves.

As a light breeze sprang up to cool overheated cheeks, the anxieties and concerns that had propelled them to leave their homes in the east dropped abruptly away. Overhead, a bird of wide wingspan soared to a horizon just beginning, on this summer evening, to be tinged with the rosy light of sunset. The bird seemed to symbolize the possibilities of their own flight. Here, at the edge of the desert, they were staking their claim.

Like the forty-niners of old on the trail of gold, their eyes shone with the light of a dream and their hearts thrilled to the chords of an ambitious symphony all their own. They had come a long way, set down tentative stakes in a place that still felt foreign to them, but which would soon become home. Their Torah would make it so. History's wandering Jew had learned that lesson early: Home was wherever you perched your *shtender*.

Tova, draining the last sweet drops of soda from her cup, scanned the group until she found Shana. Her daughter had finished her toast, too, and was standing quietly along with the rest. Tova surprised a glimmer of excitement in Shana's face. The sulky, resistant, I'm-here-against-my-will attitude had slipped off those young shoulders like a silk shawl. At this instant, knitted together with the others in hope and ambition, Shana seemed to be thrilled with the significance of what they were here to do.

Nachman Bernstein, standing beside his wife, caught the look in Shana's eye and the responsive joy in Tova's. The sight added an extra dollop of contentment to his already overflowing sense of mission. He had a wonderful family to hold the lines steady on the home front, and a terrific team with which to go out and conquer the world. Right now, at the very start of their adventure, anything and everything seemed within reach of his tingling fingertips.

Tomorrow they would plunge into the sea of day-to-day life, with its challenges and obstacles and the dreary spells when nothing went right.

Tomorrow the horizon would sometimes become obscured. But for this one shining moment they stood together at the brink, reveling in the heady wine of a new beginning.

In her stroller, Layala Mandel began to cry. The spell was broken.

"Maybe she wants some soda, too," her sister Tzirel giggled.

"And maybe," her mother decreed, "she wants to be in her own crib at home."

Efraim and Etty discarded their empty cups in the trash bag Asher held out to them, then piled the rest of their brood back into their car and drove away. The others moved at a more leisurely pace, reluctant to end the day and to leave this magical spot.

"Rabbi Harris was right," Nachman Bernstein remarked to his wife as they led their children slowly toward the waiting minivan. "The lakeshore might be prettier, but it's also a good deal more expensive. Fleischmann will do well to invest in this tract instead. It's level enough down here for easy building, protected from the wind by the cliffs at our back, and just a mile or so outside the city proper."

"Will the *mesivta* be finished by the time I'm ready for high school, Ta?" Chaim asked eagerly.

Rabbi Bernstein turned to smile at his son. "It will if I have anything to say about it, *im yirtzeh Hashem*. Fleischmann says he's going to light a fire under the foreman and his crew. He's getting on in years and wants the project completed as early as possible. "

Pleasantly fatigued, and busy with rosy dreams of the future, the family fell silent as they walked along to where they had left the minivan. A short distance away, Asher and Rivi Gann got into their small Accord and drove away in the direction of town. Avi Feder's even smaller hatchback left next. Tova tried to identify the various forms of plant life they encountered as they walked. She recognized white and purple sage and thought she labeled a creosote bush properly, but the rest of the local flora eluded her. Her concentration was disrupted by the need to keep a firm hold on her share of the 2-year-old twins — her husband had the other half — as Mo and Bo made a valiant but futile effort to keep their heads from drooping in utter exhaustion. They lost the struggle in the end, of course, each twin finding a secure resting place on a solid parental shoulder.

A light wind rose with the incipient evening, to ruffle the girls' hair and make the boys clutch at their yarmulkes as the Bernsteins made their tired, sunburnt way back home.

"You should've seen those Indians!" Donny Bernstein said excitedly as he swung through the hot, dry air. They were ending the day on the swing set in the Mandels' backyard, lit with the first faint flush of sunset. "They looked like something out of a Wild West picture!"

"Shana was scared out of her wits," his brother, Chaim, chuckled.

"I'll bet. I'd have been scared, too," Shimi Mandel said frankly. "What were they doing there?"

"I dunno." Chaim shrugged.

"They said they were seeking their fortune," Donny reminded him. "After I said that we were seeking ours. Remember?"

For the first time, Meir Mandel spoke up. At 14, he tended to adopt a lofty attitude around the younger boys. He was off to yeshivah in the morning, and regarded this whole Lakewood venture as just a temporary blip on the screen of his life. Still, he was curious. "What did you mean by that?"

Donny turned to him, the ropes of his swing twisting along with him. "Well, back when our parents told us that we were going to move out here, my father said that people have to go where they're needed and where they are led to go. He said it's like seeking your fortune ... only not gold or stuff like that."

"Your spiritual fortune, he meant," Chaim clarified. "Going to the place where your *neshamah* needs to go. Where you can do the most good."

Meir nodded sagely. Shimi looked slightly perplexed, and covered this by hurling himself noisily down the slide, wincing at the metal's heat.

"What *I'm* worried about," he announced when he'd hit bottom, "is my bar mitzvah. I mean, are there even any kosher catering halls in this town?"

"Good question." Chaim swung thoughtfully back and forth.

"Meir had a *great* bar mitzvah," Shimi went on, expanding on the topic uppermost in his mind. "Mine'll be nothing compared with his. Why'd we have to go and move out here just before my bar mitzvah?"

Meir looked smug. He might have reminded his younger brother that the "greatness" of his bar mitzvah had been dependent not on the catering hall or the number of guests, but on his own superlative performance. But he didn't say it. He didn't have to. Meir's excellence — as opposed to Shimi's failings — was an old story in the Mandel household.

"Anyway, I want to get back up on that trail as soon as possible," Donny went on, reverting to the original subject. "Maybe we'll meet those Indians again!"

Chaim frowned, all at once the responsible, older brother. "I'm not sure that's such a good idea."

"Why not?"

"Those guys looked ... I don't know. There was something about them ..."

"Chaim's scared, too!" Shimi said gleefully. Because the "too" included himself, there was no mockery in the words.

"I'm not *scared*, exactly ... But they made it pretty clear that they didn't want us around."

"So what?" Donny said hotly. "Do they own New Mexico?" Kicking his feet powerfully into the air, he soared up toward the sky.

"We don't have much time," Shimi pointed out, his expression glum. "Meir's going to yeshivah tomorrow, and the day after that we start learning again, too." He brightened. "But we can do it tomorrow."

"I wouldn't want to go anyway," Meir said loftily. "I'm not interested in any stupid exploring."

"Well, par-don *me!*" his brother said, rolling his eyes. He caught Donny's eye. "We can do just fine without Meir, can't we?"

"Sure. Though he might be sorry, when we find buried treasure and divide it up without him!"

Meir sniffed. "Huh. *That's* likely." His tone was heavy with the weight of the three long years that lay between himself and Donny. Chaim and Shimi — though both, at 12, much closer to Meir in age — were relegated to the same infant category.

Stung, Chaim turned to the others. "Okay. Let's go tomorrow."

"If my mother lets," Shimi said quickly. "We've still got some unpacking to do."

"We're pretty much done with all that," Chaim said. "That's the good part about our coming out here before the rest of you. It was kind of quiet being here by ourselves, but we got the boring work out of the way."

"Well, I've still got it in front of me," Shimi said gloomily. "Some of it, anyway. My mother's making me do my room by myself, but she's going to check it afterward. Yikes!"

"It shouldn't take long," Donny consoled him.

Shimi brightened. "No ... Actually, I've got most of it done already." He launched himself onto the slide again, this time from the bottom up. His sneakers made a squeaky sound as he climbed. "And then ... freedom!"

"For just one more day," Chaim sighed.

"Freedom to waste time," Meir snapped in an uncanny, if unwitting, imitation of his mother.

"To explore," Shimi contradicted.

"That's right." Donny soared back, then swung upward again. "We're gonna get to know this place frontward and backward! Every single rock. Every single cliff. Every single cave!"

Chaim felt a momentary pang. His father had told them to stay away from strangers, Indians or not ... *But we're not going to talk to them, or anyone else,* he assured himself. *We're just going to explore those cliffs. And of course we'll be careful. I'll make sure of that.*

Conscience eased, he said, "We'll take along ropes and stuff in our knapsacks. And food, and flashlights ..."

"Yeah!" shouted Shimi. Turning at the top, he hurtled down like greased lightening, landing with a whoop of laughter that made his mother, busily sorting boxes, tending the baby and keeping an eye on dinner all at the same time, remember their existence.

"Boys, inside!" she called. "Time to wash up for supper!

Donny and Chaim leaped off their swings. "See you tomorrow," they promised. The four boys parted, two to go inside toward the family's farewell supper, and the other two to wander on home to partake of their own hearty meals. Their afternoon in the fresh air had made the picnic lunch seem like ancient history.

With the image of Donny's Indians in his mind, Shimi rendered his version of an Indian war cry as he ran into the house.

His mother flinched. *"Must* you be so loud?"

But Shimi, the Apache warrior, was too busy whooping to hear her.

V.

"The baby's acting up again," Etty said, sounding nearly as fretful as little Layala at the moment. "And just when we need to travel."

"Leave her with someone," Efraim recommended. His eyes were busy scanning the map he'd picked up to help them find their way to the airport at Albuquerque. It was time for Meir, their firstborn, to leave the nest. Yeshivah life awaited him in California.

"I'm worried about her, Efraim." Etty hefted the baby over her shoulder and patted her back in a vain attempt to soothe the exhausted sobs. "She cries far too much, and she's not gaining the way she should."

"Weren't you planning to take her to the doctor?"

"I was — and still am. I even put Dr. Sadowsky's number in my book already. There's just been so much to take care of: the house, the unpacking, Meir's suitcase to get ready and the farewell dinner to cook. I'll make an appointment for the baby the minute we get back, *bli neder.*"

"What about today — the trip?"

"I think you're right. The poor thing'll be much more comfortable with a babysitter."

Efraim looked up from his map. "Do you have anyone in mind?"

In answer, Etty strode over to the phone and, in the time-honored fashion of mothers everywhere, juggled baby and phone until she'd made the connection she wanted.

"Hello — Rivi?"

"Etty! How nice to hear from you. How's everything going?"

"Fine, *Baruch Hashem.* The thing is, we're about to take off for Albuquerque, to put Meir on his plane."

"Oh? Is he flying?"

"Los Angeles is just a short flight away, though it's many, many hours by car. And trains are so expensive that we decided he might as well fly and get there sooner."

"I see." There was a question in Rivi Gann's voice. The call had caught her with paintbrush in hand, trying — as she had been for days — to capture the sublime texture of sun on sand on her canvas.

"Here's the problem, Rivi. Layala's very cranky this morning. She's certainly ready for her nap, but I suspect she also may be coming down with something, though the vomiting has been going on for a couple of weeks now ..." She shook herself free of her distracting thoughts. "Anyway, Efraim and I were planning to take her along with us. The other kids will be camping out at the Bernsteins today ... Actually, they were all supposed to come along to see Meir off, but Shimi started a campaign last night about this being their last day before school starts, and how he and the Bernstein boys have made all sorts of plans." Her frown came clearly through the phone line. "Of course, once *he* started that train, Tzirel and Chanala jumped aboard, clamoring that they'd rather play with Gila Bernstein than spend the whole day in the car. Ora likes the toys at the Bernstein house, too. So in the end, poor Meir will have no one but his mother and father to see him off."

"That's not so bad, is it?" Riva comforted her. "He'll get plenty of attention from both of you that way."

"Maybe. But I wanted to give him a royal send-off. My Meir deserves it ..." Etty sounded almost tearful, which prompted Rivi to say, "Etty, you've been doing way too much. Don't forget that you just gave birth — what? Just over a month ago? Give yourself a break!"

"I will, when this is over ..."

"Hah. That'll be the day."

Etty smiled into the phone. "Anyway, Tova's been good enough to agree to have them all for the day. But I don't want to saddle her with the baby on top of everything else ..." She let her voice trail off.

Rivi picked up her cue. "Do you need me to babysit? I'd be happy to, Etty. Just drop her off with some instructions. What a treat!" There was genuine pleasure in Rivi's voice.

The pleasure dissolved a moment later.

"Yes, I thought it would be," Etty said, in the manner of one bestowing a gift. There was graciousness in her tone — and more than a trace of unwitting condescension. "It's a three-hour drive each way, Rivi, plus the time at the airport. You'll be able to enjoy her for nearly a full day — with our blessing!"

Thanks a lot — for nothing. The words, unbidden, rose up in Rivi's mind with uncharacteristic bitterness. Trust Etty Mandel to twist the knife of Rivi's barrenness a little deeper into her heart.

She means well, Rivi thought, in a frantic bid to regain her own good nature. *She's just lacking in tact, that's all.*

The thought provided some solace, though not much. But Rivi had nearly an hour in which to compose herself before her doorbell rang and little Layala, complete with voluminous infant paraphernalia, was delivered up to her for the day.

A treat for Rivi — compliments of the Mandels.

Etty swallowed a lump in her throat as she hugged her oldest son for the last time. Efraim had already given Meir a hearty handshake and a resounding, "*Hatzlachah!*" As he took his place in line for the security check, Meir looked solemn and pale in his new suit and hat. The next time she saw him, he would be a *yeshivah bachur,* somewhat remote, never quite their own little boy again. His eyes would have seen sights that his parents had never shared; his mind would be filled with words and thoughts that would shape his character and his outlook. He would have taken his place in the world.

She knew she ought to be proud, and she *was* proud. But the tears would not stop their dogged effort to flood her eyes, despite her best efforts to bat them away.

The minivan seemed very quiet as they drove home from the airport. With uncharacteristic discernment, Efraim said, "Try not to worry too much, Etty. He's a good boy and a smart one. He has his feet on the ground. He'll be fine."

"It's not his learning I'm worried about," Etty confessed. "It's his social life. I don't know why he's always had such a hard time making friends." She broke off, surprised at herself for betraying her anxiety. Usually she kept this particular worry well hidden, even from herself.

"I know," Efraim said.

He said nothing else. What else was there to say, really? Meir had his strengths, and he had his flaws. He would hopefully make the most of the former and learn to compensate for the latter. If he called for help, they would offer what they could. Etty knew all that as well as he did. Etty was wondering just how much they would hear from Meir. Her boy, she thought with melancholy pride, was no complainer. He might be suffering, and they would have no idea of it. She bit her lip.

The highway unwound placidly ahead of them. On either side, rosy desert shimmered in the sun. Beyond, to the right, lay a range of cliffs, jutting upward into blue sky with knifelike clarity. To the left, a lone mesa stood all by itself, flat topped and regal. Efraim glanced sideways at his wife, then returned his attention to the road ahead of him. Meir had always been the apple of his mother's eye. Maybe this move had been a good thing in more ways than one. Back in New York, they would probably not have sent him away from home at all.

"This experience will make a man of him," he told his wife.

"Yes," she said. She sounded as if she wasn't quite sure she relished the prospect.

Efraim himself was in high spirits. These days, a filament of anticipation was threaded through his every waking moment. Here was a chance for a new start, an opportunity to prove himself, to influence others, to be the teacher he believed he could be. *"Meshaneh makom, meshaneh mazal."* A new place, a new fortune … Etty heard him whistling as he sped along. Suddenly, there was a flicker on the road, a quicksilver motion hardly glimpsed before it was gone.

Efraim slammed on the brakes. The highway was empty; he pulled the car over to a complete stop and craned his neck for a better view. "A rattlesnake! Etty, that was a rattlesnake, I'm sure of it! Right there, in front of our car!"

She shuddered. "What a wilderness we've come to."

He grinned at her. "I think it's exciting."

The smile held as he restarted the engine, and he succeeded in rubbing his wife's nerves raw by whistling all the way home.

VI.

It was a merry threesome that set out from the Bernstein home at mid-morning: Chaim and Donny Bernstein and Shimi Mandel, each with a bulging knapsack and a blithe spirit. It was nearly an hour's walk to the site of the previous day's picnic but that, for the explorers, was just the appetizer before the main course. The cliff paths and their wealth of dark mysterious caves beckoned irresistibly.

When they reached the site some 50 minutes later, they were already sunburned and famished. Their first order of business was lunch.

"Good thing my mother packed so many sandwiches," Donny mumbled through a very full mouth.

"I like her sandwiches." Shimi's mouth was no less busy. "My mom always puts in healthy stuff, like *bean sprouts*." He made a face, then continued his enthusiastic chewing.

Chaim was silent, studying the terrain with a leader's eye. They would take the path they had started up yesterday, he decided. He'd noticed a few interesting-looking caves nearby. And the trail itself was interesting, too, if caves palled: Who knew where it ended? Maybe at the very top of the cliff, where stone met sky? He pictured himself standing at the top of the world, and smiled. What a perfect way to spend the last day of summer vacation.

Shimi couldn't have agreed more. A perfect last day of freedom — followed, he hoped, by a far better school year than he was accustomed to. The torture that the classroom represented for him would be replaced, here in Lakewood, with a home-schooling agenda. Until the new *mesivta* building was completed — and until he and Chaim Bernstein reached high-school age — they were to be taught by two of the *kollel* members. How this arrangement would play itself out, Shimi wasn't sure. It might prove easier than a regular school — or harder. But nothing could be worse than the agony of sitting in a crowded classroom, day after day, listening to a teacher throw words at him that he felt utterly incapable of catching.

He reflected on the impending regimen as he bit into his third sandwich. Asher Gann would be an interesting and easygoing rebbe. Shimi didn't know Avi Feder very well yet, but he glimpsed promising signs in the widower's sad passivity, which was not likely to go hand in hand with a strict classroom manner. Too bad his own father wasn't doing the homeschooling; Shimi knew from long experience how easy it was to sidetrack his father into long, fascinating discussions over a barely relevant side point.

As for Rabbi Bernstein, Shimi was secretly disappointed that they would not be learning with him. By all accounts, he was a great *maggid shiur*. Which was probably why he had been chosen to be the *Rosh Kollel* instead of Shimi's father. Boy, had his mother been mad about that!

"Time to go, guys," Chaim announced. "*Bentch*, clean up your litter, and let's get moving."

Ten minutes later, the three figures were toiling up the path, moving ever upward toward the sun. They had no idea that they were being watched. Bobby Smith owned a powerful pair of binoculars, and he had them trained on the boys at that very moment.

"It's those kids again," he muttered.

"Which kids?" Big Jim asked, although he knew. It was his automatic response to ask questions. He had learned early that this was one of the survival methods he needed to get through life with a mind that seemed about one-half as sharp as most other people's.

"The ones from yesterday. See? I told you they'd be back. Today it's the kids; tomorrow it'll be their parents, swarming all over the place. And did you see those surveyors this morning? This is getting serious, Jim. We can't have people cluttering up this area. We need privacy for what we're doing. We don't want anyone around when we find the treasure." He spoke with the binoculars to his eyes, watching the boys stop to let Shimi remove a stone from his sneaker and then move on again.

"We can hide till they leave, can't we?" Jim asked.

"Till the *kids* leave, maybe. Though I suspect they'll be back. It's those surveyors I'm really worried about. Where there are surveyors, there'll be buildings. What if they start putting up some Jew-building right here, where we're working?"

What if they did? Big Jim wrinkled his brow, straining to grasp the consequences of that scenario.

"We won't be able to go on with our search, that's what!" Bobby snapped, scowling. He looked through the binoculars again, just in time to see the trio of explorers enter one of the caves that he and Jim had been through that very morning. Here was a new and very serious worry: What if a pack of kids stumbled upon the treasure before he and Jim did?

He was distracted, and called it quits once they had submitted two more smallish caves to a thorough search. "We'll get to the others tomorrow," he muttered to his companion. Big Jim nodded, as always suiting himself to Bobby's mood. Like a lumbering shadow in the other's wake, he followed Bobby down from the cliffs and into town.

"What now, Bobby?" he asked, reaching for the bottle on the dingy kitchen counter, and the pair of glasses that they never bothered to rinse.

"We make a plan." Two straight lines were etched into Bobby's brow, perpendicular to the twin ebony curtains of hair that hung down on either side of his aquiline face. "We put our heads together, Jimmy-boy, and figure out a way to keep the field clear for us. See?"

Big Jim nodded, though both of them knew that Bobby would be the one doing the thinking tonight. Jim would only keep him company, pouring the drinks and providing a sounding board for any notion Bobby might choose to share. When it came to making plans, Bobby was the acknowledged master.

With his first glass of the evening poised halfway to his lips, Jim paused as a thought struck him. He liked the look of those kids, toiling so valiantly up the steep path. They had looked so innocent and so hopeful, with their eager eyes and the beginnings of a sunburn on skin unaccustomed to the New Mexican sun. He hoped Bobby's plans would not bring any harm to those nice kids.

Sneaking a look at his partner, he saw the cruel turn of Bobby's lip and the unfocused gaze that spoke of a brain intensely preoccupied with solving a particular problem. He knew that look, and he knew what it meant when Bobby wore it.

He sighed. *Too bad*, he thought. He had really liked the look of those kids.

Chapter 7

I.

Geronimo, that most notorious Apache of all, was Bobby Smith's hero.

"Geronimo" had been the Spanish settlers' name for the courageous Indian who had led a series of daring and devastating attacks on their strongholds in the 1880's. The Apaches themselves had called him *"Goyale"*: the smart one. Secretly, that was the name that Bobby Smith had also adopted for himself.

He was smart, too, he believed; cunning in a way that his fellow Native Americans would never be. They were living with one foot in the past or maybe, he sometimes thought in exasperation, both of them. The world, as it was presently constituted, seemed to be passing them by in a haze, like smoke from a long-handled peace pipe, spiraling up to dissipate uselessly in the shimmering air.

Bobby preened himself on his own difference. *He* knew how to seize an opportunity when it came his way and how to remove an obstacle when it threatened him. Geronimo had used his wily leadership — his *brilliant* leadership, Bobby fervently believed — to oppose United States troops bent on stealing Indian territory. Today, the battle was drawn along different lines. Still at stake was the success of the Native American, but that success was measured in dollars and cents rather than in yards of territory reconquered or pints of soldiers' blood spilled. Geronimo, the tactician and the warrior, was his hero, but Bobby's particular war was of a different and thoroughly modern order.

In dealing with the specific problem facing him, the trouble was not coming up with a solution, but weeding out the inferior possibilities so as to come up with the most efficient one of all. The solution that would put Bobby over the top, where he belonged.

He was still mulling over his options that night as, with Big Jim in tow, he stepped out of their dismal rental apartment for a breath of fresh air. They had decided to head for the reservation tonight. Bobby was in the mood for a game of pool. He prided himself on his pool, and the reservation's Eight Ball did not usually offer much in the way of serious competition. It was an easy way to make a few extra bucks.

The Eight Ball was not very crowded tonight. The place was wreathed in smoke, creating a blurred, almost surreal atmosphere. Bobby narrowed his eyes and surveyed the scene. There were a few people at the bar and a couple of old-timers sitting alone at corner tables as though painted onto the woodwork — though not Old Henry. Old Henry would never grace a barroom again. A couple of young Indians, cigarettes dangling at the corners of their mouths, were shooting pool. Bobby and his friend gravitated in their direction. While Jim went off to fetch their drinks, Bobby stood watching the game in critical silence.

"Good eye," he told the winner presently. "Play another?"

The stranger nodded.

"High stakes?"

"I'm just about wiped out, man," the other protested. "Twenty's my limit tonight."

Bobby frowned, then shrugged. "Fine. Twenty it is." That would pay for his drinks, at least.

Big Jim came back bearing a glass in each beefy hand. Admiringly, he watched Bobby shoot. Like everything he did — in the opinion of his faithful shadow, at any rate — Bobby played like a pro. Jim sipped his drink and enjoyed the show.

Bobby was poised over the table, eyes fixed on his target ball and the cue rigid in his hands. The way his hands looked these days bothered him. The fingernails were encrusted with dirt, the palms calloused and blistered from his endless digging in caves. So far, the digging had produced nothing but dirty hands and an aching back, but he was not about to give up. Not by a long shot. The treasure was waiting. It was calling to him …

He took his shot almost absently, his mind busy with a vision of entering still another cave with a pickaxe over his shoulder, and encountering the dazzle of gold … He was jerked abruptly back to the present when a word from a nearby table caught his ear. He froze and listened, his concentration ruined.

Turning, he saw the tall kid who'd lost the previous game, and who was now seated at the table with a drink in front of him. He'd been joined by a couple of his buddies.

" … Jews." That was the word Bobby had caught, and that had wreaked havoc with his concentration. "There it was, in letters as big as your face," the tall kid chortled. "'JEWS GO HOME.' Bet that shook them up some."

"Where's 'home'?" speculated a pimple-faced youth nursing his second beer. "Where do Jews live, d'you think, Al?" It was clear that he had never encountered a Jew in his life.

"Bobby?" Big Jim asked, concerned. "You okay?"

"Hey!" Bobby's opponent spoke up from the other side of the table. "You playing, or what?"

Bobby made a shushing motion with his hand. He wanted to hear this.

Nineteen-year-old Al Barker — for that was the identity of the tall pool-player — let his limp black hair fall forward over his brow and smirked in a know-it-all way that would have been intensely annoying had his friends not been so used to it. "Somewhere over on the other side of the world — the Mideast, they call it. Deserts and camels and stuff." With a shrug, he dismissed the entire question of the Jewish homeland.

"Why'd you do it for, anyhow, Al?" the pimply faced one asked. His curiosity seemed boundless tonight.

"Hey, I thought we were playing *pool* here!" Bobby's opponent said loudly.

Bobby turned to glare at him. There was something in his eyes that made the other guy back off, palms up. "O.K., O.K., never mind. Whenever you're ready."

At the table, Al looked more knowing than ever. "My boss, see, he says someone once told him that you can't trust a Jew." Al worked as an apprentice mechanic for a local gas station. "He says he met a few of them one time, and he don't want them out here. So me 'n — me 'n a buddy, we decided to give those Jews a message they wouldn't forget. See?"

His companion nodded solemnly and took another long swig of beer. The third young man with them, shorter than the other two and of sullen demeanor, broke his silence to ask, "What happened? How'd they react?"

Al shrugged. "They made sure to wash the words off right away, before it made much of a ruckus." He frowned as a memory came back. "Steve Birch heard about it, though. He came around, asking a lot of nosy questions."

"Good guy, Steve," pimple-face offered tentatively.

"Maybe. But nosy as an old woman."

Another silence fell. More beer was consumed. Slowly, Bobby turned away and resumed the game. His next shot was off.

"Tough luck, Bobby," Big Jim said sympathetically. With a ferocious scowl, Bobby threw himself back into the game. He'd show these jokers a thing or two about shooting pool.

He made a nice comeback. Twenty minutes later, when he and Jim left the Eight Ball, Bobby Smith was $20 richer.

"Nice game," Jim commented as they ambled beneath the star-studded sky toward the car.

"Ssh. I'm thinking."

"Whatcher thinking about, Bobby?"

A slow smile lit Smith's face. "That kid back there gave me an idea."

"An idea? 'Bout what?"

At Bobby's disgusted look, Jim hastily backtracked. "Uh, I mean, what's the idea?"

"I was looking for a way to scare those Jews away from here, right? To leave the coast clear for us ..." Like a teacher accustomed to dealing with a particularly slow student, he was resigned to the need for curbing his impatience when explaining things to Jim. "We don't want a bunch of Jews poking their noses where they don't belong, cramping our style and maybe even finding the treasure before we can get to it. Right?"

"Ye-eeah … right." Jim's brow furrowed as he followed his friend's train of thought.

"So … I've got a plan that'll scare them off so they don't bother us anymore. A kind of warning signal. Ever hear of 'in-ti-mi-da-tion'?"

Ponderously, Jim shook his big head. As they drove slowly back to Lakewood, Bobby defined the word in vivid detail.

Bobby checked his watch for the sixth time in a minute, scowling. Jim was supposed to meet him here with the car, so that they could make a quick getaway the minute the deed was done. So far, there was no sign of him.

He had decided not to involve Jim in the actual plan. The big guy had a soft spot — a fatal soft spot, Bobby had always thought — that balked at the kind of ruthless behavior a person needed to survive. Bobby had been halfway through explaining his plan when he'd seen the look in Big Jim's eyes, and stopped talking.

"What *about* the synagogue, Bobby?" Jim had asked, incomprehension and anxiety mingling in his dark eyes. "What're you gonna do?"

"Nothing, Jim. Forget it. Just meet me over at the synagogue at midnight, okay?" Bobby's own car had been totaled on the highway several months earlier, but he hardly felt its loss. Jim was such an accommodating driver.

"But what're you gonna *do* over at the synagogue?" Jim persisted. He could be annoyingly dogged at times. It was all Bobby could do not to snap his head off. Drawing on his dwindling reserves of patience, he said nonchalantly, "I've become interested in the Jews, seeing as how they're starting to move into these parts in bigger numbers, see? I just wanna get to know what they're all about, that's all."

Jim relaxed. "Okay. Fine, Bobby. I'll be there at midnight."

Bobby was at the synagogue long before that. A silvery fingernail of moon cooperated in keeping his presence secret as he hovered in the shadows, watching the last of the worshipers leave the building. The last one out locked the door, and with a final backward look to make sure all was snug for the night, got into a navy Ford Escort and drove off. Bobby watched him go with satisfaction. Time to get to work.

Or, maybe not. Maybe he'd better wait for Jim to get here, to make sure he had his escape route ready before he committed himself to what he had in mind. No sense in leaving himself high and dry when the police showed up ... and the fire department ...

Jim was late. The numbers on Bobby's watch crept on past midnight, and still no sign of the decrepit vehicle Jim drove these days. Each time he had to step into it to get anywhere, Bobby winced. *Never mind*, he thought. *We'll hit the jackpot soon enough, and then I'll have enough money for ten brand-new cars.*

At the thought, he lifted his head impatiently and stared again at the empty street, as though willing his friend to show up. The moon hid its modest radiance behind a cloud, plunging the street into a deeper darkness. Conditions were perfect for the job. He checked his watch yet again. Twelve-thirty. *Where was Jim?*

A footfall behind him nearly made him jump out of his skin.

"Bobby Smith? Is that you?"

Slowly, Bobby turned. He was standing face-to-face with another Native American, one he'd met before and was not eager to meet again.

"Steve Birch," he said, in a tone that made no pretense of being glad to see him. "What're you doing out here so late at night? In fact, what're you doing here in Lakewood anyway? I thought you lived out at the reservation."

"I could ask you the same thing," Steve said quietly. He was still dressed for the office in a lightweight tan suit and brown-and-tan striped tie. An immaculate white shirt glimmered in the night, like pearls on velvet.

"I've got a place here in town now." Bobby was sullen. He didn't like to account for himself to anyone, least of all someone as successful as this Indian lawyer. But there was something about Steve Birch that made it impossible not to answer.

"Oh? Got a job?"

"You could say that ..." Bobby took the offensive. "What about you? What're you doing here so late?"

"I have a place here in town, too, Bobby. Have had one for a couple of years now. I was working late and decided to stretch my legs." Steve omitted mention of the brief catnap he'd taken at his desk, a nap marred by the old nightmares. Fresh air had seemed vastly preferable to remaining indoors where the dreams still hemmed him in.

"I wanted a walk, too. How's that for a coincidence?" Bobby laughed a touch too heartily. "Well, nice seeing you." With a last look up the street, Bobby made as if to go.

"Hold on a second, Bobby." Steve's voice was still quiet, but it held the note of authority that Smith hated. He stopped walking. "What brings you to the Jewish synagogue tonight? I wouldn't have thought you'd find this place interesting."

Bobby made a great show of surprise. Looking around him as if becoming aware of his surroundings for the first time, he exclaimed, "Oh, is that what it is? I thought it was a — a community center or something." He thanked his lucky stars that he had hidden the can of gasoline and stacks of newspapers in the bushes while he waited for Jim.

Steve seemed to weigh this response. With a shrug, he said, "These are decent people, Bobby. They don't hurt anyone. I'd take my walks elsewhere if I were you."

"Will do. No problem, man!" With a last would-be airy chuckle, Bobby waved good-bye and headed off down the street.

At the corner, he waited for Steve Birch to leave. This, to his chagrin, took longer than he would have expected. Birch remained where he was for a long time — hours, it seemed to Bobby, though probably no more than 10 minutes actually passed — staring at the synagogue wall.

There was a six-pointed star adorning that wall, a three-dimensional shape that emerged from the brick surface of the building as though it had a life of its own, and cast its own six-pointed shadow in the moonlight. Steve Birch gazed at this star for 10 long minutes, while Bobby Smith, poised on his corner, chafed at the delay. At last, Birch moved on, sauntering slowly on down the block and out of sight.

Only then did Bobby hurry back to the synagogue to retrieve the kerosene and newspapers. With a lash of anger, he acknowledged the necessity of abandoning his plan for tonight. For one thing, there was no Jim to provide the getaway car and, for another, that nosy Birch might afterward remember Bobby loitering at the site in the middle of the night.

To add insult to injury, he was forced to carry the kerosene can (the newspapers he dumped in the nearest trash receptacle) beneath his arm all the way home.

It was nearly 1 a.m. when he started the long walk. With each step the can grew heavier, and his fury hotter. He was very eager to learn just why his pal Jim had let him down.

Geronimo, he was sure, had never been saddled with such a dismal second in command!

II.

With little fanfare but much enthusiasm, the new study-year began.

Until the new building was completed, the *kollel* was to be housed in the shul. Nachman Bernstein, with his larger class, taught in the *beis midrash* itself, while his three colleagues used the smaller rooms branching off the hall at the building's rear. From his office at the very end of the long corridor, Pinchas Harris listened with pleasure to the tramp of feet in the usually silent halls, to the eager babble of voices rising in friendly greeting as neighbor met neighbor at classroom doors, and most of all, to the words of Torah emanating from each of those improvised classrooms.

The first week progressed beautifully, with each night seeing more potential students flocking into the shul to learn. Householders and businessmen, professionals, retired people and those just starting out in the workforce — all were curious to see the *kollel* in action, and to taste its offered fare. Until now, their Jewishness had been a home-brewed affair, with each individual or family weaving his own identity out of the cloth of tradition, vague associations, and a sprinkling of practical instruction by the rabbi. With the onset of regular, structured classes, those who were interested in taking their religious observance to the next level were being offered a helping hand. Others, not yet certain where they stood in terms of committed observance, but curious about the philosophy of Judaism, found scope for their interests, too. It was an exhilarating beginning, heady with promise: the fine wine of learning, diluted to suit the beginner's palate.

Some sipped more cautiously than others. The ranks of the observant had been fixed early in the community's history; they had been very slowly swelling ever since. The new *kollel*, it was hoped, would increase the tempo of commitment. And, during that first week, these hopes seemed justified. Whether from idle curiosity or the acknowledgement of a long-banked inner spiritual fire — for many, it was both — housewives abandoned their kitchens and families, to commune for an hour with their Jewish souls. In Avi Feder's practical *halachah* class, many of these women found themselves dreaming up matches for the widower who greeted them and the world, with a smile that did not touch his eyes.

The community's professionals — among them attorney Nate Goodman, forensic psychiatrist Abe Rein, and pediatrician Ben Sadowsky (with difficulty tearing himself away from his ubiquitous medical journals) — flocked to Nachman Bernstein's high-level *shiurim* in Talmud and Jewish thought. Nate Goodman, in particular, kept a high-voltage current running between himself and Rabbi Bernstein, arguing incessantly and learning beautifully. Abe Rein was heard to remark that the lawyer had missed his calling. "You ought to have been a Rosh Yeshivah, Nate."

"Hah! In another lifetime, maybe," said the *ba'al teshuvah*. But the others noticed the way he flushed with pleasure.

Other householders, not as far along as these, chose instead to attend Efraim Mandel's less-demanding *Chumash* class. They settled down in their seats for an hour of interesting but uncomplicated lecturing, and emerged at the end of class feeling comfortably enlightened and more than ready for their beds.

The teenagers, for a lark, decided to drop in on the first night, and stayed on, most of them, to wrestle in thought and sparkling debate with a vibrant Asher Gann.

They were still debating as they poured out of the room an hour later. Efraim Mandel, stepping out of his own classroom, saw the young people clustered in a tight circle around Asher, as though drawing energy from his very essence. His words, effervescent despite the seriousness of the subject matter, rang out like bells. The sound was hypnotic. Down the hall Efraim stopped short, listening despite himself. A student threw out a question; Asher turned the lighthouse-beam of his personality on him and answered. Efraim studied the attentive group. The faces of these teenagers and young men, in the habit of looking out on the world with superior or indifferent eyes, were suffused now with a deep interest, and an almost adoring intentness, as they listened to Asher talk. Watching, Efraim suffered a pang as sharp as any that could be inflicted by sword or lance.

This was how he used to feel when watching Nachman Bernstein, back in the New York yeshivah: the sense of being on the outside of a magical circle too sweet to include him. Like bees to honey the students would cling to Nachman then; these New Mexico students were repeating the performance now, with Asher.

Nachman, at least, was *Rosh Kollel* here. Efraim had resigned himself to being eclipsed by the head of the operation, and the sight of Nachman's popularity would (he hoped) be less painful here in tiny Lakewood. But Asher! Asher was a colleague, an equal, and younger than himself by a good few years. To see Asher stepping so effortlessly into Nachman's shoes, to watch him acting as a magnet to draw and focus these young people's spiritual ardor, was more than Efraim was able to bear. With a curt "Good night" to the one or two lingering students who'd walked out of the room with him, he quickened his step and soon passed them.

The late September night, so full of promise when he'd entered the shul, seemed flat now, and meaningless. He hurried through the parking lot at the rear to find his car, then drove listlessly down streets that were slowly becoming familiar to him. Walking up to his own house, he was enveloped by the same sense of rejection and failure that had impelled him through his days and nights back in New York.

The house was quiet, the children in bed. Etty was at the kitchen counter, mixing up something which would doubtlessly reside in the recesses of the freezer until resurrected that Shabbos. His wife was a marvelous cook, but a possessive one, keeping her treasures to herself until the moment came for the grand unveiling. Well, he was in no mood for fanfare tonight. He was tired of waiting for permission to start enjoying life. He was ... tired.

"Efraim! I didn't hear you come in," she said, turning to greet him with an unusually eager smile. The *kollel's* official opening had infected her, too, with the optimism of fresh beginnings, resulting in a sense of well-being that was unusual for her. "Well? How did it go?"

He forced himself to speak pleasantly. "It went fine. We had a pretty good turnout for a first night. Every class was full."

"That's wonderful! And how was *your* class?"

"Pretty good. I've got a nice bunch of students." He walked over to the refrigerator and looked inside, rummaging. "Is there any of that chocolate mousse left from Shabbos?"

She stared at his back. "Efraim ...? What about your diet?"

"Or those delicious oatmeal lace cookies. Any of those around?"

With a sinking heart, Etty heard the old gears slip back into place with a dreary little "click."

III.

Asher Gann turned his key in the lock and burst into the house like a gust of wind shot through with sunlight. He was whistling a jaunty tune when Rivi hurried out to meet him. "Asher! Welcome home."

He studied her. There was a dab of color on her chin, the same on her index finger, and a familiar, abstracted look about the eyes. "You've been painting."

She nodded, smiling. "Guilty as charged. Well, tell me everything. How was it?"

He threw his hat into the air, missed it coming down, and nodded in approval as his wife caught it for him. "Good catch!" He threw himself into his favorite chair, a leather Laz-E-Boy that Rivi had bought him two birthdays ago. "Rivi, it was beautiful! Couldn't be better. We've got a really good group of people, all interested in learning. A curious, argumentative, *involved* group. Beautiful!"

She was glad to see him so happy. "I'm glad, Asher. You're a great teacher." She paused. "You know, between homeschooling the boys, these evening classes and your own learning, you're going to have a very full plate this year."

He shot her a quick glance. "Is that a problem?"

Another smile. "Not at all. I'll be busy, too. I've got the house to finish setting up, and my painting ... and I absolutely *love* teaching."

"So you've mentioned." He abandoned his recliner for the kitchen, where he sat facing her. A plate of cookies waited on the table. Rivi poured them both a cup of tea. "Funny, I never saw you as a teacher."

"Neither did I," Rivi confessed. "But this is different. This is art. I don't have to stand in front of a bunch of students lecturing on some subject that they have no interest in, forcing them to write down every word because I'll be testing them on it later. That — that feels almost antagonistic, somehow."

Asher grinned, remembering his own school days. "I'll say it is!"

"Art class is different. Mostly, the kids enjoy being there. All I'm really doing is helping them draw and paint better, and most kids naturally like doing those things or would, if they weren't being graded on it. I'm going to try to reduce the pressure and keep it fun. So far, it's worked."

"So far? It's been one day!"

"I love teaching," Rivi said, cupping her chin in her palms and gazing dreamily past Asher's shoulder. "The children are like blank canvases, waiting for me to touch them with a delicate paintbrush — to color and shape them — to turn them into something that they weren't to begin with ..."

"We both know where all of this is coming from," Asher remarked quietly.

Rivi glanced up sharply, flushing. Then she relaxed, and managed a small smile. "How well you know me, Ash," she sighed. "You know, most people wouldn't make a crack like that to a woman in my situation."

"I'm not 'most people,'" her husband retorted. "I'm in the same boat, right? I just refuse to let it get me down. We've got a great life, Rivi. And, with Hashem's help, it'll continue being great. We've both got a lot to give, and we can have lots of fun giving it. When Hashem decides that the time has come for us to give to our own children — well, that's when it'll happen!"

Rivi's vision suddenly blurred. Asher's words had touched off an upsurge of emotion, some of it painful but the rest of it sweeter than the honey she had just stirred into her tea. She looked across the table. He was contentedly chomping on his second cookie, washing it down with a swig of tea.

"You know something, Asher?" she said impulsively. "Some things should not be reserved just for special occasions. Special things, I mean — the special words you reserve to say at high moments, like an anniversary."

He tilted a questioning brow at her.

"So I want to tell you, right here and now — unspecial as this occasion may be — how very, very happy I am being married to you."

He smiled, both at her words and at the wave of boyish embarrassment that flooded him at hearing them. Gruffly, to cover the embarrassment, he said, "Well, ditto that — in reverse. But, Rivi, this *is* a special occasion: the first day as a teacher, for both of us. Can it get better than that?"

It could, and they both knew it. But for now, they were content to let things be: to drift into a peaceful silence as they polished off the plate of cookies together. When it was empty, Rivi got up to rinse their teacups, and then returned to her canvas while Asher went eagerly off to the tiny "den" where he kept his *sefarim*. Someone in his class — hardly more than a kid, really — had asked a whopper of a question tonight. Asher had tried to answer as best he could on the spot; but now he was going to research the subject down to the bottom. Next time they met, he would be prepared!

He reached for a certain volume in his bookcase, then arrested his hand in midair. *Avi.* He had forgotten that he'd meant to phone Avi the minute he got home. With a remorseful pang, he picked up the extension on his desk.

"Avi? Is that you, old friend?"

"And who else should it be?" came the dry answer.

"Good point. Just checking in to see how your first night of class went."

"It went well, all things considered."

"All things considered?"

Down the line, he heard his friend chuckle. "The *halachah* lesson went down well. It was what happened afterward that shook me up."

"Meaning?"

"Meaning that at least four different well-meaning women came up to me after class to suggest a *shidduch*. I had to practically gnaw off my own leg to escape them, like an animal in a trap!"

"C'mon, Avi. It couldn't have been that bad." Asher paused, choosing his words carefully. "You know, it might not be such a bad thing. You could at least think about it."

Another laugh, more brittle this time. "Don't bother with the sales talk, Asher. My mother's already been through all that with me. I've agreed to go home for Succos, where she has a lineup of girls waiting to meet me."

"Avi! Are you serious?"

"Never more so." A sigh. "I just wish I weren't."

"Why not? Don't you feel ready to go out a little — see some new faces? It can't be easy for you …"

That, Avi thought, was the understatement of the year. Perhaps Asher realized it, too. "Well, I'm glad to hear you'll be going East for Succos. We'll miss you, of course, but who knows? This could be a good move."

"That's what you said about my coming out here!"

Asher grinned into the phone. "They're all good moves, Avi. The important thing is to keep moving."

That, Avi thought as he hung up a minute or two later, might indeed, as Asher had said, be the important thing. But for him, still caught up in the paralysis of grief, it felt like the hardest thing of all.

IV.

"*H*eidi? Is that really you?" The words burst out of Tova in a gasp of surprise and relief.

"It's me. Thanks for all your messages, Tova. And sorry about the long delay in calling back." Heidi's voice sounded curiously muffled as though either the voice, or the personality behind it, had been somehow truncated.

Alarm bells ran in Tova's head. Her initial relief at hearing Heidi's voice gave way to the old apprehension, and her apprehension made her sound testier than she'd intended. "Heidi, what is going *on* with you? I've been going out of my mind with worry. Talk about being incommunicado ... And —" she remembered suddenly — "your mother! She's been frantic! Have you called her?"

"Yes. We've spoken."

"Well, thank goodness for that. I think she must have aged 10 years in these past couple of weeks. Heidi, tell me what's going on. Where have you been? And why haven't you returned any of our calls?"

Heidi sat very still on the ultramodern sofa in the living room of her West Side apartment, looking out over a Manhattan from which she felt infinitely removed. The city gleamed below her with cold detachment. It was no longer a place she knew. Certainly, it was no longer a place that felt like it belonged to her. Somewhere along the line, a disconnect had occurred, and Heidi was dangling now at the end of a wire in midair. *What's going on with me?* she echoed bleakly to herself. *Good question. Too bad I don't have any answers ...*

"Heidi!" Tova's voice was insistent in her ear. "Talk to me!"

She gathered her strength for the ordeal. "Okay, I'll talk. So how's Lakewood treating you? The *kollel* must have started. It *is* Elul already, isn't it? How's it going?"

She heard Tova suck in a long breath, always a sign that she was fighting for self-control. There was something so familiar, so solid, so steadying in the sound of that indrawn breath that it brought tears to Heidi's eyes. Good old Tova. Her best friend ... Though for all the good Tova could do for her right now, she might as well have been on the moon.

"I will tell you all about life in Lakewood, New Mexico," Tova said at last, "when I see you. Preferably, this week."

This startled Heidi out of the well of self-pity in which she'd been slowly drowning for days, in her anonymous motel room and on the long drive back to New York. Momentarily, it jerked her out of the confusion that seemed intent on devouring not only her days and nights, but her very essence. It was a bewilderment completely foreign to her.

The Heidi she knew had been able to view the world, and herself, with crystal clarity. That Heidi had been clear and decisive. Now, it was as though that former Heidi had vanished. In her place there was only a blind groping after … what?

"So, are you planning on popping back East for a visit?" she managed to ask, with lips that felt like twin slabs of lead.

"I'm talking about seeing you *here*, Heidi. Come out and stay with us a while."

Heidi emitted a short bark of laughter. "I've got a job, remember?"

"*Do you* — still?"

Heidi was silent. After her abrupt disappearance without a coherent explanation, the office had assumed illness, and they had not been far wrong. It was just that the illness had not been physical in nature. She was uncertain about returning to her desk. The office might welcome her back, but did she really want to go? Was she ready?

A wild image bubbled up inside her: the visual picture of all the hours and hours that she *hadn't* billed this week. Whom did those hours belong to? There was no client to claim them, and no senior partner to convert them into cold, hard cash. Was it possible that Heidi, for the first time in years, had actually owned a full week of her own life?

Tova was talking. It was incumbent upon her to listen. When Tova's voice stopped, she would be floating again in that nebulous pool of uncertainty that so distressed and terrified her. She strained to make sense of the words, as though they were a lifeline and the mere act of listening could save her from the depths.

"… *Yamim Tovim* are coming up. Instead of spending them at your parents' home, how about coming out here to keep us company? We'd love to have you, and (here Tova's tone became consciously tactful) you could probably use the break …"

"I *am* a break." Heidi did not know where the words came from. They bubbled up from some dark, unknowable source deep inside. From the shattered place.

"What?"

"Um … I mean … something's broken …"

"Heidi, what are you talking about? Heidi …? You're scaring me!"

"Well, guess what? *I'm* scaring me." Heidi slumped very low on the sofa, her spine nearly parallel with the cushion on which she sat. She was still dressed in the bathrobe she had put on when she'd awoken that morning, her first one home since her spontaneous sojourn in the Poconos. How long had it been since she hadn't leaped into her work clothes within seconds of rising?

Her hair was still matted with sleep, though it was 11 o'clock in the morning and she had woken at dawn. She stared out the window at the familiar city view. Somewhere in that concrete panorama, men and women were going to work. In cubicles of lath and plaster, in offices cramped or lavish, they were devising their legal strategies, meeting to talk over their triumphs and failures, and always, always, racking up those billing hours.

Those men and women were busy trying to outsmart their rivals, who were busy trying to outsmart *them*. In the process, they were all making lots of money. And at a certain desk in a certain office, the ghost of Heidi Neufeld sat in a leather swivel chair being a brilliant young lawyer. Or was the ghost seated on this sofa instead, staring dully out the window and clutching a telephone receiver as if she hoped it held the answers she needed to go on living?

"I think I'm having a nervous breakdown," she whispered. Desperately rallying her sense of humor, she added, "I always wondered what that felt like ..."

Tova heard the desperation behind the humor. "Heidi. It's just over a week to Rosh Hashanah. I'm going to make a reservation for you to fly out here. The nearest airport of any size is in Albuquerque. Please G-d, I'll be there to meet you. Spend the *Yamim Tovim* with us — please?"

A vista seemed suddenly to open up in front of Heidi: a veritable Garden of Eden, perched at the edge of a black chasm. She had a choice. She could stay where she was, wrapped in the cold fog that had descended so abruptly to conceal from her the dilemmas of her own life. In the confusion, she ran the risk of sooner or later stepping right down into that chasm ... Or she could take Tova up on her offer and spend a glorious couple of weeks being someone else. Anyone else, except this new Heidi perched over this magnificent city like a baby bird too frightened, and too fragile, to venture out of its nest.

By the time she got herself to believe that there really was a reprieve — that all she had to do was order her mouth to form a simple "Yes" — she was crying almost too hard to say the word.

Through her tears, she managed to choke out the faint inarticulate syllable. But Tova heard.

V.

Steve had fallen into a routine that was as disturbing as it was puzzling.

Night after night, when the town had curled in on itself and sunk into its midnight quiet, sleep was suddenly the furthest thing from his mind. Instead of reading a book, or listening to soft music, or climbing into bed for some refreshing and much-needed slumber, he found himself walking.

He walked always in the same direction, and always without quite knowing why he had chosen that direction. His feet carried him block after block, until he reached an intersection he'd barely known about until a few nights before. Just past that intersection, on an unassuming and otherwise residential street, stood the synagogue.

He would stop walking then, and stare at the building as though willing it to impart some secret. Most of all he gazed at the six-pointed Star of David emblazoned in the center of the brick wall, just above the congregation's name. In the warm darkness, the star seemed to call to him, like a symbol of a terribly important journey he had once meant to take, or had already taken but forgotten.

The sight of it excited and troubled him. There was a queer, sharp pain in his heart when he laid eyes on the star, and on the building it adorned. At these moments he did not think about anything. Rational thought was never farther away. He was outside himself, something other than the intellectual persona that was attorney Steve Birch. Reason had nothing to do with these nighttime treks: pilgrimages, he might almost call them.

He would stand in front of the building, and the star, until the ache became too poignant to bear. Then he would turn his back and begin retracing his steps, going home.

More and more these days, he was thinking of his Lakewood apartment as "home," rather than the one he kept in his name on the reservation. And that, he knew, was because more and more, he was drifting away from his Native American identity and toward the more nebulous and less-defined one of just-plain-American. This trend troubled him deeply. It was as though he'd let go of an anchor that bound him and held him secure, and had consequently parted from his own moorings and set himself adrift in an uncertain sea. The compass that he had once used to guide his life seemed broken now, unreliable. The trouble was, he had no other one to use in its stead.

There was still his modest legal practice, a neutral thing that offered him neither pleasure nor pain; it was a means of livelihood, no more. Until now, the lion's share of his talents and energy had gone into representing his Indian brothers when they tripped over their own weaknesses and walked head-on into the brick wall of the American jurisprudence system. As he paced the streets of Lakewood each night, attracted like a metal shaving to the magnet of that mysterious, six-pointed star, the lives of his brother Indians seemed very remote. Irrelevant. He didn't want it to be that way. He was like a creature impelled against its will, prowling and reprowling the same strange territory in search of ... he knew not what.

Bobby Smith, lurking in the vicinity of that same shul night after night, ground his teeth in frustration at the sight of the Indian attorney pacing and staring in front of *his* target. Anyone would think that Birch, himself, was out to do his own bit of no-good to the place. No more than the lawyer himself did Bobby understand Birch's strange fascination with the synagogue. All he knew was that he wanted the guy out of there.

Since the night — more than a week ago now — when Big Jim's car had failed him and forced Bobby to postpone his plan, surveyors had been busy at the site of the new Jewish school. It had been all Bobby and Jim could do to stay out of sight of the workers' inquisitive eyes and telescopic instruments while continuing their probe of the local caves. Bobby was determined to set his plan of intimidation in motion before the heavy equipment was brought in and construction begun in earnest.

Stop them in their tracks, he thought. *Stop 'em cold. Show them that they've picked the wrong place for setting up shop. Jim and me, we belong to these cliffs and rocks. They belong somewhere else.* He didn't know where those Jews belonged, but it sure wasn't here. And it was up to him to let them know.

It was only the presence of Steve Birch, appearing on the scene night after night, that held him in an agonizing limbo of inaction.

He had considered carrying out the deed earlier in the evening, before Birch came. But there was an unusual amount of activity in the synagogue these days: classes of some kind, Bobby surmised sourly. Men and women and even teenagers poured into the place each night, some of them to linger on until quite late, arguing some point with their teacher or each other. The police, too, had made its presence felt during this time, with official cars casually patrolling this and nearby streets as the students came and went. No, he didn't dare make his move before midnight; and he couldn't make it then because of Steve Birch. Waiting Birch out was a tactic he'd tried only once. Steve had nearly startled him out of a year's growth by reappearing unexpectedly just minutes after he'd left, to stand riveted before the building for another endless half-hour.

And there had been one Saturday night when Bobby had watched in dismay as a horde of people streamed into the synagogue for some kind of postmidnight service. These Jews were unpredictable, that's what. To his relief, the service was not repeated on the following night — but Steve Birch put in an appearance as usual.

The safest thing to do would be to wait for a night when Steve didn't show at all. How soon that would come, Bobby had no clue. His patience was fast evaporating. Those surveyors were scurrying about the site like a bunch of nasty ants, sticking their noses where they had no business being and getting ready to draw up their plans. Up above their heads, there were still a good many caves waiting to be investigated. And somewhere deep in the shadows of one of those caves — if Old Henry could be believed — lay a fortune with Bobby's name on it.

And so, grinding his teeth and clutching his can of kerosene, he waited.

VI.

Shimi Mandel was having a wonderful day. He was surprised to find that such days were possible; even more, they filled him with a certain awe.

Always before, school had been a place where frustration was *de rigueur* and anguish not uncommon. In the rigid structure of the classroom, Shimi's restless spirit, combined with mild learning disabilities, had prevented his scintillating mind from expressing itself fully. The teachers' reactions had been negative, for the most part, and his parents' expectations colored accordingly. To make matters worse, there was always his brother, Meir, in the background: Meir to be compared to and contrasted with, always to Shimi's detriment.

Now, with the suddenness of a miracle, the picture had changed.

Meir was out of the reckoning, away at his yeshivah where, as far as his brother was concerned, he could shine to his heart's content. Shimi did not mind people lavishing praise on his big brother, as long as they did not use their admiration for Meir as a bludgeon with which to beat Shimi.

As for Shimi's school year, young as it was, here was the real miracle. School had changed from an ordeal to an adventure. And Shimi, in the process, was becoming what he had never in a million years envisioned himself becoming: a successful student.

I love this homeschool thing, he thought as he made his way happily home from the shul that served as the *kollel's* headquarters as well as the boys' temporary schoolroom. In addition to their own learning and preparing their evening classes for the community, Asher Gann and Avi Feder had assumed *rebbi* duties during the daytime hours. Their only pupils this year were the Bernstein brothers and Shimi Mandel. Rivi Gann was filling out their general-studies program, working around her own art classes in the Jewish day school. The younger children — Gila and Yudi Bernstein, and Tzirel and Chanala Mandel — were presently attending that same day school, under the efficient guidance of their kindhearted principal, Mrs. Simi Wurtzler. Three-year-old Ora Mandel attended a playgroup in Mrs. Rein's house and seemed very happy there.

Perhaps it was the intimate teacher-student ratio that had helped Shimi begin to blossom. There was also the boon of Asher Gann's effervescent personality, and Avi Feder's quiet tenacity in bringing out the best in each boy under his tutelage. Shimi found himself for the first time volunteering answers in class, and poring over texts with real interest. Even more astonishing, he found himself jumping out of bed to greet each new day. His father, Efraim, was too busy with his own new teaching and *kollel* responsibilities to notice the change in his son. As for Etty, if she thought about it at all, it was merely to breathe a thankful sigh that Shimi was not causing them headaches — yet. Based on his past history, she knew they would not be long in coming.

"Hi, Ma!" Shimi burst into the house. "I'm home!" He threw his book bag onto the floor, waited for the inevitable, "Put away your bag," from his mother, and cheerfully did so.

He sauntered into the kitchen, where Ora was coloring at the table and Layala was half-asleep in her infant seat, mercifully quiet for once. He had never known such a baby for crying! It was squall, squall, squall, all day long and half the night. His mother thought it might be "colic"; all Shimi knew was that it made his ears hurt. And when she wasn't crying she seemed sleepy and unresponsive, even for such a small infant. And the vomiting! After every feeding, regular as clockwork. It had become a standing joke among Layala's siblings, though her mother wasn't laughing …

"Hello, Shimi," Etty said absently, her hands moving with lightning efficiency to prepare dinner before the time came for her to leave. "How was school?"

The question was automatic; unfortunately, the ear at which her son directed his answer was set on automatic, too. Instead of the usual, "Fine," he launched into the equivalent of a sonnet, a rainbow, a chorus.

"School is just amazing, Ma! I'm learning up a storm — Rebbe Asher says so; and Rebbe Avi praised a question I asked in Gemara this morning! I'm even doing O.K. in math, and my composition was the best I've ever written! Mrs. Gann really liked it, I could tell."

He stopped, partially for breath and partially to receive his mother's lavish compliments. They never came. She nodded absently, gave the pot a final stir with a long wooden spoon, and bent over the baby, murmuring, "It's time to get ready. We'll be late."

"Late for what?" asked Tzirel, wandering into the kitchen in search of a snack.

A moment ago, Shimi had been feeling hungry, too. For some reason, his appetite deserted him. His mother said, "I've got to run out and buy us a new microwave. Our old one just went *kaput* ... Mrs. Gann has offered to babysit. To make it easier for all of you to do your homework, she's going to come over here instead of your going to her place."

"Great! I love Mrs. Gann," Tzirel said, her hand hovering between an apple and a granola bar.

"Take the apple," her mother ordered.

"Ma," Shimi said desperately. "Did you hear what I said? I'm doing great in school these days!"

"That's nice," Etty murmured. "It's about time we saw a little *nachas* from you. Your brother Meir never gave us a moment's worry."

Meir again! Even hundreds of miles away, he haunted the house and cast his long-distance shadow over everything Shimi did. Even the successes felt like failures ... Shimi saw himself as one of those blackened, silver candlesticks he had seen in an antiques store once: the kind that no amount of polishing would ever help. There might be shining silver underneath, but on the outside, only tarnish. That was how Shimi felt: permanently tarnished.

He left the kitchen and went up to his room, slamming the door just a little harder than he had to. His mother winced. Would Shimi never settle down? Sometimes she didn't know what was going to become of that boy.

Layala awoke fully. She began to whimper, then to cry. Etty scooped her up to prepare her for their outing. She'd been planning on a visit to the doctor's, then had to cancel the appointment at the last moment when their cranky, old microwave had decided to give up and die. Unable to imagine an efficient kitchen without the use of a microwave, Etty was on her way to purchase a new one. She'd call the pediatrician for a new appointment in the morning.

Upstairs, Shimi clapped his hands over his ears against his baby sister's howls, wishing that the gesture could block out the rest of the world, too. A few short minutes earlier, as he'd walked home from the shul where he had his lessons, he'd been feeling on top of the world. Funny how suddenly things could change.

Ma was right, he guessed. She'd always said he was moody.

VII.

Heidi Neufeld had flown dozens of times before. She'd worn the same kind of chic-but-comfortable business suit that she was wearing now, and carried the same leather luggage and matching hand-bag. But she'd never felt the way she felt tonight as she boarded her plane. Where the accordion walkway met the aircraft, she caught a fleet-ing glimpse of a smoke-colored sky, sunset's last light touching the outer rim with a final flush of rose. Then she had one foot inside the plane, and then both of them, and a stewardess was greeting her with a smile and wishing her a pleasant journey, and Heidi was praying that she would make it to her seat before she collapsed.

Brittle; that was the way she felt. Not the kind of weakness that comes with a flu or debilitating illness; this was a new thing, a fragility that turned her entire being into an eggshell, ripe for the cracking.

Thankfully she settled into her window seat, stowing her hand lug-gage beneath the seat in front of her. She looked out the window. A few early stars had appeared: rather sad-looking specimens, their shine dulled against the faded backdrop of the metropolitan sky. What were the stars like out in New Mexico? Finding out was something to which she could look forward. A tiny something, which was about all she could handle just now. Figuring out the larger questions of her life required far more energy than she was able to muster presently.

A woman of indeterminate age stopped in the aisle to peer at seat num-bers. Having found what she was looking for, the passenger launched into a fury of arranging and stowing her possessions away: coat and bag in the overheard compartment, voluminous handbag beneath the seat in front, and finally, depositing herself with much shifting and creaking in the seat beside Heidi's. After all that was squared away, she glanced at Heidi as though to assess the possibilities for passing the time on the flight. Hastily, Heidi closed her eyes, folding her hands neatly in her lap like a kindergartner composing herself for sleep. She heard her neighbor reach for the in-flight magazine, and the disappointed rustle of pages.

Heidi kept her eyes closed. There was plenty to think about, though thinking was not an easy thing for her to do these days. With Yom Kippur just around the corner, introspection was in order. She resolved, rather feebly, to make a stab at it during the flight; the rest, she hoped, would be more easily accomplished in the haven of Tova's house at her journey's end.

Both she and Tova had hoped to be together for Rosh Hashanah, but here Mrs. Neufeld, Heidi's mother, had stepped in with tearful but surprisingly steely opposition. "You've been through such a hard time," she told her daughter when Heidi at last paid a long-overdue visit to her anxious parents. "I'm not sure what's going on, but I do know one thing: This is a time when you should be home with your family. A friend is fine in her place, but there's no one like a mother to help you when you're not … feeling like yourself."

Heidi disagreed, but she didn't tell her mother so. In her opinion, Tova Bernstein would be like a breath of fresh air through an open window, while her mother was a warm, stifling blanket, lovingly wrapping her up to the point of suffocation. Unwilling to hurt her mother's feelings, she had compromised: "I'll spend Rosh Hashanah at home, Mom. But I fly out to Tova for Yom Kippur and Succos." There was a note in her voice that her mother recognized from many a childhood battle, and therefore, she gracefully — and gratefully — retreated. If Heidi could produce that particular note of iron, she might not be quite as … troubled … as her mother had feared.

In her tentative way she had urged Heidi to see a doctor, a mental-health professional, anyone who might bring her daughter back to her old, familiar self. Heidi had refused. Her malaise was more spiritual in nature: an identity crisis of the highest order. This was nothing that a pill or series of well-meant homilies could cure. Therapy might be in order, but she wanted to see first what some time spent away from the invisible, barbed-wire constraints of her powerhouse job might accomplish — and, of course, the company of the dearest and most sensible friend in the world.

So here she was, sitting very still though with an inner trembling that matched the plane's strengthening vibrations as it began to move down the runway. Gathering speed, the aircraft retracted its wheels and set sail for the sky. Heidi let out her breath and cautiously opened an eye to peek out the window.

Sky and earth swirled crazily above and below her, but no more crazily than the thoughts inside her own head. Once, her rational mind had been her best friend. It was her tool, her weapon, her saving grace. It had betrayed her now, turned disjointed, subdued by emotion. She felt a familiar clutch of panic — familiar, because panic had become an old friend during her self-imposed isolation in the Poconos motel room — and willed it to subside. Her mind may have turned to slush, but her willpower seemed blessedly unimpaired. She might stand in need of a major overhaul in whatever cosmic garage catered to dislocated lawyers, but her engine was still running.

"Wait," Tova had commanded in their last conversation today. "Wait till you get out here. Don't think, don't feel, don't worry. I'll be there to meet your plane when you arrive."

Those, Heidi reflected drowsily as she pulled the scratchy airline blanket up to her chin and tucked a hand beneath her cheek, had to be some of the most comforting words ever spoken.

Chapter 8

I.

"I t's fun to get away, isn't it?" Tova remarked as she and Nachman sped in the direction of Albuquerque.

"Sure." Nachman sounded abstracted. *He has so much on his mind,* Tova told herself. She resolved to let him have his silence, to offer it to him as a gift, as it were. After all, silence could be very relaxing. She would play the sweet, understanding wife and allow him his time to think.

Thirty minutes later, sweetness had begun to pall, as had the silence. A charcoal infinity of road unwound ahead of them, and she was beginning to feel bored.

"Nachman? Hello?" she called.

He tore his eyes from the road and his thoughts from his *kollel.* "Hm?"

"As I was saying, it's fun to go away together with your husband. Get the operational word here? 'Together,'" she said meaningfully.

"What? But I'm here ... Oh, I see what you mean." He grinned at her. "You'll have to excuse me, Tova. It was hard leaving everything today to make this trip. Of course, I don't begrudge it to you — I wouldn't have wanted you to make the six-hour round trip on your own — but ..."

"But your mind is still back in Lakewood." Tova shook her head. "Well, I'll give you 15 more minutes to finish thinking, Nachman. Then I'll want some attention!"

Naturally, because he knew she was waiting for him to "finish thinking," he couldn't focus on his thoughts at all. Instead, he relaxed his grip on the wheel, chatted with his wife and eventually popped one of their favorite music tapes into the car's cassette player. Tova glowed. She supposed she should feel some compunction, but not a sliver of guilty conscience ruffled her contentment. It was good for Nachman to get free of the *kollel* for a few hours. It would give him perspective on the various issues and problems he was grappling with in these early days; it would refresh his spirit and recharge his batteries. That decided, Tova set herself to wholeheartedly enjoy the rest of the trip to Albuquerque's airport to meet Heidi's plane.

Nachman, watching her, knew exactly what she was thinking. Tova believed this trip was good for him. Well, that was nothing new: Tova tended to think she knew what was best for everyone! This tendency would have been annoying, except for the fact that she was usually right. In any case, he was prisoner in this car for the duration of the drive to Albuquerque and back, so he might as well enjoy the ride. The remainder of the journey was very pleasant for both of them. It seemed like no time at all when they discerned the airport lights twinkling ahead of them.

"It took us nearly three hours to get here," Tova mused aloud. "Back home, in New York, a three-hour drive is a big deal . A trip to the country in the summer. An ordeal. Out here, where everything is so spread out, time just sort of melts into space so that you hardly feel it passing."

"Very profound," her husband told her, twinkling. "Melting time and space — I like that."

She lifted her chin. "Well, I try."

"All kidding aside, Tova, what's our approach going to be with Heidi? I'm still not sure what happened to her —"

"Neither does she, frankly," Tova broke in. "She thinks she suffered some kind of nervous breakdown or something. A break of some kind, certainly. Suddenly, she simply could not bear the thought of going to that office of hers, of spending all her days and nights trying to rack up billing hours for those lawyer bosses of hers, of 'wasting her life not living,' as she put it. Nachman, it hurt my heart to hear her talk like that. Heidi, who was always so successful, so ambitious, so bursting with energy."

"She never married," Nachman remarked.

"*Yet*. Now that she's taken a step out of the box, I'll bet marriage will be the next step. You have to be free to start moving in a new direction. And Heidi's a real catch. She just has to decide that being a wife instead of a hotshot lawyer is what she *really* wants."

He glanced at her, then back at the road. "So you think she's free of the job?"

Tova hesitated. "I think she's flirting with the idea," she admitted. "It's been her life for so long, I think it's hard for her to picture herself doing anything else. And she *likes* practicing law, Nachman. She's good at it, and it stimulates her mind. If only it wasn't so — so all consuming. It just about swallowed her up."

They were silent on the last few miles of the airport access road. Around them, dusk had deepened into rich, dark evening. Stars popped out in a navy sky like bright pins poked through paper.

It was the stars that Heidi noticed first, as she stepped from the plane and inhaled her first breath of New Mexico air. The stars, and the fact that the air was as dry and heady as a glass of champagne. *It was like stepping onto the moon*, she thought. *A different feel, a different world*. If she tried really hard, she might jump clear up to touch that sky.

Then she remembered Tova, waiting for her inside the terminal, and quickened her pace so abruptly that she bumped into the well-heeled passenger stepping along just ahead of her.

"Excuse me," she gasped, slowing to a decorous pace. Only her heart continued to trip along with unaccustomed rapidity, as if the taste of that champagne air had filled her with a sense of celebration. Though what there was to celebrate in her present state, she hadn't a clue.

No, that wasn't exactly true, she thought with an inward smile. *Tova was waiting. That was a very good start*.

The first rapturous greetings were over. Heidi's luggage was safely stowed in the back of the Bernsteins' minivan and they were on the road again, nose pointed southeast this time. Homeward.

For the next hour or so, Tova's neck was twisted into a permanent pretzel as she chattered to Heidi in the seat behind her. Her friend, she thought, looked surprisingly well for someone who had just emerged on the other side of a life-crisis — until you looked at her eyes. There was a depth to them, a darkness that hadn't been there before. An air of uncharacteristic fragility surrounded Heidi, and it emanated from something far less tangible than her recent weight loss. Tova didn't like it.

"It's a good thing you agreed to come out here," she said briskly. "We're going to talk our heads off, and you're going to eat well and sleep well and figure out your life!"

"If you say so, doc." Heidi's smile was strained. She was beginning to feel tired; physically, she was two hours ahead of the others, on Eastern Daylight Time. And, as was common with her these days, physical fatigue brought on the other kind: the core-deep emotional exhaustion that had been taking such a severe toll.

It was Nachman who heard the new note in her voice, and who tactfully suggested to his wife that they give their guest a chance to rest. "We've still got a two-hour drive ahead of us," he told Heidi. "Might as well close your eyes and have a nap."

But closing her eyes was just what Heidi found it impossible to do. She felt jumpy as a drop of water hopping over a hot surface. Propping a chin on her fist, she gazed out the window at the passing scenery.

The country was flat under a vast expanse of sky, with the stars she had admired earlier blazing in proud profusion. Here and there a flat-topped mountain — a mesa, Tova had said they were called — jutted up to break the monotony. Occasionally they drove through a small town, where Heidi had a glimpse of lighted windows and dimly seen figures as the car flashed past. *Who were those people?* she wondered dreamily. Sitting in their living rooms, or eating a late dinner at their scrubbed kitchen tables, they had no inkling that such a person as Heidi Neufeld existed. They neither knew nor cared that she was at a crossroads in her life, and that her mind and heart had very nearly shattered in the effort to get her there.

Rather than depressing her, the notion brought her a strange peace. Her problems were not, after all, of such earthshaking importance as her emotions would have her believe. After all, right here before her were dozens — hundreds — of people going about their lives just as though she didn't matter at all. How refreshing!

"Only an hour to go," Nachman called out presently.

"Heidi, I'm so thrilled that you're here," Tova said for the umpteenth time. "This is going to be the best thing in the world for you. You're going to have a peaceful, restful vacation at *Chez Bernstein*. How clever of you to come!"

Heidi smiled wryly. "Did I have a choice? You can be mighty persuasive when you want to be, Tova dear." Both women chuckled and Nachman smiled.

All three were to remember Tova's optimistic prediction — "peaceful, restful" — with acute poignancy, only 24 hours later.

II.

The sun sank in a fiery ball over the western horizon, officially ushering in Yom Kippur eve.

Tomorrow would be a busy day, Pinchas Harris thought as he went out to his car. Apart from his personal sojourn to greet the Day of Atonement, as the town's only Orthodox rabbi he would be besieged with phone calls from his congregants as well as being over his head in shul arrangements. His wife might call him an impractical idealist, but Pinchas was extremely hands-on when it came to his beloved shul. Everything from the seating to the melodies used in the various prayers came under his watchful eye. The still-young congregation, like a child, was ever growing, ever evolving, and it was up to him to ensure that the movement was always in the proper direction.

His trusty *gabbaim* — attorney Nate Goodman and pediatrician Ben Sadowsky — did a marvelous job. If a person could be said to have two extra right hands, these men served in that capacity for Rabbi Harris. But that did not prevent him from holding numerous late-night sessions to pore over every detail of the High Holy Day services. Rosh Hashanah had come and gone without a hitch and, Pinchas thought with modest pleasure, with a sense of definite uplift for the worshipers as a whole. A good number of people had come over to him afterward — in supermarket aisles, parking lots and in shul itself — to offer a word of approbation. Rabbi Harris, old hand that he considered himself, was not immune to praise. It pleased him, mostly because it meant that he'd done well by his congregants. He had successfully guided his flock. The memory of that jolt of pleasure only spurred him on to outdo himself next time around.

Penina, his wife, would use her day off from her high-school principal's job to scour the house in honor of the big day. She would be slightly on edge because she never fasted well. Pinchas had extracted a promise that she'd remain at home, preferably in bed, if she felt weak, and not make an attempt to come to shul in the heat. The hot dry air often made her a little dizzy even when she was not fasting. The last few days had been exceptionally dry and searing, even for New Mexico. With a sigh, Penina had promised.

In his small, pleasantly decorated but far-too-cluttered house around the corner from the shul, *gabbai* Nate Goodman reviewed his seating chart a final time. Tomorrow morning he would tack it up in shul, where it would become as immutable as a law of nature. Everyone knew that seat changes were out of the question once Nate had posted the chart. He expected a few calls tonight as people belatedly realized that they would be spending all of an evening and a day perched on the same chair in the same spot, and would become anxious to make sure that spot was to their liking. Nate was used to this, and took it in stride. In dealing with this, as with all problems he encountered in his professional and personal life, his astute, legal mind joined forces with a unique, creative flair all his own, to produce solutions that worked. In the case of the High Holy Days seating, he had become a master at leaving enough wiggle-room for last-minute changes and adjustments. But after he hung up the chart at Shacharis tomorrow, he knew and they knew: absolutely no more wiggling.

Ben Sadowsky, pediatrician and second *gabbai*, sat in the well-worn armchair that his wife had used when entertaining Shana Bernstein with Indian lore a couple of weeks earlier. In his lap sat a medical journal, but Dr. Ben wasn't reading. His hands lay idly on top of the open journal as his mind wandered ahead to the upcoming year. At the forefront of his mind was little Layala Mandel, whom he had examined that morning.

He'd tried to disguise his concern from the child's mother, but Etty had picked up on it at once.

"What is it? Something's the matter, doctor — I can tell. What's wrong with my baby?"

"It could be one of several things," Dr. Ben had said with his most reassuring bedside manner. "The best thing to do is to run some tests. Actually, the simplest test would be an ordinary sonogram: the same kind of ultrasound that you had when you were expecting this little princess. That will eliminate several possibilities."

"But what do you think it is, doctor?" Etty Mandel had pressed. Her face had been white and strained as she clutched the baby to her chest, ready and willing to battle any force in the known universe on behalf of her child, but helpless in the face of her own ignorance. "Tell me what you think!"

He had told her what he thought. His sensitive fingers, palpitating the baby's abdomen, had found the telltale "olive" that led to his tentative diagnosis. Layala, he suspected, suffered from a condition that affects the immature digestive system of some infants. "That could be why she cries so much, especially after she's eaten. She's in considerable discomfort."

"Pain? Is she in pain?" Etty's face had become even paler. Layala, responding to the tension in the arms holding her, began to whimper. Why had she put off bringing the baby to the doctor these past couple of weeks? She'd had good enough excuses. She'd been drowning in a sea of responsibilities: unpacking her family's worldly goods after a major, cross-country move; getting her oldest son ready to fly off to yeshivah; preparing her other children for new schools in a new city. But what use were justifications, when her own, guilt-ridden heart was declaring: "Unexcused!"

"She may be in some discomfort," Dr. Ben said again. "The condition I'm thinking of is called pyloric stenosis. Would you like me to explain?"

Etty gripped her hands together, willing her panic to subside so that her brain could function. "Please."

"The stomach has an opening at the bottom that leads down to the intestines. That's called the pylorus. When the muscle around the pyloric valve grows too thick, it can cause a blockage. That's what's causing Layala to vomit so violently after each feeding. You say the symptoms started at about 3 weeks of age?"

Etty nodded. "When we landed at the airport, to be exact. In the ladies' restroom ..."

"That sounds about right, in terms of timing. If we find that she *is* suffering from pyloric stenosis, we'll have to perform a procedure to help her feel better."

"Procedure?"

"Surgery, Mrs. Mandel. Layala would need an operation to correct the problem in her stomach. There's a good man in Roswell who's an expert at this kind of surgery. That's just about 50 miles away — an hour's drive. I'll set things up for you, if it turns out to be necessary."

He performed a quick blood test right there in the office, to check the baby for dehydration. By the looks of her, he judged that she did not yet need to be fed intravenous fluids. Given her frequent bouts of projectile vomiting, however, it was only a matter of time before dehydration set in. He scheduled an ultrasound for her at a local facility, for three days hence, the day after Yom Kippur.

Presently he sent Mrs. Mandel home, with her mixed bag of hope and fear. *A procedure that could help her ... A good man in Roswell ...* What a prospect to carry with one into Yom Kippur ...

Dr. Ben's eyes closed. In the kitchen his wife rustled quietly, preparing something for the prefast meal, or perhaps the post-fast one. The familiar sounds comforted him, and he dozed. But his dreams were troubled by specters of women with chalk-white faces and little babies who wouldn't stop crying.

III.

Etty and Efraim hovered between anxiety and hope as they monitored their youngest child's progress. Since Layala's appointment with Dr. Sadowsky, every wail, every grimace, and every blessed interval of quiet was closely registered by her vigilant parents. When she passed a few peaceful hours, Etty was convinced that Dr. Sadowsky had misdiagnosed Layala's complaint, and that the sonogram would prove it. Then the baby would start crying again — a feeble whimper at first, as though she was tired of her mixed-up insides and wished it would all just go away — but soon mounting to a crescendo of heartrending sobs and then piercing wails. Another feeding, and another bout of violent vomiting. Then Etty's worried eyes would meet Efraim's equally anxious ones, and her belief in a negative test result would fast ebb away.

She patted the baby's back as Layala drifted in a merciful sleep on that *erev* Yom Kippur night. When all was quiet, she got out her well-worn *Tehillim* and tried to lose herself in its pages. Though her prayers drove straight up from the heart, it was not easy to concentrate with one ear ever on the alert for the first plaintive sounds from the baby's room.

At the Bernsteins, *erev* Yom Kippur was hardly distinguishable from any other day of the year; at least, not the evening part. Tomorrow, Tova thought as she mechanically folded laundry, she would try to institute an air of penitent reflection. Nachman would review the laws of Yom Kippur with the boys, and she would pay special attention to Shana and Gila. It was a time for heart-to-heart conversation, when wellsprings of introspection rarely tapped during the rest of the year temporarily gushed forth.

Tova paused with a half-folded shirt in her hands. Memories of tender talks with a younger Shana rose up now in a kind of mockery. Would Shana let it happen again this year? The flash of belonging that she'd felt at the picnic that day, when paper cups had been raised high in a toast to their mutual futures, had receded again into sullenness. Though Shana did not actively dislike her school, and despite the fact that she had made a couple of tentative friendships and enjoyed her occasional meetings with Mrs. Sadowsky to plumb the depths of New Mexico's history, she still refused to be happy. Shana seemed determined to withhold that vital spark of joy that every mother longs to see in her child's eye. To Tova, who had been longing in vain for months, this was intensely frustrating.

"She's your first teenager," Nachman had told her, in what he genuinely believed was a comforting outlook. "Get used to it."

Well, she *wouldn't* get used to it! Tova was determined to break through her daughter's resistance, to make her see how wonderful life could be — here in tiny Lakewood in the Southwest United States, or anywhere — if only one allowed it to be. Shana was simply unwilling to let it, and Tova could not, for the life of her, think of a way to get her to step up and open that particular door.

But that didn't mean she was about to give up trying.

Heidi greeted the approach of the Day of Atonement with something surprisingly close to excitement. It was a remote kind of excitement, like water churning sluggishly through a too-narrow channel, but it was the first strong emotion of any kind that she had allowed herself to feel since the day she decided to head for the Poconos instead of her office. The excitement was a herald to the introspection she must undergo before tomorrow. Though she knew it would hurt — though it hurt already — she knew with a deep-down certainty that this was what she needed most of all: a reckoning. What better time to look inward, to reassess the course of one's life, than on Yom Kippur?

And if that course was strewn with boulders and pitfalls, what better place to map out a new route than in Tova Bernstein's house?

She was in a safe place. She had her best friend to help her. Here, on the twisting trail of her own fog-ridden landscape, she would search for a way out. For the first time since she had turned her car onto an unfamiliar highway and landed in a strange motel room, she almost believed that she would find it.

"Aunt Heidi!" It was young Yudi, coming for his bedtime story, a nightly ritual whenever she was a guest in his home. "Aunt Heidi, where are you?"

Heidi sat up in bed and switched on her bedside lamp. Time to rejoin the land of the living. She was tired, so tired … but she could not, even now, resist a child's plea.

"Here!" she called back.

"Where?" Shouting up and down stairwells was a way of life at the Bernsteins.

To herself, in a whisper, she added, *Right where I need to be.* Aloud, she called, "In my room. Come on up, Yudi!" She listened with pleasure to the patter of eager feet making their way to her, as if the owner of those feet knew she had a special story waiting for him. Hastily, Heidi began to spin the rusty wheels of her mind, trying to think of one.

For Rivi Gann, Yom Kippur was a two-day affair. *Erev* Yom Kippur found her already launched into an intensely reflective state of mind. Setting aside paints and brushes, lesson plans and domestic affairs, she took her soul out the day before Yom Kippur and gave it a thorough airing.

Asher knew better than to speak to his wife about anything mundane or trivial on this day. Rivi was absorbed in a profound, personal experience that he — of a more extroverted, matter-of-fact type of mind — could scarcely comprehend. For him, Yom Kippur was a day of penitence and prayer, when he could cleanse his soul and start over again with a fresh slate. He would bumble and stumble along as best he could over the course of the ensuing year, with the memory of that cleansing experience to keep him on track.

For Rivi, it was more than that. It was a profound communing with her Creator, and with the parts of herself that only He knew about. It was a probing as thorough as that of a surgeon's tool, delicately extracting a buried malignancy.

The introspection began as night fell. Rivi sat in the little room she called her "studio," but she did not think about art. She sat in darkness, gazing out the window at the immensity of Hashem's world, in the grip of feelings too deep for words. At some point, the everyday world intruded in the form of a remembered responsibility: She recalled that she had once again agreed to watch little Layala Mandel tomorrow. The child gave Etty no peace, and there was so much cooking to be done for her large family before the holiday began. Rivi herself, of course, had far less to keep her busy. She was glad to help. Layala had taken possession of a special piece of her heart: a piece that had long been reserved, in silent waiting, for a certain, tiny someone who had yet to put in an appearance ...

The dark and the quiet were just right for Rivi's soul work, but she was finding it hard to focus tonight. She was distracted by anticipation, relishing the fact that tomorrow she would be tending a baby just like any other Jewish mother. Maybe she would even find herself feeling a bit frazzled as she tried to accomplish the day's tasks around the infant's demands. What bliss!

The phone rang. Dimly, she heard Asher pick it up. From the imperceptible shift in his tone, she knew that it was Avi calling. Avi, who would be spending his first Yom Kippur alone. January would mark Yocheved's *yahrtzeit*, the first anniversary of his wife's death. A milestone of sorts would be achieved then, and along with it perhaps the beginning of genuine healing. But tonight had to be difficult for Avi. She closed her eyes, hearing the low hum of her husband's voice as a backdrop to her thoughts.

IV.

"**A**vi, how's it going?"

"Well, I've been annoying my neighbors with my violin practice," Avi confessed. "But, on the credit side, my cooking's improving."

"What's your speciality?"

Avi hemmed and hawed before finally admitting that it was spaghetti and meatballs. "Nothing fancy, you understand," he hastened to add. "But solid, hearty fare."

"So when are you going to invite us over for a test run?"

"Patience, my friend. The culinary art requires a long honing. A slow simmering, you might say …"

"You'll be here for the *seudah hamafsekes* before the fast, right?"

"If it's all right with your wife —"

"It was her idea, you ninny! How long will it be before you realize that we actually want you around?"

Avi sighed. "Thanks, friend. I'll try to remember that."

There was that note in Avi's voice again; time for a quick subject change. Asher reminded himself of a question he had been meaning to ask his friend in relation to their *kollel* outreach classes, and the two men were soon engrossed in a discussion that, had Asher but known it, helped carry his friend across the terrifying chasm that had opened up before him a few minutes earlier.

Avi was used to being lonely — or thought he was. But when full night had set in, always his most difficult time of day, and he realized that Yom Kippur loomed just ahead, he experienced the sharpest pang of grief that he had felt since getting up from *shivah*. Yom Kippur had always been a special time of closeness for the two of them; an occasion to share their deepest dreams and hopes for the upcoming year.

There was no Yocheved to share his dreams now. There was no one to share anything. And, anyway, he was no longer sure there were any dreams left to share ...

"So you'll be here for the *seudah*, right?" Asher asked again, as a way of winding down their talk. It was nearly time to leave for shul and the class he taught there.

"Right. Thanks, Asher. For ... everything."

Asher waved this aside with characteristic briskness. "Never mind that. You're the best, Avi, you know that? We just recognize that fact, that's all."

"I'm lucky to have you guys as friends."

"We're the lucky ones. Don't you know anything?"

Avi laughed shakily, as the chasm retreated even further. "I guess I don't know as much as I thought. See you in shul?"

Asher checked his watch. "In about 10 minutes. Bye!"

"Bye ..."

Ten minutes later, the quiet building had undergone its nightly transformation into a hive of Jewish outreach and education. Pinchas Harris, sitting in his office putting the final touches on his post-*Kol Nidrei* and pre-*Ne'ilah* speeches, listened with pleasure. The *kollel* was the best thing that had happened to this community — after the founding of this shul, of course.

Their hard-won school programs catered to the children, but these evening courses were for everyone. Housewives, laborers, and businessmen could venture from their homes and whatever spiritual niche they presently occupied, and set out on a journey of learning that might, with time, nudge them into someplace entirely new. Nachman Bernstein was an excellent fellow, just right for the position he filled; his colleagues, with whom Pinchas was less well acquainted at this juncture, also seemed to be working out well. The voices emanating from the various classrooms sounded to his ears like the humming of a well-oiled machine, a Torah machine.

Smiling at his whimsy, he bent over his papers again. He'd better get to work on those talks of his and add his own couple of drops to the river of Torah that the *kollel* was pouring out over his little flock.

Two hours later, the shul was quiet again. Teachers and students had departed, leaving a peaceful silence in their wake. As usual, Pinchas Harris was the last one out. He moved from room to room, switching off lights, and then walked outside, carefully locking the door behind him.

Less than hour after the rabbi's departure, Steve Birch showed up for his usual nocturnal interlude, communing in the dogged but inexplicable way he'd developed of late with the Star of David adorning the shul. Clouds covered the moon tonight, and the star was dull against the bricks, its luster dimmed. Steve peered at it through the darkness, lost in a vortex of confused memory and vague hope, before finally turning away to seek his bed and the solace or mystery of his dreams.

It was less than an hour after *that*, after Steve had long since disappeared and the rest of Lakewood lay slumbering and quiet, when Pinchas Harris sat up abruptly in bed. He had woken from a sound sleep to an overwhelming urge to return to the shul he had left such a short time earlier.

V.

The synagogue had still been lit up when the battered white car drove slowly past earlier in the evening. Bobby and Jim saw men going in and out, wearing jackets despite the heat.

"Say your prayers, guys," Bobby said softly. "You're gonna need them."

They waited in enforced patience until the last worshipers had left. Still the lights blazed on. Their patience began to wear thin. An eon seemed to pass before the lights were finally doused and the rabbi came out, locking the front door behind him. They watched him enter his car and drive slowly away, content in the knowledge that the building was safe and secure for the night. The last of the rabbi's headlights had scarcely disappeared around the corner when Bobby and Jim slipped through the shadows to the rear of the shul.

The pair knew they could not begin their nefarious undertakings just yet. Sure enough, right on cue, that two-faced Steve Birch showed up to commune with who-knows-what. He took his own sweet time; but just when Bobby felt he would burst from anxiety, Steve departed as quietly as he had come.

Bobby had finally decided to include Jim in his plan and, despite inner misgivings both voiced and unvoiced, Jim had agreed to play his part. Bobby handed him a pair of latex gloves that he'd picked up at the reservation's pharmacy and slipped on a matching pair himself. Jim was put in charge of crumpling the newspapers, but it was Bobby who placed them strategically in the most likely spots. And it was Bobby who then poured the gasoline liberally over the newspapers wedged up against the shul walls, the wooden window frames, and the front and rear doors.

"Get back to the car, Jim," he whispered as he took out the matches. "Be ready to drive away the minute I'm inside. Go!"

He waited to see Jim safely in the car, with the engine switched on, before he struck his first match. In its small glare he saw his dreams lit up in glorious technicolor. There were just one or two minor obstacles to remove before his way would be clear again: the road to glittering fortune.

Flame kissed paper. The blaze was even more satisfactory than Bobby had hoped. Where darkness and silence had been an instant before, hissing orange flames reached for the sky. Five seconds later Bobby Smith was in the car and speeding away at Jim's side.

The engine groaned and the seats creaked. Bobby could no longer hear the steady crackle behind him, as red-hot tongues of flame devoured wood and plaster. But he could imagine it, and that was nearly as good.

Pinchas Harris — already under the covers and half asleep himself — felt a sudden, overwhelming impulse to return to the shul.

His wife opened bleary eyes and asked why in the world was he was putting on his shoes and jacket. "You've spent all evening at the shul. You have a couple of exhausting days ahead of you. Why don't you get some sleep?"

"I will, Penina," he promised. "As soon as I get back." There was no use trying to explain why he felt impelled to return to the shul. The urge was as pressing as the one that impels a mother to lean over her infant's cradle again and again to listen to its quiet breathing. With tender hands she tucks the blankets more securely around her baby, laughing at herself even as she knows that she'll be back again, sooner rather than later. Pinchas Harris felt an inexplicable need to make sure that his "baby" was safely tucked in for the night. It was as simple — or as incomprehensible — as that.

Penina fell back on her pillow, too tired to argue further. She was asleep before the front door closed behind her husband.

Pinchas drove slowly down the quiet streets, windows rolled up and the air-conditioning at full strength on this very warm night. The air felt dry as tinder. Afterwards, he could never reasonably explain how he caught the acrid tang of smoke without opening a single window. It was as though his nose had developed a super-sensory ability, or perhaps he'd just been listening very closely to some message delivered in the silence of the soul.

However it happened, Rabbi Harris later claimed that he smelled the smoke half a block away, through the window glass and the blast of frigid air blowing at him from every one of the car's vents.

Pulling up outside the shul, he no longer needed the evidence of his nose. He was perfectly able to see the flames now, licking at all four of the building's walls in long ragged lines, as though the shul were a painting and the flames a grotesque, living picture frame.

As his heart began to do a clumsy two-step all over his rib cage, he yanked out his cell phone and dialed for help. His finger was shaking so hard that it took four attempts to get the simple, three-digit number right.

VI.

"**A**rson," said Sheriff Ramsay.

Nachman Bernstein wrapped his arms, in shirtsleeves but no jacket, around himself as though he were cold on this stifling night. As if the desert heat were not enough, the flames had added their bit, making beads of perspiration pop out on Nachman's face. Pinchas Harris, standing nearby, looked like a wilting leaf. He was wearing a jacket over his pajamas and seemed utterly oblivious to the ludicrous spectacle he made.

Normally a man with his feet firmly on the ground, Nachman felt as though he had stepped into somebody else's bad dream. When Rabbi Harris's call had come over his cell phone — even in his shock and distress, Pinchas, considerate of the Bernsteins' sleep, had avoided dialing their home number — Nachman had been just barely awake enough to answer it. Hovering at the edges of sleep, the rabbi's words had sounded horribly surreal: "There's been a fire, Nachman. The shul. I thought you'd want to know ..."

"Fire?" Nachman had shaken his head to dispel the mists of sleep. "At the shul? *Now?*"

"Even as we speak," came the heavy answer. "I put in a call to the fire department. They're on their way." A pause. "There's the siren now ..."

Nachman, several blocks away, heard it, too. In a weird, stereophonic effect, the sound reached his ears through the line at the same time. The siren's wail jolted him awake as nothing else could. "I'll be right over."

And here he was, watching the firemen douse the last of the flames, and listening to the sheriff pronounce the unthinkable.

"Arson? Are you sure?" The words came thick and strange off Nachman's tongue.

"It has all the signs," Jack Ramsay said patiently. "Did you ever hear of a natural fire — due to an electrical short or simple carelessness — breaking out all around the perimeter of a building at the same time?"

"I see your point. Has anything like this ever happened in Lakewood before?"

The rabbi and the sheriff exchanged an uneasy glance.

"You didn't tell him?" Ramsay asked.

"Tell me what?" Nachman demanded.

Pinchas Harris cleared his throat. "I didn't want to worry you. It — it seemed like a one-time thing — a flash of hate that flared up and died down again ..." Haltingly, as though he were ashamed of the episode instead of angered by it, Pinchas told Nachman about the "JEWS GO HOME" spray-painted over the shul walls months earlier.

"And there's been nothing since then? No anti-Semitic incidents at all?"

Another exchange of looks. "Nothing you could put your finger on," Ramsay said slowly. "One or two little incidents that may have had its source in anti-Jewish feeling — or not. Petty crime can strike anywhere."

Nachman sensed that the sheriff believed this no more than he himself did.

"This may be premature," he said heavily. "But do you have any idea as to the perpetrator of this arson?"

"We have ideas," Ramsay said. "But —" He shrugged. "Police procedure, you know."

"I know." Nachman pulled out his cell phone. "I'd better call my wife. She'll be frantic. It was all I could do not to let her come out here with me tonight."

Pinchas watched him dial. "I'm not calling mine," he said heavily. "Let her sleep. There'll be time enough in the morning to spread the bad news ..."

The "police procedure" that the sheriff had mentioned was of the small-town, informal variety. First, having seen the last of the smoldering flames safely doused, the firemen sped away with his thanks. Ramsay went back to his office, where he sat at his desk laboriously filling out the paperwork attendant on the incident.

There had been little real damage to the synagogue, he thought with relief. The rabbi had discovered the fire before it traveled far enough to do much harm. Mostly smoke damage, the firemen believed, and not very much of that. The fire had been started, as Ramsay had mentioned, around the building's perimeter, and it had been working hard to make headway against mortar and brick. Had the arsonist done the job inside the synagogue, Ramsay shuddered to think of the extent of the likely destruction.

An amateur, he decided, thankfully signing his name at the bottom of the incident report. Yawning, he glanced at his watch. The next step in the investigation would have to wait for morning. There was no reason to wake Steve Birch from a sound sleep. Time enough tomorrow to sound him out about possible suspects within the Native American community. He would also be putting his men out on the streets with feelers among other possible criminal elements. A flicker of anger shot through him. Lakewood was a nice, peaceful town. No one was going to turn it into a nest of big-city crime — hate or otherwise — on *his* watch!

He considered a cup of coffee, then prudently opted for the couch in his office instead. If he was lucky, he would catch a couple of hours of sleep before morning.

Steve Birch was asleep — and dreaming. It was *the* dream again. Only this time, there was something different about the girl silently pounding her maize along with the other Apache women.

Around her neck — tucked into the folds of the skins she wore for warmth, so that no one but a visionary or a man in a dream could possibly have seen it — was a six-pointed Star of David.

As she leaned over the cookfire to settle the maize pot, the flames highlighted the glitter of tears in her hazel eyes.

There were matching tears in Steve Birch's hazel eyes when he awoke.

Chapter 9

I.

Shimi couldn't sleep. He was accustomed to sharing a room with his brother. Now that Meir had gone away to yeshivah, the room seemed twice as big and ten times as dark.

It was not that he was really afraid of the dark. Before, darkness had been his friend, lulling him to sleep by removing the distraction of seeing things. But now, with Meir gone, Shimi felt suddenly uncomfortable in his own, familiar space. His bed was a jail cell, with the darkness and the silence the grim manacles holding him prisoner. He was an innocent man condemned to solitary confinement.

At last, when it became impossible to lie there another second, Shimi got out of bed. Off in the distance, the sound of sirens rendered the night even spookier. He opened the door quickly and stepped out onto the upstairs landing, which was dimly lit by a modest, single-bulb fixture. He still felt a jolt of surprise, sometimes, that this was not the landing he had grown up with. The wallpaper was different, the carpet was different, the positioning of the stairs and bathroom were different when he stood outside his bedroom door.

It was not an unpleasant jolt, just a startled one. Shimi did not regret their move out west. He felt freer here, somehow. Maybe it was the immensity of the sky and the sparse, ageless landscape, so much more personal than any city block could possibly be. No, this had not been a bad move. Too bad Meir had to leave for yeshivah before they had a chance to settle in together. The thought reminded Shimi of how he'd felt just now, in the room they no longer shared. He hesitated, unsure of his next move.

The Mandel house was not one of the rollicking places where people start waking up when the sun goes down. His mother had strict rules about bedtime, and her offspring were tucked in just when they ought to be. Normally, Shimi didn't mind. His bedtime was a reasonable one, and even when Meir was allowed to turn in later than he was, there was always the knowledge that he would be along soon, a knowledge almost as comforting as his brother's actual presence. But now there was no Meir, and no hope of Meir opening the door and walking in. He was alone, and he'd better get used to it. He leaned over the bannister railing to see if there was any chance of communing with another living being in this house tonight.

There was a light on in the kitchen. That meant that either his mother or his father was still up: his mother, probably. Tatty was either learning in the "study," or already in bed. After another brief hesitation, Shimi made for the stairs and started down. Anything was better than facing that room again.

His mother, as he might have expected, looked unpleasantly surprised to see him when he walked in. She was quick to smooth the frown of annoyance, but it had been there on her face. Any change in Etty's mandated routine rattled her sense of order. Children needed a certain amount of sleep in order to function well. Never mind that Shimi was usually the first one up in the mornings; never mind, either, that he seemed possessed of a nearly inexhaustible energy supply. Children needed their sleep! And their mother needed her "downtime"; a precious dollop of solitude to smooth out the emotional creases that the daytime had pressed into her psyche.

"What's the matter?" Etty asked sharply. "Don't you feel well?"

"I'm fine, Ma." Shimi strolled over to the table and sat down facing his mother, who had been nursing a cup of tea and enjoying the silence. "I can't sleep, that's all. It's hard to get used to Meir not being around."

At the mention of Meir's name, Etty's expression softened. "I miss him, too. But you're going to have to get used to being alone in the room sometime, you know."

"I know." Shimi looked meaningfully at his mother's teacup. "Can I have a midnight snack? That might help me sleep."

"Nice try," she said with a reluctant smile, grudgingly enjoying his resourcefulness even as a part of her was wishing for the return of her peace and quiet. Had it been one of the girls, now, she would have resented the intrusion less. Shimi was another story. He was like a stone thrown into a calm pond. Restless and chatty, this son always had an unsettling effect on her. Efraim understood him better; always had. For Etty, from the start, this boisterous, outgoing child had seemed cut from a different cloth than she was. She preferred her string of relatively manageable, and certainly more comprehensible, little girls — and her Meir, of course. When Shimi had begun to display problematic behavior at school, she'd retreated even further from her son, in bewilderment and disapproval.

He clutched his stomach. "I'm sta-a-a-rving!" he announced with overdone pathos. His broad grin was an invitation: *Share the joke with me.*

She stood up, unsmiling. "Oh, all right. Just one cookie. But you have to brush your teeth afterward."

"It's a deal." Eagerly, Shimi accepted the proffered treat and savored it in the quiet kitchen, unaware of — or at any rate unfazed by — his mother's patent discomfort in his presence. It was a look he was used to: Etty always seemed to be a little uncomfortable inside her own skin. There was an ever-present tension just beneath the surface. Everyone in her family was familiar with it and hardly gave it a thought anymore. If she seemed just a little extra tense around Shimi, he had long ago developed the self-protective capacity to ignore it.

He finished his cookie, flashed his mother a smile, and said, "Well, it's been nice talking to you."

"Yes." She smiled back mechanically, uneasily aware that they had not talked much at all. What did she ever say to him, really, except to make critical remarks about his behavior or schoolwork? Any other kind of conversation would have felt — unnatural. Guiltily, she made a stab at it.

"Uh … How are you doing these days, Shimi? Do you like it out here?"

"Love it. Lakewood's fine. Me 'n the Bernstein boys are planning to explore all the caves just outside town."

"You be careful," Etty said automatically.

"And school's a million times better than it was back east. I'm actually learning something!"

For the first time, she smiled. "That's good. Maybe you and Meir can learn together when he comes home."

"Will he be here for Succos, Ma?"

"No, how could he? He just left. We don't have the money for plane tickets every other day. He'll be staying with the cousins for Yom Tov."

"So when do we get to see him again?"

She hesitated. "Pesach, probably. Unless we can swing a visit to L.A. for Tatty or myself before then."

"We kids wouldn't get to see Meir, though."

"No, I guess not. We don't have that kind of money, Shimi."

"That's okay." Money had been the bogeyman of the Mandel household for as long as Shimi could remember. He reached casually for another cookie. "Well, I can always talk to him on the phone. We've got unlimited long-distance calling, right?"

She nodded, eyes on the cookie in his hand. "Don't think I didn't see that, young man."

He crammed the cookie into his mouth. "See what?"

A laugh bubbled out of her, startling Etty herself as much as it did her son. He had a way of slipping past her guard, in negative ways usually, but sometimes in the most delightfully positive way, too. If he could rub her nerves raw, he also possessed the capacity to tickle her funny bone; to startle her, for just a moment, out of her sober demeanor and all-too-serious view of life. It felt good to laugh. It felt good for Shimi to see her laugh.

Then, too quickly, the moment was over. Briskly — the perfect mother again — she reminded him to brush his teeth and wished him a good night.

"Are you coming up soon, Ma?"

"Yes. Why?"

He shrugged. "I just like to know that everyone's in bed at the same time. It makes the house feel less lonely, somehow."

She looked at him, and there was a flash of understanding in her eyes. For once, she knew exactly how he felt. She, too, liked to know that her family was safe and snug in their beds when late night closed in.

The flash lasted for just an instant in time. Shimi hardly noticed it. But it stayed with Etty, warming her even more than her sudden burst of laughter had, or the second cup of tea she poured herself after her son had returned upstairs.

II.

*E*rev Yom Kippur is hectic at the best of times. Between *davening*, *kapparos*, preparing meals and getting ready for the holiday — not to mention any precious interlude snatched for self-reflection — there is scarcely a moment not accounted for.

This particular Yom Kippur eve was a nightmare.

Penina Harris woke early that morning to the news that there had been a fire at the shul — "Arson, the sheriff says," her husband laconically informed her as he tried to dress with hands numb with fatigue.

"What damage?" Penina asked sharply.

"Nothing very serious, *Baruch Hashem*. Mostly smoke. Ever try breathing real close to a campfire? That's what the shul smells like right now. The actual fire damage can be repaired at our leisure, being external to the building. But no one can *daven* there until the place has been thoroughly aired out. The interior walls need to be repainted, too. Luckily, the *Sifrei Torah*, inside the *aron*, managed to escape the worst of the smoke — but the rest of the place is reeking."

"How long do you figure it'll take?"

He shrugged. "We'll need an expert's opinion on that." The first article on this day's agenda was finding a substitute location for Yom Kippur services. Then, if there was time, he would line up a repair crew for the day after tomorrow.

Pinchas rang up his *gabbaim* for an emergency meeting to consider the question of temporarily relocating the shul.

Nate Goodman showed up first, dark eyes flashing at the thought of someone having the nerve to harm their shul! Tall, dark, and powerfully built, the lawyer looked ready to take on whatever dregs of society were responsible for this outrage. Dr. Ben Sadowsky was less effusive in his dismay, but no less indignant. The two were eager to spend their meeting with Rabbi Harris discussing the arson and its ramifications.

Nate wanted to get after the police at once, to make sure they caught the perpetrators without delay. He wanted to personally take up a paintbrush and make the shul look as good as new. But, like the rabbi, he understood that — in religious life as with everything else — the rule of "first things first" reigned supreme. And the first thing, as Pinchas Harris told them the moment they sat down together at his dining-room table, was to find a place to *daven* on Yom Kippur.

The Jewish Community Center was considered as an option, and then rejected. Given the dry, punishing heat, the distance to the JCC was simply too far to be walked with any comfort, especially by fasting people. Nate Goodman suggested his own house, but this was judged too small for the purpose.

"My basement is large. I live close to the shul," Pinchas Harris declared. "And I'm the rabbi. We'll have it at our place."

Penina, recruited to the task, looked first startled, then panicked — and then grimly resolute. Picking up a notebook and pen, she proceeded to make a comprehensive list of everything that needed to be done to turn her home into a temporary shul.

All morning long, a host of volunteers carried folding chairs and tables down into the spacious, Harris basement. A makeshift *bimah* was set in place in the designated men's section; on the other side of the *mechitzah* (a hastily strung pair of sheets on a clothesline) were rows of seats for the women. Bathrooms were allotted to each group, with a sign affixed to respective doors to avoid confusion. The *Sifrei Torah* were brought over and laid reverently in a corner until they were needed. The easy chairs and Ping-Pong table that usually resided in the basement were unceremoniously shoved out of sight in the laundry room. Penina had been planning on doing a load of laundry that morning; she abandoned the idea in deference to a higher cause.

Word of the arson was passed by phone among the shul's membership, which comprised the whole of tiny Lakewood's Orthodox community. There was an upwelling of outrage, which was then set aside for the moment. Right now, every ounce of emotional energy must be directed toward preparing for the fast-approaching holiday.

Tonight and tomorrow they would pour their hearts out in prayer; even more earnest, perhaps, than they would otherwise have been because of this unexpected and frightening development. There would be time enough to deal with the repercussions of the crime afterward.

In the cramped sheriff's office, however, it was business as usual.

Jack Ramsay was seated at his cluttered desk, facing Steve Birch, who had come at his summons. When he heard the location of the crime, Birch's face twisted in a strange dismay.

"What's the matter, Steve?" Ramsay asked, watching him closely. "You look upset."

Steve rallied his wits. "Naturally, I'm upset. Who wouldn't be? We don't want a rash of hate crimes in this town. And torching a synagogue is a particularly heinous form of it."

The sheriff tilted his wooden armchair precariously back on its hinges, until he seemed to be addressing the ceiling. "Steve, I hear that you've been hanging around that synagogue yourself, nights."

Birch waited until Ramsay had set down his chair with a thump and then met his gaze squarely. "I may have taken a walk in that direction now and then."

"Pretty late at night, from what I hear."

"You've got good sources, sheriff."

"I train my men to keep their eyes open." A pause. "Well? What's the story behind these midnight strolls of yours?"

Steve shrugged. "Insomnia?"

"Was that a question or an answer?"

Steve stood up and began pacing the cramped room in an agitation unusual for him. His calm, Indian inscrutability seemed to have abandoned him for the moment. "I can't explain it, Jack. When I can't sleep at night, something keeps driving me toward that synagogue. It's like I'm — I'm mesmerized or something."

Ramsay stared at him a moment longer, then relaxed. "Well, that's your business. Seen anyone interesting while you were out strolling?"

Steve was about to reply in the negative when he stopped.

"I did see someone, one night," he said slowly. "Bobby Smith. A Mescalero, from the reservation. He seems to have moved here. I met him outside the shul — 'taking a walk,' he said."

"Well, you can't fault him for that," the Sheriff said with heavy humor. "You were doing the same thing, weren't you?"

Steve ignored this. "He acted jumpy. I didn't like his loitering there. I remember that I even gave him a little speech about the synagogue being a place where decent people come to pray. He was very casual — lighthearted, even." Steve frowned. "Maybe a little *too* lighthearted ...""

"Care to talk to him? Or do you want to leave that pleasure to me?"

"I'd better see him first," Steve said. "He'll talk more readily to a fellow Native American."

Ramsay eyed him curiously. "Know the guy from the reservation?"

"Only vaguely. But he was friendly with my stepfather. We met in the hospital once, before Old Henry died."

"What's he like?"

"My stepfather? Not a very ...""

"Ha, ha. I mean your friend — Bobby."

"He's no friend of mine. What's he like? Your typical lowlife. Charming enough when he wants to be, but he'll stab you in the back — or the ribs — in a second if you get in his way."

"Nice character."

"Exactly. Which is why I want to have a little chat with him about the fire at the synagogue."

"Think he'll talk?"

Steve stood up. "I have a bit of a reputation in the community. The Indians know I'll work hard to defend them if it comes to that, so they generally cooperate with me when it's a question of collecting information."

Ramsay stood, too. "You won't let on that he's a suspect?"

"I think that would be counterproductive at the moment, don't you? Let's keep him nice and comfortable."

"And if you learn something to make you think he's the one behind the arson?"

A cloud fell over the Indian lawyer's face. "If that happens, I'm going to press him — hard. So hard that he'll wish he'd never thought of taking a walk down to the Jewish synagogue."

Ramsay nodded. "What about the kids we suspected were behind the hate message spray-painted on the synagogue wall half-a-year back?"

"I'll talk to them, too. Don't worry, I'm going to leave no stone un-turned within the Indian community. I want to get to the bottom of this as much as you do." He slanted a look at the sheriff. "Planning to do any questioning among non-Indians?"

Ramsay grinned. "Of course. But that's not your turf, is it?"

"Guess not. I'd appreciate if you'd keep me posted, though, Jack. No sense in duplicating our efforts."

"Will do."

Both men got to their feet. Ramsay shook Birch's hand and said, "Good luck, Steve. As always, I appreciate your help. Keep in touch."

"No problem." Steve's tone was affable, but the preoccupied look on his face told the sheriff that his thoughts had already taken him far from this cramped office. Jack Ramsay sat down to do some overdue paper-work. When he next looked up, Birch was gone.

III.

"Shana?" Nachman Bernstein called up the stairs.

His daughter's voice floated back down to him. "I'm up here."

He waited. Presently the door of her room opened and Shana poked her head out. "You wanted me, Ta?"

He nodded. "We're having a meeting about the shul at Rabbi Harris's house in a little while. I'm picking up Dr. Sadowsky, since both his own and his wife's cars happen to be in the shop. He mentioned on the phone just now that his wife would be happy to see you, if you'd care to hitch a ride."

Instantly, as though a switch had been pulled, Shana's face lit up. It had been a long Yom Kippur, and after a quick meal to break her fast

Shana had been planning to spend the evening in her room, moping. A visit with the fascinating librarian was a much brighter prospect.

"Sure, I'll come!"

"Fine. I'll be leaving in about 10 minutes. After the meeting, I'll pick you up when I drop the doctor off at his place, and we'll go home together." Shana disappeared into her room to get ready. Ten minutes later found her hovering impatiently by the front door, like a moth straining at the light. She was quiet in the car, and her father respected her silence enough not to intrude on it. As they neared the Sadowskys' home, however, he murmured, "You really like the librarian, don't you?" Shana nodded in the dark. "She's nice. And she knows things! She knows just about everything there is to know about this area — past and present. She's fun to talk to ... and she listens, too."

"No good advice about adjusting and getting to like Lakewood?"

Shana flushed. "No advice. Just interesting talk."

"And good listening."

"Yes. That, too."

"Sounds like a pretty lethal combination to me," Nachman said with a smile. Shana glanced at him, hesitated, then grinned sheepishly back. For some reason, she found it much easier to maintain her barrier of cool resentment with her mother than with her father. Nachman, less intent on making sure she was happy, had the ironic effect of making her feel relaxed enough to actually be open to the idea.

She was happy right now, or as happy as she was going to be in this one-horse town. She was happy because they had pulled up in front of the Sadowsky house and she was piling out of the car. She pictured the casual furniture in the living room, where she would soon be comfortably ensconced. Moving up the front path at a near-run, she felt like a little kid pulling the ribbons from a birthday package. Warmth waited inside, and interesting conversation, and a sense of fierce, shy independence. This — even more than her own room at home, right now — was *her* place.

Ben Sadowsky met her at the door on his way out.

"Good evening," he told Shana with grave courtesy. "My wife is waiting for you with bated breath. *And* homemade cookies." He waved to Nachman and started down the path to the curb.

He had left the door wide open. After a moment's hesitation, Shana stepped inside. She stood in the front hall, wondering if she ought to take the liberty of sitting down in the living room that stretched invitingly on her right, or wait here for her hostess.

Her dilemma was solved by the sound of brisk footsteps from the direction of the kitchen. The librarian emerged, bearing a tray of cookies and two mugs, the rising steam of which told Shana that hot chocolate was on the menu. The sense of joyous anticipation, that had been building up inside her all the way over, exploded in a crescendo of something that felt like a homecoming.

She smiled a shy "Hi" at her hostess and then, without waiting to be asked, entered the living room and sank into her favorite easy chair.

Sheriff Ramsay scanned the assembled group seated around the Harris dining-room table. This room seemed more fitting, Pinchas Harris had thought, than the casualness of the living room. They were here on serious business. Arson was about as serious as you could get.

In his jeans and checked shirt, Jack Ramsay looked a world away from the soberly dressed Orthodox men. Most were still in their holiday suits, though some had removed jackets and loosened ties. They were pale from the just-ended 25-hour fast, and the anxiety that had brought them here. The four *kollel* men sat grouped together at one end of the table, with Rabbi Harris and his two *gabbaim*, Nate Goodman and Abe Sadowsky, at the other end. Also present were Sammy Cohen and Dr. Abe Rein, board members and pillars of the community in general and the shul in particular.

"What's the good word, sheriff?" Pinchas prompted.

Ramsay's somber gaze rested on the rabbi. "Nothing very good so far, I'm afraid, rabbi. We've questioned several people in connection with the arson, but there are no new leads at the moment. Steve Birch, our liaison with the Native American community, has been busy tracking down various 'persons of interest,' both in the reservation and here in town. So far, no one's cracked."

"Are there any strong suspects?" Nachman Bernstein asked quietly from his end of the table.

The sheriff hesitated. "We're tending toward the Apache line of thinking."

"Never thought I'd hear those words outside the pages of a Western," Asher Gann murmured to Avi Feder, who grinned and shushed him.

"Any special reason?" Nachman asked mildly. The *kollel* head sounded concerned but not accusatory or demanding. Ramsay felt some of the tension go out of him. He'd been afraid that this would be a lynch-the-sheriff session, with the Jews at his throat for not protecting them well enough. He hadn't had a chance to become acquainted with Rabbi Bernstein since the Bernsteins had moved here in the summer, but he had heard good things about him. Meeting him now, he found himself addressing a man with a steady gaze and a disarming openness.

"Yes, actually, there is," Ramsay told him. To the table at large, he expanded, "About half-a-year ago, maybe a little longer, there was that other incident at the synagogue. The hate message ..." He trailed off questioningly.

Heads nodded, to indicate that the others were aware of the episode. The notable exceptions were Asher, Avi, and Efraim Mandel, who seemed to have been left out of the loop. Avi and Asher leaned forward with interest. Efraim frowned.

"What hate message?" he asked, a touch too loudly.

The sheriff blinked at the belligerent tone. "Someone spray-painted some nasty words on the wall of your synagogue. 'Jews go home,' something like that. Birch believed he had pinpointed the perpetrators, though without any hard proof: a couple of youths from the Mescalero reservation. He gave them a talking-to, put the fear of G-d into them, so to speak — and they haven't poked their heads above water since. Least as far as we know."

"There have been other incidents ..." Pinchas Harris ventured.

Jack Ramsay nodded. Patiently, he rejoined, "Yes, but no proof that they were anti-Semitic in nature."

"But the victims were Jewish," Sammy Cohen insisted. "The grocery, the smashed windshield ..." Cohen had graying hair and an iron eye that tolerated no nonsense. It was not in his nature to tiptoe around an issue.

"That's correct," Ramsay agreed. "Still, there's no proof."

"Proof, shmoof." Nate Goodman, the lawyer, was in no mood for tiptoeing either. "We all know what's going on here. The question is: What're we going to do about it?"

The sheriff spent the next half-hour telling the worried Jews what he was planning to do about it. "Namely, nothing," Nate pronounced in ill-concealed disgust, when he was finished.

Ramsay flushed. "Now, that's not fair. The investigation is ongoing. However, since there was no danger to human life and minimal damage to the building, you'll understand that we have to deploy our forces as we see fit."

"Of course," Nate said dryly. "We understand fully." He turned to address his fellow coreligionists. "Guess we'll have to take matters into our own hands, guys."

The sheriff lifted a warning hand. "We'll have no vigilante groups operating in *this* town."

"Wouldn't dream of it," Nate said. There was something in his tone that made Rabbi Harris chime in hastily, "Of course not, sheriff. But you'd have no objection to our being — er — proactive in our own de-fense?"

Ramsay found his feet. "Any help to law-enforcement agencies from members of the Lakewood community is always welcome. Just make sure you know your bounds."

Rabbi Harris stood up, too. Shaking the sheriff's hand, he thanked him for coming and began walking him to the door.

"Excuse me."

Turning, Ramsay saw Rabbi Bernstein at his back.

"I was wondering — all in the line of helping ourselves and our law-enforcement agencies, you know — if I could meet this liaison man of yours."

"Birch?" Ramsay lifted an eyebrow.

"Yes, that's the one. Perhaps he would agree to meet with us, or with me personally if he doesn't relish a mob scene." Nachman smiled at Rabbi Harris to rob his words of offense. "That is, if you don't mind, Pinchas?"

Nachman, it was clear, had decided to take at least some of the reins of this investigation into his own hands. Pinchas, the man of vision, stepped gratefully back to leave the stage to the far more capable man-of-action.

"Certainly, certainly, Nachman. By all means!" Both men turned to look at Ramsay.

The sheriff nodded slowly. "I'll pass the word to Birch. I imagine he'll be willing to meet with you. He may not be of any help, though."

"That's all right. I'd just like to get to know all the actors in this little drama."

Ramsay shook Bernstein's hand at the door, nodded again at Rabbi Harris, and left. Nachman had a glimpse of a clear, black, star-sprinkled sky as he closed the door behind the sheriff. So much beauty there; such a large, expansive peace. Why did hateful people have to come along and harm other people's places of worship? Didn't we all live under the same sky?

He shook off the momentarily bleakness. "Well, time to get my daughter home. Tomorrow's a school day."

"Oh? Where is she tonight?"

"At the Sadowskys, visiting with his wife. I'm serving as Ben's limo service at the moment."

He collected Dr. Ben, who was standing in a knot with the other local men as they discussed the state of the shul, the criminal investigation, and their future as a community. Gently but firmly, Nachman pried the pediatrician away from the others and led him out to the car.

He was once again overwhelmed by the immensity of the night sky, and its distance from human concerns large and small. This was no petty incident that concerned them tonight. Someone had set fire to the town's only synagogue. That sent a very harsh and frightening message to the community, one that could not be ignored or glossed over.

But the stars shone on, serene and remote, spots of light in a sky that hung over the town like a canopy. Nachman threw a quick, silent prayer in its direction, begging the One Who had spread that canopy over His world to keep a close eye on the tiny band of the faithful in Lakewood, New Mexico.

IV.

"**I** found something interesting," Mrs. Sadowsky told Shana over their cocoa and cookies. "Did I tell you I've been doing some research into the Jewish historical presence here in the Southwest?"

"I think so." Shana looked up, her fingers curled around the mug's warmth. "*Were* there any Jews here? It seems so unlikely."

"Unlikely, yes. On the other hand, where have we Jews *not* been? That's the stark meaning of the word '*galus.*' Exile has a painful way of sending you places you'd never have dreamed of visiting ..." She grimaced.

Shana grinned at her expression. "Even this hole-in-the-wall town."

Mrs. Sadowsky smiled at her, saying without words that she knew how Shana felt: as though she had been sent into a personal exile of her own. Her smile also said that she would not try to talk her out of the feeling. This was exactly the kind of attitude that made Shana so grateful to her, and so comfortable in her company. It was the thing that kept her coming back time and again.

"Oh, Lakewood's not so bad — now," Mrs. Sadowsky said. "It was a different story in the old days, though. Plenty of hardship and deprivation for the old-time settlers in these parts." She paused a beat. "Danger, too."

"Indian attacks, you mean?"

"Among other things. Poverty, illness ... But mostly — yes. That *is* what I mean."

Shana leaned forward. "You said you found something."

The librarian held up a finger and struggled out of the chair in which she was so comfortably sunk. On her feet at last, she hurried out of the room; presumably to fetch something from the cluttered, intriguing room she called the "den." Shana had seen the room briefly when she first made Mrs. Sadowsky's acquaintance and been given a tour of the house. The room had held an instant attraction for her, except for the fact that the place was so overflowing with books and papers that there was no room for the kind of cushiony chairs so conducive to comfortable conversation. That, Shana supposed, was why they spent their time in the living room instead. She sipped her cocoa, waiting. Mrs. Sadowsky was back a moment later, holding a slim volume in one hand and her mug — which she was still holding — in the other.

"What's that?" Shana asked.

"A diary. Did you know that pioneer women often kept diaries? Especially out here in the wilds of the West, where the nearest neighbor might be 60 miles away." Mrs. Sadowsky collapsed back into her armchair, peering at Shana. "You look surprised."

"I — I didn't think ..."

"You didn't think they were literate? Some, I'm sure, were not. But a surprising number of pioneer women came from the East, where they'd had good educations. They came out here to be married, usually, and spent the rest of their lives very far away from the kind of places they'd known when they were young. Many of them probably never saw a big city again."

"So, they kept diaries?"

"Some of them did. There's a whole new genre of literature for you, if you're interested, Shana. Journals, diaries: personal accounts written by individuals, mostly women, that provide a really fascinating glimpse into what their day-to-day lives were like."

Absently, Shana reached for another cookie as she thought about this. She imagined herself in a checked, gingham apron (what *was* gingham, anyway?), wearily setting aside her broom at the end of her workday and, with a spurt of eagerness, picking up a dog-eared notebook and a little stub of a pencil. As the wind howled about her windows (a husband was absent in these scenarios, presumably out doing the chores or hunting their supper), she sat at a homemade wooden table and arduously scrawled down the events of her day.

She looked up at the librarian. "What events? I mean — what did they find to write about?"

Mrs. Sadowsky laughed. "You think their lives were boring, do you? Well, I'd suggest you read one or two of the diaries before you judge. Droughts, tornadoes, Indian rampages, horse-thieves — what *didn't* they have to cope with in those days?"

"I wouldn't mind reading it," Shana admitted, tilting up her cup to get at the dregs of her cocoa.

"Want some more?" At the girl's negative headshake, Mrs. Sadowsky rushed eagerly on. "Well, I was looking through some old diaries from this part of the country, and I found a reference to Jews!"

"Really? What kind of reference?"

Mrs. Sadowsky opened the slim volume. "This was written by a woman named Jane Willard. She was 27 years old and the mother of three. She was one of those who'd been educated in the East, married, and come out West with her husband at the height of the California Gold Rush. Like so many others before them, they realized that the lure of gold was far stronger than their ability to find it. Wisely, the couple decided to pull out before they became completely broke. Her husband, Joshua, had heard about opportunities in the Southwest, and moved his family here to Lakewood, then a tiny outpost near the Pecos River."

Shana hugged her knees. "What was it like? What does she say?"

"Listen. I'll read it to you."

There was a very good reason that the librarian had, for the past decade or so, run a very popular story hour for children. She opened the diary to the page she wanted and pitched her voice thrillingly low, yet able to carry clearly to her audience of one. Gently Shana set down her mug, ignoring the lure of the cookie plate as Mrs. Sadowsky began to read.

"June 23, 1849. Joshua chopped the wood today; sky looks like rain before too long. I've put up my sourdough and the butter's done. The beans are soaking on the stove, so I'll write now, before the baby wakes.

"Fear is in the air — the Apaches are on the move. Nights disturbed by war cries. Rumors of an attack, the kind they had at Brownsville, where only a handful survived. Joshua's prepared the cellar with candles and provisions in case we have to hide. He's camouflaged the trapdoor so that you can't tell there's a cellar there at all. Everyone's staying close to home today ...

"Some strangers came to town yesterday — two women, wearing kerchiefs. One of them spoke a little English. They knocked at my door, asking for a bite of food. Wouldn't touch my stew but accepted some dried apples, turnips and a day-old loaf. Looked haggard and worn; said they'd been on the road since early spring. Before that, they came in a big boat all the way from Europe — Poland, I think they said. They were on their way to California. The woman who was doing the talking saw my Petey, and said that she had two children, a boy and a girl, just a little bit older than Petey.

"I told her not to bother about the gold, that very few struck it rich and too many died in the attempt. She looked sad, and said that death comes in many shapes ... then shivered as though she didn't know why she'd said that. She tried to laugh it off, saying in her broken English, 'We Jews are good friends with the Angel of Death. That's why we talk about him so much.' Then she changed the subject, admiring my curtains and asking about the tatted lace at the fringes. She spotted my diary sitting on the table, and lit up — seems she used to keep one, too, back in the old country.

"We talked about the Apaches, and I offered to let her stay in our cellar with her husband and youngsters if an attack is heading our way, the way people are rumoring. It would be cramped, but I knew Joshua would agree with me that we ought to save whoever we could. But she said no, she would stay with her own people and share their fate. Such a wild, dark look in her eyes as she said that, as if she'd been to the edge of despair and back again ...

"I said good-bye with a heavy heart. 'You be careful, now,' I said. I don't know why, but I liked the look of her. I hope they find a place to be safe if the Indians do come ..."

Mrs. Sadowsky turned a page and looked somberly up at Shana. The homey sofa and armchairs had faded away, replaced by a wooden homestead, a butter churn that had seen much use, and "beans soaking on the stove." Outside, the evening stillness was ripped open by war cries, issuing from the throats of invisible, painted Indians. The cries, and what they forebode, shredded the peace as though with a knife. Shana hugged her knees more tightly, willing Mrs. Sadowsky to go on.

Gravely, Mrs. Sadowsky did so.

"This is dated the next day. It isn't pretty, Shana."

"Go on. Please!"

"The Apaches came yesterday, just as Joshua and I feared. We spent hours in the cellar, huddled up like sheep in a pen with the slaughter knife hanging right above our heads ... The baby wouldn't stop crying. I must have fed him two bushels of dried apples before he would settle down ... Johnny and Katie were quiet. Scared. Even deep down in the cellar, we could hear the screaming — harsh and brutal, like wild animals on a ram-

page. There were other screams, too. I could hardly bear to listen. Joshua didn't say much. I cried a little, and waited.

"Finally, things got quiet. When the quiet had gone on for long enough, Joshua went up to the trapdoor first, then called down that it was safe for the rest of us to come. He wouldn't let me go out into the town. He went, along with some of the other menfolk. When he got home later, he wouldn't tell me what he'd seen there — but there was a smear of blood on his hand where he'd missed it washing up. All he would say was, 'Most of the locals had their hideyholes and were safe. But not all ... And then, there were those strangers in town. We dug a heap of graves, Jane. The coyotes won't get them, anyway ...'

"Later, after I'd finished crying, I asked Joshua if they'd buried any children. He said no. I wondered where that Jewish woman and her family had gone. Could they have escaped? It didn't seem likely — but then, where are the children? My mind went round and round the question, like buzzards circling a corpse, until my head ached and I couldn't think anymore. I cried again that night, in my pillow, until little Katie woke up and tiptoed up to me and asked in a hushed, trembly voice why I was making those funny noises. So I stopped. I held Katie until she fell back asleep, and then fell asleep myself, to dream of that nice, sad-eyed woman, who wouldn't stay here and be safe because she wouldn't leave her people ..."

Mrs. Sadowsky closed the book softly and looked up. Tears stood in Shana's eyes, glistening like small, bright beads in the low lamplight.

"Those poor people ... Jews, just like us. Why didn't they go inside, where they'd be safe?"

"Maybe there was no place to hide that was really safe, Shana. The Apaches invaded homes, too. It was Joshua and Jane's good fortune that they had a deep cellar with, presumably, a door that was well hidden so no one would suspect the cellar was there. I'm sure that many others were killed along with the Jewish 'strangers.' But it was only the travelers who had no family to bury them." She sighed. "I wish I knew more about them. Who were they? They were heading out to California, the diary says. What led a group of immigrants — right off the boat, apparently — to start such a long and dangerous journey out West?"

"Gold," Shana said simply.

The librarian considered this. Finally, she said, "Maybe. But maybe there was more to it than that. Maybe those poor immigrants were searching for the better life they'd been longing for, and that they'd traveled across the world to find. Every step they took down that dusty, westward road brought them a little farther away from the pogroms of their hometowns ..."

"*And* there was the gold," Shana reminded her.

Mrs. Sadowsky smiled sadly. "Yes. There was certainly the gold. People have done stranger things for the security that gold can bring."

A small silence filled the living room. Shana shifted in her armchair, finding another position to ease her cramped legs. In a faraway voice, she said, "I wonder what that Jewish woman's name was. Jane Willard said that she was wearing a kerchief, so maybe they were religious. Poor things — to be buried in a strange town, so far away from everything and everyone they had ever known. Right in the middle of nowhere." She made a face, instantly spanning the years to the present. "Which is exactly where I am, right now!"

"Do you still hate it so much?" Mrs. Sadowsky asked gently.

"I don't hate Lakewood. It's the change I hate. Being uprooted. I miss my friends. I miss the *way* we were friends. Everything's different out here."

"Aren't the girls in your class friendly?"

"They're fine. I'm just not very interested in them right now, that's all." The sullen mask had fallen over Shana's features again.

"Are they interested in you?"

Grudgingly, Shana confessed that several of the girls had invited her to their homes. "Sometimes, I go. But mostly I say no. I say that I'm busy. And I am!" She glanced up at Mrs. Sadowsky, eyes brimming with shamefaced laughter. "Busy hating the fact that I have to be here at all!"

"That'll pass," Mrs. Sadowsky said in her brisk way.

"That's what my parents say. But how do you, or anyone, *know* it'll pass? Maybe I'll hate it here forever."

"There must be a reason Hashem brought you here, Shana. Have you ever thought of that?"

Shana was silent.

"Shana?"

"It all seems so random!" Shana burst out, her whole face burning with passion. It was clear that this was something she'd been brooding over for a long time. "One day I'm in Brooklyn, New York — and the next day, in Lakewood, New Mexico. It seems to make no difference *where* I am! I'm — I'm like a leaf blown in the wind. I could land anywhere. Who would care? What difference would it make?"

The echo of her questions hung in the air, which seemed to vibrate with the pain they held.

"But our lives are not random," Mrs. Sadowsky told her quietly. "Hashem guides them. You know that as well as I do, Shana. It was His Hand that guided you here. To me, the very fact that you've ended up in such an unlikely place proves that."

"But — *why*? I was doing fine just where I was!"

"Maybe you'll do even better here."

"Huh." The syllable held so much skepticism that Mrs. Sadowsky winced. "Not likely."

Before she could return an answer, the light tap of a horn came to their ears. At almost the same moment the front door opened and Ben Sadowsky — Dr. Ben — walked in. "Your father's waiting outside in the car, Shana," he called.

Shana got up, thanked Mrs. Sadowsky in a wooden voice, dashed a stray tear from her eye, and went out to her father.

Inside the house, the phone rang. Mrs. Sadowsky took one last glance out the window at Shana's retreating form, sighed, and then went into the kitchen to answer it.

A moment later, she called her husband's name. "Ben, it's for you!" Dr. Ben lifted himself from the armchair in which he'd just settled himself. In an undertone, hand held over the receiver's mouthpiece, she added, "It's Mrs. Mandel. About little Layala."

She was surprised, when her husband took the phone from her, to catch an expression of very un-Ben-like dismay on his face.

V.

"**D**octor? This is Etty Mandel. I hope I'm not disturbing you ..."

Dr. Ben refrained from the obvious reply, that calling a pediatrician up at home in the late evening might be dubbed a "disturbance" by any standard. He merely said, in his mild, patient way, "Not at all. What can I do for you?"

"Have you set up the ultrasound test for my baby, doctor?"

"Mrs. Mandel, I wasn't in the office today, remember? It was Yom Kippur. I'm planning on seeing to it first thing in the morning. How is Layala? Does she seem any different?"

"Not really. The vomiting's still going on, and she seems as uncomfortable as ever. I just want to find out what it is, for sure — so we can deal with it and get it over with!" The words burst out of the distraught mother with all the force of something suppressed for interminable hours.

Dr. Ben closed his eyes. "I'm so sorry. You were my last appointment, day before yesterday, and it was too late to make the call then. I meant to arrange for the sonogram first thing next morning — *erev* Yom Kippur — but things became so hectic. The day just before a Yom Tov usually is, though the day *after* is even worse, with parents bringing their children in for every kind of ailment you can imagine — and some of them *are* more or less imagined, I'm sorry to say! — that they didn't have time to take care of earlier." In his guilt, the doctor, usually a man of few words, found himself babbling. "It was nonstop patients all morning, with an emergency appendicitis case thrown in for good measure, and my receptionist was out sick, so things got really bogged down. And then it was time to go home and get ready for Yom Kippur. Sometimes I go into the office on a *Motza'ei Yom Tov*, just to catch up on paperwork, but tonight we had the meeting about the arson at the shul. I saw your husband there."

"Yes, yes," she said impatiently. Even an inferno paled beside her concerns for her baby.

"In any case, I can't arrange anything till the morning. I'll do it first thing, *bli neder*."

"Please. I'm going crazy, not knowing what's what."

"I can understand that," Dr. Ben said sincerely. Inwardly, he cursed his own forgetfulness. He'd had a lot on his mind yesterday, but she'd had a crying baby on *her* mind for weeks now.

Dr. Ben wasn't a particularly imaginative man, but as he sat at his ease in his comfortable living room, he couldn't help seeing Mrs. Mandel in his mind's eye, fretting along with her baby as she wondered what sort of medical mystery might be taking place inside the tiny creature she had brought into the world.

Please G-d, first thing in the morning he would take care of it.

Avi Feder followed Asher home from the meeting with Sheriff Ramsay. Rivi was preparing a second break-fast meal for the three of them — the first had been hardly more than cake and coffee — both to assuage hungry appetites and to allow the Ganns to say good-bye to Avi. Their widowed friend was booked on an afternoon flight to New York, where he would be spending Succos with his family.

"Ah," Avi groaned. He twisted in his chair and stretched out his long legs so that they reached nearly to the center of the kitchen. "Now, *that* was a meal! I can hardly move."

"So don't," Asher said drowsily. He had likewise consumed a very hearty meal and that, taken on top of the long fast, had put him in a mood for sleep. "*I* don't intend to."

"Not even to help clear up?" Rivi said with a pout, though her gray eyes twinkled. "Don't tell me you're planning to leave it all for me to do! And don't tell me to leave it for the morning, either. I wouldn't sleep a wink knowing that this whole mess was waiting for me."

"You are to sit there like a queen," Asher commanded, abruptly wide awake. "Avi and I will do the clearing away *and* the washing up." He yawned elaborately. "Just as soon as we can move."

A contented silence descended on the small kitchen. The curtains were drawn against the night and the flower-shaped fixture suspended from the ceiling shed its golden light over the table and the remains of the feast. Dishes, placemats and even the various ceramic ornaments adorning the counters were artistically matched in coordinated colors. Rivi had created an oasis of peace and beauty out of that most mundane of rooms: an ordinary kitchen. Admiring the decor, Avi thought it no wonder that neither he nor Asher felt like budging. Why bother stirring from your place when that place is so perfect?

Except — here the sadness fell again, not softly, but hard and clanging as prison bars — because the perfection, the beauty and the serenity were not his own. They belonged to Asher and Rivi, together. In a little while, he would go home to his empty apartment and face his empty existence. Unwittingly, he let out a sigh.

"Thinking about how much you're gonna miss us?" Asher kidded. His friend's ongoing sadness hurt him so much that he couldn't stand to bear witness to it. At every glimpse, he would try to josh the sadness away. Usually, he succeeded. He succeeded because Avi had no desire to inflict his own pain on anyone else, least of all on his very best friend in the world.

"Sure," Avi said lightly, matching his tone to Asher's. "Even my mother's cooking doesn't hold a candle to your wife's."

Rivi glowed. Asher beamed. Avi said, "Besides, after the wide-open spaces we have out here, I'm going to find it hard to get used to New York again. Just thinking about it makes me feel as if I'm crowded into a sardine can with a billion other sardines."

"Oh, come on. It's not that bad," Rivi smiled.

"No," Avi admitted. "But I think I really will miss Lakewood, New Mexico. This place has become home, in a way."

"Will you be dating in New York?" Asher asked in his direct way. Rivi flashed him a look. She had been dying to know the answer to that very question, but would have sunk into the earth rather than tackle Avi so bluntly.

"My mother's lined up no less than three prospects," Avi said, tilting back his chair and closing his eyes. "A social whirlwind, that's me."

"You don't sound very happy about it," Asher remarked almost accusingly.

"Why should he be?" Rivi jumped to his defense. "It's not as if dating is fun. Meeting a total stranger, having to make small talk even when you sense off the bat that this one is not for you ..." She let the words trail off with a shudder. Then she came to herself with a guilty start. This was no sort of talk for Avi Feder to be hearing right now. "You said you'll be going out with three women? Isn't that a little — counterproductive?"

With eyes still closed, Avi shrugged. "Safety in numbers."

"So that's what this whole trip is about? *Safety?*"

He opened his eyes. "My mother was nagging me to death about starting to date again. She said she had a whole lineup of girls waiting to meet me. Finally, I couldn't fight her any more. So, I said yes."

"To three women."

"Why not? If one doesn't pan out, there's always the other two."

Asher studied his friend thoughtfully. "You have no intention of getting serious about any of them, do you?"

Avi didn't answer.

"Think about it," Rivi said earnestly. "Don't you *want* to meet someone and — and have the possibility of happiness again?"

Still he didn't answer. What could he say? That he wanted someone in his life the way a freezing person wants warmth ... That the silence in his little apartment oppressed him almost to the point of insanity? That he sometimes played the violin for hours at a time, just to hear a different voice than his own in that silence? That he longed with all his being to walk into his apartment and sense a loving presence waiting for him, the way a starving man longs to sniff his dinner cooking on a stove behind the kitchen door? That this was the most all-important and all-consuming dream of his life? And that he was absolutely terrified of going after it?

Again, it was Asher who said it out loud. "He's scared. Aren't you, Avi?"

And because the words had been spoken, they suddenly seemed less shameful. "Sure. Wouldn't you be?"

A shadow crossed Asher's face. "I wish I could take your place, kid. I'd pluck a girl-in-a-million out of the air for you, and see you happy again."

Avi felt a lump rise to his throat at this uncharacteristically emotional speech. "Thanks, Asher. Just let me find the right someone, so I can be happy."

"You'll have to find her yourself," Rivi said softly. "Don't be afraid. Just *daven* hard — and go for it. She's waiting for you. I know it." She paused, then added delicately, "But maybe you should tell your mother to focus on just one woman at a time?"

The mere thought of knocking on a strange door to meet a stranger who was not his Yocheved made Avi cringe with a wild, bashful terror. He shook his head, looking for the moment more like a scared schoolboy than a grown man with tragedy behind him, about to embark on the quest for a partner for the second time in his life.

"You know what they say," he murmured, closing his eyes again to stave off any further argument. "Safety in numbers."

VI.

Nachman Bernstein heard the front doorbell chime, but paid no attention. His mind was fully occupied with arson. Not the arson that had been perpetrated on the shul, but a second crime: more recent and, for the *kollel* which he headed, even more ominous.

The surveyors had been hard at work at the site of the planned *mesivta-kollel* building. They had set up temporary quarters — ordinary camping tents, mostly — to accommodate them during their brief stay. Just yesterday, Nachman had received a report from the head surveyor, saying that they were nearly through and would have their figures ready in another day or two.

The men on the site had spent a peaceful night and then embarked on a final morning's work — "tying up the loose ends," as the chief surveyor laconically expressed it. It was then, while they were away from camp, that someone methodically torched three of the four tents.

It was the smoke that brought the surveyors back, curious at first, then alarmed — and then enraged. Though they managed to put out the flames on their own, three of the tents and most of their supplies were all but decimated by the flames.

"Again!" Nachman had exclaimed when he heard the news, his dismay vividly tinged by fear. The *kollel* seemed to be cursed! First the shul, site of their temporary classes, had been the victim of an attack that was, according to the local grapevine, unprecedented in the community. And now, this. Was the "curse" nothing more than ordinary, garden-variety anti-Semitism, as dismally familiar as it was virulent?

More phone calls had quickly followed: to the sheriff, to Rabbi Harris, to his fellow *kollel* members. Nachman had just completed his round of calls and collected various reactions — from a tight-lipped, "We'll get on it right away," from Ramsay, to Asher Gann's almost flippant, "Looks like someone around here doesn't like us very much" — when the doorbell rang. A moment later, Tova poked her head through the study door to inform her husband, rather round eyed, "There's an Indian here to see you. Steve Birch, he says his name is."

"Oh?" With an effort, Nachman pulled himself together. "Oh, that's right, we're due to meet tonight. It slipped my mind completely. Though, actually, the timing couldn't be better." There was a grim expression about his mouth as he spoke. "Please show him in here."

Steve Birch followed Tova down the hall to her husband's study, admiring the comfortable decor and studiously ignoring the frankly curious stares of the younger Bernstein children. At the study door, Tova left him with a courteous, "I'll bring some coffee. Or would you prefer tea?"

"Coffee's fine, thanks. I take mine black."

Tova scurried off to the kitchen. As he prepared to meet Rabbi Bernstein, Steve was suddenly, unaccountably, nervous. He entered the study with a sense of stepping into a different world — more, a different medium, in which he was not certain he would be able to breathe. Then Nachman lifted his head to smile a greeting, and the tightness in Steve's chest began imperceptibly to ease. The two men eyed each other.

Nachman's first impression was a startled one. For the first time in his life, he was face-to-face with a genuine Native American, the features and figure conforming with cowboys-and-Indian images from his own youth. He saw the archetypical coloring — the hair coarse and dark, though the man's complexion was considerably lighter than the deep red-brown he would have expected — broad shoulders, prominent cheekbones and a rock-steady gaze. At the same time, there was a jolt of familiarity as he met the stranger's gaze, as though he were recognizing an old friend. Looking more closely, he noted something about Birch's eyes that seemed out of place. They were a curious color, not the unfathomable black of the Native American at all.

Steve, in the meantime, was studying Nachman Bernstein with equal intensity. Apart from a few distant glimpses and the casual encounter at the gas pump, this was his first close-up encounter with a real Jew. An observant Jew, judging by what the sheriff had told him and his own eyes endorsed. He saw a full brown beard, features that were pleasantly symmetrical if not strikingly handsome, and eyes that, behind wire-rim frames, held an innate warmth and a reservoir of hard-won wisdom. They were good eyes, eyes that you wanted to have gaze at you with approval. For some reason, it was suddenly very important to Steve that Rabbi Bernstein approve of him.

"Come in," Nachman said, collecting himself after a few seconds that seemed, to both of them, to have lasted a century. There was a sense of something vital having shifted in those seconds, like the subtle realignment of snow on a mountain slope, invisible now, but hinting at a possibly cataclysmic avalanche to come. "Please, have a seat." He indicated an armchair facing his desk.

Steve sat. In an effort to stop staring at his host, he let his eyes sweep the room. They rested on the bookcases that lined three of the four walls, one each to the right and left of where he sat, and two narrower ones flanking the window that stood directly behind Nachman's head. The shelves were filled with volumes, leather bound for the most part, of which — and this surprised him — the vast majority appeared well used. Clearly, this was no showcase study, but a room that saw a lot of living. He eyed Nachman again, speculatively. He didn't *look* the academic type, but if he were not the reader of these books, then who was?

"Thank you for coming to see me," Nachman said, reaching out belatedly to shake his visitor's hand. Steve's grasp was cool and quick. "Perhaps it was a 'chutzpah' for me to ask that you meet me here. It's just that I've been extremely busy, what with the *kollel* start-up and being smack in the middle of our holiday season."

"Yom Kippur," Birch pronounced carefully. "I know."

With a smile, Nachman nodded. "And Succos is just around the corner." The smile vanished. "It's supposed to be a time of joyous celebration, but it's going to be a little hard to feel very joyous with all this going on."

"The arson at the synagogue, you mean?"

"That — and the most recent attack."

Steve sat up straight. "What attack?"

"I suppose you haven't had time to hear. It only just happened — about an hour ago, from what I've been told." Quickly, Nachman filled him in on the morning's events at the surveyors' camp.

"This is intolerable," Steve said, a flash of anger lighting the curiously colored eyes. "One act of arson is a nasty prank. Two makes it a campaign. A criminal campaign."

Nachman studied him. "Do you think there's more to come?"

"Someone," Steve said, in unconscious mimicry of Asher Gann earlier, "doesn't seem to like you people very much."

"That seems obvious. But — why? Is this simple, generalized anti-Semitism, or something more pointed?"

Steve pondered the question before offering an answer. "It's a little too much of a coincidence, I think, having these crimes take place shortly after a new infusion of religious Jews into the community — Jews who have bought a large tract of land right outside of town and are planning an ambitious construction project. Some person, or persons, may not like that."

"Again — why? Were there competing bids for the land? Or do they object to our building on principle ... bringing us back to our garden-variety anti-Semitism?"

"I'm not sure. But I don't like the look of things, Rabbi Bernstein. There's something evil about all of this. If the reasons are practical ones, then the perpetrator or perpetrators are choosing to achieve their goals through violence instead of legitimate, free-market manipulation. And if it's the other ... Well, purposeless hatred is always ugly."

"I couldn't agree more."

A brief silence fell, during which Nachman sadly pondered the age-old tendency of hatred to rear its ugly head even in the most civilized of countries. Steve was thinking about a different kind of prejudice, a much more personal one, directed at a young boy who just didn't fit in. Maybe he and this bearded rabbi had more in common than might seem likely at first glance ...

He shrugged off both the memories and the speculation. He had a job to do.

"I've been sniffing around in the Native American community, both here in Lakewood and over on the Mescalero reservation. So far, everyone I've spoken to denies having had anything to do with the fire at the synagogue. I'll start over again now, with this second crime to add a touch of gunpowder to my questions."

"Do you have any strong suspects?"

He thought of Al Barker, then of Bobby Smith. "One or two. As I say, so far nothing has panned out. Unfortunately, through either good luck or good management, the perpetrator left no clues at the synagogue."

"No fingerprints?"

"Nothing. But wearing gloves will do that." Steve prepared to take his leave. "I'll be in touch with the sheriff, rabbi, but please keep me updated on any developments at the site. Maybe we'll have better luck there."

"I'll certainly do that," Nachman said warmly. "In the meantime, I guess all we can do is pray." He picked up a small *siddur* that lay on his desk. "My trusty companion ..."

It was a casual remark, lightly made, with no intended overtones of any significance. Steve Birch's reaction was anything but what he would have expected.

Steve stared at the *siddur* in Nachman's hand, the face beneath the deep tan turning pale. "What — what is that?"

"A prayer book. In Hebrew, a *siddur*."

"May I?"

Wondering, Nachman handed it over. Steve took it gingerly, as though it were red hot or possibly capable of biting his hand. Slowly he turned it over, and then over again so that the gilt letters faced him. On the cover a Star of David leaped to his eye, mesmerizing him the way the same symbol on the synagogue wall had done on so many sleepless nights.

"Is anything the matter?" Nachman's voice seemed to be coming from a great distance.

"N-nothing." Steve forced his eyes away from the *siddur*, and met Nachman's curious glance. An overpowering impulse came over him, to divulge his history to this man with the warm, wise eyes — to pour his life into this rabbi's lap, so to speak, and see what he might make of it ...

Decades of reticence came to his aid. With a cool smile, he shook his head and handed back the *siddur*. He felt an odd regret as he saw it pass back over the desk, as though he were standing on shore, bidding a forlorn farewell to a ship bound for open seas. Resisting the urge to snatch the *siddur* back, he rose to his feet and extended his hand.

"Thanks again for coming," Nachman said, shaking it. "You know, I had intended to urge you to do your best to solve these crimes — to reiterate the urgency we feel, and our need to know we're safe to go about our peaceful, legitimate business. For some reason, I don't believe I have to do that."

"No. Quite apart from your own urgency, I feel a good deal of pressure of my own. I've been working with the Mescaleros all of my adult life, often to the detriment of my private law practice. It hurts to see one or more of them crossing the line in such a blatant way. Such a hateful way. I want to stamp it out as much as you do."

"We're agreed then," Nachman smiled. He walked his guest to the door. "I'm sure we'll meet again sometime."

"Yes." From his mother, the gentle, gentle-eyed Alice, Steve Birch had inherited a kind of "second sight" — a little-understood trait that had set both of them apart from the others in the tribe, and which, he suspected, had given rise to his recent spate of strangely troubling dreams. As a boy, this extra sense had helped him out of sticky spots on more than one occasion. It told him now, with a certainty he had learned not to question, that he would be seeing more of Nachman Bernstein in the future. Even more — that they were fated to know each other well. How or why this would come about, he hadn't a clue. But his intuition never lied.

He said good-bye in an almost mechanical manner as both Rabbi and Mrs. Bernstein saw him out of the house. The trip back to his own apartment was made in the same automaton-like fashion. It wasn't until he walked through his own front door that he was abruptly galvanized into purposeful, almost frenzied action. Dragging a chair over to his bedroom closet, he climbed it and reached as far back as his hands would go, until his fingers touched a small package at the very back of the highest shelf.

This he took down. Climbing carefully down from the chair, he carried the package over to his desk, where he laid it down. For a moment he stood staring at it, almost afraid to untie the string that held it together.

Finally, with a shrug, he reached out and tugged at one end of the string. The knot fell apart. He pulled open the paper, to reveal a single item.

The *siddur* could have been a twin to the one that Nachman Bernstein had handed him in his study just now, except that this one was smaller and the gilt letters were nearly rubbed away. The thin pages were yellowed with age and emitted a musty smell. On the worn leather cover was another Star of David, eroded to a pale replica of its original brightness by the frequent touch of loving, long-ago hands.

Steve Birch sat at his desk, gazing down at the *siddur* with unseeing eyes. His mind soared to unknowable realms as he communed with the small book, occasionally touching it with hesitant, butterfly fingers. Hours winged past, unnoticed. Outside, the world plodded on, but it was a world that he neither sensed nor cared about.

It was with an almost physical pain that he finally wrenched himself back to the present, and to the reality that held him as fast as any prisoner.

Part Three:
Inferno Of Fear

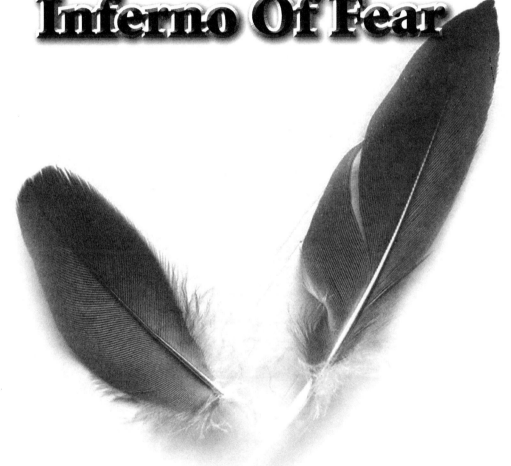

Chapter 10

I.

Reactions to the second arson were varied.

The Lakewood Examiner speculated at length as to the perpetrator's identity, postulating everything from juvenile high jinks to virulent anti-Semitism. Letters to the editor included some messages of sympathy and a few veiled grumbles about "outsiders" coming in and buying up property for "foreign institutions."

At the *kollel*, an atmosphere of gloom and apprehension clouded what had begun with such sunny hopes. Asher Gann and Efraim Mandel were jumpy and anxious. Avi Feder, when Asher called him in New York with the news, sounded remote. "I'm sure it's all going to work out all right in the end," he murmured.

"It's not the end I'm worried about," Asher said. "It's the present, which includes someone who clearly doesn't want us around."

"You guys have my sympathy," Avi said absently. He paused. "I'm meeting my first *shidduch* prospect tonight. *Erev* Succos — shouldn't I be doing better things?"

"What could be better than looking for someone to share your life?"

"Anything … Asher, how am I going to get through this? I hardly slept a wink last night, and I'll be babbling like a drunken fool by this evening."

"You'll be fine. But, if it helps … you have my sympathy."

"Ouch. I guess I deserved that."

"Seriously, Avi, take it easy. Just go with the flow. If this doesn't work out —"

"There's always Prospect 2 or 3. Safety in numbers. I know." Avi did not sound very happy at the thought. "Why did I let myself in for this? As if meeting one person wasn't enough, I had to go and commit to three! Am I crazy?"

"I'll assume that's a rhetorical question, buddy. Anyway, with any luck you may never have to go past Prospect Number 1 … We'll be rooting for you tonight. Keep us posted, O.K.?"

"I'll do that, *bli neder*. And good luck catching our pyromaniac. Do they have any better idea who it could have been than they did when I left?"

"I don't know. Nachman's our liaison-man with the authorities. He'll be the first to know …"

Nachman Bernstein was worried, and when he was worried he talked little and did a great deal. He was on the phone on an almost-hourly basis with the sheriff's office, with the fire chief whose men were sifting the second arson site for clues, and with Steve Birch for updates on the Indian angle. He made sure to stay in touch with his fellow *kollel* members as well, more to encourage them than to provide actual information, which was still in pitifully short supply.

"It's like a curse," Efraim grumbled to his wife as he foraged in the fridge for a snack. With Succos just around the corner, he found himself with plenty of free time on his hands. The succah — largely thanks to his son Shimi's inexhaustible energy — was already up, and the girls were busy preparing homemade decorations. "It's almost as if we weren't meant to be here in the first place."

"What do you mean by that?" Etty shot back. She had been up half the night with the baby, her Yom Tov cooking was only half done, the house was a mess by any standard — far less than her own exacting one

— and she was a bundle of nerves over Layala's impending surgery. She was awaiting word from Dr. Sadowsky before she and the baby would make the 50-mile trip to Roswell. What with jumping every time the phone rang, trying to squeeze in a little cooking during Layala's brief fitful naps, outfitting her children for the holiday and lending a hand with the decorations, she had neither the time nor the patience for her husband's pessimism.

"What I mean," Efraim said, deciding on a wedge of chocolate cake hidden at the back of the fridge, presumably by his wife to prevent his questing fingers from finding it, "is that I'm beginning to wonder if we made a mistake coming all the way out here. Look at what we've got: a maniac on the loose, torching the shul and our building site within days of each other. And who knows what he has on his mind next?"

"Focus on your students," Etty advised distractedly. Was that Layala she heard, waking from her sleep to the inevitable tummyache and tears? "That's what we came for, isn't it?"

"Not that they're interested in anything *I* have to say," he grumbled. "Not with Asher Gann around to upstage me every step of the way."

"Asher? What does he have to do with anything?"

"Oh, nothing." Efraim was in no mood for a tongue-lashing, which was exactly what he would get if Etty heard him complain about Asher. *Give it all you've got!* she would tell him, in that impatient tone that said she wondered where his gumption was. *Stand up there and give your all to those students. Don't worry about Asher Gann or anyone else. You have what it takes!*

The trouble was, he wasn't sure that he did. If he lacked the gumption to make something of himself, even out here where Torah teachers were so scarce, was there any hope at all? He had started out on that first day with rare confidence, pouring out his knowledge for the benefit of his adult students and basking in the genuine interest he saw reflected back in their faces. But it had taken no more than a single glimpse of Asher's charismatic ease, as he had stood surrounded by that admiring circle after class, to bring a sense of his own shortcomings rushing back to bury him. He had continued on after that, but the magic was gone. He knew that by his own lackluster presentation and by his students' wandering attention.

"Efraim," Etty said. She had stopped listening for the baby and was directing all of her considerable concentration on him. "You aren't doing it again, are you? After everything we've talked about? After this enormous move to give you a fresh start?"

"Doing what?" he asked blandly.

"Digging a hole and burying yourself in it."

"You've got a sense of humor, you know that?" He picked up the cake, mumbled the blessing, and shoved a third of it into his mouth in the first bite. His manner declared, loud and clear, "No Trespassing. Keep Out!"

Etty hesitated. She had a great deal more to say, but the baby was definitely awake now, and wanting her. Besides, she knew from bitter experience that Efraim, in this mood, would not be receptive to her well-meaning advice. With a last exasperated look at him over her shoulder, she hurried out of the kitchen. She wished Efraim would pull himself together, once and for all. She wished he would finally realize what a fine teacher he could be, if only he got past that paralyzing sense of inferiority.

Most of all, she wished she had done a better job of hiding the cake.

"What's the matter, Asher?" Rivi asked with concern. She was folding laundry on the gleaming dining-room table. Asher, a *sefer* propped open in front of him, was keeping her company. However, while she was industriously folding, she gradually became aware that he wasn't doing much learning.

He confirmed her suspicions by closing the *sefer* with a snap. "It's that Efraim Mandel," he growled. "I got a call from another one of my students this afternoon. Seems that Efraim's been contradicting much of what I've been teaching my class."

"Oh, come on. That sounds like an exaggeration!"

"It's true. Whenever an opportunity arises to contradict something I've taught, Efraim's jumped at it. I've been bombarded by questions from my students, who are naturally confused."

"So am I, actually. Don't the two of you teach different subjects?"

"He manages anyway. I'm at the end of my rope, Rivi. That man has no right to undermine my authority in the classroom. I know he's older than I am, but who is he to criticize what I'm teaching? If he has something to say, shouldn't he come over to me first, privately?"

Slowly, Rivi nodded, a half-folded blouse forgotten on her lap. "Yes, that would have been better. But he probably didn't stop to think, Asher. He probably just thought of something on the spur of the moment and spoke out about it."

"Half a dozen times? Feels like a campaign to me."

"That's nonsense, and you know it."

"I'm not so sure." Asher launched himself to his feet and began to measure the length of the dining room with his long, irritated stride. "Efraim seems to be jealous of me. Why, I don't know. He's just as good a teacher as I am when he tries, and he certainly knows as much as, or more than, I do. So why does he keep trying to trip me up and make me look bad to my students?"

"I'm sure it's not a conscious thing," Rivi said quickly.

Asher was silent.

"And I'm not so sure you're right about his being jealous. Maybe he's just ... insecure," she went on.

"Insecurity and jealousy. Don't they go hand in hand?"

Rivi sighed. "Let's not go all psychological now, Asher. I'm too tired. Besides, this is no time to be criticizing the Mandels. They've got enough on their heads right now, with Layala's surgery and all."

Asher stopped his pacing, surprised. "Surgery? What surgery?"

"Didn't I tell you? It's not scheduled yet, but it should be within a matter of days." Rivi told him about the baby's condition. "They need to widen her stomach opening or something. Poor thing." Her eyes misted over.

"Well, I'm sorry for the baby, and for the Mandels, of course. But that doesn't excuse what Efraim's doing!"

Rivi saw that her husband was genuinely troubled, as anyone would be, with a disgruntled colleague making his job harder and the academic year just beginning. Still, she was sure he was misreading things. Efraim's comments had probably been well intended. Anyway, he was probably not thinking very clearly right now, with little Layala's ordeal looming just ahead. Her heart twisted as she thought of that sweet baby under the surgeon's knife. She had been babysitting Layala a great deal since they moved out here, an arrangement that suited her just as well as it suited Etty. Secretly, she had to admit to herself that she had fallen head over heels in love with the baby girl.

As she reached for the next article of clothing to be folded, she sneaked a glance at Asher. He was wearing the mulish look she knew all too well. No point trying to smooth things over now; he was clearly in no mood to listen.

And it was certainly not the right time to tell him that she planned to abandon him the minute surgery was scheduled, and spend most of Layala's hospital stay right at that baby's side.

II.

The boys were beside themselves with excitement. It was not every day that they got to see arson and sheriffs and deputies up close. Crime and mystery were in the air, as evidenced by the endless closed-door meetings and the whispered rumors and the lingering smell of smoke in the shul. Things were happening.

They had a certain sense of outrage, too, that some person or persons unknown had had the temerity to tamper with their property. Donny, especially, waxed eloquent over the various lurid punishments he would like to see meted out to the perpetrator when he was caught.

And behind it all was the hidden voice of fear: of an unseen enemy who used fire as his weapon.

Being youngsters, it was the excitement that overpowered the rest. They held a meeting of their own in the boys' bedroom: Chaim and Donny Bernstein and Shimi Mandel, with little Yudi Bernstein hovering at the outskirts of the huddle, trying to keep up.

"It's like this," Chaim said importantly, taking charge of the proceedings as befit his slightly elder status. "Someone's out to get the *kollel*, and has to be stopped."

"Why?" Yudi asked.

"Why's someone out to get the *kollel*, or why does he have to be stopped?" Shimi asked, before Chaim could tell his little brother to go away and leave the situational analysis to older, sager heads.

"Why both?"

"Well, we don't know exactly the reason someone's out to get the *kollel*. Maybe someone doesn't like Jews."

Chaim headed off another "Why?" by interjecting quickly, "And he has to be stopped because we want to have our *kollel* in a nice, new building on the site that Tatty showed us. O.K.?"

Yudi nodded uncertainly. "Isn't the *kollel* in the shul now?"

"That," Donny told him, "got burned, too."

Yudi was beginning to look frightened. "Why's everything getting burned? Why doesn't Tatty make it stop?"

"Tatty's trying to stop it," Chaim said impatiently. "The Sheriff is, too. Yudi, if you can't stop asking questions you're going to have to go play somewhere else. O.K.?"

Yudi thrust his hands into his pockets and sat down. Shimi felt sorry for the younger boy, and would have said something reassuring had he not felt Chaim's eyes boring into his back. He decided to change the subject. "Vacation'll be over soon. Let's do something."

"Let's take a hike!" Donny suggested, bouncing on the bed in a burst of excess young energy.

"We could go up to the cliffs again," Chaim said. "Remember the hike we took at the picnic that time? When we met the Indians …"

"That's right. You told me about them," Shimi recalled. "Were they scary?"

"Yes … and no. They started out sort of unfriendly, but then that changed."

"What were they like?"

"One of them was kind of tough looking. The other was big, but harmless."

"He was flabby!" Donny giggled.

"An Indian came to *our* house," Yudi announced suddenly.

The others' reaction could not have been more gratifying. "When?"

"This morning. When the fire happened. I saw him come in. I was hiding up on the landing, behind the banister."

"I'm sure he never noticed you," Chaim said sarcastically.

"Eagle eyes, that's what they have," Donny announced, having crowned himself the official expert on Indian lore. "You shouldn't have spied on him, Yudi."

"I wasn't spying. I just happened to see him standing there when Ma opened the door, and decided to watch."

"Well?" Chaim prompted. "What did he do?"

"He came inside and went into Tatty's study. They were in there a long time. Then he came out, thanked Ma and Ta, and left."

"Exciting." Donny sounded disappointed.

"I'll ask Ta about him later," Chaim decided. "Meanwhile, who wants to go out to the site and climb up to the caves?"

There were no dissenters. With school out until after Succos, they had the afternoon free. Shimi was especially eager, having missed the chance to hike with his friends that other time. Chaim armed himself with a flashlight despite the blazing sun, and Donny made sure to take along a couple of candy bars for sustenance. As for Shimi, he spent the next few minutes convincing little Yudi that the hike would be too much for him, and promising that he would tell him all about it when they got back.

Tova heard the front door slam below. Chaim had stuck his head into the master bedroom, where Tova was sitting with Heidi, to inform his mother that he, Donny and Shimi were going out for a while. Tova had nodded vaguely, her mind still very much on her friend and not overly concerned with what games the boys might be playing on this sunny afternoon. "Be home in time for dinner," she called, and let it go at that.

With the echo of the slammed door still ringing in her ears, she turned back to Heidi. "Headache any better?" she asked solicitously.

Heidi rubbed her temples. "Too soon to say. The aspirin hasn't kicked in yet. Then again, I don't think the headache is physical in origin. It started up the minute we began this conversation. Or rather, the minute *you* began it. So maybe we'd better postpone our talk for another time, and —"

"Nope," Tova broke in. "We're going to have it now. Tomorrow will only bring on another headache, so what's the point of putting it off?"

Heidi's fine legal brain produced no rebuttal for this argument. With a sigh, she assumed an attitude of resignation. Tova dove right in.

"I want to know about this so-called 'nervous breakdown' of yours, Heidi. It didn't just spring up out of nowhere. Every storm is formed someplace — sometimes miles away and over a long period of time — until the right conditions come together, and the storm breaks."

"I wasn't aware that you've had meteorological training."

"Don't try to distract me, Heidi. Let's get to the point. The storm."

"It was some storm," Heidi admitted ruefully. She rocked in the cushioned glider, eyes straying to the window as though seeking escape. Tova herself had taken the less comfortable straight chair at the desk she had asked Nachman to install beneath the window when they moved in, and which was utterly devoid of any sign of "work"; Tova attended to the bills and her correspondence in a cluttered niche in the kitchen. Her back was very erect, as though she intended by her posture to underscore the gravity of her inquiry.

"Tell me about it," Tova ordered.

Heidi rocked back and forth, resigned to the inevitable. "It's hard to explain what happened. One minute I was a successful attorney, commuting to the city each day dressed for success. I had a briefcase bulging with legal briefs that I took home with me every night and worked on till the wee hours. I had a fairly active social life, too, though the activity was of the treadmill type: pumping hard but going nowhere. I didn't think I was unhappy. I thought I *was* happy. And then, one morning, I found myself behind the wheel of my car, driving — not to the office — but to the Poconos.

"I spent nearly a week vegetating in a motel room, living on tuna and tomatoes. I didn't spend the week thinking through my life; I spent it not thinking about anything at all. I ignored frantic calls from my parents, my sister ... you. I ignored everything because, suddenly, it was all too much for me to handle. Before that, I could juggle a dozen difficult cases and still look and feel fresh as a daisy; now I felt as though rinsing a single coffee cup would break me. My nerves felt as though they'd been worn ragged and were about to snap in two. Sometimes, I thought they already *had* snapped in two. The result was that nonperson, lolling around that motel room."

Tova's eyes swam in tears. Eliciting pity had been the last thing on Heidi's mind, but her matter-of-fact recital had touched a deep wellspring of empathy in her friend's heart. More than anything in the world, she wanted to help set Heidi's life right again. If she could have waved a magic wand, she would have given it all to her: a happy marriage, a satisfying career if that was what she wanted ... children, a home, and inner peace.

But there was no wand, and no magic formula. "It's going to take time," she said finally, trying to keep her voice from cracking and betraying the profound compassion that fueled her words.

Heidi nodded. "That's why I'm glad I came out here. Time seems to move more slowly here. I don't know why."

"Maybe it's just because you've stepped out of your own life, your own responsibilities. You're on vacation."

Heidi met her friend's eyes squarely. "That's no solution. It's just temporary. A Band-Aid."

"Sometimes, when you're physically sick, the best thing you can do is simply rest, to give your body a chance to heal itself. I think that's what you need right now, Heidi. To rest, and — and give your soul a chance to heal."

A lifted brow. "My soul? What's that got to do with anything? This isn't a spiritual crisis, Tova."

"I don't know about that. The emptiness you've described ... the non-being, almost ... that sounds like a spiritual ailment to me. As though you've been somehow disconnected from your innermost self ..."

"We're getting into deep waters," Heidi laughed, suddenly self-conscious.

"Too deep for me, maybe," Tova agreed. "I'm no psychologist. I'm not even particularly insightful. Nachman could probably run circles around my analysis. But I'm your friend, Heidi. I've known you — forever, it seems. And that's how it strikes me."

Heidi sighed. "You're probably right."

She lapsed into silence, which was abruptly shattered by a sound at the door. This swung open, making both women jump. Nachman stood there, apparently as surprised to see them as they were to see him.

"Oh, I'm sorry, ladies. I didn't know you were in here, Heidi. I was looking for Tova."

Heidi made to rise. "I'm the one who should be sorry. I'm intruding. I'll just —"

"Stay right where you are," he ordered. "I was just looking for Tova to tell her that I've called another meeting about the arson — at our house."

"Tonight?" Tova asked.

He nodded. "With Succos coming up, I want to put our heads together now. Maybe we can come up with some sort of strategy to keep our interests in this town safe ..."

"Will the sheriff be there?"

"No, nor the Indian liaison-man, that lawyer who came to see me — Steve Birch. It'll be just us: the *kollel* — minus Avi, of course — Rabbi Harris and some of the more active members of his shul. As I say, we'll put our heads together and see what we come up with."

"Will the wives be there?"

"Any of them who wants to be. I know Asher Gann mentioned that his wife plans to come. After all, this issue impacts on all the families."

"Coffee and cake?"

"Sounds right to me." He smiled at his wife, nodded pleasantly and turned to go.

"Excuse me?" It was Heidi. Nachman turned back to the room.

"Yes?"

"Would it be all right if I sat in on the meeting? Seeing as other women are going to be there and all."

Tova said quickly, "Are you sure you're up to it, Heidi? I thought we said you needed rest."

"If I rest any more, I'm going to really go out of my mind — with boredom!"

Nachman laughed. "You are certainly welcome to attend the meeting, Heidi. Feel free to put in your two cents, too. We could use a lawyer's perspective."

Once again, he started to leave — and then thought better of it. Addressing his wife, he said, "Chaim around? I thought we might do some learning. Hectic as things have been around here, I've been neglecting him a bit."

"He went out with Donny and Shimi. I don't know where."

"Well, never mind. I'll catch him when he gets back.

This time he made it all the way through the door, which he closed gently behind him. He still had a few more calls to make, to set things up for tonight.

III.

"**B**oy, it's hot," Donny complained. He lifted the baseball cap from his head, wiped his forehead with his sleeve, and replaced the cap. "We should've gone later in the day, when it cools off."

"Quit grumbling." Chaim took a long drink from his water bottle.

Shimi took a drink from his own bottle. Nothing — neither the heat, nor thirst, nor the sometimes-jagged rocks beneath his sneakered soles — seemed to daunt the boy. His enthusiasm for this hike, as for any project in which he found himself involved, was undiminished by outside circumstances. Shimi was one of those rare souls who live purely in the moment, throwing every bit of his focus and energy into whatever he happened to be doing *now*. It made him a pleasure to be with, Chaim thought, especially as his own brother had never stopped complaining the whole way here. Donny was always the first to want to do anything — and the first to complain when the going got tough.

As Donny had pointed out, it was hot, and the climb into the stony hills wasn't easy. All three boys hefted their backpacks more securely on their shoulders and plodded on. They poked their heads into one or two of the smaller caves that lined the trail like a row of primitive motel rooms. The caves were bare and uninteresting, but they did provide the boys with temporary shade and some relief from having to squint in the never-ending glare of the sun.

"C'mon," Chaim urged, back on the trail. "I see another cave up ahead. Maybe it's a bigger one."

"I've got a rock in my sneaker," Shimi announced. He sat down on a large egg-shaped boulder just off the trail. "You guys can go on ahead, if you want. I'll just be a minute."

Donny, eager for another rest himself, was all for waiting with Shimi, but his brother wanted his company up the next stretch of the trail. "We're getting high enough to have a good view of the building site," Chaim said. "Don't you want a bird's-eye view of the new *kollel*?" A piece of gum helped sweeten the deal. Donny went.

The Bernstein boys were soon out of sight around the next bend in the trail. Shortly after that, the noise of their passage had faded as well. Shimi sat very still, letting the sun and the solitude envelop him in a sweet, surreal haze. He was never alone, not like this. He felt like the only human being for miles and miles. His mind knew that this was not so, that Chaim and Donny were not far away, but his heart was suffused with a strange, deep sense of solitude. It made him a little nervous, but only a little. He bent to untie his shoelace and retrieve the stone that had lodged itself in his shoe.

As he straightened up, shaking out the sneaker, a sound reached his ears. It seemed to be coming from slightly below him and to the right. A clink … a rattle, as in a shower of pebbles … and an indistinct murmur. A human voice.

Thrusting his foot back into his sneaker and tying a hasty knot, Shimi stood up and, without stopping to think, went to investigate the source of the unexpected sounds.

They were issuing, he decided, from one of the caves they'd passed on their way up. It was not a very interesting-looking cave, its mouth yawning wide to reveal an uninviting emptiness, and the boys had given it a miss. Shimi hesitated, and then stepped in out of the sun.

The temperature in here was at least 10 degrees cooler than in the sun-baked air outside. For a moment, Shimi stood still, enjoying the coolness on his overheated skin. The noises came again, from the depths of the cave: another clink, more falling rocks, a sharp-edged comment with an overtone of anger. Shimi was just beginning to back away when the noises stopped and a face suddenly appeared in front of him. Then two faces.

He thought he recognized the pair from the Bernsteins' description on their previous excursion on these trails: the two Indians who had so fired their imaginations. That time, to hear the boys tell it, the men had looked peaceful, almost friendly. One had been tough looking, Chaim had said. The other, according to Donny, was flabby. Yes, there was no question about it: These two matched.

Right now, the first man — with the shoulder-length black hair, high-angled cheekbones and hawklike black eyes — looked anything but friendly. His companion was as large, clumsy and bearlike as Chaim and Donny had painted him. Consternation was stamped on the heavy features, but the big man said nothing, clearly content to let his companion do the talking.

"What are you doing here?" Bobby Smith asked, the words slicing through the dim cave like a knife.

"Nothing," was Shimi's automatic reply. He edged back another inch. How far in was he? Wasn't the entrance supposed to be just a couple of yards behind him? It felt like a couple of miles.

"Did you follow us in here?"

"'Course not!" Indignation made Shimi braver. "We were just hiking on the trail, that's all. It's a free country, isn't it?"

"Maybe — and maybe not." Bobby stared at Shimi, and it was like no stare Shimi had ever encountered before. The black eyes were fathomless and stone sharp at the same time. They made Shimi very uncomfortable. They made him want nothing more than to find his way out of there, fast. He turned and began to run.

A wiry hand shot out and clamped itself on his shoulder. Viselike, the grip brought pain that made Shimi gasp and sent tears springing into his eyes. "Lemme go!"

"I'll let you go if you swear not to say a word about meeting us here."

"Why? What're you doing here, anyway?"

Unexpectedly, it was the big man who answered. "Nothing," Big Jim said, with unconscious humor parodying Shimi's earlier reply. "We done nothing. You seen nothing."

"O.K., so I seen nothing. *Now* will you let me go?"

"One word to anyone — *anyone* — about meeting us here," Bobby hissed, tightening his grip on Shimi's shoulder, "and you're going to wish you were never born. Got it?"

Shimi nodded, wincing. "Why would I want to tell, anyway? I didn't see you doing anything."

Bobby exchanged a swift glance with Jim. He let go of the boy's shoulder and shoved him toward the cave's mouth. "Go!"

Shimi half-ran, half-stumbled out of the cave. His heart was pounding so hard that his chest hurt. Only now, in reaction, did he feel the symptoms of shock that the rush of adrenalin had held in abeyance before. His legs trembled uncontrollably, his heart seemed to skip a few beats, his head ached fiercely. Not daring to look back over his shoulder, he scrambled up the trail in pursuit of his friends.

The silence was his enemy now. The vast blue canopy overhead mocked him because it offered no barrier from hostile eyes. He felt very exposed: as vulnerable as a newborn baby. Like his sister Layala, soft and helpless and unprotected. He wanted to crawl into the nearest hole and cower there, knees to his chin, until he felt safe again. But he had to keep moving. They were at his back, probably watching every move he made.

Ahead of him, somewhere, were his friends. Why hadn't he come across them already? It felt as though he had been climbing for hours. With a sinking feeling, he wondered if the Bernstein boys had left without him. Alone on a mountain with no one but *them* for company ... He shuddered, closed his eyes for a moment in half-panic and half-supplication, then forced himself to climb again.

It wasn't hours, but just minutes later that Shimi found them. A surge of relief washed over him in a great healing wave as his straining ears caught the drone of Chaim's voice just ahead. Shimi quickened his pace: a mistake on that narrow, rocky trail. Down he went, among the stones and the dry, greenish-gray things growing among them. A sharp pain shot up from his knee; upon inspecting it, he found it marred by a large but unalarming scrape. Scrambling to his feet again, he continued up the trail, ignoring the pain. He swung around a last bend, one hand on the rock wall to steady himself, and let out his breath at the sight of the Bernstein brothers, sitting on a rock and sharing a bar of rapidly melting chocolate.

"Hey, Shimi," Chaim said placidly. He held out the bar. "Want some?"

"N-no thanks." Breathless, Shimi sank down on the boulder beside them.

"What's the matter with you?" Donny demanded, staring at Shimi's white face and wide, stricken eyes.

"Nothing." Shimi's hand went to his shoulder, rubbing the spot where the viselike grip had taken hold in the cave. Chaim's eyes were not on Shimi's shoulder, but on his left knee.

"You ripped your pants," he said, pointing. "And your knee's bleeding."

"I know. I slipped." Shimi struggled to recapture his breath, and his equilibrium.

Chaim peered more closely into his friend's face. "Are you sure you're O.K.? You look funny."

Shimi rubbed his shoulder. "I'm fine. C'mon, let's go home."

"Already? But we didn't finish our hike!"

"I'm hungry. I want to go home."

Donny took up the cry. "And I'm *starving*! Come on, Chaim."

Chaim studied their faces to see if he had any chance of getting them to change their minds. The prospects didn't look good. Outnumbered, he shrugged his shoulders and accepted reality with good grace. "All right, let's go." He stood up, and the others followed suit. In near silence they began the return trip down the trail which they had climbed in such high spirits just a short while before.

When they passed the spot where Shimi had stopped to take the rock from his shoe, he broke out in a cold sweat. It was all he could do not to turn and stare directly at the cave mouth, a few feet down and slightly to the right. Were the Indians still inside? Would they wait until the boys had passed and then come out and pounce on them in their soft-footed way, with no whisper of warning?

"Hurry," he urged, moving as quickly as he could with one leg already stiffening at the injured knee joint. In his haste he slipped again, just past the cave's entrance, and scraped his other knee. He kept going.

It was with twice-ripped pants, two aching knees and a profoundly thankful heart that he stood at last on solid ground, his back to the cliffs and his face turned toward Lakewood as it dozed in the afternoon sun.

IV.

Nachman stood at the door to greet each new group of arrivals as they arrived. Rabbi Harris was first, accompanied by his wife, Penina, and *gabbai* Nate Goodman. The tall, lanky attorney seized Nachman's hand in a strong grip. "We're going to catch those arsonists and put them behind bars," he promised grimly. "Don't you worry."

"I wasn't aware that you've been elected sheriff," pediatrician Ben Sadowsky joked, coming up behind them. Sadowsky, the shul's other *gabbai,* smiled at Nachman and gave him a much less fervent handshake in greeting.

"I don't see that Sheriff Ramsay is doing all that much," Nate grumbled as the group, at Nachman's urging, moved in a knot toward the dining room. Tova was there, setting out the last of the coffee cups and plates of cake. Beyond her, in the open kitchen, Heidi was arranging packets of sugar and Splenda, and lemon slices for those who preferred tea. Before the first arrivals had finished finding seats around the large oval table, the bell rang again. Nachman opened the door a second time, to admit Asher and Rivi Gann.

"Avi Feder sends his regards — and his regrets," Asher told Nachman as they shook hands. "I've been invested with voting rights on his behalf."

"This isn't a board meeting, Asher," Nachman said, ushering the couple inside. "I don't think we'll be voting on anything."

"How is Avi?" Nate asked curiously. "He gave me a call before he left, but I couldn't talk for long."

"He didn't tell me much," Asher admitted. "He's going on *shidduchim,* and doesn't sound too excited about it. I'm not sure he was ready to take the plunge yet."

"Everything in its right time," Nachman murmured. "I'm glad you could come. Come in, come in, both of you. We'll be starting in just a minute. I think everyone's here."

Unfortunately, Efraim Mandel walked up to the half-open door just in time to hear these last words. They produced a cold jolt to the heart that froze him in midstep. Flushing, he forced his hand up and knocked loudly on the door to announce his presence. Nachman swung it fully open again with a hearty, "Well, here's Efraim! Now we can start." He shook Efraim's hand, oblivious — or pretending to be — to the other man's discomfiture. There are some people who are accident prone in a physical sense; Efraim Mandel seemed to be socially unfortunate that way. Unerring as the bumblebee to a flower's heart, he consistently found himself in the wrong place at the wrong time, and reaped all the stickiness of honey, without any of the sweetness.

Rivi leaned forward to ask about Layala. "Any word about the operation?"

Efraim Mandel glanced diagonally across the table at Dr. Sadowsky. "He's the one to ask, not me." If he sounded curt almost to the point of rudeness, Rivi put it down to worry over his child. Ben Sadowsky smiled his pleasant smile and said quietly, "I'm waiting for the green light from Roswell. The surgeon there is trying to fit the baby into his schedule as soon as possible. If the situation were more acute, she would have had the operation by now."

"Seems pretty acute to me," Efraim muttered down at the table.

"It is hard listening to a baby cry in discomfort, day after day," the doctor agreed sympathetically. "Still, a few more days won't harm her, and we want the best man in the area for the job."

Rivi was on the point of commenting again when Nachman Bernstein, at the head of the table, cleared his throat. The low-voiced conversations ceased as all heads turned toward the *Rosh Kollel*.

"Thank you all for coming on such short notice," Nachman began. "As I told each of you when I invited you here, I'd like to have some sort of working plan in place before Succos comes — and it's coming fast."

"Tomorrow night," Rabbi Harris nodded. "And my succah's not even up yet. Who's had time, with all this going on?"

"You'd think he was personally leading the investigation," his wife, Penina, said in jest, her eyes fixed half in affection, half in exasperation, on her husband.

"I'll help you put it up, if you want," Asher Gann said. "Mine's ready, and I've got all this free time on my hands. *Bein hazemanim* drives me crazy."

"I can vouch for that," Rivi murmured, to general chuckles.

The rabbi thanked Asher for his kind offer, and Nachman moved along with the agenda. "Before we get down to the business at hand, let me thank my wife, Tova, for the delicious refreshments you see on the table. Please, everyone, help yourselves ... And I'd also like to introduce our guest, and my wife's very dear friend, Heidi Neufeld, from New York." He slanted a glance at Nate Goodman. "Heidi is a lawyer, too."

Nate's interest quickened slightly at this. He looked down the length of the table to where Heidi sat, wearing an old sweatshirt and an air of being a polite spectator. At the others' murmured greetings, Heidi raised a mechanical smile, then reached for a slice of cake just to give her hands something to do. She was beginning to regret her impulse to join this meeting. What did she have to do with any of the crises, large and small, taking place in this town? She was an outsider. Worse, she was an outsider still scrambling back, inch by inch, from the edge of a precipice that she had not noticed yawning before her and that had very badly shaken her.

Heidi Neufeld, from New York. Her former life seemed to belong to someone else now. Some other ambitious young lawyer belonged at her Manhattan desk, making clever decisions aimed at helping rich corporations grow richer. It was another woman who would be striding down the busy downtown streets toward a power lunch, heels clicking a tattoo of self-importance, a Morse message which, deciphered, said: "I've got vital matters on my mind. I'm going somewhere in a hurry, and I'm going to be paid magnificently for being there. Time is money, you know ..."

Tearing her mind away from her own issues, she looked around the table from beneath half-lowered lids, surreptitiously studying the others. She saw concerned faces, solemn faces, faces mostly unknown to her. To her right, Tova was a familiar landmark in a foreign terrain. Nachman was another. She steeled herself to listen to what he was saying: to pay attention, to care. If she was indifferent to her own life, she should at least muster a modicum of concern for what these good people were going through. Right now, it was the only thing that felt real.

"... no progress of any real significance," Nachman was saying. "The sheriff says they're still interviewing possible suspects and continuing to comb the site of the arson for clues. In the meantime, I think it would be a good idea for us to map out some sort of overall strategy, both in terms of our response to these two crimes and in terms of our readiness to meet any future incidents of this kind."

Dr. Sadowsky looked up sharply. "Have the police definitely linked the two crimes?"

Nachman looked surprised. "I'd have thought it was obvious. The shul, and the site of the new Jewish high school and *kollel*. Is there any question in anyone's mind that the two acts were perpetrated by the same party or parties — and for the same reason?"

"Anti-Semitism," Nate said, brows snapping together with a frown.

"Not necessarily," Pinchas Harris objected. "We could be dealing with a gang — young kids looking for a little excitement ..." Even in his own ears, his words sounded weak.

"With all respect, rabbi," Nate said, "I think that's wishful thinking. There have been hardly any cases of arson in Lakewood in recent years. Why the sudden spate of 'excitement' among our town's youth? And why now? It can't be a coincidence that these things happened just after the new *kollel* arrived and bought a nice tract of land right outside town."

"A competitor?" Asher mused aloud. "Maybe someone else had his eye on that property."

"Fleischmann looked into all of that before buying," Nachman said. "There were no other outstanding bids. No one's shown any interest at all in that piece of land — and it's been on the market for years."

Goodman drummed his fingers on the table. "I say we all agree, here and now, that the crimes *were* linked and that they are anti-Semitic in nature. You can't ignore the words that were painted onto the shul: 'Jews go home.' Nothing very subtle about that, is there?"

"I agree with Nate," Nachman said. "Everyone?"

Around the table, heads nodded in slow agreement. A heaviness seemed to descend, as though the bald statement of their problem had made it more solid — and more ominous. Asher reached absently for a cookie; Nate poured himself a cup of tea. Someone passed the sugar. The grim truth had a few seconds to sink in, and those present used those seconds to gear themselves for the next stage in their deliberations.

"O.K.," Nachman said, aiming for a brisk note but ruining the effect by letting a sigh creep into the word. "O.K. We're agreed. Now, what do we do about it?"

"About the crimes," Ben Sadowsky asked, "or the anti-Jewish feelings?"

"Both, I suppose. If we find the arsonist, we'll have eliminated our most pressing problem. We can deal with the larger picture later."

"We don't want to rile up our other neighbors," Nate said slowly. "Right now, we're dealing only with an individual or individuals who have it in for the Jews of Lakewood. Let's not let this thing snowball into a them-versus-us thing."

Nachman nodded. "That's the last thing we want. And yet, in order to prevent these crimes, we need the support of the general community. The police, of course ... Sheriff Ramsay has been cooperative so far."

"What about the media?" Heidi spoke up suddenly.

Nachman looked at her. "Excuse me?"

"The media. Newspapers, radio, TV. They can be very useful allies. You can use them to let the people know what's going on and to solicit their support against hate crimes of this nature. If you create a positive enough climate — and a sufficiently vigilant one — it might be enough to deter the arsonist from striking again."

"That's the *worst* thing we could do!" Nate Goodman said forcefully from the other end of the table.

Heidi eyed him frostily. "I beg your pardon?"

"You're from New York, right? In the big city, the answer to everything is: Make as much noise as you can. Rant and rave and get everyone in a dither about your cause." He shook his head. "It won't work here. Lakewood's a sleepy little town. We don't take well to that kind of 'noise.' The people don't want to be exhorted, and they'll take it badly if we try to do it. No, we've got to go about this in a different way. Raise neighborhood consciousness about the crimes: yes. Solicit community support: yes. But discreetly, behind the scenes. That's what's needed here."

"Where has discretion got you so far?" Heidi snapped. "Nowhere at all. You've got to enlist the support of the people, of the man in the street who has nothing against Jews and everything against criminals who set fire to public buildings. You've got to let him know that his house could be next!"

"We've all agreed that this is a hate crime —"

"But it's still a crime! And people — even in 'sleepy little towns' — fear and hate crime. It's in their best interest to know about it, and fight it together with you!"

Asher said thoughtfully, "She's got a point, you know." To which Penina Harris retorted, "So has Nate, actually!" Tova bit her lip and threw an anguished glance at Nachman.

Across the expanse of the table, the two attorneys glared at each other. Heidi was breathing hard, pink splotches high on both cheeks. Nate's face relaxed into a small, ironical smile. He inclined his head. "You know best, of course, being from the big city and all." He paused, then added, with no trace of amusement this time, "But I'm afraid you don't know the first thing about small-town life."

"No loss," Dr. Sadowsky said, in an obvious effort to defuse the sudden tension. "We're not all that interesting ..."

"I don't need to know about small-town life in order to know that you're on the wrong track here," Heidi snapped at Nate, holding onto her temper with difficulty. "You're being small minded and provincial. A crime is a crime, wherever it takes place!"

"True. But the wrong kind of handling can double the damage. And that includes responding with a roar when a whisper will suffice."

Nachman decided it was time to take up the gavel again. "Let's move on now, folks. Leaving aside for the moment the question of involving the media, what are your thoughts about hiring a private watchman for both the shul and the building site?"

The discussion continued, winding more or less purposefully through the maze of fear-driven possibilities. A decision was made to ask Sheriff Ramsay for extra manpower to guard their institutions; should police protection prove either unavailable or inadequate, a special fund would be started to cover the cost of hiring private watchmen. Tactfully, Nachman suggested that the local media had made a fairly large to-do over the arson in any case, and that nothing further was needed at the moment. "To be reassessed after Succos," he added, with a glance at Heidi. Her color was still high. She had not said another word throughout the rest of the meeting, and just as assiduously avoided meeting Nate Goodman's eye.

As for Nate, the Lakewood lawyer had curiously little to contribute after his clash with his counterpart from New York. How had things escalated the way they had? He had his views, certainly, but he hadn't meant to turn them into weapons of open warfare. When the meeting broke up he hesitated, wondering if he ought to go over to the Bernsteins' house guest and apologize for any ill feeling his comments might have engendered. But by the time he had made up his mind to move, Heidi had escaped from the room and was nowhere to be seen.

He started for Tova Bernstein next, intending to ask her to pass on his apologies. But Tova was already on her way out, hot on Heidi's heels.

V.

The first thing Asher did on his arrival home was to pick up a phone and call Avi Feder in New York, to apprise him of how the meeting had gone. He had promised to do this, and though there was nothing of real substance to report, a promise is a promise. Besides, Avi's emergence on the *shidduch* scene interested him intensely. He believed he knew Avi better than anyone, and knew, too, just what kind of wife he needed. Someone not too different from poor Yocheved, but with an extra dollop of maturity to understand the pain he had been through and the practical sense to help him over it.

In the last couple of days he had already debriefed his friend after Avi's meetings with *Shidduch* Prospects 1 and 2, both of which had ended in polite good-byes after a single time. *Shidduch* Number 3 had been imminently pending the last time they'd spoken, the day before. While Rivi still held to her belief that meeting so many different women all at once was just a waste of effort, Asher was reserving judgment. Everyone has his own style, he figured, and after what Avi had been through, he deserved to do whatever felt right for him. The niggling suspicion that Rivi was right, and that his old friend was essentially doing nothing more than seeking "safety in numbers," he chose to ignore for the moment.

"So, how'd it go?" Avi asked when he heard Asher's voice.

"I was just about to ask *you* that, buddy. I assume you met with the third young lady on your list last night?"

"I did."

"And ...?"

"You, first. How'd the meeting go?"

Asher decided to be patient. "You didn't miss much. We batted around the whole thing for a while and got nowhere. The Bernsteins have a guest from New York, a woman lawyer, who got pretty hot under the collar because Nate Goodman wants to keep a low profile about the hate crimes and she thinks we ought to blare it out to the media. That added some excitement to the meeting. Otherwise, it was more of the usual: round and round the mulberry bush, with no real progress. It's up to the police, I guess."

"So you didn't decide on any course of action?"

"We're going to ask the police for more protection for the shul and building site. If they don't come through, we'll look into hiring a private guard. That about sums it up." A pause signaled a shifting of gears. "And now it's your turn, buddy."

He heard Avi suck in his breath as though steeling himself for an ordeal. "I met with Number 3, as you call her, last night. She was very nice."

"Do I detect a 'but' on the way?"

"But — I'm not interested."

"Why am I not surprised?" Asher made no effort to conceal his disappointment.

"It's still early, Asher. I'm still raw at this game. Give me time."

"Do I have a choice? When are you flying back here?"

"Right after Succos, *im yirtzeh Hashem.* I'm looking forward to getting back to teaching."

"So what'll you do with yourself for the next nine days or so? Now that you've fulfilled all your *shidduch* obligations." He shook his head, though Avi couldn't see it. "Three girls in your first week home, and nothing at all for the rest of your stay. I call that lopsided."

"Oh, I'm sure I'll find some way to keep busy," Avi said vaguely. "Well, gotta run. Talk to you later, Ash."

"I'll try to call again on *erev* Yom Tov."

"Great. Bye now."

Avi Feder flipped his cell phone shut, but did not immediately clip it back onto his belt. He kept it in his hand, fingering it absently as he stared without seeing out the window of his parents' spacious living room.

He had not been perfectly open with his best friend on the phone just now. While it was true that he had met Numbers 1, 2 and 3 this past week, there was a new development that he had not shared with Asher — interested as he knew Asher would have been to hear about it. Perhaps he had withheld the information precisely *because* Asher was so interested. Why get his friend excited over nothing? And "nothing," Avi was certain, was just what he would find when he met *Shidduch* Number 4 this evening.

This one had been an afterthought; a last-minute addition by his mother when she had seen which way the wind was blowing with the other candidates on the list she'd provided. Her Avi had politely but firmly declined a second meeting which each of the three lovely women that she had so carefully, and so eagerly, selected for him. Rather than face the prospect of sending him back to the wasteland of New Mexico with a failed mission behind him, she had extended herself to even greater heights, taking time out from her monumental Yom Tov-cooking schedule to make a series of urgent phone calls.

The young woman she ultimately came up with was a young widow who had lost her husband in a freak accident while driving cross-country with his family to his parents' home in L.A. He had been driving with his window open to enjoy the spring breeze, when a large bird suddenly flapped at the window, wings practically brushing his face. Startled, he lost control of the wheel. Unfortunately, this loss of control happened just as a massive tractor-trailer was passing in the next lane. The impact had been horrific. The driver of the car was killed instantly, with his wife and 6 month-old baby, in the back seat, shaken and bruised but otherwise physically unharmed.

Now, a year and a half later, Shiffy Taub was unsure whether she was ready to start trying to rebuild her life. She was a strong young woman, and a courageous one, but the trauma of losing her husband and finding herself having to raise her first child on her own had shaken her to her depths. There had been no time for a leisurely recovery: She had a baby to care for.

Her mother claimed that Shiffy *was* ready. Shiffy herself was not as certain. But when the matchmaker said that Avi Feder — fine family, fine *talmid chacham*, fine character — would be flying west right after Succos, something seemed to relax inside her. This would be a fairly uncomplicated way to ease into the *shidduch* game again. Here was a man whose life belonged somewhere else, who would be a transient visitor to her life, as she would be to his. It was a safe bet, if anything was safe in this world. She could dip her big toe into the water and then snatch it out again, secure in the knowledge that Avi Feder would be halfway across the country before the water had the chance to chill her.

So she said, "Yes," and waited by the phone for Avi to call. Given his tight schedule, the call and their actual meeting would be separated by just one day.

It was a good call. So good, in fact, that she found herself strangely eager as she got ready for their meeting that evening. Here was someone, at any rate, who would not bore her. She clutched her young son very tightly as she kissed him good-night, then relegated him to the tender ministrations of his grandmother. Living with her parents as she did, Shiffy had the luxury of built-in babysitters, though this was a luxury rarely availed of until tonight. She was wearing her high-heeled shoes and her best custom wig that had scarcely been out of its box since the accident. The sound of Avi knocking at her parents' door would be her cue to re-enter the great swimming pool of life.

You're just dipping in your big toe, remember, she told herself in a last-minute pep talk aimed at lifting her flagging courage. But, "safe bet" or not, as she waited for the knock she was conscious of a trepidation that had nothing to do with safety at all. She felt as though the cold waters were about to close right over her head.

As for Avi, he was not quite sure why he'd agreed to this last-minute change in plans. He had consented to seeing three women on this trip back to his ancestral home: three more than he had wanted to meet. That ought to have placated his mother, his father and all the various other do-gooders so anxious to provide him with a substitute for his lost Yocheved.

But his mother hadn't been satisfied, and Avi hadn't had the strength to fend off her persistence. So he had agreed to Number 4. At worst, it would be another story to share with the Ganns when he got back. At best, it might be a not-too-unpleasant way to spend an evening. She had sounded nice enough over the phone. Articulate, funny and interesting. And, unlike the trio who had preceded her this week, she had something in common with him. Bereavement may not be a recommended topic of conversation for an ordinary first meeting, but this "first date" would be no ordinary event for either of them. Shiffy, if anyone, would understand that. And so, he found himself looking forward to hearing about her experiences and comparing them with his own.

At any rate, he would not be bored.

At the appointed hour, he checked the tilt of his hat in the mirror, tightened his tie an infinitesimal notch, and went out to the car his father had loaned him for the duration of his visit. A moment later he was driving through the darkening streets — guided by a scrap of paper on the dashboard — to an unfamiliar address.

As he drove, he was pleasantly conscious of having done his duty. A few hours from now, he would be a free man. Free to throw off the stiffness, the discomfort, the unresolved pain of the *shidduch* game, Round 2. Free to enjoy the upcoming Succos holiday in peace.

Free to welcome back the loneliness that had become his closest companion.

He stifled a sigh. A tiny voice in the back of his mind asked, "At what price freedom?" But he didn't listen, because he didn't want to hear. Besides, he already knew the answer.

The price he was paying for this tenuous freedom from pain was a complete absence of pleasure, or the hope of pleasure in the future. He was robbing himself of the very things he needed to make his life a thing of joy. But, for the moment at least, those things paled in comparison with the pain he had suffered. He was willing to do anything to avoid the terrible hurt of loss again.

Even wrap his own heart up in mothballs and put it into indefinite storage.

VI.

"What's the matter?" Nachman asked his wife. It was after midnight, and the first chance he'd had, since the meeting around their dining-room table had broken up hours earlier, to really look at her.

He didn't like what he saw. Tova, still in her apron after hours of Yom Tov cooking, appeared drawn and preoccupied. Before she could answer his question, he launched into a well-worn lecture, the chiding tone overlaid with genuine concern.

"You're overdoing things again, Tova. You don't have to cook enough food for three armies, *or* have six choices for every course. Keep it simple, O.K.? I'd rather have a wife with a smile on her face than a state banquet."

"I know," Tova aimed for a smile, but fell slightly short of her goal. "I think you've told me that before."

"Once or twice."

"Or 500 times. Actually, too much cooking's not the trouble tonight. I've been finding it therapeutic, in a way. Soothing to the mind."

He hitched up a wooden kitchen chair and sat down. "So why does the mind need soothing tonight?"

With a sigh, "It's Heidi."

"I thought you said she was getting better. Opening up, facing things, trying to find her way in life. That sounds pretty healthy to me."

"To me, too. In fact, just her flying out here was a sign of health. Heidi's not giving up on herself so fast, Nachman."

"Good! Then what's the problem?" What was giving his wife shadows under her eyes and making her move as though someone had wound her up and forgotten to turn her off? He watched as she began tidying up the kitchen. Her movements were automatic, her mind clearly somewhere else entirely. Presumably, with Heidi, upstairs in the guest room. But why?

Suddenly, understanding dawned. "You're not upset about what happened at the meeting, are you? Heidi did come across as the high-powered New Yorker, but it was clear that her intentions were pure. She wanted to help. I don't think anyone held it against her."

"Nate Goodman certainly seemed to."

He waved this away. "A difference of opinion, that's all. I'm sure Nate didn't give it another thought. You know what lawyers are like."

I know what my friend Heidi is like, Tova thought with a touch of bleakness. Heidi had surprised her by venturing out of her self-constructed shell today by offering to attend the meeting, and then going so far as to volunteer her advice. It had been sound advice, whether you agreed with it or not. Certainly not the vapid mouthing of a power-hungry New York attorney bent on having things her own way. But that was exactly the way Heidi felt she'd portrayed herself tonight.

The admission had not come easily. When Tova hurried after her at the meeting's end, she had found a Heidi seething with fury. "Who does he think he is? What makes his opinion more valid than mine? What right did he have to speak so condescendingly, as though there's no way in the world I could ever understand the gentler, kinder pace of small-town life? *What gave him the right?*"

She'd been beside herself for a long time, and nothing Tova said to calm her had the slightest effect. And then, abruptly, Heidi had spun jerkily around to face her — she'd been pacing the little guest room like a caged panther — and sunk down onto the bed. All the air seemed to go out of her, as though she were a pricked balloon. As her fury deflated, depression swam in to take its place.

"Who am I kidding?" Heidi said, staring down at the nubbly carpet. "I'm just sounding off to distract attention from the real facts of the case."

"What facts?" Tova had asked, bewildered.

"The fact that I shoved my oar in where it wasn't needed and definitely wasn't wanted. That Nate Goodman had every right to his opinion, because he lives here and I don't. He has a stake in what's decided at such meetings. I'm just the visitor: the jet-set lawyer dropping in to dispense my wisdom, then flying out again to glittering Manhattan and my high-stakes lifestyle." She gave Tova a brief, bitter smile. "If he only knew ..."

"Heidi! Everyone at that table wanted to hear your opinion. You have plenty of experience that can help us with a situation like the one we're dealing with. Would you please stop beating yourself up?"

But beating herself up seemed to be exactly what Heidi wanted to do. Her outburst at the table seemed to her, in retrospect, to have been in the poorest of poor taste. She'd been overbearing, intrusive and insensitive. Worst of all, she'd made a fool of herself in front of a fellow lawyer. "I called him small minded and provincial! Do you believe that, Tova? Just like a little kid, I threw a tantrum because he wouldn't see things my way."

"You didn't!" Tova protested. "You just voiced your opinion. Come on, Heidi, snap out of it!"

It was no use. Heidi was determined to brood about her shortcomings, and there was nothing Tova could do about it except wish her a warm good-night and hope that sleep would straighten out the kinks in her friend's point of view.

As she was about to pass through the guest-room door, Heidi called out from behind her, "Tova?"

"Yes?"

"Would you — I know this is asking a lot, but I'm asking you as a friend — would you call that guy up and apologize for me? For the things I called him, I mean. They weren't very nice."

"I don't mind doing that. But I still don't see —"

"Good-night, Tova. And thanks." She was dismissed.

Tova looked at Nachman now, and said simply, "She wants me to call Nate up and apologize. She can't forgive herself for what she calls her 'tantrum.'"

"Nate expressed himself pretty strongly, too, you know."

"Yes. But he didn't call her names. 'Small minded' and 'provincial' were her exact words, I believe."

"I see what you mean. Well, call him by all means, if it'll make you feel better." Nachman shook his head in mock-exasperation. "Whew! What a pair!"

Tova froze. Her eyes widened. Slowly, she turned to stare at her husband. "Nachman? Do you think ... maybe ...?"

Vigorously, he shook his head. "Don't even think about it, Tova. It's much too soon for Heidi to be thinking along those lines."

"It's not Heidi who's doing the thinking," Tova murmured. "It's me."

"Well, it's a free country. I can't stop you from thinking. But if I were you, Tova, I'd keep my fantasies in check. The way those two went at it today, it'll be a miracle if we can even get them to talk civilly to each other next time. It was like — like fire and water!"

Tova smiled, the shadow banished from her eyes. But whatever thoughts had brought on that smile, she elected to keep them to herself.

Chapter 11

I.

Shimi was acting up again.

Etty, his mother, gritted her teeth and willed herself to be calm. Still, the messages kept creeping into the unarmored crevices in her mind, a whining litany of grievance: "This is all I need! The baby's not well — due for surgery any day now! — and *this* is how he chooses to behave? If I can't count on my own son to cooperate at a time like this, who can I count on?" The answer, of course, was "no one," and it filled the edgy mother with resentment, which perched on top of her already-overflowing tension like a crow brooding over a heap of refuse.

The change had come over her son quite suddenly. She'd noticed it the moment Shimi came home from a hike with his friends the day before.

The Shimi who had left home had been sunny, equable, willing to tame his high-spirited nature if it would make his mother happy. After years of negative reports from his schools back East, Etty had begun to breathe easier and to dare hope that Shimi had rounded the bend into conformable behavior. For the first time in his young life, he was learning well. Maybe all he had needed was the kind of personalized attention he was getting at the hands of Asher Gann and Avi Feder, here in their tiny, home-brewed "yeshivah" in the shul.

But the Shimi who had walked through the back door after his outing with his friends was a white-faced, wild-eyed boy with the air of being about to explode from some inner tension. He'd hung around the kitchen for a while, getting in his mother's way as she had tried to cook the family's evening meal while keeping an anxious eye on the baby. Again and again, Shimi had opened with a tentative, "Ma —," only to break off and stare gloomily down at the tablecloth.

"What is it already?" Etty had asked impatiently. Stir the soup, chop the cucumbers, add a sprinkle of paprika to the chicken. "You keep starting and stopping. If you have something to say, then say it!"

"Say it! Say it!" 3-year-old Ora echoed gleefully, looking up from her coloring book to grin at her brother across the kitchen table. "Shimi, say it!"

Shimi opened his mouth again, then closed it with a snap. "I can't. I mean, I have nothing to say."

"Now, *that's* intelligent," his sister Tzirel remarked, having wandered into the room just in time to catch Shimi's words.

He scowled at her. "You stay out of this! Ma, tell her to stay out of it."

"Out of what?" Etty was confused. A full-blown quarrel seemed to be blowing up right here in her spotless kitchen, but she could not for the life of her have said which wind had ushered it in.

"Out of my life! Out of my business! *Tell her to keep her dumb, old comments to herself!*"

All three of them — Tzirel, Ora and their mother — turned to stare at him. His face was bright pink now, as though lit by some mysterious source of heat from within. It was as if he was working himself up into a towering rage, as a defense against some threat which left him helpless. A pitiful defense, bluster, but it was the only one he had. Though his words were loud and they were angry, the eyes that blazed above those pink cheeks held something that was not anger. Had she looked more closely, his mother might have recognized that something else as fear.

But Etty was not looking closely. Stir the soup, stick the baby's pacifier in her mouth, restore peace to the kitchen ...

"Shimi, I'll thank you to lower your voice. You're scaring the baby."

Shimi might have said a bitter word or two on the subject of being scared. But another voice was sounding in his mind.

"One word to anyone — anyone — about meeting us here, and you're going to wish you were never born. Got it?"

So Shimi said nothing. As he began to stomp out of the kitchen, Tzirel taunted softly, "I *told* you he didn't have anything intelligent to say."

In response, Shimi tweaked her pigtail, and had the gloomy satisfaction of hearing her wail in indignant pain. His mother promptly sent him to his room, which suited his mood just fine.

That had been only the beginning. Last night, this morning, and now this afternoon, Etty had spent the intervals between cooking and cleaning for the swiftly approaching Succos holiday, acting as referee in a series of fights between Shimi and his sisters. The shrill, raised voices that had alerted her to this latest fracas was the last straw. She didn't know about its breaking any camel's back; all she knew was that it had definitely snapped her own last shreds of tolerance. Frankly, she'd had her fill.

"Shimi!" she scolded. "How many times have I told you to leave your sister alone? Tzirel, if he teases you again, you come to me. He'll be punished." To Shimi again: "Take that as your last warning."

Shimi lowered his head until he resembled a bull preparing for attack. Instead of charging, however, he walked in silence out of his sisters' room and into his own. Etty heard the slam of his door, loud enough to wake the dead.

The person it did wake was Layala, who had just dropped off to sleep after what seemed like hours of fretful squalling. Wearily, Etty closed her eyes. She wished she could shut her ears, too; just blot out the crying and pretend it wasn't happening. And while she was at that game, she could pretend that her infant daughter was not about to be scheduled for surgery; that her son was not reverting to the troublesome old pattern that their move seemed, temporarily, to have broken; and that her husband was not busy snacking his way to oblivion in an attempt to anesthetize the pain of feeling himself inferior in his chosen profession. *And* that she wasn't living at the edge of nowhere as she was trying to cope with all of this.

A mighty sense of grievance filled her. When were things going to get easier? When was her family going to behave to her satisfaction, well mannered and healthy, all the pieces falling into place as in a chess game she couldn't help winning?

The answer, of course, was "never." The knowledge greeted her like an old, if not particularly beloved, friend. She was long used to life's refusal to conduct itself along the lines she'd laid down for it. Most aspects of her life felt like enemies, lurking in ambush to trip her up if she dared let herself feel even momentarily content. If this feeling of enmity impoverished her spirit and kept the corners of her mouth perpetually turned down, that was nobody's business but her own. When things went well, *then* she would smile! In the meantime, who had a better right to dissatisfaction than her?

Her eyes opened. Her ears, despite her wistful longing, had never been shut. With a sigh she didn't bother to stifle, she walked out of the girls' bedroom and into her own, where Layala was now howling in earnest. From down the hall she heard the machine in Shimi's room switch on, blaring his favorite CD at least 10 times louder than the human ear ought to be able to stand. Etty hesitated, wondering whether to confront him.

Instead, with another sigh that seemed to tear her already-raw nerves into long, fragile shreds, she kicked her own door shut and went to tend to the baby.

Steve Birch checked the address jotted in his little notepad. Yes, this was the place. Not a very appetizing place to live, judging by the odor of rancid spices and stale cigarette smoke that pervaded the narrow corridor. A welter of sound reached his ears from the various apartments in the squat building: two voices raised briefly in argument, a dull, throbbing melody blaring from a radio, a clatter of pots. From behind Bobby Smith's door there was no sound at all. Yet the super had assured Steve that Bobby and Big Jim were home. "They usually are, this time of the morning. Sleeping it off, y'know."

Steve knew. He knew all about the plague of alcoholism that was rife among the Native American community he had pledged himself to help. Too many in the community had turned to the bottle for solace. In Bobby's case, this was a pity. Whatever Steve might think of the man's lifestyle or morals, he had a certain strength of personality that could be sensed as soon as one entered Bobby's orbit. Steve recalled their brief vigil together at his stepfather's hospital bed. Bobby had given off the aura that belongs to an individual of steel will. What Bobby wanted, Bobby made sure to get. If only someone had taken the trouble to teach him to want the right things ...

Steve shook his head to shake off this train of thought. It was not his job to teach Bobby, or to rehabilitate him. If Bobby expressed an interest in either of those things, Steve would be more than happy to help. Right now, he was on a mission of a very different kind. He was here to interrogate a suspected arsonist.

He lifted his fist to the scarred door and knocked.

It was a full two minutes and several additional bouts of knocking — each round louder than the previous one — before a shuffle of feet told him that someone was coming. The face that greeted his own through a crack in the door was not friendly.

"Whaddayou want?" Bobby growled. He had not shaved that morning and his breath, even at a distance of a couple of feet, did not bear closer acquaintance. He wore gray sweat pants and a very grimy T-shirt that had once been white.

"Mind if I come in, Bobby?" Steve asked pleasantly. "I've got a couple of questions to ask you." He paused. "Jim, too, if he's here."

Bobby hesitated, as though weighing the option of slamming the door in the lawyer's face. Finally, with a grunt, he swung it open and stepped aside to let Steve enter.

Big Jim was there, a mountain of a man in a shabby armchair beside the room's only lamp. The lamp was switched on, despite the bright sunshine outdoors. With the shades drawn, the whole room was plunged into an artificial gloom hardly alleviated by the lamp's feeble, yellow gleam. Lamp, table, floor and every other visible surface sported a generous coat of dust. More dust specks danced in the dim light.

"May I sit?" Steve asked. Big Jim blinked at him, still only half awake. It was obvious that he'd fallen asleep in that chair — and in his clothes, which were extremely rumpled and emitting an interesting odor all their own.

"Suit yourself," Bobby said ungraciously. The eyes above the stubbled cheeks narrowed. "What kind of questions?"

Steve settled himself comfortably in another armchair, facing the one at present very fully occupied by Big Jim. Still addressing himself to Bobby, he said, "As you may have heard, there have been a couple of cases of arson in this town. Both of the targets were Jewish institutions. First the synagogue — remember the night we ran into each other there, Bobby? — and now the site of the new Jewish high school, just outside town." He paused, waiting.

"What's any of that got to do with me?" The words emerged in a snarl.

"Well, that's just what I don't know, Bobby. Suppose we start by you telling me what you were doing down by the synagogue that night."

"I told you — I was taking a walk. Any law against takin' a walk in this town? If there is, I never heard of it." If Bobby's sarcasm aimed for a jocular note, the deep-set eyes told a very different story. They were still as stone, watching Steve carefully as adrenalin coursed through his veins in an instinctive fight-or-flight response to the line of questioning.

"No law that I've heard of, either," Steve said, still affably. "The trouble is, the fire broke out at the synagogue not long after you were there, Bobby. Coincidence?"

"Sure, that's what it is. A coincidence!"

"I'm not so sure." Steve leveled his gaze on the other man's, and suddenly his manner was not affable any more. Their eyes met and locked. Coldness met coldness, the one coming from an innate directness and integrity, the other calibrated for survival.

"I was right here with Jim that night," Bobby said flatly. "Jim can vouch for that. Can't you, Jim?"

"Sure," Big Jim said at once. "Sure, I can vouch for that all right." He sank back in his chair, pleased with himself for proving so helpful to his friend.

"And which night would that be?" Steve asked. "I don't recall mentioning any dates."

"Keep your trap shut," Bobby hissed at his well-meaning friend.

"No, don't do that," Steve said, turning to smile with a degree of warmth at the big man with the eyes of a simpleton. "Talk to me, Jim. Tell me about that night."

"We-e-ell ..." Big Jim's forehead creased in his effort to remember. "I was supposed to pick Bobby up in my car by the Jewish building one night ..."

It was all Bobby could do not to leap on Jim and muzzle him. It was with a monumental effort of will that he restrained himself. His only comfort was that Jim seemed to be confusing the night when Bobby had met Steve with the night the arson had actually been committed.

"Pick him up? Why?" Steve was alert.

"It's a long walk back here."

Bobby clenched his fists in impotent fury. Would Jim mention the kerosene that Bobby had taken with him? If he did, the game was up. They would both be behind bars before you could say, "buried treasure."

"I see." Steve slanted a glance at Bobby. "Do you usually take your walks so far from home?"

Bobby shrugged, inwardly breathing a sigh of relief. But the relief might still be premature. He had to get Big Jim to keep his mouth shut. Maybe, if *he* did the talking, the lawyer would stop focusing on Jim.

"I couldn't sleep. You know how it is. I had no idea the place was a — what'd you call it? Synagogue? I was just walking. Jim ... Uh, Jim knows how it is when I can't sleep. He was going to come get me if I wandered too far away from home. He's nice that way, Jim is. A real pal."

"And suppose I were to ask your pal if you had anything with you that night?"

"Why should I have anything with me?" Bobby said hastily. "A guy doesn't carry stuff around when he takes a walk, does he? If you asked Jim that question, he'd just say, 'No, not a thing.' Wouldn't you, Jim?" The black eyes fixed themselves on Jim.

The big man shifted nervously in his chair. "Uh, sure, Bobby. That's what I'd say, all right."

"I'm sure you would," Steve said. He shifted gears. "Let's talk about the fire at the surveyor's camp."

"The what?"

"There's a team of surveyors mapping out the site where the Jewish school's going to be built. Someone set fire to three of their tents the other day. Know anything about that?"

Bobby tensed. "No. Why should I?"

"I wouldn't know. Spend any time in that area, Bobby?"

"Now and then. Me 'n Jim like to hike."

"How do you earn your living, Bobby?"

"Jim 'n me, we do some odd jobs for folks around here. Sometimes Jim uses his car to drive people places — what you might call a car service, know what I mean? We get by."

"Plan to spend much more time in this place?" Steve left the question deliberately vague, so that Bobby wouldn't know whether he was referring to "this apartment" or "this town."

Bobby shrugged. "I couldn't say. We take it day by day, know what I mean?"

Steve stood up, heartily sick of the musty, odoriferous room and the unsavory pair inside it. "Then I'll be sure and find you here when I want to talk again?"

"If you say so ... " Bobby shrugged.

"Good-bye for now, Bobby. You too, Jim. Nice chatting with you."

With that, he let himself out.

Bobby held his breath until the door had closed behind the lawyer. Then, with a whoosh of expelled air, he sank into the nearest chair and ran a forearm across his damp forehead.

"That was close," he muttered. He turned to Jim, lips tightening. "Now, listen here, Jim. There's a few things you got to remember. Or rather, things that you got to forget."

The sun shone brightly in the world outside, but in the shabby living room the lamp did its feeble best to illuminate the impromptu schoolroom in which Bobby Smith set himself to teach his hapless friend a thing or two.

II.

Avi drove up the Flatbush street that exuded a disturbing sense of welcome. He did not have to look far to pinpoint its source.

It was not that the houses greeted him with any particular friendliness. They were as impersonal as they'd been the first time he drove up this block, stately behind their attractive brick facades and the occasional scrap of lawn. Nor did the row of shade trees — black shapes against the night sky — welcome him with any special warmth. The house before which he eventually pulled up — grateful for the miracle that had afforded him a parking space just where he needed it — did not roll out a red carpet in his honor. It rested on its modest lot exactly the way it had on his last two visits, the curtained windows giving away nothing, the whole place coolly self-contained in typical New York fashion.

No, the source of the feeling — the odd and disturbing sense of homecoming — came not from bricks or trees, but from the person waiting for him behind those windows.

It was a strange feeling, being waited for. It gave him a pang of pleasure, quickly suppressed. He was not courting that kind of feeling these days. He was not courting pleasure. He was not courting. Not really.

If that was the case, he asked himself as he climbed out of the car and started for the front door, *what in the world am I doing here?*

My mom made me do it, he thought in his own defense. But that had been true only the first time. His first meeting with Shiffy Taub had been a matter of honoring his parents, no more and no less. He had already met a string of other prospects on this visit back home, and this encounter would be just another bead on the same string.

Somehow, the bead turned into two beads, and now here was a third, come to join the first two to form the beginning of a bright, hopeful necklace to hang around his befuddled neck.

He shook his head to shake it free of these unwanted images. This was the next-to-last day of *Chol HaMoed*. Tomorrow night would be Yom Tov again, and after that he would be winging his way back to New Mexico, to his *kollel* and his bachelor apartment and his real life. This meeting —

this *third* meeting — and the young woman who waited for him behind that door, was as meaningless as all the others. Shiffy was just a little more congenial than the rest of them had been, that's all. If his mother insisted on forcing him to jump through these hoops, why not relax while he was doing it?

He had told Shiffy right off the bat, on their first meeting, that he was unready for a second marriage. She might (as he, himself, had silently done a moment ago) have asked him what, in that case, he was doing at a lounge with her tonight. She didn't ask. She merely listened with her grave, attentive air, nodded slowly, and said, "I can understand that. You're still hurting from the loss of your wife. How can anyone be expected to jump into something new, and especially something as life affirming as marriage, under those conditions?"

"You do understand," Avi had said gratefully. With a sudden sense of release, he had held up his hand to order another set of Cokes. He realized with vague surprise that he wanted to prolong the evening. As long as they both knew this was going nowhere, he was free to appreciate Shiffy's company. And he had to admit that he did appreciate it, if only for the pleasure of sharing their respective tales of suffering; like a couple of kids after an ordeal at the playground, comparing skinned knees.

Shiffy Taub had experienced as much pain as Avi in the recent past. More so, perhaps, because the tragic accident that took her husband had been so unexpected. Avi's Yocheved had wasted away over the course of many months of illness, until the woman he buried was only a shadow of the one with whom he'd stood beneath the *chuppah*. Shiffy's husband, in contrast, had been taken from her in the full flush of health and strength. As she described the experience, it was like riding a bike along what seemed to be an obstacle-free road only to smash full tilt into a brick wall that suddenly materialized out of nowhere. The impact stole her breath away and left her gasping and doubled over in agony for a long time.

"You have a son," Avi had said, stating the fact more than asking. His mother had provided him with a full resume before he made that first call to Shiffy.

"Yes. Tzvi was just a baby when my husband was killed. He's 2 now."

He shook his head in sympathy. "That must've been tough. At least I didn't have anyone to be responsible for when my wife died. I had only myself to take care of." And I didn't even do a very good job of that, he added inwardly.

"You've got it all wrong," Shiffy had told him. Though she spoke calmly, an intent look had leaped into her brown eyes, a signal for his attention. He was learning to recognize that look: It meant that what was coming next touched a deep place in her.

"It was Tzvi who kept me sane during those first months," Shiffy went on. "Both before he was born, and after. When Heshy died, I felt as if I had nothing to live for … but then I realized that I did. I had this baby who was totally dependent on me to create a good life for him. He was always there, a reminder that I was not allowed to slide into the black hole of grief that I so much wanted to hide in. I had to live — for him.

"Before the accident, I knew he depended on me. After, the sense of being responsible, of being needed, became a thousand times stronger." She paused, then finished simply, "There's nothing like knowing that someone needs you to make you feel your life is worth living."

Avi listened in silence. What was *he* living for? His Torah, of course. He was making great strides in his learning, and this afforded him enormous satisfaction. His family and friends, of course … indirectly. They had their own lives to lead. None of them were dependent on him, not the way Shiffy's child was on her. He thought further. There were the boys he was homeschooling this year, Chaim and Donny Bernstein and Shimi Mandel. They needed him, didn't they?

Somehow, he didn't think that any of these things were what Shiffy had in mind. She was gazing at him in that same intent way, waiting for his reaction. Waiting for a sign that he'd heard her.

He was not able to give her much. "I guess I'll take that on faith," he said slowly. "I don't have any children. Nor, at the moment, do I have a wife. Nobody really needs me as much as all that." It was a painful admission.

Later, back in his old room at his mother's house, staring at the ceiling as the sleepless hours ticked past, Avi had realized that he was going to do something completely unexpected. He was going to break his own rule and see Shiffy again. He had a sense of a conversation unfinished between them. He would meet her a second time, just to prove to his mother that he *was* trying.

Their second meeting had taken place on a sunny, *Chol HaMoed* afternoon. They went to the New York Aquarium. They had talked easily, mostly about what they were viewing. Avi proved adept at imitating the funny fish-faces they observed, and Shiffy, though generally of a rather serious demeanor, turned out to be capable of giggling in a lighthearted way that refused to acknowledge past suffering. They ended the afternoon with a stroll down the boardwalk, nearly deserted on this October day. A couple of elderly women, muffled to their chins, sat on a bench in silent companionship. Young people rattled past, almost horizontal on their 10-speed bikes.

"I love the ocean," Shiffy had remarked as she neatly dodged a couple of speeding bikers. "When I'm breathing in the sea air, I can't see anything wrong with the world."

Avi took an experimental breath. "It *is* an optimistic sort of smell," he agreed. The comment took him by surprise. He was not usually of a whimsical turn of mind.

Shiffy nodded, delighted with his insight. "The breeze off the ocean seems to carry happiness on its back and scatter it everywhere, like seeds." She glanced at him sideways. "Am I making sense?"

"Terrific sense. Though there's more than just happiness there, I think."

"Optimism, you said."

"Yes. It's the smell of the future … a good future. And the smell of distance, where the things that are hurting you don't really matter anymore."

"That's right! That's exactly what I do sometimes, when I'm feeling low. I think of some faraway place, where people are walking around completely oblivious to my pain. If they don't even know about it, how bad can it be?" She laughed.

He laughed along with her, recklessly ignoring the fact that he was behaving completely out of character. It must be the influence of this unexpected young woman, bringing out hidden aspects of him. He drew in another deep lungful of sea air, reveling in its clean, cool tang. They walked along in silence for a while. Somehow, it seemed enough.

Later, when he remarked diffidently to his mother that he thought he would ask Shiffy out for a third time, she became nearly air borne with excitement.

"Relax, Mom," he said with a wry twist of the lips. "This is just a third meeting, that's all. Don't make any assumptions. It doesn't mean anything."

"*Why* doesn't it mean anything?" Mrs. Feder had demanded.

"Just … because." He sounded ridiculously childish in his own ears. "I told you I wasn't ready, Mom."

"In that case" — her eyes grew stern — "it's wrong to see her again."

"Oh, she's not ready, either. We clarified that on our first meeting. So it's all right."

Mrs. Feder pursed her lips as though to cast doubt on the "all rightness" of this move. But, having her private doubts about some of the other things her son had said, as well, she held her tongue.

And so, here he was, hand poised to knock on Shiffy's door for the third time in this extraordinary week. His projected departure had made the speeded-up schedule mandatory. In all probability, this would be the last time he would see Shiffy Taub. He would fly back to Lakewood on the day after Yom Tov, carrying with him the memory of an interesting and comfortable companion with serious brown eyes that could light up like the flaring of a match when she laughed ...

The door opened at his knock. The house belonged to her parents, but at the moment they were nowhere to be seen. Mr. Taub had interviewed Avi with fatherly punctiliousness on their first meeting; the second one had been preceded by a few minutes of small talk with Shiffy's parents before he'd whisked her away. Throughout both, he had sensed a wariness in them, an almost suspicious vigilance. They seemed very anxious to safeguard their daughter's happiness, as though, having suffered what she had till now, she would not easily be dislodged from their protective wings so soon. Avi was the first person she'd agreed to meet since becoming widowed.

"Hi, Avi," Shiffy said. To his surprise, she seemed underdressed for a night out on the town. Her skirt and blouse were neat but casual, her heels low, her face nearly devoid of makeup. "There's been a snag."

"A snag?" he repeated stupidly. "What do you mean?" He felt acutely conscious of his formal attire, the suit and hat and carefully selected tie.

"It's Tzvi. He's running a fever and feeling very unhappy. I've spoken to the doctor and he suggested that I bring him in tomorrow. In the meantime, though, I can't just go out and leave him. My mother's willing to tend to Tzvi, but he keeps calling for me. I don't feel right going out tonight."

"Oh." His heart became heavy as lead, sinking down to the level of his freshly polished shoes. "But I'm leaving right after Yom Tov. I wouldn't be able to give you a rain check ..."

"I know." She looked sad. Then she peeked at him uncertainly. "Unless ..."

"Unless what?"

"How do you feel about a sit-in date?" The words emerged in a rush, tumbling over each other in her eagerness to get them out.

"Sit-in?" He seemed to be doing nothing but echoing things she said tonight. He made an effort to collect his wits.

"My mother can keep an eye on Tzvi, and if he really needs me I'll just take him out of his crib and let him join us. We could talk, and maybe play a board game or something ..." She trailed off, waiting for his reaction. When it didn't come at once, she added quickly, "Of course, if you'd rather just cancel and go home, I'll understand."

Of course she would. She always did. Belatedly, Avi offered a reassuring grin. Why was he standing on the doorstep like a fool? He stepped inside, and she moved to close the door. "I like Stratego, if you have it. If not, Scrabble's fine."

She relaxed. "We have both. But I've got to warn you, Tzvi may need to join us at some point."

"No problem. We'll let him play, too."

He was rewarded by a big smile. Shiffy looked not only reassured, but happy. To his own astonishment, that made him feel the same way.

"Lead on," he said, removing his hat.

"The game room is right this way," she murmured, showing him into her parents' big, comfortable living room, where several board games were already waiting on the coffee table. Among them, he saw to his wonder, were both Scrabble and Stratego.

They were deeply absorbed in a Stratego competition when Shiffy's father wandered into the room to get a *sefer* from the bookshelf. He directed a vague, amiable smile at Avi and murmured something about a question he needed to research for school. He was a yeshivah high-school rebbi and the kids, he confided, sometimes came up with the most marvelous stumpers. Sometime later, Shiffy's mother came in carrying little Tzvi. She left the room, only to return again almost immediately with a tray of coffee and cake, and a cookie for the toddler enthroned on his mother's lap.

Tzviki's arrival more or less ended the game session; the child displayed a definite penchant for the red Stratego pieces, and there was no chance of proceeding with any safety while the board was anywhere in the reach of those pudgy little fingers. "Veekee play!" he announced, his illness forgotten in the thrill of the game. Avi noted the pink splotches on the boy's cheeks, and the glassy look in his eyes that betokened fever. Rescuing the Stratego pieces, he set himself to entertain the child with some of the funny faces he'd practiced at the Aquarium. Tzvi tried to imitate the faces while his mother looked on, smiling. There was a lot of conversation, some laughter, and a desultory stab or two at starting another game. Somewhere in the course of the evening Avi dispensed with his jacket and loosened his tie. By the time Shiffy got up to put a now droopy-eyed Tzvi back into his crib, Avi was surprised to find that it was after midnight.

As he stood up to go, a strange reluctance weighed down the hand that reached for his jacket and hat. Though it was only October, the night outside this snug living room seemed very cold and uninviting. Here, inside, the air was suffused with a glow, as though someone had poured molten gold over everything. He was inside one of those plastic bubbles which, if turned upside down and shaken, turn into a snowy wonderland. Only it wasn't snow that danced in the air like current-driven dust motes. It was contentment.

There was a sudden flash of memory. The last time he'd felt this way, comfortable and safe in a lamp-lit living room with the vast, dark night held at bay beyond his windows, had been the week before Yocheved was diagnosed. That had been the last time he'd felt truly content with himself and his life. The last time joy danced invisibly through the air around him, for no special reason except that he was in his own snug home, and his wife was near, and life was good.

He didn't want to be feeling that way now. He *couldn't* be feeling that way now.

With a surge of something that was three-parts guilt and one-part panic, he bid a surprised Shiffy — who had just returned, minus Tzvi — a hasty good-night, and all but ran out the door.

Three nights later, he was on a Southwest Airlines flight bound for New Mexico. He had not spoken to Shiffy again.

III.

"**I**t never rains but it pours." Etty Mandel could almost hear her grandmother saying the words: her mantra in times of trouble. The consensus in the family had long been that Etty was a chip off the old grand-maternal block; in their approach to life's problems, they were virtually identical. Whenever some difficulty arose to tilt the ground beneath her feet, Etty would clutch her seat and wait for more. Because something more, in her experience, was always waiting to happen.

So she was not surprised — dismayed, but not surprised — to hear her cell phone ring in Layala's hospital room that afternoon, with her husband's voice at the other end. Some sixth sense — an intuition long attuned to the frequency that broadcast unexpected trouble — heard something in his voice that he was trying to disguise.

"How're you holding up, Etty? And how's Layala?" He already knew, from calls to and from his wife earlier in the day, that the operation had been a success. Little Layala was asleep now, with her mother hovering nearby ready to pounce if she woke to any sign of pain or discomfort. Already, Etty Mandel had half the ward nurses jumping through hoops to reassure her, every hour on the hour, that the baby was recovering nicely.

"Layala's fine, *Baruch Hashem*," Etty said sharply into the phone. "What's the matter, Efraim? What's wrong?"

"Wrong? What should be wrong?"

"Efraim ..."

A sigh. "I didn't want to worry you. You've got enough on your hands, what with Layala's surgery and all ..."

"But?"

"But — it's Ora."

"Ora?" Etty stood up, clutching the receiver as an image of her curly-haired 3-year-old rose up before her mind's eye. "What's wrong with her?"

"She's got a fever. I thought she looked flushed after her nap, so I took her temperature. It's 102."

"Does she have any other symptoms?"

"No. I called the doctor," Efraim went on, anticipating her next question. "And he said to keep the fever down and bring her in if she complained of any pain or seemed especially out of sorts."

"Is she? Out of sorts, I mean."

"Well, that's the problem. She keeps asking for you."

Efraim had his strengths, as Etty knew. They included playing games with his kids, listening to their complaints and offering simple "kiddie" foods to keep them happily, if not particularly healthfully, nourished. What he was less good at was nurturing a sick child. Illness made Efraim jittery, and Ora was very attached to her mother in any case. Etty bit her lip. Her eye traveled to the baby, peacefully asleep in her bassinet and hooked up to equally somnolent monitors. There was a stir at the other end of the line, and then her husband's voice, saying, "Here. Ora wants to talk to you."

"Mo-o-o-mmy ..." The thin wail tore at Etty's heart. "Mommy, come home."

"Soon, darling," Etty said, her brain spinning furiously to find a solution to this dilemma. "Soon ..." Could Efraim find someone to stay with the kids while he and Etty switched places? The thought of leaving her husband with Layala made her bite her lip again. He was not at his best with infants, tending to handle them like fragile china and transmitting his own trepidation to the baby. What to do?

"Please put Tatty back on the phone, Ora," she said soothingly.

"Are you coming home? I'm sick!"

"Soon ... Is Tatty there?"

At last, Tatty was there. "Efraim, I'm going to have to call you back. I need a few minutes to think."

"All right. Take your time, Etty. I'll be here."

They hung up. Etty checked the baby again, then the monitor. With the *kollel* still in vacation mode until *Rosh Chodesh*, Efraim had been conveniently on hand to cope with the other children while Etty ushered poor Layala through her ordeal. Ora's illness was an unforeseen and unwanted complication; a rogue wind to blow away all of Etty's carefully laid plans.

Her mind scrambled to figure out her next move. The upcoming 24 hours loomed like a jigsaw puzzle with all the pieces scrambled. She had only a limited time to get them in order if the picture was to make any sense at all.

There was no choice. She would have to send her husband to Roswell in her place. Layala was recovering nicely, and Ora needed her at home. The thought of leaving her baby was an agonizing one, but logic told her that it was the only solution. Efraim would just have to cope.

She was just reaching for her cell phone to inform him of her decision when there was a hesitant knock at the door.

"Come in," Etty called.

A head poked its tentative way around the door. Rivi Gann. Rivi had driven all this way to see Layala.

"Hi, Etty! I heard from Efraim that the operation was a success, *Baruch Hashem*!"

"Yes. The doctors are pleased. How nice of you to come all this way, Rivi. Don't you teach today?"

"I gave a few art classes this morning, but there's nothing on for this afternoonp; it's my easy day. So I figured I'd use the free time to see how Layala is doing." As Rivi's eyes strayed to the sleeping infant, her expression softened.

Without any premeditation, Etty found herself blurting, "Rivi? I never would have asked you to drive to Roswell in the first place ... but since you did anyway, I wonder if you'd be able to do me a favor ..."

"What is it? I'd love to help."

Quickly, Etty outlined the situation. "Efraim can be here in a little over an hour, if I leave now. Would you mind keeping an eye on Layala for me? I don't like leaving her alone here even for that amount of time."

"Of course!" Rivi's face brightened like the sun. "I'll be happy to. If Layala wakes up, she'll recognize me. We're old friends, she and I."

"Thanks, Rivi. I knew I could count on you. Efraim's not going to know what to do with himself here," Etty said, briskly gathering her things. "He's hopeless with small babies, and dealing with one who's just had surgery is probably going to put him over the top!" Her look was troubled. Then another thought struck her. "I wonder if he'll be able to find a *minyan* here for Minchah and Ma'ariv? And if he does, who'll stay with Layala while he *davens*?"

Rivi moved closer to the distraught mother. "Etty, listen to me. There's a very simple solution to all of this. There's a reason Hashem put it into my head to make the trip to Roswell this afternoon. I'm obviously needed here. Efraim doesn't have to come. I'll just call Asher to let him know I'm staying here for as long as necessary."

"But it'll have to be all night! Ora's running a fever. She'll probably wake up in the night ... I won't be able to leave her."

"Not a problem," Rivi said serenely. "Come on, Etty. You know and I know that this is the ideal solution. I don't have any kids who need me at home. I have some experience with Layala already, and I'll take great care of her until you get back. If you like, I'll call you often to let you know how she's doing." She paused. "Well?"

"It's too much to ask."

"Let me be the judge of that!" At that moment, it would have been hard for an outsider to know who was the supplicant. There was something close to pleading in Rivi's eye. Etty, gazing worriedly at the sleeping Layala, didn't notice. Since their move to Lakewood, Rivi had become an almost built-in babysitter for Layala. She was familiar with the baby's habits, and Etty knew her to be a capable caregiver. As long as her needs were adequately met, Layala was still too young to mind her mother's absence. It really was a perfect solution.

Still, Etty hesitated.

"Let me help, Etty," Rivi urged. "I'll take good care of Layala for you."

Etty hesitated a beat longer. As a solution, it seemed almost too good to be true. "She doesn't take a bottle," she murmured. "I'd have to get hold of a pump."

"What better place than a hospital?" Rivi asked blithely.

"Well, if you're sure ..."

"I'm positive."

"What if Ora's still sick in the morning?"

"You stay with Ora as long as you think she needs you. Layala will be in good hands."

A moment later, Efraim heard his wife's voice on the phone. "You're off the hook, Efraim. Rivi's here."

The jigsaw puzzle was falling neatly into place. Etty peered through the windshield as she moved out of the hospital parking lot, strangely bereft without her baby. She watched the play of sunlight on the white stucco walls of the houses, and later on the scrub brush growing along the highway. The sun was harsher here than the one back East. It was a desert sun, reigning supreme in a pitiless end-of-summer sky. Was this the kind of sky under which the fledgling Jewish nation once trekked through the wilderness, on their way to the Promised Land?

As she drove, Etty thought of her own journey, from her childhood home in a Chicago suburb to her married home in Brooklyn, then on to — of all places! — this tiny town in New Mexico that few people had ever heard of. In a sense, she, too, was always traveling, heading for some mythical Promised Land of her own. A place where all the various elements of her life would come together and she could finally be content. When would that magical moment come? When would it all be perfect?

Then she was turning the key in her own door, and stepping into her own immaculate front hall. Efraim hurried out of the kitchen to greet her, the towel tucked into his belt liberally spattered with pizza sauce.

"Ora!" Cupping his hands to his mouth, he roared in the direction of the back bedrooms. "Ora, Mommy's home!"

"Mommy!" The eager, little voice spurred Etty down the hall even before she took off her coat.

She had been waiting a long, wistful time for her life to become perfect. For all she knew, the wait stretched beyond the visible horizon — and then some.

Just now, though, the quest for perfection would have to wait. Her daughter needed her.

IV.

Mrs. Simi Wurtzler stepped out of her car, straightened her jacket and adjusted the strap of her no-nonsense shoulder-bag. She was parked in front of the day-school building. *Her* building, was the way she always regarded it — and with some justification. Not so many years before, the day school had been no more than a dream in the collective mind of Lakewood's tiny but burgeoning Jewish community. It had been largely due to Simi's devoted efforts that it had become the successful institution it was today.

Her efforts, and those of Penina Harris. But the rabbi's wife had moved on, after a time, to create a girls' high school, leaving the still-fledgling day school to Simi's tender ministrations. The school was the fruit of her mind and heart: her baby. For a middle-aged woman with a nurturing nature and a manager's practicality whose own children had already flown the nest, the Lakewood Jewish Day School was a wonderfully satisfying substitute.

Simi Wurtzler was the first to arrive at the low-lying building of blond brick on this first day after the Succos break. There was no real reason to be here this early, at an hour when most of the teachers and all of the students were hardly out of their beds. She was the proverbial "morning person" who found it impossible to sleep past the sun's first rays. And because she was up with the sun and first on the scene, she was the first to see the message that some wicked hand had left behind to greet her.

The words were scrawled on the school's front wall just beside the large front doors, in foot-high letters of blood red:

JEWS GO HOME.

They were the same words that had appeared on the shul building some months before, though Simi herself had not seen them: Rabbi Harris had ordered the repugnant message washed off posthaste. With chalk-white face and splotches of crimson fury dotting both cheekbones, the principal walked right up to the wall. From this vantage point, the paint looked smeary and uneven, with ugly drips dangling from some of the thick red letters like hangnails from stubby toes. A hasty job, with no finesse to smooth the rough edges of hate. She wished that she could spread herself six feet across, to conceal the horrendous message from the children's eyes when they leaped out of cars and minivans in just over an hour's time.

If she couldn't transform herself into a human shield, she would do the next-best thing: turn herself into a human eraser. Impossible, in the time available to her, to wash away the message with soap and water — but there was another recourse. Hurrying as though pursued by demons — the anonymous demons who had defaced her beloved school — she went down to the basement, where all the leftover paint of the ages was stored. She soon found what she was looking for. Ignoring her labored breathing and the sharp pang of protest beneath her heart, she hastened back outside to the defaced wall, pried open the lid of the can she'd carried up with her, picked up a brush stiff with layers of ancient paint, and set to work.

Heedless of her good suit, she worked in a frenzy, using the black paint to draw heavy lines across the offending words on the wall. The black completely obliterated the red, as she had hoped it would. Dip, paint, and dip again, until the first of the hateful words had been turned into a dense, black oblong. Then the second word, and the third. By the time the first of the cars rolled into the parking lot, Simi was in the washroom, trying — in vain — to scrub away the dark stains on her hands. Out front, the pale building was marred by ugly rectangles of fresh, black paint. This, she knew, would raise a great many eyebrows and elicit endless questions. She was fully prepared to provide answers to those questions to any parties who might require them.

But at least her children would not be met by hate when they walked up the path on their first day back at school after the Succos break.

"Ta, it's that Indian again."

Chaim spoke in a whisper, but his father heard. Nachman lifted his head from his Gemara (what a luxury to be able to learn at his leisure in his own study at home — in the morning!) and said calmly, despite his surprise, "Send him in."

Chaim returned to the front door bearing his father's invitation. What luck that school hadn't started for him yet! With the *kollel* closed for the *bein hazemanim* break until *Rosh Chodesh*, he, Donny and Shimi Mandel were enjoying an extended vacation. Wait till the others heard that the Indian had come back to their house! This visit was connected to the rash of hate crimes that had been targeting Jewish sites in the area; that much, Chaim's intuition told him in no uncertain terms. Briefly, he considered listening at the keyhole of his father's study, then rejected the idea. A good upbringing and his own conscience ruled out such a maneuver. He could only hope that his father would agree to fill him in afterward.

Steve Birch, on entering the study, saw at once that Rabbi Bernstein had no idea of the latest anti-Semitic outrage to be perpetrated in their midst. Nachman's greeting was pleasant, with a subtle inflection that implied some curiosity over his visitor's unexpected appearance. Steve felt the same strange combination of reverence and comfort wash over him as he took the chair the rabbi indicated. Abruptly, after they'd shaken hands, he said, "I'm sorry to be the bearer of bad news. Did you hear about what happened at the school?"

A jolt of electricity ran through Nachman. "No. What happened?"

"The principal discovered it this morning — luckily, before the students got there. Another hate message. Same color, same text — this guy's not very original is he? — splashed across the front of the building."

For an endless moment, Nachman simply stared. What visions were crossing the screen of his mind Steve couldn't know, but he was certain they weren't pretty. At last, remembering to breathe, Nachman sucked in a long lungful of air. "I see. So our Jew-hater strikes again."

"Seems that way. Although she was aware that she was tampering with the evidence, Mrs. Wurtzler, the principal, had the presence of mind to cover the message with black paint before the kids arrived to see it. Then she phoned the sheriff, who eventually phoned me."

"I see," Nachman said again. His heart rate was beginning to return to normal. Fleetingly, he wondered how Jews had survived in earlier centuries, when a "hate message" might take the form of a village-wide pogrom or a bullet to the heart. He supposed he ought to be grateful that their own particular nemesis seemed to have opted for a less dramatic method of making his feelings known. Damaging as arson might be to both property and the psyche, it was fortunately not lethal.

Still, the cumulative effect of all these incidents was devastating, which was exactly, perhaps, what the perpetrator wanted. Make things uncomfortable enough, the guy hoped, and his message would sink in. JEWS GO HOME!

It was impossible to sit still, but the study was too small to make per-ambulations feasible, especially with a guest perched on a chair facing the desk. In lieu of pacing the room, Nachman tilted back his big chair and began rocking rhythmically back and forth as his mind processed their next move.

He met Steve's eye. "Any progress among the Native American popu-lation? The last time we met, you said you had some possible leads."

"I've questioned a few suspects in the arson cases. My attention is pretty firmly fixed on one man in particular, and a friend of his — actu-ally, more of a sidekick, or willing slave. So far, my suspicions fall into the category of pure hunch, minus any evidence, so my hands are tied. But I'm keeping an eye on them."

"Nothing else from the sheriff's office?"

"Nothing yet, though he's been trying. There's not much of a criminal element in Lakewood, which is why he's been focusing on the reserva-tion. But, as I say, that's been a washout, too. So far."

Nachman stopped rocking and landed on all four legs of the chair with a thud. "Then we're still where we were before. Nowhere." He sounded discouraged.

"We'll get him, rabbi," Steve said softly. "We'll get him, and we'll put him away so no one else will ever get the idea that the Jews aren't wel-come members of our community."

"Thank you, Mr. Birch. I appreciate those words."

"Please, call me Steve."

"Fine — if you'll call me Nachman."

Steve looked startled. "But — you're a rabbi!"

Laughing, Nachman said, "Don't put a halo on me, Steve. I just try my best, like anyone."

The friendliness in his tone made him seem so approachable that Steve found his hand straying to his pocket. "Uh … may I ask you something, rabbi? Of a more personal nature …"

Now it was Nachman's turn to look startled. He almost reminded his guest to call him by his first name, but refrained. Something in the Indian's manner told him that it was in his capacity of rabbi that Steve was now approaching him. He settled back in his chair and said, with an encouraging smile once again tinged with curiosity, "Certainly. How can I help you, Steve?"

Without a word, Steve took the *siddur* out of his pocket.

It was the same *siddur* that had been wrapped in paper on the top of his closet at home for years, neglected and all but forgotten until his first encounter with Rabbi Bernstein the week before. Since then, it had been burning a hole in his pocket, waiting for the right moment to emerge into the light of day. The moment had arrived.

Nachman took the *siddur* in silence and studied it. He saw that it was very old, its yellowed pages so terribly fragile that he was afraid to turn them. The front cover showed gilt letters nearly rubbed away by friction and time, and a gold *Magen David* in the same condition. He looked up at Steve. "Where did you get this?"

Steve was carefully noncommittal. "I picked it up somewhere. It's — it's just like the one I saw in this room last time, rabbi, isn't it? A prayer book?"

"Yes. We call it a *siddur*. Jews pray from it three times a day, including the Sabbath and holidays. This one looks very old: an antique. It may be valuable." He was on the point of adding, "Exactly where did you find it?" but something held him back. Something in the nature of a warning, a wall of stone, in the eyes of the man facing him.

Steve said nothing.

Nachman sensed that there was more to this *siddur* than Steve was telling, just as there was more to Steve himself than met the eye. And speaking of eyes, this Indian had the oddest ones for a man of his breed: hazel instead of the usual black, the perimeter darker than the rest. Was Steve some sort of half-breed? And, if so, what was his history?

An intriguing question. But, right now, it faded beside the present-day concerns weighing on the *Rosh Kollel*. Arson had been committed on both the shul and the site of the new Jewish institution in its earliest stages on the outskirts of town; a series of hate messages of anti-Semitic import had defaced that same shul, and today, the Jewish day school as well. There was a disquieting pattern here that could not be ignored.

Nachman waited a little longer for his visitor to speak. Had his visitor demonstrated a desire to confide further in him, Nachman would have put aside his worries and listened with all his attention. But Steve Birch, constrained by early conditioning and his own reticent nature, was waiting for the rabbi to draw him out with the right question. A question he hardly knew how he would answer, shrouded as his own past had always been in mystery.

But Nachman didn't ask, and Steve, after a moment, stood up. Nachman handed back the *siddur*, though his eye lingered on it for a long moment after he passed it over. "A special *siddur*," he said. "I'd be interested in having it dated. Would you like to donate it to a Jewish museum, or at least hand it over to experts for assessment?"

Steve hesitated. "Maybe some other time," he said. "Right now, I'd like to hold onto it, if you don't mind."

"Mind? Why should I mind? It's yours, isn't it?"

"Yes," Steve said. The word was deeply weighted. "It's mine."

They parted affably. Nachman walked his visitor to the front door, where Steve turned, strangely diffident.

"May I — may I come speak with you again, rabbi? Not about the case, I mean." There was something in the Indian lawyer's manner that was very different from the cool, hard face he showed the world. Various criminal elements among the area's Native American community would have been hard put to recognize him just then.

"Certainly," Nachman said, putting out his hand again, though they'd already shaken in the study. "Come anytime. We'll talk."

With these words ringing in his ears, Steve Birch left the Bernstein home.

In the living room, which gave a clear view of the front door, Chaim was all agog.

V.

"Something else has happened, Donny. I know it, because that same Indian came to see Tatty just now." Chaim had raced upstairs to find his brother. Quickly, he put Donny into the picture.

The boys were torn. On the one hand, they wanted to dash out and fill Shimi in with all possible haste. On the other hand, they felt silly bringing him nothing but warmed-over crimes and empty speculation. If something new *had* happened, they wanted to know what it was. It was Chaim who decided to confront his father and just ask. Whispering to Donny to stay out of sight, he knocked on the study door.

"Come in." Nachman sounded tired. Tentatively, Chaim pushed the door open and stepped inside, prepared to beat a hasty retreat if his father seemed unreceptive. But the smile that greeted him was the same warm one as always, radiating welcome. "Hi, Chaim. What's up?"

Eagerly, the boy came forward. "I hope you don't mind, Ta. I saw that Indian come to see you again. Is there — did anything new happen? You told us that he works for the sheriff."

"Not exactly. He just acts as a sort of liaison between the law-enforcement people and the Native American population in these parts, especially down on the Mescalero reservation. He's been trying to help out with the arson cases and ..."

"And?" Chaim pounced on the word.

With a sigh, his father said, "Well, I'm sure you'll be hearing about it soon in any case. You were right. There's been another incident ... anti-Semitic graffiti, this time painted on the front of the day-school building."

"Same message?"

"The very same. Somebody clearly doesn't like our presence here. But with good people like Steve Birch and Sheriff Ramsay working hard to catch the perpetrators, we all hope that episodes like this will very soon be a thing of the past." Vaguely, through the mists of a tension-induced fatigue, Nachman was aware that he was sounding like a press release instead of a father speaking with his own son. He tried to shake off the strange torpor that had enveloped him since Birch's departure. "Right now, though, there doesn't seem to be anything concrete that we can do to prevent them."

"We can help, Ta," Chaim offered earnestly. "Me 'n Donny 'n Shimi …."

"I don't really think you boys can be of much help here, Chaim, but thanks for the offer. I'd really rather you stayed out of possible trouble."

Chaim decided to beat a prudent retreat before "I'd really rather" turned into "I forbid." A moment later, he was conferring with Donny in their bedroom.

"I told you something happened!" he crowed. "C'mon, let's go find Shimi!"

Donny, as ever, was a willing partner to all of his big brother's plans. Within minutes, they were on their bikes, squinting their eyes against the wings of a fiercely beating sun as they pedaled their way to the Mandel house. The air seemed to shimmer around them.

"Boy, I'll never get used to this heat," Chaim grumbled as they rode. Even the wind generated by their movement was dry as leather.

"I kind of like it," Donny said. "It's a clean feeling; not that sticky way you feel when the air's all humid."

Chaim had to agree with his brother on that point: Humidity was virtually unknown in this part of the country. Gone were the days when his shirt clung to his back from a simple walk down his street in summer. Still, he found it hard to get used to this arid atmosphere. Sometimes he felt as if he were walking on the moon. And there was so little rain that they were rationing water this year. Homeowners on alternate sides of the street got to water their gardens on alternate days. No humidity; but also no water. There was a price for everything.

With these philosophical thoughts to keep him company, he led the way to Shimi's house.

The Mandel place soon loomed up on the right. Braking, the brothers leaped off their bikes and headed for the front door to ring the doorbell. At the last second, they changed this to a knock. It was some time before Etty opened the door for them. She looked haggard.

"I thought I heard someone at the door," she murmured. "I was in the back of the house with Ora. She's running a fever today."

"*Refuah sheleimah*," Chaim said automatically. And Donny added, "We didn't want to ring in case the baby was sleeping."

A pained spasm crossed the mother's face. "Layala's not here today. She's at the hospital in Roswell. She had an operation on her tummy. Didn't your parents tell you to say *Tehillim*?"

"Oh, right." With a guilty pang, Chaim remembered. "We, uh, were planning to do it soon."

"Maybe we can say some *Tehillim* with Shimi," Donny improvised. "Is he home?"

Etty Mandel stepped aside to let them in.

"Uh — Mrs. Mandel?" Chaim ventured as he passed her.

"Yes, Chaim?"

"Have you noticed anything … different … about Shimi lately? He's been acting kind of strange. He hardly wants to do anything anymore."

"Shimi," Etty Mandel said heavily, "is the least of my worries right now." Turning her back, she left them to find their own way upstairs.

They found Shimi in his room, propped up against his pillows and turning the pages of a book in automatonlike fashion. He hardly glanced up at their entrance.

"Hi, Shimi. Whatcha doing?" Donny asked, plopping himself down on the bed.

"Nothing."

Donny squirmed excitedly. "Well, guess what?" With typical single-mindedness, Donny had completely forgotten his own suggestion to say *Tehillim* for Layala. "We just found out that another thing's happened: a message painted across the front of the day school!"

This ignited a spark of interest. "When?"

"This morning. At least, that's when the principal found it. I wish I knew the creeps who are doing this!"

Something seemed to shut down in Shimi's face. He began to turn the pages of his book faster now, in a show of industriousness that convinced nobody.

Chaim began to pace the room. "My father's really worried, Shimi. Everyone is. Don't you think we should do something to help?"

"We *are* helping; by staying out of their way," Shimi growled. "You think the police want a bunch of kids tripping them up everywhere they go?"

Both Bernstein brothers stared at their friend. Was this the same intrepid Shimi Mandel who had forged up dusty trails with them just a few days before? Then, it had been all they could do to keep up with him. He had seemed lit from within by an inner joyousness in motion.

"You're different," Chaim said slowly. "You've been different since we came down off the cliff that day."

Shimi averted his head. "Forget it. You're imagining things."

"No, I'm not. What's going on, Shimi? Why are you suddenly so uninterested in everything? We were having fun."

"FUN?" The word exploded from Shimi with the force of a bullet. "Is that what you think all of this is: *fun*? This is serious stuff, guys, and you'd better not forget it."

His outburst spent, he sagged back onto his pillow and began rifling the pages of his book in a near-frenzy. Chaim regarded him in open puzzlement. Donny gaped.

"What's gotten into you, Shimi?" Donny complained.

"Nothing's 'gotten into' me. I'm busy. I'm tired. I'm not interested in climbing any old cliffs in the heat. And I think you guys should stay away from them, too. That's all I have to say!"

"Look," Chaim said. "We're not interested in fighting, okay? We just don't know what's gotten into you lately. If —"

"Why am I the only one around here who knows how to mind his own business?" Shimi asked the ceiling.

Chaim flushed. "This *is* our business! It's the whole town's business. Someone's been setting fire to Jewish places —"

"Setting fire to our own fathers' *kollel!*" Donny inserted hotly.

"So I think this concerns every single person here. Including you!" There was a spot of color high up on both of Chaim's cheekbones, a sure sign that he was deeply perturbed. "Shimi, don't you even *care*?"

A shiver seemed to run through Shimi, shoulder to heel. He leaned limply against the headboard as though depleted. Finally, he turned his head to meet Chaim's eyes. "I *do* care. Of course I do! I care as much as any of you. Maybe even more."

"Then, why ...?" "Those guys are dangerous," Shimi whispered.

"Which guys? The arsonists? How do you know there's more than one of them?"

With a sigh, Shimi steeled himself to tell his story. "That hike on the cliffs ...?"

"Yes?"

"Remember when I had a rock in my sneaker, and you guys went ahead without me ... " Shakily, as though the words themselves had the power to hurt him, Shimi told about his encounter with the two Native Americans, who had threatened him with vague but terrifying disaster if he stuck his nose where it wasn't wanted.

"They're doing something up there," Shimi whispered urgently. "And they don't want anyone around to see them do it. That's probably why they set fire to the surveyors' site: to scare them away."

Moved by his logic, Chaim looked at Shimi with a touch of admiration. "Do you really think that was why? Everyone else thinks it was plain old anti-Semitism."

"Haven't you noticed that it all started when the *kollel* bought the site for the new building?"

Chaim and Donny looked at each other. Chaim lifted his head with a jerk. "No, that's not really true. I remember my father saying that there were a couple of anti-Jewish incidents even before we came out here. Last winter, I think he said. Rabbi Harris told him about it."

"Well, what happened between last winter and this summer? The *kollel* moved in, that's what! It moved into the shul. And bought some land, and started surveying, just where those Indians are prowling around. And both those places got torched." Shimi's eyes were two hard, bright marbles. "I *saw* those guys. They talked to me. They threatened me! Let's not forget that."

It was obvious that *he* had not forgotten. Now Chaim understood the reason for his friend's strange, reclusive behavior since their hike. Shimi was scared out of his wits.

Uneasily, Chaim wondered if, maybe, he and Donny should be scared, too.

But Donny was parading around the room, waving his arms. "Let's go up there and catch 'em red-handed!"

"You're nuts," Shimi said flatly. "These guys are dangerous."

"They won't even see us," Donny insisted. "We'll sneak up on them when they're not looking, and —"

"You think you can outsneak an Indian?" Shimi asked with contempt. He made a twirling motion near his temple, as though to say, "Nuts!"

Chaim intervened quickly. "Well, thanks for telling us, Shimi. I can see that those guys really shook you up."

"You won't go near those caves again, will you?"

Chaim hesitated. "Well, not anytime soon. School starts tomorrow, remember?"

"Maybe if things are quiet for a while —" Donny began hopefully.

"When Indians are quiet," Shimi said with ominous emphasis, "that's when you'd better start watching your back."

On that bleak note, the Bernstein boys parted from their friend. They were as quiet as a pair of proverbial redskins on the walk home. They had a lot to think about.

VI.

Sheriff Ramsay parked discreetly behind the school building and made his way quietly to the office where Simi Wurtzler was waiting for him. At the principal's request, he had timed his visit to take place at an hour when classes were in progress, when students and teachers alike ought to be immersed in their lessons and oblivious to an outsider in their midst. Or so she hoped, anyway.

"So much for discretion," she sighed half an hour later, when the sheriff had departed and an influx of curious faculty members had begun to flock into her office in a steady stream, with a gaggle of wide-eyed schoolchildren hovering just behind. It was impossible to miss the ugly, black stain on the front of the school building, and the general curiosity the sight had engendered had not yet been satisfied. Still, Simi was not sorry she'd created that stain. A smear of dark paint was infinitely preferable to the scream of hate that lay beneath.

Now, with so many questions being hurled at her — and with the meeting with the police behind her, not that it had accomplished much — she moved at last to clear the air.

"Attention, please," she announced calmly over the intercom. "As you may have noticed, some paint has been smeared across the front of our building. That paint has been put there to cover up some ugly graffiti that appeared overnight. The building will soon be cleaned, and with the cooperation of the local authorities we hope to prevent the recurrence of such incidents in the future."

She waited for the dust to settle. When the murmurs and exclamations had died away, she added a brief, "Please resume your classes —" She was cut off by the clamor of the bell. When it fell silent again, she added dryly, "when recess is over." A wave of tension-releasing laughter met these words, and then came the stampede of young feet out to the playground.

It was just after recess that Miss Harmon, the fourth-grade teacher, noticed something odd at the window.

She blinked, trying to recapture the image that had tickled the corner of her eye. Before her, in neat rows, children laboriously copied lines from the blackboard. The teacher stole another glance at the window.

There it was again! A shadow, man shaped, blocked out the sun for an instant and then vanished.

Mere seconds later, the figure reappeared at the next window. Miss Harmon gaped, unsure whether to believe the evidence of her own eyes. She started purposefully toward the window. Gila Bernstein, in the window seat, paused in her writing and glanced up as a shadow fell over her page.

Her eyes widened. The blood rushed from her face. She opened her mouth and issued a piercing scream.

"Calm down, girls!" Miss Harmon spoke sharply to disguise her own rising panic. Several girls seated near Gila, and startled by her scream, had added their shrieks to hers. The shadow flickered at the third window — and disappeared again. Miss Harmon waited no longer. Jabbing a finger at a girl in the front row, she barked, "Go to the office and get Mrs. Wurtzler. Hurry!"

The girl was off like the wind, impelled by the twin motives of escaping the breath of danger that had touched the classroom, and spreading the exciting news of its presence.

"Miss Harmon says to come right away!" The girl stood in the doorway of the principal's inner office, heedless of the protocol that would have had her apply first to the secretary, standing agape at her side. Mrs. Wurtzler lifted her head. Dimly, from the other end of the long, low building, she heard screams. She was on her feet before her conscious brain issued the order to stand. Again, as it had that morning, her heart began to beat too rapidly. She stilled it with a hand to her chest as she began running down the hall, the entire office staff hard on her heels.

By this time, the noise from the fourth-grade classroom had attracted the attention of a number of other teachers and students. The principal found the doorway blocked when she approached, though a word from her scattered the crowd in a twinkling. She ran into the room, where Miss Harmon was standing in a defensive position behind her desk. The children were in a state of mild to acute hysteria, most of them shrieking so loudly that it was hard for the principal to make herself heard.

"Quiet, girls!" she ordered. Such was the force of her personality that fully half of them actually stopped screaming. The other half of the class, however, was still making themselves heard. She turned to Miss Harmon. "What is it? What happened?"

"There was someone at the window," the teacher told her. "A man — we could only see his shadow ... silhouetted against the bright sun outside." She prided herself on this calm recital of the facts, though her voice was pitched rather higher than usual, and noticeably wobbly.

"Quiet!" Mrs. Wurtzler commanded again. The rest of the tumult faltered and faded, giving way to a low-pitched babble. As always, the principal's presence had a calming effect. She was about to say more — with the goal of completely restoring order so that she could deal with the pressing issue of unearthing the intruder who had so frightened them all — when there came another shrill gasp from the window. She looked sharply across at the perpetrator, a dark-haired girl in pigtails. "What's the matter? Is he back?"

"N-no," the pigtailed girl said in a frightened voice. "It's Gila. She — she looks funny. Like she can't catch her breath ..."

Gila had not suffered a single asthma attack since her family's move to New Mexico. The traumatic routine seemed to have receded into the mists of the past: the waking nightmare when she could not force the necessary quota of oxygen into her starved lungs, no matter how hard she tried, and the speeding trips to the hospital, with her mother white faced beside her in the back seat and her father hunched over the wheel as though his life depended on winning a race against every traffic light. But it had not been her father's life that hung in the balance; even at a tender age, Gila had known that. It was hers.

Other times, an ambulance had taken her away instead, its siren a mournful accompaniment to her own desperate quest for air. There would be needles and masks and grave words that she wasn't supposed to hear. Then a blessed period of light again, until the next attack.

All that had changed with their move. For more than two glorious months she had lived in the world of light and ease, a world where every breath was both a thing of joy and something to be taken utterly for granted. She relished the sensation of being just like everyone else. Like a photograph too long in the sun, the fear had gradually faded.

And then she had looked up from her notebook and seen something that shot terror directly into her heart: A man-shadow at her window, black against the sun and impossibly tall from her angle of vision. It was the stuff of every bad dream she'd ever had, only there was no Mommy to hold her close until the horror had run away and comforting reality stepped in to take its place. The shadow *was* the reality. The piercing scream was dredged from the depths of her small being. And as she screamed, she felt her lungs growing stingy and mean again, refusing entry to the one thing that she must have to live: air.

Dimly aware of the press of anxious faces surrounding her, she closed her eyes, the better to concentrate on the effort to breathe. She remembered her mother telling her, over and over, "Don't be afraid. It's the panic that makes it so much worse. Just stay calm, and try to keep breathing. We'll get you help just as soon as we can." But calmness was far away from her. How could she remain calm, when all around her people were shouting and running, and just outside the room where she had believed herself to be safe there lurked a dark and mysterious menace?

Time passed in a blur. Choking and gasping for air, she was reliving the routine she thought she had left behind forever. First the haunting wail of a siren, then the ambulance doors flinging open to receive her — with Miss Harmon at her side this time, instead of Mommy or Ta. She heard someone say, "Call the parents, tell them to meet us at the hospital," and was grateful. She would have told them so, had she any breath to spare for mere words. Tears, which would normally have embarrassed her, streamed down her white cheeks. Now, she ignored them. There was only thing that mattered at the moment. *Breathe ...*

She ignored everything except the agonized effort it took to suck in the life-giving oxygen that everyone else seemed to be able to access with no trouble at all; as though the air that existed in such abundance all around her was a prize in a game that she'd never learned to play.

Chapter 12

I.

"**I** can't stand it," Tova whispered to her husband as they hurtled along the highway toward Roswell. "I thought we'd put all this behind us. Gila was doing so well out here ..."

"She's still suffering from asthma." Nachman was hunkered over the steering wheel as though urging the car to greater speed by sheer force of personality. "That hasn't changed."

"I know that. But the drier air was supposed to help her, make the attacks go away."

"They did go away, until a stranger came right up to her window at school and spooked her." Nachman's fists gripped the wheel so tightly that the knuckles turned white. He was not a violent man, but at that moment he would gladly have knocked down the man who'd frightened his little girl and stolen the very breath from her body.

"Hurry ..." Tova gazed sightlessly at the arid landscape, whizzing by in a blur broken only by the occasional mesa. The flat-crowned mountain stood impassive and hard beneath the sun, equally impervious to time and to human frailty. Nothing short of an act of G-d would shatter that arrogant rock. Here it would stand, shoulders squared against the fierce desert wind, while children were rushed to hospitals gasping for air and their panic-stricken parents hurried blindly after them ...

She remembered the first time. It was etched indelibly on the screen of her memory, which was funny, given the fact that she hadn't even been on hand to see it happen. Gila had been just 3 years old then, a seemingly healthy youngster with toddlerhood not far behind her and a rosy future lying ahead. Tova enjoyed the time she spent with her little girl, especially their nightly bedtime-story ritual. Gila was a rapt audience, round blue eyes fixed intently on her mother's face as though determined not to miss a syllable. At the scary parts, she would snuggle into her mother's side; happy endings made her laugh out loud.

Then there came a night when Tova wasn't there to read to her.

"Mommy's in the hospital, sweetie," her father had explained, holding Gila on his lap so that she would know that the chain of love and security was unbroken. "She had a little baby today — a boy. You have a new little brother now, Gila." Nachman waited for her reaction.

"I want Mommy. I want her to read me my story," Gila whispered with stricken eyes.

"And she will — in a few days. But tonight, you're going to have to make do with my reading. I promise you, I'll try to say all the words right."

As an attempt at humor, it fell flat. There was no response from young Gila apart from a deadly stillness. Nachman could feel the stillness moving in, spreading slowly to permeate the little body on his lap, like a greedy monster sucking something vital from the very core of her being. A moment later, he realized what it was that the monster was taking: air. It was sucking the air from poor Gila's lungs.

"D-daddy! Daddy!" She was coughing, and then she was no longer coughing, and that was even more frightening. She couldn't describe what was happening to her. She didn't know the word for "breathe," or, if she did, she'd forgotten it in her panic. All she knew was that there was something clogging her chest, making it impossible to draw in the life-giving stuff she so desperately needed. She choked, clawing at her skinny throat. "Daddy ...!"

He took one look at her and leaped for the phone. A Hatzolah ambulance was there in minutes. Nachman watched in horror as an oxygen mask was clamped over the sweet features he knew as well as his own. Then both he and his 3-year-old were loaded into the ambulance for the short trip to the same hospital where Tova lay cuddling the brand-new infant who would, on the following week, be named Yehuda Leib, Yudi, for short.

For Tova, it was like the intrusion of a nightmare into a blissful sleep. In an instant of time, she went from being the happy mother of a brand-new infant to the terribly anxious parent of a child gasping for the breath of life. She did not personally witness the desperate struggle in the ER before the epinephrine that the doctors injected began to work, opening up the vital air-passages and allowing Gila to breathe again. She only heard about it from Nachman afterward. In his own distress, he made no attempt to whitewash the story or paint it in less garish colors than the reality suggested. She got it straight-out, along with the full complement of fear and anxiety that her husband had experienced in those terrifying moments.

She — the whole family — was doomed to repeat that same, deadly emotional duo over the next five years. Fear and anxiety ... anxiety and fear. Gila began taking daily doses of albuterol in a nebulizer, which administered the correct dose in the form of a fine spray that she inhaled through a mouthpiece. As a young child, it had been difficult for her to hold her breath for the required number of seconds necessary for the medicine to work, but she gamely continued trying. When she was a little older she was equipped with an inhaler, to be carried around with her everywhere.

"Stress," the doctors repeated, shaking their heads. "Diminish the stress in her life. And take her away to a drier climate."

Well, that was just what they had done! They'd scooped Gila up and borne her away to a safer place. A place where the monsters weren't meant to find her. Where every breath was supposed to be a balm and a blessing. The inhaler, lugged around from force of habit for the first few weeks, was now lying abandoned in Gila's desk drawer.

Tova stared bleakly out the window as the car sped toward Roswell. Every thought seemed calculated to drive home the truth she was trying so hard to avoid: Gila hadn't escaped. Their attempts at being her heroic rescuers had been futile. Even here, so far from her earlier existence, the monster had caught up with her. All it had taken was a black shadow against a brilliant block of sun, where no shadow was supposed to be.

"Oh, why'd we come here?" she burst out, hardly knowing that she was speaking aloud.

"Tova ..."

She heard the muted pain in her husband's voice — a pain the more poignant for being powerless. "I'm sorry," she whispered. "I didn't really mean that. It's just ..."

"Gila."

She nodded. Her eyes closed. For the rest of the speeding ride, there was no more talk.

The road rolled on and on with hardly a bend. There was nothing to break the monotony of the scene, nothing to distract Tova from the thoughts that chewed at nerves that felt like pieces of frayed rope. She bit back another frantic "Hurry." If Nachman went any faster, he would be flying.

But at last, the journey did end. A bold highway sign informed them that a hospital was nearby, and then the hospital itself loomed ahead of them against the hard, blue sky. A creditable attempt had been made to beautify the grounds with the aid of a professional landscaping firm, but neither Tova nor Nachman was in any mood to enjoy them. They raced inside with a single compelling need that blotted out all else: the need to find their daughter.

They came upon her in one of the ER cubicles, with an anxious Miss Harmon in attendance. The teacher stood up at their entrance, the enormity of her relief showing clearly in her face. "Here you are!" she chirped, for the child's benefit. "Gila, your mother and father are here." She glanced at her watch. "That was quick. Why, you must have flown all the way from Lakewood!"

"Just about," Nachman said, moving forward to reach his daughter. Tova had already grasped Gila's hand and was clutching it as though her touch might impart the life force the child needed. The blue eyes above the oxygen mask were calmer now, happy that they were there.

"The doctor just left," Miss Harmon said. "He gave Gila a shot —"

"Epinephrine," Tova said, her eyes never leaving her daughter's face.

"I think that's it. The doctor said it would open her bronchial tubes and help her breathing, and it did. She's going to be fine. Aren't you, Gila?"

Gila nodded, too exhausted by her ordeal to speak. The teacher hesitated. In this still-life scene of parent and child, she suddenly felt herself superfluous. "I'll go see what I can find out," she murmured, and made a hurried exit from the cramped cubicle.

"Thank you," Tova called softly after her. Her grip on Gila's hand tightened imperceptibly. Powerful emotions swamped her, threatening to drag her away in their undertow. Profound gratitude, a bottomless love for her child, and a fear that she dared not put into words. She closed her eyes. From somewhere nearby, she heard Nachman say, "*Baruch Hashem*, she's out of the woods. She's breathing fairly normally now."

Tova's eyes opened. With a remarkable semblance of calm, she said, "Yes, I can see that. I hope the doctor gets back here soon. I want to ask him some questions."

But it didn't really matter when the doctor returned. Her Gila was in Hashem's hands, here in Roswell or back East where they used to live. He was the One Who had blown the breath of life back into those precious lungs. Tova's eyes closed again as, fervently, she said a silent little prayer of thanksgiving to Him for looking after her child, along with a plea that He would never, ever stop doing so.

Nachman had some questions, too, but — seeing the tentative peace beginning to steal over his wife's face — he kept them to himself. He had questions about the one thing that Tova seemed, so far, to have skipped right over: the shadowy figure that had precipitated Gila's attack.

Who was he? What were his intentions? Did he have any connection to the hateful scrawl discovered on the school building that morning, or was this an entirely different manifestation of the evil that lurked in sunny little Lakewood?

A great many questions and, as yet, no answers at all.

II.

Three floors above the Bernsteins' heads, Rivi Gann sat beside Layala's crib, watching the baby breathe.

"It's so beautiful," she whispered into her cell phone. "Oh, Asher, Hashem gave the doctors the ability to fix her poor little tummy, and now she's going to be all right. No more pain. No more vomiting. She can be happy now."

"What about you? Are you feeling all right?"

"Me? I've never felt better in my life! Why?"

"You sound a little strange. Overwrought."

"I'm just a bit emotional. It's so special, being here for her like this when she's so helpless. She won't be waking up for a couple of hours yet, the nurse says. I want to be right next to her when she opens her eyes."

"Rivi —"

"Yes?"

Asher hesitated. Then, with a muffled sigh, he said, "Nothing. See you when you get home."

She said good-bye into the phone, eyes already straying to the bassinet with its precious burden.

She sat in a hard, plastic chair, oblivious to the discomfort, and oblivious, as well, to her own exhaustion. She sat that way for the rest of the afternoon and into the evening, and all evening into the night. Sometime around midnight, reaction set in. Adrenalin had kept her going to this point; now her shoulders ached and her lids kept threatening to droop, but she refused to close her eyes for so much as a second. They remained fixed, steadfast and loving, on little Layala. An IV tube snaked away from one frail arm. Rivi longed to pick up the tiny hand and plant kisses of relief and gratitude on it.

Instead, very carefully, she lowered her head until her lips just barely brushed the minuscule wrist. Then she sat up again and resumed her vigil.

Back in Lakewood the next morning, Etty Mandel shook out the thermometer and smiled. Ora's fever was down! She had taken one look at the child on her return home the afternoon before, and driven her straight to Dr. Sadowsky's office. A simple test revealed that Ora had an infected throat. The antibiotics that the doctor prescribed seemed to have done the trick. The infection, though not yet fully subdued, was on its knees.

The older children were waking up now, with Efraim keeping a casual eye on them. Etty trailed through the rooms of her home all morning like a restless wind, repeatedly popping back into Ora's room to check on her progress. Though still in bed, the little girl was looking remarkably better with each passing moment. Tzirel and Chanala were in school, though Shimi's lessons would begin only when the *kollel* resumed its regular learning schedule. As he had been prone to do lately, he was keeping to his own room, strangely uncommunicative. Well, at least he wasn't getting into trouble. Etty had no time to bother her head over Shimi's antics right now — or anyone else's, for that matter. Ora was on the mend. Efraim was in charge on the home front. And Layala was waiting!

"I'm going!" she called out, almost tripping in her haste to find her husband. "Efraim, I'm going to the hospital!"

He looked up from the *sefer* he had been perusing while relaxing in his recliner. "You are?"

"Ora's fever is down, and I think she'll be all right with my going away now. She's over the worst of it, *Baruch Hashem*. You can have Tzirel read her storybooks when she gets home, and feed her a little chicken soup for supper. I'm going to zip over to Roswell and see Layala!"

"Give her a kiss from me," Efraim smiled.

"Don't worry. I'll be giving her so many kisses, she won't know what hit her! But one of them will be marked 'Special from Tatty.'"

Upstairs in his room, Shimi heard his parents' laughter. Moments later he watched his mother drive away, the car's nose pointed north, toward Roswell. He wished he were going with her. He wished he were going anywhere, as long as it took him far away from the dread with which he had been living these past few days.

But escape seemed impossible. People were burning down shuls, or trying to. A shadowy figure had scared the daylights out of the fourth grade at the day school, sending Gila Bernstein to the hospital. The world, it seemed, was full of ominous figures casting their black shadow over otherwise sunny lives. There was only one way to avoid the darkness: to crawl into one's own little corner, where one could at least pretend to be safe, and lock the door.

He sat in his fortress hideaway, waiting for the danger to miraculously disappear. He had a feeling he might be waiting a long, long time.

Etty burst through the hospital's front door and made straight for the elevators.

The ride up to the third floor seemed endless. She wanted to shout aloud to the other immobile figures standing beside her in the moving cube: "My baby's been operated on, and she's going to be fine! She comes home tomorrow!" She'd done the right thing. She had turned away from her infant in order to tend to her ailing 3-year-old. Now came her reward: the sight of her baby recovering from surgery, growing stronger, getting ready to come home. There would surely be a spark of recognition in those little eyes. Etty longed to feed Layala, to hold her and feel the sense of wholeness envelop her again. The elevator whirred to a halt. Etty's heels were clicking fast on the hard corridor tile before any of the other passengers had even stepped out.

In Room 303, a nurse had given Rivi permission to hold Layala. Very gently, the nurse picked the baby up and placed her in Rivi's waiting arms. The nurse glanced at the chart. She was new on the ward today and had not been in this room before.

"She's coming around just fine, Mrs. Mandel," she said cheerfully. "You'll be able to take her home before you know it."

Etty Mandel walked into the room just in time to hear this happy announcement and to see Rivi tenderly cradle the baby, *her* baby, head lowered to Layala's in a gesture of utter devotion.

With a muffled gasp, Etty rushed over to the chair. "I'll take her now, thank you!"

Rivi nearly jumped. "Etty!"

"*I* am the baby's mother," Etty Mandel told the equally startled nurse. "*I* am Mrs. Mandel." She leaned down and all but snatched her daughter from Rivi's unresisting arms.

"I'm — I'm sorry, ma'am. I just naturally thought ..." The nurse's words trailed off in confusion.

She had thought, of course, that the woman hovering so tenderly at the baby's bedside was the baby's mother. Etty's whirlwind entrance had come just a fraction too soon for Rivi to rid her of that notion.

Etty thanked Rivi stiffly, giving her no opportunity to say good-bye to the precious charge she had tended all night and half the day. Ashen faced, with lips set like a steel gate to hold back the words that threatened to burst from her, Rivi choked out an equally stiff, "You're very welcome," and walked out of the room to grope blindly for the nearest elevator.

III.

Rabbi Harris stood up. "Thank you for filling us in, sheriff. Don't take this the wrong way, but I think we've been seeing altogether too much of each other lately!"

Sheriff Ramsay smiled thinly. "I know what you mean. Let's hope we clear this thing up quickly. This intimidation campaign has gone on long enough."

"Is that what you think it is?" Nate Goodman asked. He had accompanied Pinchas Harris to the sheriff's office. "Intimidation?"

"What else? 'Jews go home' sure sounds like someone's trying to get a message across, doesn't it?"

"It could just be some bored teenagers trying their fathers' anti-Semitism on for size ..."

"Maybe. I don't think it is. Oh, we've had a couple of incidents before this. About half a year back, that was. A Native American kid with a chip on his shoulder was responsible for those. Steve Birch laid down the law to the kid, and the episodes dried up. No, this feels like something different. Same message, but different feel." The sheriff paused. "Grant you, I could be wrong."

Nate hoped he was. Far easier to cope with a disgruntled teenager than with whatever evil entity was stalking their community at present. At the thought of young Gila Bernstein, the lines of his strong-featured face softened in compassion. As though reading his thoughts, the sheriff asked, "Any word on the kid with the asthma? Rabbi Bernstein's little girl?"

It was Pinchas Harris who fielded the question. "I've been in touch with him. Thank G-d, they got Gila to the hospital in time. Things seem to be under control now. They'll probably be releasing her in a couple of hours."

"Good news." Sheriff Ramsay stood up and extended a hand to each of them. "I appreciate your visit, gentlemen. Believe me, we're pulling out all the stops on this one. I won't have Lakewood turning into a place where schoolkids are frightened in their own classrooms or their fathers are afraid to pray in their own synagogue. We're going to catch the culprit and make him pay!"

It was an emotional speech for the usually impassive lawman, and Pinchas took it as a sign of the tension that the crowded events of recent weeks had created in the protector of this otherwise sleepy town. He thanked the sheriff again and, with Nate right behind him, took his leave.

"What do you think?" he asked his *gabbai*, glancing up at the taller man.

Goodman shrugged angrily. "I feel utterly helpless. I hate it."

"Yes, good can feel helpless in the face of evil," Rabbi Harris said philosophically. "But, in reality, the opposite is true. It's the evil that withers and dies in the face of genuine goodness."

"That's all very well," Nate said gloomily. "But what can we do right now, to make *this* evil curl up and die?"

"We can *daven*. I want to call a gathering of our entire membership this evening, Nate. It'll be Lakewood, New Mexico's first *Tehillim* rally."

"Good idea!" At the prospect of action, the *gabbai's* face lit up. "I'll start making calls the minute I get back to the office."

"Very good. And, Nate —"

Nate, at the wheel, took his eyes off the road for a second. "Yes, rabbi?"

"I promise you this. When we catch the guy who's behind all of this, guess which lawyer's going to be our liaison with the prosecutor's office?"

Nate grinned. "Believe me, I can't wait."

Pinchas dropped Nate off at home, then drove on. He was soon driving up a familiar block. Pinchas recognized it: This was where the Bernsteins lived. He and Penina had enjoyed a pleasant meal there on Succos, an occasion only slightly marred by little Mo's spilling ketchup on his wife's new outfit. He was smiling reminiscently, when he suddenly spotted a small group beneath the spreading cottonwood tree on the Bernsteins' lawn. Shana was there, and the twin toddlers, and the Bernsteins' guest. On impulse, he pulled over and got out of the car. He'd heard, briefly, from Nachman, that Gila was all right, but he wanted to receive confirmation of that welcome news.

Also, this would be a good time to exchange a few words with the house guest. He wanted to get a better idea of what kind of person Heidi Neufeld was. It was a good thing he'd dropped his companion off when he had. This would be one conversation he didn't want Nate Goodman overhearing.

The news about Gila had reached Shana in the middle of her high-school math class, a class that she would ordinarily not have minded missing at all. This time, the reason for her absence was too frightening for her to draw the slightest enjoyment from it. Her mother had called urgently for her to come home at once, to be with the twins while Tova and Nachman sped off to the hospital at Roswell.

Mo and Bo, as though sensing the fear in the air, were especially uncooperative this afternoon. Had Heidi not been there to lend a hand, Shana did not know how she would have coped. Then Yudi came home from kindergarten, to add his particular brand of cranky anxiety to the mix. Shana couldn't really blame them for being afraid, or cranky; until her parents and Gila were safely back home, her own mood would continue that way, too. The only difference was, she couldn't show it. She had to be the responsible one. Her mother was counting on her.

Heidi was amazing, Shana thought, watching her mother's friend read book after book to the insatiable little boys. Yudi sat cross-legged at Heidi's feet while the twins leaned against either knee as though determined to pin her to her seat until they'd had their fill of stories. Heidi had decided that plunging the children into a fantasy world far removed from their own was the best antidote to fear. How could a kid be worried about his sister in the hospital when he was riding a bike with Curious George or sympathizing with a fictional animal over a nasty cold he'd caught? Mommy and Tatty might be gone at the moment, but a whole cast of friendly characters were there to keep them amused — and distracted.

Heidi had also figured out that the boys would do better outdoors than cooped up inside, where everything they saw reminded them of their absent mother. Shana leaned back in her lawn chair and let the sun press its hot hand down on her eyelids. Behind them, a pleasant, red haze filled her vision. Heidi and the twins were sitting in the shade of the single tree that adorned their lawn, but Shana preferred the sun. At least, she preferred it until she became uncomfortably hot. The delightful thing about this climate, as she had had occasion to reflect before this, was its total lack of humidity. Dry heat was so much more bearable, she felt, than the clammy bath you had to wade through just to walk down a New York street in summer. Eventually, if she stayed here long enough, she would probably get used to it, and perhaps even grow to dislike it. But for now, Shana could not get enough of this pleasantly intense, unsticky sun.

Suddenly, her eyes flew open. She heard a car door slamming right in front of the house A man emerged from the vehicle that had parked at the curb, and was making his way past the tree that was casting its shade over Heidi and the boys. Shana relaxed as she recognized Rabbi Harris. He waved at her, and she gave a bashful wave back.

"Rabbi." Heidi struggled to her feet, though doing so meant displacing the twins, who set up howls of protest. For once, Heidi didn't hear them.

"Hello," Pinchas said. "I was just passing by, and I wanted to hear how Gila's doing." He addressed the remark to both Heidi and Shana.

Wondering vaguely if she had grass in her hair — she'd spent 15 minutes sitting on the grass earlier while the twins romped around her, occasionally scattering the yellowish blades over her head like confetti — Heidi smiled politely. "How nice of you, Rabbi Harris. I'm glad to say that Gila is, *Baruch Hashem*, out of the woods. They administered epinephrine and oxygen, and she's breathing much more easily now. They should be releasing her in a couple of hours."

"Well, that's terrific news," Pinchas Harris said heartily, just as though he hadn't already heard this from Nachman some time earlier. He hesitated, uncharacteristically at a loss for words. "Uh, Miss Neufeld?"

"Yes?"

"I guess I'm also here in the capacity of a messenger. My *gabbai*, Nate Goodman, asked me to apologize to you for — well, for what happened at the meeting that night. He says he was abominably rude, and he's sorry. I should have passed the message on well before now, but things kept piling up. You know how it is. May I tell him he's forgiven?"

"*He's* sorry!" Heidi's cheeks burned. "I made a total fool of myself. I may be guilty of being a New Yorker, but I'm not usually *that* pushy. Please tell him to erase the whole thing from his memory!"

"Let's just consider the 'delete' button pushed," the rabbi said with a smile. Changing the subject with seeming casualness, he began to question Heidi about her job and her family, soliciting her opinions on various subjects in an attempt to gauge her character. Relieved to have her abysmal performance at the meeting finally out in the open and dealt with, Heidi responded openly. After a few minutes, however, Bo's patience ran out. It was time, he decided, to express his outrage at having his reading session so rudely curtailed: "Heidi, read! Bo wants a story!"

"*Mo* wants a story!" his twin chimed in.

"Well," Heidi said, with an indulgent smile for the indignant youngsters. "I guess we'll have to do something about that, won't we?"

"Go ahead, go ahead," Pinchas urged. "I've got to be going anyway. Good afternoon, ladies. Shana, please tell your mother I asked after Gila. And if there's anything you need ..."

"Thank you, Rabbi Harris," Shana said. With a brief round of goodbyes to Yudi and the twins, Pinchas took his leave. Heidi resumed her seat beneath the tree, picked up the book she'd dropped in her abrupt scramble to her feet, and placidly began reading aloud to the boys.

Despite the alarming events of this morning and recent weeks — events that had kept the rabbi tossing and turning in his bed at night, and praying with extra fervor each time he stood up with his congregation — Pinchas Harris found his heart lifting as he stepped into his car. His good friend, *gabbai* and right-hand man, that confirmed bachelor, was a hard nut to crack. Nate's standards were high and he was not easily pleased. But, as the rabbi's mind drifted back to the New York lawyer seated beneath the cottonwood tree with her storybooks and trio of attentive youngsters, he decided to have a talk with Nate that very evening. He had what he believed was a promising idea to place before him.

IV.

A vi Feder retrieved his car from its long-term parking slot at the airport and automatically headed for the exit that would take him east and south, back to Lakewood.

He had not gone very far, however, when he had second thoughts. What was his hurry? What was waiting for him back there? The *kollel* was still on vacation and his apartment would feel even emptier than usual after his busy week-and-a-half in New York. He was looking forward to seeing Asher again and, at the same time, dreading it. Asher would be full of probing questions, the questions of a good friend, a concerned friend. A friend who would believe — and not refrain from expressing — that he, Avi, was suffering from a case of temporary insanity. The worst of it was, Avi wasn't so sure he disagreed with that diagnosis. He swung his car around and executed a neat U-turn.

Ahead lay Albuquerque, shimmering in the sun. Beyond a cursory glance through his windows as he sped past on his way to the airport before Succos, Avi knew nothing of the city. Ignoring the fact that he was not really all that interested in bettering his acquaintance, he plowed determinedly into the traffic lanes leading downtown. There is no better place to lose oneself than in a large anonymous city. New York would have been ideal, but he guessed that Albuquerque would do in a pinch.

From his study of local maps, he knew that the city was deep in the heart of Pueblo country. He had never been especially interested in Native Americans, not even in his boyhood, when Cowboys and Indians had been the order of the day. He now surprised himself with a sudden fascination in them. How better to spend his day than in discovering a whole new culture, one about as far removed from his own life as it was possible to be, and therefore as effective a distraction as he could possibly find? He was nearly trotting in his eagerness by the time he entered the portals of Wright's Indian Museum.

The place was floor-to-ceiling Indian artifacts: mementos, he was given to understand, of the long-deceased Anasazi civilization. Just who or what the Anasazis were, he hadn't a clue. Nor did it really matter. He devoured every garishly colored face mask, every totem and headdress, as if he would be tested on them later. While his eyes feasted on these alien and the occasionally grotesque souvenirs of a past long gone, he was readily able to forget the more recent past in his own life. These tepees were about as far as one could get from the stately brick and stucco houses of Flatbush. Ground maize might have been all very well for the Anasazis, but they were not at all reminiscent of the sumptuous meals he had paid for and consumed with enjoyment in New York. And nothing could be farther from his companion on a few of those New York evenings than these wax women with their long dark braids and aloof black eyes.

He glanced at his watch. Nearly a whole hour had gone by as he wandered in a forgotten world. Only the rest of his life to go …

He shook his head to clear it of such thoughts. He was doing fine. He was touring Albuquerque. What could be healthier than that? Had he driven directly back to Lakewood, he would doubtless have been forced to exert enormous mental energy to banish the thought of the hurt he imagined Shiffy must have suffered at his rude and precipitous departure. By now, she would know that he had flown home. His unspoken good-bye would, by its absence, constitute the clearest of messages. How could she know of all the times, too numerous to count, when his hand had strayed in the phone's direction to try and rectify matters, only to fall back, helpless to disobey the strictures of his terror-stricken heart?

She couldn't know. And so, she would convince herself that they had simply, to use the up-to-date vernacular, not been "on the same page." She had thought their time together meant one thing; he had put it into another category altogether. Maybe she would shed a tear or two …

Avi gritted his teeth. This was exactly what he had come into the museum to forget. Abruptly, he had had his fill of Indians. He strode out, consulting the pocketful of brochures he obtained from a tourist-information center near the museum. There were a number of other sites that looked interesting. Here was one, not too far away: The Rattlesnake Museum! His step quickened.

If the Anasazis had transported him to a different world, this place was one step even further removed: The denizens of this museum were not even human. "The world's largest collection of rattlesnakes, in beautiful, natural landscapes," touted the brochure. Avi duly visited one snake dwelling after another, noting differences in the creatures' colors and design, smiling mechanically as one specimen slithered like a very long "S" from one end of its space to the other, intent on some doomed insect it fancied for its lunch. After a while, all the snakes seemed to merge into one snake: a single entity crawling on its collective belly through the artificial underbrush it called home. Avi's eyes began to glaze, and along with boredom came the return of unwelcome thoughts. He was out the door in a flash, bent on the next distraction.

The midday sun beat down on him as he made his way along the white-hot sidewalks toward the Museum of Natural History and Science. A scene flashed into memory: His mother, complaining, "Avi refuses to set foot in a museum unless I bribe him with promises of ice cream or candy. How am I ever going to civilize that boy?"

Well, Ma would be proud of me now, he thought grimly. Or perhaps not, considering the debacle he had left behind him. His mother had been outraged — that was the only word for it — at the way he'd concluded what had seemed such a promising start with Shiffy Taub. Disappointment had counted for only part of her upset. The rest was dismay that her son could have behaved in such a rude, boorish manner. If one had to end a *shidduch,* one might at least do it in a courteous way! Not disappear into the night — or, in Avi's case, into the wilds of the American Southwest — like a criminal slinking away from the scene of his crime.

But that was exactly what it had felt like to Avi. A crime. A crime against his late wife, his Yocheved, to whom he had committed himself forever. Did "forever" cease to be legally binding when one of the parties to a marriage slipped out of this world? And, if so, was the bereft spouse within his rights to leap on that legalism as though onto a lifeboat, or was he still morally bound to the departed one by ties no less strong than before?

Avi didn't know the answer. All he knew was the sense of *rightness* that he had experienced in Shiffy Taub's company, and the guilt that sense had engendered. He'd never been very good at relaxing with his own conscience. And so, rather than grapple with it in endless, escalating tension, he had chosen to walk away instead; correction: to run away.

Here it was! The usual fossils greeted him in the museum's front room, like the concierge at some grand hotel. Moving on, he walked past caves, ravines, geological depressions, an active volcano. He might as well have been walking down the streets of Albuquerque. All of it passed him in a blur as he focused on the inward scenes jostling for his attention. Shiffy's little boy, head down on his mother's shoulder as she'd risen to put him back to bed after an absorbing game of Scrabble. Shiffy's understanding expression as he described the agonies of what he'd dubbed "Round 2" of bachelor life. "It's like someone turned the clock back, and all the years that I've lived since my yeshivah days are somehow erased. Only — they're not. Because I'm a different person than I was then, with lots of memories to prove it. Some good memories, and some awful ones."

She had understood, because she had been there herself. There she was, living in her parents' home again because heaven had seen fit to pluck her husband away from her in the prime of life. Her young son was growing up with a Zaidy in place of a father: much better than nothing, but not at all what Shiffy had envisioned as she stood beneath the *chuppah* with the baby's future Tatty.

Avi stopped walking, nearly colliding with a diorama of the planets surrounding the sun. He stood stock still, waiting for the waves of furious emotion. Like a beach beaten by endless waves, he felt eroded. Worn down. A war was raging inside him, and the combatants were fear, and yearning, and hurt, and shame, and a longing for forgiveness. If he could only hear that Shiffy had forgiven him, he would be at peace. But he would not hear it. He had lost the right to that privilege.

Frantically, he whipped out the last, battered brochure from his pocket: The National Atomic Museum, featuring a detailed history of the development of the A-bomb. That ought to be far enough removed from Indians and dinosaurs and rattlesnakes. Perhaps, in the violence of atomic fission, he would find the absolution he sought. Or, at the least, a measure of oblivion.

Given his progress so far today, he was not optimistic.

V.

Blind flight. Like a wounded bird bleeding from an arrow that has struck alarmingly close to the heart, Rivi ran through the antiseptic hospital corridors. There was an elevator here somewhere; if she could only stop her vision from blurring, she might be able to see it. Dashing a hand across her eyes, she tried again. An open elevator waited patiently at the end of the hall. In a moment, she was inside.

Now that she was no longer running, the respite from motion allowed the hated picture to resurface in her mind's eye, like an afterimage planted on her retina. Little Layala, snug in her arms one moment; snatched away the next, leaving an icy void behind. It had been the baby's mother who had taken her, but not in a spirit of grateful warmth. Rivi's devotion had been repaid with hostility. She had been treated not as a helpful friend, but as an enemy. Her eyes stung, her heart ached, and the arms that had so recently held their precious burden hung limp and useless at her sides.

Blind again, she stabbed at the elevator button through a haze of tears. Presently the doors slid open with their impersonal sigh, not caring whether she was in or out. She stepped through them, almost as uncaring herself. Another brush at her eyes cleared her vision enough to help her find the lobby's exit.

There was no exit. She was not, as she had thought, on the hospital's ground floor at all. Instead of the lobby, with its plastic couches and information desk and gift shop, she saw another corridor stretching away on either side. She had gotten off at the wrong floor.

Hanging on the wall directly facing the elevator was a black-and-white directory. Like a punch to the heart, she read the words: "Dr. Ethan Kennedy, Dr. Anne Dominic. Fertility Specialists. Room 104."

She stared at the words, mesmerized. *Fertility.* The word had haunted her from the first year of marriage, and it continued to haunt her days and nights like a tortured, restless spirit. She was barren, bereft of that which she most ardently craved. With a swallowed sob, she stared at the sign and thought of all the specialists they had seen back East. She had planned to visit the clinic at Memorial Hospital just as soon as they were settled. Rivi felt an insane urge to laugh. Settled? They had been settled even before they came: settled in despair, in hopelessness. They were just going through the motions now. A person couldn't live with unfulfilled hope for so many years without paying a price. For Rivi, that price was a resigned acceptance of her fate. And along with that acceptance, something vivid and animated had leaked away from her.

Still, she and Asher were pledged to keep trying. Dr. Ethan Kennedy and Dr. Anne Dominic, Fertility Specialists. This hospital had a fine reputation, and it was less than an hour's drive away from home. Why not? On impulse, she followed the pointing arrow to Rooms 100-110. The doctors' names greeted her again at the door of Room 104.

Raw with the memory of the 24 hours just past — the pretending game she'd been playing with Layala Mandel, and its heartrending outcome — she pushed open the door and walked inside.

With Gila out of danger and released to their care, the Bernsteins had been on the point of leaving the building when Tova suddenly remembered: "Isn't the Mandel baby still here following her surgery? In all the excitement over Gila, I forgot that I'd meant to call Etty and hear how the night went." She was chagrined at the oversight. "Layala must still be upstairs, on the children's ward. Let's stop in for a minute and visit."

Nachman was amenable. As the three of them rode the elevators up to the third floor, Tova thanked Hashem silently for the fact that Gila was standing on her own two feet beside her, breathing normally and looking healthy and happy. She thanked Him for the blessing of modern medicine, which could literally restore the breath of life. And she pleaded in her heart for a reprieve for her daughter; preferably, one that would last the rest of her life.

In the pediatric ward, the nurse manning the desk directed them to Room 303. They found the door open, and walked in on a charming scene: Etty Mandel seated in a comfortable armchair, holding the slumbering infant in her arms.

"Hi, Etty," Tova began — then stopped short. The face that Etty turned at their entrance was gaunt with strain. There was a haunted look in her eyes, and Tova saw now, an unnatural rigidity in the way she held the baby. Alarmed, she asked, "Etty? Is everything all right? Didn't the surgery go well?"

With an effort, Etty nodded. "It went fine, *Baruch Hashem*. Layala's going to be fine now." In an almost spasmodic gesture, she clutched the child closer to her chest.

"Then what's the problem?"

"Problem?"

Tova moved closer, leaving her husband and daughter hovering tentatively in the doorway. "Etty, you don't look so good. Is there anything wrong?"

Etty hung her head and swung it from side to side in an almost bovine gesture of mute anguish. Tova's alarm grew. Pulling up an orange, plastic chair — was there a single furniture supply house for every hospital in the world? — she leaned close and asked in an urgent undertone, "What is it, Etty? Please tell me."

"Rivi." Etty's voice was strangled.

"What?"

"Rivi was here ... She watched the baby ... until I took her away."

"Took her away — from where? I don't understand."

Drawing a deep, shuddering breath, Etty turned her head to face Tova fully. Her eyes held a blazing shame. "I was horrible to her, Tova." The story, once begun, unfolded in a tumble of words. "She offered to stay with her for me yesterday afternoon, because Ora was sick and needed me at home. She stayed with her the rest of the day and all of last night ...."

Tova mentally unscrambled the pronouns, trying to follow the story line without interrupting. Etty continued, eyes on the floor now. "Ora's getting better, so I hurried to come back here. I saw Rivi holding her. The nurse called her 'Mrs. Mandel' ... I grabbed Layala. Grabbed her ... as if Rivi was trying to keep her from me. That's how I felt ... like something had been stolen from me. Rivi left ... You should have seen the look on her face ..." At this, Etty hid her own face so that it was nearly buried in the baby's blanket. Layala squeaked in her sleep, a protesting sound. Her mother lifted her head slightly to ease the unwelcome pressure.

Tova waited, but there was nothing more. Hesitantly, she attempted a response. "You think you may have hurt Rivi's feelings?"

"I know I did! I was terrible. I did a terrible thing. After what she did for me, for us, for my family ... I treated her like — like a criminal!" The self-contempt in Etty's voice was difficult for Tova to hear without wincing. Instinctively, she glanced over her shoulder. The doorway was empty. Nachman had whisked Gila away from the unfolding scene. Tova was on her own.

"I'm sure Rivi understands," she offered in solace. "You were under stress. Your baby had just undergone surgery; you were worried and upset. Just apologize to her. It'll be all right."

"Right after Yom Kippur, too," Etty said tonelessly, as though she hadn't heard a word Tova had just said. "It's just over two weeks ago that I stood in front of Hashem and asked Him to make my soul as white as snow. And now, what a horrible stain ..." Her eyes, wide and anguished, fixed themselves on Tova. "How can she possibly forgive me, Tova? Ever?"

"Rivi's a very forgiving person. But you've got to take the first step, Etty. You've got to make it right."

Etty shuddered. She looked scared to death.

VI.

"**E**verybody's acting strangely today," Tova complained to her husband later that night, as they prepared to put an end to the seemingly endless day. Every 24-hour period in her life was crammed with activity: each chore, each responsibility, folded away like laundry and stuffed into its allotted drawer in Time's great dresser. But this day had felt longer than most. The earlier part of the morning, before Tova received the call that sent her flying over to the school and then the hospital, was lost in the mists of the past. The rest, however, stood out clearly in her mind. Strange: that was the word she would have to choose. Everyone seemed to have behaved out of character today.

Nachman nodded to indicate that he'd heard her, but he was preoccupied. He had plenty on his mind, with the *kollel* due to reopen soon and some unseen predator doing his best to send every Jewish institution in town up in flames and terror. Tova, recognizing the signs of inaccessibility from long experience, held her tongue. Nachman was the best of husbands and his ear was usually open to her, but there were times when she had wisely learned to keep her own counsel.

Anyway, what was there to put her finger on? Nothing but a series of odd scenarios, each one slightly troubling in its own way but none of them obvious enough, or sufficiently concrete, to consider in any coherent fashion. They were just enough to disturb her peace with their niggling question marks.

She scrubbed restlessly at the kitchen counter, as though her sponge could erase her lingering unease. It was long past the time when she should have been in bed, but she felt too wired to sleep. First, there had been that scene with Etty in the hospital. Tova wasn't sure what, exactly, had transpired between her two fellow *kollel* wives in little Layala's room, but as the *Rosh Kollel's* wife she felt a responsibility to see that the situation was properly addressed. She made a mental note to call Etty in the morning — and Rivi, as well.

The drive home had been uneventful, but she'd found a series of mysterious, almost furtive faces on her return. Shana had been sitting in the living room, curled up in a favorite armchair, scribbling in a dog-eared notebook. Tova, recognizing it, felt her heart leap up in cautious joy. It was Shana's writing notebook.

The girl had a knack with words, and in happier days had written many a story or poem in that notebook. She didn't share many of them, but the fact that she was engaged in creatively expressing herself had always pleased her parents. Since their move to Lakewood — no, long before that: since the decision to move to Lakewood — the notebook had lain abandoned in the bottom drawer of Shana's desk. Tova thrilled to the sight of it in her daughter's hands now.

"Hello, darling." A kiss planted on Shana's brow was accepted without reaction. "Writing something interesting?"

Shana looked up, her gaze unfocused. "It's so sad," she murmured. "She was a Jewish woman, too. A mother. She could've been anybody."

"What? Who are you talking about?" As in the encounter with Etty in the hospital, Tova had an odd sense of floating in the dark, of just missing the point.

At this, Shana looked up and finally saw her. "Oh, hi, Ma. I didn't realize you were there. I was just sort of talking to myself." She gestured vaguely at her notebook, embarrassed.

"But which Jewish woman — mother — were you talking about?"

"Just someone I read about with Mrs. Sadowsky. Something historical."

She was being evasive. Playing the understanding mother, Tova did not press her. "Well, enjoy." Shana nodded vaguely, eyes already back on the written page. Tova moved on down to the playroom.

She found the younger boys there, happily occupied with a floor puzzle, over which they were scooting what looked like a hundred Matchbox cars. "Hi, guys," she called, brightening up as the twins scrambled to their feet and hurled themselves at her in an ecstasy of reunion. Yudi, abruptly sullen, remained where he was.

"What's the matter, Yudi? Don't I get a hug from my big boy?"

Grudgingly, he abandoned his highway and submitted to his mother's embrace. "It's not fair," he declared. Tova's heart sank at the familiar opening gambit to so many a childish complaint.

"What isn't?" she asked.

"Chaim and Donny get to do all the fun stuff because they share a room together. Why do I have to share with the twins? I never have any fun."

"Looks to me like you're having a ball right now." Tova pointed at the floor.

"Oh, that's baby stuff. Chaim and Donny are doing the really fun stuff." "And what kind of fun is that, if I may be so bold as to ask?"

"They're talking secrets. About Indians and stuff."

"Well, if you're nice to them, I'll bet they'll play Cowboys and Indians with you, too."

It was no use. Yudi was in no mood to have his spirits lifted. Philosophically, Tova left him to his gloom. The realities of life dictated that some siblings be older than others. This was something that Yudi would have to learn to live with. And, judging by the way he'd been playing as she walked into the playroom, she had no doubt that he would get over his sulks much more quickly if she were not present.

Accordingly, she backed out of the room, taking a suddenly clinging Bo with her. Soon enough, soothed by a snack and a drink and a few minutes of concentrated Mommy-time, the toddler was off her lap and back in the playroom. Tova started up the stairs to see what state the rest of the house was in. And where was Heidi?

Chaim and Donny's room first. She paused outside and tapped on the door. A muffled, "Who's there?" reached her ears.

"It's your mother. May I enter, O great cowboys?"

It was Donny who opened the door for her. "Why'd you call us that, Ma?"

"Something Yudi said. He's not very happy that you won't play with him."

Chaim looked up in surprise. "What does he want to play?"

"Cowboys and Indians, I presume."

The boys exchanged a bewildered look. "We haven't played that game for ages," Donny said.

Tova shrugged. She had done her bit for Yudi, and there were more pressing things on her mind than children's games anyway. Pleasantly, she asked, "Did you boys have a nice day while we were gone?"

This reminded them of the reason their parents had been away. With a guilty start, Chaim belatedly asked how his sister was.

"She's fine now, *Baruch Hashem*."

"Sorry I didn't ask sooner, Ma. I just assumed, because you came in here looking so normal ..."

"That everything is back to normal. Well, it is, *Baruch Hashem*! So you guys can resume what you were doing. I'm going to see what I can do about supper."

"Hey, that's right. I'm hungry!" Donny sounded surprised.

"Just another hour or so," she promised, and left wondering what in the world she was going to serve her hungry family. It was too late to defrost anything, and they had already eaten spaghetti twice this week. Not for the first time, Tova bemoaned the loss of a convenience she had taken serenely for granted back East: take-out food.

She was tired, and there was dinner to make. But before going into her own room to kick off her shoes and change into more comfortable clothes, she went into Gila's room.

Her 9-year-old was lying in bed, ostensibly reading, but with her head turned toward the wall as though she'd been on the point of dropping off. "Hi there, sweetie. Feeling all right?"

Gila nodded without turning her head. "I'm fine, Ma. Just a little tired."

"Get some rest, then. I'll call you when dinner's ready. It'll be about an hour."

"Okay, Ma."

Gently, Tova closed the door. Gila was safe and sound in her own room, breathing in and out just like she should. With a renewed sense of elation, Tova stepped out of the room. It did not occur to her until much later that it was unlike Gila not to turn her head at her mother's entrance, and to greet her with a smile. There was something remote and forlorn about the view of her daughter's back that Tova, thrilled to see her out of danger and worried about what to cook for dinner, had entirely over-looked. She moved down the hall and tapped on Heidi's door.

Her old friend had extended her stay in their home far longer than she had originally intended. She seemed to be soaking up the sunshine, the relaxed pace — the *differentness* — of their little New Mexico town. Tova couldn't have been happier. Remembering the haunted look in the woman she and Nachman had picked up at the Albuquerque airport some weeks earlier, she could not help but feel a sense of complacency. Inviting Heidi out here had been a stroke of genius. Her friend was look-ing more at peace than Tova remembered seeing her for a long time.

If she still seemed restless now and then, she was taking it in stride. New York, and her old life, were waiting for her whenever she was ready for them. When her boss, head of the law firm where she worked, had phoned last week to ask about her plans, Heidi had murmured some-thing about needing to tend to her health. "I'll get back to you as soon as I can," she had promised, though when that would be was anybody's guess. By this time, Tova could not imagine life without her dear friend and house guest at the breakfast table, playing with the little ones, chat-ting with her over the dinner dishes.

"Hi, Heidi," she said, poking her head through the door. "Thanks for helping Shana hold down the fort here. I take it everything went smoothly?"

"Just fine." Heidi was standing at the guest-room window. She was doing nothing else: just standing and looking out. There was a curious energy in her very immobility, as though she were a runner crouched at a starting line, waiting for the gun to go off. "How's Gila?"

"*Baruch Hashem.* Resting. This was a scary one ..." Tova shuddered. "And we don't even know who or what it was that triggered the attack. Some sort of intruder, maybe? I hope they catch him soon, whoever he is."

Heidi nodded in empathy, but her mind seemed far away.

"Anything happen while I was gone?" Tova asked, in an effort to keep the conversation going. Usually, Heidi needed no prompting.

"Not much. The boys were great. I must've read them a hundred stories. They just eat them up. Oh, and you had a visitor. Rabbi Harris stopped by to hear how Gila was doing."

"Really? How nice of him. What else did he have to say?"

Heidi hesitated. "He apologized for his *gabbai,* the one I insulted. And I apologized back. So that's over with." She looked relieved.

Tova was relieved, too. She still had her long-term worries about Heidi, but her mind was already moving on to the more immediately urgent items on her agenda, including dinner and tidying up the house she'd abandoned in such frenzied haste earlier that day.

Now, hours later — with dinner over, the dishes done and the children in bed — Tova scrubbed her counters and pondered the oddities she had encountered in family and friends that day. The phone rang.

"Hello?" It was rather late in the day for anyone to be calling.

"Mrs. Bernstein! I hope I'm not calling too late. This is Pinchas Harris."

"It's rarely too late in this house, Rabbi Harris. Do you want to speak to my husband?"

"Actually, it's you I wanted to reach. There's something I wanted to ask you. Are you sure this is a good time? I'm afraid I was too busy to get to a phone till now."

This sounded interesting. "No problem at all, rabbi. What is it?"

"Nate Goodman, our *gabbai* — do you remember him from our meetings? Tall fellow, beard, an attorney — came to see my wife and me this evening, at my request. We had a long talk. I have an interesting suggestion to make … about your friend, Miss Neufeld."

"Heidi?" Tova groped for a chair and sat down.

"Yes. Do you have a minute?"

"Rabbi," Tova said fervently. "I have as many minutes as you want. Go on, please. I'm all ears."

Chapter 13

I.

G ila had not been dozing off when her mother walked into her room. She had been crying, and it was only by virtue of her mother's aching feet and her preoccupation with dinner that she hadn't noticed.

Gila had been crying because it was all her fault.

Ever since she could remember, it had been all her fault. Her fault whenever the family's peace was so rudely shattered by one of her sudden attacks. Her fault that her mother looked so drawn and anxious and her Tatty so serious, his heartwarming smile nowhere in evidence. Her fault that trips had to be canceled, outings postponed and parties unattended because her lungs refused to take in air the way they were supposed to.

Everyone else was able to breathe without any trouble at all. "As natural as breathing," went the expression. But for Gila, drawing breath wasn't natural at all. When the attacks came, it was like being at the top of a very tall mountain, where the air was so thin that there just wasn't enough of it to fill her lungs, no matter how hard they worked. And so, the ambulance would be called, and Gila rushed away amid a blaring of sirens, flanked by her worried parents and gnawed by the knowledge that she had once again upset everyone and turned all their plans upside down.

If she'd felt badly before, it was a hundred times worse now. The whole family had pulled up roots and moved across the country to this little town in New Mexico because of her. At first, Gila had let herself nurse a cautious hope. Maybe this really was the solution. It hadn't been an easy move — especially for Shana — but if they settled down and were happy here, and if her attacks stopped, then there might be a happy ending after all.

But evil people had set fire to the shul, and then the surveyors' tents at the site of Tatty's new yeshivah. Everyone was scared and worried. Because of her, the family was in a dangerous place. She knew that, because she'd heard Donny say that until the bad guys were caught, no Jew in this town was safe. And then, today, she had seen the shadow of the bad guy: a glimpse of evil that had literally stolen the breath from her lungs. Speeding along the highway to the familiar siren's tune, Gila had been conscious, through her labored gasping and heaving chest, of a sinking despair. It was happening all over again. Traveling all this way had done not a bit of good. She was still sick, still disrupting her family's peace of mind, and with a horrifying dollop of fear to poison the mix even more.

That was why Gila was crying in her bed, as she waited for a supper she had no appetite to eat. But by the time she made her way downstairs to the dining room, her eyes were dry and her young face composed. The least she could do for her family was to keep them from worrying even more about her than they already did. The last thing she wanted to do was ruin their dinner or what was left of their day. She was carrying a large enough burden of guilt already.

With a start, she realized that she was being spoken to.

"What's that, Ma?"

Tova laughed. "I was just asking you to pass the potatoes … for the third time. You've been daydreaming, sweetie."

"Oh. Sorry, Ma." A flush rose to Gila's rounded cheeks. With a sheepish smile, she passed the dish of mashed potatoes to her mother.

"Shana?" Tova said. "Can I please have the salt?"

There was no response. Shana's elbow was on the table, chin resting in the heel of her palm and eyes fixed on the indeterminate distance.

"Guess I'm striking out today," Tova remarked. This, too, elicited no reaction at all. She caught Gila's eye, and they both giggled.

Gila reached past her sister for the saltshaker and passed it to her mother, feeling for once as if she'd gotten something right.

Shana was quiet during dinner, but that was not unusual these days. In her previous lifetime — back East — she'd been something of a chatterbox, at times much to her brothers' annoyance. The move to Lakewood seemed to have subdued her, turning her inward so that she communed more often with herself than with those around her. This change worried her mother. But Shana was looking happier these days. She had made a couple of friends at school and was spending a lot of time with the librarian — the doctor's wife, Mrs. Sadowsky. All of which, Tova hoped, were harbingers of a gradual recovery of good spirits and healthy outlook in her eldest child.

The reason Shana was quiet during this particular dinner — though her mother didn't know it — had nothing to do with her contentment, or lack of it, in Lakewood. Her mind was elsewhere. It was locked in the past, on a day when a band of pale, courageous Jews had made their last stand in this very town. She couldn't stop thinking about that poor "woman with the kerchief" who refused to abandon her people when danger threatened. Doom, it seemed to Shana, had accompanied the group of Eastern European Jews across the ocean and onto the shores of a foreign land. Or had doom stepped in only when they decided to leave the security of the settled East Coast for the Wild West reaches?

It had been gold that lured them away from safety and into a deadlier danger than any they had known in their native villages. Shana was fascinated by the strange twist of fate that had led two such disparate cultures into a head-on clash; one which, almost inevitably, had ended in tragedy. On the one hand, a band of pious Polish Jews, on a journey of hope to America, land of opportunity, and, on the other, a tribe of Apache Indians, angered at the theft of their ancient hunting grounds, displaced and dispossessed and on the warpath because that was the only way they knew of to make things right again. The high, pale foreheads and suffering eyes of one group had come face-to-face with the red skins and hard, sculpted features of the other. Heartbroken words of *Tehillim* had countered bloodthirsty machetes. And Hashem, in His infinite wisdom, had permitted the machetes to have their way. Might had triumphed that day, with a terrible loss of precious life.

But that, Shana thought fiercely, *was only the way it seemed.* Might and cruelty could never really win. Those long-ago Jews had died proud in their Jewishness, their bearing to the very end a sanctification of Hashem's holy Name. Even Jane Willard, a simple pioneer wife, had been touched by the Jewess's innate dignity and the rocklike strength of her faith. That unknown traveler was her nameless sister in history, and Shana was proud of her.

Later, climbing the stairs to her room after a stint at the kitchen sink, the girl's thoughts touched again on Jane Willard's diary. The account Mrs. Sadowsky had found was their only source for any knowledge they had of the Apache attack that had spelled the end of that pitiful band of Jews. In it, Jane Willard had mentioned that the Jewish woman was delighted to see that Jane kept a diary, as "she kept one, too." What, Shana wondered, had become of that other journal? Shana would have loved to be able to learn, firsthand, what had been in the mind and heart of that faithful and intrepid Jewish woman who lost her life in this very part of the world more than a century and a half earlier.

With rising excitement, Shana resolved to speak to the librarian about the possibility of tracking down the diary of the "woman with the kerchief," the memory of whom had begun to haunt her thoughts even as it plucked the strings of her tender, young heart.

II.

"This is unacceptable!" It wasn't often that Nachman Bernstein raised his voice, but Sheriff Ramsay was now privileged to witness that phenomenon in person. "It's simply not good enough to say you're 'working on it.' There are residents of this town — Jewish residents in good standing — whose lives are at risk because of these perpetrators. We need answers, and we need them now!"

The sheriff's office was small and cluttered. A stale aura of cigarette smoke hung in the air, though there was no sign of either ashtray or cigarettes in sight. Nachman wondered if the smell was a residue of a previous era. He wondered, too, if the oppression he felt in this stuffy room was due to a different kind of residue: the ghosts of old crimes, hovering in the air and turning it rancid.

The sheriff leaned back in his leather chair; both the man and the chair looking rather the worse for wear this morning. "Rabbi Bernstein, please believe me: I understand how you feel. I'm not just saying that; it's the honest truth. I don't like what's going on any more than you do. Lakewood's been a peaceful place for years. Why do you think our law-enforcement arm is so tiny? We really are doing the best we can. I've got my men — and there's few enough of them — out canvassing the streets, trying to pick up anything they can, any clue to the identity of the person or persons behind this string of crimes." He paused, then added in a far-less-official tone, "How's your daughter feeling today?"

"Gila's all right now, thank G-d. But what happened at school yesterday has brought this thing very close to home."

"I'm sure it has." Ramsay rummaged in a pile of papers on his desk until he found what he was looking for. "We hired a competent forensic psychiatrist — a Jewish fellow, maybe you know him? Dr. Abe Rein's the name — to create a psychological profile of the criminal for us. Want to take a look?" He held out the sheaf of papers. Nachman leaned forward and fairly snatched them from his hand.

Dr. Rein was a neat worker. Setting aside the professional jargon, Nachman emerged with a clear picture of the man whom the psychiatrist believed had committed the string of hate crimes against Lakewood's Jewish population.

> "... a personality that includes elements of what psychiatry terms a 'hysterical' neurosis, in which the ego is overly dramatized and led to seek the glare of the spotlight even at the expense of his own best interests. This man is after glory, fame, wealth — and believes himself entitled to them all. He was probably poor in childhood, leading to frustrated dreams of someday "making it big" or "striking it rich." This kind of personality may choose acting as a career, which will in some measure satisfy his crav-

ing for the spotlight. He may, on the other hand, through lack of ability or unfortuitous circumstance, be forced out of the limelight he so desperately craves ... but will never stop seeking.

"However, in even the most mundane situation he will come across as a dominant figure who must have his way at all cost. Such a personality will often have a 'sidekick,' usually a weaker or less-intelligent friend or family member to serve as admiring audience, ego-stroker and willing accomplice.

"The perpetrator should be fairly young, but not too young: an educated guess would place him somewhere between the ages of 25 and 35. He would have a strong will and a masterful manner that camouflages the painful hollowness within ..."

Nachman looked up from the report to find Sheriff Ramsay watching him. He felt a sudden sense of kinship with the man, whose deep-set eyes held a twin burden of responsibility and helplessness that struck an all-too-familiar chord with the *Rosh Kollel.*

"Good stuff here," he said, tapping the pages with his finger. "At least, it looks that way to my untrained eye. What do you think?"

"I think Dr. Rein knows what he's talking about. Steve Birch has his own ideas about this. Even before the report came in, he's had his eye on a guy who might fit the bill. A Native American, from the reservation but living in Lakewood at the moment. Right age, right kind of personality. He even comes along with a sidekick — the kind of number two man that Dr. Rein mentions."

Nachman recalled something Steve had told him at their last meeting: *My attention is pretty firmly fixed on one man in particular, and a friend of his — actually, more of a sidekick, or willing slave ...*

Noting the other man's rising excitement, Jack Ramsay held up a warning hand. "We've got to tread carefully. As in any case, we'll need proof. On top of that are the sensitivities involved in our dealings with the Native American population. We don't want to go stirring up a hornet's nest."

"Doesn't Birch represent the Indians — legally, I mean?"

"Sure. Does his work *pro bono*, too. Good man."

"Why do you think he's taking such an interest in helping the Jewish community, when one of his own might be implicated in the crimes?" The question tapped into Nachman's deeper curiosity about the man called Steve Birch. He freely admitted that he was drawn to the fellow, but he just as frankly could not figure out what to make of him.

Ramsay took his time about answering.

"Birch is an odd one," he said at last. "Neither fish nor fowl, as the saying goes. He's obviously got some mixed blood in him somewhere. Ever notice those eyes?" At Nachman's nod, the sheriff continued, "I don't think he's fully accepted by the Native American community, despite his ongoing efforts to help them: efforts that they're all too eager to accept, seeing that it's effective and it's free. At the same time, he doesn't really fit in with non-Indians, either."

"Sounds sad."

"I guess it is. But Birch is strong. He doesn't come around whining or looking for pity, just does his job as he sees it. And right now, he sees his job as putting that arsonist behind bars ... whoever it is."

"I'll give him a call," Nachman said.

"No need. I'm sure we'll be hearing from him if he has anything new to report."

"I'll call him anyway. I've got to feel like I'm doing *something*."

"Gotcha." Ramsay stood up and leaned across the cluttered desk to shake Nachman's hand. "Nice talking to you, rabbi. And don't worry about our slacking off around here. We're just as anxious to get those guys behind bars as you are. Believe me."

"I do. Thank you, sheriff." Nachman stepped into the outer office, a room not much bigger than Ramsay's inner office had been. A bored-looking secretary with a head of tight gray curls sat staring at her computer screen, varnished fingertips tapping an occasional letter on the keyboard. She did not look up as Nachman passed. Idly, he wondered whether it would take a gale-force wind to tear her eyes away from her monitor, or perhaps a full-scale shoot-out right outside the door.

The corners of his mouth lifted in a grin as he found his car parked outside at the curb. He started the engine and drove slowly past a jeweler's, a children's wear shop and a dry cleaners, before taking the right turn that would lead him away from the commercial center of town and toward his own home. The cell phone in his pocket rang.

"Hello?"

"Hi, Nachman." Asher Gann's voice sounded strained. "Got a minute?"

"Actually, I'm on my way home, so you've got my ear for at least the next six minutes or so. What's up?"

Uncharacteristically, Asher let a few beats of silence elapse before launching into speech. Nachman felt his antennae spring to attention. Something was troubling this usually effervescent young man, and he had chosen to turn to his *Rosh Kollel* for guidance. "What is it, Asher?"

"It's my wife. Rivi. She's — very unhappy."

"Are we talking about a *shalom bayis* problem?"

"No! Not at all, Nachman. That's not it ..."

"Then what?" Patience was the key to this kind of dialogue. He waited, steering the car down streets that were becoming as familiar to him as the ones he had driven along every day back in Brooklyn.

Asher began to tell him a somewhat convoluted tale about Etty Mandel, Etty's baby, and his own wife. Rivi, it seemed, had been asked to babysit for the child on numerous occasions, and had grown very attached to her. When the little Mandel girl had come down with a virus on the day of Layala's surgery, Rivi had agreed to pinch-hit for Etty, staying with the infant in the hospital at Roswell and serving *in loco parentis* all night long.

"What Etty Mandel did after that was unforgivable," Asher said, seeing in his mind's eye his wife's white face when she arrived home, and hearing again the ominous silence that hinted at emotions too deep for words. "She burst into the baby's hospital room and just about snatched the kid out of Rivi's arms — as if Rivi were a kidnaper trying to steal her precious baby. My wife was devastated. She came home looking like a zombie. I've never seen her like that, Nachman." He stopped, then added in a strangled voice. "I don't know if I can forgive Mrs. Mandel for this. She hurt Rivi deeply. My wife hides these things, but I know her well enough to see that she's bleeding inside, Nachman. Bleeding."

"I'm sorry," Nachman said soberly. "Asher, let Tova and me come by tonight to talk this thing through with you and your wife. All right?"

"With all respect, I think it's the Mandels you should be talking to ..."

"We'll get to that. We *kollel* members need to get along, Asher. That's an imperative. I'd like to start by hearing Rivi out. I'll get to Mrs. Mandel later." He waited a beat. "Can we come?"

"Of course." Asher's tone was heavy. "Maybe it'll do Rivi some good to get this off her chest. Air things out."

"I'm sure it will. See you about 8 o'clock, O.K.?"

"Fine."

Scarcely had he disconnected from Asher, when his phone rang again. Nachman flipped it open and saw his home number on the readout screen. "Hi."

"Nachman. How'd it go at the sheriff's?"

His visit to Ramsay's office seemed to have taken place ages ago. He sighed. "I'll tell you about it when I get home. How's everything going over there?"

"That's what I was calling about. You've got a visitor."

"A visitor?"

"It's that Indian again." Tova had lowered her voice to a near-whisper. "Steve Birch. He wants to see you. What do I tell him?"

For an instant, Nachman was speechless with surprise. The very man he wanted to see! If he wasn't careful, he was going to start to believe there was some sort of telepathic bond between himself and Birch.

"Please tell him to wait. I'm on my way."

Nachman flipped his phone closed and stepped on the gas.

There were things to be done; important things, all of them. Beginning with a talk with that enigmatic Native American with the oddly colored eyes and a mysterious old *siddur* that had come into his possession from heaven only knew where.

III.

One of the bookcases in Rabbi Bernstein's study had sliding-glass doors. Steve paused in his pacing to stand in front of these doors and study his reflection, superimposed against a long dark row of books written in a language he didn't know. It was the language of his little prayer book.

The titles, most of them gold embossed, looked like symbols from another world instead of ordinary words in a foreign tongue. He stared at them for a long moment, as though sheer force of will might squeeze from them the secret of their meaning. Then his eyes traveled upward, to the reflection of his own face.

In the glass, his features hung in eerie suspension, floating in a black pool. How many thousands of times had he seen this face in the mirror: as he shaved, brushed his teeth, swiped at his hair with a brush? It was as familiar to him as anything could be. And yet, as he gazed at his own reflection, it was like looking at a stranger. No ... that wasn't it, exactly. It was rather as though a stranger were inside him, knocking at the gates of his consciousness and begging for permission to step into the light of day.

Steve did not know who the stranger was; he only knew that he wished he were a stranger no longer. Whoever he was, that stranger was the true owner of the unusual pair of eyes that met him in the mirror every morning and of the dreams that had for so long haunted his nights.

The eyes continued to look impassively back at him, giving nothing away. He put his hand in his pocket and felt the reassuring bulk of his little prayer book with the Jewish star on the cover. The star that his grandmother had spoken about, in a dream that had woken him in a cold sweat at 4 o'clock that morning.

In the predawn darkness he'd lain rigid with pounding heart, trying to recapture the dream while sensing that, in some inexplicable but very real way, it had already captured him.

Grandma had died when he was only a boy. Through her daughter — Steve's mother, Alice — Steve had inherited his grandmother's eyes, and also her inward, thoughtful nature. The little paper-wrapped package he kept in his closet had been handed down from Grandma to Alice, too, and then on to Steve in lieu of a daughter.

They had not talked much, he and Grandma; at least not with words. But everything that she'd ever said to him was etched in his memory: precious markers in an enigmatic landscape. She had enjoyed taking him outside to gaze up at the stars. According to the stories he read in the Bible, G-d had done the same with Abraham, hadn't He? He had shown

Abraham, the first Jew, the stars, promising that Abraham's progeny would be as numerous.

Young Steve would follow Grandma's hand as she pointed out various landmarks in heaven's vast terrain.

"That's Betelgeuse," she would say. "And there's Cassiopeia — she's shaped like a long 'W', see — and Orion's Belt ..." And the stars seemed to leap to life as she spoke, becoming in his boyish imagination his allies in an often hostile world.

"Follow your star," his grandmother would tell him before she led him back into the house. "Never be afraid, Steve, to follow your star ..."

Those were the words she had spoken to him in the dream last night. Only, instead of "Follow your star," she said, "Follow *the* star." He had woken with beads of cold perspiration on his face and a question in his mind: Follow what star? Which star?

He had fallen back into an uneasy sleep. And when he woke again, to broad sunlight streaming through the curtains he'd neglected to draw the night before, the first thing he saw was the Jewish prayer book lying on his bedside table. A prayer book emblazoned with the six-pointed Star of David on the cover.

Follow the star?

A landmark in heaven's vast terrain ...

There and then, he decided that he had to see Rabbi Bernstein again. Now. Today.

At the sound of the study door opening, he turned away from the bookcase. The rabbi's wife stood in the doorway, bearing a tray containing a steaming mug and a plate of cookies. The cookies looked homemade.

"I'm sorry about the wait," she apologized, walking into the room and setting the tray down on the desk. "My husband should be home any minute ..."

"That's all right," he said quickly. "I don't mind waiting." He gestured at the book-lined walls. "This is a good place to wait."

Though they'd been spoken by a 21st-century man with a law degree and a suit to match, the words struck Tova as being inscrutable and old, like the Indians themselves. *A good place to wait.*

"I won't argue with that," she smiled. With a farewell nod she retreated, closing the study door behind her.

Steve prepared to resume his wait. This time, however, he had company: a mug of coffee, home-baked cookies, and a sudden overwhelming feeling that could only be described as *coming home*.

Home had lately become an ambiguous word to Steve. He'd grown up on the reservation, and had pledged the lion's share of his adult energies to helping his Indian brethren navigate the choppy waters between the old practices and the modern world. Many, sadly, were failing to stay the course. Their heritage had lost its power to sustain, while the new world offered the gamut from cool indifference to outright rejection.

Though he'd owned his Lakewood apartment for years, he still thought of the reservation as "home." While he could not honestly say that he passed through its gates these days with any sense of warmth, there had at least been the familiarity of old associations, and acceptance as one of their own.

Until today.

This morning, quelling the impulse to race directly to Rabbi Bernstein's house, Steve had taken a drive out to the reservation. There were some outstanding cases he wanted to follow up on, not to mention the continuing search for the arsonist who had rattled Lakewood's tiny Jewish enclave. He'd walked into the Mescalero reservation with both of these things on his mind, so preoccupied that he didn't see the group of young men until he heard their voices.

"Hey — there goes the Jew lover!"

Lifting his head with a jerk, Steve saw Al Barker, perpetrator of the anti-Semitic graffiti on the synagogue wall some months back. Steve had helped him stay out of trouble then. In return he'd expected, if not gratitude, then at least tolerance. But tolerance was the last thing on Al's mind today, or that of his friends'.

"Jew lover!"

"Why don't you go back where you belong? In the syn-a-gogue!"

"Yeah. Go pray in the synagogue with your Jew friends!"

He listened in uncomprehending shock. Where was all this animosity coming from? There was no question in his mind that animosity was what he was hearing. His own people were spewing hatred at him because he was trying to help the Jews identify the criminal who was terrorizing their community.

The world — confusing enough before — suddenly ceased to make any sense at all.

He felt no urge to respond to them. Their taunts were of less significance than the cawing of a flock of ill-tempered crows, squabbling over crumbs. What *was* important — what shook Steve Birch to the depths of his being — was his reaction to them.

"Go pray in the synagogue with your Jew friends."

In a daze, he realized that this was exactly what he would have liked to do. Pray … with his Jewish friends.

Reeling like a drunkard, he did an about-face, sweeping past the hostile insolence of Al and his cronies, past the crumbling adobe buildings, through the dusty shimmering heat, back to his car.

Back to Rabbi Bernstein, and the book-lined room that was as warm, as safe, and as real, as "home" is supposed to feel.

IV.

A vi Feder could put it off no longer. He had to phone home.

"Call me the minute you get there," his mother had commanded. "So I'll know you've arrived safely."

But he hadn't called the moment he arrived. He had spent the day roaming the streets and museums of Albuquerque instead, like an insatiable tourist in place of a *kollel* man with a guilty conscience.

That conscience had been bothering him ever since. And though he'd managed to ignore it last night — pleading exhaustion after his flight and the long round of sightseeing, followed by the three-hour drive down to Lakewood — he was forced to heed its clarion call this morning.

She answered on the second ring.

"Hi, Ma!"

"Avi! So you finally remembered to pick up a phone."

"I didn't forget, Ma." Amazing, the power she possessed to put him on the defensive within the first three seconds of any conversation … "I was just, uh, busy."

"Too busy to call your mother?"

His heart sank. Bravely, he decided to take the bull by the horns. "Actually, I put it off for a good reason. I knew I was in for a scolding."

"A scolding? What for? For running away like a thief in the night and hurting a young woman's feelings? Do you think you deserve a scolding for that?"

She had him neatly cornered. "I explained it to you, Ma. It just wasn't right."

"You're the one who's not right — in the head!" Having got this off her chest, Mrs. Feder softened. "Listen, Avi. I know it's not easy for you. Starting up with *shidduchim* again, after you'd already been married and settled; how could that be easy for anyone? But you need a wife. You can't deny that, Avi. And you and Shiffy hit it off so beautifully. Why did you have to run away?"

Because I panicked. Because I'm not ready to be happy again. He did not share these thoughts with his mother. He had been prepared to endure a lecture — even a harsh one — because he knew he deserved it. Compassion and understanding he couldn't handle. Trying for a mature note, he said, "It wasn't 'running.' I broke off an unsuccessful *shidduch* — albeit with some regrets. She seemed like a nice girl ..."

"She's an *amazing* girl! And you're a fool!"

He almost smiled. This was much easier. "Well, all I can do is try to learn some wisdom, then ... Sorry, Ma, I'm in a big rush. Talk to you later ..."

She wasn't fooled by the pretense of busyness, but she let him go because she'd had her say and also, apparently, her fill of frustration.

Avi stared at the silent phone for a moment, replaying the conversation in his mind as bleakness settled over his heart like an ill-fitting suit. Then, abruptly, he reached for his hat and jacket and started for the door. Perhaps it was the memory of the frenetic social life he'd led in New York that made him feel utterly incapable of facing this evening alone It was only 7:30, early enough to drop in on the Ganns. Asher would be glad to see him. He would offer a sympathetic ear, and Rivi would provide the comfort food to go along with it. Suddenly, Avi couldn't wait.

He rang the Ganns' doorbell somewhat nervously. After the reception he'd been accorded by his mother, he was not sure what to expect at the hands of his friend especially after he'd described, in the detail that Asher would demand, the fiasco named Shiffy.

No, that wasn't right. The fiasco named Avi. *She'd* done nothing wrong, nothing at all. If anything, Shiffy was the wronged party. In a blinding flash, he remembered how she'd looked as they said good-bye after their last meeting. Witnessing his abrupt departure, a forlorn uncertainty had crept into that face to dim what had been, just moments before, unmitigated serenity. He had been the one to dim the switch of her joy, and his own, at the same time. Like an old-fashioned electric circuit-box, he'd been incapable of handling the current of joyous possibility. And so, he had blown a fuse and done an escape act.

"Avi!" The door was flung open and there was Asher, beaming with pleasure at the sight of him. "You actually dropped in without announcing yourself first. Will wonders never cease?"

"I hope it's not an inconvenient time ..."

A flicker of chagrin crossed his friend's face. "Actually, we're expecting the Bernsteins here in a little while. It's not a social get-together. We have a little problem to discuss."

"Oh? Then maybe I should come back another time."

A firm hand shot out to grab his sleeve. "You're coming right inside. Rivi and I have been waiting at the edge of our seats to hear how it went in New York."

"And when the Bernsteins come?"

"I don't mind if you hang around, though Rivi may feel differently. This is really about her."

"I'll just say hello to Nachman and then scoot out of here the minute they come."

"Fine." Asher pulled the door open wider and ushered his friend inside. "Come in, and talk fast. We've got a lot to catch up on."

Obligingly, Avi started talking the minute he got inside, and was still going strong when the doorbell rang again to herald the arrival of Nachman and Tova Bernstein.

Etty Mandel bustled about the house, thrilled to have little Layala back where she belonged, her insides functional now and her mood miraculously sweetened. No longer did feeding time herald a crying jag that wore out the baby and her mother in equal measure. Layala was a happy girl now. No need to worry about her any longer. Etty was free to turn her mind to other things: such as her own abominable behavior toward Rivi in the hospital the other day. The one subject on which she had no desire to dwell ...

"Ma! Would you please tell Ora not to steal my colored pencils? I need them for school!" Tzirel was aggrieved, cheeks flushed and hands planted on her hips.

"Ora did not 'steal' anything," Etty said automatically. "Ora, please return Tzirel's colored pencils. Why don't you use your own?"

"I don't have colored pencils," the 3-year-old declared. "I only have crayons, like a baby!"

Etty restrained herself from peppering that indignant, adorable little face with kisses. Small children, small problems ... How indescribably sweet, when a lack of colored pencils looms as the largest problem in a little girl's life — one which her mother can so easily, as though with the flick of a magic wand, solve for her.

She crouched down so that she was at her daughter's eye level, and asked, "Would you like your very own package of colored pencils, Ora?"

Ora nodded solemnly.

"Fine. Next time I go to the store — maybe even tomorrow — that's just what I'll get you. Okay?"

Ora's face cleared. She offered a toothy smile and trotted off to play. Tzirel reclaimed her box of pencils in silence. In her crib, Layala slept the sleep of the just. Efraim was learning in the dining room, and Shimi was upstairs in his room, probably wasting his time as usual.

The phone rang.

In a rosy glow over the childish squabble successfully hurdled, Etty was smiling as she picked up the receiver. The sound of her oldest son's voice was like frosting on a scrumptious cake. "Meir!" she exclaimed. "How nice to hear from you! How's everything at yeshivah?"

Yeshivah was fine. Meir, himself, was more than fine. He had called, ostensibly, to pay his respects, but mostly to pass on the various accolades he had garnered from the rebbi, *mashgiach*, and even the Rosh Yeshivah that week. Meir was doing again what he did best: carving out a shining place for himself in the corridors of yeshivah life. Etty's heart lifted, soared, sang.

With her cup of *nachas* overflowing, she passed the phone on to her husband. "Efraim, it's Meir." She hesitated. "Please let me know when you're done. I need to make a call."

She stared at the floor, wondering what had prompted those words. She needed to make a call: to whom? She had made no plans to call anyone. She hadn't thought about what to say or not to say. She was totally unprepared. But something in her fast-beating heart told her that the time had come. There was only so long one could avoid the inevitable. When you made a mistake, there was a price to pay, and the earlier you paid it in full, the better you would feel afterward.

And so, the moment Efraim called, "I'm off, Etty," she retrieved the receiver and settled herself soberly in a kitchen chair, as though facing an invisible tribunal. The house was momentarily quiet. She really should wait till the kids were in bed, when she'd be sure of uninterrupted time.

By then, however, her courage would surely have deserted her.

Right this minute there were the good feelings generated by Meir's call to keep her rooted in her own reality. She was not an awful person. She had raised a son like Meir, hadn't she? All in all, she was okay. She had simply made a mistake with Rivi, just one day after Layala had undergone surgery. Given the stress of the moment, was it any wonder she'd snapped?

Armed with these consoling self-justifications, she picked up the phone and dialed Rivi Gann's number.

"Hello?" To her surprise, the woman's voice at the other end did not sound like Rivi at all. "This is Etty Mandel. To whom am I speaking, please?"

"Etty! Don't you recognize my voice? This is Tova. Rivi was busy in the kitchen. She asked me to pick up."

Now Etty could hear the murmur of men's voices in the background. Nachman Bernstein, no doubt, chatting with Asher Gann. Actually, from the sound of things, there were more than just the two of them. What would any Gann affair be without Asher's faithful sidekick, Avi Feder?

"Sounds like quite a party," she murmured, feeling an ugly flush mottling her cheeks with the stain of humiliation.

"It's not a party," Tova tried to explain. "We — Nachman and I — just came over to discuss something with the Ganns. Avi happened to be here when we came." Tova paused. "Actually, I was planning to call you just as soon as our discussion was over."

Etty gave a harsh bark of laughter. "Don't worry about it. Efraim and I are used to being left out of the loop."

She sensed further explanations on the tip of Tova's tongue, but refused to submit herself to any more mortification. "Oops, is that the baby crying?" she exclaimed, though not a peep had been heard from Layala's room. "Gotta go, Tova. Send my regards to everyone. Bye."

In the space of 10 seconds, the roles had been reversed. Before, Rivi had been the injured party, and Etty the debtor. The apologies had been primed to flow in one direction.

With this abortive phone call, Etty once again became a victim. Abandoning her decision to beg Rivi's forgiveness, she went instead into the dining room to inform her husband that, once again, there was a party on and they hadn't been invited.

V.

Indians were the topic of conversation in the Bernstein house that night.

Shana was in the laundry room, folding laundry for her mother. Heidi, bored, came in and lent her a hand. As they folded, Shana found herself sharing the sad saga of the unknown Jewish woman who had perished, along with her family and a band of old-home companions, in an Apache attack in this very town.

"Mrs. Sadowsky showed me the diary of a woman who lived on a farm around here. She had met one of the Jewish travelers, a woman wearing a kerchief, and wrote about her. The woman was part of a group that had come from Europe. They planned on settling in the East, but the gold fever got them. They made it as far as Lakewood, when the Apaches attacked and killed a lot of townspeople, including those Jews." Shana's hands stilled as tears brightened her eyes. This happened every time she thought about that long-ago wife and mother, and her fellow travelers, who had perished on the cusp of adventure, on the trail of gold in America, the Land of Opportunity.

Heidi stopped folding, too. "How brave," she murmured, her face going soft and distant. "Imagine, picking up and leaving the only home you've ever known — the people and places you're so familiar with — and going off to a strange land to start all over again. That takes a special kind of courage."

"Jews have been doing that throughout the ages," Shana pointed out, unconsciously paraphrasing what the librarian had told her.

Heidi's eyes refocused on Shana. "That's true. But not all of us have the same quality of courage. Some of us are stick-in-the-mud stay-at-homes!"

"Unless you have no choice." Shana was thinking of a certain move from East to Southwest, and of a certain girl who practically had to be dragged there, kicking and screaming.

"Yes," Heidi said absently. "Unless you have no choice." What she was thinking of, Shana couldn't guess.

They resumed their folding and pairing and stacking. Heidi's thoughts had wandered far away. Shana wondered about the final thoughts of that band of brave, doomed Jews who had spent so short a time in this town before meeting their bitter end ... Abruptly, she moved back into the present. Was that a honk?

"Where are you going?" Heidi asked, startled.

"Someone's picking me up. I've gotta go."

"Where to? Mrs. Sadowsky's?"

Shana blushed. "Actually, it's a school friend this time. We're going to work on a project together."

Ignoring the astonished look that Heidi bestowed on her, Shana fairly ran from the room to fetch her sweater and schoolbag. Apaches and pioneers and long-ago dramas faded from her mind as she flew down the stairs toward something that she hadn't realized, until now, how deeply she missed: simple camaraderie with girls her own age. The calm, unhurried dance of friendship. In New York or New Mexico, she knew now that she couldn't survive without it. She'd hung back, reluctant to admit her need. But she was admitting it now. It had been long enough.

She threw open her front door just as the horn sounded a second time. "I'm here!" she called breathlessly, and ran toward the car's open door. She slipped inside and slammed it shut, her own laughter mingling with the other girl's to form a sweet melody that has been nourishing young and old alike since time began.

"That's his house," Bobby whispered. Big Jim nodded, the movement of his head all but swallowed up by the darkness. A moment later, he asked, "Whose house?"

"The rabbi's. Weren't you listening to anything I said?" Bobby said impatiently. "The rabbi who bought the land for a new Jewish school — right where we've been searching for the treasure. Turns out he's the one behind all our problems. Right?"

"Right!" This time, Jim's nod was emphatic. "So this is his house?"

"Yes. Steve Birch came here today. I get the feeling it's not the first time, either. He's been helping the sheriff — and the Jews — trying to track us down." Bobby's lip curled.

"But he won't find us. No one finds us unless we want them to. Right?" Jim sounded as if he were reciting a well-known mantra.

"You got that right, Jimmy. Ssh." He peered through the bushes as the front door slammed. The Indians watched a smiling teenage girl fly down the path to a waiting car. "That must be his daughter."

Jim thought about this. "The rabbi's?" he ventured at last.

A couple of boys came into view at the end of the block. Lightly they ran past the bushes that concealed the two men. They continued on to the house and through the front door that the girl had just exited.

"And those," Bobby added thoughtfully, "must be his sons."

Bobby's brow was knitted in thought. Maybe it was time to make things a little more personal. Setting fire to empty tents and buildings was one way of sending up a warning. When that was ignored, it might be time to step up the action, to raise the stakes.

He stood up cautiously, silent as a shadow. With a jerk of his head, he indicated to Jim that they were leaving.

He had seen all he wanted to see for now. Time to get back home — or to the decrepit apartment he was temporarily calling "home" — and do some serious planning.

Chapter 14

I.

Heidi's thoughts, as Shana raced out of the room and down the stairs, were not on long-ago dramas. They were focused exclusively on her own, very current one. And on the question of just what kind of stage the curtain would open onto when the next act of her life began.

That a new act was about to begin, she was certain. There had been something irrevocable in her flight to the Poconos that day. Call it a breakdown; call it finally heeding the voice of sanity. Call it the cry of a drowning career woman. But she'd done it. She had broken the chains that had bound her to her desk at Flaxen, Domb and Tremaine. She might take up the yoke again but, if she did, she knew that it would not be in the exact same way as before. Something inside her had changed. She had moved into a different place from which there was no going back.

For weeks now, she'd been soaking in a long, warm bath of friendship and family life. There were no pressures, none of the adrenalin-producing stresses that had once defined her life — more, that had made her *feel* alive. In this place of ageless rock and regal mesa where time was measured in centuries, she was learning to move more slowly, too. To notice things, and to notice people. To think more about her Creator and wonder why she had relegated Him so terribly far into the background. Had she really thought a legal file more fascinating, or more vital, than her bond with the Almighty? And, if she had, how had it happened?

"Heidi doesn't like facing the dark," her father had said of her. "It forces her to think."

She had pooh-poohed the idea when she first heard it. Her father — much as she adored him — had not, she believed, understood her at all.

But she had been forced to think, once she severed her ties to everything that had prevented her from thinking before. With no reason to leap out of bed and join the rush of humanity that swirled through Manhattan like a never-faltering current — no reason to link herself by phone, e-mail and fax modem to other legal eagles like herself — she found herself strangely disconnected and, even more, strangely free. Free to examine things she'd shied away from before.

Things like her own life.

She considered the direction of that life now, as her hands moved automatically, continuing the laundry-folding where Shana had left off. Tova would be home soon, and she would want an answer for Rabbi Harris and his extraordinary suggestion.

Her hands fell into her lap as she mulled over that suggestion. Extraordinary? What an understatement! It would be a clash of two cultures. A war of worlds. Was she, the ultra-urbanite, supposed to seriously consider a *shidduch* with a hick-town lawyer whose shingle hung proudly in Nowheresville, New Mexico?

Somewhat to her own astonishment, she *was* taking it seriously.

Unable to sit another moment as the pressure of her thoughts built up inside, she began to pace the room. Soon she was patrolling the kitchen and living room, pausing at the windows to look out at the dark, empty street and the limitless, black sky above. She enjoyed the panoply of stars, much more vivid here than back in New York, but missed the soar of skyscrapers. There was a lot that she missed about New York. The noise, the charge, the adrenalin high that rushed through her veins every time she stepped outside — these had been her drugs.

She listened to the silence. It was a restful silence. Tova's house, despite its usual quota of childish bickering and familial tensions, was a restful house. A loving house. She compared it to her cubicle of space high above the Manhattan streets ... a world away. A lifetime away. What had she done within those four sterile walls? How had she lived? Could it really be called "living" at all?

Considering that that life had precipitated what amounted to some sort of emotional breakdown, was she mad to even consider taking up the reins again?

On the other hand, the only thing she was trained in was the law. The only place she had ever lived — had ever even considered living — was Manhattan. Her job was still waiting for her, her boss had assured her in their most recent phone conversation — though with an edge in his voice that promised that both he and the job would not wait forever. Did she want her old life back? And, if she didn't, what did she want instead?

That was the question. What *did* she want?

As she made her way slowly along the upstairs landing to her own room, the troubling question accompanied her with every step: What did she want? Ever since she applied for law school, there had never been any doubt. Now she was all doubt. What, at this juncture of her suddenly disjointed life, was her goal, her aspiration, her dream-come-true?

Nate Goodman was waiting for an answer. Was it insane to agree to a meeting with someone so far removed from the only world she'd ever known?

The *Yamim Noraim* were behind her, but she felt a sudden urge to pray the way she had prayed then: from the deepest place within her, and with a burning intensity that made her close her eyes in the privacy of her room. "Hashem, I need Your guidance," she whispered. "I've always been a know-it-all. I had answers for everyone. Now, I have no answers. I'm alone in the dark and I don't know which way to go. Please, be my Light."

The words spent, she sank into a chair by the window, gazing through the pane but seeing nothing. She was waiting. Gradually, a sense of profound peace stole over her. It had nothing to do with the tranquil landscape or the quiet house. This was an inner peace, a divine peace. She sat very still, relishing it, clinging to it with bated breath lest it depart before she was ready to let it go.

By the time Tova and Nachman returned from their visit to the Ganns, her mind was made up.

"Hi, Heidi," Tova called. She was pleasantly surprised to be greeted by tidy piles of folded laundry. "Thanks for folding."

"Shana did a good chunk of it."

"Well, thanks for your part." Tova sat down and yawned. "So what's the good word?"

She had meant it casually, as a simple conversation-opener. What she got in return made her eyes fly open in stunned delight.

"The good word is: yes," Heidi said, and laughed at the surprise on her old friend's face. Then the laughter faded into an anxious but hopeful little smile as Tova, recovering fast, made a lunge for the nearest phone.

The die was cast now. She was on her way to someplace she had never been before. As Heidi listened to Tova speak to Rabbi Harris, it was a toss-up which emotion dominated: excitement — or sheer terror.

While she was at it, Tova decided to make another call as well: this one to New York, where a mother sat and fretted over the future of her grown-up son.

"Hello — Mrs. Feder? You don't know me, but I've often heard your son Avi speak about you. This is Tova Bernstein. My husband —"

"Is the head of Avi's *kollel*. Did you think I wouldn't know that? How nice to hear from you, Mrs. Bernstein." She was gracious, but her puzzlement came clearly over the line.

"Please, call me Tova. You're wondering why I called. I'll tell you. I saw Avi tonight, Mrs. Feder. He looked as though he could use a helping hand."

"He can use a whole bunch of helping hands! Did he happen to tell you what he did here in New York? He went out three times with a lovely young woman. She lost her husband, poor thing, and has been raising her baby all by herself. Well, not exactly by herself; she's living with her parents. But without a husband. Such a fine person! Smart, pretty, accomplished, and a devoted mother. I was really hoping that she would be the one for Avi."

"But ...?" Tova prompted.

"*But* — the silly boy ran away! That's right, Tova. He just upped and ran when he saw that Shiffy liked him. And that *he* liked *her*! Believe me, I could tell. I saw his face when he was getting ready to meet her. It was the face of someone who was starting to live again. And now ..." The words trailed off in a sigh of pure frustration.

"I see." Tova perched at the edge of her bed. "I had a word with Asher and Rivi Gann after Avi left their place this evening, and they corroborate what you've just said, Mrs. Feder — I mean, the fact that Avi really did like Shiffy. He admitted that he 'ran away,' as you put it, because he just doesn't know if he is ready to handle another relationship. It seemed too frightening to him, after all the pain he's suffered ... losing his wife ..."

"I understand all that. But what else can he do but take the plunge? What did his great-grandparents do when they lost everything in the war? What does a Jew always do? He cries a little — or a lot — and then picks himself up and starts again!"

"I couldn't agree with you more," Tova said warmly. "And that's exactly why I'm calling. If Avi is afraid to get up and try again, maybe this thing needs a friendly, little push. Hm?"

A spark of interest perked up the older woman's voice. "That sounds interesting. What do you have in mind?"

Tova told her.

II.

*I*n the dream, he was a hunter. An untrained hunter still: a boy standing on the cusp of manhood, about to embark on his first, solo hunting expedition to prove himself worthy of the tribe.

He felt young and old at the same time, alternately quaking with fear and thrilling with pride. His moccasined-feet made no sound at all on the forest floor. Squirrel and deer lifted their heads at his shadowlike progress, but few were startled into running. The air itself hardly seemed to be displaced by his presence. Which was just as it should be. A true Apache warrior did not leave behind so much as a bent twig to mark his passing. The boy would learn the age-old secrets of the ancestors. He would not let them down.

He had been walking for some two hours when there was suddenly a most un-Apachelike crackle up ahead. The boy stopped short, scarcely breathing. He spotted the bear.

It was a big bear, overstuffed and clumsy in preparation for the long winter's sleep. It lumbered heavily on all fours, completely absorbed in finding its lunch on the branches of a blackberry bush. Still, the boy knew, when threatened, the creature could move with deadly swiftness. He must not let his guard down even for an instant.

Eyes trained steadily on the foraging beast, he lifted his bow with agonizing slowness. There must be no glimpsed movement, no flash of color or whisper of sound to alert his prey. He saw the big black paw fumbling for the last of the fat berries hidden deep inside a tangled bush. With the bear half-turned away from him, the boy seized the chance to fit his notched arrow quickly into place. His hand was rock steady as he took aim. He was not afraid any longer. He was neither eager nor proud. He felt nothing, for emotion would only distract him. There was nothing in the world except himself and his target, and the arrow being drawn slowly, ever so slowly, back to its maximal catapulting position.

TWA-A-A-ANG! The arrow sailed through the air in a swift, graceful arc. It caught the bear as the animal was in the act of spinning around, a roar of rage halfway out of its throat. The arrow struck it full in the chest. Two more quickly followed, the last one piercing one enraged, little eye. The bear collapsed with a thud that shook the forest.

On silent feet, the boy walked up to examine his prize. It was a worthy prize, and one that would win him full initiation into the world that had reared him. He would be a man among other men. He would be Apache, through and through. This was his moment of triumph.

Why, then, as he squatted at the dead bear's side, did he begin to weep, the sounds in his throat so harsh and uncontrolled that the birds in their treetops fled at the noise?

He was still crying when he awoke: a tired Native American lawyer in a small bachelor apartment, teetering on the cusp between his old identity and the new. Right now, he owned neither. Like a baby bird banished from its nest, he found himself flapping his wings frantically in the air, untutored in the skills he needed to survive and unfamiliar with the lifesaving currents that might save his life. The security of his nest was no more than a memory now, and memories do not make a particularly nourishing meal. Was he destined to starve before he found that which he was seeking?

Bewilderment and sadness wrapped around him like a shroud as he lay in his narrow bed, remembering the dream. He lay unmoving for a long time.

At last, turning his head, his eye fell on the little prayer book on the nightstand. In a stray beam of sunlight, the faded gold star seemed to wink at him. "Take heart," it seemed to say. "In this false world, nothing is as it seems to be. Open my pages and begin your journey ..."

Why or how he should feel this intense connection with all things Jewish, he hadn't a clue. Nor did he know where this prayer book had come from, which his gentle mother, on her deathbed, had given him. There had been no explanations, except to say that it had belonged to her mother and *hers* before that. But it belonged to him now. Though he had paid it scant attention for a long time, relegating the book to the obscurity of his closet's top shelf, these days it seemed to be burning a hole in his mind.

He had looked up the records at the town hall. There was no mention of Jews having ever lived in Lakewood, New Mexico or anywhere within a hundred-mile radius. No indication that any Jew had been native to the area a century or more ago. But if that were so, where had the Jewish prayer book come from? How had it come into the possession of a modern-day Indian living on the Mescalero reservation?

Steve got out of bed and sat at his desk, the prayer book in hand. He sat there, turning pages and staring at the incomprehensible words, until he felt a new heart flow back into him. He was truly the hunter of his dreams, but not a hunter of living beasts. He was on the trail of his own self: past, present and future. Like the dream-arrow that had flown swiftly and unerring toward its prey, he would seek out a new kind of weapon with which to slay his doubts.

Steve Birch got up, washed his hands as the rabbi had mentioned that a Jew did in the morning, and prepared to face the day.

"I'd sure like to get my hands on those bad guys," Donny fretted as he turned over in bed on their last night of freedom. Classes were scheduled to resume at the *kollel* in the morning. "I wish we could do something to help, Chaim."

"I don't know ..." Chaim had had time to think things over. "Ta said it's a matter for the police. And remember what happened to Shimi? It could be dangerous."

"It was dangerous for Gila," Donny remarked soberly. "Remember what happened to her?"

Chaim clenched his jaw. He would never forget the sight of his mother's strained white face, all the times she'd rushed off to the hospital with Gila. This kind of stuff wasn't supposed to happen to them any more. They had come here to get away from it. Gila's asthma attacks had become a thing of the past, or so he'd thought.

"Yeah," he said heavily. "I remember."

Donny turned over again. "I wish there was *something* we could do."

Chaim didn't answer. His own secret wish was that he could turn the clock back and be a carefree kid again, before arson and asthma and sinister strangers had come along to mess up his life.

When Chaim didn't answer soon enough, Donny flopped over in bed one last time and was instantly asleep. It took Chaim a while longer to follow suit.

III.

With the start of the new *zeman* at the *kollel*, the Yom Tov season was officially behind them.

As if to mark the change, the weather turned perceptibly cooler. Chaim and Donny, sitting in their makeshift classroom in the shul/*kollel* for their lessons with Avi Feder and Asher Gann, found themselves barely able to concentrate on the subject matter. Their thoughts were up in the hills, walking trails and searching caves for a sign of the "bad guys" who had upset the even tenor of their days. Shimi, sitting in preoccupied silence at their side, refused to be drawn into any sort of discussion of the situation. Keeping avid track of Sheriff Ramsay's progress in the case became the sole purview of the Bernstein boys.

Along with his official deputies and Native American liaison, attorney Steve Birch, Ramsay was busy coordinating his investigation. Birch had tried again to make contact with the two men at the top of his private list of suspects: Bobby Smith and "Big Jim" Littletree. Unfortunately, at the moment neither man was to be found. The landlord of the apartment complex where they lived — and where Steve had visited them once before — claimed that the pair had not moved out. Their belongings were still inside and they had paid their monthly rent on time. But of the tenants themselves there was no sign — and hadn't been, according to the landlord, for the past couple of days.

They're hiding out somewhere, Steve thought. *But where?* He did not ask "Why?" The very fact of the men's disappearance seemed to point to their guilt. There might be an innocent explanation for their absence, but Steve was inclined, when it came to these two, to presume guilt unless the facts proved otherwise.

He kept his suspicions to himself. No use getting the sheriff and his men into a lather over what was only, after all, an unfounded hunch. Steve had learned to trust his intuition, but Ramsay couldn't be expected to do the same. Not unless Birch brought him some hard proof.

Meanwhile, measures had been taken to safeguard the town's Jewish institutions. The day school now had a guard posted just inside the front door — a temporary measure, until the sheriff felt that the situation had been brought under control. The Bernsteins had taken measures to protect their daughter, as well: Gila's inhaler was to stay with her at all times, her parents ordered. Gila had meekly accepted the device — a talisman of her parents' love for her, and a comfort at those moments when she was visited by an all-too-vivid recollection of those panic-stricken moments when her lungs had labored in vain for the air she needed to live.

Apart from the guard posted at the day school, the shul now had a night watchman on board, as did the site where the surveyors were finishing up their job. Construction crews were due to begin their work very soon. Local firms had been signed on for the bulk of the labor, with an architectural team from Albuquerque to draw up the plans and oversee construction. Nachman Bernstein was on the phone with this team virtually every day, as well as with the building contractors, finalizing details and firming up work schedules. With the whole town feeling the beneficial effects of this ambitious new project, there was mounting sentiment that the arsonist responsible for jeopardizing it ought to be behind bars. Rabbi Harris, his *gabbaim* and his congregation could not have agreed more.

"Bye, Ma!"

"Good-bye, boys! I love you both!"

"Bye!"

"Bye-bye! Have a great time!"

Tova kept waving until the twins were out of sight. It was the 2-year-olds' first day at play group. Of the three of them, it was Tova who seemed to be the most seriously plagued by separation anxiety. Without her youngest two children to keep her busy all day long, she felt suddenly off balance, bereft of her mandate. A minister-without-portfolio.

Nachman was to drop Mo and Bo off on his way to the *kollel*. The play group was being run by Adele Rein — wife of Dr. Abe Rein, forensic psychiatrist. Tova kept meaning to ask him what, exactly, a forensic psychiatrist did. It had to do with criminals; that much she knew. Imagine delving into the murky depths of the criminal mind! It would be, she speculated, like diving into a slimy, green swamp. She shuddered. Her attitude toward the entire field could be summed up as, "Better him than me."

Dr. Rein's wife, at any rate, seemed a capable enough woman. Adele, who'd been running this play group for years, had been happy to welcome the Bernstein twins after Succos. Tova had resisted starting them in September, claiming that the boys needed time to acclimate themselves to their new home.

Actually, the twins had acclimated within their first two weeks in Lakewood; it was their mother who needed the extra time. Time to grow accustomed to the desolate empty-nest feeling that enveloped her any time she thought of home without that rambunctious, double-trouble duo to fill the house with noise and mess and their private, mysterious games. Time to build some structure into a day gone suddenly structureless. Time to cry a little, and then to wipe her tears and figure out what to do next.

As it turned out, the next thing appeared almost before she'd finished waving Mo and Bo on their way.

Heidi was still upstairs, presumably asleep. Tova sat down to a solitary breakfast, wishing someone had invented earplugs to drown out the sound of silence. She had poured her first cup of coffee when the phone rang.

She jumped to answer it. "Hello?"

"Mrs. Bernstein? Good morning. This is Dr. Rein."

"Oh, hello, Dr. Rein." Too late, she realized how surprised she must have sounded. "How are you?"

"*Baruch Hashem*. And yourself?"

"Just fine, doctor. My twins are starting in your wife's play group this morning. They were very eager to go."

"That's exactly what I'm calling about," said Dr. Rein. "I'll get right to the point, shall I?"

"Of course." Where was this heading?

"I heard a rumor that you have a background in medical billing?"

"Yes, I have. Back in New York, before the twins came along, I billed for a couple of doctors. I worked part-time, out of my house."

"Perfect! Here's my proposal, Mrs. Bernstein. I've been in touch with Dr. Sadowsky, the pediatrician. He and I are both in need of an experienced person to help with our billing. You'd be able to work at home or at either of our offices. Make your own hours. Does the idea appeal to you?"

Tova looked around at her empty kitchen, heard the ringing echo of silence. A slow smile started in her eyes and gradually spread to the rest of her face.

"It certainly does, Dr. Rein. It speaks to me loud and clear! Of course, I'll have to talk it over with my husband, and put my own ideas in order. May I call you back tomorrow?"

"Absolutely. I'll look forward to hearing from you. Thank you, Mrs. Bernstein."

"Thank *you*, doctor."

Tova hung up, but left her hand resting on the phone for several long minutes as her mind began busily working out possibilities. With a start, she realized that she had not yet shared the news with her husband. She didn't want to move an inch further along this road until she had consulted with him. The impulse came as natural as breathing: Apart from the relationship they shared, there was no one whose judgment and acumen she respected more. She wanted Nachman's advice about what sort of time commitment he thought she could handle, and what she ought to charge for her time. Eagerly, she punched in his cell-phone number.

As she listened to the busy signal, some of her excitement faded. If there was one thing she hated, it was being forced to wait when she had something on her mind that she was anxious to share.

The busy signal persisted into a second try, and then a third. With a sigh, Tova gave up. If Nachman was on the phone this long, it must be an important call. She decided to empty the long-neglected refrigerator and give it a good scrubbing while she waited. That ought to pass the time, if not in an especially pleasant way, then at least in an undeniably useful one. She would while away the minutes with roseate dreams of herself at a computer keyboard, diligently billing away to the doctors' and her own satisfaction. The extra income would certainly come in handy, too.

Sponge in hand, she gave herself up to pleasant daydreams. Not a bad way to spend her first day as a Mommy-without-portfolio.

IV.

Nachman Bernstein *was* on an important call. He was speaking to Rabbi Greenfeld, his Rosh Yeshivah in Brooklyn. The Rosh Yeshivah had made the call as a routine gesture: a desire to be updated at the start of the new *zeman*, and an opportunity to tender his wishes for their success. He was startled, and considerably dismayed, by the story he heard from the *Rosh Kollel* he'd appointed to head the venture.

"Nachman, why haven't you told me any of this before now?"

Apologetically, Nachman explained. "I didn't want to worry the Rosh Yeshivah. At first, the sheriff seemed confident that he would catch the shul arsonist pretty quickly. Then came the other incident, at the building site ... and what happened to Gila."

"Gila? Your daughter?" Rabbi Greenfeld's voice sharpened. "What happened to her?"

Briefly, Nachman described the episode involving the shadowy intruder at the day school, and Gila's terrifying reaction. "She's all right now, *Baruch Hashem*. We make sure she carries her inhaler wherever she goes. She used to do that, but stopped taking it with her once we moved out here and the asthma attacks seemed to have ended."

"They will stop again," the Rosh Yeshivah assured him firmly, responding to the note of helplessness in Nachman's voice. "The perpetrator will be caught, and your daughter will be healthy."

"As they say, rebbi — from your mouth to G-d's ears!"

The Rosh Yeshivah chuckled. "Now, tell me about the *kollel*. Has the new *zeman* gotten off to a good start?"

Nachman listed the various community-outreach classes that he and his colleagues planned to teach this *zeman*, some of them a continuation of previous classes while others were new offerings. "We've been trying to listen to the people, to get a feel not only for what they need to learn, but also for what they want to learn. Kabbalah is a big draw, but so far I've resisted the demand. I've impressed upon them the need for having a solid foundation of *Chumash* and Jewish *hashkafah* under their belts before they can even think of tackling the mystical world."

"Good. And the four of you — and your families? How are you all doing, personally?"

Here Nachman was forced to pause. There was much that he could tell the Rosh Yeshivah, but he was hesitant to stir up waters that might, given time and patient effort, calm of their own accord.

Sensing his reluctance, Rabbi Greenfeld pressed harder. "Please tell me everything, Nachman. I have a big stake in seeing that the *kollel* is successful. Anything that might undermine its success is of interest to me. And maybe I can help."

With his back against the wall, Nachman launched into the story in his usual, forthright way. "It's Asher Gann and Efraim Mandel, reb-bi. The old jealousy thing, on Efraim's part, and now, a coolness on Asher's. Seems Mrs. Mandel did something to hurt Mrs. Gann's feel-ings, and now the husbands are on the outs even more than they were before."

"Why is Efraim jealous?" Rabbi Greenfeld asked, homing in on the first point that Nachman had raised.

"Asher is very popular with the students. As you know, he has lots of natural charm and a fairly magnetic personality. After class, the young people cluster around him, asking questions and hanging on his every word. While Efraim ... "

"Yes? How is Efraim holding up? How are *his* classes?"

"His *classes*," Nachman replied, "are fine. Inside the classroom, he comes into his own in a way that I can really appreciate. The walls are not very thick in the shul, rebbi, and if I listen carefully I can hear him teaching. He's good. He holds their attention and gets them thinking. No problem there."

"Then the problem is ...?" "The old, green-eyed monster rearing its ugly head *after* class — when Efraim watches Asher's students making a big fuss over him while Efraim just says good-bye and goes home. It's really his own lack of confidence that turns him sour, I believe. There's nothing inherently wrong with Efraim, either as a teacher or as a person. But if he *thinks* there is ... "

"Exactly. You've got good intuition, Nachman." Rabbi Greenfeld seemed pleased with this proof that he'd chosen wisely in appointing Nachman Bernstein to represent the yeshivah in New Mexico.

"I may be able to see the problem," Nachman said frankly, "but I'm at a dead loss when it comes to figuring out the solution."

"The first thing to do is to have the wives patch things up between them." The Rosh Yeshivah hadn't forgotten Nachman's second point.

"I agree, rebbi, 100 percent. Tova and I went over to the Ganns the other day, to see what we could do."

"And?"

"So far, no luck. Rivi's too hurt, and Asher's too angry on her be-half."

"Have you tried talking to Efraim?"

"No ..." Nachman strained to get in touch with the intuition Rabbi Greenfeld had spoken about. "No, I haven't. Efraim is so sensitive to criticism ... I think that things are going to come to a head, rebbi. Sooner or later, something's going to crack this thing wide open. Someone's going to make a move, and after that things will resolve themselves under their own steam."

"That may be so," Rabbi Greenfeld said gently. "But if it doesn't happen that way, you may have to take a more active role. You know that, don't you?"

"Yes, rebbi. I'm just hoping that I'm right about this."

"I hope so, too, Nachman. About this, and about the attacks in the community. If you think it would be helpful, I'm prepared to fly out there to be with you. Anytime."

"Thanks, rebbi. I really appreciate the offer. Right now, though, I don't see the need. We're holding up."

"Good. I'm going to have the Brooklyn yeshivah say some special *Tehillim* on behalf of the *kollel*, our little brother in the Southwest. May we see much *nachas* from you — soon!"

"*Amen,*" Nachman answered fervently.

"Stop looking at me like that, Tova," Heidi complained, as she pulled yet another outfit from her closet, considered it briefly, and then tossed it onto her bed to add height to the ever-growing pile of clothes heaped there. "You remind me of my mother."

Tova grinned. "Right now, I *feel* like your mother. I'm *shepping nachas,* Heidi."

"Why? Because I'm going out with somebody?"

"Because you're going out with Nate Goodman. He's special — as I hope you know. I thought so the minute I met him. Remember the meeting at our house?"

"How could I forget?" Heidi made a face. "I made an utter fool of myself that night. Please don't remind me about that night. Or, for that matter, remind him!"

"He obviously doesn't hold it against you. Besides, I don't think you made a fool of yourself at all. You just expressed an honest opinion."

"In a pompous, overbearing and totally insensitive way. Don't try to whitewash it, Tova. I goofed. I only hope I manage to hold my tongue when I meet him this evening; at least, long enough to keep my foot out of my mouth."

Tova laughed. "I wouldn't worry. So, have you decided what you're going to wear? He'll be here in half an hour, you know."

With a tiny shriek that would have stunned her erstwhile colleagues at Flaxen, Domb and Tremaine, Heidi snatched up the outfit at the top of her pile and ran to finish dressing. Tova gazed after her, bemused and delighted at the change in her old friend.

This was not the Heidi who for years had frustrated Tova with her hardheaded insistence on pursuing the fast track from her Manhattan high-rise. Nor was she the shattered woman, fragile as cracked glass, who had stepped off the plane at the Albuquerque airport weeks ago. This Heidi was different: softer than the other one, and glowing with renewed emotional health. The very fact that she'd agreed to see the small-town lawyer gave Tova reason for hope. It was a delirious hope that made her feel like cheering as she headed for the kitchen to throw together a late potluck supper for her family.

The twins and Yudi had already eaten — macaroni and cheese, their favorite standby. She had no patience for cooking tonight, not with this excitement taking place in her own home. Once she and Nachman had greeted Nate Goodman and seen the pair on their way, she would pull a few leftovers out of the fridge and make do. Her family would understand.

Unfortunately, this was the evening that Shana chose to invite a friend over for dinner.

She informed her mother of this fact in an almost casual way, catching Tova on her way out of Heidi's room.

Tova blinked. "A friend? For dinner?"

"Yes, Ma," Shana said, holding onto her patience in the face of her mother's inexplicable slowness in grasping the situation. "I invited Dassi over to eat with us tonight. Afterward, we're going to study for a test together. I just wanted to know if it's all right with you, Ma."

Tova seemed struck dumb by the fact that Shana had a friend. "Dassi?" she managed at last.

"Yes, Ma. Dassi Tepper. I went to her house the other day to do our homework, remember?"

"Uh, not really ..."

"It was the night you and Ta went over to the Ganns, I think," Shana said impatiently. "Anyway — can she come?"

"Of course!" Tova exclaimed, belatedly recovering her wits. First Heidi, and now Shana. Would wonders never cease?

Then a shadow of worry crossed her face. What in the world was she going to serve, with a guest at the table? A very important guest, judging by the eagerness in her daughter's face.

Watching that face, Tova's heart melted. She would head to the kitchen and begin foraging in pantry and cookbooks until she found something wonderful. She could be a pretty creative short-order cook. Just now she felt a surge of energy — fueled by happiness — that would lift her up to meet any challenge. Even the question of what to make for dinner, with nothing much in the house and the weekly shopping trip still days away.

V.

Nachman came home from the *kollel* early in order to be on hand to greet Nate when he arrived at the house. He smiled into his beard as he drove home. He had often pictured the moment when he would see Shana, his oldest daughter, off on her first *shidduch* encounter — the first step in losing her to a husband of her own — as an emotional one for him. Heidi Neufeld seemed to have pre-empted that moment, putting him in the curious position of acting as surrogate father to his wife's 30-something friend. He had never envisioned his hostly duties as extending quite this far, but he liked and respected both Heidi and Nate, and he wished them nothing but good. If he could help in any way to grease the wheels of this unexpected match, he would do so gladly.

He opened his front door to an air of suppressed excitement. From upstairs came strange bustlings and gaspings as Tova and Shana ran circles around Heidi, presumably in the process of helping her get ready. There was no smell of dinner cooking, but Nachman wasn't that hungry anyway. He called up the steps, "Tova! I'm home!"

"Oh, thank goodness!" Tova's face appeared, flushed and smiling, over the banister rail on the landing. "I was beginning to worry that I'd have to greet Nate all by myself."

"How's Heidi doing? Is she nervous?" he asked as his wife tripped lightly down the stairs to join him.

"Is she ever! To tell you the truth, I'm nervous *for* her!" She lowered her voice. "This is a big moment, Nachman. A turning point."

"You think so?"

"Absolutely. You should see her. She's a different person from when she first came here."

Smiling, he said, "I give you the credit for that, Tova."

"Nonsense. She just needed to get away — to tear herself away from that artificial world that was stifling her. To get back to reality, and to real people ..."

A yell from the family room, followed in quick succession by a furious scuffling, an ominous thud and a noisy wail, made Nachman lift his brows. "Sounds like we've got some 'real people' right here in our midst ... a bit out of control, wouldn't you say?"

"No one's had any time to pay attention to them." As Tova rushed off to discover the source of the disturbance, she called over her shoulder, "Oh, by the way — Shana invited a friend over for dinner tonight."

Nachman stared. Like his wife a short while ago, he echoed blankly, "A friend? For dinner?"

"That's what she says! Her name's Hadassah Tepper — Dassi for short. Isn't it wonderful?" Beaming, Tova dashed to the door of the family room.

"So what are we having?" he called after her.

With her hand on the doorknob, his wife afforded him a dazzling smile. "Haven't a clue!" With that, she disappeared into the room to play judge to her battling boys.

"Doesn't she look wonderful?" Tova sighed, watching through the window as Nate opened the car door for Heidi and waited for her to settle herself inside before shutting it again. "Poor Nate looked so terribly nervous. I had to hold myself back from giggling."

"Heidi seemed all right," her husband remarked.

"She knows how to put on a good show. Her years of training as a lawyer probably taught her how. Inside she was quaking, believe me."

"I do," Nachman assured her. "And now ..." he glanced meaningfully at his watch. "What time do you think we can eat?"

"Oh my gosh — dinner!" Without a backward look, Tova sprinted for the kitchen. Smiling into his beard — he seemed to be doing a lot of that tonight — Nachman went to his study to catch up on his learning until the meal was ready.

Just over an hour later, Tova did them all proud. She had managed to throw together a very creditable shepherd's pie out of ingredients dredged up from various previous meals plus some freshly cooked and mashed potatoes. Shana helped toss the salad, which she served with her favorite dressing. "Hope you like it," she told Dassi. "It's sort of my own recipe. I adapted it from one I found in a cookbook."

"It looks great." Dassi Tepper turned out to be a girl with polite manners and a shy smile. Shana was very solicitous, passing her things in a steady stream. The parents exchanged a pleased look. The daughter they had dragged from Brooklyn, figuratively kicking and screaming, seemed to have come into her own at last.

"I ran into Mrs. Sadowsky at the post office today," Nachman remarked. "She says she hasn't seen much of you lately, Shana."

Shana had the grace to blush. "I've been meaning to go over there. I've just been so busy ..."

"That's all right," Tova said quickly. "I'm sure she understands." Turning to Dassi, she explained, "Shana and Mrs. Sadowsky have been making a study of this area's history. Haven't you, Shana?"

"That's right." A quick look to see how her new friend was taking the information reassured Shana that Dassi did not perceive anything either childish or pathetic in her spending time with the town librarian. "Mrs. Sadowsky knows practically everything there is to know about Lakewood. She told me some really interesting stuff about the Indians."

"Really?" Dassi said. "Like what?"

"Well, for one thing, she found a diary written by a pioneer woman who lived on a farm right here, outside of Lakewood. Her name was Jane Willard." Shana paused dramatically. "And guess what? Jane met a Jewish woman — a *frum* woman, it seems — who'd come all the way from Europe!"

"She came here all by herself?" Dassi was bewildered.

"Of course not. She was with a group of new immigrants, just off the boat. They were planning to stay in New York, where they'd landed, but they got gold fever. You know — the California Gold Rush? This was in 1849, just when it was all happening. Thousands of people were heading out west to try and find gold. And this group of Jews decided to try their luck, too!"

Dassi's eyes were very wide. "So what happened? Did they find it?"

Shana became aware of her father's intent gaze. "Yes," Nachman echoed. "What happened to those Jews, Shana?"

Shana's face grew long. "It was very sad. A bunch of Apaches went on the rampage the next day and massacred them all."

"Did anyone survive?" Nachman asked tensely. Tova shot him a questioning glance, which he didn't see. "Anyone at all?"

"Not according to the diary," Shana said. "But there *was* one strange thing … The Jewish woman Jane Willard met? She said she had two children. Jane didn't see them that day. But her husband said afterward, when they'd buried all the bodies, that there was no sign of any children. That's strange, isn't it?"

"Very strange," Nachman said. There was an odd gleam in his eye, which Tova made a mental note to ask him about later. Meanwhile, there was the food to pass around and the guest's comfort to see to. Not to mention the pleasure of watching Shana talking so animatedly to a girl her own age — at last! *Mrs. Sadowsky*, Tova thought, *had served her purpose well*. She made a second mental note, to call and thank the librarian, first chance she got.

The moment the meal was over, Nachman pushed back his chair. "Well, this has been great. But I've got to get back to the *kollel* now. It's late; classes start soon."

Outside, the rectangle of golden light from the house vanished abruptly as the front door closed behind him. In the resulting darkness he walked over to his car, slipped behind the wheel and started the engine.

He hadn't lied: it *was* late. He really ought to hurry back to the *kollel* and his myriad responsibilities, with all possible speed.

But before he did, he pulled out his Palm Pilot, where he recorded the many details and appointments necessary to the smooth functioning of his own and the *kollel's* life.

"Talk to Mrs. Sadowsky," he typed in. "Apache massacre. Jewish kids."

With that, he snapped the device shut, shifted gears into "Drive" and set off at a far-from-decorous pace.

In the shadows, a pair of thoughtful eyes watched the car speed away. Then they returned to the house they had been observing this past hour or more. The eyes had a speculative gleam: the kind a housewife may have as she stands in front of a fruit display, squeezing melons to check which one is ripe.

VI.

Efraim was conscious of a great weariness as he pulled up in front of his own house. This had little to do with the hour: Though it was nearly 11 o'clock and he'd been learning all day and teaching all evening, he had always been something of a night owl, blessed with a second wind well after sundown.

No, the feeling came from someplace far deeper. It was both more, and other, than sheer physical exhaustion. His *soul* felt tired.

He switched off his headlights and gazed at his home. His castle! More and more often, these days, he was finding home a beacon and a lure, calling to him when his other life — his professional life, so to speak — persisted in disappointing him. He craved sleep, to temporarily erase the sense of strain and futility that lately seemed everpresent. And food, in its own way, served in the same capacity.

He was overweight, out of shape, and gnawed from within by twin monsters of jealousy and fear of inadequacy. Because each fed on the other, a diminishment in the jealousy might have boosted his sense of his own abilities. The trouble was, he had as yet found no sure-fire method of banishing the jealousy.

Why envy was associated with the color green was beyond him. For Efraim, it was black, black, black; a fathomless pit into which he repeatedly stumbled and fell. Each time he set eyes on Asher Gann, the dark emotion consumed him like a devouring, black flame. And before Asher, it had been Nachman. Like a person genetically predisposed to a certain illness, Efraim Mandel was predisposed to envy.

It was a gut-wrenching feeling, almost a physically nauseating one. He hated it, and hated himself for being weak enough to fall victim to it. Yet so far, he had not — despite valiant, if sporadic, efforts — discovered a cure.

Etty understood. And why shouldn't she? She was the same way, always measuring herself against others to see where she stood on the scale of success in life. Her own personal "cure" was tireless and unrelenting labor; a regimen of perfectionism that provided her with a sense of having her life under control, and thus balanced favorably against the lives of others. Efraim was not cut out that way. How could he push himself to work harder, when his every effort was undermined by a personal conviction that he would never, however hard he tried, ever really measure up?

In her unsentimental way, his wife was supportive. She understood the pain he suffered over his own lack of stature. She was, in a very real sense, his biggest fan. She had always propped him up back in Brooklyn, though they'd both hoped that things would be different here. But nothing had really changed. Perhaps, if Asher Gann weren't in the picture ...

Here, he abruptly pulled the brakes on his train of thought. Whatever else he might do, he was determined to be honest with himself. Asher Gann made no difference. If it weren't Asher, it would have been someone else. Efraim Mandel was fated to feel perennially insecure. Popularity was not his forte. The pleasant tenor of his classes notwithstanding, he was aware that he lacked the charm, and therefore the attraction, of many of his fellow educators. There was nothing he could do about this — except wallow in his misery. And sleep. And eat.

Having come full circle in his unhappy musings, he got out of the car and made his way into his castle, a king with bowed head and weary soul.

"Etty, I'm home." He was surprised at her absence from both the kitchen or living room at this time of the night. Could one of the little ones have woken up? Was anyone sick, *chas v'shalom*? Raising his voice slightly, he tried again. "Etty?"

A moment later she emerged from their bedroom, wan and listless. With a jolt, Efraim realized that his wife had not been looking or acting like herself lately. With the worry over Layala behind them, he had thought she would perk up and attack the household routine with her usual energy. Instead, she was drooping around the place like a wilted flower.

Efraim took off his hat and jacket as she moved slowly in his direction, a vague greeting on her lips and a preoccupied look about her eyes. *She'd been this way a great deal lately*, he thought with a guilty start. He had hoped for a little wifely sympathy tonight — an encouraging word or two to stave off the blues that bedeviled him. Instead, it looked like *he* was going to have to be the comfort-dispenser tonight.

He straightened his shoulders and deliberately looked away from the kitchen, where refrigerator and pantry waited.

"Etty, are you feeling all right? You don't look so well."

"I'm fine, *Baruch Hashem*," she responded without much conviction. She roused herself to add, "How are you, Efraim? How was your day?"

Here was his cue to pour out all his troubles. Valiantly, he ignored it. "Sit down, Etty. You've been working too hard. Go on, take a load off your feet. I'll keep you company." Like a docile child, she allowed herself to be coaxed into the living room, where she took a seat on the couch and he sank into his favorite armchair. His wife's uncharacteristic passivity heightened his alarm.

"Now," he said briskly, as though she were one of his children instead of a woman with a personality so forceful as to occasionally border on the intimidating, "tell me what's wrong."

"Wrong?" Her voice was too high, too determinedly perky. "Nothing's wrong. What should be wrong?"

"That's what I was hoping *you'd* tell *me*. You're not looking well, Etty — and you're not behaving like yourself, either. Has something happened? Tell me. I guarantee, you'll feel better!"

To his utter dismay, she began crying.

As these things go, it wasn't much of a show: hardly more than a few large, slow tears rolling down Etty's pale cheeks, to end their journey at the corners of her quivering mouth. But they had a dumbfounding effect on Efraim. Etty so rarely wept.

"Now you *have* to tell me," he said, trying with a twist of humor to lighten her mood and allay his own fears. "What's wrong, Etty?"

"I'm such a bad person," she sniffed. "I never realized it before ..."

"What are you talking about? You're a wonderful person!"

"No, I'm not." Her tone sharpened, as though to say, *Don't contradict me.* "If you do something awful, that means you're an awful person." She spoke in a monotone, as though reciting a lesson long-ago learned by heart. "I can't stand it. I can't stand being who I am ..." She covered her face with her hands. The sound of dry, muffled sobs filtered through to Efraim.

"Please don't cry ..." When there was no response except for more of the nearly silent sobs, he probed in puzzlement for the reason. "Why don't you tell me about it? First, because I'll explode from sheer curiosity if you don't. And, second, because it'll make you feel better. O.K.?"

She lowered her hands and met his eyes at last. Her own were unfocused, swimming in tears still waiting to be shed.

"Remember the day Layala had her surgery?"

"How would I forget? It was just last week!"

Doggedly, she plowed on. "Remember when Ora was feeling better, and I drove down to Roswell to be with the baby? To take over from Rivi ..."

He nodded. Rivi had been such a help, stepping in when Etty couldn't be there for Layala. "Sure, I remember. What about it? Did something happen?" Thinking back, he realized that he could date this change in his wife's demeanor from Layala's surgery. What was it all about?

"I was terrible," she said, in the same dead monotone as before. "I grabbed the baby from her as though she were trying to kidnap her or something. Not even a real thank-you! I shamed her in front of the nurse. I was churlish, ungrateful and cruel. I—"

"Etty, stop it. You were overwrought. Your child had just undergone surgery. Between Layala and Ora, you had been up for most of the past two nights. You weren't thinking straight."

"I wasn't thinking at all. I was just reacting — like an animal in the jungle. I saw Layala in Rivi's arms. I heard the nurse call her, 'Mrs. Mandel,' and I pounced like a ferocious beast. 'That's *mine*! Don't you dare touch what's *mine*!'" Down went her face, burying itself in her hands again.

Efraim was at a loss. "I don't understand. If you behaved badly to Rivi, why didn't you call her that night, or the next day, and apologize?"

"I did, but she was having some people over, so I never got to say my piece." Etty didn't mention the "party" to which she and Efraim had apparently not been invited. "The next few days, I realized that I still had to say I was sorry, but I was too ashamed." The words were muffled through her hands. "I'm still too ashamed. I can never look Rivi in the eye again, Efraim. She was so good, and I was so awful ..." To his horror, the tears renewed themselves, spilling through the cracks between her fingers.

Best let her have her cry, Efraim decided. He waited, leaning back in his armchair with his eyes fixed on his wife. When the shudders grew less pronounced and she lowered her hands at last to reveal a blotchy face and red-rimmed eyes, he cleared his throat. "That's your *yetzer hara* talking, Etty — telling you that you're just too terrible to do *teshuvah*. You know what you have to do, don't you? You have to go over to Rivi, and beg her forgiveness. Then you have to figure out why you had that reaction, so you can avoid having it ever again. And then you have to ask for Hashem's forgiveness, as well!" He leaned forward, willing her to step out of her private agony long enough to hear what he was saying. "That's the *teshuvah* process, Etty. There's no way around it."

"I know ..." She hiccuped. "I don't know if I can do it, though. How can I ever face Rivi again?"

"How can you face her *without* having apologized from the depths of your heart? Once you've done that, you'll have peace. I mean that, Etty."

Her voice was low. "I know you're right. I'm just — scared. It's hard to admit how awful you've been. What a monster can be hiding inside ..."

"Seems to me it won't need much of an admission. You're just human, like the rest of us. We all have our personal monsters ... Rivi will understand. Why not just confront the fact that you made a mistake, apologize sincerely, and move on?"

"You make it sound so simple ..." And maybe it was, she through drearily. Painfully simple. She produced a watery smile. "Thanks, Efraim." *Thanks for being strong for me*, she meant, but did not say. It was a role-reversal rare enough for the two of them. Had she not been so fully caught up in the present crisis, she would have relished this feeling of being nurtured, of problems being taken from her shoulders. She was usually the burden-bearer in the family.

With a shuddering sigh, the kind she remembered at the end of childhood bouts of tears, she said, "I guess ... I guess I'll go over tomorrow."

"You could call her now."

"I need to do this in person. And it's too late for that now. No, it'll have to be tomorrow."

A few minutes later, they got up. Etty made a beeline for the kitchen, expecting her husband to follow. But Efraim found, unexpectedly, that he wasn't as hungry as he had thought. In fact, he might dispense with his nightly snack this evening. It certainly wouldn't harm his waistline any. He harbored a sense of things having changed somehow tonight. There had been a seismic shift, both in Etty's emotions and perhaps in the balance between them as well. Too tired — as well as too unexpectedly euphoric — to explore the thought tonight, he made a mental note to reflect on this evening's events tomorrow, when his mind was fresh. Meanwhile, he would do a little more learning before calling it a night.

On his way past his son's room, he heard strains of soft music coming from Shimi's CD player. *Shimi's been acting out of sorts lately, too*, he thought guiltily. *It might not be such a bad idea to have a little talk with him as well. Might as well strike while the iron's hot.*

He pushed open the door a crack and peered inside. Shimi was lying in a ball under his covers, shoulders rising and falling with his even breathing. Too even? Efraim wondered if his son had decided to feign sleep at his entrance and if so, why?

He hesitated, then let the door close again. Etty would have his head if he woke his son at this time of the night just to have a little talk.

As his wife had done moments earlier, he decided to put the delicate task off till tomorrow.

Part Four:
Flickers Of Hope

Chapter 15

I.

T he funds of the treasure hunters having run perilously low, Bobby Smith and "Big Jim" Littletree were forced to temporarily dim the garish lights of their dream-driven world and engage in basic survival skills.

The bottom line was, if they wanted to keep eating, they needed to work.

Bobby almost immediately found a job as a grease monkey in a Lakewood auto-repair shop, which entitled him to wear oil-stained overalls and spend most of his day, wrench in hand, lying under ailing cars and pickup trucks. It took Jim a little longer to find employment. After two days of fruitless knocking on doors, the manager of the local Taco Bell franchise took him on board as a busboy and kitchen help in exchange for a minimum-wage salary and all the tacos he could eat. The manager soon came to regret these terms, as Big Jim was capable of consuming enough tacos to tilt profit margins dangerously toward the red. However, the boss had taken an inexplicable liking to the big easygoing man, and let him stay.

The money thus earned kept Bobby and Big Jim solvent for the time being. Bobby paid the next month's rent on the apartment, and stocked up on food, water and camping equipment. As soon as they were sufficiently above water, he intended for him and Jim to quit their jobs and move back into the hills. There was another promising line of caves that Bobby wanted to explore.

Big Jim was beginning to think otherwise.

In the plodding way that his mind processed things, Jim was growing restless. His was not a nature that easily gave way to an emotion as extreme as impatience, but they had been hunting gold for a long time now and coming up empty-handed all the time. He liked his job at the Taco Bell. He could eat all the tacos he wanted, and he took pride in being thorough in his work and polite in his dealings with the customers. He liked his fellow workers, liked trading jokes with them and laughing out loud at every one. It was not a good idea to laugh around Bobby. Bobby was a serious man. A driven man. He expected Jim to be the same — and to obey him implicitly. Being a natural follower rather than a leader, Jim didn't often mind this arrangement. But he was starting to mind now.

"How 'bout we put off treasure hunting till the spring?" he asked one evening, his courage sparked by another good day at the fast-food outlet.

"Hm?" Bobby, hunched over one of his terrain maps, was hardly listening.

Big Jim swallowed, shifting his mammoth feet on the threadbare rug. "I said, maybe it'd be a good idea to put off this treasure hunt for a while. Now that we've got jobs and all …"

Slowly, Bobby lifted his head. His slate eyes pierced Jim like a snake's fangs, their bite just as sharp and twice as toxic. "Do I hear what I think I'm hearing?" he asked softly. "You backing out on me, Jim?"

"No, no, Bobby. I wouldn't do that." The big man raised his hands. "I just thought it might be nice to eat regular for a while, and sleep indoors instead of in a cave. Just for a while, you know?"

Bobby's head snapped back into its former position. "You can do what you like, Jim. I'm getting close now, real close. Old Henry's treasure is waiting for me … so near, I can smell it. You stick with me, you'll be a rich man. Or you can eat tacos for the rest of your life. Your choice."

I like tacos, Big Jim thought plaintively. He shuffled his feet again, trying to think. Finally, he said, "How 'bout if we give it a deadline? Say, a month? How 'bout if we say we'll give it one more month, and then — if we don't find it — we give up?"

"Two months," Bobby said, without looking up from his map.

"Ol' Henry might have been ... what's the word? When your head goes funny because you're sick ..."

"Delirious. I've thought of that. He wasn't delirious. He spoke as normal as you or me. He was sane, Jimmy-boy, and he knew exactly what he was talking about. He knew about a treasure in one of those caves out there — and he wanted me to have it!" Bobby's eyes blazed with dark fire.

Big Jim stepped back, as though scorched. Still in retreat, he mumbled, "Okay, then: two months. But that's it, okay?"

"We're gonna find it long before then." Bobby spoke confidently, but inside he seethed with a furious worry. Why hadn't they come across the treasure yet? How much longer was he going to have to search? With each passing day, the chances of that Jewish building site being overrun with construction crews loomed closer. And once all those people were in place, it was going to be hard — very hard — to search properly, and with the freedom and privacy they needed.

It was a race now: them or us. Bobby gnashed his teeth at the delay the need for money had imposed on them. But it wouldn't be much longer. They would soon have enough to hit the trail again. They would start on the new line of caves he had marked on the map. Likely they would also find some other caves that were not marked on any map at all. And in one of them his future waited, glowing like a sun in the midnight of its stone tomb. He, Bobby, would unearth it, and free its light to illuminate his life to the end of his days.

Bright imaginings, to keep him company in the gloom of a jeep's underside by day and his dingy room at night. Big Jim wasn't smart enough to see what he saw. But, if Jim played his cards right, Bobby just might be nice enough to let him come along for the ride.

Meanwhile, he had ideas. One of them involved a small reminder to the rabbi-man who was behind the construction, and all of Bobby's troubles.

II.

Earl Flaxen was becoming impatient. Though he prided himself on treating his subordinates well — or what passed for "well" in his cutthroat profession — he was beginning to consider his flexibility in the matter of Heidi Neufeld to have gotten out of hand. Heidi was a promising lawyer. She billed high, and was both efficient enough and personable enough to charm her clients into shelling out huge sums in return for the tax shelters she so cleverly devised for them. In the six years of her employment, Earl had not heard a serious word of complaint against Heidi Neufeld. That explained his incredible kindness (as he put it) in the matter of her … well, her nervous breakdown.

Because that, despite her evasive answers, was what it boiled down to. Never mind. She had cracked under the strain; nothing new in that. The important thing was the answer to a single question: Was she fit and able to come roaring back into the station she'd left behind in such a hurry? He was willing to give her a chance to prove that she was — that the weakness, whatever its source, was behind her. Trouble was, how could he give her that chance, when she insisted on burying herself in some hole out in New Mexico?

In their last phone conversation, Heidi had assured him that she was completely recovered. She'd sounded it, too: crisp and confident, her voice very unlike the rambling, almost frightened one he had heard several weeks earlier. She was back to her old self: good! In that case, she ought to be back at her old desk!

The moment had come to bring things to a head. It was ultimatum time.

"Andrea?" he said into the intercom on his desk. "Would you get me Heidi Neufeld on the phone? If she's not at her current number — the New Mexico one — try her cell phone."

Less than 60 seconds later, he heard Heidi's breathless, "Yes?"

"This is your boss speaking," Earl Flaxen intoned with heavy humor. "That is, I presume that's still what I am. If I may have a few moments of your valuable time, Heidi?"

Heidi had been terribly nervous, that first day, but watching the way Nate's hand shook as he tried to fit the key into his car's ignition had brought her to the staggering realization that he was in even worse shape than she was.

"Relax," she said with a quiver of laughter. "I promise I won't snap at you this time …" The oblique reference to their quarrel at the Bernsteins' dining-room table was dropped deliberately. Lawyerlike, she decided it was better to get everything out in the open, where it could be dealt with and — hopefully — disposed of. "Cards on the table," as her father used to say.

Nate's response to her remark was to drop his keys entirely. In the few seconds that it took him to locate them under his seat, he recaptured his composure — and his sense of humor. "Agreed," he said with a grin. "All future arguments to follow debate-system rules. Might as well be civilized."

"Why argue at all?" she had asked lightly. To which he tossed back, "Why, indeed? Now, where would you like to go?"

He offered two choices: a quiet lounge in Lakewood's (admittedly not very impressive) tallest building — or dinner in Lakewood's only kosher restaurant, which happened to be a dairy one. Heidi suggested that the view from the lounge would be better after dark, whereas Nate countered that, in the absence of a panoply of city lights, the view of the surrounding landscape was actually more interesting by day. "This is not Manhattan, you know."

"You don't have to be in Manhattan to enjoy a night view!" Heidi retorted.

A startled beat passed. Nate slapped his forehead. "Look at that! An argument already!"

Heidi laughed, shaking her head. "You decide," she said. And nothing would prevail upon her to change her mind.

In the end, Nate opted for a quick dinner at the dairy place, followed by a visit to the lounge, where the spacious windows offered them the tail end of a magnificent sunset. "The best of both worlds," he declared.

As darkness descended on their tiny corner of the Southwest, Nate and Heidi had settled down to get to know each other.

He was interesting, there was no question about that. As Nate shared his thoughts and his history with her, new facets of his personality continually emerged. She found much to admire in his character, and most of his opinions — the ones she didn't find herself arguing vociferously against, despite her best intentions — were sound.

Best of all, she wasn't the tiniest bit bored. If there was one thing Heidi loathed, it was tedium. Too many of the *shidduchim* over the too-many years that she'd been "on the market" had bored her nearly to tears. Here, in Nate, she'd discovered someone whose company she could actually imagine not only tolerating, but actually enjoying, for longer than a single evening. For her it was a novel experience.

On the way back to the Bernsteins' house, he drove past the small cottage-style building that housed his tiny law offices. "NATE GOODMAN, ATTORNEY-AT-LAW" read the copper-plate sign that hung, slightly askew, in front.

"I'm impressed," Heidi told him. The cottage looked almost picturesque — and certainly far more modest than the imposing skyscraper that was home to Flaxen, Domb and Tremaine.

"Not a scratch on New York," Nate said simply. "But it's home."

It was, literally, his home. Nate's living quarters were above the office. He kept Heidi laughing with anecdotes about his domestic skills, which were, by his own admission, negligible. "But I'm a whiz of a lawyer, and not a bad *gabbai*, either," he said modestly. "I figure, you can't be great at everything."

He dropped her off and waited while she fumbled in her purse for her key. FInding it at length, she opened the door to let a wash of light spill out onto the lawn. With a last wave, she went inside and closed the door, taking the light with her. Nate started the car and drove away.

She sat beneath the cottonwood tree next morning, looking around at the peaceful street, slumbering in the baking sun of the United States Southwest. Such peace and quiet! A torrent of memory came at her out of nowhere: the rush and tumble of a typical Manhattan street corner. She saw the lights and heard the noise — a babble of voices in different languages — and sniffed the aromas of 20 different ethnic foods competing on the air. How her blood had quickened in the mere act of walking down one of those streets! She remembered towering buildings and roaring buses and phones ringing, ringing, ringing. She recalled power lunches and dinners and conferences, acts in a cat-and-mouse game where everyone knew the script and the final curtain was the bottom line. In her memory, she breathed in the money-soaked atmosphere of a high-ticket law firm, as familiar to her as the scent of her childhood home.

Tova poked her head through the back door. She had been wearing a new look, harried but happy, ever since she started her new, medical billing job. Right now her hands were floury as she tried to get a head start on her Shabbos baking. "Heidi! Phone for you. I think it's New York."

"New York" was her euphemism for Heidi's law office. If it had been anyone else — Heidi's mother, for instance — Tova would have said so. Heidi rose to her feet, shaking out the cramps in her legs. As she stepped out from beneath the shade of the tree, the full force of the sun struck her like the flat side of a blinding sword. A few rapid steps brought her to the kitchen, where she picked up the receiver and offered a breathless, "Yes?"

Earl Flaxen's voice was at the other end of the line. Heidi pictured him at his desk, stocky in his well-cut suit, long jowled and silver haired, with a figurative pair of dollar signs stamped on his retinas.

"This is your boss, speaking," Earl Flaxen intoned with heavy humor. "That is, I presume that's still what I am. May I have a few moments of your valuable time, Heidi?"

Heidi drew in a long, quivering breath. It had come: decision-making time. The ring of steel in Flaxen's voice told her that he would not be put off any longer. She thought briefly of Nate Goodman, and then she didn't think about him anymore.

"I think it would be best to discuss that in person," she said, in an approximation of her old businesslike manner.

"Precisely what I had in mind," Flaxen said with approval. "I'd like to personally welcome you back home, Heidi. The office has missed you. Your clients have missed you. Your desk is piled high with the files of clients impatient for your return."

"Didn't you tell me that Lisa Evans has been handling my clients?"

"Sure," he said easily. "But Lisa's not you, Heidi."

"No one's indispensable."

"Not unless you make yourself so!" There was a rustle of paper as he examined his appointment book. "So ... when can we expect to see you again?"

"Thursday," Heidi said, running her eye along the calendar page that hung beside Tova's fridge. "I'll catch a flight out of Albuquerque tomorrow."

"Good, very good. We'll have lunch. One o'clock?"

She wished she were in a position to refuse lunch with her boss. Given her upbringing and religious values, the prospect made her uncomfortable. In her years with Flaxen, Domb and Tremaine, she'd usually managed to avoid the two-hour "working lunches" that her colleagues seemed to revel in. Under the circumstances, however, she thought it more prudent to fall in with her employer's plans. "That'll be fine," she reluctantly agreed.

"See you then," her boss said heartily. "Have a pleasant flight back, Heidi."

"Good-bye, Mr. Flaxen." Heidi hung up. She turned away from the phone to meet Tova's accusing stare.

"Don't," she begged, walking straight past her friend to the foot of the stairs.

"Heidi! You're leaving? Just like that? What —"

"Don't," Heidi said again. "I have to do this, Tova. I have to see ..."

"See what? Heidi, you don't belong there anymore! Don't you see *that*?"

But Heidi was not seeing anything just then. Blindly, she put one foot in front of the other and let them carry her up to the sanctuary of the guest room that she had been calling her own for all these long weeks.

And after that, it would be time to start packing for the trip that would determine the course of the rest of her life.

III.

Etty Mandel did not attempt to see Rivi Gann on the day after her talk with Efraim, as she said she would. The reason she didn't go was because, in the morning, she woke to a raging fever and chills. She had caught a virulent, draining, and long-lasting flu.

"I must have picked it up in the hospital," she murmured, lying weakly in bed with Layala tucked in beside her. "You go in healthy and walk out with all sorts of germs. Go figure!"

Tova, who came by to pay a get-well visit, nodded sympathetically. She glanced at the baby, waving her arms contentedly in the air beside her mother. "How's Layala doing?"

"She's like a different child, *Baruch Hashem*! That surgery really did the trick. I'm so grateful to Dr. Sadowsky for arranging it. She's so cheerful these days! Gaining weight, too."

"That's good." Tova smiled. "And the others? We haven't seen much of Shimi around our house lately. He used to be in and out all the time."

Something closed down in Etty's face. She found it hard to handle Shimi in the best of times; now that she was under the weather, her son was like a dragging weight on the heart. If it had been Meir, now ... But Shimi was not Meir, and never would be. While he was "acting up" less frequently these past few days, he remained a shadowy, antisocial presence in the home. Looking back, she realized now how different he'd been at the start of the year: noisy and rambunctious as ever, but eager, happy, filled with laughter. What had happened to cause the change?

Worried as she was, she lacked the strength to confront her son, and Efraim was too busy coping with the twin burdens of *kollel* and the home front — with his wife laid low, he was forced to tend single-handedly to everything from cooking to homework — to draw him out, either. For both of them, Shimi was relegated to a mental drawer labeled, "To Be Dealt With Later" — as soon as either of his parents had the time or energy to deal with anything beyond the daily round.

Tova left soon afterward, without bringing up the subject uppermost in her mind: Rivi Gann. The rift between the two women — and, consequently, the two couples — pained her deeply. Why, this meant that half of their tiny *kollel* was at odds with the other! Not a very heartening record.

But Etty was clearly in no shape for either confidences or scoldings. All that would have to wait for later, when Etty had recovered her strength. Meanwhile, Tova found time in her busy schedule to cook nourishing meals for the Mandels, as she had done today, and drop them off in person to see how the patient was coming along.

Rivi was cooking for the Mandels, too. She did not deliver her handiwork in person, preferring to send Asher instead. Her reluctance to face Etty made her feel terrible, like a stranger to herself. Never before in her life had she found herself feeling such aching antipathy toward another human being. She hated it. She longed to change it. But something within her had frozen that day in the hospital, and nothing Rivi might do had managed to thaw it yet.

Not that Rivi was trying all that hard. Mostly, she chose to ignore the whole subject, much as a small child will avoid hot stoves after experiencing the pain that results from touching one. Where that child might have come away with a smarting finger, it was Rivi's soul that smarted, scorched by the flame of Etty's unkindness. Rivi didn't know where to find the balm that would soothe it. So she soothed her conscience instead, by cooking enormous tasty meals for the Mandels several times in the week that Etty was ill, and sending them over with Asher. Sometimes, as she stirred and chopped and simmered, she longed for wings that would allow her to rise above her own emotions.

Apart from this ugly stone sticking its head above ground, the garden of her life was lovely. She enjoyed teaching art at the Jewish day school and was beginning to form a real bond with one or two of her pupils. Asher was happy in the *kollel* and was demonstrating a genuine aptitude in the realm of adult education. At every hour of the day and half the night, the phone rang with unfamiliar callers — earnest teens or adults — asking for "the rabbi." Asher spent hours on these calls, explaining, guiding, touching hearts. Rivi's own heart expanded as she listened to him. Under his tutelage, these individuals were blossoming into completely new creations.

The experience, she sometimes thought, *must not be so very different from that of bringing a child into the world.* Not that she would know … The thought brought her around full circle, to little Layala, now barred from her life by the rift with the baby's mother. Once again, hateful thoughts whirled through her mind: thoughts that could only be banished either in the depths of her *Tehillim,* or in the frenzied stroke of brush across canvas.

She was in her backroom "studio" one day, painting by the clear, steady northern light that came through its windows, when her doorbell rang. She looked up from her easel, wondering who her caller might be. She was expecting no one. Asher was away at the *kollel*, and Rivi — not scheduled to teach until afternoon — had decided to use the morning hours to pursue her favorite hobby. On the canvas, a softly beautiful, autumn landscape was taking shape and color — so very different from the harsh, sun-scorched view from her window. She was tempted not to answer. The bell sounded again. With a sigh Rivi put down her brush, wiped her hands on her paint-spattered smock, and went to see who it was.

A glance through the peephole in the door showed her a woman's hatted head, bowed over a baby in her arms. The image was distorted through the lens, but Rivi didn't have to see the woman's face to guess her visitor's identity.

Slowly, swallowing a rush of something near panic that had risen up in her throat, she unlocked the door.

"How are you feeling?" Rivi asked, every other emotion momentarily taking a back seat to surprise. Etty looked pale and very fragile. Even the weight of the small baby seemed to be too much for her. "You probably shouldn't be out yet."

"The doctor said I could get out of bed today," Etty said with a wan smile. "And that was all I needed to hear. I ... I knew where I needed to go, first thing ..."

Belatedly, Rivi realized that she was being remiss as a hostess. With a rush, she also remembered who her visitor was. Opening the door wider, she stepped back and said in stiff monotone, "Won't you come in?"

Etty moved past her, shifting the baby in her arms as though they ached. Rivi longed to take Layala from her, but she pressed her lips together and didn't say a word. It seemed to her — wishful thinking? — that Layala met her eyes with something akin to recognition.

She collected herself. "Can I offer you anything? A cup of coffee? Tea?"

Etty looked at her smock. "Were you in the middle of something?"

"I was painting. It can wait."

"I've never seen your studio," Etty said on sudden impulse. "May I see it? Maybe we can sit there ..."

They made a bizarre procession, the three of them, walking down the short hallway to the back bedroom where Rivi kept her easel and canvases. Etty went first, with Layala gazing over her shoulder at Rivi, who followed with an odd sense of walking onstage in a play in which she had never been told her lines. *Etty started this,* she thought uneasily. She would take her cues from her.

Etty moved around the "studio," openly admiring the finished canvases that lined the walls. Rivi wondered if the paint fumes might be harmful to the baby. She went to the window and pulled it open.

"They're stunning," Etty said at last. She turned, spotted a futon that had seen better days, and asked, "May I?"

"Of course." Rather than sit beside her, Rivi pulled up her painting stool to face Etty and the baby. Etty laid Layala on her knees, where the infant gazed solemnly around her.

"You're — you're probably wondering why I'm here." Etty listened to the echo of her own words and grimaced. "Actually, I'm sure you know why. The real question is, why I've taken this long to come."

"You've been sick." Rivi spoke automatically, her tender heart always quick to set another's mind at ease. But her eyes, resting on Etty, remained watchful, guarded.

"I should've come before I got sick. I should've come ... the next day." She didn't have to specify which day she was referring to; nor did Rivi need to ask. "And I wanted to, Rivi. I wanted to, so badly. But," she drew a breath and offered a ghastly imitation of a smile, "I was scared."

Rivi didn't know what to say, so she said nothing. This was Etty's show.

"Anyway, I came today ... to say I'm sorry. I treated you horribly in the hospital that day, after you'd been so kind to Layala and me." Absently, the mother's hand stroked her baby's head. Layala emitted a low gurgle and blinked her clear blue eyes. Etty looked up again with fresh urgency.

"Those are not just words, Rivi. I mean them from the bottom of my heart. I — I've been trying to do *teshuvah* for what I did to you that day. I've been facing the dark places inside myself, where such a thing could come from." She lowered her head, to cover the fact that her eyes were watering. "Please forgive me ..."

Rivi's heart melted. "Of course I forgive you. I ... I've been struggling to do that, all this time. I *wanted* to forgive right away, but I just couldn't ..."

"I hurt you too much."

Rivi met these words honestly. "Yes. You did."

Etty made a gasping sound, half-sob and half-inarticulate murmur. Quickly, Rivi said, "Please don't feel bad about it any more. It was a very hard time for you. Your baby had just undergone surgery, and you couldn't even be with her. You were wrung out and overstressed. I understand." She recited the words as she had rehearsed them in her own mind innumerable times before. This time, though, she tried to say them without feeling an instant wall of rejection spring up inside her. *Could* she say them without sinking into the old hateful resentment? Had she really forgiven?

With blinding clarity, a memory seven years old flooded her mind. She was newly engaged, gazing raptly down at the ring on her finger — the diamond that Asher had just given her.

"Do you like it?" he'd asked eagerly.

"I more than like it. I love it." She hadn't loved it for its size or its sparkle, though those were pleasing enough. She had loved that diamond for what it symbolized. The purity of its lines, its honest translucence, spoke to the depths of her soul.

She would live up to what this diamond represented, she had vowed silently. She was going to be more than merely Rivi now. This ring meant that she was part of a pair, responsible to somebody and, please G-d, to a whole family of future somebodies. That called for a largeness. It insisted that she never again sink into pettiness, never fog the crystal clarity of what this stone demanded of her ...

"Do you really forgive me?" Etty whispered, echoing Rivi's silent question to herself.

Rivi shook off the memory, but not its message. Meeting Etty's eye, she nodded firmly. "I do. Really."

Etty was silent for a long moment, absently playing with her baby's wispy curls. Her next question took Rivi utterly by surprise.

"Can — can you help me figure out where it came from? So it won't ever happen again?"

Rivi stared at her guest in astonishment. When had she ever heard Etty Mandel ask for help in anything? Or admit to any sort of weakness? Never, that's when. Impressed by this proof of how deeply the incident had shaken her, Rivi was moved to say hesitantly, "I do have a thought, Etty. But please stop me if you feel I'm treading on too-personal ground."

Etty glanced around, as though to indicate that *she* was sitting on Rivi's personal ground that very minute. The northern exposure of the studio windows was conducive, Rivi had always thought, to clear thinking as well as good painting. She ruminated a moment in its light. Then she said, quietly, "Here's my opinion, for what it's worth. I think it's all about security."

"Security?" Etty echoed blankly.

"That's right. It's all about feeling secure. Lots of people think it's a positive thing to be *insecure,* as though feeling that way provides a fail-safe protection against arrogance or something. But it's not true. Insecurity leads to so many evils: jealousy, resentment, imagined slights — you name it."

Etty took a moment to digest this. "You think I'm ... insecure?"

"What do *you* think?"

At Etty's dismayed look, Rivi instantly regretted having embarked on this track. "You don't have to answer that, Etty. I'm sorry —"

"No, no, I want to hear. You think I'm insecure? How?"

"Think back, Etty. When you came into Layala's hospital room that day ... How were you feeling just before you walked in?"

Etty thought back. Rivi could see the wheels of her mind turning, turning ... and coming to a stop at a place that, judging by the involuntary wince, was none too pleasant to recall. She waited, neither prompting nor really expecting an answer. All she had really wanted to do was prod Etty into figuring it out for herself. To her surprise, Etty spoke the memory out loud. It was obvious that the admission, like the memory, raised intense discomfort.

"Just before I walked into the room, I remember thinking that people wouldn't think I was a very good mother ... leaving my own infant with someone else when she was recuperating from surgery. I wondered if I *was* a good mother … And then I walked in, and saw you holding Layala, and heard the nurse call you by my name. She thought you were the baby's mother … It was like I'd suddenly lost something infinitely precious. I snapped …" Rivi nodded to show she understood. Fully committed now, she plunged recklessly in up to her neck. "You've got to let go of the guilt, Etty. And the feeling that you have to have everything under control. At home … with people … even with your own kids. Maybe if you'd been feeling more secure about Layala, you wouldn't have reacted the way you did."

It was Etty who nodded now, a slow, ponderous motion that seemed weighted down with pain. "I see."

Do you? Rivi wondered. She leaned forward and added, earnestly, "Please don't think I'm being presumptuous, Etty. I just want to help. I — I want to be your friend. A real friend."

"That's all right. Go on … Please."

"I just think you'd be so much happier if you'd — let yourself be happy. And that comes from feeling secure. From knowing that everything is all right, just the way it is. That *you're* all right. Even if things are less than perfect …"

They talked on — 20 minutes more, 30 — until Layala, who had fallen asleep across her mother's knees, woke suddenly and began crying. The sound roused the two women to the demands of real life. While Etty prepared to nurse her baby, Rivi went to the kitchen to fix something to eat. In the kitchen later, the talk was lighter, inconsequential, less intense but more comfortable. Etty complimented Rivi on her pretty, matching dishes and place mats, patterned with wildflowers in an array of pastel colors. Rivi told a funny story of how she'd acquired the set. Etty smiled and Layala gurgled, as though glad to see her mother happy.

Throughout it all, a part of Etty held itself in reserve, mulling over what Rivi had said.

There was truth here. "Insecure": a small word, to describe a big attitude. A damaging attitude. At some point down the years, something in Etty had become twisted. Something sweet and good had gone sour. At peace with Rivi at last, she yearned to achieve the same truce with herself. It was time — though only heaven knew how she would do it — to straighten what had been bent. To sweeten what had gone bitter and unwholesome. She had a feeling that figuring out the "how" would be the major goal of the next phase of her life …

It was time to go. Etty got to her feet, hesitating. Then she held out her precious bundle. "Want to hold her?"

Rivi smiled broadly. "I thought you'd never ask!"

As she took Layala in her arms, both she and the child's mother knew that whatever measure of forgiveness had been asked for and offered today had been the genuine article. And if it was not yet a thousand percent complete, it was well on its way to becoming so.

IV.

T ova's day started out badly, and it did not improve as the hours wore on.

First, Bo woke up tugging at his ear and indicating in a wordless but all-too-clear fashion that it was time for a visit to the doctor. Bo, like his twin, was prone to ear infections.

The change in plans meant that Tova would have to send Mo to his play group alone, something she knew he would not relish. Also, it meant missing a day of work for Drs. Sadowsky and Rein. She enjoyed the bustling atmosphere of the pediatrician's office, where she generally did her billing, with its underlying mission of offering care and protection to its patients and the occasional medical crisis to get the adrenalin pumping. For this reason, she'd opted to work in the office rather than at home. Bo's ailment would necessitate neglecting the billing during the daylight hours and spending long hours at her computer tonight — not a pleasant prospect. But what choice did she have?

As expected, Mo put up a fuss at being dropped off at play group without his twin. With his protests still ringing in her ears, she bundled Bo back into the car for the trip to the doctor's. As a professional courtesy to his newest employee, the pediatrician had invited her to come in first thing that morning.

"It's an ear infection, all right," Dr. Sadowsky said, putting down his light. "I'll prescribe an antibiotic. Bo should be fine in no time."

Comforting words. They sustained her on the trip to the pharmacy, where she handed in the doctor's prescription, and then home, to settle Bo in his bed for an unaccustomed nap. Worn out with discomfort and excitement, the little boy fell asleep at once. This left his mother free to address her own affairs. At the top of her to-do list was: Worry about Heidi.

What was that girl up to? She'd been doing so well, settling into a calmer, saner lifestyle than the one that had nearly driven her over the edge. She'd even agreed to a *shidduch* with a fine young man, right here in Lakewood. And now — this! A ticket to New York on this afternoon's flight from Albuquerque.

Refusing all offers of a ride for the long trip to the airport, Heidi had boarded a Greyhound bus right after breakfast. She'd hugged Tova hard, and thanked her repeatedly. But Heidi had turned a deaf ear to Tova's pleas that she change her mind.

"I have to do this," was all she would say as she filled her suitcase. "I have to see …"

"What about Nate Goodman?" Tova had demanded. "You saw him only once. It seemed so promising …" She waited, but Heidi said nothing. "And now, you up and run with hardly a minute's warning! What am I supposed to say about all that?"

"Have a good trip?" Heidi said, with a comical uplift that reminded Tova of the way Shana and her friends talked: every statement a question.

"Very funny," Tova muttered, morosely watching Heidi lift another pile of clothes neatly out of a drawer. "You notice that I'm not offering to help you pack."

"Duly noted, thanks."

"That's because I disapprove of this whole thing. Are you sure you know what you're doing?"

Heidi had turned to her at that, her expression suddenly somber. "I think that's for me to decide, don't you?"

Tova flushed. "I'm sorry. I overstepped."

"Don't be sorry. But, Tova, you've got to let go. You've got to let me live my own life. I love you dearly, and I've loved being here, and you guys basically saved my life — well, my sanity, anyway. But this is something I have to do before I can go on with my life. O.K.?"

What answer was there to that, except an echoing, "O.K."?

But it was not O.K.; it would never be O.K. Heidi had departed for Albuquerque with a suddenness that made Tova dizzy — not to mention heartsick. She missed her friend terribly before she was gone five minutes.

In desperation, Tova had even put a call in to Rabbi Harris the night before. She asked him if he'd heard about Heidi's decision, and what he thought about it all. To her chagrin, his answer was essentially identical to Heidi's. He said that Tova's job was to stand aside and let her friend get on with her life. "Heidi's a smart woman," he said gently. "She'll make the right decision. You need to stop worrying. That won't help anyone."

Stop worrying, the rabbi had advised. As though she could press a button and turn it right off …

With a sigh, Tova trailed through her quiet house and into her empty kitchen, where she poured herself a cup of coffee.

An hour later she was desultorily scrubbing the breakfast dishes with a sponge, her mind miles away — in Albuquerque's airport lounge, with an increasingly remote Heidi — when she was roused by the ringing of the phone.

"Hello?"

"Tova! I'm glad you're home. It's me — Rivi."

"Rivi. How are you?"

"I'm fine. More than fine." There was something in Rivi's voice — a note that Tova hadn't heard much of lately. "Something good happened today, Tova. Etty came over. She apologized. We talked things out. We're all right now."

"Rivi! That's wonderful!" Instantly, Tova's mood lifted. The dark clouds evaporated, letting in the sun of a bright new day. "I'm so glad. I've been so worried." "That's why I called, you old mother hen. Did anyone ever tell you that you worry too much?"

"It has been mentioned … But I'm glad you've relieved my mind of one thing, anyway."

"Oh? What else is on your mind these days? Apart from arson and other nasty stuff?"

"Heidi." Briefly, Tova updated Rivi on her friend's departure. "Things were going so well, too. I never expected her stay here forever, of course. But when she agreed to see Nate Goodman, I couldn't help hoping …"

"We all did," Rivi admitted. "But what can you do? A person's gotta do what a person's gotta do."

"That's what Nachman says. And Rabbi Harris."

"I'm in good company, then. Don't worry, Tova. Everything'll turn out all right in the end. You'll see. If Heidi and Nate are meant to be together, they will be!"

"And how's that supposed to happen, if they're at opposite sides of the country?"

"Ever heard of airplanes?"

"Yeah, I've heard of them. Unfortunately, Heidi's on her way aboard one even as we speak."

"I know you'll miss her, but try to cheer up, Tova. Enjoy my little piece of good news, anyway."

"I am! I will! I'm going to call Nachman right now and tell him." Nachman had been concerned by the ever-widening circles of tension that, with Rivi and Etty at its center, had quickly engulfed their husbands as well. Surely the *kollel* would run more smoothly for having this quarrel patched up. Nachman would be very glad to hear it.

But Tova, eagerly punching in her husband's number on her speed-dial, never got the chance to share her story. Nachman, it turned out, had news of his own.

"Hello?" He sounded distracted.

"Nachman, it's me," Tova said breathlessly. "Listen, I just got a call from —"

"Excuse me, please ..." There was the sound of muffled voices in the background before her husband came back on the line. "Sorry about that, Tova. I've got a — situation — here."

Instantly she was on the alert, every nerve tingling. "A situation? What do you mean?"

"I came to the *kollel* this morning and parked in my usual spot. Just a few minutes ago, I remembered that I'd left a *sefer* that I needed in the car. I came out here to get it — and found all four of my tires slashed."

Tova gasped. "Who ...?"

"I don't know," Nachman said heavily. "But whoever it was doesn't seem to like me very much."

"You — or Jews in general?"

"Good point, Tova. That's what we have to find out. sheriff Ramsay's on his way over right now."

V.

The street in front of the shul quickly filled with vehicles. There was Ramsay's distinctive car, with the word SHERIFF blazoned across both sides, a second police car with strobe lights flashing, and a van bearing Lakewood's modest "crime team." Because this was the latest in a series of incidents targeted at the town's Jewish populace, the sheriff was taking this seriously — more seriously than an ordinary case of tire-slashing might warrant.

"Rabbi Bernstein, have you had any threatening calls? Letters? Even a nasty incident on the street or in a store?" Ramsay asked.

"Nothing. I haven't been singled out from the rest of the *kollel* — or the rest of the Jewish community, for that matter. Until this." Nachman's eyes fell on the wheels of his car, now flat as four deflated balloons, and looking about as disheartened as Nachman was feeling at the moment.

"You do think this is aimed at the community?" Pinchas Harris asked the sheriff. Alongside the police personnel, all the *kollel* members as well as Rabbi Harris, his secretary, the Bernstein brothers and Shimi Mandel — the last three temporarily reprieved from their lessons — stood in a concerned knot near the mutilated car.

"I think it's part of a pattern," Ramsay said slowly. "First, the arson incidents, here and at the construction site just outside town. Then the intruder at the Jewish day school. When the man responsible for both the new building and a future influx of Jewish residents gets all four tires slashed right in front of the synagogue, I tend to think there's a connection."

"Hm. I see your point." Rabbi Harris looked intensely unhappy.

Ramsay was no happier. His peaceful town was turning into a hotbed of anti-Semitism ... or not quite. This might be the work of a single perpetrator, perhaps working with a buddy as Dr. Rein had suggested in his report, acting on a personal grudge against the Jews. Catch the perp, and you slammed the lid on the trend. His eyes roved the area around the car and came to rest on an elongated object lying abandoned in the gutter. It was the gleam of sun on glass that had caught his eye. Two long strides brought Ramsay to the curb. Stooping, he used his handkerchief to carefully lift the object from the curb.

He held it up. "Do you usually have empty bourbon bottles lying around in front of the synagogue?"

Nachman Bernstein and Pinchas Harris shook their heads simultaneously, for a moment resembling a pair of puppets manipulated by invisible strings. The sheriff took his find over to his car and deposited it carefully inside.

"You think the guy who did this to my tires ...?" Nachman let his sentence trail off.

"There's a chance," Ramsay nodded. "We'll run it for fingerprints, anyway. Can't hurt to try."

"That was an easy one," Jack Ramsay said with satisfaction. "That's the kind of crime work I like to see. Less than two hours from discovery to arrest."

"You've got the man behind bars already?" Nachman asked incredulously. He, along with Pinchas Harris, Steve Birch and the sheriff himself, were crowded into Ramsay's tiny office on Main Street.

"Yes, sir, we do." Ramsay beamed with modest pride. "That bottle I found in the gutter in front of the shul? We ran it for prints, found some that belong to a Native American derelict by the name of Willis. About 55, usually to be found on a stool at the Lakeside Pub — a fancy name for a dusty old bar on Francis Street — when he's not drinking out at the reservation. My men picked him up for questioning about half an hour ago. He confessed less than 10 minutes after that."

It was Willis's confession that had brought the present occupants of the sheriff's office running over to Main Street. Nachman Bernstein and Pinchas Harris exchanged a look in which cautious hope vied with skepticism. It was Nachman who voiced the latter aloud.

"Sheriff? Doesn't this look a little — fishy — to you? I mean, the tire-slasher conveniently leaving a bottle for us to find right near the car ... and then sitting around in his usual bar, waiting to be picked up?"

"He wasn't waiting, exactly," Ramsay explained. "He was drinking up some courage before hitting the road. Told the barkeeper he was planning to 'lay low' at the reservation for a while. Hinted that Lakewood was a bit 'too hot' for him right now. My men caught up with him just as he was about to leave."

Nachman nodded thoughtfully. "And he confessed, you say?"

"Didn't take much pushing. The guy was half-drunk and terrified. Started talking almost as soon as we got him into the interrogation room. My men promised leniency if he told them who put him up to it."

"Why do you think anyone 'put him up to it'?" Rabbi Harris asked curiously.

"Instinct, mostly." Ramsay shrugged. "Willis is not your typical, violent criminal — and tire-slashing is a violent crime, make no mistake about that. In this case, the violence just happens to be directed at things instead of people. Luckily for us."

All three of the other men in the room nodded, silently echoing that sentiment.

"Willis is not a violent type. Timid as a kitten, really. The real love of his life is his bottle. My men asked around in the bar. No one recalls him ever lifting a hand to anyone or even raising his voice. A gentle soul." Ramsay paused. "Just to make sure, I spoke to Dr. Rein, our forensic psychiatrist. Same guy who wrote up a profile on the arsonist?" He tilted a questioning brow at Nachman, who nodded.

"And?" Nachman prompted.

"And he says that Willis does *not* fit the profile: no way, no how. Just as I thought."

"Good instincts," Pinchas Harris murmured. Ramsay colored slightly at the praise.

Nachman asked, "So, he was hired to do it?"

"Seems that way. He was scared to death to admit it, though. Understandable, under the circumstances."

"Did your men get anything concrete out of him?" This from Steve Birch, who'd been silent up till now.

Ramsay turned to the lawyer with a question of his own. "Do you know Willis, Steve?"

"Vaguely. He was up on vagrancy charges a few years back. I helped get him registered for the dole, straighten himself out a little."

"He has a petty criminal record: misdemeanors, no jail time served. That's how we happened to have his prints on record," the sheriff said. "Some modest pilfering over the years, to finance his drinking. To answer your question, Steve: yes, my men did get something out of him. Not a name." He looked regretful. "But a definite story. Seems that someone told Willis he was looking to buy a car — your car, Rabbi. He said that if Willis slashed the tires, it would bring down the asking price. He promised to share a percentage of the difference with Willis."

"Ingenious," Steve Birch remarked. "Not to mention manipulative."

"My own thoughts exactly," the Sheriff agreed. "But no amount of talking — or threatening — has managed to pry a name out of the guy yet. He seems much more terrified of whoever hired him to do this than the prospect of spending a few nights in a nice, warm jail cell. Can't really say that I blame him ..."

"What's going to happen to him?" Nachman asked.

"If you choose to press charges, he'll be a guest of the county for the next 30 days or so. Three square meals a day, though no bourbon, I'm sorry to say."

"The bottle will be waiting for him when he gets out, I'm sure," Rabbi Harris said dryly.

"Sure it will. And there may be something else waiting for him when he gets out: payment for slashing those tires. We'll keep an eye on him then, see if there are any signs of sudden prosperity." Ramsay shook his head in frustration. "But, like I said, that's more 'n a month away."

Nachman fixed Ramsay with a direct look. "Sheriff, do you think our arsonist is the man behind this?"

"I hate to say it, but the odds are high. Like I said, we did have one or two minor anti-Semitic incidents in the past — isolated incidents. Now that we're seeing a definite pattern of crime and intimidation, we can't pretend that this incident is unrelated. We can hope it is. It may even *be* unrelated. But, like I said, the odds are high that it's part of the same package, rabbi. Someone doesn't like you people, or your plans. Or both."

"I see." Nachman stood up and extended a hand across the desk. "Thanks, sheriff. You'll keep us posted on any new developments?"

"You know I will, rabbi." Ramsay glanced at his watch. "Unless I miss my bet, your car should be ready by now — equipped with four brand-new tires. Joe — who owns Tire World — works fast. Want a lift down there?"

"I'll drive him," Steve Birch said before Nachman could answer. "I'm passing that way."

Nachman shot a look at him, but Birch's face seemed to be carved of wood, as inscrutable as an old-fashioned Indian mask. With a quick good-bye to Pinchas Harris, Nachman accepted Birch's offer.

He waited until they'd pulled away from the curb, seat belts buckled and engine purring softly, before saying, "You wanted to talk to me about something, Steve?"

Steve glanced at him, then back at the road. "Actually — yes. I've been having more of those dreams, Rabbi. I keep seeing that Indian boy and his sister ... and a Star of David, among other things. It's confusing me. I — I don't know where I am these days."

"I can sympathize with that, Steve. Confusion is a terrible thing. The *Gemara* — our Talmud — says that there's no greater joy than resolving doubt."

"I can't imagine a greater joy than that," Steve said simply.

Nachman hesitated. "Something has come to light lately, though with everything that's been going on I haven't had a chance to pursue it. A Jewish connection with this area, that may help explain these dreams you've been having. Not to mention the *siddur* you have in your possession. I'd like to hear more, Steve. A lot more, about your past, and your mother's. Maybe when things settle down — when the arsonist is caught and behind bars — we can dig really deep and discover what this is all about."

"I'd like that, rabbi." For a moment the impassive mask cracked, and a suffering soul peeked through. Then Steve schooled his face to its usual expressionlessness. "Thanks for your help. I mean that."

"I haven't done anything yet. But I will," Nachman promised. "With G-d's help, I will."

Joe at Tire World was as efficient as Ramsay had painted him. Nachman's car was ready and waiting with, as the sheriff had predicted, four spanking new tires affixed to the chassis. Nachman paid for them, thanked Joe, and drove slowly home to apprise his wife — who was doubtless bursting with curiosity by this time — of the situation.

Something had happened, he would tell her, that was really nothing at all. It was just a blip on a radar screen — an insignificant scribble in a larger and ominous pattern.

Just a little reminder, so to speak, from their community's anonymous enemy, to let them know that he hadn't forgotten them.

VI.

Bobby Smith threw down his wrench in disgust. This was the last straw. His sense of his own worth, already outraged by the work he was forced to do as a garage mechanic, had hit an all-time low. It was bad enough having to crawl under other people's cars to tend to the grimy underside of car repair. But when black, greasy oil began spurting out of nowhere, covering his jumpsuit, face and hair as he lay supine and helpless on the ground beneath, something snapped.

"I've had it," Bobby snarled. His dark eyes burned. He deserved better than this. There was a fortune waiting for him somewhere, and he had a feeling — a prickling, creeping, crawling-up-the-spine feeling — that he was getting close. Real close. But how was he supposed to pursue hidden treasure when he was buried under cars all day, taking orders from a nobody and earning hardly enough to keep body and soul together?

He was done with all that. It was over. History. Somewhere up in those caves, his future lay waiting, lighting up the darkness just for him. He would uncover the gold and finally start living!

He unzipped the jumpsuit, grimacing as black oil touched his fingers. Out came his handkerchief, to wipe it off. Underneath he wore faded black chinos and a white T-shirt. He started for the gate.

"Hey, Bobby! Where're you going?" The "nobody" who paid his wages came running out of the garage, a dirty rag dangling from his hand.

"I'm outta here, Joe. Mail me what you owe me. You have the address." Bobby did not break stride.

"Whaddaya mean, you're outta here? You work for me, Bobby! Take your lunch break later. It's only 11:15!"

"This isn't lunch, Joe. It's o-ver." As his erstwhile employer stared, Bobby swung through the gates of the garage lot and vanished up the street.

It was time to get hold of Big Jim and get back on track. They had enough money now to pay next month's rent and to eat, too, if they were careful about how much they ate. Who needed food, anyway? Bobby felt a wave of energy surge through him as though powered by an unseen electrical source. Every nerve ending tingled with the desire to act. He had wasted enough time tinkering around with other people's cars. He'd had enough of taking orders. He would keep his eye on the ball now — on the round yellow ball that was his own personal sun. His light, his future, his fortune …

Fifteen minutes' concentrated walking brought the Taco Bell sign into view. Three minutes after that, Bobby walked through the front door in search of his partner.

"I don't know, Bobby." Big Jim was fretful. "I kinda like this place. I like the food, and the people are nice, too."

"You'll be able to buy all the tacos you want when we strike it rich," Bobby reminded him. They were sitting at one of the tables in the rear, Jim having been granted an early lunch break by the franchise manager. The busiest time of the day was yet to come: noon through dinnertime. Jim would be through with his break by then and back on his enormous feet, sporting his good-humored grin as he wiped down tables and swept taco crumbs from the floor.

"I don't have to buy them," Jim pointed out. "I get them free."

"Free? You get them by selling yourself into slavery!"

"I'm no slave. I get paid a salary for what I do."

"Well, stick with me and you won't need a salary. You'll have everything you want — a hundred tacos a day, a thousand! — without having to lift a finger!" Bobby was growing increasingly agitated.

Abruptly, his face shut down. He had reached his limit at the garage, and he had just gone over the top here, too. "Listen, buddy," he said softly, leaning closer to Jim so that their faces were only inches apart above the orange vinyl table. "This is it. It's decision time. Either you come out to the caves with me tomorrow, or we're finished. We're washed up. I'll keep the gold for myself, and you can keep your precious tacos."

Jim hesitated. His body was clumsy and his mind felt the same way. Analyzing a situation, weighing the advantages or disadvantages to himself, was a feat he found difficult to handle. Longtime loyalty to Bobby Smith urged him to follow wherever Bobby went — to embrace his friend's dream and share in the good fortune that was bound to come eventually. Bobby was too smart for that not to happen.

On the other hand, Jim's limited imagination led him to live very much in the present and, at present, his happiness was bound up in this congenial Taco Bell.

He furrowed his brow, trying to think of a way out of the impasse.

Then the broad brow cleared, and the beginnings of a big smile spread across his face. "Tell you what, Bobby. Today's — what? Wednesday? Thursday's always pretty slow around here. How 'bout if I take the day off tomorrow and go up to the caves with you? I could call in sick. People do that all the time around here."

"We'll need more than just tomorrow, Jim."

"Well, let's take it one day at a time." That's what Bobby was always saying: "One day at a time."

Bobby eyed the big man speculatively. "All right, then. Tomorrow. We leave early, before dawn. I want to try that line of caves northeast of town. We haven't checked those yet."

"There must be dozens of caves up there. How'll we do them all in one day?"

"We won't." Bobby's voice was grim. "It's going to take longer than that. You're going to have to decide, Jim — one way or another. Either you're with me or you're not. You'll have all day tomorrow to make up your mind."

Jim chewed his lip sorrowfully. "Why can't we keep working at our jobs awhile, Bobby? We could use the money, and —"

"I'm through with the garage. I just quit the place."

"Quit? And ... and you want me ..."

"To do the same thing. Yeah, that's right. But you don't have to make a decision right now. Sleep on it, Jim. Come out to the caves with me tomorrow. Then you'll decide."

It was a reprieve, albeit a brief one. Still, Jim could look forward to the rest of today at his beloved Taco Bell, and he had all day tomorrow to make up his mind. Who knew? Maybe they would strike it lucky, and he would never be forced to decide at all. Miracles like that sometimes happened ...

"You got yourself a deal, Bobby." Beaming, Jim checked his watch. "My break's almost over. We better have something to eat. How do you want your taco? And don't worry about paying: this one's on me." His pleasure was obvious.

Bobby was about to say that he wasn't hungry. Then he changed his mind. Might as well keep Big Jim happy; he was going to need him tomorrow. With a thin smile, he said, "Plenty of cheese on mine. Thanks, buddy."

"No problem," Jim said happily. "What are friends for?"

Thursday seemed primed to be Chaim and Donny's lucky day.

Their mother took two phone calls the night before. The first was from Asher Gann, one of the boys' teachers.

"I'm sorry to have to do this to you, Mrs. Bernstein," Asher said. "But Rivi and I have an appointment at the hospital over in Roswell in the morning."

"Oh? I hope everything's all right?"

"We're fine, *Baruch Hashem*. It's a new specialist Rivi found, that day she was there. Might as well do our *hishtadlus* with him, too ..." He sounded curiously ambivalent, as though hope and despair were struggling to achieve an uneasy truce inside him.

"Good luck with that," Tova said sincerely. "We'll be *davening* for the two of you."

"Thanks. Anyway, I'm calling to let you know that there'll be no morning classes at the *kollel* for the boys tomorrow. Lucky kids — they get a day off from school."

"What about Avi Feder?" Avi was the boys' other teacher.

"He just called me. He's under the weather, running a slight fever and generally feeling miserable. He'll be in touch with you himself, I'm sure. But I'm afraid he'll also be out of the picture tomorrow. So there go the boys' afternoon classes."

Sure enough, Avi phoned just minutes later to confirm Asher's message. His fever was negligible but he had a full-scale head cold. He would be taking a sick day tomorrow.

Tova filled her husband in on the situation. Nachman might have been able to stand in for the missing teachers, except that he was due to meet the building contractors at his *kollel* office tomorrow morning. "It's going to be a long one," he said. "It's a series of meetings, actually. We're having the plumbing firm, the electrical people and the landscaper all down on the same day, to meet with the architect and the contractor. That way, we hope to be able to coordinate all our efforts and start the ball rolling smoothly."

"Good luck with that," Tova said, for the second time that night. It looked like the boys were going to be her headache tomorrow. She would have to stay home from work again and try to get through the day's quota of billing from the house.

But Chaim and Donny had another idea. "Ma, we're perfectly capable of staying home alone," Donny declared. "Chaim is 12 and I'm already 11 ... well, pretty soon, anyhow. You don't have to miss work just because we have no school."

Chaim nodded vigorously to indicate his full agreement with every word his brother was saying. "We'll be fine, Ma. No problem. You've left us home before, right?"

"I suppose so ..." Tova thought out loud. "I can be in phone contact. Maybe I'll cut my hours short ..."

"There's no need for that, Ma. Don't you trust us?" Donny tried to look as virtuous as possible, no easy feat considering the fact that he was plotting insubordination even as he spoke.

In the end, Tova decided to trust them. She would go to work as usual, and call home every now and then to see if the boys were all right. Bo's ear infection had yielded to treatment and he and Mo would be at play group all morning. Shana, Yudi and Gila would be at school. Her big boys were ... well, big boys. Big enough to leave unattended for a single morning, anyway.

"A day off from school!" Donny crowed. "Let's go hiking!"

Chaim looked at him in amazement. "Donny, every time we go up to those cliffs, you *kvetch* endlessly. And now, you want to go up again?"

Donny had a short memory. He waved his brother's objections aside. "It's not so hot these days. Let's take along some sandwiches and chocolate and stuff. It'll be fun!"

"Shimi said it's dangerous," Chaim said slowly. "He met those two Indians up there, remember? They threatened him ... Maybe we'd better stay home."

But Donny had his heart set on a hike. Unblushingly, he used the time-honored weapon of young boys everywhere. "Chicken?" he taunted.

Red crept into Chaim's cheeks. "Of course not," he said with dignity. "I just think that maybe —"

"You *are* scared!"

"No, I'm not!"

"Prove it. Come on a hike tomorrow. How often do we get a day off from school, just like that?"

Chaim hesitated. The cliffs called to him like a magnet. Back East, the only time he had ever been able to strike out into the heart of nature had been in summer camp. What better way to spend an unexpected school holiday? On this sunny morning, it wasn't too hard to push Shimi's shadowy menace from his mind. "We'd have to be back by the time Ma gets home." It was their tacit understanding that they wouldn't be sharing their plans with their mother.

"No problem," Donny agreed. "Wanna call Shimi? Maybe he'll want to come along."

"And maybe not," Chaim predicted dryly.

A quick call to Shimi ascertained that Chaim's assessment was right on the mark. There had been no change of heart since their last conversation on the subject. Not only was Shimi emphatically uninterested in hiking past the town limits, but he seemed intent on changing his friends' minds about going, too.

"No way," Donny said, on the extension. "We're going. *We're* not chicken!"

"It's just a hike, Shimi," Chaim added. "We're not going to be hunting for crooks or anything stupid like that."

"They may come hunting for *you*," Shimi said darkly.

Chaim chose to ignore this. "We'll be starting out first thing in the morning, as soon as our mother leaves for work. We have to be back by the time she gets home, around 2 o'clock. Last chance: Do you want to join us?"

"You know I don't. Why bother asking me all the time?"

"Too bad." Donny was pitying. "We'll tell you all about it when we get back."

"*If* you get back ..."

"Shimi, quit that," Chaim said. "We'll be careful. Nothing will happen."

"I hope you're right. Be really careful, you guys ..."

"We will," Chaim promised. And Donny chimed in, "If we see those two guys, we'll sneak away so quietly that they'll never even know we were there. We'll be like shadows. We'll be like — like Apaches!"

In his bedroom in the Mandel house, Shimi shivered.

In the room that she shared with Shana, Gila Bernstein shivered, too. She shivered with excitement over what she had just inadvertently overheard, when she'd picked up the receiver to call a classmate and heard her brothers on the phone with Shimi Mandel.

The gist of their talk had so captivated her that she never even thought of replacing the receiver and restoring their privacy. Instead, she listened spellbound as her brothers described their plans to hike up into the hills next day. She heard Shimi warn them away from the area, talking about some Indians who had threatened him. Were they the ones who had burned Tatty's building site, and who'd scared the daylights out of her in the schoolyard? She remembered the terror of not being able to catch her breath, so familiar to her from her New York days, and the bizarre circumstances that had led to her first asthma attack in Lakewood.

If her brothers were going up into those hills, she would have to be there, too.

She wasn't naive enough to think that she could confront them and make them change their minds about going. Boys had a thing about appearing brave, and an appeal to their native caution would probably backfire. But she wanted to be on hand to make sure that Chaim and Donny were all right. Her family was always looking out for her. Here was a chance for a tender-hearted younger sister to give something back to the people she loved.

A stomachache tomorrow morning should do the trick, she thought as she carefully replaced the receiver in its cradle. Ma would want to stay home with her, but there would be no need, Gila would tell her. What better babysitters than her own big brothers?

Tomorrow, Donny whispered, as he and Chaim climbed into their beds later.

Tomorrow, thought Gila, hovering at the edge of sleep in her own bed down the hall.

What Shimi thought would be impossible to say. He spent a good part of the night working very hard at *not* thinking about what the next day might bring.

Chapter 16

I.

Manhattan was *loud.*

Heidi had forgotten how incredibly noisy the city could be. The contrast to Lakewood, New Mexico was so startling as to be almost painful. Her ears — grown accustomed, over the past weeks, to a desertlike hush, where the voice of the whispering wind could be heard sighing through the trees and stirring up the dust — felt assaulted by the clamor that was New York. She had also grown used to a sky that stretched like a canopy from horizon to horizon, and felt cheated now by the niggardly slivers of blue that the city's skyscape doled out.

Focus on the positive, she told herself, as she walked briskly along the crowded street — an operation far more complex than she remembered. It involved dodging pedestrians and fending off vehicle fumes while straining to cross the street ahead of the eager taxis and oversized trucks that bore recklessly down on her and the rest of the hurrying pack. She was engulfed by a cacophony of blaring horns, cell-phone conversations in a plethora of different accents and the roar of mammoth buses plastered with vivid, life-sized posters that constituted an assault of a different kind.

Her feet, having fallen out of the habit of high heels, were beginning to ache. Heidi found herself longing for the scratchy feel of the sparse grass under Tova's cottonwood tree, where the whirr of a fly's wings might be the only sound to disturb the peace. For a precious instant, she was *there*. The dry Southwestern heat swept through her, and she could almost believe she heard Tova's laughter floating out to her from the house ... Then an unwary shoulder brushed hers in passing, an uncaring voice muttered an insincere apology, and she was back in New York. It was an effort to drag her attention back to the bustling street around her, and the business at hand.

At least she had had one night of relative peace before entering the fray. Last night, after navigating her way out of the airport and into a taxi, she had leaned back tiredly and wondered how her apartment would look and feel after having been away for such a long time. Walking into it some 45 minutes later, she confronted a space grown alien to her. The four walls — that for years had sheltered her — had grown unfriendly in her absence, turning a cold shoulder as though they resented her intrusion.

"Look," she said aloud. "I'm not so sure I want to be here, either."

There was a great deal of which she still wasn't sure. But on this one night, she was determined to put decisions aside. She'd had the forethought to pack a picnic dinner back in Tova's house, and she proceeded to eat the slightly soggy sandwiches at a kitchen table suddenly turned inhospitable. The bedroom, in which she'd passed an impatient few hours nearly every night in recent years, seemed equally uninviting. Only her desk, with its view of the twinkling city lights, offered a bridge of continuity to her old life. She sat on the comfortable, executive chair and, without turning on the desk lamp, reached for the phone.

"Ma?"

"Heidi, is that you? How are you, dear?" Heidi had enjoyed a number of brief conversations with her mother in the past weeks. She wondered if she was going to enjoy this one.

"I'm fine, actually. I'm also back. Here, in New York."

"You're back?" Incredulity and pleasure struggled for supremacy in Mrs. Neufeld's voice. "When did this happen? And why didn't you let us know you were coming in? We could have picked you up."

Heidi gave a shrug that her mother couldn't see. "I figured, I left without warning, I might as well do the same thing on the return trip. Besides, I need to be in Manhattan in the morning."

"I'd love to see you, Heidi. You could have spent the night here."

"Thanks, Ma. Maybe another night. I've got a few things to take care of right now."

Her mother sucked in a hopeful breath. "What's the story, Heidi? Are you — are things back to normal? Are you home for good?"

Starting with Heidi's unexpected break for the Poconos, Mrs. Neufeld had alluded to this strange interlude in her daughter's life only indirectly, and always with the vaguest of euphemisms. If she didn't talk about it, so her reasoning went, maybe it would go away. And now it looked as though it *had* gone away. Proof: Her Heidi was back where she belonged.

Well, not really where she belonged. That would be in a home of her own, presided over by a good man, her husband, and graced by the presence of Mrs. Neufeld's future grandchildren. Still, barring that miracle, she was pleased to see her daughter in functioning mode again — back on track, so to speak.

"For good?" Heidi repeated thoughtfully. "Whether for good or the opposite is something that still remains to be seen ... But I'm here, anyway. I just wanted to say hi. I'm kind of exhausted from the trip, so I'm going to crawl into bed and catch up on my sleep."

"And tomorrow? What are your plans?"

"Tomorrow," Heidi said, gazing through the glass at the mesmerizing lights of a city whose possessive tug was already beginning to make itself felt, "I'm having lunch with my boss."

"Good luck with that," her mother said. With an AWOL Heidi facing her superior after so many weeks, she assumed there might be a difficult scene in store for Heidi.

"Thanks, Ma. I think I'm going to need it ..."

She was brought back to the present by a sort of sixth-sense intuition that told her to stop walking. Looking around, she saw that instinct had not erred. Her feet had carried her directly to the place they'd taken her virtually every weekday for the past eight years. The weeks-long gap in her working life might never have happened.

Her apartment had turned its back on her, but the office seemed to welcome her with wide-open arms. Sleek and tall, the building opened its mouth to swallow the steady stream of men and women passing through its glass portals. Heidi took a deep breath and became one of them.

She walked through a lobby as familiar as her own kitchen at home, and straight up to the black information board beside the elevators.

FLAXEN, DOMB and TREMAINE read the legend beside a familiar trio of numbers. Heidi stepped into the elevator, its doors gaping open to receive her. They say you never forget how to ride a bike, or how to swim. Walking into this building felt the same way. There was a sense of smoothness, of familiarity — of a path being paved for her to ease her way. Without warning the old adrenalin rush returned, accompanying her swift ascent to the third floor. Her step was noticeably more rapid as she strode out of the elevator and along the hall to the room she wanted.

FLAXEN, DOMB AND TREMAINE, read the sign affixed to the door. It might as well have read, WELCOME HOME, HEIDI.

She pushed open the door and walked inside.

II.

Sunlight poured through the spacious window to flood the principal's office. It was purely a trick of the mind, Simi Wurtzler knew, but she always felt extra efficient with the morning sun shining on her shoulders. It was as though its heat was a solar cell, energizing her. In this first hour of the morning, she tore through a stack of work in half the time it might have taken her during the last hour of the day. Then she sat back and thought about the upcoming hour, which she planned to devote to classroom observations.

Mrs. Wurtzler harbored vivid memories of her own teaching days, and the trepidation she had always felt whenever the principal walked in to observe her. In those days, she had complained — along with most of her fellow teachers — that such observations were nerve racking and stilting and unfair. Today, from the other side of the desk, she viewed matters differently. It was her responsibility as principal to ensure that her teaching staff functioned at peak form; the only way to do that was by firsthand observation of her faculty's teaching methods and classroom-management skills. Still, every time she opened the door and walked inside, she could almost feel the temperature drop as dismay frosted the air with an invisible patina of ice.

Today was Miss Harmon's turn. The principal had originally been scheduled to visit the fourth-grade classroom the previous week — a visit that had been abruptly canceled by the schoolyard intruder and young Gila Bernstein's terror-induced asthma attack. As she walked down the hall toward Miss Harmon's room, she thought with pleasure that that incident seemed to have passed without leaving too much damage in its wake. Gila seemed to be on an even keel and her parents had assured the school that their daughter now carried an inhaler with her wherever she went. The asthmatic girl was still on her mind as Mrs. Wurtzler tapped on the door, pushed it open and greeted the teacher and students with a pleasant, "Good morning. Mind if I sit in for a few minutes?"

At the expected, "Not at all," she took a seat in the back of the room and let her eyes roam the rows of students. Almost subconsciously, they sought out a certain blond head of hair and the slightly stocky form still clinging to its baby fat. Simi didn't see either one. Gila was not in class today.

Fifteen minutes later, with a guilty pang, she realized that she'd hardly heard a word Miss Harmon had said. The classroom seemed under control; the girls were participating and the teacher was clearly on top of her subject. *That*, Simi Wurtzler supposed, *was all that really mattered.* Surely, even if her mind was preoccupied, she'd have noticed if something were wrong.

I can always come back next week to observe her again, she thought. But even as she considered the idea, she rejected it. That would not be fair to Miss Harmon. Was it her fault that the sight of Gila Bernstein's vacant chair had led her mind back to the series of sinister incidents that had befallen their little community these past weeks — ending with the one that had Gila speeding to the hospital in Roswell to the accompaniment of ambulance sirens?

No, it wasn't Miss Harmon's fault at all. In any case, the principal was not yet ready to make plans for next week. She was wholly occupied with her plans for the next few minutes, which included returning to her office and phoning the Bernstein house to make sure Gila was all right.

She did this on occasion, if a child was absent from school. Usually, it was because the child had been out a number of days, or was known to be suffering from a serious flu or other ailment. In Gila's case, the decision stemmed from nothing more than a protective feeling. The memory of the 9-year-old's pathetic face, as she had gasped for air while waiting for help to arrive, made Simi want to spread her wings and bear the child right out of harm's way.

Gila was probably home battling nothing more serious than a sniffle or a sore throat. But she intended to call anyway, just to ease her own mind. She even went so far as to lift the receiver.

Then she replaced it again. Almost before she heard the monotonous drone of the dial tone, Simi regretted the impulse. *There is such a thing as being too protective*, she thought ruefully, *too ready to worry over nothing.* A student was entitled to a day off for a minor ailment without having the principal calling her first thing.

There were plenty of other matters clamoring for her attention. After a moment, Simi Wurtzler turned away from the phone and addressed herself to them.

Mrs. Wurtzler's assumptions notwithstanding, Gila was not suffering from a head cold that morning, but from a bad case of cold feet.

She had managed, though riddled with guilt as she did it, to feign being just sufficiently under the weather for her mother to agree to let her stay home.

"Chaim and Donny are home anyway," she said ingenuously. "They can stay with me."

Tova smiled at her 9-year-old. "Oh, is that the reason for the sudden stomachache? The fact that your brothers have a day off from school?"

"Of course not! Why would I —?"

Tova leaned down and pecked her daughter on the cheek. "Relax, Gila. I don't suspect you of wanting to 'play hooky.' You're entitled to a sick day now and then." Gila was a good student; even more, she was a brave and patient sufferer. There was little that her mother wouldn't do for her. Even so, Tova had no reason to doubt that Gila had actually fallen victim to some mild virus. She told Gila to stay in bed as long as she liked. "I'll pop in again in a little while to see how you're doing," she promised.

"Don't you have to go to work?"

Tova misinterpreted the reason for Gila's dismay. "I would have, if only Chaim and Donny were home. As it is, Tatty's going to drop the twins off at their play group, and I'll run out later this morning to pick up some work so I can do my billing at home. I'm not going to abandon you, sweetie. Don't you worry." She blew another reassuring kiss before leaving the room.

Gila lay in bed, racked with misery under her covers. Everything she was doing, and everything that she was about to do, would have made her mother very upset had she known. But Gila couldn't let her brothers go into possible danger without keeping a protective eye on them. Like her principal, the fourth-grader was an instinctive nurturer, with a deep need to ensure that those she loved were safe. Mrs. Wurtzler had nearly 80 students to care for; Gila had only her family. But for them, she would do anything.

She harbored a tiny hope that their mother's change in plans would induce her brothers to abandon their own. There was nothing she could do right now but hunker down under her covers, and wait and see.

Gila's dismay at learning that her mother was planning to work at home that day was mirrored — and multiplied — by her brothers'.

In the privacy of their room, they debated their options hotly. Chaim was resigned to putting off their hike for another day. For Donny, there *was* no other day. "It's now or never," he insisted. "When are we ever going to get such a good chance? When's our next day off from school? Not for ages, that's when! We just got one dumped right in our laps. We have to use it!"

"But Ma's going to be home."

"So? Since when can't we go out when she's home? She'll *expect* us to play outside! Besides, now that she has Gila to worry about, she'll focus even less on us. It's perfect."

Chaim was not so certain. On the other hand, he agreed with Donny that this opportunity was not likely to repeat itself in the near future. At last, reluctantly, he agreed to stick to the plan. "But let's wait until Ma goes to her office to pick up her work. That way, we won't have to explain where we're going."

"Okay," Danny agreed. "Let's leave her a note, though. So she won't worry."

"It might be better to just leave a message with Gila ..."

The next couple of hours dragged — for the Bernstein kids, at any rate. Tova hummed a tune as she worked in the kitchen, getting a head start on supper and chatting on the phone with her sister-in-law back East. There was something comforting in having her children home with her today. They were quiet this morning, Gila presumably resting while her brothers played or read in their room.

She turned off the oven and checked the clock: nearly 11. Time to run out to the medical center for the day's quota of billing work. She checked on Gila, threw a quick word of explanation to the boys, and was out the door.

Gila was lying in bed, listening to the silence, when a footstep in the hall made her quickly shut her eyes.

"Hey, Gila. You awake?" It was Donny.

"Mmm." She opened her eyes, pretending to have just woken from a light doze. "I am now. What's doing?"

"Nothing. Just wanted to make sure you're okay."

"It's only a stomachache. I'm fine."

"That's good." The look on Donny's face belied his words. "Uh, you don't want to overdo things, you know. Better get some rest."

"I *have* been resting."

Chaim poked his head in next. "Hi, Gila. How are you feeling?" Like his brother before him, he seemed very interested in her answer.

"All right. Getting a little better, I think."

"Well, I think you should spend the rest of the morning in bed. Take it easy. Read a book. Listen to a tape. Take a nap, if you want ... Me 'n Donny are going out for a while. You'll be okay till Ma gets back, right?"

"Where are you going?"

"Just out. We have a day off, we might as well use it."

"Outside, in the yard?" she pressed.

"We'll probably walk around a little — *if* you don't mind, Your Highness." Chaim gave her a quizzical, pursed-up face that made her laugh — as he'd intended it should.

"I don't mind," she said, not quite truthfully. "Have fun." She waited a beat. "What'll I tell Ma?"

"Just say we went out." Ma would be annoyed with them for leaving Gila on her own, but not nearly as annoyed as if she knew where they were headed.

"I'm not really supposed to be home alone," Gila tried.

"It'll only be for 10 minutes or so! Ma'll be home before you know it."

"Anyway, you have her cell-phone number. You can always call her if you get nervous." This from Donny.

"What's your rush?" Gila asked, struggling to conceal her rising apprehension. "Can't you wait till Mommy gets back?"

"We've got things to do," Donny said.

"Boy stuff," Chaim added, by way of explanation.

Gila's allegedly upset-stomach lurched. They were going ahead with their plans; that much was crystal clear. Which meant that she was going to have to go ahead with hers ...

They were gone. She heard them clattering down the hall, and then silence. Chaim had closed her door behind him when he went, so she didn't hear the rustle of backpacks being slung over shoulders — but she could imagine it. She could imagine it very well. Straining her ears for the sound of the front door closing behind them — or would they choose the back door? — she hardly realized that she was clenching her covers with both fists, so tightly that her hands hurt afterward.

There it was: the faint thud from downstairs that signaled the boys' departure. Gila sprang out of bed, raced over to her closet and began dressing at a frantic pace. She thrust her feet into her sneakers and ran a perfunctory brush through her hair. Then she flew out of the room and slammed through the front door like a hurricane wind.

The block that they lived on was long and level, and it was not hard to spot her brothers making their way toward the far end. After that, she knew, they would turn right toward the open area at the edge of town. The building site was about a mile past that, an easy walk on flat ground. Beyond stood the hills and canyons, Chaim and Donny's destination.

As they made the turn that would carry them out of sight, she quickened her pace almost to a run. She was glad that there were no pedestrians strolling the quiet streets at this hour, to witness what she was doing. Her stomach was really beginning to hurt now, with nervous tension. Her lungs did not like the exertion she was demanding of them; so far, however, they were cooperating.

She patted her pocket, to make sure her inhaler was there. After the last terrifying episode, she had promised her parents — and herself — to take it with her everywhere she went.

It was right where it belonged … which was more than could be said for Gila. Uneasily, she wondered what her mother would think when she came home to an empty house. Mommy would worry. Gila felt bad about that. But she couldn't turn back now.

She touched the inhaler in her pocket again, as though for luck. On she trotted, with only that paltry weapon in her pocket to protect her against whatever might lie ahead.

III.

If there was anything worse than having a miserable head cold, Avi reflected as he shuffled around his bachelor apartment in bathrobe and slippers, it was having a miserable head cold with no one around to feel sorry for you.

Avi had been devotedly feeding himself large portions of self-pity since the night before, when his cold had taken a turn for the worse. But there's no medicine like a friendly face: some congenial soul to ask how you're feeling and to offer tea, or chicken soup, or even just a smile. Someone to be there when you're at your lowest physical ebb. Someone to share the burden of simply living your life.

Someone like … a wife.

He winced at the thought, because for the first time, the word "wife" did not conjure up his lost Yocheved. This morning, he envisioned a different face. In his present weakened state, he lacked his usual resistance. He recalled Shiffy Taub as he'd last seen her, walking him to the door of her parents' house and never dreaming that, in passing through that door, he would be walking right out of her life. She had been laughing at some remembered antic of Tzvi's, he recalled, and was still smiling as she held the door open for him. She'd been relaxed, prepared for a leisurely good-bye. Instead, Avi's had been brief to the point of curtness. He had hurried away as though every creature in childhood's monster gallery was after him, but not before he caught a glimpse of her stunned face as she watched him go.

Gritting his teeth, Avi wrenched his mind away from the memory. Here he was with a whole day ahead of him, to spend any way he pleased. He ought to rest during a portion of it, he knew, but surely he would have enough energy to get in some good learning time. He might also catch up on phone calls to old friends back East.

Thinking of phone calls reminded him that he owed his mother a call. He had been avoiding her ever since his cowardly flight from New York, but it wasn't right to cause Ma pain just because he had cut and run. He stood for a long moment in frozen immobility, then walked to the phone and picked up the receiver. The number was one he knew by heart, of course, and his fingers dialed it almost by rote.

She answered on the second ring. "Avi? Is that you?"

"It's me, Ma."

"How are you, Avi? I've been worried about you."

I've been worried about me, too …

"I've got a cold, but it's nothing to worry about." Pause. "Ma?"

"Yes, Avi?"

"I'm sorry I haven't been in touch. I've had some things to work out. In my head, you know …"

She waited.

"Ma?"

When he didn't go on immediately, Mrs. Feder prompted. "I'm still here. What is it, Avi?"

"Do you …" The question trailed off in a paroxysm of coughing. Avi choked out an, "Excuse me," went to the sink for a drink of water, and returned to the phone.

"Ma?"

"Still here."

"I wanted to ask you something …"

"So ask already. What is it?"

"Ma … D-do you still have her number?"

A three-second silence met his words. Then it was his mother's turn to clear her throat. "Her number? You mean, Shiffy Taub? That nice girl you treated so badly?"

He closed his eyes. "Yes. Can you reach her?"

"Why should she want to hear from either one of us, after the way you acted?"

"Because I want you to give her a message from me, Ma. I … want you to tell her that I'm sorry. That I was … scared."

"And?" Relentless, she pressed him to the wall.

He gave up. "And that I hope she'll forgive me …"

"*And?*"

He hesitated, but only a second. "And … and … If she'll agree to forgive me, I want very much … to meet her again."

"Ah …" There was relief and jubilation in his mother's voice. Then a cautious note crept in. "Avi? You won't hurt her again, will you? You'll be a *mensch*?"

"Whatever happens, Ma," he sighed, "I'll try to be a *mensch*."

"Good. I'll call her right away."

The line went dead even before Avi could tender his farewell or his thanks. He stood with the receiver in his hand for quite some time, his cold forgotten. His brain felt dazed. But something was happening in the inner regions where his heart was supposed to be. In the long winter of his grieving, he had scarcely remembered that he still had one. But it was certainly making its presence felt now, in exhibiting all the signs of a slow, and sometimes excruciatingly painful, spring thaw.

The moment he cradled the receiver, the silence was shattered by a shrill ring. Still feeling slightly shell shocked, he picked up the phone again.

"Avi? Is that you? You sound different."

He recognized the voice of his new friend, Nate Goodman. "Yes, it's me, Nate. Chalk it up to a stuffy nose ... How are you?"

"Great, *Baruch Hashem*. I didn't see you at Shacharis this morning, and Nachman Bernstein told me you're not coming in to the *kollel* today. What are you doing home?"

"It's this cold. I gave the boys the day off and stayed home to rest."

"Oh, that's too bad. Hope you feel better soon ..."

"Actually, I'm already feeling a lot better." Thinking of his recent call to his mother, and of its possible consequences, Avi's heart felt capable of soaring right out of his chest. Cold symptoms seemed trivial in comparison.

"You do? That's terrific. Listen, Avi. A meeting just got canceled and I've got itchy feet. It's such a gorgeous day that I thought I'd drive out to the site of the new *kollel* and have a look around. I haven't been there yet, you know."

"I didn't know that."

"I'd like to see where the arson was perpetrated. And it's so pleasant outside that I thought I'd take advantage of the opportunity to get a little fresh air and exercise, too. Maybe hike up into the cliffs, where all those caves are. Care to join me?"

Avi was about to return an automatic "no." He had stayed home with a cold, hadn't he? What good would traipsing about outside do him?

All the good in the world, he suddenly realized. The four walls of his home seemed suddenly as confining as a prison cell. His newfound hopes had expanded his consciousness to the point where remaining inside a limited space was unbearable. At the thought of clean, dry air and blue sky bisected by red cliffs, he was besieged by an overpowering influx of restless energy.

"A little fresh air would do wonders for a cold, wouldn't it?" he murmured. "Give me 15 minutes to pull myself together, Nate."

"You've got it," Nate said. "Bring a water bottle, if you've got one."

"Will do."

"See you in a quarter of an hour, then. Listen for my honk."

Shimi had not slept well. Luckily for him, there were no classes that day, so his mother let him sleep in relatively late next morning. His own thoughts proved more potent than any alarm clock, however, and he was out of bed and into his clothes long before Etty had expected to see him downstairs.

He *davened* and gulped down the breakfast that his mother insisted he eat, though everything tasted like paper this morning. Afterward he wandered up to his room and tried, unsuccessfully, to settle down to some activity or other. An hour later, his bed was littered with books he hadn't bothered to read and games he hadn't been able to muster the interest to play. What were Chaim and Donny doing right now, this very minute? Had they decided to go through with their plan to hike up into the cliffs? If so, he ought to stop them. He ought to tell their parents about the intended hike, and the danger it posed for his friends.

But something in him cowered at bearing tales. Maybe Rabbi and Mrs. Bernstein would blame him for not stopping the boys when he had the chance. How could he explain that he had tried, but they wouldn't listen? As determined as he was to keep them out of trouble, they seemed equally set on ignoring any possible danger. But then, *they* hadn't come face-to-face with those horrible Indians that day, and heard their threats …

He tried to block out the memory, as well as his worries about Chaim and Donny — to pretend that nothing was happening, and enjoy the rare freedom of a day off from lessons. But his enjoyment proved elusive. He couldn't pretend he was having fun, especially not to himself. His friends were headed for possible disaster, and no one knew about it but him. How could he sit around and do nothing?

He couldn't. By 11:15, he was dialing the Bernsteins' number.

No answer. So they *had* gone. Shimi's insides clenched with a sudden escalation of the nervous tension he'd been battling all morning.

"Bye, Ma!" he shouted as he sprinted to the door.

"Where are you going?" Etty's voice, coming from the rear of the house, sounded disembodied.

"Out. I'm going to try and find Chaim and Donny."

It was only much later that Etty would remember her son's odd turn of phrase. He hadn't said, "I'm going over to Chaim and Donny's." He'd said, "I'm going to *try and find* Chaim and Donny" …

But she was busy diapering Layala at the moment, so the words eluded her conscious mind and lodged deep in her subconscious one, to be held up for scrutiny later, at a time when Etty Mandel's mind would be focused exclusively on Shimi in a way that it hadn't been in a long while.

IV.

*I*n the dream, he sat unmoving for a long time, until sun peeked over the rim of the desert and the boy — by now, a sturdy youth — finished his soldier's meal before the big annual hunt. He watched as, like the other hunters of the tribe, the boy mounted his horse. The riders set forth in clouds of dust across the plain. Along with the women and children, Steve gazed after the horsemen until they were nothing but tiny black specks in the distance. And then the long, waving grasses swallowed those specks, too, and there was nothing to be seen but the rippling prairie.

The last one to turn away was the girl, sister of the youth who'd just galloped away with the others. Taller now, and more graceful, but with the same sad eyes, she rejoined the other young women at the water hole. Steve stayed where he was, heart aching, gazing at nothing. With a deep and grieving certainty, he knew that when the hunters returned, triumphantly bearing their haunches of bison and piles of fur to last them through the winter, there would be one — a youth with eyes that were different — who would not be returning with them.

Steve Birch woke up with dry mouth and pounding heart. The dreams were driving him crazy. They were coming more frequently now, and their power seemed to have increased to the point where he found it hard to shake them off even during the daylight hours. At odd moments of the day he would catch glimpses of the nighttime scenes, like flashes of poignant memory. These glimpses left him feeling sad and haunted for hours afterward.

He climbed out of bed and poured himself a glass of water from the pitcher in the fridge. The air outside his window was the pearly gray of incipient morning. To the east, had the window been facing that way, he would have seen dawn's rosy glow filling the horizon like red wine pouring slowly into a wide, wide goblet. Where he stood, facing west, sunrise came only as a lightening of the dark, with white turning to gray turning to a pale, pale blue. As he gazed out, he had a sudden longing to witness the sunrise. Watching a new morning unfold would, he hoped, banish the disturbing visions that had been haunting his nights. Besides, he knew he would never get back to sleep now.

Dressing took just minutes. He picked up the little Jewish prayer book. His fingers traced the faded gilt star on the cover, then the words in their unknown tongue on the brittle pages inside. Rabbi Bernstein had told him that Jews pray facing toward Jerusalem, in the east of the world. Putting the book down, he went downstairs to a silent street and stood in the first light of dawn, his face to the sun. There were certain blessings, according to Rabbi Bernstein, that a Jew recited to G-d every morning. Steve didn't know what those blessings were, nor could he have recited them in Hebrew even if he'd known where to find them in the prayer book. So he stood with the pale early sun on his face and thought a private little prayer in his mind: *G-d, if You're there, please show me my way. I'm about as lost as a person can be. So lost that I don't even know who I am anymore ... Just point Your finger at the right path, and that's the path I'll take. O.K.?*

He didn't really expect an answer, so he wasn't disappointed when none was forthcoming. But the deepening color in the eastern sky seemed answer enough. Compared to the faith he was just beginning to explore, the Mescalero myths with which he'd been raised seemed like fairy tales beside a mighty epic, a childish watercolor next to the work of a Renaissance master. It seemed there was a Creator, and He had put all of this together — the sun and the sky, the desert and the majestic mesas that paled to insignificance beside His glory — so Steve wanted to find out more about Him.

Maybe he would go see Rabbi Bernstein again today. The rabbi had said he might have some news for him soon. Steve wondered what it was, and how it would change his life. Because it seemed pretty clear to him that his life was poised for change, perhaps in a very big way ...

Things had been changing in Lakewood, too. He frowned, thinking of the arson and the other incidents, culminating in a tire-slashing by some ridiculously pathetic drunkard. Who had set him up to do it? A face flashed into Steve's mind: Bobby Smith's. On some instinctive level, the attorney had been growing increasingly convinced that Smith was the force behind these ugly happenings. There were just too many coincidences unaccounted for, too many times that Bobby had appeared where he was not supposed to be, too much sly evasiveness when questioned. On impulse, Steve decided to drive over to the reservation. Maybe he could find someone there who was close to Smith, and who might shed some light on his recent activities.

He climbed into his car, turned on the ignition and listened to the engine shatter the early-morning stillness. All around, people were still sleeping. Things should be stirring, he hoped, by the time he reached Mescalero. Pointing the car west, with his back to Lakewood and the distant Jerusalem of his rudimentary prayers, he started down the familiar road that would lead him back to the place he had always called home.

As the miles rolled away beneath his wheels, a dream he'd had a few days earlier replayed itself irresistibly in his mind. It had not been about the sad-eyed girl that time, or the boy on the cusp of manhood. Once again, he'd dreamed of his grandmother.

Grandma Hook, he used to call her. Everyone had called her that, for some long-forgotten reason. If she'd once had a different name, Steve didn't know what it was.

In the dream, Grandma Hook again took him by the hand and led him outside. This time, she didn't point out the constellations. She stared soberly out at the limitless sky, its blackness mirrored in her eyes.

"Alice is a dreamer," she said abruptly, startling the dream-Steve so that he clutched her hand and said, "What?" Alice was Grandma's daughter, and Steve's mother.

"Alice," she said again, clearly, "is a dreamer. Don't you be like her, Stevie. You keep both feet on the ground! You've got to look into things — find things out — change direction if you have to." A deep sadness filled the ancient, dark eyes. "Alice never knew how to do that. She dreamed her way through life until she married that no-good Henry Jones, who was and will always be married to his bottle. A miserable life he led her — except for you. You were always the light in her life, Stevie. Don't let the light go out ..."

And the stars themselves seemed to echo: "Don't let the light go out ..."

Even in recollection, the dream retained a strange power. Steve gripped the wheel tighter, as though his own two hands could find the way to steer his life's course. *Don't let the light go out ...*

But all his hands on the wheel could do right then was lead him back to the place where he'd grown up, and from which he'd escaped as soon as he was able. Words he vaguely recalled floated into his mind: "There is no light without darkness, and it is essential to know the night." *Perhaps,* he thought whimsically, *it's necessary to walk in the shadow for a while before you can step out into the full light of day.* The reservation, if nothing else, had been the precursor, the jumping-off point, for the remainder of his life. From its shade, he was still straining for a glimpse of the light on the other side.

The place looked just the same as ever: a collection of grayish, dilapidated buildings that appeared discouraged even in the light of the new day. Tumbleweed balls drifted down the street past tired-looking cars. Steve parked in the shade cast by a scrawny oak and got out. He wasn't sure what he was looking for, so he started strolling, letting his feet guide him.

They had taken him past one row of houses to the start of another, when he heard a voice calling out to him from a window. It was an old woman's voice. For a startled instant, Steve had the unreal sensation that he was back in his dream, being hailed by his Grandma Hook.

"Hey, you!" The voice held a curious combination of frailty and strength. A moment later, a figure came hobbling out of the building to make its slow but determined way to where Steve stood.

She was old, older even than his grandmother in the dream, who had looked about the age she had been when she passed away: 85. Her skin was like dry leather, her limbs wizened though retaining an almost youthful wiry strength. She planted herself in front of Steve, grasped her walking cane with both seamed hands and glared at him with eyes that were half-angry, half-pleading.

"Where is my grandson?" she demanded.

"Pardon me, ma'am," Steve said politely. "Who might your grandson be?"

"You know who he be, Steve Birch," the old woman glared. "You *are* Steve Birch, aren't you? The fancy lawyer?"

"I don't know about 'fancy' — but, yes, I am a lawyer. And your grandson is ...?"

"Jim Littletree."

"The one they call Big Jim?"

She nodded, sending wisps of thin white hair flying about her head. "That's him. My grandson. Do you know where he is?"

"I'm sorry, but how would I be expected to know that, ma'am?"

"He's been living in Lakewood — with that no-good Bobby Smith. I thought you might have seen him there. You have your office in Lakewood, don't you?"

Steve acknowledged the truth of this fact. "But I haven't seen Jim around lately. I did speak to him about a week ago, but not since then."

"Well, what's he been up to?" Every wrinkle in the walnut face deepened in consternation. "He's a good boy, my Jimmy. Never been too strong up top" — she pointed to her forehead — "but his heart's in the right place. But ever since he hooked up with that Bobby, he's been acting strange. Going off all hours of the day and night, and finally moving off the reservation altogether. Temporarily, he told me, but I know better. Once they get a taste for city life, they're gone."

Steve suppressed a smile at her conferring "city" status on tiny Lakewood.

"City life ruined that Bobby Smith," she went on, glaring at him. "I won't let that happen to my Jimmy!"

His voice was calm, reassuring. "I'm sure he's doing fine, ma'am. If I run into him, I'll be sure and let you know." He waited a beat. "In fact, I've been hoping to run into Bobby Smith myself. Any clue where he might be?"

"How would I know?" she spat. The walking stick tapped a frustrated tattoo on the sunbaked ground. "It's my Jimmy I'm caring about, not that so-called friend of his."

"These days, Big Jim tends to be wherever Bobby is," Steve reminded her gently.

She shook her head. "I don't know. I don't know ... Nobody tells an old woman nothing ..."

"Well, I'll give Jim your regards if I see him."

"Tell him to visit his old grandma. And you tell him" — the old woman's eyes welled with sudden tears — "tell him to mind his step. I don't trust that Bobby Smith far as I can throw him."

Neither do I. Steve kept the thought to himself. "Good-bye, Grandmother," he said softly, using the traditional Apache honorific.

She nodded her own good-bye, and turned away.

Half an hour later, he was back in his car. Apart from his encounter with Jim Littletree's grandmother, he had met no one at this early hour of the morning with any useful information to offer. The drinkers were still sleeping off last night's excesses; family men were home, getting ready for the day's work; housewives were tending to their children. Later, the reservation's idlers would make their appearance in pubs and on street corners; right now, they were busily doing nothing in the privacy of their own homes. The smoke of many chimneys curled into the sky across the reservation. It was practically the only sign of life that Birch saw.

He headed back to Lakewood.

Just before entering the town proper, he swerved off to the left. Another impulse: to visit the site of the arsonist's work. His personal quest for an identity that he could believe in seemed to have become all mixed up with his search for the perpetrators of the recent spate of anti-Jewish crimes. He was letting himself be guided by blind instinct ... or perhaps by the One G-d that Rabbi Bernstein had mentioned to him. Either way, he felt incapable of stopping. He must keep moving, keep following the inner voice — Divine or otherwise — that urged him onward.

He found the narrow road that ended in a dirt track, which in turn led directly onto the building site. Eventually a paved road would connect this site to the town. Now he was forced to abandon his car and make the rest of his way on foot.

He squinted into the strengthening sun, at the rust-red cliffs that had been crouching here since time immemorial. The cliffs were dotted with caves, staring down at him like so many soulless eyes. Why had he come here? A foolish impulse, dredged up by his desire for activity and his hatred of feeling useless. The construction site was just that, and no more: a blank stretch of land, with only a couple of signs, a portable shack and one lone bulldozer to show that building was slated to begin in the near future. Whatever he had expected to find, it wasn't here. He turned to go.

Out of the corner of his eye, he saw something move.

There was a flash of color and motion high up on one of the trails that led to the ragged line of caves. A figure was toiling up the trail. It looked too small to be an adult.

What was a kid doing out there, on his own? Steve had been blessed with particularly keen eyesight, and when the trail twisted at a certain angle he could see something that had eluded him before. The boy was wearing a yarmulke on his head.

Without an instant's hesitation, Steve started up after him.

V.

"Well, well, well!" Earl Flaxen shook out his napkin and spread it across his ample lap. "Just like old times, eh?"

Heidi could not remember ever having had lunch with her boss, but she nodded dutifully and offered a polite smile to match his own. With what the firm liked to refer to as its "religious sensibility" toward its employees, the restaurant of choice was dairy and it was kosher.

Heidi had little appetite. It was odd sitting here, facing her boss across the small table, while other diners clinked fork to plate all around her and Manhattan roared by outside. Beneath the geniality, Flaxen was all steel. His sharp gaze made her feel like an experimental animal pinned under a lab light, with the threat of dissection lurking ominously in the wings. Not a very comfortable image to take to the table ...

Somehow she placed her order, though a moment later she could not recall what it was. This was crunch time: the moment when she picked up her old life and subjected it to a good, hard look. And right now, that life was represented by silver-haired Earl Flaxen, who offered an avuncular smile that showed every one of his shark-white teeth.

"Bet you've been missing all this, eh?" Still the jovial-uncle manner, calculated to put her at her ease. Heidi wished he would draw off the velvet gloves and get down to the business of this lunch: her future, if any, at Flaxen, Domb and Tremaine.

He kept up a patter of inconsequential chatter as they waited for their food to arrive. Heidi did her best to hold up her end. Flaxen seemed determined to put her at her ease, which boded well, Heidi thought, for her chances at reinstatement. On the other hand, she was still not really sure that reinstatement was what she wanted. It was a relief to see the waitress bearing down on them, at last, with two loaded plates.

Flaxen speared a piece of salmon with his fork and directed a look at Heidi that was abruptly all business. "So," he said — the geniality suddenly boasted a thin coating of ice — "tell me about it."

"About what, sir?" She was hedging, and they both knew it.

"About why you disappeared on us these past weeks. You were very vague on the phone. Were you ill?"

"You could say that, sir. Only — not physically. It was more of an ... emotional overload, I suppose you could call it."

"Were we working you too hard?" The words were concerned, the tone less so. Associates could never work too hard. That would contravene natural law, as laid down by Earl Flaxen and partners.

"I'm not sure how to answer that. All I know is that I snapped. I needed a vacation, and I took it. I deeply regret if the firm was inconvenienced. Believe me, that was not my intention."

"I do believe you, Heidi. However, you look fine to me now. Are you completely recovered from ... whatever it was?"

"Yes," she said simply.

A relieved smile overspread her boss's face. "Good! Good! Then when can we expect to see you back at the office? Tomorrow would not be too soon as far as we — and your clients — are concerned."

"I'm afraid tomorrow would be a little too soon for me. May I have 24 hours to think things over, before I commit myself?"

Disappointment turned Flaxen's face to stone. "I don't really see what all this talk of 'commitment' is about, Heidi. You're already committed. You're a Flaxen, Domb lawyer. And the lawyer, I may add, with the most impressive billing sheet it has ever been my pleasure to see!" He handed her the compliment like a king rewarding a serf — or, Heidi thought, a man throwing a bone to a dog.

Impassively, she said, "I still need the time, sir."

He leaned forward. "Heidi, I'm going to tell you something in strict confidence. We've been looking at some of our associates and talking about who's next in line to make junior partner." After a pause for dramatic effect, he lowered his voice to a near-whisper: "Guess what, Heidi? You're next in line!"

"Uh, thank you, sir." She felt sandbagged.

"Junior partner in Flaxen, Domb and Tremaine, with added income, benefits and a nice little bonus package to boot. Not to mention a stellar future waiting in the wings for you." He spread his arms with a broad smile. "Now, tell me — does it get better than that?"

Does it get better than that? The words boomed like a death knell in her brain. *Yes,* she thought suddenly. *I think it does get better. Lots better …*

She looked at him. "Twenty-four hours, sir?"

"Oh, all right." He sat back in exasperation. "You've got your 24. But after that, I want to see you back where you belong, racking up those hours for the firm!"

Heidi smiled noncommittally, before finally addressing herself to the meal she couldn't remember ordering.

Another couple was having a meal of sorts at that same hour, thousands of miles away, in a hospital cafeteria in Roswell, New Mexico.

Asher and Rivi Gann, having concluded their appointment with the specialist, felt strangely reluctant to get into their car and simply head for home. The doctor's words had been so encouraging, the entire meeting so heady with hope, that neither of them could bear the thought of returning to routine so soon.

"Let's see what we can pick up to nosh on in the cafeteria," Asher had suggested.

To their delight, they found — in addition to fresh fruit — an entire wall of prepackaged snacks and baked goods, many of which sported acceptable kashrus symbols. Like children let loose in a toy store, they filled their tray with all sorts of goodies, though Rivi insisted that they not neglect the fruit counter. A single orange sat in lone splendor amid Asher's trayful of snacks and cakes, while Rivi had opted for a large red apple.

They sat facing each other across a tiny table in the corner. All around them, weary orderlies and harried nurses snatched a bite to eat, while patients' relatives forced down a meal with the dogged air of those for whom time in the world outside has lost its meaning. Watching them, Rivi felt a pang of guilt at her own wonderful life. The only thing that was missing to complete her happiness — children of her own — had just been nudged a little more closely into the realm of the possible by the doctor upstairs. He had done some impressive research in his own right, and the new regimen of treatments he'd recommended was different from the others. This hospital, tucked into its dry, Southwestern setting like an egg in a nest, felt different, too. And "different" sometimes spelled "change" ...

She looked at her husband. "You know how I found this doctor?" she asked softly. "It was the day of Layala Mandel's surgery — when Etty came in, and I was so hurt. On my way out of the building, I got off on the wrong floor and found myself facing a sign that said, 'Fertility Specialists.' After that episode with Etty's baby, the sign was like a slap in the face ... or a hand stretched out, offering comfort ... I took it as comfort, and went in. And now," she looked around the cafeteria, then back at her husband, "here we are ..."

"As far as I'm concerned," Asher said staunchly, "we have never stopped hoping or *davening*."

Rivi had to smile at Asher's matter-of-factness, which robbed even such a fraught area in their lives of much of the emotional tension that might have choked and strangled it. It was this trait, among so many others, that made him such a pillar of strength for her.

"Whatever happens," she said, "I'm glad you were my *bashert*."

"Well!" He leaned back in his seat, feigning outrage. "I should hope so! Where could you possibly find a more amazing husband than me?"

"Nowhere," she said meekly.

"And don't you forget it!"

Laughing, they fell to their wacky meal as though they hadn't eaten in days.

Heidi walked away from the restaurant through a blur of noise and traffic, stopping briefly in a favorite store to browse. After weeks without any real shopping, she'd had the vague idea that she might buy herself a little something, to celebrate her recovery from whatever it was that had left her an emotional basket case for a while. But nothing appealed to her. She didn't have the patience, today, to look further.

The thought of her unwelcoming apartment made the thought of going directly home unpalatable. Her own four walls seemed intent on punishing her for her prolonged absence. Or was it she who was punishing herself? To put off the moment for as long as she could, she wandered in the direction of her favorite park instead, the small green square that seemed to breathe defiance in the face of the surrounding skyscrapers.

She found "her" bench, thankfully unoccupied at present. Wishing she could kick off her shoes, she leaned back and closed her eyes. The city receded into a faint blur of noise, like white static on the radio. Was that all it had ever been?

She wondered when, exactly, the city had ceased to exert its old fascination on her. Perhaps it had happened beneath the cottonwood tree on Tova's front lawn, where silence and blue skies had shown her a different reality. The buildings and excitement and ambition that had lured her so powerfully for so long had lost their ability to tempt her. The magic had been stripped from them. Sometime in recent weeks, Manhattan had imperceptibly changed from "home," to "a nice place to visit." How had it happened?

Her sojourn away from the bright lights had changed her, she realized. It had taught her that there was greatness that didn't depend on size, and accomplishment that didn't have an hourly price tag. She was gazing into the face of a different map now; one whose topography was less soaring and dramatic, but which offered a worthier destination.

If she looked past the glittering skyscrapers, she could just glimpse a different sort of life, and a different sort of future. While the details were still vague, she knew it would be life where the tempo was slower but the rewards more real. A life where her mind might not be as keenly challenged, but her heart would be at peace.

A life in which she would be needed, not for her ability to inflate the revenues of an already-bloated law firm, but simply for who she was and for what she might bring to others.

It was also a life that would finally offer the time she so desperately needed to address her inner self: the soul she'd neglected for too long.

Too many years had been wasted already, in the vain worship of the career god. Belatedly, she could turn her attention to the real thing: to the Creator Who had been patiently waiting for her to remember Him.

Her eyes dimmed with remorseful tears. He had been so good to her, and she'd repaid Him by putting emptiness before substance, and vanity before truth. Three-quarters of the life she had led up to this moment had been as fleeting and insubstantial, she knew now, as the lights she loved to watch reflecting off the river at night. She had been in hot pursuit of an illusion.

Was it too late to change?

Resolutely, she opened eyes and rose to her feet. There was only one way to find out. The Heidi Neufeld she'd known for the past 35 years was resolute and resourceful. Till now, she'd put those hefty weapons to use in fighting empty battles. Here was one war she would be able to embark on with joy and from which she hoped one day, with Hashem's help, to emerge victorious.

The message light on her phone was blinking when she got home. She pressed the appropriate button to glean more details.

"Hello." The voice teased the edges of her memory with a pressing familiarity, though she could not immediately identify it. "I hope you get this message. This is Pinchas Harris."

Rabbi Harris. Her heart picked up speed. She leaned closer to the machine, straining to catch every syllable.

"I've had a long talk with Nate, and he asked me to call to let you know where he stands." A pause for the rabbi to draw breath — and for Heidi to simmer with nervous impatience. "He'd very much like to see you again. If you feel the same way, he says it's his turn to visit you on your turf. Today is Thursday; he's prepared to get on a plane *Motza'ei Shabbos* and be in New York on Sunday. Please call back to let me know if this works for you."

The voice recited a number, then clicked off. Heidi found herself grinning foolishly at the empty room. She stood quite still beside her desk — the desk that had seen her burn the midnight oil on so many solitary nights — and her eyes moved to the window, where Manhattan lay spread out for her admiration, like a map of a fantasy land she had visited once and never forgotten.

The visit, she realized with dawning clarity, was over.

She faced the window, and the dazzling panorama no longer had the power to touch her.

"Manhattan," she whispered, "you're history."

She picked up the phone, and with great solemnity, dialed Rabbi Harris's number. In a few quick words, she agreed to the plan.

"Good. That's very good. Wonderful, in fact!" The rabbi's elation was apparent in every syllable. "Nate will be thrilled." A pause. "He *is* concerned about one thing. Except for Sunday, he'll be in New York during the workweek. He knows what a big-city lawyer's life is like. He hopes you'll be able to find time to meet with him."

"Don't worry, Rabbi." In her cubicle of space high above the city, Heidi smiled. "It turns out I'm going to have plenty of free time next week. Lots and lots of free time ..."

She had needed only one of the allotted 24 hours to make her decision, after all.

VI.

"This is it," Avi said, brandishing an arm at the modest sign announcing the purpose of the planned construction project. "Welcome to the new *kollel* and *mesivta* building ... one day."

"That day shouldn't be too far off, from what I hear," Nate remarked. "Your *Rosh Kollel* is doing a fine job of getting the ball rolling."

"Nachman Bernstein is one of a kind," Avi agreed absently. He was finding it hard to keep his mind on the conversation. All his thoughts were centered in New York, where his mother could be making that all-important phone call at that very moment.

"He sure is," Nate agreed. He, too, was distracted. How could he not be, with a plane ticket on his desk at home waiting to whisk him off to New York.

"Ready to hike?" Avi's voice penetrated his thoughts as though from a great distance.

"Sure." Nate turned to the rust-colored cliffs and led the way to the foot of the trail. Each hot, dry breath seared the lungs. Midday was not the best hour for a hike; but this was the only time he had. Seize the moment ...

The two men weren't halfway up the first curve of the trail, when a chance remark by one of them led to a spate of confidences and a confession of deeply cherished hopes. Deep in conversation, neither Avi nor Nate had any idea that they were not alone on the trail. They didn't know that Chaim, Donny and then Gila Bernstein had launched themselves on these trails before them; lost to sight at the moment but very much present. They were also unaware that Shimi Mandel was following hard on their heels.

Nor, had they known, would they have paid much attention. Both had far more pressing things on their minds at the moment.

Though summer was over, the day promised to be a scorcher. As the temperature climbed, even in this dry climate Chaim felt the sweat beginning to trickle down his back under his knapsack. It was uncomfortable, to say the least.

Even more uncomfortable were his gnawing fears. He would never have admitted as much to his brother, but Shimi's warnings had induced in him a more-or-less permanent state of nervous tension. For two cents, he would have turned right around and gone home.

But nobody offered him two cents, and Donny was insistent that they forge ahead. The prospect of action — any action — was always more attractive to Donny than inaction. As for consideration of the risks involved — his mind simply didn't "go" there. If anything, Shimi's warnings had only whetted his appetite for adventure. Donny was primed for a morning's fun. He moved ahead of his brother, eager to explore the next bend in the trail. Somewhere above their heads, a line of caves waited with hungry, open mouths. For Donny, the sight was a challenge and a lure.

For Chaim, they spelled something else, something that sent a shiver up his spine. But big brothers can't admit to having shivers, not when their younger brothers are being so brave and persevering. So he squared his shoulders, wiped the perspiration from his brow, and trudged along in Donny's wake.

Behind them, Gila was having a hard time of it. Unlike her brothers, she did not spend most of her free time playing ball and engaging in other activities that promote muscle strength and endurance. It was with labored breath and gasping lungs that she toiled along behind Chaim and Donny, trying as much as possible to stay out of their line of sight. From time to time she fingered the inhaler in her pocket, as though for reassurance.

It was growing hotter. Gila saw the boys stop to take a drink, and wished she'd thought of bringing a water bottle along. Part of her — the sensible part — thought, *You silly! Why not just catch up with them and ask for a drink? Or, better yet, just go home!*

But there was the memory of a sinister shadow in the schoolyard, and the determination in her brothers' voices as they planned this outing. It bade her stay hidden — to hold herself in reserve, so to speak, for such time as she might be needed. She didn't know how, and she didn't know when, but something told her that she had a part to play in today's events.

And if that "something" turned out to have been speaking nonsense — well, she could always go home and have her drink then.

On she plodded, making sure always to keep her brothers in sight. When the heat and her own exertions finally forced her to stop and rest, she closed her eyes momentarily against the punishing sun. She opened them again and blinked. Her heart skipped a beat. Her brothers had vanished.

Then reason resumed her throne: They had probably started up the trail and were lost to sight around a bend. Her eyes moved up the cliff wall, with its line of caves waiting like open mouths. She stood up and started walking again, making for the foot of the most visible trail, the one she and her siblings had taken in the summer.

Whatever happened, Chaim and Donny would not be alone.

"This trail is going nowhere," Donny said in disgust.

He and Chaim had chosen a different route this time, and despite a promising beginning they found this trail far less interesting than the one they had taken the previous summer. For one thing, it was more difficult to follow, being nearly obscured in places by tumbled rocks and dry growth. And, for another, instead of carrying them upward, it seemed to traverse the cliff wall almost horizontally, so that the boys soon found themselves moving in a circuitous path that ran roughly parallel to the caves above.

Chaim agreed with his brother's assessment. Their hike was turning out to be no fun at all. He was hot and perspiring and his feet were beginning to hurt. They had planned to picnic in one of the caves, but the way things looked now, they would have to find their way down and start all over again on the other trail in order to do that. It didn't seem worth the effort.

A bird wheeled and shrieked right above his head, its slanting shadow blotting out the light for an instant. The cry, overly harsh in the silence, jangled Chaim's nerves, and the sudden shadow sent a shiver up his spine. Abruptly, he stopped walking. He looked around him as though yanked from a deep sleep.

What am I doing here?

He had left Gila alone at home. He'd probably induced, if not panic, then certainly a degree of worry, in his mother. And for what? For an adventure that was really no adventure at all. The spice of danger — that Shimi's warning had once added — had gone flat. He had absolutely no desire to meet those Indians again. Coming out here like this, with bad guys running around loose in the area, was like sticking your head in a noose. Just plain stupid. Which meant that *he* was being stupid. Standing on the pebble-strewn path, watching his brother forge on ahead of him, Chaim experienced an acute sense of his own failing. He had acted irresponsibly: he, the older one. He should have known better than to let Donny's reckless enthusiasm be his guide.

Donny was walking on, oblivious to both the bird's raucous call and his brother's state of mind. Tightening his mouth into a thin line, Chaim hurried to catch up. He had a thing or two to tell Donny before either of them took another step. Taking command, he decided that the next few steps they would be taking, would be an "about-face" and a "forward march" — right back down that trail toward sanity, safety, and home.

Shimi Mandel, having started out some 20 minutes after the Bernstein boys and 15 minutes after Gila, was bringing up the rear in this little procession.

He was angry. Angry for being so helpless to deter his friends, and angry with himself, too, for the compulsion that had him sweating his way to the outskirts of Lakewood in the broiling sun. What use would he be if any of them ran into those Indians? The previous time, he had simply frozen in fear. In the aftermath of that little encounter, he had spent days and nights holed up in his room like a wounded bear. After all his efforts to dissuade Chaim and Donny from taking this foolhardy step, they'd decided to ignore his warnings and go ahead anyway. It was with a sense of fatalism that he followed them now. There was nothing he could do to prevent another nasty encounter, if those Indians were still skulking in the cliffs. Nothing, except bear witness. And that, in itself, called for more courage than he was certain he possessed.

Shimi was far enough behind so that neither the boys nor Gila was visible to him. He was moving on instinct, making for the same trail that he and his friends had taken the other time. It was the most accessible of the trails winding up from the foot of the ocher cliffs, and he was all but certain that this was the one they would take.

Like Gila, he was regretting the impulsive haste that had made him leave his water bottle at home. His mouth was parched, the palms of his hands incongruously damp. Sharp pebbles dug into the soles of his sneakers as he plowed on, moving ever higher up the cliff face. Above, the sky was a piercing blue, and the rock walls had never glowed so crimson in the sun. He squinted up the trail; a pair of sunglasses would have come in handy, too. He started to climb.

Below, the ground spun away in descending spirals. He fixed his eyes on the trail, which required attention if he was not to stumble and rip yet another pair of pants. Some minutes later, he was approaching the curve in the trail startlingly similar to the one where he had run into the Indians that day.

His pulse began to jump. There was no sign that anyone was nearby but, then again, he had seen no sign that other time. Imperceptibly, his step slowed. It was an effort to lift his feet. A leaden weight seemed to be dragging him back, urging him to full-scale retreat.

Chaim and Donny. I can't let them down, he thought fiercely. If he had been more effective in his warnings, they wouldn't be out here today, vulnerable to danger. If he had told his parents ... Well, if he'd told his parents, none of them would be here. They would be safe at home, and those sinister Indians would be free to rampage to their heart's content. Not that he wanted them to be free to rampage against his community or anyone else. He simply felt powerless to do anything to stop them.

Sucking in a lungful of dry, hot air, he forced himself forward. Three steps brought him to the bend in the trail, and two more rounded it.

He sat down to rest a moment and as he did, he heard the sound of someone approaching from behind. Up the trail came a stranger. As he lifted his face to the boy's, Shimi had a glimpse of tanned, Native American features and unusual hazel eyes narrowed in surprise.

The man was wearing a well-tailored shirt and pants, very different from the way the other pair had looked in their grimy jeans and T-shirts. But he was undoubtedly an *Indian*. Shimi went as rigid as the rocky ground on which he stood.

It was like the repetition of a nightmare. He longed to run away as fast as his feet could carry him, but his feet refused to cooperate. *I knew it, I knew it*, droned a fatalistic voice in his head. He stood rooted to the spot, staring at the stranger in speechless terror.

Steve Birch — for it was he — opened his mouth to speak. But before he could say a word, both he and Shimi were startled and shaken by a sound from above.

It was a girl's piercing scream.

Chapter 17

I.

Man and boy froze.

The cry did not repeat itself. But a desperate scrambling above their heads told them that someone or something was making its way down the trail in their direction.

Shimi's nails dug into the palms of his hands. Every nerve shrieked, *Danger!* but where was the danger coming from? Not this well-dressed man, Indian or not, gazing anxiously up the trail for the first glimpse of the approaching figure. What, then? And who was the girl, and what had made her scream that way?

Sobbing breaths and scrabbling feet … Shimi saw the girl a fraction of a second before she — head down to find a toehold on the slippery slope — saw him. "Gila?"

Gila's head snapped up, blond curls flying around a face taut with panic. "Who —? Sh-shimi? Is that you?"

"Yeah, it's me. Was that you who screamed just now? What happened?"

Gila threw an uncertain look at the man, who said quickly, "My name is Steve Birch. I've seen you before, I think. You're a Bernstein, right?"

Gila nodded without speaking. Her breathing was ragged and she trembled with reaction, cheeks pink with exertion and the heat.

"I'm friendly with your father," Birch said. "I've been to the house …"

As memory dawned, Gila's face cleared and she nodded again. "That's right. I remember you."

Steve crouched down so that he was on her eye-level. "Mind telling me your name? Unless you want me to call you 'Miss Bernstein,' like a teacher?"

If this was calculated to put the 9-year-old at her ease, it worked. With a wan smile, she said, "Gila."

"Okay. Gila, was it you we heard scream just now? What happened up there?"

Instantly, terror seized the girl again. "Oh, please! You have to help them! Those Indians …" Realizing that she was addressing another of them, she blushed an even deeper rose. "They looked so mean. One of them, especially. They dragged those other men into the cave …"

"Whoa! Just a second, Miss — I mean, Gila. Who shoved who into which cave?" Steve's heart began to slam against his ribs in slow, painful strokes.

As the girl attempted to formulate her thoughts into coherent sentences, Steve decided it would be useful to back up a bit. "Maybe you'd better start at the beginning. What are you doing up here, Gila?"

The words tripped off her tongue as small fists clenched in her effort to make him see the scene through her eyes. "I was following my brothers. I — I wanted to make sure they were safe."

"Hey, where *are* Chaim and Donny?" Shimi asked in puzzlement.

"I don't know! I was following them, and then I sat down to rest, and when I looked up again they were gone. I thought they took this trail — the one we took last summer — but I guess they didn't. I haven't seen them at all …" She faltered, anxiety over her brothers momentarily displacing the trauma she'd just experienced.

"Go on," Steve urged quietly. "About the men you saw."

Gila blanched. "Well, like I said, I couldn't see Chaim and Donny anywhere. I was about to turn back, when I heard voices … There were two people on the trail above me. One of them was Rabbi Feder, who belongs to my father's *kollel*. I don't remember the other one's name, but I've seen him in shul and at our house ... Just then, those two Indians came out of a cave. At least, I think it was a cave. They had to go around a big, prickly cactus bush to get out ... They saw Rabbi Feder and the other person, and started talking to them, real quiet, and looking real mean. Then they grabbed Rabbi Feder and the other guy and dragged them into the cave. The other man tried to put up a fight, but one of those Indians — we met them in the summer — is really *big*. The mean-looking Indian pulled Rabbi Feder into the cave, while the big one practically picked the other man up and carried him inside ... I got scared and screamed. And then I couldn't breathe ..."

"Are you all right now?"

"I ... I think so." She began to hyperventilate, the tears streaming down her sunburned cheeks. "They're bad men! Someone has to help Rabbi Feder!"

Breath gave out. Her eyes opened wide with a deeper, more immediate terror: her asthma was on the attack again. As Steve, alarmed, started toward her, she groped in her pocket.

"It's — O.K.," she gasped. She put the inhaler to her mouth and pressed the button.

Anxiously, Shimi watched Chaim and Donny's little sister battle for breath. He had to do something ... get help. For Gila, and for Rabbi Feder and the other man in the cave with those Indians. His mind was in a turmoil as the twin demons of urgency and indecision tore him slowly to pieces. Then he heard a calm voice — a calm, *adult* voice. The voice of someone who was prepared to take charge. In the enormity of his relief, Shimi nearly stopped breathing himself.

Steve Birch was talking to Gila.

"Good girl. You'll be all right now?"

Gila nodded jerkily, sinking down with her back against a boulder as she struggled to keep her breathing even. Some color had returned to her cheeks, but her eyes still brimmed with anxiety. "They're bad men," she whispered again.

"We'll get help." Steve turned to Shimi. "Now, what's *your* name?"

"Shimi Mandel. I *knew* there'd be trouble if we came up here! Those Indians threatened me once — and now they've got Rabbi Feder and someone else in that cave. We've got to get help!" Horrified, he felt tears spring into his eyes.

Steve didn't seem to notice. Slapping his pockets, he muttered, "This would be the morning I leave my cell phone at home ..." He turned back to Shimi. "You're younger and faster than I am. I want you to run back down to town. Do you know where the sheriff's office is?"

Shimi nodded.

"Good. Get Sheriff Ramsay and any men he has available, and tell them to get up here as fast as they can."

Behind him, Gila gasped. Steve spun around. "What...?"

"My brothers! There they are!" She pointed an eager finger at the ground far below them. Now both Steve and Shimi saw what she had just glimpsed: two small figures moving slowly away from the cliffs, on a roundabout route back to town.

"They must have taken a different trail," Gila exclaimed. "That's why I didn't see them!"

"*Baruch Hashem*, they're safe," Shimi said. He felt as though a huge boulder had just rolled off his shoulders.

"Yes, they're safe," Birch agreed. "But those two men up there aren't. Go get the sheriff, Shimi."

"Will — will you try to help Rabbi Feder in the meantime?"

Steve Birch gestured toward Gila. "As soon as I've made sure she's all right. You might try to get hold of her parents after you've spoken to the sheriff. You've got to run like the wind, Shimi. Go!"

Shimi spun around like a top, and vanished in a clatter of pebbles.

For a few minutes the others could hear him scrambling and sliding down the trail he had climbed so laboriously just minutes before. Finally, there was silence. Gila craned her neck, eager to spot Shimi farther down the trail, on his way to town for help.

Help. She turned urgently to Steve. Her color was better now. "Oh, don't worry about me. I'll be all right. I can breathe again, see? Just help those men — please!"

Steve hesitated. "You won't try to go anywhere? I don't think you're strong enough to make it down on your own yet."

"I'll stay right here," Gila promised. "Please — go to them! Who knows what's happening in that cave?"

The trust that this little girl had in his power to save the situation both touched and disconcerted him. He dearly hoped it wasn't misplaced. Frankly, he didn't feel equal to the task of confronting a couple of angry Indians — Indians who'd already proved that they did not draw the line at violent behavior — in the confines of a dark cave, especially in the presence of vulnerable hostages. But did he really have a choice?

Steve looked up the trail, letting his eyes rest on the spot where it curved and disappeared. Just above the next bend was a cactus bush which, according to Gila, effectively concealed the mouth of a cave. And inside that cave were two Jews ... and the "bad men" who had so badly frightened her.

He had a feeling he could name those two men, sight unseen.

He bade Gila a grim farewell and started up the trail.

"Who was that?" Bobby Smith snarled, as the last echo of Gila's scream died away on the still air.

"Sounded like a little girl." Big Jim sounded baffled.

"Get her," Bobby ordered. "I'll deal with these two." From his belt he whipped a long knife.

Beside him, Nate sensed Avi stiffen. Wild thoughts were flying helter-skelter through his mind. It was his fault they were in this pickle. It had been his suggestion that they take this hike in the first place. When he'd poked his head curiously around a flowering cactus and seen the entrance of a cave just behind, he should have turned right around and left. Instead, he had called Avi to come exploring with him and before either of them knew what was happening, they were struggling in the iron grip of a pair of Native Americans who dragged them into the cave's cool, dim interior. He didn't like the knife in the long-haired one's hand or the look in his eye as he hefted it. He had to find a way to get them out of this mess ...

The question was, how? How to fight such a wicked-looking weapon, especially in the hand of someone who could move so silently and quickly that you didn't even hear him coming? That was how the Indians had managed to take them by surprise. One minute, he and Avi were standing at the mouth of the cave, and the next, they were facing two Indians and a knife …

The odds were stacked against them. No use trying to fight their way out of this — not unarmed, and not against that knife. There was only one other option. He turned to Avi. "RUN!"

Nate could almost feel the Indians' breath on the back of his neck as he and Avi took off in the semidarkness. He wished he'd brought a flashlight with him. But who would have expected to need one on a hike up a sunny trail? With Avi at his heels, Nate led the way deeper into the cave's interior. How far did it go? Would they run into a stone wall and be cornered like rats?

No time to think. All he could do was run, and hope for the best. And *daven*. A whispered prayer ran through his fevered brain: *Hashem, please help us. Free us from the clutches of these evil men …* Through his supplication came a fleeting image of a silver plane winging its way eastward, toward the rising sun. With an inner wrench, he wondered if he would be on that plane, or if these cold, stone walls spelled an end to all his hopes …

"Nate!" Avi's strained whisper reached him through the darkness. "Over there — looks like a crevice or something. Maybe we can hide."

Nate had no breath left to answer him. He just nodded and followed Avi's pointing finger.

It was more than a crevice. It was a wide, deep drop in the cave floor; a kind of natural depression they had nearly overlooked in their desperate flight. Only a few dozen yards beyond the drop was the very thing that Nate had been so fearful they would encounter: the end of the line. The cave's rear wall.

But all wasn't lost. There was still the crevice: a place to hide. Without spending a beat of extra time in thought, he motioned urgently for Avi to follow. They reached the edge of the drop. Nate peered down in the darkness, trying to gauge its depth.

They were out of time. Their pursuers were already upon them. In the light of the bobbing flashlight in Jim's hand, Smith's knife flickered and gleamed. Bobby had ordered Jim to go after Gila, but his partner, ignoring the order, had joined him in pursuing the runaways instead.

Bobby twisted his head to look over his shoulder. *"Get the girl*, I said! We don't want any witnesses!"

"Witnesses? To what?" Jim sounded bewildered and close to tears himself. "She sounded like just a kid, Bobby!"

"So what? Get out of here, Jim. Find her!"

In a burst of speed surprising in a man his size, Big Jim bypassed Bobby and ran instead to the lip of the depression where Nate and Avi stood facing them, fear and desperate courage mingling on their faces. Exasperated, Bobby stared briefly at his friend's back, then moved forward in his wake to face their unwelcome guests.

"It was a mistake for you people to get mixed up in our business," he snarled. "A big mistake."

"What business?" Nate blustered. "Are you the ones who set those fires? Are you the arsonists?"

Bobby's answer was to advance another step, calmly brandishing the knife in front of him. Avi took an involuntarily step backward — into empty space. In his panic, he had forgotten all about the drop in the cave floor behind him.

There was a horrible thud as he tumbled and landed in a heap on the rock-strewn bottom many feet below.

II.

"**A**vi!" Nate shouted, peering into the gloom. He could just make out a huddled form on the stone floor of the crevice.

Glancing back over his shoulder, he saw the one called Bobby moving slowly closer. With a muttered prayer, Nate heaved himself over the edge of the precipice and let himself half-slide, half-fall, down to where his friend lay.

He landed, scratched and bleeding, in the center of the depression. Every bone was jarred in the landing, but as far as he could tell they were all intact, for which he thanked his merciful Creator. Far above, two heads peered down at him. Without intending to, Nate and Avi had managed to render themselves temporarily inaccessible. They were safe from that long knife — for the moment.

Nate crouched beside Avi, shaking him. "Avi? Are you okay? Avi, talk to me!"

The other man stirred. A muffled groan made Nate sigh with relief.

Above, Bobby was issuing orders. "Jim, we need rope. Stand guard here while I get it from my pack."

Big Jim nodded heavily. Bobby turned and vanished into the darkness, turning on his flashlight as he went. Jim's own light was trained on the men in the hole below.

"Are you okay?" he called down softly.

Nate glanced up. "Why should you care? You're planning on finishing us off anyway, aren't you?"

"Maybe *he* is. I won't do it. It's one thing to look for treasure ... but this here's another thing. I don't hurt little kids ... and I sure don't kill people."

Here, Nate sensed, was a possible ally. "Can you help us get out?"

"I'm not sure how. The rope's in Bobby's pack ..."

Stifling groans as his bruised bones protested every move, Avi pulled himself into a sitting position, his back against the wall of the depression. His left wrist seemed to be useless, and was radiating waves of pain he had to force himself to ignore. Inching painfully sideways to find a smooth resting-place for his aching back, Avi felt the wall slope inward. There seemed to be a sort of ledge or shelf in the crevice's rear wall — a niche formed by a natural outcropping of rock. Idly, Avi groped inside. "Hey, what's this?"

"What's what?"

"I don't know. There's a kind of space in here, beneath this ledge. I feel something inside ..."

Nate moved closer. "Let me see." He knelt beside Avi and felt around in the shadowy niche. His fingers touched something flat and rough. He took hold of as much of it as he could reach and slowly dragged it out. Avi caught his breath in excitement, aches and pains momentarily forgotten.

It was a wooden box, weathered but intact: The cave's cool temperatures and lack of exposure to the sun had helped preserve the wood remarkably well. Avi's eyes goggled.

"Buried treasure!" he blurted.

The words reached Jim's ears. "Treasure!" he repeated incredulously. "You mean, *you* found it?" He let the momentous discovery sift through the sands of his slow-moving mind, then crooned, "Oh, Bobby's gonna be so-o-o mad ..."

Another thought, more disturbing, supplanted the first one: Bobby would want to dispose of these two more than ever now. Jim scratched his head in frustration, bereft of ideas. How he wished he had a rope!

"Wait," he called to them. "I'm going to reach down. I have long arms. Maybe I can get to you ... pull you out ..."

Nate eyed him doubtfully. "Pull out the treasure, you mean," he muttered. But Avi shook his head. "I think he means it," he whispered. "He's not as bad as the other one. I think he wants to help."

As they watched, Nate in lingering doubt, Avi with growing hope, the big man suited word to action. Sprawling at the edge of the precipice, he inched forward until his arms and shoulders were dangling in the void. Slowly, slowly, he inched even further, angling for that one point where he would have maximum reach while still maintaining his equilibrium.

"Careful!" Avi called softly. This might be one of the bad guys, but he *was* trying to help them. "You're going to tip over!"

"I'm — being — careful," Jim grunted. "Just — another — few inches ..."

Below him, he saw two faces upturned in hope. If Nate stood on tiptoe, he found that his upstretched hand ended just inches from Jim's downstretched one. Jim pushed himself forward just a little more, and his thick fingers brushed Nate's.

"*Jim!*" Bobby yelled. He was still some distance off, but moving fast. "Hold on, I'm on my way!"

The shout galvanized Big Jim Littletree into a last, extreme effort. With a grunt, he stretched himself a last few inches — inches that proved his undoing.

"Watch out!" Nate shouted.

The delicate equilibrium was lost. For a fraction of an instant, Jim seemed to hover on the lip like a huge, ungainly bird poised for flight. Then, with an anguished cry that echoed and re-echoed through the cave like the call of a tormented soul, he toppled headfirst into the hole.

By dint of a very adroit leap, Nate just managed to avoid being crushed by the falling figure.

When the last quivering echo of the crash had faded on the cool air, Nate met Avi's stunned gaze. On the ground beside them, the big man lay perfectly still, eyes closed. Jim's flashlight had tumbled down with him and, astonishingly, still shone. With caution, Nate inched closer and directed the light at the man's face. In the faint beam he saw a thin trickle of blood seeping from the Indian's hairline; just a slender trickle, no more.

Crouched in a dark crevice in the dark cave, Nate felt as remote from the world as he would have been on the moon. The silence was deafening. The very air he breathed felt cold and unfriendly. Not far away, somewhere above their heads, Bobby Smith was on his way back with a rope ... and his wicked knife.

"What do we do now?" Avi whispered.

Nate just shook his head.

This must be it: a large overgrown bush planted halfway across the trail. Pushing some of it aside with care — the thorny plant formed a great natural defense — Steve made out the black shape of the cave mouth. He strained his ears for the sound of voices, but there was none. Either the men had all gone elsewhere — unlikely, for he surely would have heard them leave as he'd climbed up to this spot — or else they had penetrated deeper into the cave.

He hesitated. For the 10th time that morning, he wished he had a weapon of some kind. By nature a peace-loving man, the impending confrontation was not something Steve Birch viewed with optimism. What chance had he, unarmed, against the likes of Smith (if that's who it was)? His best move, he decided, was to stay put. He would guard the cave entrance to make sure no one left it unobserved. That way, Ramsay's men would be sure to find their quarry trapped inside when they came.

When they came ... There was the rub. How long would it take Shimi to track down the sheriff? And how much longer for Jack Ramsay to mobilize a team and hotfoot it up here?

It could take a long time. Maybe too long for those men in there.

Gila's strained face and pleading eyes seemed to rise up before him on the superheated air. At the very least, he could reconnoiter; check out the lay of the the land. If he found the captives to be in no immediate danger, he would discreetly withdraw and leave the job to the law-enforcement people who, he fervently hoped, would be on the spot shortly. And if danger did threaten … well, then he would do what he could.

He pictured his Jewish prayer book, with its faded Star of David. Wasn't that star displayed on the shield that King David carried with him into battle? He wished he had the book — or some of King David's courage — to bolster him now.

In the absence of either, he drew a long breath, pushed the branches of the sprawling bush further aside, and stepped into the cool mouth of the cave.

Shimi's lungs were about two seconds away from bursting. He felt as though he hadn't caught his breath in 15 minutes — the amount of time it had taken him to scramble down the trail and start the mad sprint for town.

The sheriff's office, Shimi knew, was situated on Main Street. It was about halfway down the long block, tucked between a pharmacy and a barber shop. What if the sheriff wasn't in? What if he didn't believe his story? Anxiety almost made him stop running.

He forced himself to go on. Rabbi Feder and another Jew were in trouble, and Gila wasn't in great shape, either. What was happening up on the cliff right now? And in the cave? A spate of shivering took hold of him — a delayed reaction. By the time he burst panting through the door of the modest office with "Lakewood Township Sheriff" stenciled on the glass front, he was shaking like a man suffering from palsy.

The middle-aged woman behind the front desk glanced up from her typing, bored. She took one look at Shimi and half-rose in her seat, every tight gray curl on her head abounce. "Mercy! What in the world is the matter with you, child?"

When Shimi obviously couldn't answer immediately, she led him to a wooden chair and bade him sit still. "Catch your breath. Then you can tell me what the problem is." People didn't burst into the sheriff's office looking like demons were nipping at their heels unless they had a good reason.

Shimi struggled to catch his breath. "We need … the sheriff," he gasped. "Is he … here?"

"He might be," she answered cautiously. "What do you want him for?"

It took another moment for Shimi to master his breathing enough to make his little speech. "We need him," he said finally, speaking slowly and clearly to transmit the weight of the message, "to help rescue two men from some Indians who've got them up in a cave."

"Indians?" She looked blank.

"Mr. Birch sent me."

The secretary gaped at him. "Steve Birch?" With an effort, she collected herself and made for her desk — and the radio. "You just sit tight, now," she snapped over her shoulder. "I'll contact the sheriff."

Under other circumstances, Shimi would have been fascinated by the crackle of static emerging from the radio, and the disembodied voice that responded to the woman's query. But these were not other circumstances. Shimi had a vivid imagination, and right now it was operating on all four cylinders, sending gruesome images of the trapped men directly from his brain to his entire nervous system. He sat at the edge of his seat, fingers interlocked as he waited for the woman to look his way again.

When she did, it was with a tight-lipped smile. "Sheriff's on his way. Now, suppose you tell me the story."

"Story?"

"What's been going on, and how you happened to see that these two men — you haven't told me their names yet, by the way — are up in a cave with a couple of Indians."

Shimi hesitated. "I'd rather tell the sheriff himself, if that's all right," he said in a small voice. His recent herculean efforts seemed to have drained him. He sat hunched in a plastic chair, trying to appear confident but only succeeding in looking very young and scared.

"Sheriff's orders. It'll save time, he says. I'll be able to radio him the details while he's on his way back."

"Is he far away? How long till he gets here?" Shimi's mind lurched into high gear again, frantically turning over other options for finding the help they needed. If Sheriff Ramsay was going to be long ...

"He's over at the Three-Star Ranch, a little ways down the Pecos River. A couple of ranchhands got into a nasty fight and the law had to step in. Shouldn't be too much longer."

Shimi nodded with relief, willing himself to calm down. Then he drew a breath and began. "Well, it's like this ..."

He had just reached the part where he'd run into Steve Birch on the cliff trail, when the radio crackled back to life. The secretary, who had introduced herself as Stacy Rhodes, spoke into it, filling the sheriff in on some of what Shimi had just told her. Over her shoulder, she asked, "You say Steve Birch is out there?"

"Yes. I was a little scared at first, but he's not one of them. When Gila screamed —"

"Whoa there, son. Slow down. Who's this Gila?"

"She's Rabbi Bernstein's daughter. She's 9, and she has asthma. She could hardly breathe, but she managed to tell us that Rabbi Feder and another man are in trouble. She saw a couple of Indians hustle them into a cave ... Mr. Birch sent me down here for the sheriff, and he stayed behind to make sure Gila was all right. Then he was going to go on up to the cave to see if he could help."

Stacy Rhodes nodded, and turned away to speak into the radio again.

Shimi's fists tensed, the knuckles turning white. The wait was unbearable. At this very minute, those Indians might be doing — anything! *Where was the sheriff?*

Just when he thought he'd explode if forced to wait another second, the sheriff's white car pulled up at the curb in a screech of brakes. A second later he strode through the door, eyes going directly to the boy sitting like a coiled spring at the very edges of his seat.

"You the kid with the story about Indians in a cave?"

Shimi shot to his feet. "Sheriff! We've got to hurry! Rabbi Feder's in bad trouble ... And Gila had an asthma attack ..."

Ramsay was halfway out the door before Shimi finished talking. "Let's go. You'll tell me about it on the way."

Then they were in the sheriff's car and speeding back to the cliffs, taking the same route that Shimi had just covered in such breathless haste, on foot. When the road petered out, they left the car and half jogged, half ran, to the foot of the cliffs. An overwhelming thirst was raging in Shimi's throat, but he ignored it. Every nerve, every sinew, was riveted to the reddish stone walls rising ahead of them.

Somewhere in those cliffs, Rabbi Feder and another Jewish man were trapped in a cave with a couple of characters straight out of a nightmare. Gila was languishing on a rock in the aftermath of an asthma attack. And Steve Birch was … where?

III.

Steve Birch was wishing he was anywhere but where he was: hidden in the shadows of a dark cave, as he strained with all his might to hear what was happening deeper inside.

He heard voices. Very faint and muffled they were, as though reaching him from a great distance or even underground. He hesitated, as prudence fought with curiosity. It would be easier to simply back away and wait for help to arrive. A lot safer, too.

He couldn't do it.

Even more powerful than his curiosity was his sense of responsibility. The mere thought of terrified hostages, held against their will, hardened his resolve and spiked his courage. He had to see for himself what was happening. It was highly probable that Gila had read the scenario wrongly and that this was all a false alarm. Establish the facts, and react accordingly: the lawyer's credo. Cautiously following the voices, he made his way deeper into the interior of the cave.

He almost collided with Bobby Smith's back.

Groping along in the darkness, he glimpsed the faint gleam of a flashlight at the same instant that he nearly bumped into the man holding it. It was Bobby, and he too was headed toward the sounds that had attracted Steve's attention: sounds which, as Steve came closer, resolved themselves into a set of muffled voices. Bobby Smith heard them, too, and was goaded into quickening his step.

"Jim!" Bobby yelled. "Hold on, I'm on my way!" It was only his complete absorption in what lay ahead, Steve surmised, that had prevented the Indian from catching the noise of his approach till now. His shoes made no sound on the hard stone floor; nevertheless, Steve held back, standing perfectly still and letting the space between them grow to a safer distance. In the now-feeble glow of the receding flashlight, he saw Bobby stop and look around.

"Jim?" Bobby called, impatiently. "Where are you?"

Steve, watching from the shadows, saw Smith lean over some sort of rocky ledge or precipice in the cave's depths. "JIM!"

From the depths of the drop beyond the ledge, a different voice rose waveringly into the air. Steve strained to catch the words.

"He fell," Avi Feder called. "He — he seems to be unconscious."

"Yeah, and we found what you were looking for," Nate shouted, with more bravado than wisdom. Avi shushed him, horrified — but the damage was done.

Cursing under his breath, Bobby reached into his pack. His tone was surprisingly mild as he said, "Well, you'd better let me get you out of there. We'll deal with Jim later."

For the first time, Steve noticed the faint gleam of a long dagger thrust through Bobby's belt at the back. A shiver passed through him. His instincts had not been wrong, then. There was foul work at hand. The Jewish men were in definite danger.

What had Bobby been looking for — now, apparently, found? And where was the sheriff? Steve prayed that Shimi Mandel had found him in good time, and that help was on its way. Meanwhile, all he could do was stay close and keep an eye on developments here. With Feder and his friend out of reach in that deep hole, Bobby Smith's intentions, whatever they were, appeared to be stymied. He couldn't get at them down there.

Bobby, however, had a different idea. He pulled a coil of rope from his pack and began to unravel it. As he did, he looked around in the darkness and found what he wanted: a heavy boulder. This he dragged — not without much grunting effort — to the edge of the ledge. The

Indian tied one end of his rope carefully around the rock, testing the knot to make sure it would hold. Then he slung the rest of the rope over the stony ledge.

"I'm coming down," he called, more softly now. "I'm coming to see about Jim. He's hurt. He needs help. Make room for me down there …"

The sharp intake of breath from the bottom of the depression reached Steve clearly. All of his attention was riveted on Bobby's form, crouched at the lip of the ledge as he prepared to climb down.

Steve clenched his fists. Was Bobby legitimately concerned about his friend, as he claimed? Perhaps the knife was not intended for the trapped men at all.

On the other hand, could he take that risk? Once Bobby entered the confines of that narrow space, any violent intentions he might be harboring would find scope for full expression. There would be no place for the captives to run.

His thoughts were interrupted by a light, slapping sound, which puzzled Steve until he heard Bobby snarl, "Leave that rope alone! There's no way you're going to be able to throw it back up. Besides, I'm just coming down to see to Jim, all right?"

In his mind's eye, Steve saw the men frantically trying to get rid of the rope that would bring Smith down to them. The Indian had one leg over the ledge and was gripping the rope with one hand. In the other was the long knife, which he'd just plucked from his belt at the small of his back. Steve stared at the gleaming blade, momentarily mesmerized.

But there was no time to stare. No time for anything but action. *G-d*, Steve prayed silently. *Those are Jews in there. You're the G-d of the Jews, aren't You? Please — help me help them!* In a single, smooth motion he went from a crouch to a lunge, catapulting himself like a missile directly at Bobby Smith's back.

He caught the other man off guard, one leg slung awkwardly over the ledge. As Bobby tried to twist around to face his assailant, whatever balance he had managed to sustain in the assault was lost. With a furious yell, he lost his grip on the rope and tumbled into the gloomy depths below.

Steve was down the rope after him in seconds, heart hammering as he prayed he was not too late. In his zeal to stop Smith, he'd sent him hurtling down to the very place he'd intended to prevent him from reaching. His palms smarted from his too-rapid descent, but rope burns were a distraction he couldn't afford to consider right now. From the dimness below came an agonized grunt and a muttered epithet. Steve reached the end of the rope. He launched himself off at the nearest half-seen figure, and landed on top of Bobby.

"My leg! It's broken!" Bobby bellowed, clutching his leg below the knee. Steve's weight, pinning him down on the stone floor, was clearly adding to his agony. "It's broken! Get off me *now*, you idiot!"

Steve didn't get off. He stayed where he was, breathing hard, perspiring freely, and doing the only thing possible under the circumstances: sit tight and wait for the cavalry to arrive.

It took considerably longer than Steve would have liked, but they came at last: Sheriff Ramsay and two of his deputies. Shimi Mandel, on Ramsay's orders, was chomping at the bit just farther down the trail.

Shimi had completely forgotten Birch's suggestion that he find Gila's parents and bring them back to see to their daughter. He exchanged a quick word with her as he passed her on his way up to the cave with the sheriff. Gila wanted to join the posse, but Ramsay was firm in his refusal. "You stay put, little lady. We'll fetch you on our way down." He turned to Shimi. "You stay with her."

Shimi would have protested, but the plea in Gila's eyes made him close his mouth. He had a feeling the sheriff would not allow him into the cave anyway. "All right," he said, dropping to the ground beside Gila.

Ramsay eyed him with approval. "You did good today, kid." With this brief accolade, he motioned his men higher up the trail.

The lawmen entered the cave cautiously, guns held at arm's length in front of them, only to find it seemingly deserted. Wielding police-issue flashlights, Ramsay and his men moved deeper into its interior until they came to a spot just a few dozen yards from the rear wall of the cave. There they found a rope, tied around a boulder and running over the lip of a deep depression in the cave floor.

Steve Birch was in that depression, just managing to hold down a furious Bobby Smith, in obvious pain from a disabling injury. Beside him on the ground lay an inert Jim Littletree, with a considerably shaken Avi Feder and Nate Goodman, crouching with their backs to the wall near them.

Avi's eyes were closed. The look he wore was almost peaceful as his lips moved in constant prayer. Nate had said some *Tehillim*, too, but he was not feeling peaceful at all. He was in a state of high alert, ready on an instant's notice to take over for Steve, if the lawyer should tire of holding Smith down. He had offered to take over, but Birch had been afraid that Smith would manage to fight himself free in the exchange.

"Just stand by," Steve had said with a faint smile. "I'll let you know if and when my batteries run down completely ..."

The sheriff took in the scene for one astonished instant. Then, summing up the situation, he ordered his men to drop more lines into the crevice to allow Nate and Avi to climb up. Trembling with exhaustion, Steve held Bobby down for the extra few minutes that it took for the Jewish men to scramble up the ropes — Avi traveling slowly and awkwardly on account of his injured wrist and battered frame. Then the deputies went down to relieve Steve of his burden. He sighed with relief as he heard the welcome click of handcuffs closing over Smith's wrists.

"Careful! My leg's broken," Bobby growled. He sat up gingerly, wincing. Both manacled hands went to his torso with a groan. "Everything hurts ..."

"I wouldn't be surprised if you got yourself a coupla broken ribs, too," one of the deputies remarked laconically.

"It's all Birch's fault." He tacked a few choice epithets onto the name of his nemesis. "He landed on me like a ton of bricks."

The second deputy was bent over Jim Littletree, his flashlight beam playing over the big man's face as his fingers found the carotid artery.

Jack Ramsay peered over the top of the ledge. "What about the other one?" he called through cupped hands.

There was a brief silence as the deputy took another moment over Big Jim's prostrate form. His answer came back in a single, laconic syllable: "Gone."

Avi gasped. Brokenly, he said, "We thought he was just unconscious!"

Nate turned away to hide his shock. "He lost his life trying to save us," he whispered.

IV.

"We're going to take these folks out of here," Ramsay called down to Smith. "We'll be back for you in a little while."

Bobby shook his head violently. "You're not leaving me down here with ... that." He rolled his eyes at his friend's inanimate body.

"O.K." Ramsay's sudden capitulation surprised Bobby. "You can come up if you like. Think you can manage it, with your busted leg?"

"*And* cracked ribs, most likely," his deputy reminded him with gloomy satisfaction.

"I can manage."

"With your hands cuffed?"

Bobby scowled. "Take these things off. I won't run. I can't, can I — with this leg?"

Ramsay pointed his gun at Bobby and called softly down to his deputies to do the same. "Uncuff him — and stand back. One false move, Smith, and you'll be joining your pal in more ways than one ..."

The scowl deepened, but Bobby did as he was told. Hands freed, he used them to make the agonizing trip up the rope with one leg dangling at a grotesque angle all the way. The Indian strained and sweated his way over the lip of the ledge, then collapsed on the stone floor, his face covered with a sheen of perspiration and contorting in pain. Ramsay jerked Smith's arms behind his back and cuffed him again, then left him where he was to make a panting recovery from the ordeal.

When Bobby was able to walk — or rather, to hobble — he was escorted at a snail's pace back to the cave mouth. In minutes, the whole group emerged into the sunlight.

Sheriff Ramsay led the way, walking beside Steve Birch, with Avi Feder and Nate Goodman right behind them. The deputies came last, gripping both arms of a sullen Bobby Smith. He wasn't going anywhere, but he needed their help in order to navigate the trail on one foot.

Jim Littletree's body would be brought up later, when the proper equipment could be obtained. As the sheriff had said, gazing down into the depths of the crevice, there was no hurry.

Big Jim — overgrown, slightly stupid, with a fatal, doglike devotion for the wrong friend — would never need to hurry anywhere again.

Nate looked over at Avi, who was gingerly cradling his right wrist in his left hand. "You okay?"

"*Baruch Hashem.* I'm glad to be out of that place," Avi said thankfully. "But I'm one big sore spot all over. And my wrist seems to be sprained or something."

"Broken, more likely," the pessimistic deputy threw in from behind.

"My *leg* is broken!" Bobby Smith called loudly from the rear. Beads of pain and perspiration dotted his face. "Doesn't anyone care about that?"

Sheriff Ramsay turned to look at his prisoner. "We're going to take you down to the ER real soon," he promised. "And after that, you'll have a nice, long rest — in the county jail."

"Jail? What'd I do? I was taking a hike and exploring a cave — just like they were." He jutted a belligerent chin at the two Jews.

"I believe they'll have a different story to tell." Ramsay had already confiscated the knife with the long wicked-looking blade that his men had found on the lip of the ledge. It had, according to Birch, clattered out of Bobby's hand when Steve tackled him.

Bobby directed a malevolent glare at his erstwhile captives, but they hadn't a glance to spare for him. Nate breathed deeply, swinging his arms at his sides as he walked along, delirious with joy at being away from the cave's dark embrace, a free man again. "That little escapade ought to atone for quite a bit," he murmured, amid visions of a silver plane shooting through a velvet sky. He glanced over at his companion in the recent ordeal.

Avi's eyes kept closing as the pain in his wrist escalated with each jarring step. The pain vied with a profound thankfulness in his heart. And, despite his bruised and aching body and the sense of having been worked over by a steamroller, there was no question that the gratitude was winning.

It was a long, slow trek down the cliff path to where the lawmen's cars were waiting. About a third of the way down, they paused to pick up Gila and Shimi. They found the children standing tensely in the path, peering up at the spot where it curved out of sight.

"*Baruch Hashem*! They're all right!" Gila exclaimed softly when she caught sight of Avi Feder and Nate Goodman. Shimi ran over to them, a broad smile splitting his face. Gila followed more slowly, slanting a glance, half angry and half scared, at Bobby Smith, bringing up the rear with his honor guard. The slow journey down the mountain continued.

Some minutes before the group reached the bevy of police cars waiting at the foot of the trail, another vehicle came roaring up in a cloud of dust to join them. There was a squeal of brakes, and then the slam of four doors as one driver and three passengers, one carrying an infant, popped out of the minivan like a company of distraught jacks-in-the-box.

Gila squinted into the sun. She began to wave wildly. "Ma! Ta!"

"My parents are here, too," Shimi said, in a rather diffident tone.

The sheriff led the group down the next bend in the trail.

It had been Tova who started worrying first.

Coming home from the doctors' office with her day's work in hand, she'd been surprised at the silence that greeted her. The house had a certain sound when it was empty; she was familiar with that sound, and she was hearing it now.

"Chaim?" she called out experimentally. "Donny? Are you here?"

Clearly, they weren't. She wasn't worried — not yet. The boys often went outdoors to play. She didn't hear them in the backyard, so they must have gone further afield to find their fun. She'd have preferred to have had them wait until she returned home, so that she could hear where they intended to go and they could hear when she expected them back. But this was not the first time her boys had slipped the leash. She wasn't seriously concerned. Not yet.

It was only when she realized that Gila, too, was gone, that her heart lurched into a crazy dance that was not to let up until she had her daughter safely in her arms again.

She phoned her husband, but reached only his voice mail. Nachman was giving his daily *shiur* and had turned off his phone. Frowning, she dialed Etty Mandel's number next. The most likely person to know where her boys were — and, by association, her daughter — was Shimi Mandel.

"Shimi?" Etty repeated. "He went out some time ago. He said he was going to get together with your boys."

"Well, maybe they did get together — but where did they go? And why did they take Gila along with them?"

"I thought you just told me that Gila wasn't feeling well."

"She wasn't. At least, that's what she said. In that case, why is she traipsing around outside?" The tempo of Tova's frenzied cardiac dance picked up in tempo.

"I'm not sure I like this," Etty said slowly.

"I'm positive that I don't! I'm going to make some more calls." For lack of any other option, Tova called the Ganns, before remembering that Asher had taken the day off to go to Roswell with his wife. Avi Feder, whom she tried next, seemed to be out as well — unless he was napping and not answering his phone. In desperation, she finally managed to reach the shul secretary.

"They didn't stop in at the *kollel* by any chance, did they?" Tova asked without much hope.

"No, I'm sorry. I thought their classes were canceled for today."

"They were. It's just that my kids seem to have disappeared."

"I'm sorry, I have no information. Have you tried calling your husband?

Which brought her full circle.

It wasn't that they were being overprotective, she and Etty assured themselves when Tova entered the Mandels' place a few minutes later. But with all the strange and ominous incidents that had been taking place in their community in recent weeks, it simply made good sense to keep tabs on their children.

"Especially Gila," Tova murmured, biting her lip to keep from screaming out loud in her anxiety. Her chubby cherub-faced girl who had to fight her own lungs for the right to breathe. Why had Gila left the house with her brothers? It was unlike her. Gila preferred more sedentary activities: reading, needlework, paint-by-number. Why was she outside in this heat? And where had they all gone, anyway?

In the end, the two women drove down to the *kollel*, where Rabbi Bernstein was just winding up his *shiur*. They took Etty's car because it was equipped with a car seat for Layala. It was the work of seconds to apprise Nachman and Efraim of the facts — or rather, the absence of them. Nachman thought for a moment, and then gave a tight-lipped nod. "We can't take any chances. Let's drive around town and see if we can spot the children. If not ... we'll stop in at the sheriff's office."

"We won't find them," Tova predicted frantically. "I know we won't." Her mother's intuition had gone into overdrive. But she allowed her husband to convince her that it would be prudent to search anyway.

The search proved fruitless, as Tova had known it would be. The hot streets were devoid of children on this school day, and the few pedestrians they interviewed were of no use to them. At last, Nachman pointed the car in the direction of Main Street and Sheriff Ramsay's office.

Stacy Rhodes, the sheriff's middle-aged secretary, was not her usual unflappable self. Excitedly, she informed them that a boy had come in to report that some Jews were in trouble. "Shimi, he said his name was."

"Shimi!" Etty gasped.

"He was looking for the sheriff, poor thing. It was a good few minutes until Sheriff Ramsay came in, and the kid sat here like a cat on hot bricks through all of them. The sheriff talked to him briefly, and then they drove off together. I sent the deputies right along after them."

"Where to?" Nachman asked tensely.

She frowned. "I'm not sure. Some cave, he said. Couple of no-good Indians, apparently, startin' up trouble. There was some talk about a girl, too. Some kind of breathing problem, I think he said ..."

Nachman Bernstein met his wife's eyes. They were out of the office like a hurricane wind, with the Mandels puffing along anxiously in their wake. Little Layala bobbed up and down in her mother's arms as Etty ran.

They made the by-now familiar drive to the building site in near-silence. Only Etty Mandel broke it periodically to moan, "Oh, what are they up to? What could they be *up* to?" Efraim seemed to be murmuring snatches of *Tehillim*. In the front seat, Nachman concentrated on driving, and Tova listened to the insane patter of her heart as they rapidly approached their destination.

They had hardly pulled up at the foot of the cliff — scene of the celebration picnic that seemed to have taken place eons ago, in another lifetime — when they spotted figures, still hardly more than specks, high up on the trail. There were shorter figures interspersed among the taller ones, but it wasn't until they were much farther down that Tova, holding her breath until she ached, was able to distinguish their features.

She exhaled with a joyous *whoosh* at the sight of Gila, waving both arms high above her head. Both she and Shimi sported fine sunburns as they marched along with the men, as proudly as though they were on parade. Leading them was the sheriff, walking beside Steve Birch. It was a Birch rather worse for the wear, his shirt smudged and rumpled, trousers ripped at the knee. He was holding his hands awkwardly away from his body, as if they hurt.

Next into view came Avi Feder and Nate Goodman. Avi was cradling his wrist but smiling, while Nate strode along the winding, stone-strewn trail as though it were a city sidewalk. Last of all was a group of three men, two of them sporting deputy's badges and escorting the one in the middle: black eyed, hawk nosed, with features so still they might have been carved of stone. An Indian. As they drew near, Tova saw that the man in the middle wore manacles on his wrists. Her heart skipped yet another beat.

At last, the moment came: Gila was snug in her arms. "Are you O.K., honey?" she asked, hugging her little girl tightly.

"I'm fine, Ma." Gila looked up with bright, happy eyes. "I got help for Rabbi Feder and Mr. Goodman. They were in big trouble …"

"You'll tell me all about it later. First, tell me about the asthma. Did you use your inhaler?"

"Sure. I had it in my pocket the whole time. I remembered to take it along. And I also remembered to think calm thoughts and not get in a panic. I got better real quick, Ma."

"So I see. *Baruch Hashem.*" Tova hugged her daughter again, illogically blinking back tears now that tears were unnecessary. Past Gila's head, she saw the Mandels hovering over an embarrassed-looking Shimi. Unobtrusively, Tova maneuvered closer. She was unabashedly curious to hear what Etty was saying to her son.

Etty wore a look that Tova had never seen on her face before. It took her a moment to identify it, but then she had it. There was a jumble of emotions in that look, but the predominant one — the one that Etty so rarely allowed the world to see — was love. Her heart was in her eyes.

"I wish you'd told me where you were going, Shimi," Etty was saying. "I was so worried about you ..."

"Aw, why'd you worry, Ma? You know I can take care of myself!"

"That's right," Efraim said, regarding his son with a smile that positively glowed. "I've known that for a long time, Shimi. The sheriff's been telling me about the part you played in all of this. I'm proud of you."

"So am I," Etty said. " I just wish you'd shared it with us. That's what parents are for."

Shimi looked up at her doubtfully. "I thought you'd be mad."

Etty hesitated, and then sighed. "Maybe I would have been. But you should have told me anyway."

Efraim leaned in close to his son and whispered, "I guess there won't be a single person in this town who wouldn't be honored to be at your upcoming bar mitzvah, Shimi."

It was Shimi's turn to glow.

Sheriff Ramsay signaled his deputies to start herding people toward the cars. "It's hot out here, folks. And we've got to get some people over to Memorial to have things looked at."

"Avi, what did you do to your wrist?" Nachman asked. He had already shaken Nate's hand, but had to settle for a warm thump on his *kollel* colleague's back.

Avi produced a wry grin. "Nothing too good, I'm afraid. I'm just glad to be alive."

"*Baruch Hashem!*" Tova exclaimed softly. "We'll want to hear all about it: every last detail."

There were urgent questions burning on many lips, but all that would have to wait until the doctors determined that the various characters in the recent drama were fit to answer them.

It was then that the cell phone in Tova's purse jangled. Absently, almost, she pulled it out. The caller screen read, "Home."

"Yes?" she said into the phone.

"Ma?"

"Chaim! We've been looking everywhere for you. Where in the world have you and Donny been?"

"Oh, around ... But we're home now. And what we want to know is: Where *is* everybody?"

V.

Bobby Smith's X-rays confirmed that he had indeed fractured his tibia. In addition, he had two cracked ribs and had suffered numerous abrasions in the fall and the ensuing struggle with Birch. He was to be kept in the hospital overnight, under guard, followed by a stay in the town jailhouse pending further investigation into his activities.

"What we need here," a frustrated Sheriff Ramsay told Birch, "is a confession."

Steve grimaced. "Good luck."

"I know. A more closed-lip type would be hard to find."

"He had pretty loose lips down there in the cave. I was embarrassed at some of the things that came out of his mouth ..."

Ramsay shook his head. "He's gonna be a tough nut to crack. I've got most of the pieces, but the puzzle's not finished yet. We still don't have *proof* that he set those fires."

"What about searching his place? He rents a run-down apartment on Euston Street."

"Judge Diamond is my next stop. Once I have that warrant in hand, I'll be making tracks over to Euston Street so fast it'll make your head spin."

Steve slumped against the wall, suddenly overcome by a monumental fatigue. His body was not in the habit of being used the way he'd used it today, and every bone was protesting loudly. The palms of his rope-seared hands were burning steadily now, and would continue to do so, he gloomily predicted, for some time to come. Once he'd had them looked at, he longed to head home to the shower as soon as humanly possibly. His prolonged proximity to Bobby Smith had left him feeling soiled. It was unclear, however, whether the sheriff was going to let him go.

"Do you need me around right now?" he asked, trying to straighten up and largely failing.

Ramsay looked at him with pity. "You took a beating today," he said, "and I'd sure like to let you get some shut-eye. But I'm afraid you'll have to answer a few questions first. It's standard procedure. Sorry, Steve."

Birch stifled an enormous yawn. "That's okay. All part of the job …"

He felt a deep satisfaction with the way things had turned out and, especially, with his own role in today's events. By some amazing confluence of fate, he had been in the right place at the right time when two innocent men had desperately needed help. Some of the people standing around him right now would, he suspected, go so far as to call the chain of events downright miraculous. He'd been there when he was needed and, though not a fighting man, had come off creditably in his encounter with Gila Bernstein's "bad men."

Avi's wrist was badly sprained, but fortunately not broken. He wore his Ace bandage like a badge of honor. When it was his turn to be examined, Nate tried to protest that he was fine and didn't need to have a doctor look at him. But, as every single person in authority disagreed with him, he was forced to submit.

"A bit scratched and scraped," Dr. Meynard said at last, straightening up, "but sound as a nut. You were lucky." The doctor turned to his next patient. "As for you, little lady, I can see that you're breathing just fine now. Mind if I have a little listen anyway, just to make sure?"

Gila submitted to having her lungs listened to, as she had done so many times in her short life. Her eyes still carried the afterglow of the morning's adventures. To her gratification, the doctor pronounced her sound as another nut.

"Looks like we're all a bunch of nuts!" Avi grinned.

"Speak for yourself," Nate said. He was happy but utterly exhausted. All he wanted was to drive home so he could take a nap, a practice he had abandoned when he was about 3 years old. There's something about having your life hang at the end of a thread to make you feel as if you've lived a hundred years in a single hour.

Nachman noticed. "These men are beyond exhausted," he told the sheriff. "I hope you're going to let them get some rest before you start the interrogation."

"It's called 'debriefing,'" Gila said importantly. "Sheriff Ramsay told me so."

"All right; before the debriefing, then. I hope it can wait."

Unfortunately, it couldn't.

"I'm sorry," Ramsay told Avi and Nate. He sounded as if he meant it. While they and Gila were being examined by the doctor, the sheriff had spent the intervening time arranging for Bobby Smith to be admitted to a hospital room for overnight observation — with two armed deputies standing guard outside his door to see to it that he stayed there. "Time is of the essence; I'm sure you can understand that. This is our first break in the case. You two may have learned something through your experience with Smith and Littletree in the cave that'll help us pin the arson on them. We've got Smith on threatening harm with a deadly weapon, but there are those other crimes waiting to be solved. I'd like to see him locked up behind bars for a considerable spell."

"Wouldn't we all?" Nachman Bernstein murmured. He, for one, was ready to scoop up his family and head for home. He'd had enough of both hospitals and crime scenes to last him a long, long time.

But Ramsay had other plans. He wanted to debrief Shimi and Gila, as well. Their part in the proceedings, he promised, would be quick. Shimi had mentioned that he'd encountered the Indians before; the sheriff wanted to hear about that. And Gila had witnessed the Indians' forcible taking of Feder and Goodman. Their parents were obliged, though not happily, to yield their own authority to that of the law.

Their kids, on the other hand, didn't seem to mind at all. Now that it was all over, they were eager to be part of things. From their point of view, it was all part of the adventure.

Fifteen minutes later, after all the players in the recent drama had been temporarily, if inadequately, refreshed by cans of ice-cold Pepsi from the machine in the hospital lobby, Nate and Avi sat facing the sheriff's desk in Ramsay's cramped office. His secretary perched in a folding chair at the side of the desk, taking shorthand notes of everything that was said. At one side of the small room, Nachman and Tova Bernstein stood in a protective knot with Gila, while on the adjoining bench, Efraim Mandel (Etty had taken the baby home for an overdue feeding) stayed close to Shimi. Steve Birch leaned against the rear wall, fighting off an intense weariness as he listened to every word.

The sheriff had Shimi Mandel recount his story first. Shimi described his brush with the pair when they caught him alone on the cliff trail. "I remembered Chaim and Donny telling me that they'd once met those guys, when our families were having a picnic. But they said they seemed friendly then."

"Was there a difference this time?" Ramsay asked.

Shimi nodded. In a low voice, he said, "They threatened to hurt me if I told anyone I'd seen them there."

"And did you?"

Shimi shook his head. "Not at first. I was scared to. Later on, I told Chaim and Donny, because I didn't want them going out on the cliffs if those guys were there."

His father placed a hand on the boy's shoulder and squeezed. Shimi gave him a smile, wan but grateful. He peeked up at the sheriff. To ward off the lecture he guessed was coming, he added quickly, "I know I should have told a grown-up. I did try to warn Chaim and Donny not to go there today, but they wanted to hike anyway."

Ramsay nodded without speaking. He turned to address Gila, assuming a hearty avuncular matter calculated to set her at her ease. "And what's your part in all of this, little lady? Why were you out of school and up on those cliffs this morning?"

Gila had the grace to look shame faced. In a few quick words she described how she'd feigned a stomachache in order to stay home from school. "I had to," she explained earnestly, with a sidelong look at her mother. "I knew that Chaim and Donny were planning to take a hike, and I had to make sure they were safe."

All the adults exchanged incredulous glances at the temerity of this pint-sized creature with the weak lungs, who had undertaken the role of her big brothers' protector. Tova found herself blinking back tears, her heart a confused mass of emotion that she was past untangling. She just wanted to get her little girl home and keep her safe forever.

"Thank you," Ramsay said. "It's been a long day, folks. I appreciate your help." The Bernsteins and the Mandels were dismissed.

The room seemed much larger after they'd gone. "Now, you two," Ramsay told Avi and Nate. "Talk."

"There's not much to say," Nate said slowly. "Until today, I knew nothing except what everyone else in town knew: that someone had been going around committing arson and trying to intimidate our community. The first I saw of those Indians was when they suddenly popped out of that cave and grabbed us." Ruefully, he shook his head. "Sorry I can't be of more help."

The Sheriff looked questioningly at Avi, who shrugged and said, "Ditto, I'm afraid."

"Think back, both of you," Ramsay ordered. "Did either of those men say anything that could shed any light on their plans? About what they were doing in the cave in the first place, or why they didn't want you around to witness it? Some sort of criminal activity, maybe?"

Nate and Avi thought back. Slowly, Nate said, "He — the big one — talked about looking for treasure. He said, 'It's one thing to look for treasure. But I don't hurt little kids, and I sure don't kill people.'"

Suddenly, Avi sat up. "The box!" he exclaimed.

"What box?" Ramsay leaned forward tensely.

"When we were down in that hole … when I fell and hurt my wrist? I crawled as far back as I could go, and there in the wall was a kind of overhang, with a deeper area further back. When I reached inside, I felt something. Nate pulled it out. It was a long box … pretty heavy …"

"Did you get a chance to see what was inside?" The Sheriff's interest was sparked.

Avi shook his head. "Couldn't. It was too dark, and my wrist was hurting too bad. And they were coming back to finish us off …"

"Can someone go back and get it?" Nate asked. "I wonder what it is. It looked pretty old, though the wood was in decent shape."

"Oh, we'll get it, all right," the Sheriff promised him, rising to his feet. "When we get Jim Littletree's body out of there, we'll make sure to keep our eyes peeled for that box of yours. It'll be interesting to see what's inside."

VI.

Stacy Rhodes, Ramsay's secretary, poked her curly head through the doorway of the tiny office.

"Sheriff, Sam Forbes just radioed in from the hospital. Seems Bobby Smith is kicking up a fuss. He's demanding a lawyer."

Ramsay shrugged. "He's entitled to one. Let him make his phone call and round one up."

Stacy hesitated. "He says he knows who he wants. Him." She nodded at Steve Birch, who was leaning against the back wall of the office in a state perilously close to semiconsciousness. The secretary's last word had the effect of rousing him more effectively that a dousing of ice-cold water.

"Me?!" Steve was incredulous.

At the same instant, Ramsay said, "Him?"

Stacy Rhodes nodded, gratified at the stir she had created, but disapproving at the same time. "Isn't that just like some people? First he beats up the poor man, then he demands that he represent him in the law."

Steve stirred as his mind began, with difficulty, to work again. "If there's one thing Bobby Smith has in abundance, it's brazenness. Guess I'd better get on down to the hospital and hear what he has to say."

Avi couldn't restrain himself. Staring at Birch, he asked, "You're not really going to be *his* lawyer, are you?"

Birch's response was a quietly enigmatic, "What do you think?"

This did not satisfy anyone in the room; least of all, Steve himself. As he slipped out of the sheriff's office after the briefest of good-byes, he wondered why in the world Smith wanted him. Even more challenging was a different question: Was he going to do it? Until now, he had never turned down a plea for help from one of his Indian brethren.

He was still groping for answers as he sped down Main Street toward Memorial Hospital.

As he swept through the revolving glass doors, he was struck by a flash of memory. He had been in this hospital before — with Bobby Smith. They had met at the bedside of Steve's stepfather, the hard-drinking Henry, who'd staggered into the street one night in a state of advanced intoxication, and a few months later ended his life in this very hospital.

His brow creased as he tried to remember Bobby's reason for being with Henry that day. As far as he knew, the two had been only remotely acquainted, if that much. Bobby had been reticent and Steve had not really felt all that curious.

Nor was he especially curious now. Old Henry was long dead and buried, but a Bobby Smith very much alive was demanding that Steve represent him in the law. Steve frowned, trying to shake off the cobwebs of fatigue that were making it difficult to think clearly. Like a web, sticky strands of memory were wrapping themselves around his brain, confusing past and present. He struggled to throw them off, but was only partially successful by the time he reached Bobby's door.

"Afternoon, Mr. Birch." The deputy on duty in the corridor greeted him with a respectful bob.

"Hi there, Sam. Is it afternoon already? I seem to have lost track of time."

"Well, you've had a busy morning … I'd say, rounding up miscreants is one surefire way of makin' the time fly!"

Steve chuckled, then nodded at the door. "How is he?"

"Physically? Fractured leg, coupla cracked ribs. Nothin' that time and the right care won't heal. Mentally, though, I'd say he was still ailin' something terrible."

"Ailing? What do you mean? Is he angry?"

"That, too. But there's more. He's been rantin' about that cave … talkin' 'bout something he says belongs to him down there. And he's been askin' after you — 'bout every three seconds or so. Glad to see you, Mr. Birch."

Heaving a sigh, Steve rolled his eyes ceilingward. "Well, I guess I'd better go see what he wants."

"Want me to come in with you?"

"No, thanks, Sam. I think I can manage."

"Well, I'll be right out here if he gives you any trouble."

Steve thanked him, pushed open the door and walked in.

Bobby was lying down, one leg in a plaster cast elevated several inches above the bed and his chest obscured by a crisscross of thick white bandages. He turned his head at the sound of the door opening and fixed a baleful eye on Steve. "You took your sweet time about getting here, didn't you?"

Steve decided to ignore the belligerent note. Taking a chair, he said mildly, "Came just as soon as I got your message. What's the story, Bobby? Why'd you want to see me?"

"You know why. You're supposed to represent us out at the reservation. You speak the white man's language, wear the white man's suit. They say you're good. So, I want you to be my lawyer."

Steve was taken aback at the sheer audacity of the man. Did he not remember that it was Steve, who just a short time before, had caught him in the act of threatening harm to two innocent people, and who had risked his own skin to secure him until the sheriff's men arrived?

Whether Bobby remembered or not, he had the gall to act as though he didn't. "Well?" Bobby demanded. "Will you do it?"

Slowly, Steve shook his head. "I don't think —"

Bobby cut him off. "Wait. I got something to tell you. Something that'll interest you."

"What could you possibly tell me that would interest me? Apart from a full confession to the arson and the other incidents, of course."

Bobby waved that aside. "It's about the cave," he said in a hoarse whisper. "And it's about your stepdad. Old Henry." The black eyes peered at the lawyer, daring him to deny his curiosity.

Steve didn't deny it. He stared at Bobby. "What about Old Henry?"

"Remember when we sat with him in this very hospital, less than a year ago?"

"I remember. Well?"

"He asked me to come down here 'cause he had something to tell me. A secret. He told me, but he didn't want to tell you ..." Bobby taunted the other man, shamelessly ignoring the fact that he was a prisoner manacled to a hospital bed and Steve was the lawyer whose help he needed to save his skin.

"I'm not surprised that he didn't tell me," Steve Birch said calmly. "He and I never did talk much. Is this going anywhere, Bobby?"

"It sure is. Right down to that cave Old Henry told me about."

"Cave ...?"

"*The* cave. The one you found me in today." Bobby's voice dropped even lower, taking on a grotesquely secretive hush. "*The one where the treasure is ...*"

Steve eyed him blankly. "What treasure?"

"Ssh! Hold it down, will you? Want that oaf by the door to hear you — or some passing nurse? I've waited long enough for that treasure, ever since Old Henry told me about it. He wanted me to have it, see. He said so. Me 'n Big Jim spent the past half-year or more searching for that treasure. And today, one of those Jewish guys stumbled right onto it. Onto *my* treasure! I would have found it for sure, if they hadn't gone poking around where they didn't belong ..."

Steve noticed that Bobby asked no questions and displayed no grief over the fate of his erstwhile friend and treasure-hunting partner. It was this omission, unlike the man's more deliberate taunts, that sent the first flickers of real fury coursing through him. There was a hint of steel in his voice as he said, "I can see that you're all broken up about Big Jim. The nurse tells me you've been crying into your pillow."

"Never mind that now." Bobby's eyes glittered, feverish with gold-lust. "I want that treasure, Birch. By rights, it's mine. Old Henry wanted me to have it. I deserve that gold. I been combin' those caves for months to find it!"

Steve shrugged, still angry. "That's not my business. Tell it to Sheriff Ramsay. If you can claim legal right to the treasure — if that's what it is — then you'll get it. *After* you get out of jail." He half-rose from his chair.

"Don't go, Birch. I got something to tell you." Bobby looked around the room, as though suspicious that someone might be hiding under the bed or hovering beyond the drawn window blinds. "You get me that treasure — and I'll split it with you. Say, 60-40. You'll be a rich man, Birch, not just a two-bit lawyer trying to hustle between the red man's world and the white one. As my attorney, you'd have the right to keep it a secret. Just between the two of us." He tried to raise himself on one elbow, wincing as his cracked ribs protested. "Well? What do you say?"

"If I'm only a 'two-bit lawyer,' why do you want me?" Steve was on his feet now, eyes blazing, exhaustion forgotten.

Bobby shrugged. "Don't know no other lawyers. And you're Mescalero, like me. It's your duty to represent me. Besides, it was Old Henry's money, so it's only right that some of it goes to you. I never felt quite right about taking it all for myself ..."

At this sanctimonious hypocrisy, Steve's rage boiled over. Typically, however, the heat of his anger found expression only in the increased coldness of his manner.

"Sorry, Bobby. I'm not for sale. Besides, I think you're guilty as sin. I wouldn't represent you if you paid me a fortune — which you don't have."

"Yes, I do! Or I will, soon as I can get over to that cave and see what's waiting down there." Bobby's refusal to accept defeat was, under the circumstances, staggering.

"Whatever's down there is going to be brought up very soon — along with Jim Littletree's body. Have a nice day, Bobby." Steve went to the door and pushed it open.

"*You get back here!*" Bobby yelled. The inscrutable mask had slipped, showing the feral beast behind it. "Get back here and act like a lawyer! You have to protect what's mine! I got my rights!"

The closing door cut off the tirade in midstream. In the corridor, Deputy Sam Forbes met Steve's eye sympathetically. "Rough interview?"

"You could say that. He wants me to represent him. I turned him down."

"Can't say that I blame you. Nasty piece of goods, that one."

"I couldn't agree more."

You're Mescalero, like me.

The words echoed and re-echoed inside Steve's head as he made his way down the steps to the lobby, too roiled up to wait for the elevator. Even before he stepped out into the sunshine, he knew where he was headed next. There was someone that he had to see … and a lot of things that it was high time he figured out.

You're Mescalero, like me …

He slipped behind the wheel, slammed the door and turned the ignition with a sharp twist of the wrist. The engine sprang to life.

Seconds later, he was on his way out of the hospital parking lot with a roar, headed west.

Chapter 18

I.

At the last possible moment before the road veered left to take him away from Lakewood and toward the reservation, Steve made an abrupt turn and headed in the other direction.

He was acting on impulse again. This disturbed him. He had been acting on impulse too often in recent days. Legally trained, with a measured, analytical mind, he was not usually prone to fits and starts. Yet here he was, speeding along the sleepy streets of this sunbaked town, making an unplanned stop on his way to an unscheduled destination. None of this was like the Steve Birch he knew.

Then again, he wasn't sure if he knew Steve Birch at all anymore ...

The stop was at his own apartment, and it took all of one minute. Thirty seconds to sprint up the stairs and unlock his door; 10 to grab what he had come for; and 20 more to hurtle back downstairs and into his waiting car.

He sat very still for a moment, waiting for his breath to catch up with him. Then he opened his bandaged palm to reveal the frayed little *siddur* it was clutching. He gazed at it in silence for a moment, then placed the *siddur* gently on the seat beside him.

After that, the drive was uneventful. The sky was a perfect cerulean blue, the brush still summer-dry, the stunted elms and cottonwoods stoically enduring the heat. He had made this drive countless times, rushing to and from the reservation to save one of his red-skinned brothers from the consequences of his own folly. Like a colossus straddling two worlds, he had belonged to both.

He'd been raised on Apache lore, surrounded by adobe walls and his people's history, but educated, in young adulthood, in the minutia of the American legal system. In the process, he had absorbed the larger culture. If he hadn't precisely left the old tradition behind, it was certainly no longer a driving force in his life.

And yet, as the outskirts of the reservation came into view, he had a sense of overwhelming familiarity. Childhood is where we pick up the ABC blocks that spell out "normal" and "home." For Steve, the Mescalero homestead — however leached of meaning and color, however drab and pointless to him today — still spelled those things.

He drove in with old-new eyes, seeing the things he'd always seen but with a different impact. What, really, besides a mutual upbringing, did he have in common with these people? With a start, he realized that it had been a long time — long before Rabbi Bernstein and his crew came to town — since he'd felt that he had anything in common with them at all.

Faithfully, he had worked hard to fulfill his commitment to them. But for a considerable period now, he'd been acting only from habit — and pity. Whatever higher ideal he may have begun with had long since evaporated under the harsh New Mexican sun.

He drove through the reservations gates and slowed down even further. Other than a stray dog ambling dispiritedly in the shade of the weather-beaten buildings, there was no one to be seen on this searing afternoon.

It took him exactly 10 minutes to find the person he was looking for.

More accurately, *she* came looking for *him*. By some strange connection or mental telepathy, Jim Littletree's old grandmother came hobbling out of the three-story adobe structure she called home just as Steve was approaching that same building. Peering ahead, hand to her eyes, she sighted him striding up the street in her direction.

A moment later, Steve saw her, too. He stopped walking, giving her the courtesy of taking the last few steps toward what she probably already suspected would be a painful encounter.

She came to a halt three paces away from where he stood. Her cane tapped the hard earth with finality. The black eyes, rheumy with age and holding just a hint of fear, looked up into his own paler ones.

"Jimmy?" she croaked.

He shook his head. "I'm sorry, Grandmother. So very sorry ..."

"H-how?" The black eyes dimmed with tears.

"Your grandson died trying to defend two innocent men against Bobby Smith. In the end, Jim chose the honorable path. You can be proud of him."

"I was always proud of him." The words were almost barked at Steve, as the old woman tried valiantly to regain her composure. "The minute he took up with the no-good Bobby Smith, I knew it would be bad. I knew it ..." The lined brown face lifted to his, and now the eyes were clear and hard. "When can I get him back? For burial here on the reservation."

"As soon as I can arrange it, Grandmother," he told her. "We'll give Jim the funeral he deserves."

The old woman nodded. With one work-roughened hand, she smoothed back the wispy strands of white at her temples; the other clutched her walking stick. She was silent for a long moment before meeting his eyes again. "Thank you."

"For what? I did nothing."

"You came to tell me. For that, I thank you."

"He was a good man, Grandmother. Never forget that."

"How can I forget? But my memories are worthless. They will sink into the ground with me when I go. There is no one to remember my Jimmy now ..." A tremor of pure pain quivered at her lips.

Steve waited a beat before answering, as though to underline the words.

"I'll remember, Grandmother," he said sincerely. "I won't forget."

Something new came into the wrinkled face; a tiny easing of the ache that would never leave her again. She seemed on the verge of saying something more, then changed her mind. With a silent nod she turned away, to make her slow way back to the shade of her adobe shelter.

Steve watched her go. When she had disappeared into the shadow of her doorway, he turned as well. He was finished here. It was time to find his car and leave. Time to leave the reservation in his dust. Time to bid this place — and his own past — a symbolic farewell.

Some five miles later, he pulled over onto the shoulder of an otherwise deserted road. He dialed Nachman Bernstein's number and waited in suspense as three, four and then five rings sounded in his ear. Finally, the rabbi picked up.

"It's Steve Birch, rabbi. I just wanted to hear how things have been going."

Nachman sounded as warm and relaxed as usual. What was it that gave these people their inner strength? This was a question that Steve had entertained before, after each of the arson attacks and Gila Bernstein's high-speed visit to the Roswell hospital on the heels of a brutal asthma attack. This time, the question did not sadden him, as it had before. It did not reinforce his sense of himself as an outsider, straining to catch a glimpse of some truth sheltering on the far side of a padlocked gate. Rather, it heartened him — because he was standing just outside that gate and had both fists raised to knock …

"Everyone's fine, thank G-d," Nachman was saying. "Apart from Avi Feder's injured wrist and my kids' insisting on telling anyone who'll listen about the 'adventure,' they all seem to be recovered from the ordeal."

"And your daughter?"

"We're very proud of how Gila handled herself today. It gives us hope that she's going to get this asthma thing under control, once and for all … with G-d's help, of course."

"Of course," Steve echoed. He paused. "Rabbi? Didn't you once tell me that Jews pray three times a day?"

"Yes. Once in the morning, once in the afternoon and a third time, at night."

"I thought so. Thanks … Uh, I know that things are kind of hectic right now, but I'd really like to see you soon, rabbi. We need to talk."

"That will be my pleasure, Steve. Say, 9 p.m.? At my house?"

"Perfect. Thank you, rabbi."

"See you then …"

Steve disconnected and sat back in his seat, staring, without seeing the panorama he knew so well. This portion of the country was steeped in its own history. Dramas had been staged here, the battles both large and small. Growing up, this tiny corner of the world had been the only thing Steve had known — though not all that he had wanted to know.

He still knew so little. But he would learn. That was something he promised himself firmly: He would learn.

Maybe some of the answers lay between the pages of the little book he'd snatched so impulsively from his room on his way out to the reservation. He hadn't needed it on his way over. On his way there, he had still been Mescalero.

In the few miles he had driven since leaving the reservation, he had said his private farewells to his past. It was time to start forging a new path into the future. He picked up the *siddur* and began turning the pages reverently, fingers shaking slightly as they touched each fragile, yellowed page. Drawing a deep breath, he murmured aloud, "Well, this is a first."

Jews prayed three times a day, Rabbi Bernstein had said. This morning he had murmured a little plea to G-d, but that hadn't been what he would call a genuine prayer, out of the pages of a genuine prayer book. This would be his first time today. His first time. Ever.

He didn't know what he was saying, but it felt good to be saying it from the pages of this *siddur*. Though the words were still indecipherable to him, the pipelines to heaven were wide open.

As he closed his eyes and blotted out the physical world, he sensed a billowing expansion that he had never felt before. A largeness … Something very, very big was opening up in front of him; something that he didn't need his eyes to see. It filled the vastness of the universe and crept in to fill up the cracks in his own soul as well.

With his eyes closed tight, he felt as though he were just beginning to see. He stood quite still, mouthing his own still-ignorant prayer, and knowing that the One he was addressing would understand just what he meant.

II.

Shiffy smiled nervously. "Do I look all right?"

"You're beautiful." Impulsively, Tova gave the younger woman a hug. "The kids are already in love with Tzviki. They'll be glad to take him off your hands whenever you're ... otherwise occupied."

"Thanks." Shiffy gazed into the flames of the candles she had just lit. She still couldn't believe she was actually here in Lakewood, New Mexico. The trip out west with her toddler had been one long blur of boarding gates, liftoffs, landings, and vague hopes. "This is all your doing, you know. I want to say thank you."

"Me? What did I do?"

"You called me that night ... all those weeks ago, after Avi flew away without a word."

"Oh, that. It was nothing —"

"You went out of your way to get my number from Avi's mother," Shiffy went on, ignoring the interruption, "and called me, a total stranger, just to make me feel better. 'He didn't leave that way because of something you said or did,' you told me. 'In fact, just the opposite. He's just scared ... very scared. Please give him time, Shiffy. He may come back ... And when he does — please, please don't turn him away. Please give him another chance.'"

Shiffy turned to smile almost tearfully at Tova. "You have no idea how low I was feeling that night. A person never knows what's going to happen with a *shidduch*, but this one seemed so promising. And then ... to leave like that, so abruptly, without a word. It was a blow." She paused, unconsciously grimacing at the memory. "Like a blow to the heart ..."

"Well, that's all in the past," Tova said briskly. "Whatever happens now, you'll both know you gave it your best shot."

"Yes." Shiffy smiled radiantly. "Thanks to you. You're an angel, Tova Bernstein."

To cover her embarrassment, Tova glanced at her watch. "The men'll be home from shul soon."

"Already?" A spasm of alarm crossed Shiffy's face. Clearly, she was both dreading and longing for the moment when the front door would open and Nachman Bernstein and his boys would come in, ushering their guest in before them.

A flurry of phone calls between Mrs. Feder, Shiffy Taub, Tova Bernstein and an experienced travel agent had resulted in a flight from New York to nearby Roswell that had required Shiffy and little Tzvi to switch planes twice, but had eliminated the three-hour drive from Albuquerque at the flight's end. Avi Feder, when Nachman spoke to him just before Shabbos, had sounded nearly as nervous as Shiffy looked.

"How will I find the words to apologize to her?" he'd asked Nachman, anguished. "I can't believe she came all this way after I ran out like that. What can I possibly say to make it up to her?"

"I think you'll find the right words," Nachman told him. "The fact that she agreed to come here at all is proof that she's ready to forgive. Relax, Avi. It'll be all right. In fact" — Nachman's eye had held a twinkle that his friend, at the other end of the line in his bachelor apartment, couldn't see — "I predict that it's going to be much more than all right."

"Will you and your wife cover for me at the Shabbos table? If there are awkward silences, I mean."

"Don't worry. We'll cover."

As things turned out, there was not much need for Nachman or Tova to say much of anything. The children were in such high spirits, and the girls in such transport over Tzvi, that they produced a nearly nonstop spate of chatter that successfully carried a tongue-tied Avi and a bashful Shiffy through the meal. Avi was still morbidly consumed with guilt over the way he had left after Succos. He was also self-conscious about the wide Ace bandage on his wrist. Young Yudi loudly insisted on hearing Avi's version of events in the cave, which didn't help any. As the story unfolded, he was conscious of Shiffy's horrified reactions and obvious relief at the happy outcome, but he kept his remarks addressed to the children. It was only afterward, with the table cleared and the family dispersed to their various post-*seudah* activities, that Avi stammered out an invitation to take a walk.

Shiffy excused herself, put Tzviki to bed, and emerged minutes later with a light sweater and a shy smile. The moment they left the house, the family exploded.

"Ma! Is he going to marry her?" Yudi demanded.

"I like her," Gila declared. "I hope he does."

"I adore that Tzviki," Shana said. "I get to watch him if Mrs. Taub wants to go to shul in the morning."

"I'll help," Gila added, doing a happy little pirouette around the room.

"The twins are down," their father observed, smiling down at his own 2-year-olds. Both Mo and Bo had their thumbs in their mouths and their eyes at half-mast.

Tova scooped up one sleepy little boy and her husband took the other. As they proceeded down the hall to the twins' room, Tova murmured, "Well? What do you think?"

He didn't have to ask her what she was referring to. With the practiced ease of the long-married, he replied, "I like what I see. Let's *daven* for them and hope for the best."

"What a blessing it would be for Avi."

"For Shiffy, too. Raising that little boy with no father …"

"I know." Tova's grip on her son tightened. She placed him tenderly on his bed, thankful that he was already wearing his pajamas. A warm kiss on the forehead elicited an inarticulate murmur from Bo, curled up beneath the covers. Smiling, she crossed the room to plant an identical kiss on Mo's cheek. Then she followed her husband out of the darkened room, closing the door behind her as she went.

The lunchtime *seudah* was a festive meal. A sense of deep gratitude suffused the Bernsteins and their guests as they sat down to the table that Shana and Gila had beautifully set, in between keeping an eye on Tzvi and the twins. Apart from Avi (who had walked home from shul at Nachman's side, chattering in exuberant spirits all the way) and Shiffy (walking discreetly behind with Tova), their group included Dr. and Mrs. Sadowsky. The latter greeted Shana warmly on her arrival.

"And do *not* apologize for not coming around to visit me much these days. I perfectly understand. If you've found yourself some friends your own age, no one could be happier than I am."

"Thank you," Shana whispered, cheeks burning. "I — I want you to know that I didn't just use you for … I mean —"

"We 'used' each other," the librarian said. "You were a stranger to this town and needed some companionship, and I needed a young face around the house again. It's kind of lonely, with my own kids grown up and the grandchildren so far away."

"I'll come again," Shana promised impulsively. "And I'll bring a friend along — if that's O.K. with you?"

"Perfect! You make sure to remember that promise, now, because *I'm* certainly going to. Just give me a little bit of notice, and I'll have fresh-baked cookies waiting when you come."

That hurdle successfully overcome, Shana went contentedly about her duties as her mother's right-hand girl. There were various courses to be served and youngsters to be supervised. She was walking into the dining room bearing a platter of succulent chicken cutlets, when the conversation suddenly took an electrifying turn. Setting the platter in the center of the table, Shana took her seat and gave Mrs. Sadowsky her full attention. Her father was — if possible — listening even more intently than she was.

"Jane Willard's diary mentioned that the townspeople buried the immigrant Jews who'd been massacred by the Apaches," the librarian was saying.

"Yes, you told me that the last time we spoke. Did you find any clue as to the whereabouts of those graves?"

Mrs. Sadowsky shook her head. "Not in the diary. But I've been busy these past few weeks. There are old historical archives at the town hall, and I've been going painstakingly through them all. I think I found what we've been looking for."

"A Jewish cemetery?" Donny broke in eagerly.

"Not an actual cemetery, Donny. More like a group of rough graves dug in proximity to one another. The townspeople seemed to have had the sensitivity to bury the Jews together — and separately from the massacred gentiles. It makes sense to think that they must have found some isolated spot outside the town limits."

Nachman leaned forward. "And you've found that spot?"

"I may have. I'm not sure, but the indications are hopeful. There's a small plot of ground at the foot of the cliffs, outside the town, but not too far away from it. The oldest map I found had the spot marked with a tiny 'J,' and an odd-looking star that may be meant to represent a Star of David."

"That must be it!" Nachman's eyes shone. "I've got to let Steve Birch know about this. Do you have the coordinates of the place?"

She nodded. "I wrote them down. It may not be easy to get out there ..."

"Steve will find a way. He's convinced that he's got Jewish antecedents." He went on to share, in brief, the remarkable series of dreams that Steve had told him about — dreams in which his own unique eye-color as well as the Jewish Star of David had made their repeated appearance. "He's also got a genuine *siddur*, very old but well preserved. It's apparently been handed down from mother to daughter — and finally to Steve in lieu of a daughter — for generations."

"Wow!" Gila breathed. "Then he *must* be Jewish!"

Her father smiled at her, and continued. "The *siddur* — and the dreams — are the only clues he has to an identity that might be other than the one in which he was raised."

Shana let the voices flow over and around her. Her mind was fully taken up with the intriguing mystery of this Indian who was not an Indian or, at any rate, not fully so.

"I've always sensed something about him," Tova confided to the table at large. "He seems to have — oh, I don't know — call it inner depth."

"I couldn't agree more," her husband said.

"I'll be glad to supply the coordinates," Mrs. Sadowsky offered. "Imagine praying at the graves of ancestors you never even knew existed!"

"We may never know that for sure," Nachman reminded her soberly. "He's spoken to me about converting. It seems probable that he'll have to go through a formal *geirus* if he wants to live as a Jew."

"Steve Birch ... a Jew?" Chaim spoke for the first time, testing the notion out loud. It seemed utterly incongruous at first: the clashing of two disparate worlds. The more he thought about it, however, the less strange it seemed. There was an integrity, an innate decency, about Birch that made itself felt wherever he went. No, it would not be all that surprising to discover that a Jewish soul resided within that Native American exterior.

"I'll let him know about the graveyard after Shabbos," Nachman said. "There's something special about that man. He's all torn up inside, searching for wholeness, and has felt pretty much the same way all of his life. If this information helps him any, I'll be glad."

"Me, too," Mrs. Sadowsky seconded.

Platters were passed and the conversational channels switched. Neither Avi nor Shiffy, seated across from each other at the large table, noticed the change in topic. On the other hand, they hadn't really been listening to the earlier talk, either. Though unable to exchange more than a polite, "Please pass the salt," over the course of the meal, they seemed to be linked in a silent conversation from challah to dessert. It was a conversation that took place in the silent spaces where mind touches mind and heart speaks to heart.

Nachman and Avi spent the afternoon in the *kollel* study hall, reviewing the Gemara they were learning. They returned to the Bernstein home for *seudah shelishis.* Soon after Ma'ariv and Havdalah, no one was surprised when, after quickly putting Tzvi down for the night, Shiffy agreed to join Avi for another walk.

"Have a nice time, you two!" Tova called softly after them, though it was doubtful whether they heard a word she said.

Nachman Bernstein left his study in search of his wife. He found her in the kitchen, flipping through the pages of her newest cookbook in a random way while a cup of tea cooled at her elbow.

She looked up at his entrance, and smiled. "Join me in a cup of tea?"

"No, thanks." He glanced at the clock above her head. "They've been out quite a while."

"That's a good sign, don't you think?"

"I don't know what to think."

"Oh, Nachman. It's not always necessary to compute all possible permutations with your rational mind. Why not just let your intuition take over? What does your *heart* think is happening with Avi and Shiffy right now?"

"Hearts don't think. And intuition," Nachman grinned, dropping into the seat facing her, "is a woman's domain. But I do have a good feeling about this *shidduch*."

"Me, too." Her smile faltered slightly. "I just wish things would go as well for Heidi. I wish she hadn't gone to New York just now. I wish I knew when she was coming back."

"That makes three wishes in all," Nachman grinned. Nonchalantly, he added, "Would it help if I told you that Nate Goodman is flying to New York tonight?"

Tova's incredulous stare was everything he could have hoped for. She groped for words and found none. Her joyous, staggered silence was a perfect cue for what came next.

There was a rattle at the front door. (The Bernsteins had given Shiffy a key to use for the duration of her stay; the same key, in fact, that Heidi had reluctantly returned when she left.) As Tova and Nachman sat as if glued to their chairs, they heard the muted murmur of voices, and two pairs of feet crossing the living room's hardwood floor. A head — two heads — poked through the kitchen doorway.

"Oh, good," Shiffy said, her smile radiant. "You're up."

"Up," Tova said, "and waiting."

"Waiting for Shiffy?" Avi asked, walking in. "You didn't have to do that. You knew I'd get her back safely."

"Waiting for both of you," Tova said pointedly. "So, how was your evening?"

The glance that the couple exchanged set Tova's heart beating far more rapidly than its customary pace. Nachman, too, felt the slow rise of excitement as Avi said slowly, "Our evening was … magnificent."

"Perfect," agreed Shiffy. The smile didn't seem capable of leaving her face. Tova held her breath.

"We talked things over," Avi said, "and realized that we have something in common. Oh, we actually have a lot of things in common, but this one is a biggie." He stopped.

"Well?" Tova breathed.

"After what we've both been through, we're both absolutely terrified. Of the future. Of life itself … or rather, of what life can throw at you."

A somberness touched his eyes as he spoke, as if the shadow of past sorrows had flitted through the softly lighted kitchen.

"It's not easy to trust that things can ever be good again," Shiffy added softly.

"But," Avi went on, turning to face the Bernsteins fully, so that Tova for the first time could see the blazing pools of light that were his eyes, "we realized one simple thing. We realized ..." Again, he broke off. To everyone's amazement — his own, most of all — his eyes filled. "We realized," he managed to choke out, "that we can be scared ... together."

Shiffy looked a little teary eyed herself. After a single frozen instant, Tova jumped to her feet and threw her arms around her. Nachman grabbed Avi and hugged him hard, then shook his hand like a pump gone berserk. "Avi, you *meshuggeneh*! You did it! You asked her to marry you!"

"And she said yes," Avi whispered. The tears fled, replaced by a fierce, grateful joy. "Nachman, would you believe it? She said yes!"

"Of course she did!" Tova exclaimed. "Oh, mazel tov, mazel tov, you two!"

"I'd better go check on Tzvi," Shiffy said, wiping her cheeks with the palms of her hands and laughing at the same time. "Did he wake up at all since I left?"

"Not a peep out of him," Tova assured her. "I checked on him every 20 minutes or so."

"Thank you so much ..." Shiffy started for the door.

"Hurry back," Nachman ordered. "We've got a 'l'chayim' to make." He was already on his way out of the kitchen as he spoke.

"And after that," Avi said, "I've got to call my mother."

"So do I," Shiffy's voice floated back to them.

Nachman made for the breakfront, where his small stock of liquor was stored. Avi stood dazed in the middle of the kitchen as Tova began throwing together a plate of cakes and cookies. Then she stopped what she was doing and asked, "Did you say something, Avi?"

Avi Feder turned to stare at her, jubilant and stupefied in equal measure. "Would you believe ...?"

Avi's hand trembled as he pushed the buttons to reach his mother. "Ma," he said when she answered the phone, "I know it's late, but — "

"Yes, Avi?" she said. "Quick, tell me the news."

"Shiffy and I —" He choked up and tried again. "Shiffy and I are —"

"Engaged!" his mother shrieked. "Oh, Avi, you've made me so happy!"

They spoke joyfully for a few minutes, and Shiffy in turn collected her "Mazel tov" from Avi's mother, along with a promise to go see her the minute she returned to New York. Then Avi took the phone again.

"Ma," he said quietly, "please call Yocheved's parents and tell them. I don't want them to find out from strangers."

"Of course, Avi," she answered, with emotion that matched his own. "They've been so concerned. Painful as it is, I know they will be delighted for you."

Avi thanked her, and hung up the phone. For a moment he stood very still, letting past and present wash over him and then wash away again, leaving him clean and peaceful as white sands after the tide has rolled out. With the beginnings of a deeply grateful smile, he rejoined the others. It was time to celebrate.

III.

There was rejoicing in the *kollel* the next morning and indeed, all the next day and into the night. As various students and community members flocked to the shul for *davening* or classes, they were regaled with the happy news of Avi's engagement. Each announcement was the signal for a new round of "Mazel tovs!" usually followed by yet another cycle of hearty song and dance. It was a euphoric Avi who taught his evening classes that night. As Efraim went through the motions with his own group, he felt an answering joy in his own heart, like the echo of a distant yodel flung back from some remote Alp. Avi had certainly known his share of suffering. He deserved some happiness at last.

When was the last time I felt that happy? Efraim wondered.

On his wedding day, certainly, and at the births of his children. But the more recent past — his years in the Brooklyn *kollel*, and the months since their move to New Mexico — had been more ambivalent. There was still the enormous contentment he felt in the study and teaching of Torah. This was what he wanted to do; this was what he was meant to do.

But there was a deadened area inside him, like a neglected garden that refuses to flourish, or an airless vacuum incapable of supporting life. He knew the exact source of this unjoyful deadness: jealousy. Always, gnawing at him with greater or lesser intensity, was the sense of envious comparison to others which led, in turn, to the burning sense of failure that had become his most constant companion.

Back in Brooklyn, he had been terribly jealous of Nachman Bernstein. Nachman's elevation to *Rosh Kollel*, however, had neutralized the jealousy by the simple expedient of removing him from Efraim's orbit. But that didn't mean that he was free at last of the tangled coils of envy. He'd simply transferred the focus of his envy to Asher Gann.

He could hear Asher's voice now, booming out in its confident way and, as always, completely mesmerizing his students. Efraim felt himself shrinking in comparison, as though there were only so much psychic space in the world and the more space Asher's personality took up, the less there was left over for him.

Like a tiny but vicious predator, the jealousy nibbled away at his vitals. His wife tried to soothe the pain that gave rise to these feelings or that were created by them. But nothing that Etty said helped for long. It was as if Efraim and his envy were locked in a sick, unbreakable partnership: a macabre dance that could lead only to slow paralysis and the death of joy.

But something was different tonight. There was a sense of exaltation in the air that would not be opposed, and that even Efraim found it impossible to ignore. Perhaps it stemmed from the relief of knowing that the arsonists who had threatened their tiny community seemed to be out of commission at last. That easing of worry had come hard on the heels of his own more personal salvation, in terms of Layala's successful surgery.

He was filled with relief over Shimi, too. His most difficult child had emerged from the ordeal on the cliffs with a renewed sense of self-worth, which had begun to translate into unusually cooperative behavior at home. Etty was beside herself with pride and satisfaction. She and Efraim were both basking in a belated sense of *nachas* from their second son, whose light had always been effectively hidden behind Meir's more dazzling bushel.

And now, to top off the general joy, was Avi Feder's engagement. It was impossible not to share in his happiness, or to wish him every good in the world.

Buoyed by an unaccustomed sense of well-being, even the sound of Asher's hearty voice down the hall lost some of its sting. If life could be good for others, it could be good for him, too. In fact, looked at objectively, it *was* good. He could be happy ... if he only allowed himself to be.

Like an isle of sanity in an ocean of raging emotion, the thought raised its head clearly in his mind. *I can be happy, too. I don't have to be jealous. That's just a choice I make — but I can unchoose it any time I like. I can be happy!*

How he managed to teach his class he didn't know; but teach it he did, and apparently successfully, if one judged by his students' friendly good-nights when it was over. He left his own classroom and moved blindly down the hall toward the beacon that was Asher's voice. This was not in teaching mode now, but speaking with practiced ease as he answered questions, related anecdotes and diffused general good cheer to the small but eager cluster of students who always seemed to flock around him when classes were over.

Efraim watched and waited, willing the virulent insects of envy to still their wings. This he found an almost impossible task. The insects whirled and stung; they refused to be silenced. Clenching his fists in the slowly emptying corridor, he uttered an inward cry. *Hashem! I can't do this alone. Please help me. Help me not be jealous anymore. Help me stop tearing myself up this way. Help me find peace ...*

When the last of the students had drifted away, Asher turned — and was surprised to see him standing there. An instant guardedness crept into his manner.

"Efraim? You wanted to see me about something?"

Efraim winced inwardly at the caution in Asher's voice. Not that he blamed him; the Mandels and the Ganns had a difficult history behind them. Well, maybe it was time to start rewriting history.

"Yes, I did," he said, mustering the necessary courage because he had to. Because he could not go on even one more day living with the festering sore that was his own soul. "I wanted to repeat what I said to you on *Erev* Yom Kippur. Only this time, I really mean it."

"*Erev* …?"

"I asked you then to forgive me if I'd done anything to hurt you," Efraim plowed on. "I asked it because that's what you're supposed to do before Yom Kippur and, of course, you said you did. But you weren't aware — at least, I don't think you were — of where my … hostility, I guess you'd call it … has been coming from."

Asher was looking increasingly uncomfortable. "Look, Efraim. There's no need to —"

"Yes, there is a need. I need to tell you how incredibly, stupidly jealous I've been of you. Of your charisma, of your way with the students — of everything. That, and nothing else, is what's been motivating me to treat you in ways that I shouldn't have. You haven't done a thing wrong; it's all me. And I guess my attitude has filtered down to my wife, too. So I'm apologizing on behalf of us both …"

"Efraim. I don't know what to say."

"Then let *me* say it. I want to start over," Efraim said. "I want to stop being jealous of you. I want to make the most of myself, and of this experience out here in New Mexico. I want for us to work together to build this *kollel*, and eventually the *mesivta*, too, into something great."

"Those are goals we can definitely agree on." Asher seemed relieved to have the conversation move into more practical channels. "Yes, let's start over. I've been just as silly, letting this thing drag on for so long. I should have confronted you a long time ago — asked what was eating you. But I'm glad you came over just now. That took guts."

Efraim considered various responses to this, then settled for a simple "Thank you."

The two men walked down the hall and out the door. As he looked up at the sky, awash in silver stars, Efraim realized that he could not remember the last time he had felt so … free. If he had owned a pair of wings, he could have unfolded them right there and then and soared up to visit those distant suns. He couldn't wait to get home and share this moment with Etty.

He could predict her reaction. She would hear him out in silence, and then shrug and declare in her tart way, "You should have done this a long time ago, Efraim. But better late than never, that's what I always say."

And he would agree with her, with all his heart.

IV.

Getting Big Jim's body out of the crevice proved a more daunting project than anyone had expected. Sheriff Ramsay phoned various police jurisdictions to request the loan of the necessary equipment. But for one reason or another, nothing seemed to be available until after the weekend. In one county, it was the equipment itself that was in use elsewhere; in another, the operator was off duty till Monday.

"Can I count on Monday, then?" Ramsay asked impatiently. He guessed — hoped — that the cool, dry air in the cave would preserve the body till then.

"Monday it is."

Meanwhile, the sheriff and his men were busy collecting evidence in their case against Bobby Smith. The debris of arson that they found in Smith and Littletree's rental apartment was deemed sufficient to get an indictment. A snag developed when the lawyer the county had assigned to Smith declared his client unfit to stand trial by reason of an unstable mind.

It was Dr. Abe Rein, forensic psychiatrist, to whom Sheriff Ramsay assigned the unsavory job of delving into Bobby Smith's mind to see if he was, or was not, capable of standing trial.

General opinion among Lakewood's law enforcers held that Smith was as sane as anyone. But Bobby put on a convincing show. Swaying, chanting and shouting by turns, he kept the guard at the tiny two-cell jail in a state of constant annoyance. It was imperative that he be examined by a competent professional, and Dr. Rein wasted no time in doing so.

Medicine contains many gray areas; the law does not. Legally, the issue was black or white: Either Bobby Smith was capable of standing trial, or he wasn't. In the latter case, he would be committed to a state mental facility for treatment until such time as he was deemed fit to be tried for the crimes for which he'd been indicted.

Abe Rein met Bobby Smith in his cell, with the guard within call. Smith was docile during the meeting, withdrawn as a schizophrenic or a small child. But Rein knew his job. Three times he came back to conduct his interviews, which were aimed at ferreting out any possible psychopathy in the prisoner. When he was done, he wrote up the results of his evaluation and presented them to the judge at a pretrial hearing.

Judge Horace B. Nelson read the report and concurred with it. His large head, crowned with a mane of white hair of which he was inordinately proud, bowed for a moment before he announced his ruling.

"Bobby Smith is of sane mind and capable of assisting in his own defense. Therefore, he is deemed fit to stand trial. So the court orders!"

Bobby was given the news at midday on Wednesday.

At dusk that same day, he had a visitor from the reservation.

Like bees to honey, the Bernstein boys were drawn to the tiny holding cell next to the sheriff's office. Sometimes Shimi Mandel joined them, but mostly he preferred to stay away. Donny, in particular, enjoyed swaggering about in front of the jail, taking immense pleasure in the fact that his little sister was one of those responsible for placing the prisoner inside its sturdy brick walls.

The site exerted a morbid fascination for Chaim. The thought of so much evil locked away and neutralized was both comforting and frightening. Comforting, because Bobby Smith was under the watchful eye of the law now, and thus rendered harmless. At the same time, there was a sense of playing with fire that Chaim couldn't quite shake. Until Smith was behind bars in some extremely secure state prison miles away from Lakewood, he would not feel completely safe.

On the day that Bobby Smith received his visitor from the reservation, Chaim and Donny were hanging around the jail again. They did not see Bobby's visitor arrive, but they witnessed his departure. Though they didn't know it, the Indian they watched exiting the jailhouse and slouching down the street was Al Barker, from the Mescalero reservation; an Al Barker a few months older and even more streetwise than the youth Steve Birch had visited at home in an attempt to reform the young man's increasingly antisocial ways. He was wearing grubby khakis and his usual expression of surly arrogance, tinged now with a certain secretive excitement. Chaim and Donny spotted him when they were still some distance away, approaching down Main Street. By the time they arrived at the jailhouse, the street was quiet again, and all but deserted.

The brothers loitered out front, staring at the single cell's high, narrow window and chatting in a desultory fashion. Classes were over for the day, but enough daylight still lingered in the sky for the boys to see the cell window and to picture the prisoner languishing inside. They found a real satisfaction in both the actual sight and the mental image. It would be suppertime soon, and their mother would be expecting them. They had, by their estimation, about five more minutes before it would be time to head for home.

Four of those minutes had passed without incident, when a sudden clamor from within the jailhouse electrified the brothers. There was a shout, the sound of violent scuffling, and then the startling report of gunshots. Abruptly, the door to the street was flung open. Donny surged forward, excited and curious. Chaim had just grabbed his arm to pull him back when, at precisely the same instant, they both recognized the figure swaying in the doorway.

It was Bobby Smith. He was unkempt, the ruler-straight black hair longer than ever, and the black eyes hard as steel. Most startling of all was a spreading stain in the center of his prison uniform.

One of Bobby's hands clutched at the source of the stain. Chaim watched in horror as blood gurgled up over Smith's fingers, staining them bright red. With a strength born of desperation, he practically dragged Donny into the shadows of the narrow alley that ran between the small jailhouse and the sheriff's office beside it.

In the waning light, Smith looked like a figure out of a nightmare. The chiseled cheekbones seemed more prominent, accentuating the flat dark eyes beginning to glaze with pain. He lurched a step forward, and then another, head flicking right and left as though looking for someone or something. On cue, a figure came running down the street toward the open jailhouse door. It was the Indian they had seen slouching away just moments before. He reached the jailhouse door just seconds after Bobby appeared there. He flashed right past Chaim and Donny, huddled in the shadows, without seeing them.

Go the other way, Chaim prayed silently. *Please, please, go the other way ...*

Al Barker caught sight of Bobby swaying in the doorway, lightheaded with blood loss. "You crazy, man? *Move!*" he snarled. "My car's over there ..."

He pointed west — away from the sheriff's office. As the two men started in that direction, Bobby moving slowly and with exaggerated care because of his wound, Chaim tugged at his brother's sleeve. "We've got to get the Sheriff," he hissed. "Hurry!"

"Let's follow them," Donny urged. "If we find out where they're going, we can —"

"NO!" Weeks of tension exploded in the single whispered syllable. "We are *not* going to follow them. We're getting help — grown-up help — and we're getting it *now!*"

Donny turned to his brother to protest, only to be met by an unexpected and blazing determination. Reluctantly, he surrendered his dreams of glory. They burst into the sheriff's front office like a double implosion, scaring poor Stacy Rhodes nearly out of her wits.

She collected them again in a hurry. "What are you two kids doing, barging in like that? You nearly gave me a heart attack!"

"The prisoner ... He's escaped!" Chaim shouted.

"The prisoner ...?" She stared. "You're kidding, right?"

"No joke."

"Then why haven't we heard the alarm? What's the guard doing over there — taking a nap?"

Then, hearing her own words, she paled. Her finger jabbed down on the buzzer on her desk. "Sheriff," she said in a voice that was suddenly hoarse. "There's a couple of kids here saying that the prisoner's escaped."

The inner door flew open almost before she finished speaking. Sheriff Ramsay's brows met in an enormous scowl as he glared at the boys. "What's going on?"

He had addressed Chaim, the elder brother, and Chaim responded instantly. "We heard noises from inside the jailhouse — sounded like a fight. There were gunshots ... Then the door opened and Bobby Smith came out. He was bleeding ... Another Indian came running up the street and ran away with him. He said he had a car." Chaim quickly reviewed his own story to inspect it for holes, then ended with a decisive nod. "That's all."

Ramsay was already halfway out the door. Over his shoulder, he shouted, "Which way did they go?"

"West!" Donny called back, glad to be able to make a contribution, however meager, to the drama.

Ramsay flung himself into the driver's seat of his car and sped away into the sinking sun, one hand on the steering wheel, and the other busy radioing for help.

The sequel to the episode filtered back to Lakewood's Jewish community in bits and pieces, and was finally confirmed by a phone call from Rabbi Harris to Sheriff Ramsay.

Thanks to the Bernstein brothers' timely alert, Ramsay had been able to mobilize the necessary manpower for the chase in an astonishingly short time. Smith and Barker, speeding westward in a cloud of dust, were overtaken by a police vehicle approximately 20 minutes after leaving Lakewood's town limits — on the point of entering Mescalero territory. Al Barker opened fire on the police but was soon captured by a couple of very angry policemen when his ammunition ran out.

Bobby Smith, though severely weakened by loss of blood, attempted to escape into the brush while Barker was fighting it out with the police. With the sheriff in hot pursuit, he managed to cover several hundred yards of rough terrain before collapsing. He died — en route to the hospital — of the gunshot wound he had sustained while breaking out of jail.

The guard had been left seriously injured in the jailhouse, shot by the gun that Al Barker had slipped to Smith in the course of his visit. How or why the guard's vigilance had become so lax as to allow the weapon transfer to happen, no one was ever able to learn, for the guard never regained consciousness. He, too, passed away in the small hours of that night; yet another victim sacrificed to one man's unquenchable hunger for gold.

V.

"**H**old 'er steady … Here we go!" The rasp and whirr of the lifting apparatus filled the cave with a deafening din.

Jack Ramsay stood back, letting the experts wield their machinery. A winch had been set up as close to the ledge as possible, with storm lanterns scattered at intervals around the rear of the cave to illuminate the area. With the aid of ropes, two men had descended to the floor of the depression and were now busy securing the corpse in a specially designed sling and buckling it in for the ride up to the top. When all was in place, one of the men yelled, "Ready!" The winch operator, a dour-looking string bean of a man, yanked a lever.

Pulleys revolved; cables rose and fell; the motor whined. "Big Jim" Littletree was drawn slowly up from the depths. A van was waiting to transport the body to the police morgue.

"There's something else down there," Ramsay told the operator.

The sour look deepened, but the man was under the Lakewood sheriff's orders today. He waited morosely for more.

"It's a box," Ramsay explained. "I'm going to have my men search for it in the place where we were told it was found. When they give the word, I want you to haul it carefully — very carefully — up to the top."

With a nod, the operator turned his back on the sheriff. Ramsay had already given his men their instructions. Presently, to his satisfaction, he heard the call rise up from below: "Got it, chief. Should we use the same sling?"

"Only if it's a secure fit. This is some sort of antique, boys. Let's be careful how we handle it, okay?"

"We'll handle it with kid gloves, chief!" one of his deputies called back cheerfully.

"Or we would, if we had any …" the second rejoined. There was the echo of a chuckle, and then silence as the deputies saw to the serious business of securing their find.

Five minutes later, Sheriff Ramsay was gazing down at the box at his feet.

It looked very old, with a hand-carved precision to the molding on the lid that was rarely seen anymore these days. As Nate Goodman had remarked, the wood seemed to have weathered the years surprisingly well. Like Nate, Ramsay surmised that the cave's cool, dry atmosphere had helped preserve the wood of which the box was made. The question was: Had its contents enjoyed the same good fortune?

Ramsay stooped to lift the box. It was heavy, but a careful experiment revealed no rattling of its contents. That meant that whatever was in there was large enough to fit inside without much extra space.

"No point in speculating," Ramsay said aloud. "Let's get this thing back to the office and have a look."

It was with an air of ceremony that he supervised the transfer of the old box from the police car to his desk. In honor of the occasion, he had the surface of the desk swept clear of everything else, goading his long-suffering secretary, Stacy Rhodes, into a pointed, "So *that's* what color it is …!"

Stacy and the two deputies stood respectfully by as Ramsay tenderly pried the lid open with the aid of a screwdriver. The lid was not locked or even latched; it was only the effects of time and weather that prevented it from lifting with ease. Ramsay, working with exaggerated care, inserted the tip of the screwdriver at intervals around the rim, between box and lid. When he judged the latter to be sufficiently loosened, he took hold of it from both sides, and lifted.

Four pairs of eyes stared at the object lying inside. Two sets of wooden handles protruded at the top and bottom, the color of the wood paler than that of the box, but by its appearance, deriving from the same era. The object was wrapped up in rather threadbare velvet, but Ramsay didn't have to unwrap it to know what the velvet hid. He had seen a similar object when investigating the torched synagogue some weeks before.

"Stacy," he said, without looking up from the box. "Please call Rabbi Harris and Rabbi Bernstein and ask them to come down here at their earliest convenience. I think they're going to want to see this."

"I don't believe it," Pinchas Harris said raptly, gazing at the velvet-wrapped object lying in its box like a baby in its cradle. "A *Sefer Torah!*" For the others' benefit, he explained, "A Torah scroll. How old is this one, I wonder? We'll have to have it analyzed. And a *sofer* — a scribe — will have to inspect it …" It was clear that he was talking to himself, mind flying ahead with plans for this amazing find.

Nachman Bernstein stood beside him. With one finger he touched the velvet, then glanced at Pinchas. "May I?"

The rabbi hesitated. "Do you think we ought to move it?" Then, recklessly, "Oh, go ahead, Nachman. Pick it up. I'm dying to hold it myself …"

Nachman reached inside. As tenderly as a father picking up his newborn child for the first time, he lifted the *Sefer Torah* and cradled it in his arms. Pinchas Harris moved closer, eyes shining, and planted a kiss on the worn velvet.

"It's so old," he said reverently. "I wonder what this *Sefer Torah* has been through? And how did it end up in that cave, of all places?"

"Mrs. Sadowsky's band of immigrants," Nachman said suddenly.

All eyes turned to him in surprise. The sheriff said, "What?"

"There's evidence that a small group of Jewish immigrants passed through here during the Gold Rush of 1849 … Or rather," he amended soberly, "they intended to pass through. A horde of Apaches swept into town and massacred a number of people — including those poor newcomers …"

"They must have put the scroll in the cave for safekeeping," Ramsay surmised. He eyed the burden in Nachman's arm with an almost shy respect.

Pinchas Harris shook off the pall of the past. Energetically, he said, "Nachman, I can't wait to get this over to a *sofer*. That is," he turned to the sheriff, "if you'll release it to us?"

"The box was found on public property," Ramsay answered slowly. "If I report it to the proper government agencies, there could be months of red tape until the whole thing is untangled." He saw disappointment spring into both of the rabbis' eyes.

"But," he continued, "seeing as how this is clearly a Jewish religious artifact, and therefore of primary interest only to the Jewish community, I think it would be appropriate to release the box and its contents into your custody, don't you? Call it a little bit of compensation for what you people have been going through lately, with the arson and all."

"Thank you, sheriff!" Rabbi Harris beamed. "There's surely a reward waiting for you for this!" Seeing the sheriff beginning to formulate a protest, he added hastily, "In heaven, of course."

"Of course," Ramsay agreed, smiling broadly. "Need any help transporting this thing to wherever it is you're taking it?"

Pinchas and Nachman exchanged a look. "I think we can manage, Sheriff. Thanks," Nachman said. To Pinchas, he added, "My minivan?"

"Perfect. We'll take it to the shul. Then I'll start making some calls."

Nachman planned on making some calls of his own: to librarian/historian Mrs. Sadowsky first. And, second, to Steve Birch.

Every Jew in Lakewood was going to take a special interest in the contents of this historic box, unearthed in a cave right outside their town. But, if his guess was right, Birch's interest would be the greatest of all — and of an extremely personal nature.

VI.

Bobby Smith was laid to rest in the Mescalero graveyard on the day after Jim Littletree's funeral was held.

Jim's grandmother had flatly refused to permit a double ceremony. What little comfort she could derive from the sorrowful occasion came from the sight of the dozens of respectful mourners who came to pay their last respects to the benevolent giant who had tragically strayed into the most dangerous territory of all: bad company. Now Big Jim lay peacefully beside his ancestors beneath the hard New Mexico sun. His days of toil and friendship were over.

Whether Bobby Smith's rest was as peaceful is doubtful. Only a handful of people attended his funeral the next day, and they came out of curiosity rather than love. One of these was Steve Birch.

Another was Big Jim's grandmother, who walked silently up to the fresh mound of earth when the brief ceremony was over. For a moment, Steve thought she was going to make some sort of sign: some gesture to express her grief, her outrage, her contempt.

But all she did was stare at the mound for a long moment in piercing, wordless reproach. Then she turned her back on the new grave and hobbled away, the tip of her cane leaving a trail of pale indentations in the dust.

A sentence came unbidden to Steve Birch's mind: words he'd read just the night before in the annotated, English-translation book of Psalms that Rabbi Bernstein had given him, a token to mark the start of his long journey toward what Steve believed were his roots and knew was his destiny. *"Better for me is the Torah of Your mouth than thousands in gold and silver."*

Bobby Smith had died in pursuit of a dream of material riches. Steve Birch hoped to live in pursuit of a very different kind of dream …

It was a new word for him — "Torah" — but one that held enormous significance. That was the name of the scroll that had been found in the cave in the cliffs, hidden there with devotion by a band of weary but hopeful Jewish immigrants. They, too, had been on the trail of gold. And they, too, had perished in the quest.

Perhaps, he reflected soberly, *a Jew's time is better spent searching out the meaning of G-d's Word than the gold dust swirling in foreign rivers.* They had not learned that lesson in time, those far-from-hardy travelers. He would take up the search where they had left off.

He checked his watch. If he didn't hurry, he would be late for his next class with Rabbi Bernstein. These lessons in Jewish law and lore were quickly coming to eclipse everything else in his life. His step was vigorous as he walked to his car and slipped inside. Without a backward glance he drove away from the cemetery and the reservation on his way to a place where he could finally belong.

It was very late, but Tova was too wired to sleep. She and Nachman sat in the living room, facing the picture window. Moonlight, flooding the room, provided the only illumination. Through the window they could see the nearly full moon skimming froths of cloud-waves in an indigo sea.

"Is it really over?" she asked. "Are we safe now?"

He waited a beat before answering. "It's over," he said, "or as over as things can be, in a world where 'Eisav hates Yaakov' forms an integral part of reality. Safe? We're in Hashem's hands, Tova. That's safe enough for me."

She nodded. Around her in the silvery darkness, the house seemed to breathe in time with the rhythms of her children's sleep. She would go upstairs soon. Maybe, with this newfound sense of security to bolster her, she would finally find the rest she craved. A deep, contented yawn took hold of her.

She caught Nachman's smile. "Go ahead," he said. "You must be exhausted."

"I am. I think I'll sleep now."

"Good." He gazed out at the velvet sky, where tiny stars were sailing around the frigate of the moon. "I guess I'll learn for a little while ..."

"I guess you will," she said fondly as she rose to her feet. They would each take this peace that they had been given as a gift, and use it to fill their greatest immediate need: She, to catch up on the slumber that had been in such short supply during these tension-filled weeks, and Nachman to nourish his soul with the words of Torah that made up the rock-sturdy foundation of his world.

"Good night," they said at the same moment.

Laughing, Tova watched her husband head in the direction of his study. Then she drew the curtains to blot out the moon and took the stairs two at a time, eager to get the night over with, so that tomorrow would come more quickly.

Epilogue

EIGHT MONTHS LATER

It was June, and summer had returned to the Southwest. On the outskirts of Lakewood, not far from the foot of the brooding red cliffs that had seen so much drama the previous autumn, a group was gathered to celebrate.

They had gathered once before, for a similar reason. That occasion had been in high summer, and the celebration had taken the shape of an informal picnic attended by the four families newly arrived in New Mexico to launch their fledgling *kollel*. This time, the gathering was more official in nature. The Rosh Yeshivah, Rabbi Greenfeld, had flown down together with old Mr. Fleischmann, their generous sponsor, to be present at the inauguration of the new *kollel* and *mesivta* building.

The construction of the building had been astonishingly quick. The weather itself had seemed to conspire to make the job go smoothly. Supplies came in on schedule; workers proved more reliable than not; contractors actually fulfilled their contracts more or less on time. *Heaven seemed to be smiling down on their project*, Rabbi Greenfeld thought with a pleased smile of his own. He looked around at his small but competent band of soldiers. How many of them would still be here in, say, five years' time? Would their newly fledged institution flourish as they hoped? Would Hashem shower their efforts with success?

He had no way of answering his own questions. The only thing that the venerable Rosh Yeshivah could predict with certainty was that things would not remain static. The one constant in life was change.

Right now, though, he was content to relish the joy of this special occasion, and let tomorrow take care of itself.

Tova Bernstein was also thinking about change on that festive afternoon. This inauguration was taking place nearly one full year since the Bernsteins had moved to Lakewood.

Images from the past 12 months flowed inexorably through her mind: painful images and beautiful ones, the difficult as well as the sublime. It hadn't been easy to uproot the family, but here they were, and here, please G-d, they hoped to stay as long as they were needed.

The sound of her husband's voice tore Tova from her reverie. As *Rosh Kollel* and the driving force behind this whole undertaking, Nachman Bernstein had been asked to say a few words in honor of the occasion.

He quoted from *Tehillim*: "He who bears the measure of seeds walks along weeping — but will return in exultation, a bearer of his sheaves." Smiling around at his fellow celebrants, he said, "If there's a better description of triumph after adversity, I don't know what it is. We plant our seeds, sometimes in tears, and we later bear the resulting sheaves of grain in joy. But even then, we have to remember: The job doesn't stop there. We must 'bear our sheaves' even on that blessed day. The burden, however joyful, still remains to be carried. Even at the moment of greatest celebration, let us not forget that there is still work to be done. Important work. Ongoing work. The spiritual work that this building was created for, and that we have come out here to accomplish.

"May we 'bear our sheaves' in triumph and joy, and with help from Above, for many long years to come!"

A spontaneous cheer erupted. Tova wiped a surreptitious tear from the corner of her eye.

And then the ceremony was over. It was time to pile into their cars and drive home, where children waited to be fed and a myriad of domestic details waited to be seen to. Nachman parted warmly from the

Rosh Yeshivah, who would be flying back to New York in Fleischmann's personal jet. Efraim ushered his family into their van and Asher and Rivi waved good-bye before disappearing in their car. Avi and Shiffy Feder managed, not without difficulty, to load an overtired Tzvi into his booster seat. Nate Goodman loped over to Nachman.

"My car's in the shop — again," he announced with a comical groan. "Can we hitch a ride with you?"

"No problem," Nachman said. "Hop in, we're about to leave. Yudi and the twins claim to be 'starving.'"

In no time at all, the minivan was barreling briskly down the streets of Lakewood. With the return of summer, everything looked hard baked again. Tova was still struck, even now, by the strangeness of it all. But she found she didn't really mind. For a Jew, home was where your shul was, and your yeshivah, and your *kollel*. Her people had been transplanted too many times to count, but they remained the same people. They carried their home — their spiritual center — with them wherever they went. The Brooklyn of her childhood might be a million miles away, but she was right where she was supposed to be.

The minivan slowed as it approached a small house with a metal shingle swaying lightly in front. In the last of the afternoon sun, the sign cast a moving shadow on the gravel path below. GOODMAN AND GOODMAN, the shingle read. And underneath, in smaller letters: ATTORNEYS-AT-LAW.

"That's our stop," Heidi said.

Tova twisted around in her seat to smile at her friend. "You're joining us for a Shabbos meal this week, right? You haven't forgotten?"

"Would I forget such a thing?" Heidi asked with an air of injured innocence.

"You're so busy these days, who knows?"

"I used to think I was busy back then — in Manhattan. Little did I know what it's like to run a home and a legal practice ..." She rolled her eyes in feigned dismay.

"But you can handle it, right?" Nate asked his wife, as they climbed out of the minivan amid a chorus of good-byes from the Bernsteins.

"With the right partner," Heidi told him, a smile kindling in her eyes, "I can handle anything."

They waved at the minivan as it roared away down the street. Then the Goodmans walked up the path, past the shiny new sign, and through the front door of their own sweet home.

It was very late when Pinchas Harris decided to call it a night.

His wife always chided him for being such a night owl, but he found that his mind worked at twice its usual efficiency after the sun went down. Before seeking his bed, he decided to pay one last visit to the dining room, where the *Sefer Torah* discovered in the cave on the cliffs reigned in the center of the oblong mahogany table. The *sofer* who had labored these past months to repair the historic scroll had finished the job just that afternoon. Pinchas felt as if an old friend had stepped back into his life. In a few days' time, in a gala *Hachnasas Sefer Torah* ceremony, the *Sefer Torah* would be transferred to its new and permanent home in the shul's *aron kodesh*.

He carefully raised the lid and lifted out the *Sefer Torah*, which he kissed with reverence. Idly, his eye fell on the interior of the box. Something about the bottom seemed a little … off. As though the wood had shifted somehow. Wondering, he reverently set the scroll down and started to investigate.

The wood at the bottom of the box hadn't shifted. What had shifted, Pinchas realized with a sense of shock, was a thin piece of lumber that had been placed over the bottom. Some long-ago carpenter had created what was essentially a false bottom for the box. Its recent travels had jarred the wood just enough to make it discernable.

With the tips of his fingers, Pinchas cautiously pried up the thin sheet, half-expecting the elderly wood to split with a sigh at being disturbed. He stared down at the flat object lying in the center of the rectangular box, where it had lain concealed for over a century and a half.

Two minutes later, he was at the phone.

He hesitated, wondering if it was too late to call the Bernsteins' home number. He decided to dial Nachman's cell phone instead, on the assumption that this would wake no one in the Bernstein household.

"Nachman!" he exclaimed, as his call was answered. "You're still awake. Good!"

"What's up, Pinchas?"

"I'd like you to see for yourself. Can you come over?"

Nachman's astonishment crackled over the line like electricity. "*Now?*"

"If you can. There's something here that I think you'd want to see. I know of your special interest in the Jewish immigrants who came to these parts all those years ago, and who we assume left the *Sefer Torah* in the cave. I think I've found proof ..."

"I'm on my way." Nachman was out the door almost before he'd hung up the phone.

"Look," Pinchas said quietly. "This is exactly where I found it. It was lying underneath a thin sheet of wood — a false bottom." Nachman followed the direction of the rabbi's gaze, back to the wooden container that had held the Torah.

Lying in the center of the long box was a small, brown-paper packet, a sort of precursor to the modern-day envelope. After staring at it wonderingly for a moment, Nachman lifted the packet from the spot where it had lain for so many years, tucked beneath the sacred scroll.

With infinite care, he lifted the flap and extracted a sheaf of handwritten pages. The ink was faded, but still legible.

"It's a list of names," he almost whispered. "About 25 of them. Men's names, and women's ... Eastern European, gauging by the names and the handwriting."

"Looks like a passenger manifest. Here's the name of the ship, see?" Pinchas Harris studied the page intently. "Look," he said suddenly. "There are a couple of children listed, too. It says 'Hershel Baumgarten' and 'Esther Mindel Baumgarten,' followed by two names that are slightly indented on the next line: Yaakov and Gittel Baumgarten.' The format is different from any of the others. I believe they must have been children."

"You could be right," Nachman said slowly. "I think —" He stopped short, fingers sliding around the inside of the packet. "Wait a second. There's something else here!"

Pinchas moved closer as Nachman drew out a sepia photograph.

Before studying the picture itself, Nachman turned it over to see if it had any identifying notation on the back. "It says something in some language — Polish, I'd guess, or perhaps Czech. There's a year here, too: 1849." He sounded awed. "More than a 150 years ago ..." Quickly, he turned the photograph and held it up for Pinchas to see.

It was a group portrait, taken in the stiff, unsmiling style that had been the norm in photography's early days. There were 25 figures in all, lined up in four rows and all staring fixedly at the camera with identically solemn expressions that effectively erased all traces of individuality. Some of the figures were obviously married couples, though the majority were single men. Standing in front of one such couple were two children: a boy of about 6 and a girl who appeared a little younger. Both of the mother's hands rested on the daughter's shoulders, while one of the father's hands gripped the son's.

The children's faces wore the same serious expressions as their elders, though there was a spark of something like excitement in the boy's eyes — as if his inner self refused to conform to the photographer's stringencies. The little girl, Nachman noticed upon closer scrutiny, was the only one not staring directing at the camera in front of her. She was gazing sideways, instead, at her brother.

Nachman exhaled slowly, only now becoming aware that he'd been holding his breath. "What a find!" he murmured. "The inscription on the back reads 1849. That's pre-Civil War."

"Very 'pre,'" Pinchas Harris agreed.

"Birch's dreams!" Nachman said suddenly. "A boy and a girl ... Pinchas, will you excuse me a moment?" Without waiting for an answer, he pulled his cell phone from his pocket and punched in a number on his speed-dial. To his chagrin, the phone rang and rang.

"He's not in," he said, disappointed. "I'll leave a message."

Just after sunset, Steve had followed an impulse to visit a site he had been to many times since Mrs. Sadowsky had unearthed her old maps. Ultimately, they had led Steve to this spot: the gravesite of the band of Jewish immigrants, massacred by the Apaches during the Gold Rush of

1849. Though he would never have absolute proof of it, he believed that he was standing at the graves of his ancestors.

The young boy and girl of his dreams had not been buried here. Neither he nor the librarian had been able to find a hint of any Jewish youngsters who might have been buried in the area after the horrific massacre. All he had was the mention in Jane Willard's diary that Esther Mindel, the Jewish woman Jane met so briefly before the Apache onslaught, had been a mother. Had Esther Mindel brought her children with her to Lakewood? And, if so, what had become of them in the massacre?

Steve had a private theory of his own. Tragically orphaned in the massacre, he believed that the children had been taken in by the Mescaleros: the boy, if Steve's dreams were to be believed, to eventually be killed in the course of a tribal hunt, and the girl to marry into the tribe ... but not before she took possession of the sole memento of their former life; the small *siddur* with the gilt Star of David that had rested in her brother's pocket the day the Indians came.

Somehow, she had known that her Jewishness would transmit itself to her children, and to her daughter's children after her. Perhaps, before his death, her brother had taught her that fact, dredging it up from the days when he'd sat in *cheder* with his *shtetl* friends. Though she'd been forced to become a part of the lives of the tribe that sustained her, the girl had clung to her secret agenda. She'd handed the *siddur* down to her daughter: to form the first link in a chain that culminated with Steve Birch, sensitive Native American lawyer with an unquenchable thirst for truth and an aching hole in his soul.

In just a few months' time, before the Jewish New Year, he would immerse in a *mikveh*, undergo circumcision and begin a new life as a Jew. The joy that enveloped him at the prospect was tempered by the memory of all the lost years. All the lost generations ... Esther Mindel and her compatriots had found brutal death at the end of their journey, but not before she sent her precious children away, so that they might live.

And now, the great-great-grandson of one of those children was preparing to join fully in the faith of his fathers. Full circle ...

He had repeated the story to himself so many times, and embellished it with so much detail gleaned from his dreams and his deepest yearnings, that it carried, for him, the stamp of truth. And yet, he didn't know. Not for sure. He would probably never know.

Standing at the old gravesite, he opened the *siddur* he had brought with him. It was not the heirloom *siddur*; that was far too fragile to survive a steady diet of New Mexican heat. He prayed with devotion, but also with a pain that never quite left him. When he was done with the formal prayer — reciting the Hebrew words carefully and accurately — he closed his eyes and added a deeply personal one of his own.

Please, he beseeched his Creator. *I know I should probably be satisfied. I should be grateful that I've come this far, and that I know which direction I'm meant to follow. Still ... I need something more. I need — clarity. I need some sort of confirmation that I am who I believe I am. That my dreams were not a pack of nonsense, the fruit of a frustrated mind. Maybe it's too much to ask ... but I'm asking anyway. Please?*

Afterward, Steve Birch took a long walk. Strolling the streets was a favorite method for walking off whatever ailed him.

What ailed him tonight was the thing he had prayed about at the gravesite: the gaping hole in his identity that he had come to believe would be with him for the rest of his life. As a companion, it was not acutely uncomfortable. It was more like an ever-present throb that could be ignored for a time, but that never failed to make its presence felt with renewed vigor. He ought to be used to it by now. Why wasn't he used to it?

His footsteps echoed on the quiet streets. The sky seemed very high and very dark, dwarfing the town and all those asleep within its precincts. As he walked beneath the vastness of that black-velvet dome, he found his batteries of hope gradually recharging. Whether or not he'd been born a Jew, he would soon, with his official conversion, be a halachic one. He'd have plenty of work to do to fill that role the way it deserved to be filled. There was a G-d — *his* G-d — waiting to be worshiped with every ounce of his being. What did anything matter beside that? His pain didn't matter ... his past didn't matter.

As the dark street carried him nearer to his home, he had a sense of expansion, as though he were shedding a weighty burden with every step. Lighter and lighter he grew, until he was no more substantial than a puff of cloud. The questions fell away, and the pain along with it. In sudden, fierce emotion he lifted his eyes to the starry heavens and whispered, *Whatever You hand me is okay. Even the uncertainty about who I am is okay. I don't need to know who I am — as long as I know who You are ...*

The phone was ringing when he reached the door of his apartment. As he fitted the key in the lock, it rang again. He flung the door open just as the message machine took over.

"Steve?" Nachman's voice said. "If you can hear this, please pick up. I've got some news for you. It's kind of important."

Without pausing to catch his breath, Steve ran over to the phone — and into the beginning of everything.